THE CHILDREN OF THE GODS SERIES:BOOKS 7-10

DARK WARRIOR TETRALOGY

I. T LUCAS

THE CHILDREN OF THE GODS SERIES
BOOKS 7-10
DARK WARRIOR TETRALOGY

Copyright © 2020 by I. T. Lucas

All rights reserved.
No part of this book may be reproduced in any form or by any electronic or mechanical means, including information storage and retrieval systems, without written permission from the author, except for the use of brief quotations in a book review.

NOTE FROM THE AUTHOR:
This is a work of fiction!
Names, characters, places and incidents are products of the author's imagination or are used fictitiously and are not to be construed as real. Any similarity to actual persons, organizations and/or events is purely coincidental.

CONTENTS

DARK WARRIOR MINE

Prologue	3
1. Andrew	6
2. Sebastian	11
3. Andrew	14
4. Syssi	18
5. Amanda	21
6. Andrew	24
7. Nathalie	28
8. Bhathian	32
9. Andrew	35
10. Nathalie	38
11. Andrew	41
12. Syssi	45
13. Sebastian	49
14. Andrew	53
15. Amanda	58
16. Andrew	61
17. Sebastian	65
18. Nathalie	68
19. Andrew	71
20. Nathalie	75
21. Anandur	78
22. Andrew	82
23. Nathalie	87
24. Andrew	90
25. Nathalie	94
26. Andrew	98
27. Nathalie	101
28. Andrew	105
29. Bhathian	107
30. Nathalie	111
31. Bhathian	115

32. Andrew	117
33. Nathalie	121
34. Andrew	125
35. Nathalie	130
36. Andrew	133
37. Nathalie	136
38. Andrew	139
39. Nathalie	142
40. Andrew	145
41. Nathalie	149
42. Andrew	152
43. Nathalie	155
44. Andrew	161
45. Anandur	164
46. Nathalie	167
47. Andrew	170
48. Anandur	174
49. Bhathian	178
50. Andrew	181
51. Sebastian	185
52. Nathalie	187
53. Andrew	190
54. Nathalie	193
55. Andrew	196
56. Nathalie	199
57. Andrew	202

DARK WARRIOR'S PROMISE

1. Nathalie	207
2. Andrew	211
3. Brundar	214
4. Nathalie	217
5. Anandur	220
6. Nathalie	224
7. Andrew	228
8. Nathalie	231
9. Anandur	235
10. Bhathian	239
11. Nathalie	243
12. Anandur	247

13. Syssi	250
14. Nathalie	254
15. Anandur	257
16. Carol	261
17. Syssi	266
18. Nathalie	270
19. Kian	275
20. Andrew	279
21. Sebastian	282
22. Kian	285
23. Andrew	288
24. Dalhu	292
25. Andrew	296
26. Nathalie	301
27. Carol	305
28. Sebastian	308
29. Andrew	310
30. Kian	314
31. Andrew	318
32. Nathalie	323
33. Anandur	327
34. Andrew	331
35. Nathalie	334
36. Sebastian	339
37. Andrew	341
38. Nathalie	344
39. Andrew	346
40. Nathalie	350
41. Andrew	353
42. Andrew	356
43. Nathalie	358
44. Andrew	361
45. Bhathian	364
46. Syssi	366
47. Andrew	369
48. Nathalie	371
49. Andrew	375
50. Nathalie	381
51. Bhathian	384
52. Andrew	388

DARK WARRIOR'S DESTINY

1. Carol	393
2. Nathalie	396
3. Robert	400
4. Nathalie	404
5. Andrew	409
6. Nathalie	412
7. Anandur	416
8. Carol	420
9. Kian	423
10. Robert	428
11. Andrew	431
12. Carol	435
13. Robert	438
14. Nathalie	443
15. Andrew	447
16. Carol	451
17. Sebastian	457
18. Kian	460
19. Dalhu	464
20. Kian	468
21. Sebastian	472
22. Dalhu	476
23. Kian	480
24. Dalhu	484
25. Andrew	487
26. Nathalie	490
27. Andrew	494
28. Nathalie	497
29. Andrew	501
30. Nathalie	505
31. Andrew	509
32. Nathalie	513
33. Kian	517
34. Andrew	521
35. Kian	525
36. Kian	528
37. Nathalie	532
38. Andrew	537
39. Anandur	541

40. Nathalie	545
41. Andrew	549
42. Syssi	553
43. Andrew	558
44. Nathalie	562
45. Kian	566
46. Nathalie	569
47. Syssi	572
48. Nathalie	575
49. Andrew	578
50. Nathalie	581
51. Andrew	585
52. Nathalie	588

DARK WARRIOR'S LEGACY

1. Nathalie	595
2. Andrew	599
3. Carol	603
4. Andrew	606
5. Nathalie	610
6. Andrew	613
7. Robert	616
8. Nathalie	620
9. Carol	627
10. Nathalie	631
11. Robert	636
12. Andrew	643
13. Carol	648
14. Anandur	652
15. Kian	655
16. Losham	657
17. Nathalie	659
18. Amanda	663
19. Andrew	668
20. Anandur	672
21. Nathalie	675
22. Andrew	681
23. Nathalie	686
24. Anandur	692
25. Andrew	695

26. Kian	700
27. Robert	703
28. Anandur	708
29. Losham	711
30. Dalhu	714
31. Nathalie	717
32. Andrew	720
33. Robert	725
34. Amanda	728
35. Carol	732
36. Robert	735
37. Anandur	742
38. Andrew	745
39. Anandur	749
40. Losham	753
41. Anandur	756
42. Kian	763
43. Anandur	766
44. Nathalie	769
45. Andrew	772
46. Nathalie	777
47. Andrew	780
48. Nathalie	782
49. Andrew	785
Dark Guardian	789
The Children of the Gods Series	801
The Perfect Match Series	811
Also by I. T. Lucas	813
FOR EXCLUSIVE PEEKS	817

DARK WARRIOR MINE

PROLOGUE

Harvard-Westlake High school
Studio City, California
13 years ago.

"Hi, Nathalie." Leaning his hip against the metal door of his locker, Luke Bruoker produced his seductive smile. For her.

Walk away, the voice in her head commanded.

Shut up, Nathalie thought back.

Just do it. You know what he's thinking.

As if she needed Tut to freaking tell her what was on Luke's mind as he flashed her, *Nutty Nattie*, the perfect set of teeth that had all the other girls wetting their designer panties. With his good looks and rich daddy, Luke was one of the most popular guys in school, and for giving her the time of day, he probably expected her to fall at his feet in gratitude.

Not this girl, not going to happen, buddy.

Trying to ignore her too handsome and too full of himself locker neighbor, Nathalie stuffed the books she came to retrieve in her backpack.

But what if she was wrong? What if Luke was just being nice? And anyway, even if he wasn't, she didn't want to be rude.

"Hi, Luke." Nathalie lifted the corners of her lips in a tight smile and waved goodbye.

You're not wrong, Tut snickered. *But if it's any consolation, he thinks you're hot.*

It's not.

Unfortunately, there was no way to hide things from the stowaway sharing her cranium space.

You're such a liar. Tut's laugh echoed in her head before slowly fading away.

Well, what did he expect? She was only human and couldn't help but feel flattered.

He was such a pain, but if she was lucky, for the next few hours he'd leave her alone. Tut, or *tutor*, as he'd introduced himself after chasing all the other voices away, hated math class. In fact, the ghost in her head didn't like school, or homework, or tests—which was probably the main reason she was such a good student. The only time Nathalie could be alone in her own skull was while studying.

Tut claimed to be teaching her about life.

Yeah, right, more like ruining it.

Watching TV with him was a nightmare. He wouldn't shut up for a moment with his nonstop derisive commentary about everyone and everything. And hanging out with friends or going to the mall was more of the same.

Who was she kidding? As if anyone wanted to hang out with Nutty Nattie—the girl who talked to herself.

Nathalie pulled on the straps of her heavy backpack, hitching it higher on her back as she walked faster—pretending to rush so no one would notice that she always walked alone.

Mostly, she felt invisible. No one would look at her, except maybe for some of the nicer girls who would occasionally give her a pitying smile—as if she was retarded or deformed. The best she could hope for was to be regarded as the crazy genius. Unfortunately, even though she was smart and worked harder than most, she deserved only the first part of the title.

But at least her hard work had gotten her accepted into this overpriced private high school. Trouble was, her parents couldn't really afford it—not even with the generous financial aid they'd been awarded—and she knew for a fact that they were dipping into their equity line to finance the difference. The school called the discount a scholarship, but it wasn't. None of the rich kids were getting it, not even those who were excellent students.

Still, it wasn't as if anyone was privy to that information, but it wasn't hard to guess either. Her classmates arrived at school in Mercedes and BMWs while she drove a three-year-old Toyota Corolla hatchback.

Not that she was complaining, her car was great—the previous owner had hardly driven her, and she was almost as good as new. Besides, this was the best her parents could afford. God knew they had always given her everything they could, and probably more than they should—spoiling their only child.

When she was younger, she'd thought it was her due, but lately, it was making her feel guilty. It seemed as if by giving her all of their love, her parents were left with nothing for each other.

In fact, this morning, her mother told her that she'd filed for a divorce.

Oh, God, what is Papi going to do?

The coffee shop wasn't making much, and they would not have been able to afford much of anything without her mother's government pension.

How is Papi going to survive without it?

Thank God, it was her last year of high school, so at least this expense would be gone. And since she'd gotten a full-ride scholarship to the University of Virginia, college wouldn't cost her parents anything.

But savings aside, it meant that her father would be all alone once she left.

At sixty, her mother was still a knockout, while Papi, two years her junior, looked like a grandpa. It had to do with his love of baking—and eating. He was at least fifty pounds overweight and almost bald. But he was the sweetest guy. Which was probably why his business wasn't doing so well. He had never turned away anyone who was hungry, regardless of their ability to pay.

Not fair.

The God her father believed in so earnestly should've smiled upon a man like him, rewarded him for his good heart and generosity. But instead, his beloved coffee shop was barely staying afloat, and his beautiful wife was leaving him.

Nathalie had a feeling that her mother had just been waiting for her to finish school and go to college to make her move. Eva hadn't been happy for years—even when Papi had been much thinner and still had hair. She always looked troubled, almost fearful, though Nathalie couldn't figure out why.

Maybe her mother suffered from some mental disease—like Nathalie did. Though instead of hearing voices of dead people in her head, Eva might've been anxious or depressed.

It was about time she talked with her mother and cleared things up. She was definitely old enough for a grownup conversation. Perhaps they both could benefit from psychiatric help. And maybe, just maybe, with treatment, Eva might change her mind about leaving.

But even if she wouldn't, to be rid of Tut, it was worth a try.

Problem was, psychiatrists were expensive.

Maybe that was why her parents had never taken her to one, even though they must've known that her so-called imaginary friends had been very different than those of other kids.

But Papi had said that it was harmless, nothing to worry about, and her mother had agreed. They'd cautioned her that it was okay to play pretend at home, but she shouldn't be talking to herself in public.

Nathalie had tried.

As she had grown older, she'd realized that it wasn't normal and that the people talking to her in her head were probably just elaborate hallucinations. A mental disorder and not ghosts. She'd stopped telling even her parents about it.

But here and there, she would forget herself and respond out loud—hence the damn nickname. *Nutty Nattie.*

1

ANDREW

I've just landed, taxiing in, I can be at your place in an hour. Andrew texted Bridget as soon as it was okay to turn cell phones on.

She answered. *Waiting impatiently (̔}~̔{)*

It took him a few seconds to decipher the meaning.

Cute.

For an immortal, who was born God knew when, she was surprisingly well versed in current texting lingo and etiquette. Better than he was. He'd never asked Bridget how old she was, in part because he felt it was impolite, and in part because he was afraid to find out. For a forty-year-old man, it would've been beyond weird to know that his girlfriend was hundreds of years old.

Andrew wondered how Syssi dealt with her husband's age. His baby sister, thirteen years his junior, had fallen in love with Kian before finding out that her Greek-god-lookalike boyfriend was so ancient.

The few clan members Andrew had gotten to know since he'd been sucked into their world ranged in age from nearly two thousand, like his new brother-in-law, to Amanda, who was over two hundred. Not to mention their mother, the goddess, who was over five thousand years old or more.

This was another lady who Andrew would never dare ask for her age. He was an adrenaline junkie, but he wasn't stupid enough to court certain death.

After a day of endless meetings, followed by a five-hour flight from Washington back to L.A., Andrew would've preferred for Bridget to come over to his place. Trouble was, whatever was in the fridge had probably spoiled over the two weeks he'd been gone.

True, he could've ordered takeout, but there was also the issue of his bed being messy, and probably not quite fresh smelling. He couldn't remember the last time he'd changed the linens. Not that they were all the way into the gross category, but Bridget deserved better.

He'd thought about buying her a present in D.C. but eventually had given up on the idea. First of all, Bridget was loaded, just like all other clan members, and what Andrew defined as a reasonably-priced gift, she might consider trash. Secondly, he had no idea what to buy for a woman in general and for this one in particular. Dr. Bridget's tastes gravitated toward the practical.

Except, she had a thing for red.

Damn, just thinking about those spiky red heels of hers was enough to get him hard. But it wasn't as if he could buy her shoes. And even if he were one of those guys who could guess a woman's shoe size, hers were probably the kind that cost over a thousand bucks—not something he could afford on his government salary.

So yeah, the only things he felt confident buying for a woman were chocolates and flowers.

But at least he wasn't as clueless as Bhathian, who didn't even know how to behave around one, or what to say.

The guy had been terrified of going to see the long-lost daughter Andrew had found for him. So much so that he'd asked Andrew to accompany him to her coffee shop, just so they could sit there, pretending to be customers. It hadn't been a good feeling to bail on the guy, but Andrew had had no choice. Her place had been closed on the evening he'd delivered the news of her existence, and the next day he'd been told to pack up a suitcase and hop on a plane to Washington.

The trip had been a total waste of time. He'd spent two fucking weeks in Homeland Security headquarters—stuck in boring meetings, listening to bureaucrats who believed they knew best how to devise a plan of action that could've been condensed into five paragraphs on one yellow-pad page. Actually, it was exactly what he'd brought back.

One fucking page.

They could've bloody emailed him. Anyway, no one had listened to what he'd had to say.

Fuck, he hoped Bhathian hadn't waited for him to go see the girl—correction, woman; earlier this year the guy's daughter had turned thirty.

An hour later, Andrew knocked on Bridget's door. Luckily, no one had hitched a ride with him on the elevator that had taken him from the clan's private parking level up to her floor. And by no one he meant Bhathian.

He planned to call the guy after his reunion with Bridget.

Andrew and the doctor had a lot of steam to release. The entire time he'd been away, he'd been preserving his energy for the insatiable immortal.

Today, he would show her staying power.

She opened the door, wearing a long white T-shirt, spiky red heels, and nothing else. "Andrew, you have no idea how happy I am to see you," she purred.

"Not as happy as I am." He lifted her up for a kiss, kicking the door closed behind him. She wrapped her legs around his hips.

Bridget was naked under that semi-sheer thing, every curve and shade of her generous breasts and aroused nipples clearly visible, and the bedroom was too far away.

Turning around, he pinned her against the nearest wall. "I can't wait," he groaned, holding her up with one hand and going for his belt buckle with the other.

"Let me." She pushed his hand away and opened things up for him. Freeing his shaft, she guided it into her moist heat. Bridget was drenched. He hesitated, but only for a split second, before ramming inside her with one powerful thrust.

On a groan, her head hit the wall behind her.

With the wall holding part of her weight and her thighs locked in a tight grip around his hips, he needed only one hand on her ass to keep going, and he put the other one to good use, pushing her shirt up and palming a breast.

Bridget did one better, pulling the thing over her head and tossing it on the floor. Now, she was completely bare save for the shoes.

They could stay on.

Damn, this was so fucking hot.

Thumbing one perky nipple, he pinched and tugged, taking turns and giving each the same loving attention.

Bridget's hands shot into his short hair, and she gripped his skull, bringing his head closer for a hungry kiss. As their tongues and teeth dueled, her sharp incisors were winning, and as she bit down on his lower lip, she drew blood.

Feisty immortal.

He brought his hand down on her butt with a loud slap, then gripped both cheeks and began pounding with gusto.

"Yes! Oh, dear Fates, yes!" Bridget seemed oblivious to the fact that she was being banged into the wall with such force that the plaster was cracking, and small particles of paint were flying in the air.

If she were mortal, she would've bruised badly.

Liberated by her resilience, Andrew kept going hard.

It was so fucking good to feel vital, strong, male. But as he neared his completion, Andrew had the passing thought that as amazing as this was, something was still missing.

"Now," Bridget hissed.

He obeyed her command, synchronizing his climax with hers and coming hard inside her—his shaft milked by the convulsing muscles in her sheath gripping him harder than any fist.

"God, Bridget..." He fumbled for words as he lowered her.

Her thighs trembled a little, but as her feet touched the floor, she was steady. "Come to bed." She bent and pulled his pants up but left them unzipped. "I don't want you to trip on the way. I still have a use for you." She winked and walked away.

To his relief, he saw that although her back was slightly reddened, the skin looked intact. But as she sauntered ahead of him, he noticed that one of her curvy butt cheeks still bore a faint outline of his handprint. That one, he didn't mind. Not at all.

In fact, he felt his shaft give a twitch. Good, the abstinence was paying off. Tonight, he would be able to last, hopefully for as long as it would take to satisfy the lustful immortal.

Two hours later, a Victoria's Secret lineup naked parade wouldn't have gotten a rise out of him. And if tongues could get sprains, his would've been sporting a brace.

The merry tune Bridget was whistling in the kitchen was like a slap to his manhood. She was going to kill him, pleasurably, but he'd be dead nonetheless.

Andrew closed his eyes and inhaled deeply. One didn't need an immortal's superior nose to smell the thick scent of sex on the bedding, and if he had an ounce of energy left in him, he would've gotten all domestic and taken them off for her.

Still naked, Bridget sauntered into the bedroom with a loaded tray and placed it on the side table. "Sit up. I'm going to nourish you. You look pale."

"I wonder why?" he said as he propped himself up on the pillows and took the coffee mug she'd handed him.

"Poor baby. Too much for you?"

Now, that was mean.

"Not at all. Give me an hour and I'm back up." *Not if my life depended on it...*

"Aha. Sure. Whatever you say." She handed him a pastry.

As he chewed, he was reminded of the call he still owed Bhathian. It would have to wait until he could move.

"This is good. Where did you get it?"

"I was on Fairfax earlier today, and the smells lured me into this new bakery. I don't remember the name, but it's on the box if you want to write it down. I bought an assortment to try it out, but I'm afraid this is the only one left." She smiled sheepishly.

"Oh, yeah? Who ate all the rest?"

"I did."

"How many?"

"Eleven. There were twelve in the box."

And here he'd thought that Bridget only ate veggies. With an appetite like this for baked goods, it was a miracle she wasn't fat.

He appraised her lean midsection. "Where do you pack it all?"

"Breasts and butt." She patted the aforementioned parts.

"Then by all means, eat more. I love your curves."

A sad shadow clouded her eyes, but only momentarily. She shook it off so fast Andrew wasn't sure if it had really been there or if he'd just imagined it.

She grinned. "You and the construction workers renovating that old office building on Olive. Every time I pass by, they whistle and comment."

"Want me to beat them up for you?"

She laughed. "Why on earth would I want that?"

"Some women find it offensive." He shrugged.

"I don't mind the whistling, but the comments they think I can't hear..."

"My offer is still on the table."

She leaned and kissed his cheek. "You're so sweet."

"What is it with immortal females and calling me sweet? Even my own mother never called me that."

She kissed him again, on the lips this time. "What's the matter? Your machismo got hurt?"

He crossed his arms over his chest. "Yes."

Bridget refilled his coffee mug and handed him a piece of an apple as a peace offering.

"Can you stay the night?"

And prove himself a liar when even three hours later he would remain as limp as a noodle? No way. "I wish I could, but I got to talk to Bhathian. There is something I'd promised him to do, and I didn't have a chance because of that damn useless conference my boss sent me on with barely any notice."

"You could come back later…I'm flying out to Baltimore tomorrow…"

"I thought Julian's graduation was next week."

"It is, but I wanted to spend some time with him, and he made plans with his roommates for a road trip after the graduation."

Damn, he hated to disappoint her, but he hated the prospect of staying even more. His suitcase was still in his car because he'd come here straight from the airport, and tomorrow was another long workday. He needed to go home.

Andrew pulled her into his arms and kissed her lips gently. "I'm sorry, but I just have to go home and unpack, check what alien life forms are growing in my fridge…" He tried for humor, and it worked.

She smiled. "Fascinating, save some samples for me."

"I promise to save something better than disgusting growth for you to play with."

"And what might that be?"

"Life force? Energy?" He made a face.

Bridget laughed. "After another ten days of nada, you'll need it."

"I know."

2

SEBASTIAN

Standing on top of the old monastery's newly added third-floor balcony, Sebastian leaned over the railing and glared at the cars parked outside. A damned parking lot was one more thing Sebastian realized he had neglected to plan for his new base of operation in the picturesque Ojai.

The front of the building looked like a junkyard, and in the daytime it was even worse.

From his balcony, he should be gazing at a grassy lawn and flowerbeds, not a bunch of used cars scattered on top of packed dirt.

A paved circular driveway and a fountain with a statue at its center, surrounded by rose bushes, would have made the place look grand.

But hiring workers now that the warriors were all in residence was problematic. Training would have to be suspended, and the guys would have to make themselves scarce.

The men hardly matched what one would expect of those visiting a restful *spiritual retreat*.

There was no helping the cars, though. The men needed vehicles to transport themselves to and from the clubs they were now scoping nightly in search of male clan members. Tom and Robert had gone shopping, and in a few days had managed to fill the lot with a bunch of used cars. Sebastian would've preferred to go into a dealership and lease a fleet, but Tom had insisted that buying from private owners was more discreet.

All in all, they now had twenty-nine vehicles at their disposal.

One was a big truck, for just in case, and the rest an assortment of minivans and SUVs. While the troops shared the used cars at a ratio of three to one, Sebastian had insisted that he and his two assistants each had their own brand new vehicle.

For obvious reasons, all had darkened windows.

The cars were serving dual purposes. The obvious one was transportation, but also, when needed, the back seats could be folded to provide a place for a quick fuck.

With his basement brothel's low occupancy rate, his troop's needs had to be satisfied off base.

Over the last two weeks, Sebastian had been able to find only five girls for his brothel. Not enough to take care of seventy-five immortal warriors, two assistants, and one sadist. But there was only so much he could do in a day, and snagging the right females required investigative work that took time.

Most hadn't been the right fit.

Which reminded him that there was another issue he hadn't accounted for. Human females required sunlight and fresh air to stay healthy and in a good mood. Thralling was not enough to counteract the underlying depression the lack of natural light and tiny jail rooms were causing.

He'd come to the conclusion that he couldn't keep them cooped up in the basement twenty-four hours a day.

On Pleasure Island, the women enjoyed several swimming pools, above-ground bars and restaurants, and the beautiful, tropical ocean. It was a gross oversight on his part to not realize the importance of those amenities.

Sebastian should have known that the exalted leader of *The Devout Order Of Mordth*, Lord Navuh, never did anything without a good reason. If Navuh had chosen to provide his whores with outdoor recreation, it had been only because it was crucial for the women's health and their ability to provide the exceptional services his secret island was known for.

Sebastian pulled out his phone and selected Robert's number. "Grab Tom and meet me outside."

"Yes, sir."

Sebastian rolled his eyes but didn't say anything. Robert was a lost cause. Jogging down the stairs, he glanced at the spacious recreation room. The men were done with their chores for the day, and several were taking a break playing pool or watching a movie before going to their rooms to get ready for the nightly club patrols.

There had been a lot of grumbling about the domestic chores they'd been assigned, but he had no intention of getting more humans on the premises to perform the cooking and housekeeping duties. Perhaps once the basement rooms were all filled, he would divert his attention to finding at least a decent cook. He was sick of the barbecued steaks and hamburgers the men were taking turns preparing.

Other than that, the lazy fuckers could keep on doing laundry, sweeping floors, and cleaning toilets. It wasn't as if they had that much to do during the day. Five hours of training was enough to keep them in shape, and the rest of their work was done at night.

Outside, the mountain air was crisp and cool, and other than the rumbling voices of the men inside, he could hear only the chirping of crickets and the hooting of the occasional owl. Even the coyotes didn't dare go anywhere near the compound.

"You wanted to see us, boss?" Tom said from behind him.

"Yes, I want to do something about the grounds." He waved his hand at the vehicles. In the weak moonlight, their colors were faded, all looking like different shades of gray and black. "I don't want to see this out of my window."

Robert glanced around at the gentle hills surrounding the former monastery. "This is the only flat area."

The problem with subordinates who were good at taking orders was that they didn't think independently, you had to chew everything for them.

"What do you have in mind?" Tom asked.

"I want the parking lot to be moved over there." Sebastian pointed to the side of the building. "And I want a circular driveway with a fountain in the center. The rest of the grounds need planting; grass, flowers, trees, the works." Sebastian began walking. "Come with me." He motioned for them to follow.

At some point, the back of the property had had grassy lawns with gravel paths meandering through them, but now there was nothing besides overgrown weeds and construction debris that hadn't been taken care of yet.

"I'm thinking of putting in a swimming pool over there, and an outdoor bar with shaded trellises on that side. We'll need to bring in large, mature trees to create a green canopy around the whole thing. Girls lounging in bikinis are not exactly what one expects to find in an 'Interfaith Spiritual Retreat'."

Robert looked intrigued.

"And how do you suggest we do it?" Tom asked.

"That's what I need to figure out. If it were only planting, I would've had the men do it, but for the pool and hardscaping we need a contractor with heavy equipment."

Robert crossed his arms over his chest and started pacing back and forth. "Curfew," he uttered a few moments later. "We need to coordinate several contractors with large crews to come and be done in a few hours. We'll have the men on lockdown in the house while the construction is going on."

"What about the cars?" Tom asked.

"We park them in a line on the side of the road, one behind the other."

Sebastian clapped Robert's back. "Great idea, Robert. We could tell the contractors that there are guests in the retreat and work needs to be confined to a predetermined number of hours a day. This will also explain the cars."

The guy, who was tall to begin with, seemed to grow a few inches. "Thank you, Sebastian," he said without stuttering or mumbling for the first time.

Clap, clap, clap. "Finally," Tom said.

3

ANDREW

I'm back and here in the building. Want to meet me downstairs? Andrew texted Bhathian.
Come to my place. 37 floor, #4.
I'm on my way.

Bridget's apartment was just one floor above Bhathian's, and Andrew opted to take the emergency stairs down.

They had already said their goodbyes. He'd offered to come get her and drive her to the airport, but she'd declined. Her flight was leaving in the afternoon, and she'd said that she saw no reason for him to take time off work. A taxi would do.

To his shame, he'd felt relieved. There was a big pile of files waiting for him in the office, and to catch up, he would need to not only work through his lunch break but stay overtime. His damn bosses still expected him to deliver a report despite sending him on that useless trip.

Andrew rapped his knuckles on the door and waited.

After a moment, Bhathian opened it. "Hey, my man, come in. How was your trip?" He clasped Andrew's hand.

"A waste of time." Andrew shook it then followed him inside.

The layout and furnishings were similar to Bridget's. But where hers had been personalized with all kinds of knickknacks, and everything was nice and tidy, the guy's place was typical of what one would expect to find in a bachelor's apartment.

There was an opened box of pizza on the dining table, and empty beer bottles littered every surface. It seemed that Bhathian had appropriated all that had been left from Kian's bachelor party because most of them were Snake's Venom, the expensive, super potent Scottish beer Anandur had bought for the occasion.

Bhathian followed his gaze. "Want one? I have plenty."

"Sure, why not?'

The guy ducked into the kitchen and returned with two cold ones.

Andrew took one. "I'm surprised so many were left. I thought we demolished all of them."

"There were none. But they were good, so the next day I went and bought two cases for myself."

"I thought they were pricey."

Bhathian shrugged his massive shoulders and planted his butt in a chair across from Andrew. "I have plenty of money and nothing to spend it on."

"You didn't go to see her." There was no need to specify which her he was talking about.

Bhathian winced. "The farthest I got was to stand outside her shop, but I didn't have the guts to go in."

"I'm sorry that I bailed on you."

"Not your fault."

"Do you want to go tomorrow?"

"If you can come, then yes."

"So, did you get a peek?"

Bhathian nodded. "She looks like her mother."

"Oh, yeah?"

"Beautiful." There was a definite note of pride in Bhathian's voice.

"Does she have anything from you?"

"Luckily for her, not much." Bhathian grimaced. "She has my thick eyebrows. Though, hers are pretty, not bushy like mine."

Andrew tried to picture a woman with Eva's exotic beauty and Bhathian's surly expression and came up blank.

Bhathian took a swig from his beer. "I need to find out what happened to Eva. Any idea how?"

Good question. The fact that the police hadn't found anything didn't mean much. Their investigation had probably been superficial at best.

"We can start by following the money trail. The government is still depositing her monthly pension checks into her bank account, and if she's still alive, I'm sure she is accessing it."

"And you can find out where she's making withdrawals?"

"Not easily, but yes. Unless the money is funneled through a Swiss bank. Then it's next to impossible."

Bhathian shook his head. "Just so you know, I'm forever in your debt. Whatever you need, whenever, just say the word."

"I appreciate it, but save your gratitude for when I actually find something."

"You already found my daughter, and for this alone I owe you big time. I'm not just blowing smoke up your ass, I mean it. Whatever, whenever."

"Okay, I got it, but it's really not necessary. If the roles were reversed, I'm sure you would've done the same for me." It seemed like the right thing to say, even though Andrew wasn't sure it was true. He was an outsider, tolerated only because his sister was married to the regent.

But Bhathian nodded solemnly, and leaned forward, extending his hand with the bottle. "That's what family is for."

Okay, so he might have been wrong. It seemed that Bhathian had really accepted Andrew as one of the clan. "To family." He clinked bottles with the guy.

"To family," Bhathian echoed.

Andrew emptied his bottle of Snake's Venom and put the empty on the coffee table before pushing up to his feet.

Damn, the thing must've gone to his head because he had a moment of vertigo. But it passed almost as soon as it started. It was probably only the fatigue catching up to him. "Tomorrow after work I'll come to get you, and we'll drive to Glendale. Seven okay?"

Bhathian got up and escorted him to the door. "Whatever works for you." The guy pulled Andrew into a crushing bear hug and clapped his back.

"Careful, my man. I'm still only a fragile human."

A rare smile brightening his gloomy features, Bhathian let go. "You might be a human, but from what I hear there is nothing fragile about you, tough guy."

And wasn't that good to hear.

On his way home, as he drove through the deserted streets of downtown L.A., Andrew reflected on his conversation with Bhathian.

Family.

For better or worse, the clan was now his family—independent of his decision regarding chancing the transition or not. They'd accepted him as is—the first human ever to be admitted into their tight, secret community.

He wondered if things would've been different if he hadn't brought all that he had to the table. If he were just an average Joe, with an average job, would they have entrusted him with their secrets?

Probably not.

The truth was that the clan needed him. Not that it was a bad thing necessarily, being needed was just as important as being accepted, maybe even more. Especially for a proud son-of-a-gun like him.

Which made him think of Dalhu.

The dude had done the impossible. His acceptance by the clan, however, had come at an unimaginable price. Andrew could not think of a single male that could've taken the torment Dalhu had gone through—not with the dignity and unparalleled willpower the guy had displayed.

One thing was for sure, if Andrew ever needed someone to fight by his side, Dalhu would be his first choice. Not that there was a chance the guy would be allowed to fight anytime soon. For all intents and purposes, Dalhu was still under house arrest—during his probation period as Kian had called it. True, he was no longer confined to the dungeon, and was sharing Amanda's spacious penthouse, but he wasn't allowed to leave.

The guy must be going crazy.

For a warrior to be cooped up in an apartment without the ability to release some steam must be hard. And it didn't matter that he was living in the lap of luxury with the love of his life.

Maybe Andrew should go spend some time with the dude, invite him for a sparring contest down in the gym.

Right.

Who was he kidding? As if he could offer any kind of a challenge to the powerful immortal. Even among the Guardians, Andrew suspected that only Anandur, or perhaps Yamanu, stood a chance against the ex-Doomer.

Amanda had gotten herself one hell of a protector.

Damn, it still stung.

Losing to the other guy hadn't been good for Andrew's ego. But he had to concede that despite his initial opinion of the guy, Dalhu had turned out to be the better man for Amanda.

God knew that with the kind of trouble the woman courted, Dalhu was probably the only male on earth capable of keeping her safe.

4

SYSSI

"Come here." Kian swiveled his chair and spread his knees in invitation. It had been like this since the first day she had joined him in the office. The moment Shai would leave, Kian would turn his chair around and invite her for a kiss that would often end in nookie.

As it turned out, she was more of an impediment than help.

The only thing she'd managed to achieve so far, apart from keeping her hubby happy, was to reorganize one small section of the filing cabinet. One at a time, she replaced the old, worn files with new ones and created an electronic version, including making detailed spreadsheets and scanning the supporting documents. Since Kian and Shai were such old farts they were still doing things the old fashioned way, meaning like before the Industrial Revolution, her help was invaluable. Problem was, Kian and she were too busy necking to accomplish much.

"I'm waiting..." he growled.

Syssi rolled her eyes and punched one last number into the spreadsheet before obeying his command.

"Yes, sir." She pushed out of her chair and got between his spread thighs.

"That's what I like to hear." He closed his arms around her, pulling her in and kissing her, hungrily, as if they hadn't kissed just five minutes ago.

"You know, I was supposed to be helping you, but I don't think you're getting any work done." She moved to sit on one muscular thigh.

His hand snaked under her shirt, and he thumbed her nipple over her bra. "Yes, I love coming to work now. I didn't before."

He had a point there. Well, not really, but who could think straight with arousal short circuiting cognition?

"I don't want to be responsible for your conglomerate's demise...Oh, God..." she breathed as he snapped her bra open and tugged on the other nipple.

"Nonsense, you're providing an invaluable service." He pushed her shirt up and licked the engorged peak before closing his lips around it and sucking it in.

"Fuck..." she exclaimed.

Oh no... they had a rule about her using that kind of language. Because it wasn't part of her usual vocabulary, it had become an invitation to a game that she preferred to play in the privacy of their bedroom, and not in the office where anyone could walk in at any moment. And besides, the freaking place had glass doors, so anyone passing by could see what was going on inside. Never mind that she was already half naked. But for some reason, it wasn't as embarrassing as what was coming next.

As Kian lifted his head up from her breast, he had the wickedest smile on his handsome as sin face. "My sweet, naughty girl just earned herself a spanking."

"Not here," she whispered, feeling herself blush. But this wasn't the only heat that was spreading all over her body...

"Yes, here." In a heartbeat, she found herself face down over his other knee with her jeans yanked down and her butt exposed.

"Someone might come in," she hissed, struggling to get up without much success. Even with her new strength, the arm holding her pinned to his body was as unyielding as an iron band.

"Don't worry, no one is coming, and I'll hear if anyone is out in the corridor." With a loud crack, the first slap landed on her exposed behind.

As if he can hear anything over that...

But as the second and third fell in quick succession, she stopped thinking and stopped struggling and just gave in to the sensation. By the time Kian had delivered the tenth and last, she was so close to climax she was contemplating using another f-bomb to have him start over. There was no need, though. Thirty seconds later, as Kian penetrated her soaking sheath with two fingers and then added a thumb over her most sensitive part, she came all over his hand. And his jeans.

He lifted her limp, spent body and cradled her in his lap. "I love you so much." He kissed her lips.

"I'm going to sue my boss for sexual harassment," she croaked.

"Oh, yeah? And who is that wicked boss? You can't sue yourself, you know."

"So now I'm the boss?"

"Of course, you are."

"Didn't feel like it a moment ago when you were spanking me."

"Just fulfilling my matrimonial duties as promised."

She shifted up and kissed his lips. "I love you too. But seriously, now I need to go up and change underwear. Again. And you must be really uncomfortable." She wiggled her butt over his shaft.

"No problem. I'll accompany you upstairs, and we'll continue where we left off."

"For the second time today. This can't go on, Kian. We are like a couple of horny teenagers who can't keep their hands off each other."

"What's wrong with that? I think it's great."

"Because you have important work to do, you big lug. And frankly, although playing nookie with you is super fun, I'm wasting my time here. Anyone with basic computer skills could be doing my job."

"Don't you dare quit on me. For the first time that I can remember, I'm looking forward to my workday."

"What workday? You are not doing any work. Admit it, even when Shai is here, all you do is think about the next time he leaves so you can have your hands on me."

Kian ran his fingers through his chin-length hair, brushing it back. "I can't help it. Having you near me all day long is a temptation I can't resist. I'm just a simple man with simple needs. In fact, just one, you."

He was so sweet. "I love you, and I feel the same. But we are both adults with adult responsibilities. My time would be better spent helping Amanda find more Dormants. And you could actually accomplish something during the hours you spend here."

"I don't want to." He crossed his arms over his chest, pouting like a toddler.

She caressed his cheek. "I know, my love. How about this, you bring in another assistant, someone young who will modernize your ancient record keeping and help you finish your work in less time. I'll work with Amanda, but only until four in the afternoon. That way we'll still have plenty of time to spend with each other."

"What about the other stuff I need to do, besides office work? Like showing my face at meetings and classes, and visiting with people in my official capacity."

"I'll come with you to those."

"Okay, you won. But I don't like it."

"I know, neither do I. But it's for the best. Besides, it's not like it's carved in stone. If it doesn't work, we can reevaluate and make changes. Now let me go so I can pull my pants up. I've been sitting here bare-assed for far too long."

Kian helped her up and tugged her jeans back into place.

"Yikes, I hate wearing wet panties."

His smile was conceited. "Let's go. You can take them off in our private elevator. We have some unfinished business to take care of."

5

AMANDA

"So, what do you think?" Amanda crossed her arms over her chest.

"This bedroom is definitely better than the one facing the side of the building." Ingrid pushed the second layer of drapery aside. "If we position the easel next to the window, our resident artist will have plenty of natural light to draw by. We can knock out the dividing wall between this and the adjoining room, to give him more space."

Dalhu was in need of a studio, or rather Amanda was.

Her living room was a mess. With all kinds of drawings, completed and in various stages of progress, propped against the walls and couches and the coffee table. Soon, Dalhu would be spilling his mess into the dining room. Not to mention that there had been charcoal smears on her designer throw pillows before Onidu had rushed to hide the evidence, somehow managing to remove the stains and return her beautiful pillows to their previous pristine condition.

It seemed that her emotionless butler had taken a liking to Dalhu.

Figures, even a biomechanical creation and an ex-Doomer were doing the male bonding thing.

But the mess and the charcoal dust weren't the worst of it. A number of her clansmen were waiting in line for Dalhu to draw their portraits, and some had requested a full body nude. Well, just one. Anandur.

At first, she'd thought he was joking, but he'd kept nagging about it, and today he came over, thankfully posing only half naked. She could deal with him shirtless, but she drew the line there. Anandur's junk on full display wasn't something she wanted to see, which would be hard to avoid with Anandur posing for Dalhu in the middle of her living room.

Our living room...

Damn, after almost two centuries of living practically alone, it was one hell of an adjustment to live with someone other than Onidu. Having to be considerate, accommodating...

To keep the façade going twenty-four-seven.

It was such an ingrained habit that she just couldn't drop it no matter how hard she tried.

She kept telling herself that it wasn't needed, that Dalhu loved her unconditionally, and that he didn't expect her to act upbeat and smile all of the time. But it was no use. Wherever she had an audience, even if only of one, Amanda felt compelled to put on a performance.

She sighed. Small steps, one little thing at a time.

"What else do we need here?"

"Shouldn't you ask Dalhu what he wants?"

"Nah, he wouldn't know. It's not as if he has ever set foot into an art studio. And anyway, I want it to be a surprise."

"I was wondering where he was. What have you done with him?"

"I had Anandur take him down to the gym for a workout. After all, we can't have all those amazing muscles atrophy, can we?" She winked at Ingrid.

"Certainly not. The guy is such eye candy…"

"Watch it." Amanda pointed her finger at the covetous designer. "He is mine. Eyes and hands off."

Ingrid laughed. "Yes, ma'am. But you need to hurry up and find more male Dormants for us because there is talk among the girls of going down to the catacombs and reviving us some Doomers."

"You are joking, right?"

"Give it a little time and the joking will turn into doing. I'm not kidding. Some of us are green with envy."

"Listen, Ingrid, tell your horny friends to forget about it. Dalhu is the one and probably only exception to what we know is a typical Doomer. Should I remind you what we are dealing with? Brainwashed murderers who thrive on death and suffering. Minions of evil who will target a preschool and laugh with glee when children are blown up. That's what Doomers are. Tell them."

Damn, her outburst had gotten her so worked up that she needed a drink to calm down. "I'm going to make myself a margarita, do you want one too? Or are you in the mood for something stronger?"

"A margarita is fine." Ingrid followed her to the living room. "I'll send a couple of guys to clear that bedroom. Just tell me when is a good time."

Amanda mixed the two drinks and handed Ingrid hers. "Tomorrow, same time. I convinced Anandur that he needs to take Dalhu to the gym every day. My guy will go crazy if he stays cooped up here."

"Good deal. I'm going to do a little Internet search to see what he needs. Do you want me to run it by you? Or are you okay with me just going ahead and ordering whatever I see fit?"

"I don't want to waste time, just pick the most expensive stuff. You can't go wrong with that."

"Sweet, I like an open-ended budget." Ingrid took her drink for a walkabout to check out Dalhu's various creations. She stopped in front of the large canvas Dalhu was currently working on as a wedding present for Syssi and Kian. "Oh, wow. This is gorgeous. I didn't know Syssi posed for him in her wedding dress."

Amanda snorted. "Right, as if Kian would have been okay with her posing for a *Doomer*. Heck, the Doomer thing is secondary. He wouldn't want any male looking at her for a prolonged period of time let alone drawing her. Dalhu is using one of the wedding photos. His next one will be of them together at the altar with Annani presiding over the ceremony. Here, let me show you."

Amanda walked over to the media cabinet and pulled out a small wedding album, one of the hundreds that had been sent to every guest at the wedding. She flipped to the right page and showed it to Ingrid.

Ingrid sighed and put a hand over her chest. "They are so in love. Just look at how they gaze at each other as if nothing else exists. I want that."

"I'm working on it." *Not really.* For some reason, Amanda was reluctant to go back to the paranormal research without Syssi, the traitor who had abandoned her to go work for Kian. And anyway, Amanda was so behind on her formal research that she'd decided it was more important to catch up on that and not stress herself out by trying to do too much at once.

And as to working overtime? Forget it. She wasn't about to stay longer than was absolutely necessary when there was a hunk of a man waiting for her at home.

Priorities, priorities. Amanda first, the rest of the world second.

"What are you going to do with Syssi and Kian's portraits?"

"They are a present from Dalhu to Kian. A thank you for not making too much of a fuss over us moving up here. We were expecting a war when Kian came back from his honeymoon, but, apparently, the vacation had done him good, and he was in an uncharacteristically agreeable mood. Or perhaps it was all the sex. But in any case, all we got was a frown. And a cuff. William engineered a special contraption for Dalhu."

"I'm almost afraid to ask. Is it some kind of detonation device that is triggered if Dalhu tries to leave the building?"

Ingrid was such a weirdo.

"No, silly, you read too many suspense novels. There are no explosives in the cuff, but there is a transmitter that interferes with cellular signal. Dalhu can only use a landline, and as you know, all of them go through security."

Ingrid looked disappointed. "Oh."

"Of course, Dalhu couldn't care less. It's not like he has anyone he wants to call."

Well, it wasn't entirely true. He called her at work, about every thirty minutes—to tell her how much he loved her.

6

ANDREW

*A*fter work, Andrew headed to the keep—but picking Bhathian up to go see his daughter would have to wait. Kian had called for a meeting to discuss what to do about Alex.

Fuck this goddamned traffic.

He was supposed to be there at quarter to six, but with the offices occupying most of the real estate in the less than six square mile area spewing out their employees at this time of day, downtown Los Angeles was one big fucking parking lot.

For some reason, it brought to mind an image of a flooded giant anthill evacuating tens of thousands of its little workers. Except, in this case, each ant was driving away in its own car.

Damn, why the hell had Kian picked the worst neighborhood, as far as traffic jams that is, for his fucking keep?

And it wasn't as if there were great views or anything else for that matter to recommend the place.

Just a concrete jungle, and a small one at that.

He could never understand the rich idiots who spent millions of dollars to live in a crappy Manhattan apartment with windows overlooking the next high rise building. Andrew's home had cost just a couple of hundred thousand dollars when he'd bought it, had a large yard, and the windows were not looking into his neighbors' homes.

As he finally made it down into the building's parking structure, he wished there was a valet he could leave the car with, but, of course, there was no such thing. Andrew cursed as he drove in circles down to the clan's private level. When he got all the way down, the bloody garage door blocking the entrance took forever to open as he waited for the sensor to communicate with the sticker on his windshield. The only good news was that once it finally did, he found plenty of spots available.

Wheels squealing in protest, Andrew skidded into one, threw the gearshift into park, and got out. Slamming the door behind him, he practically ran all the way to Kian's office, hoping not to be the last one.

Damn, he hated to walk into a room full of people who he had kept waiting.

But as he got there, he saw through the glass doors that everyone was already there: Onegus, William, Anandur, and, of course, Kian.

He pushed inside. "Sorry, guys. I swear, one of these days that goddamned traffic is going to give me an aneurysm." He grabbed one of the chairs surrounding the conference table and brought it to face Kian's desk.

Rapping his fingers on its surface, Kian tilted his head and lifted one corner of his mouth in a sardonic smile. "There is an easy solution and a tough one. The easy one is you quit working for Uncle Sam and come work for us full time, therefore, no more nasty commute. The other is you grow a set and attempt the transition, after which heart attacks and aneurysms will no longer be a concern."

Andrew unbuttoned his blazer and sat down. "If I quit my government work, I will no longer have access to the shitloads of information you find so valuable. And if I go for the transition and end up dead, we both lose, again. I'd rather live with the traffic and take my chances with my fragile human heart."

At his age, going for the transition was an iffy proposition at best. The only two other examples the clan had of turning adult Dormants were Michael, who was no more than twenty years old and had handled it with no problem, and Syssi, who was not yet twenty-six and almost hadn't made it at all.

So yeah, he'd rather live out his short human life than reach for the pie in the sky and drop dead.

"Can't argue with your logic." Onegus grimaced and clapped Andrew's shoulder.

"I don't know." William shook his head and shifted in his chair, readjusting his bulk to get more comfortable. Andrew could've sworn that William had gotten fatter since the last time he'd seen him, which was just a little over two weeks ago. The guy needed to cut down on the amount of junk he was eating. "If it were me, I would go for it and the sooner the better. Every day you procrastinate is another day your body ages. It would only get worse."

"I concur." Anandur winked. "There are a number of ladies who'd be very happy to get their hands on a new immortal male. You're missing out, buddy."

Anandur could stuff his opinion up his ass, but William had a point. Still, this meeting was supposed to be about Alex, and not about Andrew gaining immortality by attempting suicide.

"Okay, guys, that's enough about me. How 'bout we move on to the purpose of this chatty get-together."

"The private investigator that I hired to watch the boat has been scratching his balls for the past two weeks, observing absolutely nothing. The boat stays moored at Marina Del Rey, and Alex hasn't visited even once. His Russian crew comes and goes, but none of them bring any friends aboard, male or female. I think we need to come up with a new strategy. Unless, you think that we need to wait until something happens." Kian looked at Andrew, one brow cocked in question.

"Keep the private eye there. Stakeouts are never as exciting as they are portrayed in the movies. They take time, sometimes months, and are mostly about being bored out of your mind and eating too much pizza."

"Okay, I have no problem with that, but how about upping the ante?"

"I say we go after the Russians," Anandur said as he got up and walked over to the buffet. He grabbed a pastry from the tray that had been left there, most likely by Okidu, Kian's butler.

"Bring the whole thing over here." William waved his hand, practically salivating in anticipation. Though Andrew wondered why the guy hadn't helped himself to something before. Perhaps he was one of those overweight people who were embarrassed to eat in front of others.

Anandur stuffed the pastry into his mouth, holding it with his teeth as he grabbed the long tray by the handles and brought it over to Kian's desk.

Eh, what the hell, why not. Andrew snatched a cheese Danish.

"How do you suggest we go about that?" Kian asked.

Anandur finished chewing and wiped his mouth with the back of his hand. "Easy, seduce one of the bitches."

Onegus snorted. "You volunteer?"

Anandur shrugged. "Why not? I'll do it. I'm not too picky."

"Damn right," Onegus confirmed. "I've seen some of the skanks you've been picking up."

"As if you snag only beauty queens, you pompous bastard."

"Better looking than yours, that's for sure."

William looked uncomfortable and reached for a croissant.

"Can I go now?" Andrew asked, "I have better things to do than listening to who scores with whom."

Anandur looked like he wanted to fire up a retort, but all he did was open his mouth and then close it like a fish out of water.

Kian raised his hand. "So, let me get it straight. You are going to charm the pants off one of the Russians and pump her for information. Is that what you suggest?"

"Information and otherwise." Anandur winked.

William stuffed another pastry in his mouth.

Kian leaned forward and fixed his intense blue stare on Anandur. "How?"

"You know, I'll start with a light caress." He demonstrated on his own thigh. "Move on to a feathery kiss, right here." He tilted his head and pointed to a spot on his neck.

Andrew snorted. Onegus's shoulders shook with stifled laughter. William continued munching with gusto.

Kian didn't even blink. "I meant, where are you going to meet one of them? And how are you going to introduce yourself? Who are you going to say you are?"

"Deck cleaner." Anandur pumped out his chest and smiled. "Short, frayed shorts and no shirt, a bucket of sudsy water, and a sponge. Works for next to nothing too. You think there'll be a female in the vicinity who wouldn't want a piece of this?" His hand made a sweeping motion over his chest and lower.

Onegus groaned.

Kian nodded but then turned to Andrew. "What do you think?"

Andrew shrugged. "Worth a try."

"Then it's agreed. The Russians are yours, Anandur, do your worst. Next. William, what's the status with the surveillance?"

William swallowed the last piece of the pastry he'd been eating, licked his fingers clean, and then wiped his hands on his billowing Hawaiian shirt. "The team working on the drone will need another month at least. But if Anandur is going to infiltrate enemy territory, he can plant some listening devices for us."

Great idea. Andrew should've thought of it first, but, apparently, William's quick-thinking, brilliant mind wasn't restricted only to things related to computers and electronics.

"Do you need me to get you some? But this time, you'll have to pay for them. I can't keep supplying you with government stuff. As it is, I'm already afraid of accounting coming down on my ass for appropriating too many devices. And, potentially, they can involve internal affairs."

Kian looked irate. "Of course not. You should have said something before. You know money is no object."

"I know. At the time, it was just more expedient."

"It's all taken care of," William interjected. "After you planted that one in the Doomers' rented Beverly Hills mansion, I ordered a bunch, and I am working on modifications." He turned to Anandur. "Stop by my place tomorrow. I'll have a couple ready for you."

"By the way, Andrew, what's going on over there? Anything interesting?" Kian asked.

"Dalhu's team was sent home, and the place has been rented out again. Unfortunately, it was all done without providing us with any clues about their new center of operations. They probably communicated via email, which I failed to monitor. My bad."

"Water under the bridge. We move on."

7

NATHALIE

"A cappuccino for Melanie and a latte for Daphne!" Nathalie called out.

On their way to collect their drinks, the teenagers passed by her father and giggled, exchanging hand gestures that didn't require familiarity with the American sign language to interpret.

Nathalie sighed.

Today was a particularly bad day. Not that any of them were easy. Things were just getting worse as her father's dementia progressed. But most days, he just sat in his booth, the last one in the row, mumbling to himself quietly.

Since this morning, though, Fernando had taken a turn for the worse, or the bizarre as it may be. He was loud, arguing with what seemed like a group of imaginary people, waving his hands and pointing at the air around him.

It could've been worse. She shouldn't complain. The doctors had assured Nathalie that her father's dementia was eating up his brain at a much slower rate than the norm. She was lucky that he could still recognize her and was able to control his bodily functions, which was no less important.

She had no idea what she was going to do once this grace period ended. One day at a time, it was all she could manage. Stressing about the future was a luxury she didn't have energy or time for.

Right now, the only thing she could do to calm him down was to sit down beside him and talk to him, or rather at him. It was more the sound of her voice than the words themselves that usually did the trick.

Simple enough, but a tough one to pull off without someone to help with the customers. She was the only one here, taking orders, making coffees, preparing sandwiches, and washing the dishes. Not to mention that she'd been up since four in the morning, baking today's assortment of pastries.

Damn, where the hell was Tiffany?

At first, Nathalie had thought her one and only waitress had flaked out on her. Sometimes, Tiffany would get info about an audition and in her rush and excitement forget to call and let Nathalie know.

But when yet another day passed, and the girl hadn't shown up, Nathalie called her. The phone had rang for a long time before going to Tiffany's voicemail.

Nathalie had left a message—an angry one.

A day later, Nathalie called again and left another message—a worried one this time. Perhaps, Tiffany had gotten offended, or scared by the scathing tone of her previous voicemail, and that was why she hadn't called back.

Still, she'd gotten no response.

Since then, she'd been calling every couple of hours, hoping to catch Tiffany before being sent to voicemail. She had even borrowed a customer's cell phone, hoping Tiffany would pick up a call from an unknown number thinking it was about one of her auditions.

She'd gotten the damn recording again.

Nathalie couldn't shake the feeling that something had happened to the girl. Tiffany's address was in her employee file, so potentially she could've driven there and asked the girl's roommates what was going on. Except, what would've been easy for most anyone else, would have required a Herculean effort from her, considering the fact that she would've had to schlep her father along because there was no one she could leave him with. And leaving him alone, even for a few minutes, was a big no-no.

Whenever she needed to spend more than a moment in the bathroom, Nathalie had to lock the door from the inside and hide the key. It seemed as if Fernando was just waiting for an opportunity to run away and wander the streets.

He reminded her of a cat she'd had when she was a kid. Fritz had been a house cat who'd unfortunately refused to accept his elevated status as a beloved pet, thinking of himself as a mighty mouse hunter instead. The cat would shoot out like a rocket the moment someone opened the door.

Poor Fritz had probably ended up as a coyote snack.

Fernando would just get lost. The dog tags she had him wear at all times meant that good people would bring him back, or call her to come get him. Problem was, not everyone was good, and there were plenty of coyotes of the human kind around.

You should've put him in a home a long time ago, Tut said inside her head.

She turned her back to the pastries display and hissed, "Stop saying it. I'm never going to do it. He'll die if I do."

I know, Tut said, sounding sad, then faded away.

This was surprising; she hadn't expected him to give up so easily, or to agree. He was way more contrary than this. And it wasn't as if she herself was convinced of the veracity of her statement. Maybe an institution that specialized in dementia and Alzheimer's could actually benefit her father. But in her bones, Nathalie knew that Fernando would wither and die if she were to abandon him to some institution. He was hanging in there and doing better than other patients afflicted with the same disease because he was with her, surrounded by the familiar smells of baked goods and seeing new faces every day.

So yeah, it was tough, and she didn't have much of a life, but she was all he had, and he was all she had.

Well, other than Tut.

She wondered where her ghost, or rather the figment of her own malfunctioning brain, went when he wasn't bugging her. Was there some other dimension where ghosts and figments hung out together?

He must be lonely if there wasn't.

The only good thing about her quitting college and coming back to take care of her father was her semi-liberation from Tut. Her cerebral roommate was bored out of existence—his words—with her new life. So much so that he didn't want to hang around. Much. Luckily, he still kept enough of a presence to keep the other voices at bay.

Thinking of what would've happened if Tut had left her permanently, Nathalie shuddered. As annoying as he was, having to endure just one voice was infinitely better than the onslaught she'd suffered before he'd come to her rescue and stayed, appointing himself the guardian of the gateway to her brain and holding back all the other voices clamoring to be heard.

You're welcome.

Don't let it get to your head. You're only the lesser evil, doesn't mean that you're good.

Everything in life is a compromise, my dear.

And in death?

She heard his laugh as he began fading. *Nice try, Nattie.*

Argh, she could've strangled him if he were real. The annoying jerk never answered any questions about the other side. Using that nickname had been his way of getting back at her for asking. He knew how much she detested it.

Nutty Nattie had been buried six feet under, together with all the other unpleasant memories from high school.

College had been good. No one had known her, and she had done her damnedest not to get caught talking to herself. Occasionally she'd still slipped, especially when Tut was goading her, talking nasty about any guy she'd found attractive. But she'd managed to hide it, always having a set of earphones in her ears as camouflage. If someone had seen her talking to no one, they'd assumed she was mouthing the words of a song she was listening to.

Cellphones and Bluetooth had been a godsend. Everyone looked as if they were nuts.

"Thank you. Goodbye." The teenagers waved and stepped outside, the small bells she'd hung on the door clanging when it opened and then again as it closed. It was a precaution, in case her father tried to sneak out behind her back.

Damn, what was she, the Bermuda Triangle that people around her kept disappearing?

Her mother had been missing for six long years. But despite the pitying looks from the police detective who had been assigned to the case, Nathalie refused to accept that Eva was dead. She had to believe her mother was alive somewhere and had a damn good reason for not getting in touch with her only daughter or at least letting her know that she was alive. Though the only excuse Nathalie would find acceptable was that Eva had been suffering from amnesia.

And now Tiffany. But Nathalie didn't dare file another missing person's report. First of all, the girl might be perfectly fine and had just quit without notice. And second, if she reported another person missing, the police might start suspecting her of foul play.

Nathalie chuckled. They'd think she was doing away with people.

She noticed it had become quiet in the shop and glanced at her father. He'd stopped arguing with his phantoms and was conducting a quiet and civilized conversation with just one.

Funny, how she could relate. Though, in her case, she couldn't blame dementia. When Fernando had first started showing signs of hallucinating, she'd been sure that he was suffering from the same thing she did, and even tried to find out more about his apparitions. But she'd soon realized that what he was seeing and hearing was very different. His imaginary people had no names and didn't stick around—just random phantoms.

At the moment, they were alone in the coffee shop, and she walked over to his booth and sat down.

"Hello, my love." Fernando leaned and kissed her cheek. "You are as beautiful as ever."

It took her a second to realize he thought she was Eva. She took his hand. "It's me, Papi, Nathalie."

The fog clouding his eyes receded, and for a moment, they looked lucid as he regarded her. "Yes, of course you are, my Nathalie. Who else has a voice of an angel?"

She smiled at him through the tears prickling the back of her eyes. "Nobody, only your Nathalie." It was the answer she'd been giving him since she learned how to talk.

"That's right, my sweet little girl, Nathalie."

8

BHATHIAN

For a guy who was rarely motivated to look at his own reflection, Bhathian was spending a hell of a lot of time in front of his fucking bathroom mirror.

Not that what was staring back at him showed much improvement, despite his best efforts.

After his morning workout, he'd stopped by Anandur's barber and had gotten a trim and a good shave. Regrettably, the change was marginal.

He looked like a surly son of a bitch. Or worse.

People still crossed over to the other side of the street when they got a gander of him, and he could still clear a supermarket's aisle faster than an announcement of a free giveaway at the checkout counter. You'd think he was an ogre who ate babies for breakfast or something.

Not a charmer, that was for sure, but he wasn't all that bad either. In fact, he was a pretty decent guy, if he did say so himself.

Trouble was, he brooded—he was the-glass-is-half-empty kind of guy. Hell, the thing was more like three-quarters empty.

He couldn't understand all those bloody optimists who pretended not to see the crap around them, supergluing pink-colored shades on top of their upturned noses to obscure reality. As if everything was going to be okay with the world because they believed it, and if they didn't see the crap it didn't exist.

Lucky bastards.

He wished he could pretend like shit didn't happen. But as someone who had to swim in it time and again to fix the mess, he couldn't.

The lingering foul smell wouldn't let him.

The humans, he could understand. Their lives were short and their memories even shorter. Atrocities that had happened more than twenty years ago were a distant memory that didn't impact them emotionally, and those committed a century or more ago were completely forgotten.

Turning blind eyes and deaf ears to shit that wasn't promoted by the media was so damn easy. If it wasn't shoved down their throats because it served the agenda of someone who was willing to pay to have it in the spotlight, they had no reason to look elsewhere for much more disturbing crap.

Obliviousness was bliss.

But the same couldn't be said about his fellow near immortals, most of whom were on the-glass-is-half-full team. And the one with the biggest fucking set of pink-colored glasses was none other than their clan mother, the only surviving full-blooded goddess, Annani. How the hell could someone as ancient as she remain the quintessential optimist after all she'd been through? Annani had not only witnessed humanity's bloody history first hand, but had had the love of her life murdered by a fellow god, the insane Mordth. And if that hadn't been enough to crush her spirit for good, the fucker had launched a nuclear attack against the other gods in order to avoid prosecution for his crime, wiping out all of her people including, unintentionally, himself.

And yet, if you asked her, things were getting better. There were the occasional setbacks caused by Mordth's vengeful followers, like a Dark Age or two, but the overall trajectory was positive. Annani was convinced that her clan and their positive influence on humanity's progress was winning the long-term war against the destructive power of the *Devout Order Of Mordth*.

Bhathian suspected that Mordth's son and successor, Navuh, had a different view of things. The Doomers' fucking leader had managed to breed an army of immortal warriors that was ten thousand strong. Not to mention his *little* side business that was helping finance his nefarious activities—the brothel he'd built on some godforsaken island in the Indian Ocean.

Fuck, now he had gotten himself all worked up, and the face staring back at him from the mirror looked like it belonged to a serial killer. Bhathian wondered if it was too late to ask Kri or Bridget to do something about his bushy brows.

Perhaps, with the unibrow tamed by a pair of scissors, he could look less threatening.

Or better yet, he could try to get rid of the frown.

His phone buzzed, and he pulled it out of his pocket.

"You're coming up, or I'm coming down?" he asked Andrew.

"I've just finished with Kian. Come down to the parking garage."

"On my way." He clicked off and stuffed the thing back in his pocket.

Standing in front of the mirrored wall of the elevator, he practiced releasing the frown and even tried to smile. He better not. Instead of just a normal, run-of-the-mill killer, the fake smile made him look like an insane one.

He shrugged and adjusted the collar of his white button-down, then re-tucked it in his jeans. Should he keep the second button open? Or close it?

Why was he obsessing? It wasn't important. It wasn't as if he was going to go up to his daughter and introduce himself. All he planned to do was sit somewhere in her coffee shop where he could look at her without her noticing it and listen to her voice as she interacted with her customers. Andrew would provide the cover, pretending to talk to him from time to time so she wouldn't grow suspicious.

When the ping announced that he'd reached the parking level, Bhathian closed his eyes and took a deep breath.

Man up, asshole. You were stressing less heading out to battle.

As he got out, Andrew was waiting by his car. "Nice shirt. You look good." He offered his hand.

"Yeah, I bet." Bhathian shook what was offered.

"How about presentable, better?"

"At least it sounds as if it could be honest. I don't need a pep talk."

"Wasn't giving any." Andrew opened the door to his Ford Explorer and got behind the wheel.

As Bhathian walked over to the other side and folded himself into the passenger seat, he couldn't help but notice that unlike his own car, which was littered with empty In-n-out paper bags, crushed coke cans, and ripped candy bar wrappers, this one was spotless. The car's interior looked like it was brand new or had very recently gone through a detailing service.

"Your government provides car-washing services?"

"No, I do." Andrew backed up the car and drove up to the garage door which began sliding open.

"Impressive."

Andrew cast him a sidelong glance. "I like to keep it clean."

"As I said, impressive. Mine looks like a pigsty."

"Oh, yeah? What do you do when you need to pick up a lady friend to go on a date?"

Bhathian snorted. "What lady friend?"

"I thought all of you immortals needed lots of sex."

"We do, but it has nothing to do with ladies or friends."

Andrew rolled his eyes as he waited for a car to pass him by so he could pull into traffic. "And to think they let you teach the sex-ed class."

What the hell was that supposed to mean? Bhathian rubbed his clean-shaven chin. "Did I say something wrong?"

Andrew sighed as if he was explaining things to a clueless teenager. "Every woman who you hook up with, even if it is for only one night, deserves to be called a lady friend. Not a piece of ass, not a pussy, or any of the other creative substitutes men use. Language has power, and to think in these terms erodes your respect for women. True?"

Bhathian crossed his arms over his chest. "You keep forgetting how old I am; that's why you got it all wrong. When you say a lady, I see in my head a British matron fanning herself because she's stuffed into a too-tight corset and can't breathe. Fates know I've never hooked up with one of those. And as to friends, I'm very picky about who I regard as one."

"My apologies. I hope you still think of me as a friend."

Bhathian put a hand over his heart as he turned to look at Andrew. "For as long as I have breath in my lungs and blood in my veins."

Andrew seemed taken aback. "It sounds like a pledge."

"It is, and I do not offer it lightly."

9

ANDREW

Touching, but he hadn't done enough to deserve the guy's unending gratitude. The few hours of work he had dedicated to the search were a far cry from the kind of service that qualified for such a solemn pledge. After all, he hadn't sacrificed anything for Bhathian or rescued some relative of his from certain death.

But he wasn't about to tell the guy that finding his daughter wasn't enough of a big deal to warrant his heartfelt thanks. Obviously, for Bhathian it was.

When Andrew got off the freeway, Bhathian turned to him. "I forgot to ask you the name of her place."

"Fernando's Bakery and Café."

"That's the name of her adoptive father?"

"Yeah. Keep an eye out for the sign, it should be somewhere around here." Andrew turned into South Jonson Street.

At seven in the evening, the various shops and Cafés were still open, and judging by the number of cars parked along the street business was good.

"That one is leaving." Bhathian pointed toward a white Honda.

Andrew got behind it and waited for the driver to ease into traffic.

"You ready?" He turned to Bhathian as he parked.

The guy nodded and wiped his hands on his jeans before reaching for the door handle.

Andrew locked things up, and they hit the pavement together, walking at a measured speed that was neither fast nor slow. It must have been a hell of an effort for Bhathian, who Andrew had no doubt itched to march ahead. But even at a casual stroll, the big man was attracting attention and not in a good way. Conversations halted, and people moved out of his way, their steps getting just a bit longer and faster as they tried not to be obvious about their unexplained urgency to increase their distance from him.

Casting a sidelong glance at his companion, Andrew wondered what was so scary about Bhathian that he was provoking such strong reactions. He was well dressed, with his plain white dress shirt tucked into jeans that weren't drooping. And the guy had no tattoos or piercings. True, he was a big guy, about six four or five, with the body build of a professional wrestler, but so was Dwayne Johnson and yet people loved him. If the ex-wrestler turned movie star were to show up on the street, there would be a stampede of girls trying to get to him and not away from him. But the big difference between The Rock and Bhathian was Dwayne's big, friendly smile, as opposed to the immortal's angry scowl.

Andrew couldn't blame people for wanting to get away from a surly son of a bitch who looked like he could lift cars. A guy this size in a bad mood was bad news.

"You should try to smile more."

"Sure about that?" The dude's grimace of a smile was way worse than his scowl.

"Maybe not."

Andrew shook his head. He'd thought that accompanying Bhathian would soften the guy's impact, but it wasn't working. Probably because Andrew's presence didn't provide a strong enough contrast. True, he was shorter and less muscular than the hulking guy, but he was still over six feet tall and far from harmless. The scars on his face, although old and faded, betokened a life of violence.

Fuck, they'd better cut their visit short. With the two of them sitting in her café and scaring customers away, Nathalie would lose sales she couldn't afford to.

"Ready?" he asked Bhathian as they reached the place.

"Yeah, but you better do all the talking. I'm not good at that."

"Sure thing."

Andrew pushed the door open, and the jingling of the little bells hanging over it on the inside announced their arrival. As the few customers sitting inside the café glanced their way, their expressions changed from mild curiosity to alarm.

A moment later Nathalie emerged from what must have been the kitchen with a tray of freshly baked croissants.

The resemblance to her mother was striking. Hell, everything about her was. Andrew, who was supposed to do the talking, was rendered momentarily mute.

She put the tray down and took off the oven mitts before taking her place behind the counter.

She smiled at Bhathian and him, her lovely face showing none of the alarm her customers displayed. "Hello, what could I interest you in, gentlemen?"

Oh, boy, that deep and smooth voice of hers was doing unseemly things to his male anatomy, which was doubly embarrassing since he was standing next to her father. Mercifully, he'd headed to the keep straight from the office and hadn't changed out of what he'd worn to work—his reaction was well hidden under his blazer.

And yet, even though he knew better, he had the absurd impulse to reply *you*. Instead, he tugged at his necktie that suddenly felt too tight, then blurted out, "Coffee, two, for me and my friend."

She entered their order on her register. "Anything to go with your coffees?

I've just taken this batch of chocolate croissants out of the oven." She pointed to the tray she'd put on top of the counter to take their order. "There is nothing like eating them when they are hot—when the chocolate is still melted, and the crust is so flaky that it melts in your mouth." Her tone turned husky and suggestive as if she was talking about something completely different, and yet he was certain that it wasn't intentional. For some reason, Nathalie projected an innocence befitting someone much younger.

"Sure," he said, though she could've offered him yesterday's stale donuts and he would've responded the same.

She smiled again, and he noticed that her teeth were incredibly white. "How many would you like?"

"I'll have three." Bhathian found his voice.

Her smile got even wider. "And you?"

"The same."

Now her smile reached all the way to her beautiful brown eyes. "Big boys with big appetites. I like it." She leaned forward and whispered, "Not like all those health freaks who count every calorie." She winked, her incredibly long lashes fanning over her peach-colored cheek.

Up close, he saw that her perfect complexion wasn't the product of a clever makeup job, and the dark lashes outlining her almond-shaped eyes were not only long but also dense. If he weren't standing so close to her, he would've thought that they were fake—the kind some women glued on for special occasions. But hers were a gift from Mother Nature.

Regretfully, Nathalie's thick, dark hair was pulled back away from her face. Andrew wondered how long it was. He would've loved to see the thick waves cascading around her slim shoulders.

His question was answered when she turned and bent down to grab a pair of metal tongs from inside the display, and the heavy braid fell forward, almost brushing the floor. When loose, her hair probably reached her behind.

Using the tongs to lift the still steaming croissants from the tray, she put them on two small plates and handed them to Bhathian and him. "Here you go, and I'll bring your coffees to your table."

Andrew was very careful to take it without touching her hand, not because of some outdated notion of propriety, but because he was afraid of his reaction.

There was something special about Nathalie that affected him on a whole different level. Without her intent or even knowledge, she had planted her metaphorical hooks so deep inside him that frankly, he was weirded out.

10

NATHALIE

There was something strange about these two, but she couldn't put her finger on what it was. Nothing alarming. On the contrary, they exuded strength and confidence in the same way firefighters did. Their presence was reassuring.

The very tall one looked to be in his late twenties or early thirties, but she had her eye on the older one, a sexy man in his late thirties. If she had to guess his occupation based on what he was wearing, he was either a real-estate agent or a police detective.

Hardly anyone else still wore a tie and blazer to work.

But given the small scar over his left brow and the one on his chin, the latter was more likely.

What was strange, though, was that Tut didn't come barging in with his nasty commentary the way he'd always done whenever she had naughty thoughts about a guy. And she was definitely having them about this one.

His lips in particular... and his hands...

God, to have a man like him kiss her with that cruel yet soft looking mouth, to have him hold her to him with those strong, calloused hands...

Stop it! She needed to banish these thoughts, fast, before not only embarrassing herself by blushing like a ripe tomato but summoning the annoying voice in her head.

Perfecting her friendly yet uninterested act, she was often able to fool Tut along with the guys who flirted with her. It wasn't that she didn't want to respond, but she could never say yes, even to those she would have loved to—like this one. Because what was the point? It wasn't as if she could go on a date with anyone.

Mr. Sexy's younger friend was a huge man, with a pair of shoulders that had barely made it through her shop's front door, and a rugged face that was nevertheless very handsome.

She should have felt intimidated by his sheer size, but she wasn't. For some inexplicable reason, he made her feel safe. Not that she'd been fearful before—well, except the worry about what might have happened to Tiffany... and the old one about her mother. But as for herself, she had a sense that while this man was around, he wouldn't let anything bad happen to her. He was the kind of guy who you wanted by your side when shit happened.

It was almost palpable, the aura of a capable fighter, and one who she instinctively knew fought for the good side. Perhaps he was a Marine or a soldier in some other elite military unit. But one thing was for sure, despite his rough looks, he wasn't a thug.

Without asking how much, he pulled out a wallet from his back pocket and handed her a couple of twenties. But his friend stayed his hand.

"No, this time, it's my turn." He pulled out his own wallet and handed her a MasterCard.

She saw right through him. The only reason he offered to pay was that he wanted her to see his name on the card.

"Andrew Spivak," she read out loud and could've sworn that he blushed. But the slight flush had come and gone so fast she wasn't sure.

"Now that you know my name, could I have yours?"

Bingo. I was right.

"Nathalie Vega, very nice to meet you, Andrew." She extended her hand for a handshake.

For a split moment, he looked at her offered hand as if he didn't know what to do about it. But then, a determined expression slid over his handsome face, and he took it, closing his large calloused hand around hers.

"The pleasure is all mine, Nathalie."

As he clasped her hand for a long moment, his eyes holding hers captive, she felt something pass between them—a sort of subliminal communication that was electrifying and tantalizing.

Futile, because nothing could ever come of it.

She pulled out her hand from his grasp, and the loss of contact left her feeling bereft. "Please, choose any booth you like. It's self-seating. I'll brew you guys a fresh pot of coffee and bring it to your table once it's ready." She was well aware that she was talking too much and too fast, but she couldn't help it. She wanted him to go away so she could regain her equilibrium.

"Thank you," the other one said as Andrew just kept staring. "And if we're already doing introductions, I'm Bhathian." He extended a hand that was the size of her oven mitt.

"Nice to meet you, Bhathian." This time, as she shook the hand she was offered Nathalie only felt warmth and strength at the contact. He closed his huge hand around hers very gently, even though she had no doubt it was powerful enough to crush it with minimal effort.

"Bhathian, I've never heard the name before. Where is it from?"

He smiled and his chest inflated with pride. "Scottish." Bhathian exaggerated the accent. "It means ruler of army."

She could just imagine him in a kilt and hose, leading an army of Highlanders into battle. "Very fitting, it's perfect for you."

His smile broadened. "My mum thought so when she named me. She said I looked exactly like my father."

"Do you?"

"Do I what?"

"Look like your father?"

"Oh…" He rubbed his hand over his neck. "I don't know, never met the old bastard—" He slapped his forehead. "Forgive me, I forgot my manners."

It seemed Bhathian's embarrassed apology had shaken Andrew out from his trance, and he chuckled.

She laughed. "That's okay, I hear much worse in here on a daily basis." She leaned forward and whispered, "Sometimes, I even do it myself."

Bhathian looked relieved, even happy. "That's my gi…"—he stopped himself mid-word—"not that you are mine or anything, I just meant good for you."

"Come on." Andrew tugged on Bhathian's enormous bicep, "let's go before you put your foot in your mouth.'

The guy followed his friend. "Why the hell would I put a foot in my mouth?"

"It's just an expression, big guy."

Bhathian answered something, but she didn't hear what it was. The jingling bells were announcing the arrival of new customers she had to attend to.

11

ANDREW

Fuck, he handled the situation just great. It was a sad day for Andrew Spivak when Bhathian was doing all the talking because the amazing Andrew was fumbling for words.

Damn, this was the second time in his adult life when he'd felt like a stupid teenager again. The first had been when Syssi had introduced him to Amanda. It had taken him a while to get over the impact of her preternatural beauty. Andrew had felt overwhelmed, even intimidated, but eventually he'd recovered enough to conduct a decent conversation with his sister's stunning boss.

The second time was today.

Problem was, he was damn sure it wasn't going to get better any time soon with Nathalie, and once she delivered their coffees he would be rendered stupid again and would have nothing interesting or flirty to say.

Not that flirting with Bhathian's daughter was such a hot idea.

Fathers had peculiar attitudes about their grown daughters. And aggravating someone who could crush him like a bug was not smart.

"You did good," he told the guy. "I was surprised. You've waited to see her for no good reason. You didn't need me after all."

"No, I'm glad I waited. I would have been too afraid of saying the wrong thing. I opened my mouth only because you were having trouble."

"Sorry, I don't know what happened to me."

Bhathian hiked one bushy brow. "Yes, you do. I know my Nathalie is beautiful, and you're just a human male. I understand, and it's fine by me."

"Really? So if I asked her out on a date, you wouldn't mind?"

"Nope. But no hands, or I break them like twigs." He pulled a straw out of the dispenser and demonstrated.

Was he joking? Or was he serious? It was hard to tell with the guy. Though Andrew had to admit that he'd never seen Bhathian in a better mood. So maybe he was joking.

"What if I marry her? What then? Don't you want to become a granddaddy?"

Bhathian grimaced, some of his good mood evaporating. "Hypothetically speaking, if you end up marrying my daughter, I will not ask questions I don't want to hear the answers to."

Andrew laughed. "This conversation stays between us. If anyone we know overheard us talking like a couple of teenage girls, we would become the laughing stock of the keep."

Bhathian frowned. "I don't get what's funny about it."

"For both of us, it's our first encounter with Nathalie, and here we are discussing a wedding, if not like teenagers then like a couple of yentas. I don't know if she even likes me."

"She likes you."

"How do you know? Your experience with ladies? Or assumptions about a daughter that you've just met."

"Shh... she's coming."

Andrew clamped his mouth shut and tilted his head toward the aisle. Bhathian must have heard something with that freaky immortal hearing of his, because sitting with his back to the front he couldn't have seen her coming out from behind the counter.

Watching her sashaying toward their table, holding a tray loaded with their coffees and a tall glass of orange juice, Andrew swallowed. The lady had booty and then some, flaring out from a tiny waist and gently tapering down into generous hips and shapely thighs. And as she walked, those fabulous assets swayed from side to side in a most enticing way.

She wasn't wearing the apron she'd had on before, and behind the tray she was carrying, he glimpsed part of a breast stretching her black T-shirt. Clearly, Nathalie wasn't as endowed on top as she was on the bottom. Not that it detracted from her attractiveness in any way—Andrew considered himself an ass man.

Besides, the woman was a knockout by any guy's standards.

She stopped next to another booth first and placed the juice glass together with a napkin and a magazine in front of its lone occupant. "Here you go, Papi. I brought juice and your newspaper," she said, her tone conveying affection.

So this is Fernando, her adoptive father.

"Thank you, my sweet Nathalie," the older man said.

"You're welcome." She patted his shoulder and turned toward them, her sad smile lingering for a moment before turning bright for them.

"Two freshly-brewed coffees for Mr. Bhathian and Mr. Andrew." She placed the cups in front of each one as she said his name, then glanced at their plates and frowned. "You guys better eat these croissants before they get cold." She removed from the tray two individually sized creamer containers and placed them next to the cups.

"Yes, ma'am." Andrew saluted with two fingers, then picked up one flakey croissant off his plate. The thing was still warm, and as he lifted it to his lips, Nathalie's eyes followed his hand, staying glued to his mouth while he took a bite and chewed.

Andrew wasn't faking his reaction when he closed his eyes and moaned. It was so good that it was decadent.

"This is amazing," he overlooked good manners as he mumbled with a full mouth.

The satisfied look on Nathalie's face was worth it.

"Try it." She motioned to Bhathian, and he quickly obeyed, lifting the pastry and biting off half of it in one go.

Nathalie waited patiently until he finished chewing and swallowed, then dabbed his lips with a napkin.

Surprisingly, the brute had table manners.

"The best I've ever tasted," he agreed with Andrew. "What time do you usually bake them? I plan on stopping by every day and buying a few, or a dozen, from now on."

Sly, sly, Bhathian.

Andrew would've never expected the guy to come up with the perfect excuse for hanging around Nathalie's shop on a daily basis. But this was so good that he jumped on it as well. "You got yourself two new loyal customers. I will be joining him."

Nathalie couldn't have looked happier if they had just told her that she'd won the lottery. "I'm glad. Though if you keep your promise, I'm going to have you sample some of the other pastries. These are not even my best."

Andrew faked shock. "Noo…it can't be…"

She laughed. "The only way to find out is to try. Do you guys live nearby?"

Okay, it was time to twist the truth a little, and Andrew signaled to Bhathian to leave it to up him. "No, but we work together on a project in the area."

She moved the tray to her other side and propped it on her hip. "Oh, yeah? What kind of project?"

Andrew winked and leaned closer. "If I told you, I'd have to kill you," he said in a whisper.

Nathalie seemed unfazed. "So I guessed right, you're a police detective."

Andrew pretended defeat. "What gave me away?"

"The tie and jacket…and the scars," she added the last part hesitantly. "Don't get me wrong, you're very handsome, and they are barely noticeable, it's just that they hint at a less than peaceful past."

She thinks I'm handsome—very handsome! Yes! As he stifled the urge to pump his fist, the rest of what she'd said barely registered.

"Thank you, I'm flattered."

She looked a little confused by his thanks. "Sure thing. Anyway, I'm open from eight in the morning till eight in the evening with an hour break from two to three. I bake most of the stuff early in the morning, so the best time to come is breakfast. Today was an exception. I was running low on everything and had to bake another batch."

Poor Nathalie, at this rate she would work herself into an early grave.

"Breakfast it is, consider it a date." The double entendre was intentional, and he offered his hand to seal the deal.

She smiled and shook it, sending another electric shock straight to his groin. "It's a deal. I'm about to close, so hurry up and finish your croissants. Unless you want them to go?"

Bhathian turned to look at the display up front. "What are you going to do with those?"

"There isn't much left, but I can't serve it tomorrow, so it'll go to the trash. I have a reputation of everything freshly baked."

"Then we'll take everything you have to go. The guys back at the office will love it."

She looked horrified. "I don't want you to bring these to work tomorrow—they will not be fresh anymore."

Bhathian snorted. "Don't worry about it. When I get it to the guys, they'll demolish everything in under two minutes. There won't be even a crumb left for tomorrow. We have a bunch of piranhas back there."

She nodded. "A night shift, eh?"

Bhathian shifted in his seat. "Yeah, something like that."

"Great, let me load whatever is left into a box for you."

Aside from Fernando, they were the only ones there. Quickly devouring the remaining chocolate delicacies, Andrew washed them down with the rest of the coffee. When they got up to leave, she handed Bhathian the box.

"How much do we owe you for these?" Andrew asked.

She waved her hand. "Nothing, I was just going to throw them away."

Bhathian's face went red as he handed the box to Andrew and pulled out his wallet, placing a Benjamin on the counter. "Don't even think to argue about this." He pointed a finger at her when she opened her mouth to protest.

"Yes, sir." She saluted.

Smart girl.

"Goodnight, Nathalie, we will see you tomorrow." Andrew opened the door and waited for Bhathian, who looked like he was desperate to embrace his daughter. In the end, he just stuffed his hands in his pockets.

"Goodnight, and lock the door behind us," he said as he stepped outside.

"I will. Goodnight, guys. It was really nice to meet you. I'm glad that you stumbled upon my humble establishment." She closed the door, and they both waited to hear the lock engage.

"That went surprisingly well," Andrew said when they were some distance away from the café.

"Yeah. She even seemed to like me."

Come to think of it, Nathalie reacted to Bhathian as if he was the nicest guy and not an intimidating ogre. Perhaps she'd sensed a connection between them.

But more importantly, Andrew had a feeling that she'd been just as intensely aware of him as he'd been of her.

12

SYSSI

I need to talk to you. It wasn't late, but Syssi preferred to send a text instead of calling—just in case Amanda was busy.

After all, she and Dalhu had a lot of catch-up to do, and most of it was the kind of activity that precluded answering the phone.

A text could be easily ignored and returned later.

But she didn't have to wait long. Amanda's reply came almost immediately.

I can come over.

Syssi sent back an emoji of a thumbs up.

She had expected Amanda would rather meet at her and Kian's place. Ever since Dalhu had turned their living room into a studio, Amanda had stopped inviting people. Though come to think of it, that wasn't entirely true. Syssi had seen Anandur and some of the other Guardians come and go out of Amanda's penthouse, so maybe it was only her and Kian that Amanda didn't want to entertain.

Perhaps she was afraid that Kian would make Dalhu uncomfortable.

There was something to it. Kian no longer regarded Dalhu with outward hostility, but they were far from pals.

Though in Syssi's opinion, Amanda was making a mistake. Better to go through several uncomfortable get-togethers than perpetuate the status quo. Eventually, the men would realize that they weren't as different from each other as they believed they were, and a tentative friendship could ensue.

It could be so nice; living as they did across from each other, it wouldn't require much effort or planning for the four of them to spend time together, and the interaction would enrich their lives. It was less crucial for Amanda and her—they still hung out with each other and often also with Kri, Bridget, and Ingrid—but the men were terribly isolated. Neither had social interactions with people other than their mates.

Kian preferred it this way, claiming that the little off time he had he wanted to spend with her and nobody else, but it wasn't healthy, and she intended to remedy it. From what the guys who'd attended his surprise bachelor party had told her, Kian had had a great time and had even gotten a little drunk.

Her man needed more of that.

"Knock, knock," Amanda announced as she rapped her knuckles on the door she'd already pushed open.

"Come in. Kian is not here, so you don't need to bother with knocking."

"And where is your neglectful husband?"

Syssi chuckled. "Catching up on work that wasn't done during the day because he was too busy snogging with me."

With a pout, Amanda plopped down on the couch. "So I see you guys have oodles of fun working together."

"That's what I wanted to talk to you about. But first, can I offer you coffee? Or perhaps a drink?

"Coffee."

Syssi got busy with the new automatic coffee maker, pouring fresh coffee beans into the container. From there the thing did everything by itself. It was even hooked up to the water filter, so there was no need to fill it up with water.

"How are you enjoying your Nespresso machine?" she asked Amanda.

Amanda shrugged. "It's easy to use, which makes it perfect for me, and it makes decent coffee, but nothing compared to a commercial espresso machine."

"Let's see what you think about this one."

Syssi waited for a few more seconds until the contraption finished the grinding and the tamping and the brewing and spewed the final product into two small cups.

To go with their coffees, she grabbed from the fridge the fresh apple pie Okidu had made for dessert. There was just enough left for her and Amanda.

"Do you want ice cream with your apple pie?"

"No, I'll pass."

Syssi brought the loaded tray into the living room and put it down on the coffee table.

Amanda stirred a teaspoon of brown sugar into her coffee and took a sip.

"Well? What do you think?"

The grimace didn't bode well for the new coffee maker. "It's good, for homemade, but I miss real coffee, like what they serve at Gino's or Café Milano."

"Don't you go to Gino's for lunch anymore?"

Amanda put down her coffee and picked up the plate with the apple pie. "No, and to tell you the truth, I'm sick of eating candy bars from the vending machine for lunch."

"So busy, eh?"

"No, just not in the mood to go out by myself."

Syssi stirred in the sweetener and took a sip. It was good, Amanda was just finicky, that's all. "You used to do it all the time, what happened?"

"It's different now that I'm with Dalhu. All the attention I get from guys annoys me. I'm starting to understand why Yamanu hardly ever leaves the keep."

Syssi snorted. "You poor, gorgeous people, life is so hard for you."

"Well, I'm not complaining, but it's not always fun."

"What if I come with you to lunch at Gino's, would that make it better?"

"Of course, it would. But I can't expect you to drive there every day just so that I can eat a decent lunch. After all, I can have Onidu prepare something and bring it over. Though it could be fun if we can meet there for lunch at least once in a while."

Syssi smirked. "What if I don't have to drive there?"

Amanda arched a brow. "Skyping doesn't count as company."

Since when had Amanda become so dense?

"Not like that, silly. I'm trying to tell you that I'm coming back to work at the lab."

"Really? Oh, dear Fates, thank you." Amanda blew a kiss at the ceiling. "You've just made my day. Who am I kidding, you've just made my semester." Amanda jumped up and down in her seat.

Anticipating her next move, Syssi extended her arm, just in time to get her coffee cup out of the way before Amanda lunged to give her a hug.

When she let go, she asked, "But what happened? Don't you like working with Kian?"

"I love it, and so does he, too much. Instead of helping him get more done, I'm the reason he gets almost nothing done. All he wants to do is neck and play kinky games."

Shit, did she just say it out loud? *God*, she was so stupid. Telling Amanda something like this was like waving a red rag in front of a charging bull.

Amanda's eyes widened and then narrowed. "Oh, really? How exciting and naughty... Please, do tell."

Syssi felt the heat rising and engulfing her ears. "I'll do no such thing. Our love life is private, and the last person on earth who I want to talk about it with is Kian's sister. Well, perhaps not the last, that would be my dad, and next Andrew, but after them it's you."

Amanda lifted one corner of her mouth in a half smile. "At least I'm in good company. But have no doubt"—she pointed a finger at Syssi—"I'm going to find out one way or another."

"No, you're not. Because I'm never going to tell you, and you can forget about getting anything out of Kian."

"I have my ways." Amanda made an evil face.

Was she kidding, though? Probably. Because there was no way unless she planted a listening device in their bedroom, and Syssi didn't think even Amanda could pull this off.

"When can you be at the lab?"

Thank God, Amanda let go of that embarrassing subject.

"When do you want me?"

"Tomorrow."

"Okay."

Amanda looked surprised. "Really? I was expecting you to say something like next Monday, but I'm thrilled. Now we can put the search for Dormants back on track. I haven't done any paranormal research since I went back to work. It just wasn't the same without you."

She took Syssi's hand and gave it a squeeze. "I've gotten so accustomed to you running most of those that doing it myself somehow just didn't feel right. I kept telling myself that I need to put out an ad for more subjects, but never got around to actually doing it."

"Speaking of ads. I think we should expand beyond the limited pool of university students as subjects. We need to put out an ad, maybe even something on Facebook, that would attract people with paranormal abilities to come to us and submit to testing."

Amanda clapped her hands. "That's brilliant, Syssi. Could you do it? Come up with an idea for an ad?"

"I can try, though I've never written ad copy so I don't know if it will be any good."

"Talk to Brandon; he deals with media all of the time. I'm sure he'll have good tips for you."

Not a bad idea. "You're right. I will."

"Wonderful." Amanda pulled her in for another hug. "Welcome back."

13

SEBASTIAN

"**W**arriors, you have your assignments for tonight. Good hunting!" Sebastian sent the men off with the same words he'd been using every night.

For now, their spirits were still high, but he suspected this would change as time went by without their efforts producing results. The chance of them finding one of Annani's clansmen in the bars and clubs they were scoping nightly was slim.

He would have to come up with something else for them to do.

Unfortunately, none were capable of taking over any of his tasks, which were proving more challenging and time-consuming than he'd expected. And finding girls for his brothel was just one of many.

This morning's visit to the headquarters of Imagine Studios had been very educational. He would have to rethink his whole strategy as far as using Hollywood for his boss's agenda. Money still talked, that at least hadn't changed, but it was no longer the good-old-boys network it used to be, not exclusively. His impression was that women were running the show now.

Sebastian chuckled. It should be renamed the good-old-girls network.

And the few male executives that he'd talked with were either gay or didn't know what to do with all the pussy already available to them. So his idea of sexual bribes wasn't going to work.

Unless he could offer the kind of sex they could get nowhere else. After all, he wasn't the only one with unusual tastes. There was a wide variety of kinks to choose from, and he could arrange to provide most if not all.

If he could get his hands on enough girls, that is. Perhaps he could train his two assistants to help him out.

Sebastian cast a sidelong glance at Robert. *Nah*, this one was such a straight shooter that he barely deserved the designation of a Brother of the *Devout Order Of Mordth*. He was a good fighter, though, and not everyone in the organization had to be a cruel and underhanded bastard. After all, every commander needed someone he could trust.

That left Tom.

The guy was charming and intelligent but not handsome. Not ugly, but nothing women would drool over either. He was short, which was one of the reasons he was trained as an administrative assistant and not as a warrior, and the lack of vigorous military training meant that he wasn't muscular either. He had a good set of teeth, though, and a charming smile was sometimes all that was needed to lure a woman into a trap.

Besides, he had nothing to lose by giving Tom a chance. Worst case scenario, the guy would come back empty-handed or with a girl that wasn't all that attractive.

"Tom, a word." He motioned for the guy to follow as he headed for the stairs.

"Sure thing." Tom climbed behind him.

As they reached his upstairs study, Sebastian pointed to the chair facing his desk and closed the door.

"Is there something wrong?" There was a note of anxiety in the guy's question. Unusual, considering his otherwise flippant attitude.

Did Tom have something to hide?

Sebastian made a mental note to keep better tabs on the guy.

"Not at all." He took a seat behind the desk and steepled his hands in front of him. "I wanted to talk with you privately. I have a job for you that doesn't involve Robert or any of the other men."

Tom's face relaxed and his familiar smug smile returned. He straightened in his chair. "Whatever you want me to do, I'm on it. You know me, boss. I get things done."

"I know. That's why I chose you for this. I need help getting more girls."

For a moment, Tom looked stunned, but he recovered quickly. "Sure thing. And I appreciate that you thought of me for this, but isn't Robert a better choice? I mean, it's not like I have trouble getting myself a piece of ass, but Robert is like a chick magnet. He can do better."

Sebastian smiled. "It's not all about the size of a guy's biceps, Tom. We both know Robert. Do you think he can pull off something like this? Hell, if he were even half as devious as you, I would've at least paired you up. He could do the luring and you the catching. But the guy has no initiative and can't think on his feet. You'll have a better chance of catching flies on your own. Just use that charming smile of yours."

"You think my smile is charming? I don't know what to say, boss, I'm so flattered."

Sebastian rolled his eyes. *Give a guy one measly compliment and he thinks you love him.*

How did that human saying go? You can catch more flies with honey than with lemon? Or was it vinegar?

"Get over yourself and go get dressed. I'll meet you downstairs in twenty minutes."

"You want me to start tonight?" Suddenly, Tom's bravado went *poof*.

"The sooner, the better. I'll explain on the way. When we get to the club, I'll watch you go for it. If I think you need correction, I'll text you instructions, or if things are going real bad, I'll tell you to abort."

"Maybe I should have a bug on me, you know, so you can listen in and tell me if I'm saying the right things."

"No need. Don't worry; my hearing is excellent, and I'm going to stay close."

As Tom left to get ready, Sebastian went back downstairs and headed to the kitchen pantry, where Robert had carved a little space for himself to work. In addition to shelves loaded with canned and dry foods, it now contained a desk, a computer, and a chair.

Tom didn't mind working with background noise, and he either used the kitchen table or worked from the couch.

This was another thing Sebastian overlooked in his plans—a space for his assistants to do their jobs. Not that he'd had much choice. Most of the available space was turned into bedrooms for the warriors, and the rest was divided between the various storage and service facilities, a dining room spacious enough to serve the men in two shifts, and a large recreation room. The weapons were stored outside.

So given that his available options had been limited to stuffing three men instead of two in a room, giving up his luxurious third-floor apartment, or having his assistants work from the kitchen, he had chosen the third.

And besides, the pantry was spacious enough.

"Robert," he said as he entered the guy's domain.

"Yes, Sebastian?" Robert swiveled his chair around to face him.

"What's the status with the yard work?"

"The pool contractor is going to be here with two crews tomorrow at seven in the morning. He said he could be done in four days. And I ordered the planting material so it will arrive the day after he is done."

"What about the sprinkler system?"

"The pool contractor is going to take care of it. He needs to move pipes around to make room for the pool anyway."

"Good job." Sebastian clapped the man on the shoulder, "Tom and I are going out. You are in charge."

"Yes, sir. Any special instructions?"

"The usual. Check on the girls, see that they have everything they need, and make sure that the men who are on cleanup rotation do their job. I want to see and smell the clean when I come back."

"I'll make sure it is done to your satisfaction."

As he left the pantry and headed out, Sebastian thought about his girls. With only five available, using any of them for himself was out of the question. He couldn't have even one out of commission for the time it would take her to heal.

Regrettably, his lawyer was available no more than twice a week, which meant he'd been forced to use random subs at the club in between.

Blah, boring and predictable.

Sebastian sighed. Perhaps now that Tom was joining the effort, he could devote time to finding something better for himself.

When he got to his car, Tom was already waiting by the Escalade. Sebastian clicked the thing open.

"Want me to drive?"

"Knock yourself out." He tossed the keys at his assistant, then got in on the passenger side.

Tom turned on the ignition, then adjusted the seat and mirrors to his smaller size. "So, boss, how do I go about choosing my victim?"

"You start by selecting ordinary girls with potential for improvement. Ignore the knockouts—they get too much attention and are hard to snare. Zero in on a suitable candidate, then continue with asking a lot of questions."

14

ANDREW

"I'll see you tomorrow morning." As Andrew pulled into one of the vacant spots in the clan's private parking level, he shifted the transmission to park and cut the engine even though he was just dropping Bhathian off.

"What time?" Bhathian closed the passenger window and depressed the handle.

"I have to be at the office at nine, so right as she opens at eight. I'll meet you there."

"Good deal." He unfolded his frame and stepped out. "Thanks, man. I really appreciate what you're doing for me," he said, leaning into the cabin.

"Think nothing of it."

Bhathian gave a curt nod and pushed the door closed.

Sitting in his car, Andrew debated what to do next as he watched the guy open the heavy, reinforced door leading to the bank of elevators, then let it slam shut behind him.

It was still early, and the prospect of going home didn't particularly appeal to him. But Bridget was gone, and showing up uninvited at Syssi and Kian's, because he had nothing better to do, would spell 'pathetic' in big fucking neon lights.

So what were his options?

Hit *Barney's*?

Call Susanna?

Andrew shifted in his seat, pulling out the back of his blazer from under his butt so it wouldn't wrinkle.

Damn, even though what he had with Bridget was more or less the same arrangement he had with Susanna, it didn't feel right to call his co-worker while he was still seeing the doctor. Decency demanded that he at least keep it down to one casual friend with benefits at a time.

And then there was Nathalie.

True, there was nothing going on between them, yet, that he should feel guilty about. But he was more than tempted to give it a try. There was no doubt in his mind that he would flirt with her tomorrow, even at a risk of antagonizing Bhathian. After all, the guy owed him, and what's more, he didn't seem to be against the idea—in principle at least.

Not that Bhathian was okay with Andrew, or any other male for that matter, hooking up with his daughter, but he would be fine with a more meaningful relationship.

Question was, however, whether Andrew was fine with it.

There was something decidedly different about the way he'd reacted to Nathalie. Besides the attraction, she'd awakened a protective instinct in him that he hadn't felt for any of the other women in his life. Well, with the exception of Syssi, but she was his baby sister so that went without saying. But the women he'd dated had been capable of taking care of themselves and hadn't needed him for anything other than sex or, on occasion, his company.

It didn't make sense. Nathalie was a capable and independent woman, who was not only running a business on her own, but was also taking care of her ailing adoptive father.

And yet, deep down in his gut, he had this overwhelming need to protect her, keep her safe, make sure she was okay.

For some reason, it made him think of Dalhu. Amanda was capable and independent, and yet the guy was extremely protective of her, which given the circumstances—with Dalhu being a kept man, dependent on her for his support—didn't make much sense either.

He should go see the guy. In fact, he should've done it already. After the ordeal he'd undergone, Dalhu had needed time to recuperate, but almost a month had already gone by, and the guy deserved at least one friendly visit.

Trouble was, Andrew didn't have Amanda's number, and he didn't feel like going up and just knocking on the door. Then again, the guys manning the security desk in the lobby could make the call for him.

With that in mind, he got out of the car and headed for the elevators. He didn't bother to lock the thing, there was no need. The only ones with access to this level were clan members, and he doubted any of them would want to steal his car. It was crap compared to what was parked there.

As he got up to the lobby, one of the security guys recognized him from his previous visits.

"Mr. Andrew Spivak, how can I assist you this fine evening?"

"What's up?" He clasped hands with the guy.

"Nothing exciting, I'm happy to report."

"Excellent. No news is good news, right?"

"You got it."

"Could you please check if Dr. Dokani is home? She is not expecting me, but I just dropped off a friend and thought to go up and say hi."

"Let me check." The guy tried the penthouse, but there was no answer, and he called her cellphone next.

"She wants to talk to you." He handed Andrew the phone.

"Hi, Amanda, sorry to interrupt whatever you're doing, but I wanted to come see Dalhu, and I don't have your home number. "

"You're not interrupting, Andrew, never. I'm over at Syssi's, but I'll call Dalhu and let him know you're coming. I'm sure he'll be very pleased to see you. Oh, and Syssi says that she wants to treat you to a cappuccino from her new machine. So come over here after you're done with Dalhu. On second thought, grab him and get him to come as well. He needs to taste the difference between this and our Nespresso. And anyway, he should take a break from drawing all day long."

Andrew chuckled. "Are any of you getting any sleep with all that coffee? You sound a little hyper."

"Yeah, I am. But I'll tell you about it later." She snorted. "Over coffee."

"Good deal."

He handed the phone back to the guard and stayed a couple more minutes to chit chat with the guys about the security measures in the lobby, which were impressive, to say the least, then headed up to Amanda's penthouse.

The door was open, and he rapped his knuckles on it before walking in.

The place was a mess. What had used to be an elegant and luxurious living room was now a painter's workshop, and stunk from oil paint and paint thinners and other things he didn't recognize.

Several tall easels held portraits in various stages of completion. One was of Anandur—with no clothes on. Thank God, so far Dalhu had done only the upper body.

"I see you've been busy," he said as Dalhu walked in from what looked like washing his hands. The guy needed to clean more than just those, though. There were paint smudges all over his clothes and even some on his face.

Messy.

Dalhu came closer, and as they shook hands, Andrew observed that he hadn't regained his full strength yet. The guy was thinner than he used to be, and there was still a gray overtone to his naturally tanned skin color.

"Yeah, it seems my services are in high demand. I have a waiting list of portraits."

Andrew smiled. "How much do you charge for one?"

Dalhu looked surprised by the question. "Nothing, why would I charge for something I enjoy doing? It's a hobby, not a job."

The guy needed a reality readjustment. He was never going back to his old job, and the sooner he realized it, the better.

Andrew walked over to the bar and poured himself a glass of Lagavulin. "Care to join me for a drink? Perhaps a light beer?"

"I'll have what you're having."

"You sure it's okay? Did the doctor clear you for alcohol?"

Dalhu shrugged. "I don't need medical assessment. I'm fine."

"You don't look fine." Andrew poured the second glass.

Dalhu chuckled. "You should've seen me right after. I looked like the walking dead." He waved a hand over his face. "This is a vast improvement."

Andrew handed Dalhu the drink and walked over to the only couch that wasn't littered with various art supplies. "Amanda must've been distraught to see you like that."

"Yeah, it wasn't pretty." Dalhu lifted a wrapped pack of three canvases from one of the chairs and put it on the floor, then sat down.

"So, how are you feeling?"

"Great." Dalhu took a swig. "I started a weight lifting regimen. Anandur is helping me get back in shape. The loss of muscle was surprising. I had no idea one week of stasis could do so much damage. It's creepy to think what the others would look like after all this time."

"I bet they look like walking skeletons."

Dalhu shook his head. "If they are ever awakened, I doubt they will be able to move at all, let alone walk. Anandur and Brundar had to practically carry me here. It took me a good full day to regain enough strength to use the facilities on my own."

Poor schmuck. Must've been a hell of a blow to his ego to have Amanda help him to the toilet. Not a pleasant thought, that was for sure.

"Well, I'm glad you're feeling better. Lucky for you, painting does not require the kind of musculature fighting does."

"No, it doesn't." Dalhu grimaced.

"Listen, Dalhu, I think you should start charging for these portraits."

Dalhu shook his head. "I can't."

"Of course, you can. Who is paying for the supplies? Amanda, right?"

Dalhu nodded.

"Don't you think you should at least make enough to pay her back? I know she doesn't need it, and she doesn't expect it either, but you do—for your own self-worth. And anyway, your warring days are over, and this is probably the only day job you're gonna get. Lucky for you, this is not only something that you enjoy doing, but you also happen to have talent. Make the most out of it."

Dalhu rubbed his hand over the back of his neck. "Even if I wanted to, I don't know how to go about it. What am I going to say to the next clansman or woman—here is your portrait and you owe me a hundred bucks?"

Andrew chuckled. "First of all, you're selling yourself too cheap. You should charge something around a thousand, not a hundred. They sure can afford it. And second, you can have Amanda do the money part. Let her be your manager."

"That's actually not a bad idea. She'll have no problem charging her relatives."

Andrew pointed to the one he liked most. "You can start with this beautiful portrait of Syssi and Kian at their wedding. It should go for several thousand."

"No, this one is a belated wedding present."

"Nice."

"Yeah, I think so too."

"When are you going to give it to them?"

"The paint needs a few more days to dry. We can't wrap it in gift paper until it does."

There was a moment of silence as they both seemed to run out of things to talk about.

Andrew cleared his throat and pushed to his feet. "Well, I'm heading to Syssi's to check out her new cappuccino machine, and I was told by Amanda to drag you away from your brushes and bring you along."

Dalhu grimaced. "You go ahead. I'd rather stay here."

"Come on, I don't think Kian is there, and even if he is, you guys need to get used to each other."

Dalhu closed his eyes and breathed in. "Yeah, you're right. Let me change into something clean. But you don't need to wait for me, I know the way."

Aha, sure. As if I was born yesterday and believe he is going to show up.

"No, it's no problem, I'll wait." Dalhu shrugged. "As you wish."

15

AMANDA

Sweet Andrew. He had done exactly what she'd told him to do, and brought Dalhu with him. Except, by the look on Dalhu's face, he would've preferred to stay home. Dragging him over here had probably taken some arm twisting on Andrew's part.

Figuratively speaking, of course.

Even in his weakened state, Dalhu was formidable, and human Andrew didn't stand a chance against her man. Physically. Mentally, Dalhu wasn't there yet. He seemed anxious, his eyes darting nervously toward the darkened corridor. He was no doubt expecting to see Kian and bracing himself for his thinly veiled distaste.

Her brother was trying his best—but his best, unfortunately, wasn't good enough. Not that she was harboring unrealistic expectations of Dalhu and Kian becoming best buddies, never going to happen, but she hoped that with time they would at least become comfortable enough with each other to share a beer maybe, or tell some dirty jokes—the kind of stuff guys did with casual friends.

She sauntered up to Dalhu and kissed his cheek. "You can relax, darling, he isn't here," she whispered in his ear.

Her words worked like a magic wand. Instantly, the stiffness in his shoulders disappeared, and he walked over to the bar to examine Syssi and Kian's new coffee making contraption.

"This is one hell of a gadget," he told Andrew, who joined him for the inspection.

"It's a big fucker. There is barely any counter space left." Andrew walked around to the other side, examining the machine's back.

"Do you want to see me making it?" Syssi asked hopefully.

"Sure." Andrew stuck his hands in his pockets and shrugged.

"Cappuccino or espresso?"

"Cappuccino. I had one earlier today in a coffee shop, and it was fantastic. I'm curious to taste the difference," Andrew said.

"Dalhu?"

"The same. Amanda wants me to compare it to our Nespresso."

Syssi snorted. "Nespresso is for amateurs. When you're ready to play with big boy toys, I'll give you the name of the supplier for this beauty."

For some inexplicable reason, Syssi's comment made Dalhu uncomfortable, and he looked away. Amanda wrapped her arm around his midriff and rested her head on his shoulder. "I'm happy with the simplicity of our little machine. And in my humble opinion, there isn't that much of a difference in taste."

Andrew chuckled. "You don't have an opinion that is humble. In fact, I'm not sure you know what that word means."

Syssi giggled.

Dalhu smirked.

"What? You all think I'm a show-off?"

Andrew raised his hands. "I'm going to shut up from now on."

Dalhu nodded.

"Perhaps not a show-off, but you're definitely an extrovert," Syssi patted her shoulder. "But that's part of your charm that we all love so much, so don't take offense."

Amanda harrumphed and crossed her arms over her chest. They had a point, though. "Fine, be like that."

"This is even simpler to operate than your capsule machine. I just press this one button and voila, it does everything."

It was funny, the way the four of them were standing quietly around the thing, listening to the various noises the machine was making as it produced the first cup.

"Andrew, here is yours." Syssi handed him his cappuccino and put another cup under the machine's twin spouts. They all waited until the second one was ready and she handed it to Dalhu.

"Go ahead, mix in the sugar and tell me what you think."

Andrew forwent the sweetener and brought the small cup to his mouth.

"Hmm, really good." He took a few more sips. "But I think the one I had this morning was better."

"Dalhu?" Syssi looked at him hopefully.

"It's good. But I really can't tell the difference. I think both machines are good, and given the huge cost difference, I think ours wins." He wrapped his arm around Amanda's shoulder and brought her closer to him.

"You guys have no taste buds." Syssi wasn't trying to hide her disappointment. "Amanda? Do you want another one?"

"No, I'm all coffeed out."

"Don't stand around, take a seat." Syssi shooed them toward the couch. "I'm going to bring us something to munch on."

A moment later, she joined them and put a tray with an assortment of mismatched munchies on the coffee table. "Dig in, guys."

Amanda reached for a chunk of Brie. "How was your trip to Washington, Andrew?"

"Boring. Two weeks wasted, listening to a bunch of bureaucrats who like to hear themselves talk."

Dalhu snorted. "Yeah, I know the feeling. They all think they know better than the field guys."

"I guess pencil pushers are the same no matter which side they are on."

"Only their own, my man. Only their own. All that talk about some noble goals is nothing more than propaganda."

"And yet, you would rather fight than paint."

Dalhu shrugged. "That's what I know. It's hard to shift gears after eight hundred years of doing the same thing. But I guess I have no choice." He lifted his left arm, the one with the gleaming metal cuff on it.

"Let me see." Andrew leaned over to examine the device. "I would love to take this thing apart and see what's in it. What does it do anyway?"

"It serves dual duty; sounding the alarm if I try to leave the building, and interfering with cellular signal so I can't make cellular calls. All I can use are the landlines which are monitored by security."

"Ouch." Andrew grimaced. "I can't believe Kian still doesn't trust you. I was sure Edna's speech would do the trick."

Amanda chuckled. "I think it did, and the only reason he still insisted on the cuff was to get back at us for disobeying his orders and moving up here."

"Oh yeah? He gave you guys a hard time about it?"

"Not as bad as I thought he would," Dalhu said.

Amanda nodded. "It was just a token resistance. He came up here and informed us about the special cuff he was having William make, didn't even demand that we move back to the cell."

"Did he talk about it with you, Syssi?" Andrew asked.

"Not really. I think Amanda is right. Kian was in such a good mood after our honeymoon that he didn't want to fight with anyone. Besides, I believe that, in time, he is going to fully accept you, Dalhu. It's just that he is also an old fart who finds change difficult."

"Hey, I'm old, but not an old fart." Dalhu pretended offense.

"No, you are not. You are my handsome prince." Amanda patted his knee.

"Yes!" Dalhu pumped a fist. "I'm finally not a frog."

Amanda kissed his cheek. "You were always a prince to me, darling."

"If you say so."

16

ANDREW

"I'm fine, Andrew. You can go home. By now I'm used to long, lonely evenings of waiting for Kian to finish his work."

He pretended offense. "What? You're anxious to get rid of me?"

She slapped his arm. "Of course not."

"Okay then." He planted his butt back on the couch and stuffed another cracker in his mouth.

Syssi smirked. "You just don't want to go home because you miss Bridget."

Not really.

He must've grimaced because Syssi's smile vanished. "What happened? Did you guys have a fight?"

"No."

"Then what?"

Andrew reached for his tie and loosened it. Should he confide in Syssi? Normally, he didn't. After all, she was his baby sister and he often felt like a father to her, which precluded conversations of this nature. Then again, she'd confided in him when things had been strained between her and Kian.

"I've met someone..."

"When? Bridget left only today..." Scrunching her nose in a sneer, Syssi crossed her arms over her chest. "Don't tell me you cheated on her. I thought you were better than that."

He caught her nose between two knuckles and gave it a little squeeze, same way he'd done when she was a kid. "No, I didn't cheat on Bridget."

Syssi slapped his hand away. "Good."

"I met that someone only today, and nothing happened. She doesn't even know I'm interested. And as to Bridget, I told you before that it's not serious—for either of us."

Syssi uncrossed her arms and slumped onto the couch. "I guess that this new interest of yours is not an immortal, right?"

"No."

Well, not entirely true. She might be a Dormant. But he couldn't tell Syssi that—for a couple of reasons. First, he hadn't asked Bhathian if the guy wanted the thing with his daughter kept secret or not, and second, until they found Eva they wouldn't know for sure about Nathalie.

"Damn, now you're never going to attempt the transition."

He shrugged. "Nothing has changed in this regard. I'm just as undecided as I've been from the start."

"Yeah, but I hoped that if you fell in love with an immortal, you would have an incentive to go for it."

"It may still happen."

"So, do you want to break up with Bridget?"

Andrew sighed and popped the first button of his dress shirt open. "Here is my dilemma. I know that the next time I see that someone, I'm going to flirt with her, and I'm going to feel like an ass for doing so while Bridget still thinks that we are together. On the other hand, to break up with her over the phone is not something I'm thrilled to do either."

"Can't you wait for her to come back?"

"No."

"Wow, you got hit hard, didn't you?" Syssi tilted her head and gave him an appraising look.

Andrew scratched his head. He hadn't thought of it this way, but it was true. Nathalie's impact on him was more profound than he'd realized.

"I guess you're right. Since I first saw her, which was only a few hours ago, I felt an almost obsessive need to be with her. And it's not only a physical attraction, although she has a banging body…" Damn, Bhathian had used the exact same words to describe Eva.

"So, what's her name? And what does she look like?"

"I can't tell you her name, not yet, and don't ask me why."

Syssi rolled her eyes. "Come on, Andrew, you can't pull your national security bullshit in this case, she's just a girl."

"I know. But I can't because there is another person involved and I need his permission first." He raised a palm to halt her next rebuttal. "I'm not going to say anything more on the subject. Are we clear?"

"Argh, you're such a tight-lipped meanie." Syssi pouted and crossed her arms over her chest again.

"I promise, I'll tell you the moment I'm allowed to."

"Okay." She seemed mollified. "But if you can't wait, you need to call Bridget and let her know. Just do it gently. She's a good person."

"I know. I'll do my best."

"Do it now before it gets too late. It's already near midnight where she is. Do you want to use Kian's office? You know, for privacy?"

"I thought about calling from the car on the way home, but I guess this is better. Like ripping off a bandage—get the pain over with as soon as possible."

Syssi leaned and kissed his cheek. "You're a brave guy. Now, go." She gave him a push that had him almost topple over. "Sorry, I keep forgetting how strong I've became."

"I don't feel comfortable using Kian's office. I'll just go into the bedroom I used before. If it's okay with you?"

"Sure. Want a drink to take with you?"

He chuckled. "No, I can handle an uncomfortable conversation fully sober."

She shrugged. "Suit yourself."

As Andrew closed the door behind him and pulled out his phone, he wondered whether he should go back and take Syssi up on her offer. And the need became even stronger when he brought up the last batch of messages he'd exchanged with Bridget.

Damn, this was going to be tough.

Can you talk? He sent.

Give me a moment, I'm in a noisy place. I'll call you.

Without turning on the light, he walked over to the bed and sat down, cradling the phone in his hands and staring at the small, brightly-lit screen.

Three minutes and forty-two seconds later she called.

"Hi, Andrew." She sounded breathless.

"Hi, yourself. Sounds like you're having fun."

"I am with Julian and several of his buddies in a club. I've been dancing for the past two hours. But it's so damn noisy in there that I had to step outside."

Immediately, he got worried. "I don't want you alone on the street, in the middle of the night, in front of a club that is probably full of drunks."

There was a slight delay before she answered. "I'm not alone. One of Julian's friends was kind enough to accompany me outside."

Was he imagining it? Or was she just as uncomfortable with this conversation as he was?

"What's up, Bridget?" he asked in a tone that didn't encourage a casual answer.

"Um, I'd rather not talk about it over the phone."

So he'd been right.

"It's okay, Bridget. Did you meet someone? Is this what's bothering you? Because it's okay if you did."

"Kind of, but I can't talk about it right now."

"Is he standing next to you?"

"Yes."

Andrew closed his eyes, barely stifling a relieved breath as he let go of the tension he'd been holding in his shoulders. "Well, I kind of met someone myself. That's why I'm calling. It's not that anything happened, but I wanted to clear things up between us before anything did."

"I appreciate it."

Even though she sounded relieved, he detected a shade of sadness.

For a moment, he tried to think of what to say to make her feel better and switched the phone to his other ear. "I just wanted to tell you that you're an amazing woman, Bridget, and any guy would be extremely lucky to gain your affection. I had a great time with you. But we both felt that it wasn't meant to be, true?"

"Yeah, I know."

"I hope things will not be weird between us when you come back."

"Yeah, me too. You're a great guy, Andrew. Good luck."
"Thanks, you too."
Andrew clicked off the call and raised his eyes to the ceiling.
"Thank you, God."

17

SEBASTIAN

"How about this one?" Tom pointed to a skinny girl with long legs. A decent looking specimen, despite the red patent leather micro mini and the pair of monster platforms.

"No. She is with friends."

"So are most of them."

"Exactly. You need to search for the few that are here alone. Like this one." He pointed to a girl sitting sideways next to the bar, smiling at a guy who was using every opportunity to touch her. A hand on the knee, a pat on the hand, he was getting more brazen by the minute.

Tom raised an eyebrow. "She is with her boyfriend."

"That's not her boyfriend. A moment ago, a different guy was drooling all over her. This one just came in."

"She might be a pro."

"No, look at what she is wearing."

Tom focused on the woman. "Her skirt is short enough, and I can see part of her boob through the floppy sleeve of her blouse. That's provocative, right?"

Sebastian sighed. The kid had a lot to learn about women. "Look at her shoes."

"What about them?"

"Flats, Tom. She is wearing flats and not because she is too tall to wear heels."

Tom nodded as if he understood. "I see. And whores don't wear flat shoes?"

"No, they usually don't. Heels make a woman's ass and legs look good. They can't afford not to use every trick available to them. But that's not all. If you look closer, you'll see that her shoes are dark blue, not black."

"So?"

"Come on, Tom. I know you can't tell the finer details, yet, like the cheap quality of her clothes, or that her flats have a sticker from a discount store on the bottom. But the fact that she is wearing a black skirt and a black blouse with blue shoes that can barely pass for black is a dead giveaway. These are probably the only ones she owns, and for a girl living in the United States of America to have only one pair means that she's dirt poor."

"What is she doing in a bar, then? If she can't afford shoes, she certainly can't afford the price of drinks at this place."

"Aha, but she doesn't buy her own drinks, the men do."

"So, what do I do?"

"The guy hitting on her is getting too frisky and she is starting to look uncomfortable."

"I can see that."

"Go up to her and pretend like you're her boyfriend who is showing up late for their date. If she wants to get rid of the guy, she will cooperate. Once he leaves, you take it from there. Be nice, unassuming, and charming."

"Got it." Tom tossed back his beer, emptying the bottle.

"And, Tom…"

"Yes?"

"Keep your hands to yourself, for now."

"Yeah, I know. I'm the nice boy next door who is rescuing her from the scumbag."

"Precisely."

The good thing about Tom was that he was a quick study. And the guy could think for himself, which was a rarity among Navuh's troops.

Sebastian observed as Tom followed his instructions to the letter, getting rid of the tentacle man and dazzling the girl with his winning smile. Half an hour later, after he'd bought her two more drinks and a platter of nachos, she started laughing at his jokes. And shortly thereafter, she began touching him—a light pat on the arm, another one on his shoulder.

Tom pretended not to notice and didn't touch her in return, just as Sebastian had instructed. The best way to hook a girl was to let her think you're only marginally interested and letting her do most of the work.

A waitress approached, momentarily blocking his view. "Would you like a refill, sir?"

Nice. He liked the sir she'd tacked on at the end, much better than the honey or darling the others often used, which made him wish he was back home so he could throttle them with impunity.

He allowed himself a moment of fantasy as he looked down her impressive cleavage. Trouble was, with the amount of silicone she had in these super-sized breasts, he doubted she could feel any of the things he imagined doing to them.

"Sure, the same."

She picked up his empty glass and Tom's empty beer bottle and put them on her tray. "And for your friend?"

He waved his hand, "Nothing for now."

"Very well." She straightened, taking her huge breasts with her as she walked away.

Tom and the girl were no longer at the bar. With a quick scan, he found them on the dance floor, swaying with the rest of the cattle to the beat of the impossibly loud music.

The girl was taller than he'd first assumed, and given Tom's modest height, it was good that she was wearing flats. Long black hair cascaded in thick waves down her back, stopping short of her ample behind. Somewhat on the plump side, she was nevertheless very attractive—in an earthy kind of way. Her bright smile revealed a set of straight white teeth that contrasted pleasantly with her dark skin tone. And her large mouth, framed by a pair of lush, fleshy lips, looked like it was custom made to accommodate his shaft.

He wouldn't mind commandeering her for himself. In fact, he was getting hard just from imagining her on her knees, naked, with her hands tied behind her back, and him pumping in and out of that lush mouth of hers.

Sebastian sincerely hoped she fit the profile.

He couldn't wait to find out, but the couple kept dancing and he was getting impatient. A few minutes later he signaled Tom to bring her over.

"Sebastian, this is Letty," Tom introduced her.

"*Hola, señor.*" She offered her hand.

"It's a pleasure to meet you, Letty." He cast her a smoldering look as he took her hand and brought it to his lips for a kiss.

Even with her dark complexion and the club's dim interior, her blush was visible, and she lifted the corners of her fleshy lips in a tight, embarrassed smile.

"Please, sit down. What would you like to drink?"

She turned to Tom. "*Qué?*"

"Letty speaks very little English, and when she gets nervous she speaks even less," Tom explained before repeating Sebastian's question slowly, while using hand gestures.

She nodded and whispered in Tom's ear, "Cola."

As they sat down, Sebastian waved the waitress over and ordered a coke for Letty and another beer for Tom.

The guy leaned in, supposedly so Sebastian could hear him, not that there was any need for it with an exceptional hearing like his, but Tom seemed excited about the information he wished to share. "Letty is new here, only a couple of months. She came from Guatemala to find work so she could help out her family back home. She cleans houses for money, and also this bar."

Sebastian's smile must've been as broad as the wolf's in the fairytale about the girl with a red coat. "This is perfect because I was just looking for a pretty, young maid like you, Letty."

18

NATHALIE

Funny, getting used to good things, like having a new powerful appliance in her kitchen, was easy—not so to the things that sucked, like waking up at four o'clock in the morning.

Six days a week. Month after month. Year after year.

Nathalie hated it with a passion.

It was still night outside, and even though the window of her second-floor bedroom was tightly closed, it was cold, and she knew it would stay this way for at least four more hours. Usually, by eight, the California sun would get strong enough to bake away the last vestiges of the fog shrouding her sleepy neighborhood. From then on, it would get progressively warmer until at about two in the afternoon it would become uncomfortably hot.

After all, this used to be a desert, and without the planting and constant artificial irrigation it would still be one. The nearby Pacific Ocean did little to moderate the weather extremes.

Okay, no more stalling, one, two, three... She threw off the duvet and jumped out before her soft, warm bed succeeded in luring her back to sleep.

The pastries, breads, and bagels were not going to bake themselves.

Her regulars were expecting her to open shop at eight sharp. Like Mr. Chen, the owner of the dry cleaners down the street, who had a habit of getting there even before opening time—standing outside the door with his hands in his pockets and waiting impatiently for his morning coffee and a butter croissant.

She'd better rush.

Nathalie had hacked her morning routine so it now took her under fifteen minutes to get ready, including getting dressed and making the bed. The trick was to shower quickly, weave her wet hair into a tight braid and not bother with makeup or clothing selection. Imitating Steve Jobs's style, everything in her closet looked basically the same, jeans for bottoms and black for tops, so any combination matched.

But today she wanted to look pretty because a certain handsome guy with a sexy scar on his chin had said he would be there for breakfast.

Before leaving the bathroom, she hastily rummaged inside the vanity's top drawer until she found the black eyeliner pencil and mascara she was looking for and stuffed them in her jeans pocket. Once the first batch went into the oven, she could spare a minute or two to apply makeup in the coffee shop's bathroom.

Heading down, she stopped by her father's room to check on him. He was still sleeping.

Good.

The old building housing her shop and upstairs living quarters was perfect for their needs. After her father's condition had become such that he needed constant supervision, she'd sold their family home and closed the Studio City café so she could buy this forties era small house. It was a step down even from their modest home, but it served them well.

What used to be the living and dining room had been converted into the sitting area of the café, and the old kitchen had been renovated with modern equipment. The upstairs had three little bedrooms, which all shared a single bathroom. She turned one of them into a living room for her and her father. There was just enough room for a couch, a bookcase, and a TV. It didn't matter. After all, they were spending most of their time downstairs.

But the best part was the single interior staircase leading directly from their upstairs living quarters to the downstairs shop. This configuration made life so much easier on her. Her father had no way of wandering off without her noticing it, and the fact that she didn't need to go out at such ungodly hours of the morning, or rather night, was definitely a bonus for a single woman who for all intents and purposes was alone.

After all, the ghost living in her head and her elderly, mentally impaired father wouldn't be much help if someone attacked her.

Hey, not true, I can give advice, Tut said.

"So you decided to come back. I was hoping that this time you were gone for good."

It's true that I have to wander around in search of some action because your life is so boring, but I always come back. You missed me, admit it.

"No, I didn't, go away." Nathalie put on her apron.

Why? There are no customers—no one to see you talking to yourself.

"Fine, stay if you want to, but promise that you'll leave as soon as I flip the sign on the door to open."

I will, promise, now tell me everything that happened while I was away.

Right, as if she was going to.

"You said my life was boring, and you were right. So, how about you entertain me with tales of your many adventures?"

You know I can't.

"You see, that is how I know you're not real. If you were really a separate entity, you could tell me stuff I don't know about. But because you are nothing but a figment of my imagination, you know no more than I do."

Nathalie pulled out several batches of the dough she'd prepared yesterday from the fridge and placed them on the shelf above her work table. Next out were the slabs of butter she'd pounded into nice big squares inside ziploc bags and refrigerated overnight. Croissants were the most time-consuming pastry, and she always started with them.

I'm not a figment.

"Then prove it."

She unwrapped one of the square-shaped dough packages and dropped it on her work table, then reached for her rolling pin.

I can tell you a fascinating story.

"Humph, as if my brain isn't capable of making up tales. We've been over this before. Unless you can tell me something that can be verified by an external source, and that I have no way of knowing about, I'll keep maintaining that you are imaginary."

To shape the dough into a rectangle, she rolled her pin over it, back and forth several times to make it ready for the butter.

Damn! Her braid fell forward, but she couldn't use her hands to push it back because they were covered with flour. Instead, she tried to flip it into place by shaking and wiggling. Sporting a dusting of white powder was one thing, having a braid covered in clumps of gooey yellow substance was another.

You look ridiculous. And anyway, that braid of yours should be wrapped around your head and covered with a kerchief or a hat. What you're doing isn't sanitary. If a health inspector catches you working like this, you'll get a citation.

"Hats are not mandatory."

Maybe, but I'm sure hair is not an acceptable ingredient in croissants either.

"And who is going to tell on me? You?"

That shut him up. Nathalie placed a slab of butter in the middle of her rectangle, then folded the flaps over the butter. One more roll and it was ready for the dough sheeter.

You're getting meaner as you get older. Maybe I should look for a more amiable host.

Nathalie sprinkled more flour on her work table and unwrapped the second package of dough. "Go ahead, what are you waiting for?"

Tsk-tsk, so ungrateful. Did you already forget what life was like for you before me?

No, she didn't forget. But she hoped that after all these years of living with only one voice in her head the others were gone for good. She shuddered thinking what would happen if they came back, flooding her brain with their whining voices, their demands...

Tut had been a godsend when he'd come and closed the gate.

However, if Tut and the voices that had come before him were indeed a product of her malfunctioning brain, which was the most likely explanation, then having only him for so many years must mean that she was at least partially cured. If she managed to somehow get rid of him as well, she might be free of the voices for good.

Dream on, Nattie, without me you're guaranteed to go nutty.

Tut laughed, his nasty cackling slowly fading away.

19

ANDREW

"Good morning, partner," Bhathian greeted Andrew with a handshake as he exited his car. With the perpetual frown practically gone, the guy's face looked almost friendly this morning.

Andrew clicked the little red button on his key and locked the car, the thing doing the double chirp in confirmation. "Is there a reason why you are waiting for me on the street?"

Even this early in the morning, the only available parking spot was a few hundred feet away from Nathalie's shop, and that was where the guy had been standing.

Bhathian rubbed his palm over the back of his neck. "I'm not good with small talk. What would I have said to her?"

"How about, a coffee and a croissant, please?"

He shrugged his big shoulders and pushed his hands into his pockets. "Maybe next time. For now, I prefer for you to do the talking."

Andrew chuckled. "I'm not sure you're gonna like it much. My small talk skills are of the flirting variety." He clapped Bhathian's back, amazed anew by the amount of hard muscle on the guy's body. "What are you training with? Railroad cars? One on each side?"

That pulled a rare smile out of the guy. "Come to the gym with me, and I'll show you my routine." He appraised Andrew's slender physique with a critical eye. "You look like you're in good shape, but you need to bulk up."

As they reached Nathalie's café, the sign on the door was already flipped to open, and Bhathian opened the way. "After you." He motioned for Andrew to precede him.

Fighting the urge to check out his reflection in the window, Andrew stepped in and looked around. The place was packed, and Nathalie wasn't up front. With a quick glance, he found her serving coffee to one of the booths.

Damn, the woman had a fine ass.

Bhathian got in his face, blocking the view. "You said flirting, not ogling," he hissed menacingly, all traces of good humor gone.

"Give me a break, will you? I mean no disrespect. She is a fine woman, that's all."

Bhathian frowned for a moment longer before showing a set of scary teeth in what was supposed to be a smile. "Just messing with you." The clap he delivered to Andrew's back sent him toppling forward, making him wonder whether he should head out to the hospital to have the thing X-rayed.

Andrew regained his balance and leveled a hard stare at his companion. "You know, my sister will be very angry if you maim me. And what makes Syssi angry, makes her husband furious, you feel me, my man?"

Bhathian's face lost some of its color. "Sorry, I keep forgetting you're just a human."

"Shh, keep your voice down."

"Sorry," he whispered.

"Andrew, Bhathian," Nathalie called from behind the guy's wide back, then walked around him. "I'm so glad you made it."

"Good morning, Nathalie." Bhathian offered his hand.

She placed her small palm in his large one, but her eyes were trained on Andrew. "So, how did the guys in the office enjoy my croissants?"

As Bhathian held on to her hand, she made no move to pull it away. It didn't seem to bother her.

"Everything was devoured in minutes. I'm telling you, hearing all those groans of pleasure, someone standing outside the room would've gotten a very wrong impression—considering that they were all male."

She laughed. "Really? Or are you just saying it to make me feel good?"

Bhathian put his free hand over his heart. "I swear."

She tilted her head. "Is it true, Andrew?"

"I wasn't there, but it sounds right. Piranhas, that's what those guys are. And your croissants are out of this world."

She blushed. "Thank you, it's so sweet of you to say so."

"It's the honest to God truth." Andrew put his hand over his heart as well.

Nathalie giggled. "You guys look like you're ready to recite the National Anthem."

He winked. "Perhaps we should compose one in honor of your baked goods."

She slapped his arm. "Oh, you guys."

Nathalie looked so pleased that Andrew wanted to say more, but it would have been too much, and besides, he would've just ruined the effect, sounding insincere. He needed to gather more material.

"It looks like you're busy this morning. Do you think you can find us a booth?"

She looked back, appraising her customers. "Give me a minute. Mrs. Goldberg over there is a schoolteacher, and she's already running late. I'm going to give her a nudge."

Nathalie hurried back and stopped by the second booth to the right, bending at the waist to say something to the occupant, who must've been Mrs. Goldberg. It was hard to tell who was sitting behind the newspaper.

"Oh, dear," Mrs. Goldberg exclaimed, folding her paper and stuffing it into her large satchel. "Thank you for telling me. I was so absorbed in this article that I didn't notice the time fly. I must run." She scooted out of the booth and kissed Nathalie on the cheek. "I'll see you tomorrow, dear."

"Goodbye, Mrs. Goldberg," Nathalie called after her, then quickly collected whatever was left over from the woman's breakfast. Next, she produced a rag from her apron's pocket and wiped the table.

"Here you go, all ready."

"Thank you." Bhathian chose the seat Mrs. Goldberg had vacated, and Andrew took the one across from him.

"What would you like? Same as yesterday?" she asked.

"Yes. Coffee for both of us, and whatever pastries you think we should try."

"Perfect." She beamed. "You are my kind of customers. I'll be back as soon as I can with your order."

On her way back, Nathalie collected dishes from another booth, piling one thing on top of the other in a precarious heap while doing acrobatics with the rag to wipe the table without disturbing its balance.

"She works too hard." Bhathian frowned.

"Yeah, I wonder why she doesn't have help. She obviously needs it."

"And to think that she has already put in several hours of work to bake everything."

"I'll ask her when she comes back with our order."

Bhathian nodded and pulled out his phone.

"Are you going to call someone?"

"No, just checking the schedule of my classes."

"What are you studying?"

"Teaching."

"What?" It was hard to imagine the guy teaching anything. With the exception of combat fighting, that is.

Bhathian shifted in his seat. "Sex education to our young men."

Andrew couldn't help a snort. "You? Of all people? Why?"

The guy's lip twitched. "Why do you think? To scare the shit out of them, of course. After a class with me, the ramifications of inappropriate behavior are very clear."

"I bet, and I guess it's not about the birds and bees kind of class."

"I have no idea what birds and insects you're talking about, but the class is about consent and gentlemanly conduct."

"Okay... Is this a problem for you guys?"

Bhathian smirked. "Not anymore. But what surprised me was that the kids asked for one more class. I think it's a lark."

Might be. Or a bet between the guys to see who would have the guts to ask the ogre for one more. "What will you do if it is?"

"I'll think of something to get back at them. Perhaps force them to attend my next gig. I'm going to teach a self-defense class. Since we've started with them, the demand has been steadily increasing, and Kian asked me to join the effort."

"Here are your coffees, guys, and I brought an assortment for you to try." Balancing the tray on her hip, Nathalie pointed a finger at the plate. "There will be a test later. Make sure you're prepared."

"Yes, ma'am." Bhathian saluted.

Andrew glanced at the tray she was holding. After unloading their order, the thing still held two cups of coffee and a teapot, as well as three sandwiches and two plates of pastries. "Can I ask you a question, Nathalie?"

She looked uncomfortable but nodded anyway. "Sure."

"How come you have no help here? The place looks like it's doing well. You shouldn't be doing everything by yourself."

Nathalie sighed. "This tray weighs a ton. Let me just deliver these and I'll come back and tell you."

Glancing at his watch after she'd left, Andrew realized that it had taken longer than he'd anticipated for their order to arrive, and if he stayed to talk to Nathalie, he would be late for work.

"You have to leave?" Bhathian asked.

"I should, but I won't. I need to find out what's going on. Given her heavy sigh, there is a story here."

"Yeah, my thoughts exactly."

20

NATHALIE

Once she'd delivered everything on her tray, Nathalie put it on top of the counter. It was a quarter to nine, and since most of her morning customers had already been served, she expected to have a quiet hour or so before the next wave started at around ten o'clock.

Perhaps she could even sit down with Andrew and Bhathian while telling them about Tiffany. After all, yesterday, they had all but admitted to being some secret branch of law enforcement. They might be able to help her.

Yeah, right. As if this was the only motivation to sit down next to Andrew. Thank God, Tut hadn't come back yet. Maybe she'd be able to flirt a little.

And why would you? The voice in her head was her own.

As a soft sigh escaped her lips, Nathalie let her head drop. She might be able to have a little chat with Andrew, nothing else. Working as she did from four in the morning until eight in the evening, she was in bed by nine-thirty. Not a schedule that allowed for any social activity. And she wasn't free even during the little time she wasn't working either. Her father needed constant supervision.

Before Tiffany's disappearance, she used to leave the girl in charge and take a nap after the lunch crowd had come and gone. It had allowed her to stay open later. Sometimes, she'd even run out to take care of an errand while Tiffany had kept an eye on her father.

Now, Nathalie had reworked her schedule so she could do everything by herself.

Her only day off was Saturday, and she used it to go to the bank and purchase supplies for the coming week. God knew that doing it while dragging her father along was a nightmare. But what choice did she have?

It wasn't as if she could call a babysitter for him.

There were the adult daycare facilities she could use in case of emergency—leave him there for a couple of hours. But it would be too confusing and disturbing for him, and she was afraid of doing anything that might worsen his condition.

It was ironic, she thought as she walked over to Andrew's table, despite being surrounded by people all day long, she felt like a hermit.

"You mind if I sit next to you?" she asked Bhathian.

"Sure." He scooted to make room for her, trying to push his bulk into the corner, but still taking up most of the space on the bench. And yet, sitting so close to him that their thighs were touching felt surprisingly comfortable—the way she imagined sitting next to a brother would've felt if she had one.

On the other hand, she knew that the same proximity to Andrew would've been electrifying, even without the touching—too intense to handle. She couldn't remember having ever been so attracted to a guy.

It was better like this. Sitting across from him allowed her to see his face, look into his beautiful eyes...

"I had a waitress," she began. "Tiffany, and things were much easier with her around. But less than a month ago she disappeared. At first, I thought she was flaking out on me. She was always on the lookout for auditions, and I was sure that she was skipping work to go on some. She dreamed of a career in movies. Later, when she still didn't show up, I thought that maybe she managed to score a small role. But as I kept calling and calling and she never answered, I began worrying. I even tried calling from someone else's phone in case she was ignoring my calls on purpose, but she still didn't answer."

"Did you call the police? Maybe something has happened to her," Andrew offered.

Nathalie grimaced. "I didn't."

"Because you're not family?"

"No, that wasn't the reason. I was afraid they'd think I had something to do with it."

"Why on earth would they think that?"

"Because a few years ago my mother went missing and I filed a report with the police. What are the chances of two unrelated people disappearing on the same person?" She arched a brow and raised her hand, holding two fingers up. "I'm like a black hole or a freaking Bermuda Triangle."

Andrew seemed to contemplate the information she'd just shared, his brows taking a dip. "Perhaps I can help you with that."

Nathalie sighed. "I was hoping you would. Being a detective... or something like that."

He smiled. "Something like that. I'll look into it, but I need some more information about Tiffany."

"Sure, anything I can do. I have her address..." Nathalie lowered her eyes. "But going to check on her with my father in tow would have been extremely difficult. He has dementia, and I can't leave him alone even for a minute."

Bhathian patted her hand. "Is he the older gentleman that was sitting here last evening?" He pointed to the booth Fernando had occupied.

"Yes. He is upstairs now, still sleeping. He had an episode earlier, his hallucinations turned violent, and he was shouting, scaring off the customers. I had no choice but to give him a mild sedative so he could sleep. Hopefully, when he wakes up, he'll be better."

76

Andrew shook his head. "You don't have it easy, do you, Nathalie?"

"Nope. But I deal. I just need to find someone to help me out here. Someone cheap and part time because I can't afford more than that. I should've put a help-wanted sign in the window after the first couple of days, but I was hoping that she'd show up. Looking for someone to replace Tiffany felt like admitting that I've given up. I should, though. It's pointless to wait any longer, hoping for a miracle that is not going to happen."

"I'll try to find you someone," Bhathian said with another pat on her hand.

"You know someone who is willing to work mostly for tips?"

"I'll ask around."

A good feeling flitted through her, raising her spirits and lifting some of the weight that had been sitting on her shoulders since settling there the day her father had been diagnosed. She hadn't felt this particular sensation for so long that it took her a second or two to comprehend it.

By offering to help her, these two men made her feel like she wasn't alone in the world. The last two years had been the most difficult. With her father's condition worsening to the point where she'd been forced to shoulder the entire operation because he'd become more of a hindrance than help in the kitchen, it had taken all she had just to keep afloat while dragging him behind.

She wouldn't admit it, not even to herself, but she was exhausted, physically and mentally. Was it a wonder then that she'd clung to the first shard of hope she'd been offered?

So it might have been silly, assigning so much importance to Bhathian and Andrew's offer of help. After all, they were just a couple of kind strangers. And yet, the hope they had given her was precious. No one had done it for her before.

"Thank you." She covered Bhathian's hand with hers, closing her fingers in a light squeeze. "I welcome any help I can get."

21

ANANDUR

"Ahoy! Anybody out there?" Anandur switched the bucket of sudsy water to his other hand and reached back for the rag that was hanging out of his shorts' ass pocket to wipe the sweat off his forehead.

For his *disguise*, he'd cut off the legs of an old pair of jeans, putting them through a couple of wash and dry cycles to produce the frayed effect. Unfortunately, he wasn't all that good with scissors, and the result of his repeated attempts to get both sides to the same length was that the inside pockets were sticking from below what was a ridiculously short pair of shorts.

It was all good, though. His muscular thighs were getting a lot of attention, as was his bare chest. The shirt he had on was a short-sleeved button-down, left unbuttoned, and the gentle breeze was doing an excellent job of blowing the light fabric away from his body for maximum exposure.

He'd just finished spiffing the deck of a yacht that hadn't really needed cleaning, his physique delighting its two female occupants whose husbands had been conveniently absent. Now that his assumed occupation had been established, he was ready to take on the infamous crew of the *Anna*.

"Hello!" Anandur called out again.

A dark-haired, muscular woman walked over to the railing of the upper deck and leaned down, appraising him with a pair of suspicious gray eyes. "What do you want?"

He flashed her one of his well-practiced charming smiles and lifted the bucket. "Do you need a deck boy? I work cheap."

"No." Apparently not in a hurry to get back inside, she kept checking him out, fleshy lips pursed in disapproval.

A leggy blonde, just as muscular, joined the brunette at the railing and gave him an unabashed once-over before asking, "How much?"

"Fifty bucks for all exterior decks, two hundred for everything."

The blonde raised a brow and smirked. "Everything?"

He winked. "Everything."

A hushed back-and-forth in Russian ensued, which, unfortunately, he didn't understand. A big disadvantage for someone who was supposed to spy on a bunch of Russians. On the other hand, he had no problem reading their body language and hand gestures.

The brunette, who he assumed was the captain, Geneva, was shaking her head from side to side, while the blonde, who must've been the bitchy Lana, was trying to convince her boss to hire him. With her hungry eyes flicking over to his body every other word, he had a good idea why she was being so adamant, and helped out by flexing whatever he could without striking a pose.

Lana was practically drooling.

Perhaps he should rethink his strategy, and instead of trying to seduce the captain, who looked like a particularly tough cookie, or Marta, who was quite homely according to Amanda, he could go after Lana. The woman was easy on the eyes, and he had no problem with bitches. After all, sometimes all that was needed to cure this nasty, female affliction was a good shag or two.

The doctor is in the house, sweetheart, Anandur smirked, *and he has all the medicine you need right here.* He swiveled his hips suggestively, just in time for Lana to catch the move.

The arguing intensified and finally it seemed that the captain was capitulating.

Lana leaned over the railing, her large breasts resting on her crossed arms. "Hundred fifty, no more."

"Throw in a couple of beers and lunch, and you got yourself a deal."

"How about vodka and steak?"

He raised two fingers, then added one more. "Make it three. Do I look like a guy who can be satisfied with only one piece of meat?"

Lana laughed, a throaty, sexy sound. The corners of Geneva's lips lifted a little.

"Half bottle vodka, three steaks, one hundred and fifty dollars." Lana spelled out the conditions of the deal.

Anandur gave her the thumbs up.

"Okay, deck boy, you have permission to come aboard," Geneva pressed a button on a remote, extending the hydraulic side boarding stairs.

"Thanks." Anandur saluted. He waited until the staircase locked in place, then bounded up, careful to keep his bucket level.

"Where are you going so fast?" Geneva stopped him. "Start with the stairs. They need a good scrubbing."

"Yes, ma'am!" He turned around and started from the bottom.

"Fucking hell, I really hate cleaning," Anandur murmured as he pulled out a scrubbing brush from his bucket.

There was a little dirt trapped between the furrows of the rubberized runner covering the teakwood stairs, and he carefully scrubbed each step before going in reverse up to the next one.

All along, Lana, who'd taken a seat on one of the lounges on the lower deck, was watching his ass. Which was good for his ego, but prevented him from planting William's tiny listening device.

"Like what you see?" He glanced back.

"*Da*, you work body good."

What did she mean by that? He cast her a quizzical glance.

She mimed holding a bar and doing a chest press. "How long each day you work gymnasium?"

Aha, okay, now I get it.

"Weight lifting and other muscle work, two hours each morning. And if I have someone to spar with, I can put in a couple more."

That piqued her interest, and she sat up straight. "What you spar? Wrestling? Judo?"

Anandur dropped the brush in his bucket and sauntered toward her.

"That depends." He stood so close that her face was only a few inches away from his crotch.

For a moment, her nostrils flared as she inhaled his scent, then she cranked her head up to look at his face. "On what?"

Lana was one of those blondes who were so devoid of pigmentation that they looked almost like an albinos. Her hair, as well as her skin, was incredibly white, her eyes were a pale, watered-down blue, and her lips, although big and puffy, were only a shade pinker than the rest of her.

Not to say that she was unattractive

On the contrary, the combination of long, powerful legs with boobs that rivaled some of the best enhancement jobs he'd seen, but in Lana's case were real, and the uncommonly fair coloring was both interesting and sexy.

He ran his knuckles over the smooth skin of her cheek. "On who's my partner. I can do wrestling..." he slurred a little as his fangs filled his mouth. "I also do mixed martial arts." He caressed her other cheek.

Lana's lush lips parted and her eyes hooded. "I do wrestling," she breathed.

Anandur chuckled. "I'm game to do some wrestling with you..." he leaned to whisper in her ear. "In bed."

"You want?" She smiled, but he deduced a challenge in her eyes.

"I do."

"Why I do with a deck boy? Ha?"

"Because I'm sexy." Anandur turned around in slow motion. "And because I'll give you multiple orgasms so good that you'll be screaming my name."

"Humph, all you men think you so good." She crossed her arms under her impressive breasts, turning her cleavage into something that belonged in a porn movie.

"Ah, but I really am." He leaned and kissed her cheek, using the opportunity to stick a bug to the chair's underside, then straightened up and grabbed his bucket.

It wasn't the best of places—somewhere inside would've been better—but there were plenty more where this one came from. Next time he'd find somewhere strategically more advantageous. "If you'll excuse me. I have work to do." He spun around and began walking.

"How I know?"

He turned only his head and smiled. "How do you know that I'm the real deal? There is only one way to find out, isn't there?" He winked and walked away.

"What's your name, deck boy?"

"Anandur."
"A Scot?"
"Aye."
She grinned. "I hear Scots are very good lovers."
"As I said before, only one way to find out."
The hook had been cast, and Lana had bitten. Next step would be to reel her in.

Easy.

He was going to have so much fun with the hot Russian.

22

ANDREW

*A*ndrew glanced at the big white clock hanging on the wall above Agent Kravitz's head, willing the arms to move faster. His work day was dragging on like a stink behind a port-a-potty. Every fucking minute felt like an hour.

It had something to do with a craving for coffee. But not the watery thing brewing in the break room. Andrew wanted a good, hot cappuccino, served by a sexy lady with big brown eyes. Eyes that looked tired but full of life, hardened by experience but innocent.

Sweet Nathalie.

The moment he'd left her shop, he'd decided to go back straight after work. Without Bhathian this time. He wanted to pursue the thing that was going on between them sans her father's intimidating presence.

Problem was, Nathalie had more than one daddy.

True, her adoptive one suffered from dementia, but nevertheless, he hung around the place, and pretending like he wasn't there while flirting with his daughter would no doubt feel awkward.

Poor Nathalie, how was she supposed to have a love life while working such long hours in the café and caring for her adoptive father? It was quite likely that the last time she'd seen any action had been in college because Andrew couldn't imagine her grabbing a quickie in the kitchen, which given the circumstances was the only way she could've gotten busy with a guy.

That reminded him that he'd promised to check on her missing waitress, but staying after work to investigate would mean less time with Nathalie.

Fuck it, he could do a quick search while on the clock.

The address Tiffany had given her boss had no phone number attached to it. No big surprise there. Her generation didn't bother with landlines anymore. Everyone was using their cellphones for everything. The only information

Andrew found pertaining to that address was the name of the landlord—a corporation owning hundreds of rental units all over the country.

He emailed the main office in Seattle, asking for the phone number of the manager of Tiffany's building.

The best thing would've been to drive up there, knock on the door, and question the girl's roommates. But it would've meant more time wasted between now and finally getting to see Nathalie. Given that her café closed at eight, and the earliest he could get there was five-thirty, he wasn't about to shorten the little time he could have with her even further.

At a quarter to five, Andrew closed his computer, pocketed his keys and his access card, and said goodbye to the agents sharing his office without bothering to come up with an excuse for why he was leaving early. He'd skipped lunch so he could leave at five instead of five-thirty, and cutting an additional fifteen minutes to leave even earlier didn't require explanation.

If his boss had a problem with this, he could find another monkey to do Andrew's job.

The drive to Glendale that would've taken him twenty minutes without the damned traffic took forty-five, which wasn't too bad for L.A.'s rush hour. Thankfully, there were no accidents to bring the congested freeway to a complete standstill, and slogging along with the rest of the workplace refugees he got there, as planned, at five-thirty.

"Andrew, what a nice surprise." Nathalie's face lit up as he came in. "Where is your friend?" She tilted her head to look behind him. Funny girl, as if someone as big as Bhathian could've been hidden by Andrew's body.

He leaned his elbow on the counter to get closer. "I wanted you all to myself." He winked.

"Oh..." Nathalie blushed. "Would you like some coffee? A sandwich? I can make a custom ordered one for you. What would you like in it? There is tuna, salami, or perhaps the vegetarian, my favorite, with eggplant and roasted bell peppers. Or perhaps something else?" By the time she finished reciting the options, she was out of breath.

Sweet, her response had taken him all the way back to junior high when girls had still gotten flustered when he'd hit on them. Was she so unused to getting attention? Not likely. Nathalie was pretty and sexy and seemed like a genuinely nice person.

She was probably fending off guys all day long.

So, was it him? Was he making her nervous? Perhaps his scars were to blame, or his stupid comment from yesterday—the one about having to kill her if he told her about his and Bhathian's *secret project*. Or both.

He smiled, trying to go for friendly. But given his pose and proximity, it must've come out wrong. He probably ended up looking as if he were leering.

Her face got a shade redder, and she started chewing her lower lip as she waited for him to answer.

To give her space, Andrew straightened up and took a step back. "Surprise me," he said.

Nathalie's chest expanded as she took in her first deep breath since he'd come in. No wonder. He'd been hitting on her with the tact and finesse of an adolescent.

"Sure thing. Take a seat anywhere you like. I'll make you something that I hope you are going to like."

"No pressure. I'm going to like whatever you make."

The only vacant booth was the one at the very end of the café, and as he glanced in the direction of the one across the aisle from it, Andrew confirmed his suspicion that its occupant was indeed Fernando.

Bummer. He'd hoped to sit as far as possible from Nathalie's daddy. Grabbing a newspaper from the stand, he tucked it under his arm and headed for the back. Perhaps he'd erect a shelter using the thing.

As Andrew slid inside the booth so he could sit by the window, Fernando raised his head from his own newspaper and gave him a curt nod.

Surprised, Andrew nodded back. Did the old guy remember him from yesterday? Or did he nod at everyone who happened to be seated across the aisle from him?

He was going to ask Nathalie about it. Perhaps Fernando remembering him was a good sign. His dementia couldn't be too bad if he remembered someone he had seen only once. True, it had been just yesterday, but from what Andrew knew about the disease, short-term memory was the first to go.

Busying himself with flipping through the *New York Times* pages, reading mostly headlines, Andrew waited for his food to be served, or more to the point, for the one serving it to arrive at his table. A couple of times he lifted his head to check on her, but the place was full, and she had other customers to take care of.

It seemed like everyone had gotten their food before she finally arrived with his.

"Sorry it took me so long, but I wanted to get all the other orders done first so I could sit with you for a little while."

Now, wasn't that music to his ears. "I'm glad you did. For the pleasure of your company, I don't mind waiting."

Nathalie smiled, removing two cups of cappuccino, two tall glasses of water, and a plate heaped with mixed greens and a sandwich cut diagonally into two triangular pieces.

"Just a moment," she excused herself, turning to her dad. "Are you okay, Papi?" She put her palm on his shoulder. "Do you need anything?"

"No, sweetheart, I'm fine. You go ahead and sit with your guy."

"My..." She turned her head and cast Andrew an apologetic glance. "He is not my guy, Papi, he is just a friend."

Fernando smiled and patted her hand on his shoulder. "If you say so."

"Sorry about that," Nathalie said as she sat down across from Andrew. "I don't know why he would say something like that. It's probably his dementia."

Andrew hesitated for a moment before mustering the guts to say what he wanted to say. "I don't want to be just your friend, Nathalie. I want to be your guy."

Nathalie's cheeks got red like a couple of ripe tomatoes, and she opened and closed her mouth, then opened it again, but no words came out.

"Do I frighten you? Is that why my advances are making you so uncomfortable? I'm a nice guy, I swear. And that stupid comment I made yesterday was just a bad joke."

"I know," she whispered, then reached for the water glass with a shaky hand

and gulped down half of it before returning it to the table. "I'm not scared of you. I know you're a nice guy, it's just that I like you too."

Was there a sheen of tears in her eyes?

Andrew reached across the table and took her hand. "Is it a bad thing? Liking me?"

She nodded, dropping her eyes.

"Why? Is there someone else?"

Nothing about Nathalie suggested that she had a boyfriend, but that didn't mean that there hadn't been one in the past. Someone who had either hurt her so badly that she was afraid of getting hurt again, or someone who still exerted influence or control over her despite her breaking up with him.

God knew there were enough jerks like this.

"Is anybody threatening you, Nathalie?"

She shook her head. But Andrew wasn't going to leave it at that. She might be afraid of involving him in her problems or some other crap like that.

"Because if anyone is, you need to tell me. I'll never let anyone hurt you, and these are not empty words. I'm perfectly capable of taking care of, like in eliminating, whatever and whoever is giving you trouble."

She chuckled, but the sound was devoid of mirth. "Oh, Andrew. This is the sweetest thing anyone has ever said to me. But unless you know how to cure dementia, there is nothing you can do to help me."

That was unfortunately true, but Andrew failed to see how her father's disease had anything to do with him.

"No, regrettably, my various talents don't include miracle working. But I don't understand why your father's condition would influence the way you feel about me."

With a heavy sigh, she pulled out her hand from his grasp, and he let her, sensing she needed the distance. "I can't leave my father alone even for a moment." She whispered so quietly he had to lean forward to hear her. "He wanders off, looking for our old house—the one we sold years ago—and gets lost. Every time he manages to escape, I lose a year of my life until he is found. He has dog tags and a bracelet with my phone number on them, so I usually get calls from the nice people who find him, telling me that they have him. But not everybody is nice, and I'm afraid that one of these days he'll escape and never come back."

"That must be tough."

"It is, but I can deal with it. The problem is that I can't have a relationship, not even a friendship. I can't go out, ever. Not to a movie, not to a restaurant, not to visit someone's home. It's just my dad and me. There is no one else to step in and give me room to breathe."

"Now, there is. I'm here, and I don't care if the only way I can be with you is sitting here in this booth and waiting for you to have a few moments to spare, or hanging out at your place. I don't care about going out to movies or restaurants. All I care about is being with you and getting to know you."

"Why? You're a handsome man, you can get any woman you want. Why me and my baggage? Why settle for less?"

Her questions and her self-deprecation were starting to annoy him. "Let's get one thing straight. I don't want to ever hear you say that you're someone to settle for. You're a unicorn, Nathalie. You are rare and special, and I'm one lucky bastard to have not only found you, but to have, for some inexplicable reason, piqued your interest or even won your affection."

The shy smile that bloomed on her face was priceless. "Okay." She squared her shoulders. "So, given the limitations, how do we proceed?"

23

NATHALIE

It must be a dream, Nathalie thought, *a very nice dream, and at any moment she was going to wake up.* Things like this just didn't happen to her. A sexy guy, one who'd been starring in her very naughty fantasies last night, just offered to accept her with all her limitations because she was so fabulous that he couldn't stay away.

Right.

But if this is a dream, please don't wake me up.

"You close at eight, true?"

"Yes."

"Do you need to stay and clean up?"

Oh, God, if she had to do this too, she would've jumped off the nearest bridge. "No, I have a service that comes and cleans the place at night."

"Good, so after eight you're free, other than babysitting your father, that is."

"Yeah?"

"Are you in the mood for Chinese?"

"I'm not hungry, but maybe later. Do you want to order takeout?"

It could be nice. She was a little sick of her own pastries and sandwiches. But was she being careless? Inviting a guy she'd only met yesterday up to her apartment?

Nathalie had a good feeling about Andrew, but that didn't mean much. He was attractive and she was so lonely that she would've probably ignored any troubling signs, even if subconsciously. And anyway, with her lack of experience, she wouldn't have known what to look for.

Where was Tut when she actually needed him?

Whenever a guy would show interest in her, the ghost in her head would issue warnings or nasty comments or both, making it impossible for her to conduct a friendly conversation with anyone she found even remotely attractive, let alone anything else.

"I'll go and get us some from the Golden Palace. As far as I know they don't deliver. And I'll get a movie from the supermarket's vending machine. Anything in particular that you like?"

"Perhaps that latest *Star Wars*? I'm a big fan."

Andrew smiled broadly. "Ah, my kind of girl. I was afraid you'd go for something sappy and romantic."

"Nah, a romantic comedy yes, but I hate sad stories. I want to be entertained, not depressed."

"My thoughts exactly."

She glanced at his uneaten sandwich, and the cappuccino that was most likely cold. "Finish your food before you go."

"Yes, ma'am." He dutifully lifted the sandwich she'd made for him and took a bite, rolling his eyes as he chewed. "Delicious," he said after swallowing his first bite.

Nathalie could've gladly spent the next few minutes watching Andrew eat, but the jingle of bells announced new customers and she had to get up. "Would you like me to make you a new cup? This one is probably barely tepid."

"Thank you, but no. This is perfectly fine." He grabbed the small porcelain cup and emptied it on a oner.

"I have to go." She cast him an apologetic look as she scooted out of the booth.

"It's okay, go, take care of your customers." He waved her away.

As she rushed to the front, Nathalie sneaked a quick peek behind her at her father. He seemed absorbed in the newspaper spread out on the table before him, but the small smirk on his kind face hinted that he'd been eavesdropping on her conversation with Andrew, and that he approved.

It made her feel good, even though God only knew what scenario Papi's dementia had painted for him. He might have imagined that Andrew was her husband, or that she was someone else altogether. He had gotten confused before, thinking she was Eva. Except, she doubted he would've been happy to see his ex-wife flirting with a man.

"I'll be back shortly," Andrew said over the head of a customer who was ordering coffee and blew her an air kiss before leaving.

Wasn't a real kiss supposed to come before a pretend one? She thought it was kind of funny.

An excited flutter started in her belly, and she struggled to school her face for the sake of the older lady, who was done fumbling in her purse after having found the exact change to hand over. Never having to fake a smile for a customer before, Nathalie hoped she was doing it right and not looking like one of those plastic store mannequins.

Later, when the last customer had left, and she flipped the sign on the door to closed, the enormity of what she'd agreed to hit her hard.

God, was she nervous. Thirty years old and clueless, how embarrassing.

Everyone assumed that only the painfully unattractive or the severely socially-awkward people remained alone, never having experienced a relationship with the opposite sex. The truth was, though, that she wasn't a rare exception. Like many others—some even famous, like Jane Austen—she was a victim of circumstances. One thing had led to the next, and before she knew it, she was entering her third decade as a virgin.

And it wasn't even Tut's fault, not completely, even though she liked to blame him for it.

It might have been true in high school, but by the time she'd entered college, she'd learned to hide her *crazy*—a Bluetooth earpiece providing the perfect cover for whenever she'd slipped.

At first, thinking she had plenty of time ahead of her, Nathalie had taken things slowly, or rather not at all, too scared to start exploring the dating scene. How could she have known that her college days were numbered? That her good, reliable Papi would need her to step in and take care of not only his business, their only source of income, but also himself.

Since then, it had all been one big blur of work and more work. Andrew was like the first ray of light to penetrate the fog that had overtaken her life.

Wrong verb, Nathalie, oh, boy, really wrong.

Conjuring the image of Andrew doing a penetrating of a different sort, she felt like laughing hysterically, and she would've if not for her father. She should be excited, should look forward to finally experiencing what a woman her age should've been experiencing for at least a decade.

Instead, she was terrified.

Not of the act itself, but of admitting to Andrew that she was still a virgin. Like there was something wrong with her. Like there had been no one who'd ever wanted her.

Shit.

But that was the thing, there *was* something wrong with her—she was a freaking loon—*Nutty Nattie.* And as to not being wanted? She'd never given anyone a chance to get close enough to find out.

That being said, though, Nathalie was pretty sure that upon discovering the truth about her any normal guy would've run so fast he would've left skid marks on the pavement.

As would Andrew. And it was going to hurt like hell.

Maybe she should lock the door and pretend like she wasn't there. Andrew didn't have her phone number so there wasn't much he could do other than knock.

Eventually, he'd give up and leave.

24

ANDREW

"Nathalie, open up, it's me, Andrew." Paper bags under each arm, Andrew had no choice but to tap the door with his shoe instead of knocking.

Had she gone upstairs and couldn't hear him?

It was damn embarrassing to stand outside her shop and call her name, but there was no doorbell. And in his stupidity he'd forgotten to ask for her phone number. True, he had it written down in the file he'd compiled about her, but the thing was in the office. And anyway, receiving a call from him, when she hadn't given it, would've creeped her out.

Worse, she would've suspected him of being a stalker.

He kicked the door again, more forcefully this time, the bells hanging on the inside jingling as it rattled. She must've heard those.

"Nathalie! Open up!" he called again when another minute passed.

"Coming!"

Hearing her finally answer him, Andrew let out a relieved breath. For a moment there, a disconcerting thought had flitted through his mind that she wasn't going to let him in.

He must've been nervous. Or perhaps excited.

It was, after all, their first date, so to speak. It wasn't that he lacked confidence, or feared making a fool of himself. At his age, after having been on the dating scene for so long, Andrew had accumulated countless first dates under his belt and had it down to a fail-proof formula. He could charm the pants off a woman in less than an hour, two tops.

But there was something about Nathalie that made him feel like a teenager again. A freshness. An innocence. Which was peculiar since she was a grown woman of thirty, living in one of the largest metropolitan areas in the world, and not some young, small town girl.

Perhaps it was her character.

He'd met a few people like that over the years—the eternal Peter Pans and Pollyannas, who somehow retained their youthful disposition regardless of the date of birth listed on their driver licenses and in spite of the hardships life had thrown at them.

No, on further reflection, this wasn't it either.

True, Nathalie didn't let her troubles bring her down, but she wasn't overly cheerful either.

In any case, it was too early for him to form an opinion about her, one way or another. This was what people were supposed to do on dates, learn about each other. Although these days, it seemed as if dating was more about finding the shortest route to bed than building rapport.

Not this time.

With Nathalie, Andrew intended to be the perfect gentleman and focus on learning as much as he could about her. The exploration of her smoking hot body would have to wait for another time.

The bells on the door chimed as Nathalie threw it open. A guilty look washed over her face when she saw the paper bags under his arms. "I'm so sorry that I kept you waiting outside. I was in the bathroom and didn't hear you knocking."

A lie.

Not a biggie, it had happened to him before on other dates. Wanting to make a good impression on him, she'd probably been hard at work, straightening things upstairs in a hurry. No girl wanted a guy to know that she was messy, and that her place wasn't immaculate at all times.

"No problem." He smiled and waited for her to open the door all the way to make room for him.

For some reason, she hesitated for a moment before doing so. Was she still afraid of him?

Yeah, probably.

He didn't fault her hesitancy. A woman, who for all intents and purposes was living alone, should be wary of inviting strange men to her home.

One man, just one.

Whoa, where has that come from? Jealous, some?

Andrew shook his head. This was new.

He had no idea that there was a secret caveman living inside him. One who had been biding his time, evidently, and just waiting for Andrew to develop some sort of feelings for a woman before raising up his stupid head at the mere thought of another male with her.

Andrew used to mock his friends for this sort of thing, thinking it would never happen to him.

"Follow me." Nathalie circled the counter to get to the kitchen. "You can put the Chinese in the fridge over there."

He did as she'd instructed, taking out the various containers and putting them on a shelf inside her commercial fridge.

"This one is for upstairs." He motioned to the last bag which contained a movie, two bottles of wine, and a small box of chocolates.

"What's in there?" She peeked. "Oh, wine and chocolates…" She cast him a glance that seemed two parts worried to one part excited.

He'd better put on his most friendly, unthreatening, boy-next-door face.

Andrew shrugged and smiled broadly. "Those are just to emphasize that this is a date. If I can't take you out to dine you and wine you, I want to at least provide the second part."

"Oh... that's very sweet of you," she said in a small voice.

What is it with the sweet again? He wanted to roll his eyes. In his opinion, he was as far from sweet as a mostly good guy got.

"I got *Star Wars*." He pulled out the movie to show her.

Nathalie's eyes brightened, and she clapped her hands. "Oh, goodie, I've wanted to see it forever. Follow me." She crossed the kitchen, going toward the back door, where a small corridor led up to a narrow staircase.

Andrew had been wondering where it was hidden, assuming that it must be at the back of the building but speculating that it was attached to its exterior. He was relieved to see that the staircase to the second floor was inside the structure, so Nathalie and her dad weren't risking late night forays into the secluded alley just to go up to their apartment or down to their café.

The advanced age of the building was more evident in the back where less care had been given to appearances. The back door was small, its white paint cracked and faded, and the stairs they were climbing would not have been permitted by today's standards. For one, they were too narrow, and second, too steep—each step about a foot tall. The climb must be really hard on Fernando's old knees.

The stairs terminated at a small landing. From there, parallel to the staircase, a narrow corridor led to four doors. The last one was open, and by the intermittent sounds of laughter, Andrew guessed that Fernando was watching a sitcom.

"That's our TV room." Her smile was embarrassed. "I'll move Papi to watch his shows in his room."

Awkward.

Even though Andrew wasn't planning on any hanky panky, it wouldn't be much of a date with her father around. On the other hand, kicking Fernando out of his TV room wasn't something that sat well with him either. "I don't want to make the man uncomfortable in his own house. Perhaps he would like to watch *Star Wars* with us?"

Nathalie blushed, a pretty pink shade spreading over her high cheekbones. "It's okay, he won't mind. There's only one couch in there, and I don't think it could sit the three of us comfortably. It's rather on the smaller side."

"Okay then, lead the way." He waved his hand and followed her into the room.

Before Nathalie had converted it into a den, it must've been a bedroom, and a small one at that. Smack across from the door, he could see the back alley through its only window, and under it, two folded tray tables were leaning against the cream-colored wall—their dark cherry wood contrasting with the soft earth tones of everything else in the room. On one side was the couch she'd mentioned, and across from it a thirty-five-inch flat screen stood on its own built-in stand, and seemed much larger in the cramped space. In between, there were no more than six or seven feet of floor space.

The couch looked inviting, though, upholstered in some velvety fabric with large fluffy cushions at its back. A throw blanket was draped over one arm, and a soft rug covered the old hardwood floor. All in all, not bad.

Nathalie's den was tiny, but it exuded warmth and comfort.

Seated on the couch, Fernando lifted his head as Nathalie entered, a smile spreading across his wrinkled face.

"Papi, this is Andrew, my friend." She rested her hand on Andrew's arm and extended the other toward her father. "Andrew, meet my father, Fernando Vega."

Andrew walked over to the old man and extended his hand. "It's a pleasure to meet you, sir."

Fernando shook what he offered, his old calloused hand surprisingly strong for a man who looked quite feeble. "Yes, nice of you to come visit Nathalie, young man. She missed you, you know, while you were away."

Okay... what was he supposed to say to that? Andrew cast Nathalie a sidelong glance.

"Just roll with it," she mouthed.

"I'm here now, sir, and I'm not planning on going anywhere anytime soon."

"Good." Fernando nodded and squeezed Andrew's hand harder.

"Papi, would you mind watching your shows in your bedroom? Andrew and I are going to put on the new *Star Wars* movie in the DVD player."

"Of course, sweetheart, you know I don't like all those futuristic movies with all those robots running around." With difficulty, Fernando pushed off the couch. Nathalie offered him a hand up, and he took it, though it was clear that he was embarrassed.

"Thank you, dear. These old bones are not what they used to be. Enjoy your movie." He kissed her cheek and shuffled out of the room.

"That was easy. Weird, but easy." Andrew walked over to the flat screen, unwrapping the DVD case on the way. "Who do you think he thought I was?"

"I have no idea." Nathalie unfolded one of the tray tables and put it in front of the couch.

"Was there someone you were dating in the past that he liked? Maybe he thought I was that guy?"

Nathalie snorted. "Nope, this is purely his dementia at work."

Interesting. Fernando had either never met Nathalie's ex-boyfriends or hadn't liked any of them.

Andrew wondered why. Had Fernando been one of those overprotective fathers who believed their daughters were too good for mere mortals?

Except, in Nathalie's case, it was true.

But if Fernando imagined Andrew was that special one, he was mistaken. Regrettably, Andrew was just another nothing-special, ordinary guy.

25

NATHALIE

They were alone. At last. For the first time.

Stealing a glance at Andrew's back, Nathalie hoped to get a peek at his behind while he was still turned around, busy fiddling with the DVD.

She smirked. Instead of *Nutty Nattie*, her new nickname should be *Naughty Nattie*.

Regrettably, Andrew had come straight from work, wearing the slacks, tie, and jacket his job evidently mandated, so his assets were hidden beneath the back flaps of his blazer. At the moment, the only parts of him she could appreciate, other than his handsome face and capable hands, were his strong thigh muscles as they flexed under the thin fabric of his slacks. But then, as he bent down to insert the disc into the player, she finally got to glimpse a little more.

God, he was such a handsome man.

Were his chest and arms as muscular and defined as his lower half?

She wished he'd take off his jacket.

Bad girl, you're ogling the man like a stallion.

She didn't need Tut to feel guilty about the way she was objectifying Andrew. Go figure, apparently women could be just as bad as men when checking out the opposite sex.

Nathalie let out a soft sigh and reached into the paper bag Andrew had brought, pulling out one of the wine bottles. What had Andrew been thinking, bringing two? Was he planning on getting her drunk?

Somehow, she knew he wasn't the type. Maybe the second bottle was for him. She cast him a sidelong glance. "I don't have wine glasses."

"Do you have some downstairs? I'll go and get them." Andrew straightened up from where he was crouching.

She pulled out the box of chocolates and put them on the tray next to the wine. "No, the only thing I have we can use are tall juice tumblers."

"Perfect." He smiled, a friendly smile that at first put her at ease but on second thought worried her.

She didn't want friendly, platonic. She wanted steamy, exciting.

Nathalie wanted a hot kiss—an epic one like in the movies or in the romance novels she liked reading, one that would make her toes curl.

Last night, in bed, she'd fantasized about it... and much more...

As her cheeks heated up, she turned around to hide the telltale blush. "I'll go get them. I have some in my room." She ran out of there as if her tail was on fire.

God, she was usually so good at pushing carnal thoughts away, precisely because of the damn blushing, but she just couldn't help herself around Andrew. He was so profoundly masculine—not a boy, not a guy, but a real man. The kind every woman wished for. Strong and confident, commanding yet accommodating, respectful...

Oh, boy, hopefully, he wouldn't respect her too much. Nathalie was desperate for that kiss she'd been fantasizing about for ages, and it was about bloody time she got it.

Even if the initiative would have to come from her.

Did she have the guts, though?

The sight greeting her upon her return had her drooling, and she almost dropped the tumblers she was holding. Andrew had not only removed his jacket but had already rolled up one of his shirt sleeves and was finishing rolling the other. For some reason, his exposed forearms—strong, tanned, and sprinkled with a smattering of dark hair—were incredibly sexy.

With a hard swallow, Nathalie clenched her thighs together to relieve the sudden tingling that had started at their junction.

Lifting his head to look at her, Andrew paused the folding and frowned. "Does this bother you? I can put the jacket back on."

Shit, she must've been gaping like an idiot. "No, of course not. Um... I was just admiring how precise your folds are. Papi could never manage this, even when he was still okay. I used to always undo what he'd done and roll his sleeves for him because he never got it right."

Okay, saved, blabbering like a silly valley girl, but at least not visibly drooling.

Andrew cocked one brow and finished the last fold he'd been working on. "How did I do?" He extended both arms, bringing his wrists together so the bottoms aligned.

"Perfect." Her voice sounded breathy even to herself. Great, next she'd be singing *Happy Birthday Mr. President* in a throaty Marilyn Monroe voice.

"Good, we are almost ready for the movie. I'll just get rid of this fu..., excuse me, tie."

Oh, good, so she wasn't the only one walking on eggshells. "It's fine. I don't mind." She waved a hand that was still holding a tumbler. "I'd better put these down."

Andrew took off his tie and added it to his jacket, which he'd draped over the other folded tray table, then grabbed the remote and joined her on the couch.

"My lady." He handed her the device.

"You're giving me control of the remote? I heard that no guy would relinquish it without a fight."

Damn, had she just said *heard?* Like she'd never watched television with a guy before?

Other than her Papi, that is.

Andrew glossed over her slip. "You heard right, but when wine uncorking is involved, it takes precedence. We Neanderthals have our priorities."

Remote in hand, she watched his biceps as he unscrewed the cork and pulled it out, then poured wine into the two tumblers and handed her one.

Leaning forward, he raised his glass and clinked it with hers. "Cheers."

Up close, the smell of his cologne was doing a number on her, and she had the urge to bring her nose to where his shirt was unbuttoned and take a good sniff.

"Cheers," she said and looked away. "Is it time to press play?"

"Yes, ma'am."

Nathalie skipped over the commercials and the credits to the beginning of the movie.

She'd wanted to see this one since the first commercial she'd seen for it. But being so painfully aware of Andrew, sitting just a few inches from her, she wasn't paying attention to what was happening on the screen—it was an effort just to breathe—and if anyone had asked her what the movie was about, she wouldn't know.

Perhaps she should just turn and kiss him, get it over with so she could take a full breath again. It was too intense, this pretending to be watching because they were supposed to be on their first date and it was too soon for kissing. Nerve-racking.

"Are you okay?" He turned a pair of concerned eyes on her.

"Yes, why would you think I'm not?" She forced a smile and lifted the wine to her lips. Thank God, her hand only felt like it was shaking but didn't.

Apparently, Andrew didn't find her answer satisfactory, and as he regarded her for a long moment, she was so hyperconscious of his scrutiny that her palms turned clammy.

"I'm making you uncomfortable." It was a statement, not a question.

How the hell was she supposed to respond? Say yes? But then he'd ask why, and she'd be forced to admit things she absolutely, positively didn't want to disclose. But if she said no, he would know she was lying.

Nathalie opted to say neither. "It's just that it's a little stuffy in here. I'll open the window." She put her tumbler down on the tray table and got up on a pair of rubbery legs.

Pushing the window open, she discreetly wiped her sweaty palms on the sill and leaned out, breathing in the cool night air. Outside, a possum was grunting as it rummaged through refuse spilled from an overturned trashcan, defending its territory from other denizens of the alley. And further down, two cats were engaged in a fierce battle, probably over a similar treasure.

The scent of rotting organic matter, or perhaps it was the stink of the possum, wafted up, and she contemplated closing the window. But the truth was that her small den was indeed stuffy, and regardless of the stench, the cool air was helping calm her frayed nerves.

Suddenly, Andrew was behind her, caging her between his outstretched arms as he braced them on the window frame on each side. She hadn't even heard him approach. He leaned closer, the heat of his body warming her back and his masculine cologne scrambling her brain. Without making contact, he dipped his head so his cheek was almost touching hers. "Tell me what's wrong," he demanded in a tone that brooked no argument.

Nathalie closed her eyes and turned around. Shielded behind her own eyelids, she gathered her courage and lifted her face to his. "Kiss me."

26

ANDREW

"Kiss me," she said in that beautiful, sexy voice of hers—her lids closed and her lips parted as she waited for him to deliver what she'd asked for.

Fuck his promise not to touch her tonight. After all, she'd asked, hadn't she? And he wasn't going to say no. Nathalie seemed like she needed this with a desperation he couldn't decipher but welcomed enthusiastically. The why of it wasn't something he was about to dwell on while she was waiting for him to make his move.

She wanted to be kissed. He wanted to kiss her. End of story.

Tentatively, still bracing against the window frame, Andrew held his chest a scant inch away from her heaving breasts as he leaned into her and dipped his head. Feeling his breath on her face, Nathalie parted her lips a little more, inviting, coaxing him to plunder. But he was in no rush, and touching his lips to hers, his kiss was soft, gentle, almost chaste.

Nathalie's lids popped open, her eyes blazing with pent-up desire. A second later, her hands shot up, plowing into his hair as she smashed her lips against his.

Who knew that sweet Nathalie was a lustful little minx? And it seemed that she needed a real kiss, not a tease.

A soft moan escaped her throat as he dropped his hands to her waist and gathered her into his arms, bringing her tight against his body. Andrew didn't plunge in right away, even though she obviously wanted him to. Instead, he licked at her lips, first the bottom one, then the top, exploring, discovering her treasures one at a time.

Sometimes, delaying pleasure made it more intense.

He half expected Nathalie to take over, but she sagged into him, boneless, and let her lids drop down again. When he finally breached her mouth, it was his turn to moan, and as his hands wandered down to cup her luscious butt cheeks, he couldn't help himself and gently kneaded the firm yet giving flesh.

When he squeezed a little harder, Nathalie jerked in surprise, but then she relaxed into his palms and even pressed herself against his erection with a barely there undulation.

If she were any other woman, he would've been undressing her by now, reaching for her bra hook to release her breasts and suck on her nipples, but instinct, or maybe a subconscious hunch, was guiding him to go slow, to let her set the pace.

There was an unpracticed innocence to her enthusiasm that was giving him pause. He couldn't put his finger on it, or perhaps the clues just didn't add up. Because it was impossible that a woman Nathalie's age hadn't been kissed before. But even though his hands itched to palm her breasts, and even though he was pretty sure she would've welcomed the touch, on the remote chance that she wouldn't, he kept them down on her delectable ass as he deepened the kiss.

When he finally released her mouth, Nathalie's head dropped back on her shoulders, and Andrew had a feeling she would've crumpled to the floor if he wasn't holding her up.

"Wow, it was even better than I imagined," she said in a dreamy voice.

He chuckled. "Am I such a good kisser?"

She lifted her head and opened her eyes, her swollen lips curling up in a smile. "The best I ever had."

Now, that he didn't mind hearing. Not at all. Especially since she was telling the truth.

Still holding her close, he filled his chest with air and straightened. "Did you see that? I just got taller by an inch."

She giggled, but then shook her head and pressed her lips tight as if an unpleasant thought had just drifted through her mind.

"What's the matter, Nathalie? Talk to me."

"I wish I could," she whispered into his chest.

Andrew brought his hand to the back of her head and started caressing it gently. "I only want to know if there is something I'm doing wrong, or if there is something that you would like me to do. I'm not a mind reader, you need to tell me."

On a sigh, she closed her eyes and rested her cheek on his chest. "You're perfect, everything about you is. But I need a little more time."

Good, so it wasn't him. But what could it be? He wanted to know. The investigator in him felt a burning need to question her until she told him everything there was to know about her. But he couldn't demand it from her. After all, she wasn't a suspect, and he was still a stranger to her.

Not for long, though.

"I understand. You barely know me. Of course, you can't trust me. Yet."

"But I do. I know you. Don't ask me how, but I do, deep down in here." She pointed to her heart. "I just need more time. For me."

He cupped her cheeks in his hands and kissed her lips gently. "Whenever you're ready, sweetheart."

She nodded, but her smile looked sad, resigned.

Now he really needed to know. Perhaps he should go back to the office and dig deeper for more information about her.

Don't be a jerk, Andrew Spivak. She'll tell you when she's ready.

27

NATHALIE

Was she really going to tell Andrew all of her shameful secrets? Like that she'd never even been kissed before?

Nathalie felt bitter anger bubble up from deep down in her tummy—toward her mother, her father, the cruel fate that had her loose so many years' worth of kisses like this.

Not that there was a chance in hell any other guy could've been as good of a kisser as Andrew.

But still, she could've been enjoying this for many, many years, this and much more. If not for the damn voices in her head; if not for her mother divorcing her father and then disappearing from their lives altogether; if not for the dementia that had been stealing the pillar of strength that used to be her father away from her—one piece at a time.

For years, she'd been keeping the resentment bottled up inside, convincing everyone, including herself, that she was fine, that she was strong—a survivor. When in fact, she was lonely and scared of spending the rest of her life alone. With no one but Tut to keep her company.

Where is he anyway?

For a moment, panic gripped her. Had he abandoned her as he'd threatened he would? As annoying as Tut was, Nathalie couldn't imagine life without him. She'd be completely alone.

Lifting her head, she looked into Andrew's concerned blue eyes. Small wrinkles fanned around them, evidence of not only his age but also his propensity to smile. He was definitely a keeper, and if she had any brains at all, she'd reel him in and do everything in her power to win his heart. A chance like this wouldn't present itself ever again.

Kind of like Scheherazade, she needed to tempt him with a thousand tales, one for every night, until he would fall in love with her, or at least get so accustomed to her company that he wouldn't be able to imagine life without her.

This was so unlike her, this plotting of entrapping a hapless guy, weaving a net like some spider woman. But just like the legendary Scheherazade, Nathalie was a survivor, and survivors seized opportunities—unlike victims who let good fortune slip through their fingers while they were busy wallowing in self-pity.

She stroked a finger over the old scar on Andrew's chin. "I'll make you a deal. Every evening, you'll tell me the story behind one of these, and I'll tell you one of mine."

His broad grin was something between wolfish and boyish, adorable and dangerous. It sent tingles straight to her core.

"So, I get to come back?"

"Sure you do. You think I'm going to let you get away so easy?"

"Who said I want to get away? On the contrary, you'll find it very difficult to get rid of me. I'm a stubborn guy, and once I set my eyes on something I like, I go for it, all out."

She tilted her head a little. "Did you just tell me that you like me?"

"I more than like you. I want you." He ran his finger over her lips. "These are addictive, I could spend hours kissing you," he husked. Reaching for her braid, he brought it forward and draped it over her breast. "I'm dying to see all this beautiful hair free of the braid, cascading over your shoulders and down your back. Preferably, while you're wearing nothing, but for now I will settle for the first part."

Oh, wow, Andrew was moving fast. They were on their first so-called date, and he was already talking about wanting to see her naked. Not that she didn't want him to, but not just yet.

Don't wait too long; you've already waited long enough. The new voice in her head startled her, and she jerked away from Andrew. *Who are you?* Luckily, she retained enough presence of mind to think it rather than say it out loud.

"I was just joking." Andrew misinterpreted her sudden move.

Shit, she'd better come up with something fast before this lovely romantic moment deteriorated into an embarrassing fiasco. "I know, it's not that. I just thought I heard my father. I'd better go check on him." Nathalie forced an apologetic smile. "I need to make sure he is not trying to sneak out while I'm otherwise occupied." She winked at him before beating feet out into the hallway.

To give herself more time, she went through the pretense of opening Papi's door and peeking into his room. It was dark inside, his light snoring confirming that he was sleeping.

Who are you? she asked again.

I'm sorry, just ignore me and go back. The strange new voice sounded truly remorseful, which convinced her that it wasn't Tut playing tricks on her.

Oh, God, not again. She could deal with Tut, but not with the barrage of voices that would come flooding in if he were to leave the gate unguarded. Which was what he seemed to have done.

"Tell me who you are, please," she whispered into the darkness of the room.

For a moment, she thought he wouldn't answer her, and not because he was gone—she could still feel the foreign presence in her mind.

I'm not sure.

Great, a confused ghost, a newbie. "Do you remember who you were before?"

Before what?

Should she tell him he was dead? No, it wasn't her place. And besides, she might be wrong, and the voices belonged to something other than ghosts.

"Before now, before you popped into my head."

I can't. I thought I was dreaming, or rather sharing your dream. It began when I heard you, I mean your thoughts, debating whether to open the door for Andrew. I listened, thinking that I was dreaming someone else's dream. But this conversation between us is weird, it doesn't feel like a dream. Can you help me figure it out?

"Fine, but not now. I'm trying to appear sane, and you're blowing my cover. Wait until Andrew leaves."

I'm truly sorry for ruining your date. But I still think you should jump his bones. The man is fine, a little too old for you, but a prime stud nonetheless. Besides, you said so yourself; you've already wasted too much time.

Nathalie rolled her eyes. Was she just imagining it? Or was the new stowaway hitching a ride inside her head a gay ghost? Could ghosts be gay?

"Could you please leave?"

I'll try. Oh, here it is...I can see the exit... She heard the voice fading away.

Perhaps this was the end of it, and she wouldn't hear from him again. And yet, she had to admit that this one seemed nice, not bossy and sarcastic like Tut, or whiny like the other ones who'd invaded her thoughts before Tut had taken over.

"Is he okay?" Andrew asked when she entered the den.

"He's sleeping. I must've imagined it." Damn, she hated lying, and what was worse, Andrew didn't seem like he was buying it. In fact, he looked a little disappointed. Or perhaps she was just projecting what her guilty conscience expected to see rather than what was really there.

"I think I should go." He reached for his jacket and tie, draping both over his arm. "How about we watch the movie tomorrow?"

Andrew's tone wasn't as warm as it had been before. Evidently, his disapproval was real, not conjured by her conscience. Nathalie felt like crying. Had she blown it? Was he even coming back?

"Yes, definitely. That's a great idea. I would like that. Very much." She looked down, afraid to see reproach in Andrew's eyes, or a fake smile while he promised to come back without meaning it.

Her eyes followed his shoes as he got closer and hooked a finger under her chin. As he lifted her head, she was relieved to see that his expression had softened. "It's okay, Nathalie, there is no rush." Andrew dipped his head, his lips touching hers softly for a brief kiss. "Come, walk me down."

Downstairs, he paused at the door and put his hands on her waist. "How about a kiss goodnight?"

She nodded enthusiastically.

Andrew chuckled. "Come here." He drew her close to his body, kissing her long and hard until she was left breathless. "Sweet dreams, Nathalie." He kissed her forehead and reached for the bolt, unlocking it with the key she handed him, and opened the door.

A cold gust of wind rushed inside, and she folded her arms over her breasts, hugging herself against the chill. "Goodnight, Andrew."

He smiled. "Lock the door after me."

"I will."

Only once she was sure Andrew was a few feet away did she let out a sigh and sag against the door.

God, she was exhausted. Emotionally drained.

She'd almost blown it, and yet the hot goodnight kiss he'd given her was a good sign, wasn't it?

It didn't feel like a last kiss goodbye, more like a promise of many more to come.

28

ANDREW

Sometimes, Andrew's *gift* felt more like a curse to him. During the drive home, he replayed in his head the events that had led up to the lie.

Why had Nathalie done it?

He'd sensed that she'd been overwhelmed by the rush of desire that had swept through her. Nathalie had practically melted in his arms. And yet, she'd done nothing to hide her reaction or try to tame it. She'd even giggled at his joke. This could not have been what had had her bolting out of the room with that lame excuse. An excuse he would've bought if not for his special *gift*.

Andrew had a niggling suspicion that Nathalie hadn't been kissed much, mainly because of the way she'd been blown away by the experience. Almost like a teenager who'd been kissed for the first time. But that couldn't be. She was too old for that to be a possibility—even a remote one.

Unless she'd been in a coma for the past fifteen years, or Amish, there was no way he'd been the first guy to kiss this beautiful, sexy woman. The thought was so preposterous that it made him uncomfortable to even consider it. Maybe other men would've found a complete innocent thrilling, excited by the idea of being a girl's first in everything, but all he could think of was the terrible loss—the loneliness that hadn't been alleviated even by fleeting hookups.

For a grown woman, who appeared to have a healthy appetite for sex, it must've been plain cruel to be denied this most basic of pleasures.

Not a stranger to loneliness—hell, she was his most ardent mistress—Andrew had at least known pleasure, intimacy, camaraderie. True, none had been lasting, but there had been plenty, most of whom he'd enjoyed and remembered fondly.

Why would Nathalie deny herself? Or be denied?

Was it for religious reasons?

When he'd shaken Fernando's hand, Andrew had noticed the small golden cross hanging from a thin gold chain around the old man's neck, but the fact that the guy was religious was a far cry from proclaiming him a fanatic who'd cloistered his daughter. There had been no other religious paraphernalia around, unless it was all in Fernando's bedroom.

Nah, it didn't add up. Nathalie didn't behave like someone who wished to save herself for marriage, or who'd been brainwashed to stay away from men. She was passionate, and not shy about it either. After all, she'd been the one who had asked to be kissed. His plan had been to keep his hands to himself and try to enjoy a platonic evening with her.

So what was it?

The only other thing that came to mind was that she'd been sick. Perhaps a heart condition? Diabetes? Parkinson's?

He'd seen a movie once about a young woman afflicted with that disease. Parkinson's wasn't exclusively an old people's thing.

This, or something like it, would explain her reluctance to share with him what had troubled her. Not something one wished to disclose on a first date.

Except, this didn't make sense either—and thank God for that. Nathalie worked insane hours while taking care of her dad. There was no way a person suffering from a life-threatening or debilitating disease could've managed that.

Damn it, what could it be?

Hell, the answer was probably simpler. It wasn't that Nathalie had never been kissed, or that she was still a virgin, but that it had been a really long time since she'd been with a man. Except, even this more plausible scenario begged the question why.

The mystery had him both excited and anxious. Excited about the unraveling of secrets, anxious about what these secrets might be.

29

BHATHIAN

"Jackson, would you care to share with your friends the subject of this evening's class?"

Smirking, like he was letting them in on a grand joke, Jackson exchanged looks with his three sycophants, Gordon, Chase, and Vlad.

Damn, what had this kid's mother been thinking when she'd named him Vlad? That crazy maniac had done more damage to the clan than all their enemies combined, and the woman had named her kid after him?

"I'm waiting."

"Yes, sir. The reason I asked for another class was that your previous one was incomplete. You told us about all the things we were not supposed to do with girls, but you said nothing about what we could and should do. I thought we could all benefit from your vast experience on the subject."

Aha, so that was his game.

If the boy had thought to embarrass him, Jackson had another thing coming. By the time Bhathian was done with them, they would be blushing like a bunch of virgins, which he suspected at least two out of the four still were.

Not Jackson, the little prick had been quite active for some time now, and perhaps Gordon. But for sure not Vlad and Chase.

Bhathian leaned his butt against the edge of the desk and crossed his arms over his chest. "An excellent idea. Actually, I'm going to call your mother and compliment her on raising such a fine young man. To seek knowledge is a commendable trait, and not to be shy about asking questions even more so." Bhathian wished there were cameras in the classroom so he'd have a souvenir of Jackson's bewildered expression.

Unfortunately, there were none.

"So, Jackson, what is it that you find most difficult?"

The boy took only a few seconds to reevaluate the situation and come up with a new plan of action. He smiled and leaned back in his chair. "Let's say I'm alone with a girl and I want to kiss her. What do I do next?"

"I thought I was very clear on this the other evening. You ask permission."

"How?"

"A simple 'can I kiss you' will do."

Jackson grimaced. "Do you have anything more subtle than this lame approach? You don't know anything about girls today. I'll get laughed at."

Bhathian stifled a chuckle. Watching the back and forth between him and the boy, Jackson's friends were turning their heads like a trio in a synchronized swimming performance.

Still, he sensed that there was at least some truth to Jackson's statement. Perhaps this generation played by different rules.

"Very well. You can ask permission without saying a thing. You put your hands on the girl's waist and gently draw her to you. If she resists, even a little, you let go. But if she lets you, you go to the next step and bring your lips close to hers, without touching, and wait. Nine times out of ten she will close the distance and kiss you. Problem solved."

"What about the one out of ten?"

"Then you go to the third step. You close the distance, but very slowly, giving her every opportunity to turn her head away, or step back. If she does none of those things you can proceed."

Gordon groaned. "This will make me look like a spineless wuss; like I'm not man enough to make the first move."

Jackson nodded his agreement. "Girls like guys who are confident."

Gordon snorted. "They like assholes. The worse a guy treats them the more they want him. I don't get it, but this is the way it is."

Uncrossing his arms, Bhathian sighed. "Look, boys, I'm not an expert on female psychology, but I've been around long enough, pondering the same question, and I came up with a hypothesis. But bear in mind, this is only my opinion and not a fact, and it is not scientifically backed so I might be totally off. We all know that women are impossible to understand, and smarter men than me and you have been unable to solve the mystery."

That earned him a snort from Jackson and chuckles from the other three stooges.

"You've got that right. Let's hear it, then." Jackson straightened his back, the other boys leaning forward to listen to Bhathian's words of wisdom.

"I think it's subconscious, a survivor instinct from a time when a female who succeeded in securing a strong, dominant male as a mate had better chances of survival than others, and, of course, the benefit extended to her children as well. A nice guy wasn't a priority."

Vlad harrumphed. "And I thought Jackson's pretty face was responsible for his success with girls, when all along it was his jerky attitude."

"Hey, I'm not a jerk."

Vlad folded his arms over his bony chest. "A bully then."

Jackson shrugged. "I don't let anyone get away with shit. That doesn't make me a bully. I don't terrorize the weak and the meek. Only those who pick up a fight with me."

"So good looks have nothing to do with it?" Chase asked. "I always thought that good-looking guys got away with being jerks, and hot chicks got away with being bitches, just because they could."

The kid had a point.

"Yeah, I guess being attractive doesn't hurt, and those who get enough attention from the opposite sex without having to work for it sometimes develop an entitled attitude." He looked pointedly at Jackson. "Still, you don't have to be a jerk to project confidence, and confidence makes a man seem more attractive to women. Especially when he also has a job and makes a decent living." Bhathian winked. "No girl wants a penniless loser, not even for a hookup."

"I got it. Confidence and a job. Anything else?" Gordon glanced at Jackson, whom the boys appeared to look to as an authority on everything having to do with girls.

"You got to be kidding. Nothing is ever as simple as that with chicks. Though I have to agree with Bhathian about the job thing. It feels wrong to ask my mom for money to spend on a date. But that's just one small part. There is so much more to it."

Now, this should be interesting. A seventeen-year-old's perspective on this most difficult of subjects. The boys seemed to agree, all three staring at Jackson and waiting for him to reveal the secret to his success.

"Their expectations are insane. It's like no guy can be all of that. They want you to be tough but sensitive to their feelings; to be dominant and assertive but do what they want, how they want it, and where they want it. And the worst part is that they will never tell you anything. They expect you to guess. No wonder guys end up just ignoring their bullshit and behave like jerks."

If he weren't the teacher of this class, Bhathian would have clapped, applauding the boy's wisdom. He couldn't have put it better himself.

Women could be so frustrating.

Jackson's succinct assessment seemed to depress his friends.

Vlad threw his hands in the air. "So how do you do it? It seems impossible to please a woman."

Gordon and Chase nodded with twin dejected expressions.

Jackson shrugged. "You don't. You do the best you can and if they are not happy with it, tough."

"Are all of them like that? And why? What do they get out of making us feel like failures?" Vlad whined.

Bhathian chuckled and raised his palm to stop Jackson, who was about to respond. "First of all, you have to realize that they don't do it on purpose. This is important to remember when you get frustrated with a girl. Gender roles have changed, but not the underlying physiology. A woman's hormones, which are a remainder from a more primitive time, might compel her to seek the best protector and provider. At the same time, though, these qualities are not as desirable in modern society, and men are expected to be more accommodating and nurturing. She may crave a dominant man in bed, but not outside of it, which is confusing to us simple-minded creatures. But women don't have it easy either. They are expected to be soft and feminine but to succeed in a world that demands the exact opposite. An assertive, bossy guy is called a leader; a woman exhibiting the same qualities is called a bitch."

"Well, I'm no smarter now than I was before. I still have no clue how to behave." Vlad pushed his chair back and got up.

Bhathian motioned for him to sit back. "We are almost done. I just want to give you boys a parting piece of advice." He raised two fingers. "Communication and respect. Internalize it and repeat it like a mantra. As long as you communicate clearly and show respect, everything else will work itself out. And if not, let it go, it's not worth it. Never compromise on these two things. And, of course, it should go both ways. You should expect the same in return."

His concluding statement must've impressed the boys. Vlad was first. He got up and walked up to Bhathian to shake his hand. "This was good. I'm still clueless, but at least no longer blind." Bhathian clapped his back. "Good, I'm glad."

Chase was next, then Gordon. Jackson waited until they cleared the room before approaching Bhathian. For a moment, he just looked down at his white Converse shoes. "I want to apologize."

"Yeah?"

Lifting his head, Jackson offered his hand. Bhathian shook it.

"None of us came here expecting to learn anything, it was supposed to be a joke. You know, getting back at you for the other class when you made us feel this small." Jackson brought his thumb and forefinger together to illustrate. "But I was wrong. You're cool."

Bhathian smiled as he clapped Jackson's back. He had to hand it to the boy, Jackson had balls to come clean like this. Most people were too scared to even say hello to him, let alone apologize.

"Tell me, Jackson. Where are you going to college next year?"

"I'm not. I'm going to take a gap year. My mom agreed to let me dedicate this time to pursue my music career, but only if I find a job and work at least part time. She doesn't want me to spend all day sleeping while staying up all night, performing non-paying gigs with my band."

"Do you have anything lined up?"

"Yeah, a couple of clubs. But we have to bring the audience. Not a problem, since half of our high school will come to see us play."

"I meant job wise."

"No, not yet. I have no experience, and that's the first question everyone asks."

"I think I have something that might be perfect for you."

"Oh, yeah? What is it?"

"What time do you get out of school tomorrow?"

"I have a final tomorrow morning, and that's it. I should be done by ten."

"Wait for me outside. I'm going to pick you up."

"Where are we going?"

"It's a surprise."

30

NATHALIE

Nathalie had been waiting for Andrew to show up all morning, but neither he nor Bhathian had stopped by. She had a sinking feeling that yesterday evening had been the last she'd seen of Andrew.

He hadn't called either. So yeah, she'd forgotten to give him her number, but she was in the directory, or at least the coffee shop was.

Good job, Nathalie, congratulations on chasing another guy away, and you can't even blame me for it.

Tut hadn't been the culprit this time, but his absence had allowed that other voice to intrude, startling her worse than Tut could've ever done. So, at least partially, it had been his fault.

Where were you?

The morning rush was over, and the few customers remaining were sitting all the way in the back. Nevertheless, she was reluctant to risk addressing Tut out loud even though she found conducting internal conversations with him too intimate.

His presence alone was intrusive enough.

I've been checking out more interesting hosts.

Nathalie rolled her eyes. He'd been saying it for years, and yet he was still in her head.

I had a visitor while you were away. He was nice, not sarcastic like you. Perhaps I should invite him to stay. It was an empty threat since the new voice hadn't returned. And anyway, she couldn't imagine life without Tut. For better or for worse, he'd been a constant presence since she was a little girl. Annoying, but also reassuring.

Perhaps you should.

Damn, Tut sounded serious. Had she offended him?

"I was just joking," she whispered.

I know, but I can't stay forever, Nathalie. I've already stayed too long. I'm struggling to hold on because you need me to guard the gateway to your mind, but I won't be able to do it for much longer. Each day I'm being pulled away more and more. You must've noticed it.

She had. But she'd assumed that Tut was just wandering around, or perhaps that she was getting better, and one day the voices would stop altogether. But it seemed that Tut had been misleading her.

"Why didn't you tell me this before?"

You would have panicked.

"So why now?"

Because I no longer have a choice. The fact that someone else got through my defenses proves that I'm getting weaker.

Shit, this was serious. And he'd been right about her panicking.

"What am I going to do without you? Is it going to be the way it used to be? With dozens of different voices driving me crazy?"

Forgetting herself, she had switched from whispering to talking, and now some of the customers were looking at her. She smiled nervously and pretended to adjust the nonexistent Bluetooth in her ear, then turned around and fled to the kitchen.

You're older now. You should be able to control them better. Start with that new visitor you mentioned, practice blocking him.

"Yeah, right, as if I wouldn't have done it already with you if I could."

When you really didn't want me to know something, you did.

He was right. She'd managed to hide Andrew from him. "I think I learned how to keep some thoughts private, but that's just a small part of the problem. I don't know how to block the voices from talking to me, and that's the worst part."

Start practicing. I'll stay for as long as I can, but it seems that I can no longer keep the gate tightly closed, and some will manage to get through to you. Practice on those, and hopefully, by the time I'm gone for good, you'll learn how to control them.

God, this was just what she needed now. Even on the remote chance that Andrew still wanted to see her, she wouldn't be able to see him. Managing the voices while trying to appear normal wasn't going to work.

Perhaps a clean break was exactly what she needed— before she got used to having Andrew in her life.

Not fair. Really, really, not fair.

The bells on the door chimed, announcing a new customer. With a sigh, Nathalie wiped a stray tear away and left the shelter of her kitchen.

Her heart skipped a beat when she saw it was Bhathian. Tilting her head sideways, she tried to peek behind him, hoping to find Andrew. But the only one standing next to Bhathian was a handsome teenager with a killer smile. He kind of reminded her of Luke, the guy she used to have a crush on in high school. They even had similarly conceited expressions. Not that she could really blame Luke or this boy for their cockiness. It was probably impossible for a guy to remain humble when every woman, regardless of age, was checking him out.

"Hi, Nathalie, I want you to meet Jackson. Jackson, this is my d— dear friend Nathalie, the owner of this coffee shop and your future employer."

Jackson seemed just as surprised as she was by Bhathian's introduction, but he recovered first. Flashing her a gorgeous smile, he reached over the counter and offered her his hand.

"Hi, boss," he said.

The boy's smile was infectious, and she found herself smiling back as she took his hand. "It's nice to meet you, Jackson, but I haven't hired you yet."

"How about we all sit together and nail down a deal," Bhathian offered, pointing to the first booth on the right.

"Sure, go ahead, I'll be right with you."

Nathalie glanced at the customers sitting in the back. They seemed fine, but just so she wouldn't get interrupted later, she grabbed a coffee carafe in one hand and a water jug in the other and refilled everyone's drinks before joining Bhathian and Jackson at the booth.

"So, Jackson, have you waited tables before?" she asked as she sat across from the guys.

His confident smile turned into a slight grimace, and Jackson cupped the back of his head. "No, I have no work experience. But I'm a quick learner, and I'm good with people. And I'm willing to start cheap," he tacked on at the end.

Nathalie smiled. "You just said the magic words. You're hired. How many hours a day can you work? I assume that you're still in school?"

"I have only two finals left, and then I'm free. So the only times I can't work are next Monday and Wednesday mornings."

"How about your band? Don't you need time to practice?" Bhathian asked.

Jackson shrugged. "The guys will work around my schedule, and if we get a gig, we'll worry about it then."

So the boy had dreams of becoming a rock star. Cute, but unrealistic. Then again, at his age, dreaming impossible dreams was still allowed.

"All I can pay is minimum wage. But you get to keep all of your tips, which given your charming smile, I have no doubt there will be plenty of."

The conceited expression returned full force to his handsome face, and he extended his arm for a handshake. "When do I start?"

"How about right now?"

"Sweet."

Bhathian chuckled. "You forgot something, my boy. Your car is still at school, and I'm not going to wait for you to finish work to drive you back."

"Damn, can you drive me now? I'll get it and come back. If it's okay with you, boss?"

"No problem, and you can call me Nathalie."

Jackson got up and waited for Bhathian to slide out of the booth, which considering his size wasn't an easy feat.

"I'll be back before you know it." Jackson shook her hand again.

Nathalie was amused by the boy's enthusiasm at the prospect of working for minimum wage plus tips. He was probably overestimating his potential earnings. This was a coffee shop, not an expensive steak house, and the tips weren't that big.

As she saw them to the door, Nathalie desperately wanted to ask Bhathian about Andrew, but at the end, she chickened out.

There was just no way she could ask if Andrew had said anything to him about her. Which she imagined was something along the lines of describing how crazy he thought she was. And anyway, it wasn't as if Bhathian would have told her anything.

31

BHATHIAN

"Congratulations." Bhathian clapped Jackson's back as they exited the shop.

"Thanks, man, I owe you."

Bhathian clicked open the doors and got behind the wheel. "No problem. I got two birds with one stone. You needed a job, Nathalie needed help. Everyone got what they wanted."

Jackson scratched his ear. "I'm not sure I know what I'm supposed to do. Is it just waiting tables?"

"I suppose. Just do whatever Nathalie tells you to do. Perhaps she'll need you to work the register, take orders, clean the kitchen. I have no idea. But you're a smart guy, you'll figure it out."

"Yeah, how hard can it be, right?"

How hard indeed. Bhathian hoped this arrangement would work out, and Jackson would not disappoint. Problem was, the boy was a teenage immortal, and working with humans might tempt him to use his powers.

"Listen, Jackson. You need to be careful and remember never to use your powers. I'm sure there will be situations when you'll be tempted to. Like thralling a customer to give you a big tip, or worse…" He gave the boy a stern look. "You know what I'm talking about—girls. You're a good looking guy, and if your looks and charm get you laid, I have no problem with that. But if I even suspect that you thralled someone…"

Jackson raised his hands in the air, putting on an innocent face. "Never, I swear. I've never thralled a girl for that. I don't need to."

Was this a slip of a tongue? "Then what other things have you thralled them for? I mean, other than after the sex to erase the memory of your fangs and the biting."

"Nothing, I swear."

"Jackson!"

The boy sighed in resignation. "Okay, just once, and it wasn't a girl. I was failing math and thralled my math teacher to give me a passing grade." He seemed worried as he glanced at Bhathian's grim face. "I was desperate, my mom said she wouldn't allow me to practice with my band unless I passed math. I had no choice. Please, don't tell on me."

"Was it the only time?"

"Yes, I swear on my best guitar."

Bhathian chuckled. "Okay, I'll let it slide. But if I hear you've done anything of the sort while working for Nathalie, I'll personally whip you for it."

Jackson shrugged. "Trust me, I know, you have nothing to worry about."

32

ANDREW

*D*amn, it was after seven in the evening, and he was still at the office instead of leaving early like he'd planned. Upstairs had requested, or rather demanded, to see a progress report on his airport personnel investigation, and the fuckers wanted it by tomorrow morning.

Cutting corners left and right, he'd managed to finish it in record time, but the end product was a semi-passable thing that he would've never accepted from a subordinate. It would no doubt raise some brows—especially the ones belonging to his boss. After all, Andrew's subpar work was going to reflect poorly on him.

But to hell with it. After years of exemplary work, he was allowed one shitty report. True?

Fuck, he should call Nathalie and let her know he was running late. Not that he was afraid she would go somewhere, stuck as she was at home with her father, but she might not open the door if he arrived after eight. The coffee shop would be closed already, and she'd be upstairs.

Pulling up the file he'd compiled about her, Andrew chose to use the shop's number instead of the residence. Less incriminating, he could always claim to have gotten it from the directory.

"Fernando's Bakery and Café, how may I help you?" Nathalie answered after one ring. She sounded breathless.

"Busy day, eh?"

"Andrew." He could tell so much from just the way she'd said his name—surprise, relief, longing.

God, he was such an insensitive dumbass. Clearly, she'd thought he wasn't coming back. He should've called her ten times by now just to let her know how much he liked her.

"I'm on my way, just wanted to tell you that I'm running a little late. I hope that it's still okay with you."

"Of course, I'm not going anywhere. Take your time and drive safely."

"I will."

Poor girl, she'd sounded so relieved. Andrew felt guilty, and yet, he couldn't help also feeling a little smug.

Nathalie wanted him.

Without further hesitation, he emailed the report. Worst case scenario, his boss would chew his ass, and he would come up with an excuse, promising to do better next time. It seemed that his days as an exemplary government employee were over. He was becoming a slacker.

Andrew shrugged. He had more important things on his mind than winning the employee-of-the-month badge. Not that his department issued them.

As he drove to Nathalie's place, he wondered whether he should stop somewhere and buy flowers. It felt awkward showing up empty-handed, especially since it was only their second date and he was going to her place. But that would introduce another delay he wanted to avoid. Still, once he got off the freeway, Andrew kept his eye out for a flower shop. If there was one on the way, he would stop by.

There was one, right on Nathalie's street, and he stopped and ran out.

"Give me a nice bouquet for fifty, something for a date," he told the girl behind the counter. Andrew wasn't an expert on flowers, but he hoped that the amount would get him a decent arrangement.

"Do you know what kind of flowers she prefers?"

Andrew shook his head.

"Okay, how about color. What's her favorite?"

"I don't know. Please, I'm in a hurry. Just pick something you would've liked to receive from a guy."

The girl shrugged and headed out to the refrigerated section of the shop. A moment later she came back with a big bouquet. Too big.

"This one is nice, but it's seventy-five."

Whatever, he didn't have time to send her back for another one.

"Fine, I'll take it."

"Do you want a card to go with it?"

"No." He handed her his credit card.

Andrew didn't know what was worse, showing up empty-handed, or with a thing that was as big as some of the centerpieces he'd seen in hotel lobbies.

Damn, he hoped she would like it. The good news was that he would be arriving after eight, which meant that there would be no one in the shop to see him walk in with the flowers.

Wrong.

True, the sign on her door said closed, and there were no customers in the café, but the door was open, and as he came in he was greeted by a young guy who was wearing an apron with the café's logo on it.

"Hi, I'm Jackson, the hired help." He offered his hand for a handshake. "And you must be Andrew."

They clasped hands, and Andrew glanced around looking for Nathalie. But the only one there, other than the new guy was her father, who was sitting in his booth, busy with a coloring book. Strange.

"Nathalie is upstairs taking a shower, and she told me to entertain you in the meantime. Can I offer you coffee? A Danish, perhaps? You've got to try the Danish, man, it's out of this world." Jackson rolled his eyes.

The kid was a good salesman, that was for sure.

"Why not. Do you know how to make a cappuccino?"

Jackson snorted. "Single? Double? Whole milk? Skim?"

"Double, skim."

"Shaken not stirred?"

Andrew chuckled. "You got it."

He walked over to Fernando, who was bent over his coloring book and concentrating hard on staying inside the lines of an intricate geometric shape.

"Good afternoon, sir, how are you doing today?"

Fernando paused with his red pencil pressed firmly into the page and looked up. There was no recognition in his eyes, but he tried to bluff his way through it. "Very well, thank you for asking. And you?"

"I'm good, thank you. Well, I'll let you go back to your"— given the guy's age, it seemed wrong to say coloring—"hobby"— much better. "It was good to see you."

"Same here," the old man smiled and waved him off, then bent back down to continue his work.

"It's good for his condition," Jackson whispered as Andrew slid into the booth he'd chosen, one that was next to a window, naturally. The boy placed a plate with a steaming Danish in front of him.

"Thanks for warming it up."

"That's the only way to eat it. I'll be back with your cappuccino."

Andrew took a bite, and his eyes rolled as well. It truly was out of this world. Nathalie had a gift.

He was halfway done with the pastry when Jackson came back with the cappuccino and slid into the booth across from Andrew with a cold can of coke in hand.

"So, Andrew, Nathalie tells me that you're Bhathian's friend." Jackson raised a brow as if to ask how Andrew knew the guy.

Had Bhathian been there today, visiting Nathalie on his own? Good for him.

"We work together."

Jackson shifted in his seat, popped the coke can open, took a sip, and cupped it between his hands. The kid was trying to say or ask something and wasn't sure how to go about it. "Bhathian is a great guy. He got me this job. I had to take a class that he teaches. That's how I met him."

Andrew smiled. Jackson was telling him who he was in a way that only someone who knew Bhathian would get. Smart.

Andrew offered Jackson his hand. "I'm Syssi's brother, your regent's wife."

The kid's eyes popped wide open. "Damn, I should've recognized you from the wedding. You look different without a tux."

Andrew narrowed his eyes. "I didn't notice you there either."

Jackson smirked and looked both ways as if checking to see that no one was listening in, then leaned toward Andrew. "Me and my buddies swiped a bunch of bottles from the bar and snuck out. We got wasted in the gym."

"Aha, no wonder then." Andrew smirked. He'd pulled similar stunts at Jackson's age. Not being a hypocrite he had no intention of scolding the kid.

"Tell me, Jackson, what did you guys tell Nathalie? She doesn't know about us."

"The truth. I was a student at a class Bhathian taught, and I told him I needed a job. That's it. She didn't ask any more questions, so I didn't have to invent any lies."

"What if she asks what kind of class it was? She thinks Bhathian and I are part of some secret arm of law enforcement."

Jackson snorted. "Well, you are, kinda. And I'll tell her the truth about the class as well. Bhathian teaching a class to juvenile delinquents fits well with what she thinks of you guys."

"True."

33

NATHALIE

*A*s she descended the stairs, Nathalie's heart was beating twice as fast as normal. She was even more nervous now than she'd been the day before.

Until Andrew had finally called, she'd thought of nothing else. She kept going over every detail of their date and analyzing every word said and every touch, to either reinforce or discard her suspicion that he wasn't coming back.

Vacillating between hope and despair, by the end of the day she'd been a nervous wreck.

Problem was, even though she'd been relieved to the point of feeling faint to hear that he was still coming to see her, her high level of anxiety hadn't gone all the way down yet.

Pausing by the doorway, she took a deep breath before leaving the kitchen's shelter and stepping into her shop.

With a quick glance, she found Andrew sitting with Jackson in one booth, and her father in the one across the aisle from them. He was still busy with the adult coloring book Jackson had bought for him.

The boy had turned out to be a godsend. The customers loved him, and he'd learned to operate the cappuccino machine in one go—which was something that had taken her previous helpers weeks to do. But all of this was not as astounding as Jackson's positive attitude toward her father. The boy had even called his mother, who happened to be an occupational therapist, to ask what would be a good activity for Fernando.

She'd suggested the adult coloring books.

Immediately, he'd volunteered to drive to the nearest bookstore that carried them. Nathalie had given him two twenties, and in less than half an hour, he'd got back with three books and a box of coloring pencils. Right there and then she'd decided to give him a raise. He was definitely worth more than minimum wage. Regrettably, she couldn't afford much more than that.

Still, she was sure it would at least make Jackson feel appreciated. And besides, the way he was charming the customers, the boy was going to earn double if not more than what she was paying him in tips.

It had been impossible not to notice the look-overs Jackson had been getting all day—mostly from women, but also from some of the men. At times, Nathalie had found it disturbing to see women old enough to be his mother or even grandmother ogle the seventeen-year-old boy.

And yet, she suspected that Jackson not only wasn't bothered by the looks but was actively encouraging them—probably to get even bigger tips.

The boy was a godsend but certainly not an angel. In a few years, he was going to leave a trail of broken hearts. Come to think of it, he probably already had.

Not that she would know anything about it. The one advantage of never having had a boyfriend was that she'd never been dumped. That being said, though, she might soon find out all about it. Because if things didn't work out with Andrew...

Damn, why did it hurt so bad to even think about it?

Well, as the saying went; nothing ventured, nothing gained. She had to take a risk. Even if it terrified her.

Nathalie took another moment to gaze at Andrew's handsome face while Jackson kept him distracted.

There was something extra sexy about a man wearing a tie and blazer, a certain air of sophistication, of authority. Or perhaps it was Andrew's personality more than his professional attire that was projecting this quiet air of command. That he was a capable, dependable man was evident just from his facial expression and the way he carried himself.

Charisma, confidence, he had all of those in spades.

And for some reason, he was interested in her, a woman who was still a virgin at thirty.

With a sigh, Nathalie shook her head. It didn't make any sense. They were not a good fit. She was probably setting herself up for a heartache.

At the same moment, Andrew sensed her presence and turned his head to look at her. His eyes popped wide in a most gratifying way, and he got up, ignoring Jackson, who was still talking to him.

Her legs refusing to move an inch, Nathalie remained glued to her spot right outside the kitchen, mute, unable to even say hello as she waited for Andrew to reach her, which he did in a few long strides.

His arm reaching around her waist, he pulled her to him, his eyes full of heat as he looked down at her.

"Did anyone ever tell you how spectacular you are?" His other hand plowed into her hair, and he combed his fingers through it. "I've told you I've been dying to see you like this, imagining how you would look with your hair cascading down your back, your front—" His fingers brushed against the side of her breast, sending a bolt of desire that made her shiver.

"But the reality is even more beautiful than the fantasy. You look like a princess."

He dipped his head, and she was powerless to deny him the kiss he took right in front of her father and Jackson.

The same thought must've crossed his mind, and he pushed her back through the doorway and into the kitchen, still kissing her like he couldn't get enough.

God, the man was setting her on fire.

Nathalie didn't care that her father was in the next room, or that Jackson was probably eavesdropping and could hear each and every one of her throaty moans. All she cared about were Andrew's hands on her, and where she needed them to be. Hell, he could've stripped her naked, right there and then, and had his way with her on the kitchen floor, and she wouldn't have protested in the slightest.

Andrew had awakened in her something that had lain dormant throughout her adult life, and she felt her body come to life with sexual hunger.

The dam that she'd erected to stifle all of her yearnings and desires—never allowing herself to acknowledge they even existed because she'd had no outlet for them save for the touch of her own hand—had been breached. With last night's earth-shattering kiss creating the first fissures, weakening the structure so today it could burst asunder.

"Andrew," she breathed when he let go of her mouth, trailing his soft lips down her neck.

"Oh, God…" She couldn't help the words escaping her throat when he nipped her lightly where her neck met her shoulder. For some reason, she imagined him biting her there, piercing the skin, and was shocked to realize that she craved it.

What was wrong with her?

Was it the result of all those vampire romances she'd been devouring lately?

Must be, because no normal woman craved something so wicked.

"My Nathalie," he whispered before kissing her again.

Her name on his lips sounded so good, so right, and she didn't mind the 'my' either. She was all his, if only for these few stolen moments.

"I want to take you upstairs and make love to you," he mumbled against her lips, "for hours, and hours, until we both can't stand straight."

Shit, that was a splash of cold water on her raging libido. She probably wouldn't be able to stand straight after the first time, let alone hours.

She still had to either fess up to the embarrassing truth of her virginity or just let him discover it himself.

Or perhaps, she could bluff her way through it and say that it had just been a long time for her. After all, she was pretty sure that her hymen had been breached a long time ago by her first tampon.

What a nightmare that had been.

The tampon had gone in easily enough but refused to come out. She still remembered sitting on the toilet and trying to pull the damn thing out. It had taken her forever and hurt worse than pulling out a tooth. For years, she'd stayed away from tampons, using pads instead, until she'd figured out that they weren't all made the same. Some expanded in width, some in length, and the one she'd been unlucky or stupid enough to choose as her first had been probably one of those that expanded in width.

So yeah, chances were that she wasn't technically a virgin anymore, but she couldn't say so for sure.

Regardless of the state of her hymen, though, this was no way to start a relationship. What chance would they have of building trust if it started with a lie?

No, she would have to tell Andrew. She'd die of embarrassment, but at least she would go to heaven with a clear conscience.

Andrew must've noticed her body stiffen in his arms. "What's the matter? Did I go too far? I said I wanted to make love to you, but it doesn't mean that we have to tonight. There is no rush."

Great, now he thought that she was some kind of a prude or a scaredy-cat.

"No, it's not that I don't want to, I do. But we can't." She tilted her head toward the doorway.

Andrew sighed, his arms around her slackening their hold. "Yeah, you're right."

Damn, he sounded almost hopeless.

Nathalie's mind frantically searched for something to say, a plan, something that would give him enough of an incentive to keep coming back to her. She couldn't afford to lose him.

He smiled and touched his finger to her nose. "What are you thinking so hard about?"

"Trying to find a way for us to be together," she admitted.

"Easy, I take you to my place."

"I can't leave him alone."

"We'll bring a babysitter."

"He doesn't trust strangers. He will throw a tantrum."

"Okay, so we have half of a solution. That's already a step in the right direction. Now we only need to find him someone he likes."

Yeah, as if this was an easy feat. And there was still the issue of her confession.

34

ANDREW

"Hi, sweetheart, how is your day going?" This was the fourth time Andrew had called Nathalie today.

He just loved hearing her velvety, sexy voice. One of these days, he planned on asking her to sing something for him. Andrew had a feeling that she would be magnificent.

They were acting like a couple of lovesick teenagers.

Except, these three words were yet to be voiced by either of them.

"I miss you. When are you coming over?"

He chuckled. "Same time as every day." Since he'd met her, he'd been going to Nathalie's place every evening straight from the office. Her day started at four in the morning, so by nine she was falling asleep in his arms. The best he could hope for was to have a couple of hours with her.

The only exception had been the one evening he'd stopped by Tiffany's apartment.

Tiff's roommates had been very helpful, complaining about how she'd ditched them without notice and how they were now short on rent money. Apparently, her brother had shown up to collect her things, saying that she was going back home with him. Andrew's impression of the girl that had actually interacted with the guy was that she hadn't been suspicious. She'd said that he looked legit, knew things about Tiffany, and even had a southern accent.

She hadn't been lying.

In other words, it was a dead end. Andrew still wasn't convinced that things were as simple as they appeared, but at least it had eased Nathalie's mind.

"As soon as I can escape without getting in trouble, I'm heading to your place. I'm just going to stop by the supermarket and pick up a movie. Anything else you need from there?"

"Nope, nothing. I just want you to get here as soon as you can. I hope you're hungry. I made you something yummy for dinner."

"Starving."

"Excellent, see you at around seven?"

"You bet, goodbye, Nathalie."

Andrew had lied about being hungry. After the lunch he'd had with his boss, it would be hours before he could eat anything. But it made Nathalie happy watching him eat the special treats she was preparing for him.

Every evening, she'd have some new and exciting dish, and every time he'd put on a show for her, exaggerating wildly how much he was enjoying it and making her laugh.

He loved it, feeling a stupid sense of pride every time his shenanigans managed to get her to tear up with laughter.

Andrew sighed. Spending time with Nathalie was a pleasure, but he was suffering the worst case of blue balls since he'd reached puberty. Yesterday had been the fifth night in a row that he and Nathalie had been meeting at her place but doing nothing more than kissing. He could've taken it further, hell, Nathalie had been all but begging him to touch her, but Andrew knew that once he crossed that invisible line, he would not be able to stop.

The kissing was bad enough.

More than once, he'd been tempted to just take her on that lumpy couch in her den. But not only did he hate stealth guerrilla sex, there was something about Nathalie's fumbling inexperience that was flashing all kinds of warning signs for him to go slow and treat her with care.

So yeah, he was reliving his teenage years—of stolen kisses on the parents' sofa and achy blue balls, but also of sweet excitement and anticipation of what was still to come.

There was something to be said for delayed gratification.

Andrew wondered if the same held true for delayed orgasms. In his mind, it was a form of torture reserved for masochists, but perhaps he should give it a try, maybe it enhanced the experience the same way that delaying the whole thing did.

Although in his and Nathalie's case, it wasn't a choice or a sexual game, it was out of necessity and lack of options.

They'd contacted several agencies, but so far Fernando hadn't liked either of the two caregivers that they had invited for interviews. In fact, he'd refused to even talk to them. Maybe the old man was afraid of being fobbed off on the caregiver and losing Nathalie's constant company. To be honest, though, Andrew hadn't liked either of them.

If they were unable to locate someone both Nathalie and her father approved of, she would not be able to go out and have fun without worrying about him.

In a way, it was similar to finding a good babysitter for a kid but much worse. There were plenty of good and capable people willing to babysit a child or a baby and actually enjoy doing so. But judging by the two examples he'd seen, the same couldn't be said about caregivers for the elderly and infirm.

Since the stern reprimand he'd gotten from his boss after submitting that lousy report, Andrew didn't dare leave the office before six-fifteen. And after stopping by the supermarket and getting a movie and a bottle of wine, he'd arrived at Nathalie's a little after seven. Which meant that the shop was still open.

"Hello, my man, Andrew." Jackson was the one manning the register as he came in, and they clasped hands over the counter. The place was still full of customers even though it was nearing closing time and, curiously, Nathalie was nowhere in sight. Fernando was sitting in his usual booth at the back, still busy with the coloring books. Soon, they would need to send Jackson out to buy more.

"Where is she?"

"Taking a bath."

Andrew arched a brow. A shop full of people and she'd left Jackson alone to deal with everything? This wasn't like her.

"That's a first. How come?"

Jackson shrugged. "She finally realized that I can handle everything just fine and that she can take a breather. I told her to go relax with a bubble bath before your date." He winked suggestively.

Andrew pointed a finger at him. "Watch yourself, kid. I will not tolerate any disrespect from you. Am I clear?"

Jackson saluted. "Crystal."

Andrew relaxed his shoulders and smiled to put the boy at ease. Though by the smug look on his too-pretty face, Jackson hadn't been impressed by his posturing.

There were four new stools next to the counter and Andrew sat on one. "When did these get here?"

"Today. Bhathian got them from that yogurt place that is closing down. You know, the one over at 3rd Street?"

Andrew had no idea what yogurt place the kid was talking about, and he still didn't understand why Nathalie needed the stools in the first place. They were cramping the already tight space next to the register. "Oh, yeah? What for?"

Jackson's grin spread wide, the smugness practically dripping from him. "You're not here during the days, so you don't know. But since I started working here, the place is filled to capacity every morning and at lunch time. Nathalie needed more seats. We even had to move Fernando to the kitchen during the busy hours so we could use his booth. Let me tell you, the dude wasn't happy about it." Jackson shook his head and made a face.

Andrew could just imagine. Since he'd been spending time with Nathalie, he'd gotten acquainted with Fernando and his habits. The old guy clung to a precise schedule and everything had to be the same. The smallest of changes threw him off, and what was worse, once he got agitated over something, he stayed like that.

"How did you get him to move without him throwing a tantrum?"

Jackson winked. "I have my ways. The dude likes me. Calls me son. Probably because I'm here every day, all day long. He thinks of me as part of the family."

"That's good to hear. Makes things easier on Nathalie."

"About that." Jackson's face got serious, and he leaned over the counter to get closer to Andrew. "You need to get her out of here. I don't know how she does it, but I know it would drive me crazy to be chained to this place like she is. I can stay and watch over Freddy, no problem. And I'll even do it for free—for her. Nathalie deserves a break."

Andrew felt like kissing the kid.

Problem was, convincing Nathalie that it was safe to leave Fernando with Jackson wasn't going to be easy.

"Thank you. I really appreciate the offer, but I don't know if she'd go for it."

Jackson shrugged. "That's your job, dude. You have to convince her."

By the time Nathalie was done with her bath and came downstairs, Jackson had escorted the last customer out and locked the door.

A quick peck on the cheek was all the greeting Andrew got, and then she walked over to Jackson and kissed him too.

It was good that Andrew wasn't the jealous type—and that Jackson was still a kid—otherwise he wouldn't have liked it. Not one bit.

"Thank you, for closing up and everything. I had a wonderful time relaxing in a bubble bath."

The kid had the audacity to kiss her back. "You're welcome, and don't worry about the cleanup. I'm going to take care of it."

"I can't ask you to do this after leaving you alone in here for so long to do everything by yourself. Go home, you've done enough."

"You're not asking. I'm volunteering." Before she had the chance to argue about it, he grabbed the rag from the counter and proceeded to the table the last customer had eaten at—the only one that still needed cleaning. All the other tables had been already cleared and wiped clean. It took him about thirty seconds to be done with it, and on the way to the kitchen with the dirty dishes, he winked at Andrew as he passed him by.

Nathalie glanced around and smiled fondly at Jackson's retreating back. "Look at him, this kid is unbelievable—on his feet since eight in the morning and still going at it full speed. I guess it's his youth. His boundless energy makes me feel old."

"That's because you haven't done anything fun for ages. I'm taking you out on a proper date. Go upstairs and put on something nice."

Nathalie looked at Andrew with incredulous eyes. "And how do you suggest I do it?"

He was about to tease her and say something like '*you lift one foot and then the other and climb*' but decided to get to the point instead. They had no time to waste. Nathalie had been up since four in the morning, and she had no more than a couple of hours left in her. After that, she wouldn't be able to keep her eyes open. He needed to get his Cinderella back to bed at nine-thirty at the latest.

"Jackson is going to stay with your father."

"Jackson. You're not serious. He's just a kid."

"Yeah, but you have to admit that he is very capable, and he gets along with your father. He says Fernando likes him, calls him son."

Nathalie's expressive face showed her inner struggle, and she hadn't dismissed the idea immediately. There was hope. But then she shook her head.

"Jackson is wonderful. He works so hard. Aside from the baking he's practically taken over my job. I can sit and read a book if I want to. He handles everything like a pro. But I just can't ask him to do it. It's not fair to him. He works eleven hours a day, and even though I tell him to get here at ten, he is here already at eight to help me with the morning crowd. It's too much for him."

"It was his idea."

"Really? What did he say?"

"I told your boyfriend that he needs to get you out of here," Jackson called from the kitchen. "Oh, and thank you for the compliments."

Nathalie closed her eyes, a blush creeping up her cheeks. "The guy has the ears of a rabbit. I don't know how he does it, but he hears everything."

Andrew knew exactly how, but it wasn't something he could share with Nathalie.

"So, how about it?"

"I don't know. And what about the lasagna I made for you?"

Andrew rolled his eyes. "I'll eat it tomorrow. Stop looking for excuses."

There was another moment of hesitation, but then she smiled. "Let's do it. We can go somewhere that isn't too far away, and if Jackson needs us we can be right back."

"That's my girl. Now go. Just don't take too long, the clock is ticking."

35

NATHALIE

Upstairs in her bedroom, Nathalie felt giddy like a little girl.
She was finally going on an actual date.
But as she opened her closet and stared at her practical, everyday collection of denim and black, she realized she didn't have anything nice to wear.

Shit. She'd have to improvise.

Black stretchy jeans were good for every occasion, and she pulled them on first. A fitted black T-shirt was next, but as she put it on and examined her reflection in the mirror, she didn't like how the close fitting outfit accentuated the disparity between the size of her hips and the size of her bust.

Damn, how she wished she had an hourglass figure instead of a pear shape. There was something she could do about it, though. She pulled the T-shirt off and unhooked her bra. Looking at her breasts, she had to admit that even though they were smallish, they were nicely shaped and perky. They just needed a little boost, which could be achieved with the monster bra, as she called it, from Victoria's Secret. The thing promised to add two cup sizes, which would bring her modest B cup to a voluptuous D.

With a smirk, she put it on and reexamined her reflection. Was it too much? Now that she'd evened out her proportions, she looked sultry. Big hips, big breasts, and a tiny waist.

Perhaps the T-shirt would tame the effect.

It didn't. It kind of made it worse.

Stop fretting, you look gorgeous. You'll have all the guys drooling.

Damn, damn, damn. The new voice in her head chose a perfect timing to return. And what's worse, it was a guy, and he'd seen her naked.

"Get out," she hissed at him, trying to focus and block him like Tut had told her to.

I will. Please, don't be mad, I'm just trying to help.

He sounded so pitiful that she didn't have the heart to be mean to him. "What's your name?"

I'm still fuzzy about the details, but you can call me Sage.

"Because you're wise?"

That too, but also because I'm not sure if I'm a boy or a girl.

"You're a boy."

How do you know?

"You have a man's voice."

Can it be that you're interpreting it as masculine? I'm just a thought, I can have any voice.

He might have a point. No, it was a he, she was sure of it. "Why do you think you can be a girl?"

His masculine chuckle removed the last of her doubts. *Because I'm more excited about seeing your boyfriend shirtless than you.*

She couldn't help the giggle that escaped her throat. "Is that why you're pushing me to have sex with Andrew? Because if you think I'll let you join the ride you have another thing coming. It's just gross."

Meanie. He sounded pouty. *But I meant what I said about the bra, keep it. Add a pair of heels if you have them, and you'll look like a knockout.*

This was exactly what she was planning to do next.

Reaching up to the top shelf of her closet, Nathalie pulled down the only pair of high-heeled pumps she owned. They were brand new and still in the box they'd arrived in.

Wow, Nathalie, you look fab. Sage ended his endorsement with a whistle.

The effect was indeed impressive. She had never looked that sexy in her life. But it was also a little scary. Would she feel awkward?

Stop it. Go on, put on a little makeup, some jewelry, and out you go. Don't let Andrew wait too long.

He was right. With a sigh, she headed to the bathroom to get her mascara and lip gloss. "Okay, but I want you to skedaddle as soon as I'm done. You're not coming along on the date."

On one condition. You let me see Andrew's reaction when he sees you like this. After that, I promise to ghost out. Sage chuckled at his own pun.

"Fine." She finished curling her long lashes and smeared a little lip gloss on her full lips. Anything more than this and she would've looked like a hooker—especially with that monster bra on. A long gold-toned pendant necklace and a few bangles completed the look.

Nathalie grabbed her purse and quickly headed downstairs. Not because she didn't want to keep Andrew waiting, but because she was afraid that given another moment in front of the mirror, she would chicken out and take off the bra and the heels and replace them with something she was more used to wearing and felt comfortable in.

But as she stepped out from the kitchen and into the shop, where Andrew was waiting for her, the smoldering look in his eyes made her glad she'd had the courage to dress up for him.

Jackson whistled, then added, "You're one lucky dude, Andrew."

"I know." Andrew's voice sounded hoarse.

I bet he's so hard his zipper is about to pop.

Nathalie smiled a broad smile for Andrew while hissing in her head at Sage. *You promised.*

Have fun, Nathalie, and bang the guy. I would if I were you.

Get lost. Or better yet, get into his head. I'm not the one who's been putting on the brakes.

I bet he won't tonight, and I want to hear all about it tomorrow.

Fat chance. Now, go away.

Sage out.

She felt him fade away and concentrated on the sensation.

Perhaps next time she would be able to force him out if he refused to leave on his own.

36

ANDREW

Fuck, she looked gorgeous.

In fact, she looked so good that he didn't feel like taking her out and having all the horny bastards ogling her amazing body.

But he'd promised.

"Aren't you going to say something?" Nathalie's eyes sparkled with excitement as she sidled up to him, sashaying those luscious hips, her high-heeled shoes clicking on the tile floor.

"I'm speechless."

She kissed his cheek. "It'll do."

"Ready to go? Or do you want to say goodbye to your father?"

"No, I'd rather sneak out without him noticing it. I don't want a tantrum."

"She's right, just get out of here already." Jackson opened the door so carefully that the bells produced only minimal sound, and waved his hand to shoo them out.

He waited for Nathalie to step out and then leaned close to Andrew's ear and whispered, "You don't need to hurry back. I can stay the night."

Andrew clapped his shoulder. "I owe you, kid."

"And I'm going to collect." Jackson made the thumbs up sign before closing the door.

When he heard the lock engage, Andrew wrapped his arm around Nathalie's small waist and led her to his car.

"I can't believe I'm out. I feel free, like a prisoner who's just been released."

Andrew tightened his grip on her waist and turned her, bringing her flush against his body. "I need to kiss you, now." She tilted her head up to offer him her sweet mouth. With the heels on, Nathalie didn't need to stretch up on her toes, and he didn't have to bend as much to kiss her.

He licked at her lips and smiled. They were really sweet. The lip gloss she had on was strawberry flavored. "I'm going to ruin your lipstick."

"I don't care. Just kiss me already."

"Yes, ma'am." He took her mouth, licking inside it and exploring, his hands wandering down to cup her generous ass and press her against his aching shaft.

Nathalie moaned and gyrated her hips, adding to his torture.

God, he needed to fuck her so bad. He'd better stop right now before they ended up doing it in the backseat of his car.

"Why did you stop?" she breathed as he released her.

Reaching into his pocket for the car key, he pressed his thumb to the button and unlocked it. "I promised you a proper date, and I don't think a romp in the backseat of my car qualifies."

Nathalie chuckled. "I've never necked in a car before; it could be fun."

"I wasn't talking about necking." He lifted a brow. "And how come you never had? Did you go to an all-girl school?" That might explain some of her inexperience.

A shadow crossed Nathalie's eyes, and she shook her head. "No, I went to a regular school. Private, but coed." He opened the passenger door for her, and she slid inside, pulling the seatbelt and locking it in place without looking at him.

Had he said something wrong?

Was it a touchy subject with her?

God, it was so hard to understand women sometimes. Should he ask?

Nah, she didn't look like she wanted to talk about it. Better change the subject.

"So, sweetheart, where would you like to go?"

"What are the options? You're the expert on dating, you tell me. Where do you take your other dates?"

Yeah, he'd definitely said something that had upset her. Perhaps she was the jealous type and had imagined him doing all kinds of things in the backseat, to all sorts of girls.

"We can go to a romantic restaurant, or to a movie, or a bar, or a club, or just for coffee. What's your pleasure?"

Nathalie didn't pause to think. "I want to go dancing. Food and coffee I have every day, and if I want a drink I can have it also, but dancing… Yeah. That's what I want."

"Your wish is my command. Let's see what we have here." He did a quick internet search on his phone. "I got it." He pushed the transmission to drive.

"Where are we going?" she asked as he pulled out into the street.

"It's a surprise."

"Will there be dancing?"

"Of course, I always obey a lady's wishes."

She murmured something he couldn't hear and folded her arms over the chest—which looked suspiciously larger than usual. He stole another sideways glance. Yep, a push-up bra. Sweet Nathalie had gone all out to look sexy tonight.

Maybe she was expecting more compliments.

Yeah, that must be it.

"You look stunning, absolutely gorgeous."

She smiled and her shoulders relaxed a little. "Thank you."

Good, so he was on the right track. Perhaps a little more was needed.

"Sexy as hell."

Her cheeks reddened, and she waved her hand. "Stop it; you're making me blush."

"I like it when you blush, lets me know I have an effect on you. And anyway, it's true, you are unbelievably sexy."

She shrugged, but he could tell that she liked hearing it.

"Those stretchy pants hug your ass so perfectly that I'll be forced to dance behind you and hide these lush curves of yours from view to prevent riots."

She snorted, but her shoulders relaxed all the way.

"Is this the place?" Nathalie asked as he drove up to a valet stand with the name *Nostalgia* printed in red over its white canopy.

"Yep."

"What is it?"

"A sixties style restaurant club."

Nathalie glanced down at her jeans. "Am I dressed for a place like this?"

Andrew chuckled. "I don't think there is a dress code, but if there is, I'm going to fit in perfectly." Navy blue slacks, paired with a gray blazer, a checkered dress shirt, a tie, and brown dress shoes—yeah, a sixties club was the only place his work attire wouldn't seem inappropriate for.

"Have you been here before?" she asked as the valet opened the door for her.

Andrew joined her outside and wrapped his hand around her waist. "No, but a friend of mine from work recommended it." Andrew chuckled. "He said that it's perfect for an older crowd—like me. I hope you don't mind. If it's too staid, we can leave and find something else." He was almost ten years older than Nathalie, and her tastes might gravitate toward something more exciting.

"I'm sure it's going to be fine."

37

NATHALIE

Swaying to the sounds of Paul Anka's *Put Your Head on My Shoulder,* with Andrew's arms wrapped tightly around her, Nathalie was hovering somewhere between heaven and hell.

It felt so good, so right to be so close to him, feeling his hard body pressed against her, smelling his aftershave and his own unique masculine scent.

She was burning for more, and yet everything was so perfect that she didn't want to cut it short.

Her first date.

Nostalgia was just the right place for a romantic outing. Dim, with little round tables for two that were covered in red and white checkered tablecloths and topped with glass jars containing short fat candles. The framed posters on the walls were of the big stars of the sixties—all clean-cut and smiling brightly. A band of six guys was playing their biggest hits. Wearing tight fitting suits and hair that was slicked back with oil, they looked like they had been plucked from an old teenage romance movie.

Kind of reminded her of the prom scene from *Back to the Future.*

Surprisingly, though, the place was full of young couples and not the old farts Andrew had told her to expect.

"Are you having fun?" he whispered in her ear.

"I love it, thank you." She lifted her head to look at his smiling eyes, and he bent a little to kiss her lips lightly.

"Would you like to sit down and order dessert?"

No, she wouldn't. The steak she'd ordered had been huge, and she was still too full to even think of taking another bite of anything, no matter how good.

"I can't, I'm too full."

"Perhaps, coffee? Another drink?"

She chuckled. "Stop trying to feed me more, at this rate, my ass is going to double in size."

"This ass?" He cupped her butt cheeks and squeezed.

"Stop it, everyone can see..." she giggled.

"I can't help myself. I've been dying to squeeze it all evening long."

"Well, you'll have to wait for when we have some privacy."

"When?"

Good point. They had nowhere to go that was private unless she wanted to take up his suggestion about necking in the back seat of his car. Not that it offered a lot of privacy, tinted windows and all.

She sighed and put her cheek on his shoulder. "I don't know."

"We could go to my place."

God, it was tempting. But it was already late, and Cinderella's clock was ticking.

"I wish I could. But I have to get home and release Jackson. It's bad enough that I had him stay so late on a Friday night. Maybe it's still early enough, though, for him to catch up with his friends and go out."

"Let me text him. I don't think he would mind missing one night with his buddies. On the contrary, I'm sure that if I offer to pay him double for staying the night, he'll jump at it."

Nathalie felt a blush engulfing her cheeks. "You can't, he'll know what we..."

"So? He's not exactly an innocent lamb."

She shook her head. "I have to work with him Sunday. I'm going to die of embarrassment."

Andrew hooked a finger under her chin and tilted her head so she would look into his eyes. "I want you, Nathalie, and that's the only way we can be together. Unless you prefer me to join you in your bedroom at home. It's either this or that. Neither is a perfect solution, but you have to choose the one that's least problematic."

She didn't need to think, her place was out of the question. She was anxious enough about revealing her secret to Andrew, not to mention having sex for the first time. The last thing she needed was to worry about her father waking up and interrupting them.

But she didn't want to wait any longer. And besides, with tomorrow being the only day of the week she didn't have to wake up early, tonight was perfect.

"Okay."

"That's my girl."

Andrew's grin was almost scary—he kind of reminded her of a hungry wolf—but all she could feel was excitement.

Finally, she was going to do it! With Andrew!

As they got back to their table and Andrew texted Jackson, Nathalie waved the waiter over and ordered another drink.

Andrew arched a brow, but she shrugged. It wasn't as if she intended to sit and sip on it. The moment it got there she was going to down it on a oner. Nathalie needed the liquid courage.

"Jackson says no problem."

Nathalie wasn't surprised. She had a feeling Jackson was aware of their situation and wanted to help. Never mind that it was beyond embarrassing to have a teenage boy concerning himself with her sex life, or lack thereof.

The waiter brought her the fancy cocktail, and she tried to gulp it down, but it was too cold and too big.

Andrew clasped her hand. "Take your time, sweetheart, we have all night."

Wasn't she the luckiest woman to have a guy that was not only handsome and sexy but also considerate and patient?

She definitely was. But the flurry of butterflies in her stomach made her too restless to take her time.

Nathalie was all out of patience.

Her glass landed on the table with a clank, and she pushed up to her feet, at the same time snatching her purse from the back of her chair. "Let's go." She swayed a little, her legs not as sturdy as they were a few moments ago.

Andrew took out his wallet and put several bills on the table, enough to cover their meal and then some.

As they walked out and waited for the valet to bring Andrew's car around, the silence between them was loaded with anticipation, with sexual tension, and in Nathalie's case, with fear.

She wondered if that was how everyone felt before their first time. Probably. It was the fear of the unknown, the stories about it being painful, other stories of it being disappointing.

Doing her homework, she'd read all she could about the experience, and had even tried to watch porn, but it had been too awkward, and she logged out. It was a kind of voyeurism she hadn't felt comfortable with, even though the clip she'd started watching was from a movie done with professional actors. Not footage from a hidden camera with a long range lens catching some unsuspecting couple—which she'd unwittingly stumbled on during her search and quickly moved on to something else.

Her take home from all that research was that she shouldn't expect too much from her first time—that it was always awful, and those who claimed otherwise were lying.

Whatever, she needed to have this first time out of the way so she could have the second and the third and the fourth, and eventually find pleasure. Every woman went through this, and they still wanted more, so it couldn't be all bad.

38

ANDREW

"Here we are." Andrew cut the engine and clicked the garage door closed.

Nathalie seemed nervous, tense. She hadn't said much during the short ride to his house, answering his questions in monosyllables or nodding in response to the stories he'd told her. He was doing his best to put her at ease, but it wasn't working.

"Thank you," she said as he opened the passenger door and offered her his hand.

Damn, if she hadn't looked so anxious, he would've flung her into his arms and carried her straight into his bedroom. Instead, he wrapped his arm around her tensed shoulders and ushered her in, through the kitchen and into the living room.

"Your place is nice," she said, fidgeting with the long strap of her small purse.

"Thanks." He motioned to the sofa. "Please, have a seat. I'm going to get us some wine."

"Thank you."

Fuck, they were acting more like polite strangers than would-be lovers. Andrew was used to women who knew exactly what they wanted and weren't afraid to go for it. He'd walked away from those who'd exhibited even the slightest hesitation. After all, there were plenty of the other kind, and he hadn't had the time or the inclination to work so hard.

Wasn't worth it.

But Nathalie was different. He'd known since the first time he laid eyes on her that she was worth any effort. Because he had a feeling that she just might be the one.

Problem was, he didn't know how to go about making her comfortable.

Joking around had helped a little but not enough, and giving her space hadn't done much good either. On the contrary, it had only furthered the distance between them. Perhaps the exact opposite was needed. And if she balked he'd ease up a little.

As he came back with a bottle of wine and two glasses, he found Nathalie in the same position he'd left her, sitting on the edge of the sofa, the thin strap of her purse still nestled between her breasts. If she'd known the kind of attention it was drawing to her cleavage, she would've removed it right away.

Andrew put the bottle and stems down on the coffee table and sat down next to Nathalie. Wrapping his arm around her, he hooked a finger under her chin and turned her head so she would look at him. "What's the matter, sweetheart? Why are you so nervous?"

Nathalie swallowed audibly and tried to look away.

He held on, not letting her escape his scrutiny. "You can tell me anything. I'm not going to judge, I'm not going to criticize, or do any of the things that you're afraid I might do. I care for you, and I'm here for you. There is nothing you can do or say that will change the way I feel about you."

"Oh. God," she whispered. "Kiss me first, and then I'll tell you."

He pulled her closer against his body and brought his lips to hers, softly at first, stroking her mouth with his own, then teasing her lush lips with tiny flicks of his tongue.

Nathalie moaned and pressed herself closer to him, her lips parting in invitation. He slipped inside, sweeping his tongue against hers. When she moaned again, he slid his hand along the side of her breast then cupped it. But the damned padded bra she was wearing was like a chastity implement, robbing them both of sensation.

"This has to go," he murmured against her lips and reached behind her to slip his hand under her T-shirt and unhook the offending garment.

"Wait." She put a hand on his chest, and he halted his progress, but didn't take his hand out from under her shirt.

"What's the matter?"

"I need to tell you something."

She sounded so serious and so stricken that he pulled his hand out and concentrated on her face. For a moment, he had the terrible thought that maybe there was something wrong with her breasts—

Like a mastectomy—

Fuck, that would explain everything, wouldn't it...

Nathalie took a deep breath before lifting her head and looking into his eyes. *Such a brave girl.* Andrew braced for what she was about to reveal, promising himself to be as supportive as he could and not show how sorry he felt for her.

"Here goes, I've never done this before." As soon as the words had left her lips, her courage faltered, and she looked away.

He was about to say the words he'd prepared in his head, that it was okay and that he would find her sexy and beautiful regardless, when what she'd actually told him sank in.

"What do you mean? You've never done it in a guy's home?"

She glanced up at him with a look that seemed to question his mental faculties. "I've never had sex, anywhere. I'm still a virgin." She looked down and added in a murmur, "At least I think I am."

Fucking hell! A virgin?

He'd suspected that Nathalie was inexperienced, but not as in 'never had sex before'—just not frequent or recent.

Damn, what was he supposed to do now? He'd never been with a virgin before.

"Say something." There was worry in her voice.

"How? Why? Is it religion? Were you saving yourself for marriage?"

Shit, he wasn't handling it well at all. Instead of reassuring Nathalie, he sounded as if he was accusing her of something. So what if she was a devout Catholic or something like it? "Not that it makes any difference for me, but I'm just curious, that's all."

Nathalie shrugged, and a soft sigh escaped her lips. "I wish I could say that this was the reason—that it had been my choice—even if a weird one. The truth is that it just happened." She chuckled. "Or didn't happen as is the case."

Andrew sensed that there was a long and complicated story behind her statement, and decided that it was best to get it out once and for all and put it behind them.

Anyway, his arousal had been long gone along with his plans to finally make love to Nathalie. It had all flown out the window the moment the word *virgin* had been uttered.

He took her hand and gave it a squeeze for encouragement. "Okay, out with it, everything."

"I'm scared." There were tears in her eyes, and Andrew cursed himself for being an insensitive jerk who had no idea how to deal with this situation in a way that wouldn't make Nathalie feel even worse.

"Don't be. As I said before. I care for you, and I'm here for you. There is nothing you can do or say that will change the way I feel about you."

She snorted. "Yeah, right."

"Try me."

She looked up at him, her eyes searching his expression. He didn't look away, holding her gaze for as long as she wanted to hold his. After a long moment, she nodded.

39

NATHALIE

Nathalie had known Andrew would freak out. And she hadn't even mentioned the ghosts yet. But she was tired of hiding it from him, tired of fearing he'd run.

She was just so damn tired of it all.

In her cowardice, she hadn't been even upholding the deal she'd made with him on their first date of telling him one of her secrets in exchange for a story behind one of his scars—feeding him inconsequential little anecdotes instead.

If it ended tonight, so be it. She would cry for a month, or a year, or for the rest of her days, but if this wretched life was her fate, she had no choice but to accept it and do the best she could with it.

Screaming up to her father's God that it wasn't fair wasn't going to help her or do her any good. It was what it was, and no amount of wishing was going to change it.

"I won't blame you if, after you hear this, you want nothing to do with me."

Andrew chuckled and squeezed her hand. "Don't be so dramatic, Nathalie. It's not like virginity is a contagious disease or a handicap. It's just a temporary impediment that is easily removed." He winked.

Yeah, easy for him to say. He wasn't the one facing excruciating pain. But anyway, this was beside the point.

"That's not all. There is a reason I'm still a virgin at thirty, and it has nothing to do with religious or moral beliefs."

He nodded, but his posture revealed that he tensed in preparation for her story. God only knew what he was imagining. She'd better just spill it all out and be done with it.

"Since I was a little girl, I've been hearing voices in my head." She stole a glance at his face but was surprised to find no reaction to her statement. Encouraged, she continued.

"At first, my parents thought that I had imaginary friends, like many kids do.

What they didn't realize, though, was that the voices in my head didn't belong to children, or talk about childish things. The voices belonged to ghosts, people who had died and for some reason found me a receptive channel."

She snorted. "I'm still not sure if I'm really hearing ghosts or just crazy." Andrew still looked like nothing she'd said shocked him. He was either very good at hiding his feelings or very open minded.

"It was difficult because there were so many. It felt as if they were fighting for a chance to talk to me, but all of that stopped when Tut arrived."

"Who's Tut?"

"Just one of the voices, but he somehow managed to block the others, and since then I've been hearing only him. At least until recently, but I'll get to that later. It was a huge improvement, and it allowed me to lead a semi-normal life. But not completely normal. Kids made fun of me, calling me *Nutty Nattie* because I would often talk to myself. It made me shy and withdrawn, and I didn't have friends."

She chuckled. "Except Tut, that is. But he was a sarcastic adult, not a kid. When I went to college, it was bliss. No one knew me or my damned nickname, and a Bluetooth earpiece took care of my occasional blunder. But after years of being shunned, I was shy. I figured I had time, you know, to open up, make friends, go on dates, all the normal things a girl my age was expected to do. But time flew by, and at the beginning of my third year Papi got sick, and I had to come back and help with the shop. Since then, it was one big blur of never-ending days, working, taking care of Papi."

Andrew leaned and kissed her forehead. "You're a very good daughter, Nathalie. I doubt others in your position would've done the same."

She smiled, appreciating his compliment. "I didn't have a choice. There was no one else."

He nodded.

"So that's the whole story in a nutshell. Just one thing leading to another, and here I am—a crazy, thirty-year-old virgin."

"You're not crazy." He said it with so much conviction that she was inclined to believe that he really meant it.

"So you really believe that I hear ghosts in my head?"

Andrew shrugged. "You are not the first or the only one to communicate with the beyond. Most are charlatans, but some are genuine. There is so much out there that can't be explained, or shrugged off. I keep an open mind."

Thank you, God.

This was better than she'd ever dared to hope. Andrew, a grown man who seemed as down to earth as it got, believed her and seemed to accept her weirdness as something that wasn't completely out there.

It was nothing short of a miracle.

"You have no idea how relieved I am to hear you say that. I was sure you'd make some lame excuse and take me home, then run as far and as quickly as you could."

He leaned into her and kissed her lips lightly. "You're not getting rid of me that easily. I'm here to stay."

"And the virginity?"

He chuckled. "Again, you're not the first or the only one with that condition."

"So you don't mind?"

Andrew rubbed his neck before giving her a crooked smile. "You were so brave to tell me everything that I can do no less. The truth is that I've never been with a virgin, and I'm not sure how to make it good for you. But I'm going to do my best."

Nathalie closed her eyes and released a long breath. "So we are still going to do it?"

Andrew's voice dipped half an octave. "I promise you, sweetheart, by tomorrow morning you'll be a virgin no more."

Thank God.

Andrew pushed to his feet and before she could guess his intentions, he bent and lifted her up in his arms. "I'm taking you to bed." He paused for a moment and looked into her eyes as if asking her to confirm or deny it.

She smiled and wrapped her arms around his neck. "Just promise not to drop me on the way. I'm heavy."

He grinned like the cat who was about to eat the canary. "Nonsense, you're light as a feather, sweetheart."

She wasn't, but Andrew carried her to his bedroom as if she was.

She pressed her cheek to his and sniffed his skin—aftershave and man—the scent of a promise.

40

ANDREW

Holding Nathalie in his arms suffused Andrew with a barrage of unfamiliar feelings.

He was humming with excitement. Her confession about the voices in her head had reinforced his belief that she was a Dormant. But his joy was tainted by a dark and unfamiliar possessiveness. Because there was only one way to find out. One that he would never allow. No male was going to touch his Nathalie but him.

Unfortunately, he was still just a mortal and didn't possess the equipment necessary to inject her with the venom she needed in order to activate her dormant genes.

Andrew wondered if it was possible to extract the venom, like from a snake, and inject it with a syringe. Problem was that even if it were possible, he still wouldn't be able to let another male's venom do the work. If anyone's essence was going into Nathalie, it was going to be his.

He would have to go through the transition first, and then turn her.

But what if she wasn't a Dormant, and he ended up squandering a chance for a normal life with her?

Or worse, what if he didn't make it?

Damn, he needed to clear his head of these thoughts because he had to deal with a more immediate concern. Bringing Nathalie pleasure while taking her virginity.

Talk about impossible goals.

Well, one thing at a time. First, he would make her climax, and only then would he dare to attempt her deflowering. And if it became too much for her to bear, he would stop and take care of his own need with the help of his own hand —same way he'd done every night since he'd gotten involved with Nathalie. And thank God that he had. He wasn't as strung up and impatient as he would've been otherwise.

Causing Nathalie anguish was out of the question. If it proved to be only a little painful, then fine, he'd continue, but he would never allow her to suffer. Not going to happen.

In his bedroom, he laid her gently on the bed and turned on the bedside lamp. It bathed the room in dim light, casting a golden glow on her perfect figure. Andrew sat down beside her and cupped her cheek. "You have nothing to fear, sweetheart. We'll go slow, one little step at a time, and if it becomes too much for you, at any point, we will stop."

She nodded on an exhale, and reached for him, wrapping her hands around his neck and pulling him down for a kiss. It started slow and gentle, a kiss meant to ease her fears, but Nathalie had other ideas. Soon she was pulling him down harder and arching her back so their bodies would touch.

He wanted her naked.

Andrew broke the kiss and smiled. "You're wearing way too many clothes. Especially this medieval contraption." He flicked the side of her padded bra.

Nathalie giggled, blushing. "It makes my breasts look bigger."

Andrew frowned. "There's no need. They're perfect the way they are."

"How would you know?" she taunted, her tone becoming husky.

"Well, let's find out, shall we?" He tugged on the bottom of her T-shirt, and she leaned up so he could take it off, then lay back down, her breaths coming out in small, rapid puffs.

"You're beautiful," he whispered as he slid the bra straps off her shoulders, revealing just the tops of her breasts. But this was not the kind of bra that wanted to cooperate with slow seduction. Andrew got impatient and reached for the hook on Nathalie's back, snapping it open with the fingers of one hand while flinging it away with the other.

Finally, she was naked before him, even if only partially, and he hissed as his shaft kicked up, tenting his loose slacks.

"Damn." He couldn't help the word escaping his mouth. He should've worn jeans.

Nathalie was barely breathing as he watched her, drinking up her beauty.

"Touch me," she whispered.

He touched his thumb to the outline of her taut nipple, tracing it round and round.

Nathalie shivered. "You're torturing me."

Yeah, he'd teased her enough. His palm closing around one breast, he brought his mouth to the other and closed his lips around one sweet nipple, then sucked it in.

Nathalie mewled, her back arching off the bed. Her little nubs were so tight that he was sure they ached.

He wondered whether she would like having them pinched.

Only one way to find out.

Releasing the one he had been suckling, he closed his palm around it and moved to the other. When it was also wet, he cupped it with his other hand, letting her have a moment to relax before closing his fingers around both nubs, and pinching them simultaneously. Gently at first, but as her face showed more bliss than discomfort, he tugged harder, pulling her breasts up and away from her body.

Her hands shot up, but not to stop him. She laid them on top of his as if to tell him not to stop.

But he didn't want her nipples to become too tender. There was still a lot more he wanted to do to them. He eased up and then cupped her tender peaks, letting the warmth soothe them.

"Pfff..." Nathalie released a long puff of breath.

"How about we get rid of the rest of your clothes?" he asked gently.

"Please." Sweet Nathalie wanted him to undress her.

"With pleasure, my lady." He popped the button of her jeans open and pulled down the zipper, then peeled the tight material off her, one leg at a time.

Nathalie seemed satisfied with letting him do the honors, only lifting her behind a little to ease the way.

Her black panties were plain cotton, and for a moment, Andrew contemplated leaving them on, thinking that she would be more comfortable with a gradual progression.

But in the end, he just couldn't help it. Andrew wanted her fully nude. With one strong tug, he divested her of the panties as well.

Nathalie didn't try to hide from him, although he could see her hands fisting the bed cover as she battled against the instinct to cover the most private place on her body.

He wouldn't have allowed it.

She was his.

God, where did this come from? Andrew shook his head. He wasn't a caveman... Or maybe he was but wasn't aware of it until now.

Maybe deep down all men were still cavemen when it came to the woman they prized above all else.

As he stared at what he'd uncovered, his shaft pulsed inside his pants, begging to be released. Unlike a lot of the women he'd seen naked, Nathalie wasn't completely bare, and her nearly black, neatly trimmed pubic hair was glistening with the evidence of her desire.

"So fucking sexy."

Reassured by his compliment, she unclenched her fists and even arched her back a little.

As he traced a finger down her slit, following the wetness to its source, Nathalie gasped and jerked her thighs together.

"Sh... it's okay." He ran his palm over her thigh. "Don't be scared, I'm only going to bring you pleasure."

"I know. It was just a reflex. I couldn't help it." She tried to part her trembling legs, but they seemed to resist. "Shit, why am I such a coward? I want this, I want you, and still...it's so hard to just let it happen."

Taking a deep breath, Nathalie closed her eyes and parted her legs. Blindly, she reached for his hand. "Don't stop."

Such a brave girl, and he wasn't making it easy for her.

She was completely bare before him, while he was still wearing a blazer and a tie—his eyes roving over her magnificent body and his hands touching her in a most intimate way.

But he couldn't help himself either. There was something very satisfying in this disparity, a sense of ownership that had nothing to do with reality. And as much as his rational mind detested the idea of Nathalie still being a virgin, of all the years of pleasure she'd lost, some primitive side of him was very happy about being her first.

And if he had any say in it, her last.

41

NATHALIE

Sex was amazing, terrifying, exhilarating.

And they hadn't even done anything monumental yet.

Nathalie was discovering things about herself that were shockingly surprising. Like that she wasn't at all shy about her nudity. In fact, Andrew baring her one piece of clothing at a time had turned her on, especially since he was doing it while still wearing his tie and jacket.

Hot, hot, hot.

She loved his eyes on her, loved the passion in them, the smoldering desire. A girl couldn't help but feel beautiful when a guy like Andrew gazed at her nude body with such hunger.

Over her initial shock of feeling his fingers explore her wet heat, Nathalie wanted more; more of Andrew's hands, more of his mouth, more of his lips, more of his tongue. She wanted more of everything even though the emotional and physical storm bombarding her senses was so exhausting that she was afraid she wouldn't last under the onslaught.

She was on fire for him, so turned on that she felt like she could climax just from his gentle fingers caressing her folds. And if he thrust a finger inside her, she would for sure combust on the spot.

When he removed his hand, she barely stopped herself from grabbing it and returning it to where she wanted it.

But then, he got up and began stripping.

Finally, she was going to see him naked. Every time she'd felt his hard, muscular body—under her hands as she caressed his back and his chest, and against her breasts, as she pressed herself against him—she'd been imagining him naked. He was going to be magnificent.

First, he removed his jacket and draped it over the back of a chair, then his tie. His shirt was next. She loved watching him open the cuff buttons and roll the sleeves up, revealing his muscular forearms, which were covered in a smattering of dark hair. But, this time, there was no need for it, and after taking care of the cuffs he moved on to the buttons on the front of his shirt, popping each one slowly and revealing his muscular chest a little at a time.

Nathalie held her breath, waiting for the moment when he would part the two halves. But Andrew just left the shirt hanging open as he kicked off his loafers, unbuckled his belt, pulled the zipper down, and stepped out of his slacks.

She managed to get a good look at his strong thighs before he turned around and sat on the bed to remove his socks.

With the shirt still on.

Nathalie frowned as a chilling thought crossed her mind. Was Andrew embarrassed to show his chest or his back? Perhaps the scars on his face were just a small sample, and there were many more? Was he disfigured?

Not that she would find him any less sexy if he was scarred, but it pained her that he felt the need to hide it from her.

With the socks off, he lifted a little to pull down his boxer shorts, and at last shrugged the shirt off of his shoulders.

As she'd expected, his back was peppered with scars, old bullet holes that had healed a long time ago, but it was also heavily muscled and perfectly proportioned. Andrew was even more of a hunk without clothes than he was with them—which was saying a lot since he usually wore a professional attire that tended to enhance the looks of most men, hiding their bellies while adding width to their shoulders. But in Andrew's case, it had been hiding not flaws but sheer masculine beauty.

Then he turned around.

Oh. My. God. His shaft was huge, and dark, and it was pointing at her.

Nathalie had no idea whether Andrew was particularly endowed or whether this was what most men sprouted between their legs when aroused, but in either case, she knew it wasn't going to fit. If a tampon had given her trouble, this thing was going to split her in half.

Involuntarily, a hand flew to her mouth, and she scrambled back against the headboard.

Andrew's expression turned from puzzled to embarrassed as he glanced down at the piece of his anatomy that was scaring the hell out of her.

"I should've left the boxers on, shouldn't I?"

She nodded. Maybe if he'd turned the light off and she didn't see it...

She cleared her throat. "I'm sorry, I must seem to you like some country bumpkin. It's just that you're so big... Are you? Big, I mean? I wouldn't know."

Could this be any more embarrassing?

Andrew chuckled. "I'm probably average, but no one complained one way or another, yet." He crawled on the bed and lay sideways to face her. "Go on, touch him. It will be less scary if you get to feel him."

Tentatively she reached with an extended finger, touching it lightly. "Don't you dare laugh at me," she said, feeling Andrew's big body shake with stifled chuckles. "It's not funny."

"No, I guess it's not," he choked out. "He's not going to jump and bite your hand, you know."

Oh for heaven's sake, stop being such a big coward. She rolled her eyes at herself and reached her shaking hand forward. Andrew's abdominals clenched in anticipation, his impressive six pack getting more defined. He groaned as her hand closed around his shaft which jerked as if excited to be touched.

Well, of course it is, you idiot.

Hm, he felt kind of nice. Firm yet soft, and velvety smooth, except for the big vein running under it. Curiosity won, and she leaned closer and took a sniff. Andrew's scent was even stronger there. Very nice.

In response, he inhaled sharply, and his erection pulsed in her hand, a bead of moisture arising on the broad head.

How fascinating...

She rubbed the pad of her thumb over it, spreading the viscous drop around the mushroom head.

His hand reached for her head, stroking her hair. "Well? What do you think? Not as scary anymore?" His voice was husky, strangled.

Nathalie looked up into his hooded eyes, so full of passion, of need, and felt herself grow wet between her legs. Her lips parted, and he dipped his head to kiss her, gently, even though he must've been starving for more—such an incredible guy, giving her all the time she needed and not pressuring her at all.

"No, not scary at all. Kind of nice, actually. But I still don't think it's going to fit. In fact, I know it won't."

"We are going to try, and if he doesn't fit we are not going to force it. I told you, one little step at a time, there is nothing to fear. But I have a question."

He looked so serious that she was afraid of what he was going to ask. Though come to think of it, she had no more secrets to hide.

And wasn't that a terrific feeling? She felt at least fifty pounds lighter. "Yes?"

His eyes were smiling, the feathery wrinkles around them fanning out. "Are you going to keep calling him, *it*?"

Nathalie giggled. "What would you like me to call him? Little Andrew?"

He made a face. "I don't like the word *little* associated with my manhood."

She laughed. Even without having anything to compare it with, she was sure there was nothing little about Andrew. "Okay, how about Big Andrew?"

He shrugged. "That could work, but how about just cock? Or if you're not comfortable with that, there is dick, shaft, erection, manhood, Johnson, woody, Mr. Happy, Mr. Big, and numerous others—plenty to choose from."

She kind of liked *Mr. Happy*, but doubted Andrew would. The most common one was cock, and the least explicit one was shaft.

"I can try..." *Shit*, even this was difficult.

"Come on, go for it, say cock, be naughty," he encouraged.

It was just a word, one everyone was using, shouldn't be a big deal. "Cock," she blurted in a hurry. "Here, I said it, are you happy?"

"Yes, come here." He drew her closer to him.

"I'm really not comfortable with this word. How about shaft? Or Mr. Happy?" she tacked on.

Andrew chuckled. "Other than *Little Andrew* I'm fine with whatever."

42

ANDREW

When he'd taken off his shirt, Andrew had been worried about Nathalie's response to his scarred body, but he hadn't been prepared for her reaction to his cock.

He wasn't *that* big.

It would've been funny if Nathalie were a young girl—a disturbing thought since it would have made him a pedophile. Andrew doubted many girls reached the legal age of consent with their virginity intact.

Sixteen was probably the average age when most did away with the impediment. But not everyone. Some were left on the sidelines, getting in the game much later, and some never.

The good thing was that Nathalie seemed to have gotten over her initial hesitancy, as evident by her hand on his shaft. In fact, she seemed reluctant to let go, pressing her perky breasts against his chest and gyrating her ample hips while stroking his manhood and spreading around the drops of pre-cum gathering at its tip.

At this rate, he'd be coming in her soft little palm in no time. Not that it was necessarily a bad plan. Nathalie could take care of him with her hand, and he'd reciprocate with his fingers and his tongue, bringing her to a climax with no pain involved.

Problem solved.

Trouble was, he was pretty sure Nathalie wanted to change her virgin status as soon as possible. She seemed embarrassed by it. And anyway, it had to be done, if not tonight then the next time. Either way, it was going to be painful for her.

He closed his hand over hers and halted her up and down strokes.

She lifted a pair of worried eyes at him. "Am I doing it wrong?"

"No, sweetheart, you're doing it perfectly—too good."

"Oh..." she smiled as understanding dawned.

Andrew gave Nathalie's shoulders a little push, helping her to her back. "It's my turn to pleasure you."

"What do you want me to do?"

"Nothing. You just lie there and focus on how it feels. I'll do the rest." He palmed one breast and kneaded, then began thumbing the nipple.

"Okay..." she breathed but seemed hesitant.

"Do you trust me?" He tugged on her stiffened peak.

"Yes." It came out as a whimper.

"Good girl." He leaned and fastened his lips around it, sucking it in and licking all around.

Her back arched, and she stretched her arms above her head, bringing more of her breast into his mouth. He rewarded her with a hand on her other breast, kneading, plucking, in sync with what he was doing with his mouth.

Nathalie's hips were restless on the mattress, going up and down and side to side, and he knew she was wet and aching to be touched. Exactly the way he wanted her to be.

Hungry for him.

Releasing her breast, he trailed his hand over her soft belly down to her needy center, slowly, teasing her.

She mewled, then bit her lower lip, trying to stifle the sounds coming out of her throat.

"Don't," he commanded. "I want your moans and your whimpers and your gasps. Don't hold anything back. Don't hide from me."

Nathalie nodded, her lip still caught between her teeth.

He lifted his hand away from where she wanted it, bringing it to her mouth, and tugged on her lip. "Let it go."

"Sorry."

Andrew chuckled softly. Nathalie was so desperate for his touch that she would've obeyed any command. Which got him thinking...

Nah, not tonight.

But some day, when she was no longer such a newbie, definitely.

He repeated the journey down her body, all along keeping his eyes on her face. She was panting, her breasts rising and falling so enticingly that he took one into his mouth as his finger reached her wet folds.

"Oh, God..." she exclaimed when he gathered her moisture and pressed his thumb to her clit, her legs falling apart of their own volition.

Nathalie was drenched and more than ready to accept his finger.

At first, he just circled her opening, keeping his thumb gently pressed to her clit. She lifted her butt in a not so subtle effort to get him to push inside her.

Sweet Nathalie, wanton, greedy, needy. It was exactly the way he wanted her. He pushed his finger inside her wet, hot sheath, just up to the first knuckle.

Her breaths were coming out in rapid puffs, and again, she wiggled her sexy ass, trying to get more of it.

"You want more, baby? You want my finger all the way inside you?"

"Yes, oh, God, yes..."

Andrew pushed as far as he could go—his thumb over her clit and his finger buried deep inside her spasming sheath.

She was going to come, and the only reason she was still hanging by a thread was that he wasn't moving his finger inside her, denying her the friction that would send her over the edge.

"Do you want to come, sweetheart?" he whispered in her ear, then licked into it.

Nathalie moaned and arched her back. "Yes, please, I'm on fire…"

One, two, three… and takeoff…

Three strokes, was all it took for Nathalie to explode, her cries loud enough to alert the neighbors.

Who cares, let them call the police…

Just from watching her come, he'd almost climaxed himself. His virgin hadn't held back. She'd taken all that he'd given her with blissful abandon and without reservation.

Magnificent. Brave. Sexy.

When her quaking subsided, he cupped her between her legs.

This is mine, he said—on the inside.

On the outside, he leaned and kissed her gently, first her lips, then her closed lids. "You're amazing."

She opened her eyes. "Me? I haven't done anything. You're the one who's amazing. This was just…wow…"

"I'm not done yet."

She blushed. "I know, you haven't had your release yet."

"We'll worry about me later. I'm not done pleasuring you."

Instinctively, she closed her legs, trapping his hand. "There is more?"

"Much more."

"I don't think I can. Not right away."

He rolled on top of her, his shaft nudging her wet entrance. He shuddered with need. She stiffened.

"Don't worry, I'm not going to push inside you." He kissed her neck then trailed his lips down to her breast.

"What if I want you to?" she husked as he swirled his tongue around her nipple.

"Patience, darling. All in good time." Andrew slid further down her body, kissing her sternum, her abdomen, and then the top of her mound.

"What are you doing?"

43

NATHALIE

Andrew lifted his head and smiled. "What does it look like I'm doing?"

She'd read about it, of course. One of her favorite sci-fi romance series was all about hot aliens who loved nothing better than to go down on a woman. It had provided her with plenty of material for naughty fantasies and self-pleasuring.

She'd been yearning to experience this for so long, but now that Andrew was about to turn her fantasy into reality, she was a little apprehensive.

What if he didn't like how she tasted or smelled?

On the other hand, he knew what he was doing and must've done this plenty of times before. Chances were that she didn't taste or smell differently than the other women he'd pleasured.

Shit, thinking about Andrew with others made her angry. He was hers, whether he knew it or not.

"Do you like doing it?" she asked, hoping his answer would be the same as the aliens' in her books—that he not only loved it, but needed it, couldn't live without it...

"Of course, I do. There is nothing that turns me on more than bringing you pleasure and hearing you moan and scream my name as you climax. I love it. Now spread your beautiful legs and let me in." He applied light pressure to her knees, urging her to open for him.

This was good, not the exact same words as in her alien novels, but close enough.

Lying back on the pillows, Nathalie closed her eyes and lay back. She let her legs fall to the sides. It was so wanton and oh so naughty. But it was okay, she trusted Andrew.

"That's my girl." He slid even further down and pressed a kiss to her nether lips.

Anticipating his next move, she flooded with wetness.

Using his thumbs, he spread her wide, opening her to his eyes, his tongue. Nathalie fought the urge to clamp her knees back together and deny him access. It was too much, too soon, and yet she didn't want him to stop. She wanted this, had dreamed about it for years, and she wasn't going to chicken out. Not now, not when she was finally about to experience what was sure to be the best orgasm of her life.

"Oh..." she cried out and torqued when his tongue made contact with her wet center.

He lapped at her gently at first, just a few soft up and down swipes, then took her by surprise as he penetrated her with his tongue, thrusting in and out forcefully.

She bit her lip, trying to still her restless gyrations.

Andrew did it for her, clamping her hips as he delved deeper, fucking her with his tongue. When he withdrew and licked her throbbing clit, her head thrashed, and she heard herself mewl.

Keeping her pinned, he penetrated her with one thick finger and kept licking all around her sensitive nub. Soon, another finger joined the first. Nathalie felt stretched, uncomfortably at first, but as he kept pumping in and out of her, her sheath loosened, accommodating the extra thickness.

She was so close, and the only reason she hadn't detonated yet was that Andrew was skirting her clit, licking all around it but not touching it directly.

He added a third finger, stretching her impossibly wide. It stung, but as his velvet tongue flickered over her clit, there was an additional outpour of moisture and her sheath loosened even more. He started pumping, slowly, then faster. Greedy for those thick fingers fucking in and out of her, she moved up and down to meet each thrust.

He twisted his fingers, opening her, and as he touched a tender spot inside her, he closed his lips over her throbbing nub.

With a cry, Nathalie erupted.

He kept licking and sucking and pumping until the last of her quakes subsided. When he withdrew his fingers, a stream of wetness followed, running down her inner thighs and creating a puddle on the bed.

God, how embarrassing. Tentatively, Nathalie lifted her head and looked at Andrew.

There was a look of smug satisfaction on his face as he knelt between her legs, his massive erection fisted in his hand.

No longer concerned with the pain, she wanted to feel Andrew inside her. If her sheath had stretched for his fingers, it would do the same for his shaft. It may sting at first, but she didn't expect it to hurt as bad as everyone on the Internet claimed.

She was aching as it was, needy, empty.

"I need you."

"Do you want it inside you?" He ran his fist up and down his shaft.

"Yes."

"You don't happen to be on the pill, do you?"

Damn, she'd forgotten all about protection, though not against pregnancy. That part she had covered. "As a matter of fact, I am. I've been on the pill for years to regulate my periods."

Andrew nodded. "I'm clean. We get checked at work every three months. My last test results are from two weeks ago."

Did she trust him? Had he been with other women since they'd met? Nathalie hoped not. But she had to ask.

"Have you been with anyone since then?"

He frowned. "No, of course not." Then he smirked. "Not counting my right hand, that is. I've been with her every night, sometimes twice, fantasizing about your luscious body."

Nathalie blushed. She'd been guilty of the same. In fact, some of her fantasies about sex with Andrew had been quite shocking. She might have lacked experience, but she had one hell of an imagination.

But did she believe that he hadn't been with another woman?

He wouldn't lie about something like that, would he?

Or perhaps she wanted to believe him because she didn't want their first time together to be with a rubber membrane between them.

"Okay."

She expected Andrew to pounce on her, but instead, he bent down and resumed his tonguing. Only when he'd gotten her soaking wet and writhing again did he grip his shaft and guide it to her entrance.

"Shh... relax," he whispered as she tensed under him. "Slow and easy..." he rubbed his shaft against her wet folds, gathering her moisture and coating it with her natural lubricant.

Then he pushed, wedging in just the tip of the broad head inside, and halted.

They were both panting with the strain of it. Him—keeping still when he needed to thrust, and her—gritting her teeth against the pain.

But while the mouth of her sheath felt like a ring of fire, burning from the stretching it was forced to endure, the rest of her marveled at the feel of Andrew's big body on top of her. His sweat-slicked chest smashing her tender breasts, his rugged cheek pressed against hers, his powerful thighs cradled in between her soft ones. It felt so right. This is where he belonged—where she belonged.

"More," she breathed. "Just a little more."

As he pushed in another inch, she dug her nails into his muscular butt, not to keep him from withdrawing, but to prevent herself from bucking him off. It hurt like hell. But she wasn't going to let him stop until he was seated all the way inside her.

After tonight, she was going to be a virgin no more. Even if it meant going through hell to get there.

"A little more," she whispered again, bracing against the pain and willing her body to accept the intrusion.

He lifted his head and looked at her, his forehead beaded with sweat and his brows drawn with worry. "You're crying."

Now that he said it, she felt hot tears sliding down her temples. "It hurts, but I don't want to stop."

"Are you sure? I hate to see you in so much pain. I don't have to finish inside you. We can do this in stages, continue some another day."

This was so sweet of him, but she wanted it over and done with so the next time would be all about pleasure.

"I'm sure."

He nodded, his harsh features soft with some indescribable feeling.

Lifting his hand, he cupped her cheek and kissed her. The taste of her own juices on his tongue was for some reason incredibly erotic, naughty, and she grew wetter in a rush. The pain ebbed, turning from a burning ring of fire into a dull ache.

When he was done kissing, Andrew brought his finger to her mouth, first gently rubbing at her lips and then pushing it inside. With another outpour of wetness, she closed her eyes and sucked on it, imagining it was his shaft.

He pulled his finger out of her moist mouth with a pop, and brought it down to her clit, gently rubbing it as he pushed another inch inside.

Why was it so difficult? It no longer hurt as bad, and she would've loved for Andrew to just shove all the way in in one powerful thrust. But her inner muscles weren't cooperating, and every little push was a struggle just to get it a little deeper.

And where the hell was that barrier everyone was talking about? Was it hiding all the way at the end of her channel? But it was supposed to be near the opening and Andrew's shaft was already past that point... Perhaps it had really been that first tampon that had done away with her hymen.

For some reason, the thought relaxed her. Part of her anxiety must've been a subconscious anticipation of the tearing and the added pain it would entail. But now that she suspected that the barrier was no longer there, she felt her channel loosen a bit more.

Andrew pushed a little further. He was halfway there.

"You're so brave, sweetheart." There was tenderness in his gaze, but also something else. A possessiveness that she welcomed wholeheartedly because she felt exactly the same.

She wasn't brave enough, though, to say what was on the tip of her tongue. That he was hers as much as she was his, and she was never letting him go.

He kissed her again, deeply, passionately, and as she melted into the kiss, he drew back his hips and with one forceful thrust plunged all the way in.

She cried out from the pain, but at the same time, having him seated so deeply inside her, his shaft touching the end of her channel, felt like a victory.

They were joined.

They were one.

She wrapped her arms around him and pressed herself up against his chest.

"Are you okay?" he whispered in her ear.

"I'm great."

He lifted his head and looked at her. When he was satisfied that she'd meant it and that her eyes were dry, he withdrew and thrust again, and again, and with each subsequent push there was a little less pain and a little more pleasure.

She moaned, and lifted her hips to meet the next thrust, and the next, and the one after that.

Her enthusiastic response melted away the last of Andrew's restraint, and he turned rougher, more demanding. Grabbing her ass cheeks in both hands, he lifted her and held her in place as he drove harder, deeper, growling and groaning like an animal.

God, she loved how mindless he'd become—for her. Seeing him lose himself to the passion with such abandon sent her spiraling toward another orgasm.

His neck and chest flexing, his face contorted, he roared as he threw his head back and erupted inside her. Fiery and wet, the climax crashed over her, and she screamed his name.

Andrew collapsed on top of her, his powerful heart thundering against her chest and his ragged breaths feathering her sweat-slicked neck.

Now that it was over, and the level of endorphins and adrenaline subsided, the burning not only returned full force but expanded. Her whole channel felt like it was on fire. She couldn't bear it even for a moment longer and pushed on Andrew's chest, but it took him a second or two to comprehend what she wanted before he withdrew.

A rush of liquid trailed after his shaft. Was it blood? Or just his semen and her own wetness? She had to know.

As Andrew rolled onto his back, she sat up and looked at the big wet spot that was left behind. But it was too dark to see colors.

"Can you turn the light up?"

He chuckled, but reached to the lamp on the nightstand and turned it up a notch.

There was no blood.

"Well, I guess it was the tampon after all," she muttered.

"Tampon?"

"Long story, but it turns out that I wasn't a virgin after all. I've always suspected that my hymen had fallen victim to a tricky tampon years ago. Now I know for sure. There was no blood."

Andrew glanced at the spot and shrugged. "Does it bother you?"

"No, not really." She plopped against the pillows.

"How do you feel?"

"Sore, but wonderful. I love sex." She smiled at him. "I could use a bath, though."

"Coming right up, sweetheart." He rolled out of bed and padded away to the bathroom.

She heard him turn the water on.

A moment later he came back, holding a couple of wet washcloths, and sat on the bed.

"May I?" he asked as he brought one between her legs.

Should she let him?

Hell, why not. "Go ahead, just be gentle."

"Of course." He dabbed the warm washcloth to her sore opening.

She couldn't stifle the relieved sigh.

Andrew winced. "That bad, eh?"

She shrugged. "It was worth it."

Andrew replaced the washcloth with the other one, and just draped it over her mound. He then climbed carefully on the bed, as if afraid to disturb the mattress, and lay on his side next to her. Gently, he cuddled up to her, draping an arm around her waist.

Nathalie turned her face to him. There was worry and guilt in his eyes as if he was blaming himself for her pain.

She cupped his cheek and leaned to kiss his lips. "You were wonderful, Andrew. And I'm glad I've waited for you to be my first. I doubt any other man would've been so careful with me and so focused on ensuring I had the best experience possible."

The worry in his eyes ebbed, replaced by some tender feeling that looked a lot like love.

Could she dare to hope?

Did she feel the same?

44

ANDREW

I'm falling in love with this beautiful, fascinating, passionate, courageous, and kind woman.

Or perhaps he'd already been in love with her, but had just realized it now.

And yet, he had to consider that it might've been the result of post-coital bliss combined with awe and gratitude to Nathalie for entrusting him with such an important milestone in her life.

Caressing her soft, flushed cheek, he leaned over and kissed it. "You're precious to me, Nathalie."

"And you are to me, my Andrew." She smiled. "But I think you should check on the water. It sounds like the bath is overflowing."

"Fuck!" He jumped out of bed and ran to the bathroom, almost slipping on the wet floor in his rush to turn the water off and open the drain.

As the bath water drained, he grabbed a couple of towels and wiped the floor, wringing them out in the sink and repeating the process until the floor was only damp. He then took a fresh towel and wiped until everything was dry. In the meantime, the water level dropped to where he wanted it to be, and he closed the drain.

Taking the bunch of wet towels into his tiny laundry room, he stuffed them in the washer and then pulled out fresh ones from the linen closet.

Back in his bedroom, he found Nathalie in the same pose he'd left her in; back propped against the pillows, knees up-drawn and slightly parted with the washcloth covering her privates, and arms resting on her sides. The only difference was that her eyes were closed, and her breaths were slow and even.

She'd fallen asleep.

Poor girl, this was way past her bedtime, and the sex must've exhausted her. For a moment, he considered letting her sleep. But she was sore, and he knew the warm water would soothe her.

Threading one arm under her knees and the other around her back, he lifted her to him.

Nathalie rested her cheek on his chest and cracked her lids open. "What are you doing?" she murmured.

"Taking you to soak in a bathtub."

"Oh, okay." Her lids dropped back.

Until tonight, he'd had no use for the corner Jacuzzi bathtub the builder had outfitted the master bathroom with. Andrew preferred showers, and even if he were into bathing, to fill the big tub with water was wasteful. And yet, he was glad for it now—it was perfect for Nathalie to soak in.

Stepping inside, with Nathalie still cradled in his arms, he very carefully lowered himself into the water. When his butt touched the bottom, he rearranged her so she was cradled between his legs, her back resting against his chest.

She sighed. "This is heavenly."

"Feeling better?"

"I am. Is this a dream?"

He chuckled and hugged her closer, brushing his lips against her neck.

She shivered, and his shaft that was pressed against the smooth curves of her soft bottom got stiff again in complete disregard of Nathalie's condition.

Down you go, he admonished his misbehaving member, but the bad boy had a mind of his own,

"I'm sorry," he murmured in her ear.

She cranked her neck to look at him. "What for?"

"My cock getting ideas."

She kissed his chin, then tilted her head up, inviting a kiss. He complied with a light peck on her lips. Lifting her arms, she draped them behind his neck and laced her fingers, then pulled his head further down and invaded his mouth.

He groaned, his hands sliding up to cup her jutting breasts. On a moan, she arched her back, pressing her luscious ass tighter against his shaft and eliciting a corresponding sound from him. Without thinking, he pinched her nipples, rolling them between his thumbs and forefingers and tugging. Her butt muscles flexed, rubbing against his cock.

Damn, he could come just from the delicious friction. And what's more, he couldn't help imagining her bent over the rim of the bathtub as he took her from behind. He was such an ass. Nathalie was in no condition to be taken from any angle. Not tonight.

And yet, she seemed as needy as he was. He skimmed one hand down her slick body and cupped her sex, pressing the heel of his hand against her clit. With his other hand, he kept tormenting her sensitive nipples, first one, then the other. She was wet, dripping, and not from the bath water, but he was reluctant to penetrate her even with a finger.

"How can I be so horny so soon?' she breathed.

He chuckled. "With eating comes the appetite, and it's especially true regarding sex."

"Do you want to do it again?" she asked in a tone that was part hopeful and part fearful.

"Of course, I do. But you're sore, so the only appendage I'm going to use is my tongue." He lifted her off his lap. "Bend over the rim, sweetheart."

She cast him a hesitant glance but did as he asked, kneeling with her belly pressed to the bath's front and her beautiful ass facing him. It was shaped like an inverted heart, the two smooth globes flaring from her tiny waist. He palmed them, kneading lightly, then pushed her up.

"Lift for me, sweetheart."

She did, but only a fraction.

He gave another gentle push. "A little more."

"It's so embarrassing," she whispered as she lifted higher, finally bringing her glistening sex above the water level.

"You're beautiful," he breathed as he scooted down and got in position. "I want to take you like this so bad, but we're going to wait until you're all better." He thrust his tongue into her slit, and she jerked. "One day, I'm going to stand you on all fours, and pound into you from behind until we both see stars." She shivered, and he ran his tongue over her sex.

One hand stroking his shaft, he looped his other arm around Nathalie's ass and pressed his thumb to her clit. He tongued her trembling slit, licking all around, and then spearing it in and out of her. As he licked faster and thrust deeper, her frantic gyrations were grinding her ass into his nose, and he tightened the fist on his cock, moving it up and down to the rhythm Nathalie's luscious ass was dictating.

When she cried out, lifting up and away from his invading tongue, his seed erupted, coating her behind in thick spurts of semen.

Damn, he was quite impressed with himself, coming so hard twice in a row.

Breathing hard, Nathalie slumped over the rim, providing Andrew with the perfect angle to caress her ass cheeks under the pretense of cleaning her up.

She shook her head. "I can't stop thinking about it."

"About what?"

"What you said before about taking me from behind—it's so hot."

Andrew chuckled and playfully slapped one of her round globes. "Oh, no, I've created a monster!"

45

ANANDUR

"Oh, baby, you look so sexy. All the guys on the dance floor and around it are lusting after you. They are so jealous of me." Anandur shouted into Lana's ear as he put his hands on her hips, drawing her against his body as they swayed in sync to the loud techno music.

It hadn't taken much to convince her to go out with him, and she sure as hell had gotten all dolled up for the occasion. Her legs looked a mile long in the sequined micro mini and spiky heeled sandals she'd donned, and her braless breasts looked firm and taut under the halter top that left her back exposed—which was Lana's one wardrobe mistake. If he wasn't counting the slutty effect of the rest of her getup, that is.

Her back and arms were heavily muscled, but while her arms looked just fine, her back was corded like a bodybuilder's.

From behind, Lana looked like a drag queen.

Whatever, her front was all woman, even with the short boyish haircut. Gone was the nearly albino complexion, covered with a heavy layer of makeup, and dark eyeliner outlined her pale blue eyes. Her lids were painted in several shades of sparkly blues and silvers, and her lips in glossy pink. She must've sprayed her body with a self-tanner, or something like it because her skin was shiny like it was made from gold. The outfit and the paint job made her look like a hooker, but he didn't mind. She was hot.

With an expression even smugger than usual, Lana scanned the aforementioned males and wrapped her arms around his neck. Tall to begin with, with her high heels she was only a couple of inches shorter than him. It made kissing her easy. For a change, he didn't have to bend like a pretzel for a woman.

Fuck, the pretzel analogy got him thinking of Lana's pert butt cradled in his hands while he had her pushed against the wall—her long legs wrapped around his waist and her heels digging into his naked ass while he drove in and out of her like a battering ram.

"You like other men watch me? It makes you hot for me?" she shouted and rubbed herself against his erection, her sequined skirt catching on his zipper.

He shrugged and tried to release the fabric, but it was stuck. "Look what you've done, now we are stuck like this."

Lana swung her hips to the side, unconcerned with damaging her skirt and the sequins which went flying. "You buy me new, I don't care."

He raised a brow. As if it was his fault, but whatever, it wasn't as if he couldn't afford to buy her a new skirt. "You got it, baby."

His response made her happy, and a big grin split her face.

She sure had a big mouth, and with those fleshy lips…oh, boy, she could do some damage with those.

"You good man. You not ask how much it cost. But I tell you so you not to worry. Only twenty dollars. Even you can pay."

That's right, she was under the impression that he was a lowly deck boy. He should be more mindful of his cover story and act accordingly.

"For you, baby, anything."

"You want we sit? I need drink."

He nodded and wrapped his arm around her waist as he led her back to their table. She felt so different from other women, it was almost like having his arm around a guy, the only difference was her proportions, which were definitely feminine. Small waist, slightly flaring hips, and a butt that was small width wise but nicely rounded.

"More of the same?" he asked before heading to the bar.

"Da." She nodded.

Anandur shook his head. Vodka, and more vodka. It seemed it was true that Russians didn't consider anything else as alcohol.

Waiting for the bartender to pour their drinks, he thought about how to go about his investigation. So he had Lana interested in him, and he was sure that their date would end up in bed, but he still had no idea how to extract information from her. Or even what questions to ask without being too conspicuous. Another problem was her English, which was limited to the basics. Lana might be a great lay, but she sure as hell wasn't a great conversationalist. And he doubted she was any better in her mother tongue.

She wasn't stupid, but she wasn't the sharpest tool in the shed either. Which should've made his job easy, and perhaps it could've if not for the language barrier.

Damn, he should've asked Andrew for pointers. Not that the thought hadn't crossed his mind before he'd gone out with Lana, but he'd been too damn proud and cocky to ask for instructions—especially from a human.

Perhaps he should just thrall her. He wasn't particularly good at it, but combined with the amount of alcohol she was consuming and, hopefully, post-coital bliss he might be able to get something out of her. It wasn't ethical, but he could chuck it together with the thralling that he was not only allowed to, but forced to do. After all, there was the inevitable biting that had to be erased from her memories.

He wondered how many times that scumbag Alex had already thralled Lana, as well as the rest of the crew, and what was the extent of the damage he had already done. Who knew, perhaps Lana had been a highly intelligent girl before Alex had messed with her brain.

And now Anandur was about to do the same.

Damn, this was a bad idea. The one who should've been assigned to this task was Andrew. Rumor had it that he and Bridget had broken off their whatever they had, so Andrew was a free agent again. And as a human and an expert investigator he could get things out of Lana without causing her more irreversible damage.

Fuck, he should call Kian and ask him what to do.

46

NATHALIE

"Let's go around the back," Nathalie said as Andrew parked the car in front of her shop. It was past one in the morning, and chances were that Jackson had fallen asleep in the den. She didn't want the bells hanging over her front door to wake him up. If she were alone, she would've never dared using the back door from the alley in the middle of the night, but with Andrew by her side, she felt safe.

Andrew nodded and followed her into the narrow passageway between her shop and the adjacent house to the back alley. She'd been holding the key out since they exited the car and made a quick work of opening things and getting them inside.

Andrew frowned as she flicked on the light switch next to the door. "You really should have an alarm system here. It's not safe."

"Shh, not so loud," she whispered. "If Jackson is sleeping, I don't want to wake him up."

"I'm going to have one installed first thing Monday morning," he said in a whisper that was almost as loud as his normal voice.

"Keep your voice down. And fine, I'm not going to say no. I've been planning on installing one since I bought the place, but as with everything else, I've never gotten around to actually doing it."

"Consider it done." He followed her up the stairs.

"Thank you, but I'm paying for it." She cast him a look over her shoulder.

He shrugged. "The installation is free, and you only pay a small monthly fee."

She stopped and turned to face him. "Really? Or you just saying it to trick me?"

He rolled his eyes and grabbed her hand, bringing it to his lips and kissing the back of it. "Really. I'm not going to lie to you about something like this."

She frowned and pulled her hand back. "Oh, yeah? So what are you going to lie to me about?"

He chuckled. "Nothing."

"You better not." She pointed her finger at him.

He grabbed her hips and turned her around, then smacked her bottom. "Keep going, missy. Apparently sleep deprivation makes you cranky."

Was it?

Maybe.

She wasn't a suspicious person by nature, but she had a feeling that there was something Andrew was hiding from her, and it hadn't started tonight. It's just that until now she'd been so busy fretting about her own secrets that she hadn't stopped to think about what was it about Andrew's demeanor that had been bothering her.

It was dark on the second floor, and as Nathalie entered the den, she couldn't see if Jackson was sleeping on the couch but assumed that he was.

"I think that he's asleep," she whispered. "I'm going to check on my father."

"I'm not sleeping."

She jumped, bumping into Andrew, who was standing behind her.

"Shit, Jackson, you scared me."

"Sorry about that, didn't mean to. But Fernando is fine. I've just checked on him like about twenty minutes ago."

Nathalie fumbled for the light switch, but Jackson beat her to it, turning on the floor lamp next to the couch.

Even that dim light was hurting her pupils, that had been fully dilated ever since she'd climbed up the stairs and reached the second floor that had been steeped in darkness.

Jackson reached for his sneakers and pushed his feet inside, not bothering with the laces.

"How was he?" she asked, afraid to hear the answer. "Did he give you any trouble?"

"Nah, he was fine, we had a great time together." Jackson got up.

"Really?"

She found it hard to believe—a seventeen-year-old hotshot having a good time with an old-timer who suffered from dementia wasn't a likely scenario.

Jackson was probably just being nice. She was curious, though.

"What did you guys do all this time?"

Jackson smirked. "He asked me if I was seeing any young ladies, and we spent most of the time with me telling him stories about my various conquests, and him laughing in disbelief. I'm afraid that I'm guilty of contributing to the delinquency of an elder."

She didn't know how she felt about Jackson's admission. Mostly, though, she was glad that her father had had a good time. And as far as Jackson's stories went, Fernando would probably forget everything by tomorrow morning.

"Thank you. I appreciate what you've done tremendously, and I promise to reward you handsomely. But I think you should stay the night. It's late, and I don't want you driving home alone at this time of the night."

Jackson snorted and so did Andrew. "This is early for me. And don't worry for me, Nathalie, I can take care of myself."

"You're just a kid. You think you're invincible, but you're not. Right, Andrew?"

Andrew shrugged. "In his case, I'm not worried. Jackson could probably bench two fifty and punch a hole in the wall with his bare fist. Right, kid?"

Jackson nodded. "Three hundred."

Men and their overinflated egos. But maybe she was being overprotective. Jackson was a big boy, and despite his oozing charm, she'd sensed something dangerous in him—not towards her but as a potential. When fully grown, he would be a force to contend with.

"Fine, but be careful."

"Yes, ma'am." Jackson saluted and hugged her briefly.

"I'll walk you down and lock up after you." Andrew offered.

"Goodnight, Nathalie, see you Sunday."

"Goodnight, and thank you again."

"You're welcome."

With the guys gone, Nathalie walked over to the couch and plopped down. She was exhausted, but she didn't think she could sleep. She hated the idea of Andrew going home and her sleeping alone in her bed. Maybe he could stay, and she'd sneak him out in the morning before her father woke up. Then he could come back pretending as if he just got there.

She wondered whether she was going about it all wrong. A thirty-year-old woman shouldn't have to sneak her boyfriend into her room, and if Fernando weren't sick, she wouldn't have. But she was convinced that the routine kept Fernando from getting worse, and any big changes would affect him negatively.

On the other hand, Jackson was new in Fernando's life and yet her father seemed perfectly fine with him, embracing the boy as if he was part of the family.

Maybe she should give it a try with Andrew. If her father threw a fit because he found Andrew in her room, they would reevaluate. But it was worth the risk.

By the time Andrew came back, she had made up her mind. Reaching for his hand, she pulled him down to sit beside her on the couch. "Could you stay with me tonight?"

"I would love to, but are you sure? What about your father?"

"Let's give it a shot. If he throws a tantrum, we will rethink our strategy."

Andrew smiled and leaned to kiss her lightly on the lips. "Do you have a spare toothbrush?"

"I certainly do."

"Okay then. I hope you don't mind me sleeping in the nude."

"Not at all. But my father will if he finds you in my room. It might be too much of a shock for him."

"How about we just cuddle on the couch, then?"

That sounded wonderful. "You don't mind?"

"Are you kidding me? I would love to."

47

ANDREW

*A*s Nathalie got busy taking the big back cushions off the couch to make room for them to lie down together, Andrew went downstairs to brew them some coffee.

His girl was in the mood for cuddling, and he didn't want to disappoint her by falling asleep.

After brewing a full thermal carafe, he put it on a tray and added two cups, sugar, creamer, and a couple of leftover brownies Nathalie had put in the fridge instead of throwing away—for energy.

When he came back upstairs, the couch was ready, outfitted with two pillows and a woven blanket Nathalie must've brought from her room.

"This looks very inviting." Andrew put down the tray on the coffee table and kicked off his shoes.

"Coffee, Madame?"

"Yes, please."

He filled the two cups, leaving his own black and mixing in a little creamer and one packet of sugar in Nathalie's.

"Thank you, it's just what I need."

He wrapped his free arm around her and pulled her closer. "What you really need is to get some sleep."

"I can't."

"Want me to sing you a lullaby?"

She chuckled. "Do you know any?"

"Not any that are suitable for children. But I know an obscene one."

"Oh, yeah? Who taught you that?"

"My grandfather."

She laughed. "Get out of here, really? Your grandpa taught you a lewd song? How old were you?"

"He came to babysit me one time by himself without Nana. I was thirteen and deeply wounded that my parents still thought I needed a babysitter. My granddaddy agreed that I was too old and that they were babying me. That's when he sang me that song. He said I was old enough to have some fun, but to never let Nana or my mother know about it."

"Do you still remember it?"

"Vaguely. But it's one of my fondest memories of my grandfather. He was such a hoot."

"Did you ever tell your mother?"

"No, my father and I had a good laugh about it, but we decided that it was too crude for her. It was kind of vulgar. She wouldn't have liked it."

"Is she the prim and proper type?"

Was she? Andrew couldn't remember his mother ever cussing, not even something as innocent as *shit* or *darn*. But she had never made a big deal out of someone else cussing once in a while or telling a dirty joke.

"I guess you can say that she is proper but not prim. My Nanna, on the other hand, was definitely both prim and proper, God bless her soul. But this was how women of her generation had been raised, ladylike."

Talking about his mother presented him with the perfect opportunity to ask Nathalie about Eva. She never talked about her mother, only her father. If he hadn't known better, he would've thought that she'd been raised by Fernando alone.

"How about your mother? You never talk about her."

Nathalie sighed and lay back, scooting sideways and patting the space beside her. He lay down, threading his arm under her and bringing her head to rest on his chest.

"It's complicated. I was very close to her when I was little, and she spoiled the hell out of me, but the older I got, the more distant we became. For some reason, I was more comfortable with Papi. Perhaps it had something to do with the baking. My mom couldn't bake if her life depended on it. She could only waitress or work the register."

Nathalie chuckled. "Which was probably the only reason we made any money at all. She was so beautiful that I'm sure most of the male customers became regulars only because of her and not the tasty pastries. Once she and Papi got divorced many of them stopped coming."

Andrew ran his hand up and down Nathalie's back as he thought about what she'd told him. "Was your mother jealous of your relationship with your dad?"

Nathalie shook her head. "No. It was mostly my fault. My dad was an open book—easygoing, always smiling, and it was fun to be around him and do things together. His love for me was unconditional. My mom, on the other hand, was aloof. I always felt as if she was keeping secrets from my father and me. And the way she looked—it was kind of disturbing, to me at least."

"What do you mean?"

Nathalie snorted. "Besides making me feel like an ugly duckling? But that was only part of it. Not only was she striking, but she looked like my older sister, not my mother. Which wouldn't have been so strange if she'd had me when she was very young, but she'd been freaking forty-six when I was born and yet looked no older than thirty when I was fifteen. If not for the unmistakable resemblance between us, I would've suspected that I was adopted. Papi was younger than her by two years but looked like he was her father. It didn't make sense."

"Did you ask her about it?"

"I did, and so did others. She would say it was good genes, artful makeup, even admitting to having done plastic surgery."

"Well, perhaps that was it?"

"Trouble was, I knew she didn't. She had never even been to a dentist let alone undergone surgery. And the makeup? I think she was putting it on to make herself look older, not younger. She used to wear those long skirts and puffy blouses that made her look thirty pounds heavier. When I asked her about it, she said she liked the style and that it was comfortable."

Andrew had trouble stifling his excitement.

The evidence for Eva being an immortal was circumstantial, but it was strong. How had it happened? And why? Those were still a mystery. But immortality was the only plausible explanation for Nathalie's description of her mother.

"What do you think it was? Do you have a hypothesis?"

Nathalie shrugged. "The only thing that comes to my mind is that she'd been somehow genetically altered, probably by the government as some secret scientific project. Before she met Papi, she'd worked as an agent for the drug enforcement agency, or so she said. She might have been a Bond style assassin for all I know."

Nathalie had come up with a pretty imaginative scenario. Funny how the real explanation was even stranger.

"Do you know why they split up?"

"I have no idea. When I asked her, she said it was between her and Fernando. I've gotten the same answer from him. It almost sounded like she was implying that he'd cheated on her. And the guilty look on his face when I asked him why they were splitting reinforced that impression. But it didn't make sense. Who in his right mind would cheat on a woman that looked like her? Especially since Papi was an overweight, balding, middle-aged guy."

Andrew smoothed his palm over Nathalie's soft hair, winding a long strand around his finger. "I wouldn't be surprised if that was exactly what happened."

With a frown, she turned her face to look up at him. "Why would you think that?"

"Men have egos, even your father. And being married to a goddess who everyone is drooling over can be challenging. Especially if he perceived himself as not worthy of her, or if she implied it in some way. From your story, I gather that he was a charming and friendly guy, so it's not like he couldn't attract anyone despite his looks. He might have had a need to prove to himself that he still had it. You know what I mean?"

Nathalie's face had doubt written all over it. "I don't know. Maybe. Anyway, it's water under the bridge. I know that he loved her and was devastated when she left. The onset of his dementia happened shortly after that."

"Do you blame her for it?"

"Yeah, I do. I know that the disease must've been in his system for years prior to manifesting, but I think that it would've remained dormant for many more if not for the shock of her leaving him. And it was right at the same time I was leaving for college. He was left all alone."

Nathalie had gotten all tense, her body feeling rigid in his arms. Andrew hooked a finger under her chin and kissed her lips until he felt her muscles loosening. "I bet that part of your resentment toward her is guilt over also leaving him."

"You're right. I was so mad at her that I never called, and during breaks, I stayed with Papi, not her."

"What did she do after the divorce?"

"She worked at Nordstrom's in the men's department, and I guess dated a lot. In the beginning, she tried to maintain contact and called me every day. I would talk to her, but I'd end the call as soon as I could with the first excuse that came to mind. After a while, she got the message, and her calls became less and less frequent. Then one day she just disappeared from the face of the earth."

"Any ideas about what happened to her?"

Nathalie sighed and brought the blanket up to her neck. It was getting cold, and Andrew tucked it around them.

"God knows. She might have gone back to work for the government on some secret mission. At least I hope that this was what happened. When I hadn't heard from her for over a month, I called, but the line was disconnected. I went to look for her at the apartment she was renting at the time, but it was already rented out to someone else. She left all of her furniture behind but took her personal stuff. So I know she wasn't taken by force. Still, she might have gone on a vacation, and something happened to her then."

"Would you like me to look into it?"

"What can you do? The police never found anything."

"I'm not the police. I work for a different government agency, and I have access to information." This was as much as he dared to tell her.

"I guess it wouldn't hurt. But I'm not holding my breath. I'm tired of waiting for her to come back and hoping that she still cares for me. After all, if I find out that something happened to her, it will mean that I've lost her forever. And if I find out that she is fine but didn't bother to let me know she's alive, then it will mean that I've lost her forever anyway, because she doesn't deserve to be called my mother. Not knowing allows me to hover between the two options. I'm almost afraid to find out, so it's no longer a priority for me."

Oh, but it was, Nathalie just didn't know it. Finding Eva would provide the only definite answer to whether Nathalie was a Dormant or not. Because the other option wasn't on the table for her. There was no way in hell he would allow one of the immortals to attempt her transformation. If anyone was going to do it, it was him.

But unless he knew for sure that she was indeed a Dormant, he wouldn't risk going through the transformation. The only reason for him to put his life on the line was to facilitate Nathalie's immortality.

And if he died in the process?

Then someone else would do it for her, but at least he wouldn't be there to witness it.

48

ANANDUR

We can't switch players in the middle, and we don't have the luxury of playing nice. Go for it.

Anandur shook his head as he read Kian's text message again. This was so uncharacteristic of the guy. It seemed that Dalhu's take-no-prisoners attitude was rubbing off on their do-gooder leader.

Kian was telling him to thrall Lana.

Damn, he really didn't want to.

There must be a way to extract information from her without the help of fangs and venom. Problem was, Lana was expecting him to deliver on his promise of mind-blowing sex. Tough to pull off without biting.

Though not impossible...

Leaning against the wall outside the ladies' room, Anandur wondered what was taking her so long. Was she taking a shower in there? More than fifteen minutes had passed since she'd said she needed to pee, told him to hold her purse, and wait for her.

Bossy Russian.

In a way, it was a refreshing change from the overly polite American women. She was direct. There was no *if-you-please-could*, or *if-it's-not-too-much-trouble*. With Lana, it was *do this* or *don't do that*.

And language deficiency wasn't the problem. It was just her attitude.

A short brunette in monster platforms wobbled out of the ladies' room and sidled up to him. "Hello, gorgeous..." She gave him a once-over. "You, I want to take home with me." Leaning into him, she pressed her large boobs to his arm and lifted a long-nailed finger to touch his face.

He patted her shoulder and gave a little push. "Not tonight, dove, I'm here with someone." He lifted Lana's purse level with her face.

She pouted but refused to budge. "If she's hot, I don't mind a threesome..."

Damn, how was he going to peel her off him without shoving her? One hard push and she would fall on her ass, probably twisting her ankle on those ridiculous platforms.

He was about to say something when Lana emerged from the bathroom, her face contorted with rage. In one swift move, she yanked the brunette by the hair and shoved her against the wall. Towering over the woman, she kept a hold on her hair as she spat, "No putting your filthy hands on my man, *kurva*, you understand?" She forced the woman's head up and down in a parody of a nod.

He knew that word—it meant whore.

Lana shot the brunette one last angry scowl before threading her hand through his arm. "Let's go."

"What took you so long?" he asked as they headed out of the club.

She snorted. "If I know you in trouble I go out before."

They exited through the back door out into the club's parking lot. "I wouldn't call it trouble, baby." He opened the pickup's passenger door for Lana. "The poor things just can't help themselves, and I try to let them down gently. There is no reason to be mean when I reject them."

Lana harrumphed and crossed her arms over her chest. "Not all, I'm sure."

Anandur circled the old truck and got behind the wheel. "Of course, not. I only keep the pretty ones." He winked at her as he turned the key in the ignition and shifted the gear to drive.

The old clunker belonged to one of the maintenance guys, Rupert, and Anandur had swapped cars with him for the week. After all, he was supposed to be a lowly deck boy of little means.

His classic Thunderbird didn't fit the bill. It was one of the original Thunderbirds, and he'd had her since he'd bought her brand new in 1956. He'd been keeping her in mint condition.

Hopefully, Rupert was treating his baby well.

"By the way, I'm flattered by your impressive display of jealousy, but you didn't need to be so rough with her. She was just drunk."

Lana shrugged. "I see her hands on you, and I get angry. And it is not important that she is a woman because I am a woman too. If another man touch me, you do the same."

She had a point. Not because he was jealous, Lana didn't inspire that kind of feeling in him, but because it was his job as her date to defend her against unwanted advances. Not that Lana needed him to fend off the jerks—most human males didn't stand a chance against her—but it was a matter of honor.

"I guess you're right. It's just that I'm not used to a woman being so aggressive."

Casting him a worried sidelong glance, she asked, "You not like?"

Poor thing, she was afraid that her display of violence had turned him off. But he wasn't one of those guys who was intimidated by a strong woman, or who preferred the soft and timid types.

The truth was that he wasn't picky, and decent looks and several years of sexual experience were his only requirements. Other than that, there was little else that had any impact on his appetite.

"Oh, I like." He patted her knee, then smoothed his palm up her inner thigh and under her short skirt. When he found her little panties already moist, his shaft swelled and throbbed in response.

Lana's breath hitched, and she parted her legs to allow him better access. He pushed the panties aside and stroked her wet folds, gathering moisture and bringing it up to circle her engorged clit.

"We go to your place?" she breathed with a hopeful glint in her hooded eyes.

"Sorry, baby, no can do. I sleep on a couch at a friend's apartment. We will have to go to yours." He removed his hand and rearranged her skirt.

She grimaced. "My boss say no bring men on boat."

"Fuck. What are we going to do?"

She cast him a sidelong grin. "Many boats in marina are empty. We can go in no problem."

Driving one-handed, he reached for her and pulled her against his side. This was another advantage of driving the old truck over his Thunderbird—the front seat was one long bench. "Lana, you're a genius." He kissed the top of her head.

She put her hand on his inner thigh, her legs parting in invitation as she caressed her way up to his hard bulge. Hell, at this rate they would get each other off before ever getting to the marina.

Oh well, it was a good problem to have.

With a smirk, Anandur returned his hand to where she wanted it and tugged on her panties. He was tempted to give the lacy little thing a hard yank and tear it off her, but such a display of strength wouldn't go unnoticed, and the small thrill wasn't worth getting Lana suspicious.

"How about you take these off?"

She smiled, swinging her long legs up and stretching them, so her feet rested on the dashboard as she lifted her butt and pushed the panties down. Slowly.

"Fuck me..." he groaned and reached to cup her heated, wet flesh.

"Yes, I do, now. Stop where is dark."

It had been ages since he'd fucked a woman in a car. Not his favorite to say the least. He was just too big and wasn't into all the contorting. Doing the horizontal folded like a pretzel wasn't fun. But he was willing to make an exception for Lana, or rather for his cock that wanted out of the tight confinement of his jeans and into Lana's wet and welcoming sheath.

Anandur pulled into the dark parking lot of a small strip mall. The stores were closed for the night, and a waist-tall hedge formed a natural fence between the street and the parking area—hopefully providing enough privacy for their quickie.

"Can you move chair back?" Lana asked as he cut the engine.

"Sorry, baby, that's as far as it goes."

"Is okay." Lana hiked her skirt up and straddled him, reaching for his zipper. A moment later she had his jeans pushed down his hips. Pulling his shaft free out of his briefs, she gripped him in her strong hand.

His breath hissed out between clenched teeth as her fingers tightened around it. Normally, he loved the feel of a soft feminine palm on his sensitive skin, but there was definitely something to be said for a powerful grip.

"You so thick." Her eyes sparkled with excitement. "And so long," she marveled as her hand traveled the length of him.

Anandur smirked. "You no like?" He teased her with her own words.

"Oh, I like, *ya lyublyu mnogo*, I like a lot."

She lifted onto her knees and brushed his shaft against her wetness, coating it in her juices.

He groaned. "You're so wet for me, baby."

"Da." Lana agreed and began lowering herself on his shaft.

His hands shot to her hips, and he held her up, not letting her impale herself the way she intended. She was dripping wet, and not a small or fragile female, but he was large, and experience had taught him that a few extra moments made a big difference not only for his partner but for him as well.

"Let me. I want you inside," Lana hissed in her impatience.

His grip on her hips tightened, and she winced as his fingers dug into her flesh. "We do it my way, or not at all. Understood?"

The look of surprise on her face was almost comical.

Until now, Anandur had played the role of the easygoing bum, so she wasn't expecting him to take charge. Still, as far as he could tell, she didn't mind the switch. In fact, judging by the wetness that coated the tip of his shaft, she liked it.

"Okay, big boy. You the boss. Tell me what you want."

Hm, perhaps he could torture her for information by withholding sex...

Nah, he was so horny that he wouldn't last more than a minute before burying himself in her to the hilt.

"Just go slow, I don't want to hurt you."

An unfamiliar tenderness flitted through Lana's pale blue eyes and she brushed the back of her fingers over his cheek. "You're a good man, Anandur."

Not really, sweetheart.

49

BHATHIAN

*P*acing around his apartment, Bhathian stopped next to Patricia's portrait, the one Tim had drawn for him. He'd pinned it to the wall of his living room, next to the flat screen, so he could gaze at it from time to time while sitting on the couch and watching the dumb tube.

Eva, not Patricia, he reminded himself for the umpteenth time.

Ever since he'd gotten Andrew involved, the memories that over the years had finally dimmed and loosened some of their grip on him resurfaced full force, tormenting him anew.

He couldn't take his mind off her.

Instead of clubbing, he'd spent Friday night brooding alone in his apartment. he'd hardly gotten any sleep, and had awoken this morning before the sun came out.

Finding Nathalie had been a blessing that he still had trouble believing had been bestowed on him. Seeing her every day, spending time with her, talking with her—even though she had no idea who he was to her—had been the highlight of his every day. He lived for those mornings he was getting to spend with Nathalie at her café.

Problem was, she looked so much like her mother, he was constantly reminded of what he'd lost. And imagining what could've been was torture. If only he hadn't been such a coward, he could've had a family for all these years. He could've been raising his own daughter—not Fernando.

It wasn't that he harbored ill feeling toward the man, on the contrary. The love and dedication she was showing her adoptive father with every look and gesture, the sacrifices she was making for him, all reflected on the kind of father Fernando had been to her prior to his disease.

And for that Bhathian was grateful to him beyond measure.

He touched his finger to Eva's picture, caressing her cheek. *You must be so proud of her. Why did you leave her, though? What happened to you?*

He was losing sleep over these questions. They were going on a never-ending loop in his head.

And there was the most disturbing one—was she even alive?

In his gut, he knew she was, and what's more, he knew he had to find her. For Nathalie's sake as much or even more than his own. And he needed to do it sooner than later.

It was possible that Nathalie was already too old to attempt the transition and survive. Syssi almost hadn't made it, and she was only twenty-five...

The thought was so painful that he felt bile rise up his throat. He'd just found her, and he couldn't fathom watching her getting old and eventually dying.

He wouldn't want to go on without her.

Perhaps this was the reason Eva had fled and severed all contact with her daughter. If she had been turned without her or her partner realizing it, it meant that she had no idea how she'd become immortal and why she wasn't aging. And besides not wanting to see her own child age and die, she must've gone into hiding out of sheer fear of someone discovering her secret.

Just as the rest of them, she must've realized that once exposed she would be locked up in some secret lab at a facility that wasn't supposed to exist—living out her life as a test bunny.

Where are you hiding, my love?

He was a fool for calling Eva his love, but he was convinced that once he found her, he'd be able to make her his. After all, they already shared a child, were already a family.

For weeks now, he and Andrew had kept the story to themselves, and he was hoping Andrew would find Eva's trail. But the guy had too much on his plate as it was. Between his government job, the things he was doing for the clan, and spending every free moment with Nathalie, there wasn't much more he could take on.

Bhathian smiled at Eva's portrait. *You would like Andrew, Eva. He is the kind of son-in-law every parent wishes for.*

This was a bigger job than he and Andrew could handle themselves, and as much as he hated exposing his private life for everyone to see, it was time to get Kian and the rest of the Guardians involved. Especially if he wanted to take some time off to go looking for Eva.

Pulling his phone out of his pocket, he texted Andrew. *I want to set a meeting with Kian and tell him about Eva and Nathalie. Later this afternoon work for you?*

A moment later his phone rang.

"Why today? Shouldn't we wait for Monday to talk to him?"

"No, I'd rather have an informal meeting with him at his place than schedule one for the office. For me, it's not business as usual."

"Yeah, I get what you mean. It's just that this is Nathalie's only day off, and I'd rather not cut it short."

Bhathian chuckled. "Give her a break, she probably needs to have a breather away from you."

"You think?" Andrew sounded doubtful.

"I know that I'm not much of a ladies' man, but if Nathalie is anything like me, constant company drains her."

"Fine, text me the time, and I'll be there."

"I will."

After ending the call, Bhathian texted Kian.

Are you busy? Or can I call you about a private matter?

His phone rang a few seconds later. "What's up, Bhathian?" Kian sounded worried.

"Nothing bad, boss. If you're free this afternoon, Andrew and I have a personal matter we would like to discuss with you."

"Andrew and you?"

"Yes, sir."

"Well, you whetted my curiosity. I can't wait to hear what this is all about. How about my place, four in the afternoon?"

"Perfect. We will be there."

Bhathian let out the breath he'd been holding and texted Andrew.

Kian's, at four.

50

ANDREW

"Come in." Syssi opened the door for Bhathian and him. "Hi, stranger." She kissed Andrew's cheek after shaking Bhathian's hand.

Okay, he deserved it. Ever since he started seeing Nathalie he hadn't visited or even called his sister. Shame on him.

"Sorry." He pulled her into a hug and kissed her cheek.

"It's okay, you're going to make it up to me by telling me all about this new lady friend of yours."

He followed her inside and took a seat next to Bhathian on the couch. "Actually, that is exactly why we are here."

Syssi perked up, but then glanced at Bhathian and frowned. "And this lady friend of yours has something to do with Bhathian?"

Andrew nodded. "Where is Kian? I don't want to tell the story twice."

"He's coming." She waved her hand in the direction of the hallway. "As always, he had to take a phone call about some disaster. It's as if no one in this entire organization can make executive decisions and take care of business. They are like kids, calling daddy whenever something doesn't work out."

"You know that it's his fault. They are used to him micro-managing everything. He needs to let go."

"I know." Syssi sighed and pushed toward them a tray loaded with an assortment of small containers. "Help yourselves." The selection included roasted peanuts, almonds, olives and other munchies, along with several bottles of beer.

"Everyone is sick of me pushing cappuccinos at them, so I decided to serve beer instead. But if you guys want coffee, I can make it in a jiffy."

"Not for me, thank you." Bhathian reached for a bottle, popped the lid, and gulped half of it on a oner.

"Sorry for keeping you waiting." Kian walked in barefoot, comfortable in his weekend attire of faded T-shirt and pair of old, well-worn jeans. He looked younger and more relaxed than Andrew remembered ever seeing him.

Marriage apparently agreed with the nearly two-thousand-year-old geezer who looked like he was in his early thirties.

Kian motioned for Syssi to get up from her chair, then took her place and pulled her down to sit in his lap. She didn't object in the least, leaning back against him and resting her head on his shoulder.

It was obvious that Syssi was happy, she looked so content.

Andrew's heart swelled in a very unmanly manner, and he felt like kissing his brother-in-law on both cheeks, or at least bro-hug-and-clap him. These two belonged together, and although there would no doubt be many fights in their long future, over matters small and large, their love for each other was unshakable.

Bhathian took another swig of his beer and glanced at Andrew.

Andrew shook his head. "It's your story to tell, not mine."

He nodded. "I'm not good at this, so bear with me."

"Take your time, Bhathian," Syssi said.

"Over thirty years ago, I hooked up with a stewardess who turned out to be resistant to thralling. I somehow managed to refrain from biting her and thought it was the last I'd seen of her. A month later she found me at the same bar we'd first met at and invited me again to her hotel room. She informed me that she was pregnant and that I was the father, saying that she hadn't been with anyone else for months. I suggested an abortion, but she refused." Bhathian rubbed his hand over the back of his neck, then emptied what was left in his bottle.

The only response from their audience had been a stifled gasp from Syssi when Bhathian had gotten to the pregnancy part.

"She said she was forty-five and had given up hope of ever conceiving—which was unbelievable because she looked to be in her mid-twenties. She wanted the baby regardless of my involvement. I offered her the only thing I could, financial support. She thanked me, but that was all. She never contacted me again and never came back to the club. I went to that damned club every night hoping she'd be there, but after weeks of waiting, I knew she wouldn't and went searching for her. All I had to go on was her name and the airline she worked for. I found out that she quit her job shortly after talking to me, and moved out from the address listed in her file. I also got her social from that same file and tried to find her using it but got nowhere with it. Other than that, I had nothing else to go on."

"Why were you searching for her? She didn't want your money, and there was nothing else you could've offered her."

Syssi cast her husband an incredulous look.

"What? Did I say something wrong?"

She shook her head. "Oh, my God, Kian, sometimes I wonder about you. Think! She was pregnant with his child! If it were you, wouldn't you want to know if you had a son or a daughter? Try to help him or her in any way you could?"

Kian grimaced. "You're right. I would've."

Syssi patted his cheek as if he was a child who had learned his lesson, then turned to Bhathian. "Please continue."

"You nailed it Syssi. The not knowing has been tormenting me throughout the years. So when I heard about Andrew's access to government information, I asked him to help me find her."

He glanced at Andrew. "Perhaps you should tell this part of the story?"

"No problem." Bhathian needed a breather, and Andrew didn't mind taking over at this point.

"To make a long story short. Bhathian's stewardess, Patricia Evans, was a drug enforcement agent named Eva Paterson, who at the time was part of a long-term investigation regarding airline personnel who were suspected of drug trafficking. Following her meeting with Bhathian, she quit the agency, married a guy named Fernando Vega, and seven months later Nathalie was born. Bhathian's daughter."

"That's amazing, Andrew, do you know where they are?" Syssi sat up straight and leaned forward as if eager to hear more good news.

"We know where Nathalie and Fernando are, right here in Glendale, but Eva has been missing for the last six years. No one knows what happened to her."

Syssi cast Bhathian a sympathetic look. "Well, at least you finally found your daughter."

A mixture of pride and love shone in Bhathian's eyes as he nodded.

"Now to the reason we are here. We suspect that Eva is an immortal."

Kian harrumphed. "Impossible."

"Here are the facts." Andrew raised a finger. "One. Eva hasn't changed a bit over the years. She looked exactly the same in the composite the forensic artist drew of her from Bhathian's memories, and the picture Nathalie provided the police when she filed the missing person's report. A woman who was supposed to be in her seventies still looked to be no more than thirty."

Kian still looked skeptical, and Andrew raised a second finger. "Two. When Bhathian met her, he also thought she looked much younger than her real age. I know of no woman over the legal drinking age who would lie about being older than she actually is."

He raised a third finger. "Three. Bhathian couldn't thrall her."

"Some humans are immune." Kian waved a dismissive hand.

"Four. Nathalie talks with ghosts in her head."

"What!?" Bhathian almost choked on the olive in his mouth.

Syssi gaped, and Kian lost his dismissive expression.

Andrew smirked. "I've been seeing Nathalie, basically every day, since Bhathian and I went to the coffee shop she owns. But she only confided in me recently about the voices in her head. She isn't sure if they are real or imagined, and has tried to keep it a secret so people won't think her crazy."

"Your mystery woman..." Syssi said quietly.

"Yes."

Kian turned to look at Bhathian, who shrugged and clapped Andrew's back. "I owe him, and I like him. Andrew is a stand-up guy, couldn't have asked for a better man for my daughter."

"Oh, wow," Syssi exclaimed. "This is serious."

Yeah, it was.

Andrew raised a hand with all five fingers splayed. "Five. Nathalie confirmed that her mother looked eerily young, despite her best efforts to make herself look older with the help of makeup and unflattering clothing."

Kian moved Syssi to sit sideways on his lap. "I agree with you that the circumstantial evidence is strong. But how on earth could Eva have been immortal if Bhathian didn't bite her? And even if he did, and she happened to be a Dormant, which in itself is extremely unlikely, the transformation would've been fatal—considering her age at the time. Not to mention what it would've done to her unborn child."

Kian had been following the same string of logic as Andrew. He was going to shorten the process for the guy. "We have to assume that she was already an immortal then, but wasn't aware of it."

"There are no immortal females unaccounted for."

"Yeah, I know. Bhathian told me as much. That's why I think the only possible scenario is that she had sex with an immortal male long before meeting Bhathian, and was unknowingly turned. It must have happened when she was very young, and for years she must've assumed that she was just one of the lucky ones who were incredibly healthy and aged slowly. But as she got even older and still remained unchanged she probably freaked out and eventually ran when it became impossible to hide it any longer."

"What does Nathalie think?"

Andrew chuckled. "That during her time as a government agent, her mother participated in some secret genetic experiment, and that her disappearance has something to do with this as well. Nathalie thinks Eva returned to her old job as an agent."

Syssi pushed up from Kian's lap and grabbed one of the beers. "Her take on it is less far-fetched than Eva being turned by one of us or a Doomer, going through the transition without realizing what's happening to her, and then getting pregnant from a random hookup with another immortal."

In the silence that followed, Andrew mulled over his sister's succinct summary, and given the deep frown on Kian's face, so did he.

Bhathian popped the lid off another bottle and let it swing from between his fingers as he shook his head. "I hate to give them credit, but it must've been the Fates. The statistical chance of this unlikely sequence of events happening is so infinitesimal it's practically nonexistent."

Kian got up and grabbed a beer for himself. "What's next? I know you guys didn't come here just to share this incredible story." He arched a brow at Bhathian.

"I want to go searching for Eva."

"And I guess you came here to ask for an extended leave of absence?"

"Not yet, but I will once I know where to start looking. Andrew is going to do some research for me, but I will probably need additional resources."

Kian nodded. "Whatever you need, it's yours. But a leave of absence is problematic. You know how thinly stretched we are. We don't have enough Guardians."

"That's why I came to you before even having the first clue to follow. We need to call in some of those who left the force, and at the same time step up the training of new recruits."

"Yeah, I was thinking along the same lines, but for a different reason. There is a large contingent of Doomers somewhere nearby, and they've certainly had enough time to get organized. I expect shitloads of trouble, and soon."

51

SEBASTIAN

"Letty, Letty, Letty, I told you, if you won't hold position your punishment doubles."

The sobs got louder, but the girl lowered herself back to the bench.

Testing her progress, he hadn't tied her down this time. She wasn't doing too well even though this beating was mild in comparison to the previous ones.

Stupid girl. By now she should've known that the more obedience she showed, the more submissive and compliant she was, the sooner her torment would be over, and she'd be rewarded with a bite—the pain ceasing immediately. But apparently her brain capacity was even less than that of the famous Pavlov's dogs.

Letty was trembling all over.

At this rate, she would pass out before he got his fill.

Her screams and her begging were adequate. And even though he didn't speak Spanish, yet, the sounds she was producing were lovely.

He wasn't hitting her all that hard, and the pale welts on her ass would've faded by tomorrow even without the benefit of his venom. But the girl had a tolerance for pain of a toddler.

Damn, he hadn't even gotten hard.

Swish, with a flick of his wrist the cane landed on target.

Letty cried out but held on.

Her obedience brought a small twitch to his member. "Good girl. Just one more."

She whimpered, and he delivered the last one quickly before she lost her nerve and he would've been forced to give her more.

Sebastian was tired of her.

The problem was, she hadn't gotten him aroused enough for his fangs to elongate and for his glands to produce venom. Sebastian wanted out of this room and away from this poor excuse of a sub. For a moment, he considered calling Tom to finish the job for him. Except, the guy would lose all respect for him if he got a whiff of Sebastian's problem. And besides, he doubted Tom could get it up for the sobbing mess still bent over the whipping bench.

The guy was plain vanilla.

Reluctantly, he walked up to the girl, lifted her trembling body in his arms and sat on the bench. Cradling her, he stroked her hair and praised her although she didn't deserve it. This was an important part of her training, and he had to resort to faking tenderness.

Rocking Letty back and forth, Sebastian closed his eyes and brought up the image of his attorney. Now, that was a worthy sub. Recalling their last session did the trick, and he felt himself getting harder, his fangs elongating. Imagining that the woman in his arms was plump, short, and fair-skinned, he scraped them over her neck and then bit down.

The girl sighed, her tensed muscles going lax. He lifted her up and carried her to her room. Unfortunately, the one minute walk had defeated his short-lived arousal. He laid Letty on her bed, put a bottle of water on her nightstand, and walked out.

The question was, should he call the club and schedule a session, or go hunting again for someone he could actually enjoy?

The club won. Finding a pleasing submissive to abscond with was proving harder than he'd anticipated, as evidenced by what he and Tom had managed to snag to date. They had fifteen girls in the basement, but none was what Sebastian was looking for, and tonight his first priority was to release some steam.

Tomorrow, he would resume the hunt.

52

NATHALIE

"Hey, Nathalie, come meet my friends."

Jackson poked his head into the kitchen, beckoning her to come out. Lately, this had been the new mode of operation—him up front taking care of customers, her stuck in the kitchen, baking and preparing sandwiches.

The only times she ventured out were when she had to send Jackson out to buy supplies because she was running out. Thank God that Andrew had volunteered to do it today, so she could keep on baking while Jackson tended the front. The place had been a mad house all day and she couldn't have spared him even for a short supermarket run.

Jackson was a customer magnet—and not only of the female kind.

He seemed to have an endless supply of friends, whom he'd apparently been bragging to about her pastries. More and more of them were showing up each day to check out her baking. Better yet, they were coming back for more. More of her pastries, and more time to hang out with Jackson.

The shop was booming, there was never a place to sit, and she couldn't keep up with the demand.

Fernando had been permanently relocated to a tiny corner in the kitchen, which he didn't mind and actually preferred since she was spending most of her time in there and not up front, and besides, the crowded shop was making him nervous.

Unbelievably, she was thinking of hiring a helper for the kitchen.

Wiping her hands on a towel, Nathalie grimaced. Her poor hands were showing the rough treatment she was subjecting them to. Reddened and swollen was not an attractive look. Andrew hadn't said a word, but she was sure her touch wasn't as soft as he would've liked it to be.

"Nathalie, come on…" Jackson walked into the kitchen and grabbed a corner of her apron to drag her out.

She slapped his hand. "Let me at least take this off."

He relented, waiting for her to get rid of her flour-covered apron before coming behind her and giving her a gentle push.

Expecting Jackson's teenage crowd, she was surprised at the impressive young couple standing on the other side of the counter.

"Nathalie, these are my friends, Kri and Michael. Guys, this is the famous Nathalie."

She offered her hand to the girl. "I don't know about the famous, but it's nice to meet you, Kri."

The girl, who looked like she could play professional football, took her hand, shaking it gently as if she was handling an egg carton. "Nice to meet you too. Jackson doesn't stop talking about your pastries and we just had to come and have a taste."

Nathalie laughed. "I have no idea how he has time for all the advertising he's doing for me when he's here all the time."

Kri's boyfriend lifted his phone. "It's called Facebook, Snapchat… you name it, he used it to make you famous." He returned the phone to his pocket and offered his hand. "I'm Michael."

"Okay, now you can go back to your kitchen." Jackson *graciously* allowed her to go back to work.

She rolled her eyes. "I swear, this boy thinks he owns the place." She pointed a finger at him. "But don't forget that I can fire you anytime."

He smirked. "You wouldn't. I'm too good at this."

He was right, of course. And besides, in the short time he'd been with them, both she and her father had come to regard him as family. She wouldn't let him go even if he tried.

"You're so full of yourself." Nathalie waved a dismissive hand before ducking back into the kitchen.

Thank God it was already five in the afternoon, and that Sundays she closed at six. After this last batch of muffins went into the oven, she would finally sit down and rest. Her back and her legs were begging for a good massage.

Luckily, she had her own masseur, with strong and talented fingers. So far, only her feet and her shoulders had benefited from Andrew's incredible massage at the end of each day, but after Friday night, she hoped he'd give her a full body, sensual one.

Yesterday, she'd still been a little sore, but today she was fine—eager to find out what it would be like without the pain.

Mind blowing, no doubt.

Andrew was a skilled and generous lover, and she was so glad he'd been her first. He'd made it wonderful for her despite the unavoidable hurt, and not only because he'd been so patient and so bent on ensuring she had pleasure first. She found it beyond admirable that he'd been willing to stop at any point, and she didn't doubt for a moment that he would've even if he were a moment away from ejaculating.

Apparently, the myth that men couldn't stop once they were too far gone was just that, a myth.

A real man, a man like Andrew, could and would stop on a dime if the woman he was with asked him to.

The buzzer on her back door went off. Probably Andrew back from the supermarket.

She rushed to open up for him, and tried to relieve him of some of the many paper bags he was carrying, but of course, being the macho guy he was, Andrew refused. "I got it, sweetheart, just lock the door after me so your father doesn't sneak out."

Having Fernando in the kitchen was like having a pet who just waited for an opportunity to make a run for it, the small difference being that the door needed to remain not only closed but locked with the help of a combination lock.

Since her work table was in use, Andrew dropped the bags on the floor next to the door.

"I'll put everything away but you'll need to tell me where."

"I'll do it." She bent over the first bag and pulled out a slab of baking chocolate.

Andrew took it out of her hands. "You have enough to do, let me help the only way I know how." He kissed her lips when she pouted. "Where does this go?" He held the chocolate up.

She pointed, and he put it away then pulled out the next item. In minutes, he had everything stored, while she finished working on her muffins and stuck them in the oven.

"Finally, it's all done. And if we run out, we'll just turn people away. I'm done with this kitchen for today."

Andrew pulled her into a hug then turned her around, her back to his front, and started massaging her aching shoulders. "Poor baby, you're one big knot."

His hands kneaded just right, not too rough and not too gentle, and Nathalie closed her eyes, letting her body slump against his.

Someone cleared his throat, and Nathalie's eyes shot to her father, but he was still bent over his newspaper.

"What's up, Bhathian?" she heard Andrew ask and turned her head the other way to see the big guy blocking the entry into her kitchen with his bulk. His shoulders literally spanned the entire distance between the door jambs. In fact, he probably needed to turn sideways so they wouldn't get stuck.

"Do you guys want to come out?"

Nathalie chuckled. "Is there anywhere to sit?"

Bhathian grimaced. "Not really, but there is something I need to talk to you about and there is no space to sit in here either."

"How about we go upstairs?" Andrew suggested.

Not a bad idea. She needed to put her feet up.

"I'll just let Jackson know. You guys go up."

Andrew shook his head. "I'll tell him, you go and rest your cute butt on the couch."

Bhathian cleared his throat again.

"Sorry, my bad." Andrew apologized to him for some reason.

What was that all about? Did Bhathian have a problem with the word *butt*? He didn't strike her as a prude.

53

ANDREW

*A*ndrew gathered Nathalie's feet into his lap and started massaging her toes. She moaned, and Bhathian, who was sitting across from them on a chair he'd brought from her room, almost choked on his coffee.

Nathalie cast him a quizzical glance, but the guy immediately schooled his face into a mask of innocence. "So, Nathalie, Andrew and I have been talking, and we decided to use our department resources to help you search for your mother."

We did?

Nathalie seemed surprised. "You will do this for me? Why?"

He gave her big toe a hard squeeze. "Because we care about you, that's why."

"Ouch, I can see that." She made a face and pulled her foot away.

Andrew pulled it back into his lap. "I'm not done with this one, yet." He pressed his thumb to the arch and she moaned again, oblivious to Bhathian's discomfort.

"I told Bhathian some of what you've told me about Eva, but we need more information. Anything you can tell us about her could be a potential clue. Did she have family or friends somewhere? Did she talk about visiting a particular destination? Did she talk about her favorite places in the world from her time working as an airline attendant? Any pictures, paperwork, everything—even things that you think are trivial."

Damn, he couldn't remember if Nathalie had told him her mother's name. He was screwed if she hadn't and had noticed his slip.

But she had either told him or didn't remember if she had because she just offered him her other foot to massage.

"That's a lot. I will have to make a list and rummage through what she left behind, which isn't much, but I haven't looked at it for years."

"That's a good idea. Nothing off the top of your head, though?"

Nathalie shook her head. "My parents never went on vacations. Running a café is like slavery. But she never complained about it. She said she'd traveled enough for a lifetime and was tired of it. As far as family, she never mentioned anyone other than her parents, and she was their only daughter. Paris came up as one of her favorite places to visit, she said that Venice was stinky, and the food in Germany was awful. That's all I remember, I'm sorry."

"No worries, sweetheart. We will find a lead. The fact that she used to work for the government is helpful. I might be able to find some clues in her files. Agents, in particular, have a lot of information about them stored away in the archives, even after they retire."

"When do you think you'd be able to look through her stuff?" Bhathian pushed to his feet and stretched.

"Maybe later tonight. But I can't promise. I'm exhausted."

He bent down and kissed her cheek. "Call me when you're done and I'll come over."

"I will." She made a move to get up, but he stayed her with a hand on her shoulder.

"I'll show myself out."

"Thanks, Bhathian."

He gave her a two fingered salute and walked out, his steps surprisingly light and silent on the old stairs that groaned even under Nathalie's weight that was less than half of his.

This was one of the tricks Andrew thought he should ask the Guardians to teach him. It probably had nothing to do with them being immortal—just with their training.

"It's very sweet of you to offer to look for my mother and rope Bhathian into helping."

"He volunteered."

"I hope you'll have better luck with this investigation than with Tiffany's. I still find the story about her brother picking up her stuff fishy."

"Yeah, but it's not unlikely. If you want, I can try to find her parents' phone number and call to ask about her. But that would mean searching for her birth record to find out their first names, not a big deal, but it's work."

"No, it's okay. Finding what happened to my mother is obviously more important to me. I should go and pull out the box with her things from the attic while you're still here. It's probably full of spiders." She shivered. "I hate those nasty little things."

Andrew moved over a little, dragging Nathalie's feet with him and turning her so her back was against the armrest. "I will gladly assist with the retrieval of the spider-infested box, but I have other plans for this evening."

Catching his drift, she smiled. "And what would those entail?"

He tapped his finger on his chin. "Let's see. One bottle of massage oil, one naked Nathalie, two talented hands, and lots of moaning and groaning, with some *'Oh, Andrew, you're the greatest'* thrown in."

Nathalie laughed. "This sounds amazing, but I'm afraid we'll have to settle for a half-naked Nathalie and very quiet moaning and groaning."

"Nope. I'll ask Jackson to babysit again, and I'll take you to my place." He leaned closer and whispered. "Are you still sore?"

She shook her head. "Not at all. I'm more than ready, I'm eager for more." Her foot found his crotch, giving a new meaning to the term foot massage.

A loud stomping on the stairs must've been Jackson announcing his approach. The damn immortal with his freakish hearing had probably overheard the whole conversation and was coming to tell them that he had plans for tonight and couldn't babysit Fernando.

"Hi, guys," he practically shouted from the hallway in case his stomping wasn't enough of an alert.

Nathalie retracted her foot, but Andrew's shaft formed a bulge in his jeans that was hard to hide.

Jackson's barely contained smirk confirmed Andrew's suspicions. "I just wanted to let you know that I've locked up, and I'm taking Fernando on a looong walk to the Japanese comic store."

Nathalie turned around to face Jackson. "Why on earth would you take an old man to a comic store?"

"Well, the poor guy was cooped up in here all day, he needs to get out."

"I get the walk part, but why to a comic store?" Andrew had to ask.

"Not any comic store, a Japanese one."

"And your point?"

Jackson rolled his eyes. "Duh, comic books, of course."

Andrew chuckled. "Why would you think Fernando would want to see comics?"

With a grimace that said *'you old people know nothing'*, Jackson put his hands on his hips. "First of all, at Fernando's pace the store is an hour walk away, it has places to sit, but most importantly, it has tentacle porn."

Nathalie's jaw dropped.

"What the hell is tentacle porn?"

"Just what it sounds like—porn with tentacles. Fernando is going to love it." He winked.

"You're okay with it?" Andrew looked at Nathalie.

She shrugged. "He is a big boy. But if it freaks him out, you'll have to deal with his tantrum. Not an easy feat in public."

"Don't worry. I'm sure he's going to have fun. And if he throws a tantrum, I'll just tell everyone my grandfather has dementia. Anyway, I estimate about three hours before we are back. Have fun." He winked at Andrew.

Nathalie blushed the color of beets.

"The little devil is killing me," she whispered, thinking Jackson was out of earshot.

"No, he is being a saint. Now, what I want to know is where you hide the massage oil."

54

NATHALIE

"In the bathroom, the cabinet under the sink."

Andrew jumped up. "I'll be back in a moment."

"Wait..."

He turned around.

Nathalie cast him a sultry look. "I want to shower first."

"Need someone to wash your back?" His voice got husky.

"That's the idea."

He was back at her side in two quick strides. Snaking one arm under her knees and the other under her arms, he lifted her in his strong arms and held her snugly against his hard chest.

Nathalie giggled as he carried her down the hallway and into the bathroom. "I can walk, you know."

"I know, but I'm a full-service kind of guy. I carry and wash for the same price." He set her down on the vanity's counter and started unbuttoning her shirt.

"And the price is?"

"A kiss." He popped the last button and parted the two halves, his eyes zeroing on her stiff nipples visible even through the light padding of her bra. Regrettably, it fastened in the back.

Note to self, replace all bras with the kind that fasten in the front.

It was such a delightfully naughty thought that she felt herself getting wet between her legs. The idea of making herself easily accessible to Andrew at all times was hot.

Perhaps she should add skirts to her shopping list.

Oh, goodness, what is becoming of me?

Embrace your inner slut, girl, Sage's voice sounded in her head.

I wasn't talking to you, she thought at him. *Get lost.*

Sorry, I'm going, just wanted to tell you that I'm so proud of you that I have tears in my ghostly eyes.

She giggled.

"What's so funny, sweetheart?"

She wasn't about to tell him of Sage's brief visit. It would spoil the mood. But she could tell him about her naughty musings. "I was just thinking that I'm going to replace all my bras with the kind that open in the front."

Andrew skimmed his knuckles over the tops of her breasts, sending zings of desire down to her core. "Good idea." He grabbed her bra cups and pulled them down, folding them under her breasts.

As she glanced down at her pushed up swells—topped by nipples that were stiff and distended—the sight of her smallish breasts looking so lewd aroused her, and she wiggled her butt on the countertop to relieve the itch that had started there.

She was impatient. "Don't you want to finish undressing me first?"

Andrew's thumbs strummed over her aching peaks. "In a moment."

He licked his lips, and she arched her back in anticipation of his next move. With a groan, he leaned forward—his hands slapping the counter as he braced his weight against it—and took one nipple between his lips. Nathalie gasped, thrusting her breast out and grasping his head to get him to take more of it inside his hot mouth.

Andrew hollowed his cheeks, sucking as much of her breast inside as he could, then released it with a loud pop, capturing the peak between his teeth.

"Oh, my God," she rasped, her hands pulling on his hair to hold him to her. It didn't hurt, but there was something hot about the implied vulnerability. He could hurt her, but she trusted him not to. And that was hot too.

His tongue replaced his teeth, then he repeated the whole thing with her other breast. By the time he lifted his head with a satisfied smirk on his handsome face, she was ready to skip the shower and get down to business.

Nathalie shrugged off her blouse and reached back to unhook her bra. Next, she lifted a little to pull her pants and panties down.

Andrew's eyes were smoldering as he watched her no-nonsense, quick striptease. "Impatient?"

"Very." She made a move to hop off the counter, but he caught her before her legs touched the floor and carried her into the shower, getting in with her cradled in his arms.

"Put me down, Andrew," she commanded and reluctantly he complied.

"My turn." She reached for his belt buckle, releasing it and zipping down his jeans at the same time. He helped, grabbing his T-shirt and pulling it over his head, then tossing it out on the bathroom floor, while she tugged on his pants, pulling them past his hips together with his boxer briefs.

Kneeling to get them off his legs, Nathalie found herself face to face with his erection. "Well, hello there." She gave it a little kiss, and it jerked in response. "Miss me? I think you did." She fisted the hard length, running her hand up and down on the smooth, warm skin. When she licked the crown, Andrew groaned and swayed a little, letting himself fall back against the shower's tiled wall.

Did she make him weak at the knees?

Looking up at his face, she swirled her tongue around the mushroom head and watched his lids sliding shut, his lips parting on a pant.

"You like it, don't you?"

Andrew opened his eyes, his hand reaching for the top of her head. "I love it." He caressed her hair and then cupped her cheek. "And I hate to press the pause button, but I would prefer to be freshly showered for you."

She gave the plump head one last kiss before getting up. "You smell and taste delicious. But I get it, I'd rather be freshly showered too." She winked at him.

This was another fantasy Nathalie wished to explore. She'd been thinking about it ever since reading in one of her romance novels about a couple pleasuring each other with their mouths simultaneously. It had been one of her favorites, probably because the girl in the story was also a virgin, even though it wasn't a historical romance and the girl was in her mid-twenties. Nathalie could identify with the character.

Washing each other, they took a little too long caressing and squeezing and pinching. Nathalie was afraid they would run out of time.

She was pretty sure that if Jackson came back and realized they were still in her room, and the door was locked, he would distract Fernando. Still, better to be done before Jackson brought her father back.

Andrew grabbed one of the thick towels she had stacked on the shelf by the shower and wrapped her in it, then reached for another one to dry himself.

"Come on, gorgeous." He stepped out of the shower and offered her his hand. She took it, and he led her to her small bedroom.

Her twin-sized bed wasn't meant for a couple, and Andrew eyed it for a second before striding up to it and sitting down, then pulling her down to sit in his lap.

"Sorry about the bed."

"Why? Is it lumpy?" He bounced up and down with her still cradled in his arms. "Feels solid to me."

Was he the sweetest guy, or what?

She cupped his cheeks and kissed him lightly on the lips. "I love you, Andrew Spivak," she said, feeling like everything had just shifted, her crazy world realigning because of how right it felt to say these words to him.

55

ANDREW

Dear God Almighty, Nathalie's words, so unexpected, so priceless, hit Andrew like Zeus's mythical thunderbolt, and the shock left him speechless for about a second. Then he crushed her to him. "I love you too, Nathalie Vega," he croaked, ashamed that compared to her steady and assured tone, his delivery sounded like that of a teenage boy whose voice was still in a flux.

"You're smushing me!" She laughed.

He let go, but just a little. "Now that I have you, I'm not letting you go, better get used to it," he whispered into her hair.

She wiggled a little, forcing him to loosen his hold and free her arms.

"Look at me, Andrew," she said in a serious tone, and for a moment, he was worried that he'd gone too far.

But as he lifted his head, he saw that her eyes were smiling through a sheen of moisture.

"Now that I have found you, I'm not letting you go either. You're mine. So *you* better get used to it, buddy." She chucked him under the chin.

Her statement was meant to reassure him, but instead, it gave him pause. He was her first, and didn't most people believe that they fell in love with their first sex partner?

Nathalie was naïve and inexperienced, and surrendering her virginity to him must've been emotionally stirring for her. And it wasn't only the sex, he was also her first romantic interest. Not to mention the hope he'd given her of finding her mother. Substitute any Joe Schmo for him and Nathalie would've most likely fallen, or believed she had, for him too.

Andrew, on the other hand, had no doubt that she was the one for him. Deep down, he'd known that he'd fallen in love with her, probably from the start. He just needed to be hit over the head with her proclamation to admit it to himself.

Nathalie's finger was tracing a path down his bare torso, and he tensed, expecting her to linger on his scars, but her finger continued its downward track until she reached the top of the towel he had wrapped around his hips and gave it a tug.

"Are you going to keep it on for long?" She smiled suggestively. "Tick, tock, tick, tock... time is not on our side."

She was right, of course. And talking about whether what she was feeling was love or just infatuation could and should wait for when they were both dressed and not so hungry for each other. Perhaps when her hormones no longer ran the show, Nathalie's head would clear, and she'd be in a better position to re-evaluate her true feelings for him.

"Come here." He hooked a finger under her chin and lifted her head. Taking her lush lips in a passionate kiss, he poured his heart into it, licking inside her mouth and tasting her sweetness. She was panting when he released her mouth. With a slow hand, he unwrapped her towel. As she was revealed to him, the steam that had been trapped there rose up from her smooth skin, and he wanted to lick her all over.

"You're so beautiful, Nathalie, you take my breath away," he told her as he lifted her off his lap and laid her on the bed. "I forgot about the lotion, I'll be right back." He kissed her belly before turning to go back to the bathroom.

"Let's leave the massage for some other time." She stopped him. "Come back here, I want to taste you again." And just like that, his shaft that had been already hard from their kiss sprung up and tented his towel.

Nathalie giggled and lifted up to her knees. "Look at this..." She reached for his towel and pulled, leaving him standing in front of her with his erection standing up at attention and ready for inspection.

Dropping the towel to the floor, she took him in hand. Gently moving up and down, she then rubbed her thumb over the tip to spread the drop of moisture that had welled there.

"I love how your shaft feels, hard on the inside but velvety on the outside." She looked up at him and smiled. "The opposite of you. You're hard on the outside but sweet on the inside."

Andrew rolled his eyes. What was with that *sweet* thing? He was as far from *sweet* as it got. His internal rumblings ceased as Nathalie extended her tongue and gave it a halting lick, and then another one, then rubbed her cheek on it like a kitten on a scratching post.

He ached to bury himself in her moist mouth, but he was letting her explore.

Mercifully, she'd gone back to licking, swirling her tongue all around the head before closing her lips around it.

"Yes, just like that," he groaned, his hips surging forward of their own accord, pushing more of his length into her mouth.

She sucked it in even deeper, and he cupped her cheek, feeling his shaft on the other side. Guided by instinct, she moved her mouth and her tongue in a way that drove him wild, and it took all he had not to thrust deeper. When she moaned around him, he almost came.

But as much fun as this was, it wasn't how he wanted to proceed. It wasn't enough for him to be pleasured, he needed to pleasure Nathalie even more.

Andrew put his hand on top of her head, stroking her hair as he pulled out of her mouth.

She looked up at him with worry in her big brown eyes. "Did I do something wrong? Wasn't it good for you?"

"No, sweetheart, you did it perfectly. But even though I'm a selfish bastard, pleasuring you gives me pleasure too." He lay on her small bed and pulled her on top of him, her knees straddling his face and her mouth hovering above his cock.

She turned her head around to look at him, a blush painting her cheeks red. "Oh, God, how did you know?"

He gave her slit a lick, getting a little taste before answering her. "Know what?" He thrust his tongue in between her wet folds, finding her entry and licking all around.

Nathalie moaned. "I've been fantasizing about doing this exactly like that," she breathed and took his shaft into her mouth, going down as far as she could before retreating.

The girl was a natural. Which meant that he needed to perform magic with his tongue to have her orgasming before he erupted in that skillful mouth of hers.

Splaying his hands over her heart-shaped ass, he held her in place, stilling her gyrating hips as he tongued her.

Damn, she was hot, wild, her tender flesh quivering on his tongue, and as he pushed a finger into her wet heat, she cried out, momentarily letting his shaft slide out of her mouth.

It was good, the cool air on his wet erection was exactly what he needed to delay his climax for just long enough to bring her off first.

He added another finger, and she took him back in her mouth, groaning around him—the vibrations bringing him close to the edge again.

Closing his lips around her clit, he sucked, and at the same time scissored his fingers, thrusting them deep inside her.

Nathalie screamed, the sound muffled by his shaft, then took him so deep that he bumped against the end of her throat. With a grunt, he pulled out before his seed erupted, finishing all over her face but at least not in her mouth.

She wasn't ready for that, yet.

Rolling off him, she grabbed one of the towels from the floor and wiped her face, then sprawled next to him on the bed.

"Sorry about that," he mumbled trying to catch his breath,

"You should be." She turned her head, pinning him with a pair of narrowed eyes. "Don't you dare pull out again like that. I told you that I wanted to taste you."

"Yes, ma'am." He saluted her, barely stifling a laugh.

Who could've known that his shy virgin would turn into a hungry cougar after her first taste of sex?

56

NATHALIE

Nathalie barely stifled a giggle. Andrew could not have looked more surprised and confused if she had told him that she wanted to dance naked in the street.

Maybe she'd overdone her pretense?

Yes, she was disappointed that she didn't get to enact her fantasy to the letter, but she wasn't really mad. How could she be? Andrew had pulled out only because he'd thought she wasn't ready. No doubt he would've preferred to finish in her mouth than all over it.

Hm, she'd wiped away most of it but not all. Tentatively, Nathalie licked her lips.

Oh, yeah, there it is—Andrew's taste.

She snuggled up to him, and he wrapped his arm around her, pulling her even closer. "I wish we could stay like this."

"Yeah, me too. Unfortunately, Jackson and my father are going to be back soon."

"Do you think we have time for another shower?"

"Probably. Knowing Jackson, he will text me when they are about to come back."

"Then let's go, and take your phone with you."

This time, their shared shower was all about efficiency and not intimacy. They were out of there and fully dressed in no more than five minutes.

Nathalie took Andrew's hand and led him to the den. "Let's at least snuggle until they return."

He kicked his shoes off and lay down, then pulled her on top of him. His hands gently caressing her back and her butt.

Her cheek on Andrew's chest, Nathalie smiled. The man was obsessed with her behind—in a good way. And to think that she'd always been self-conscious about the size of her ass and her hips. Apparently Andrew counted them as assets. She giggled.

"What's funny?"

"I was thinking about my ass assets." She giggled again.

He cupped her butt cheeks and then squeezed them possessively. "I love your ass." He gave it another squeeze.

Nathalie sighed. This was so nice, and she hated that soon she would have to say goodnight to Andrew. She couldn't keep him on the couch for another night. He had to go to work tomorrow.

Evidently, he was thinking along the same lines. "We need to find a better solution for your father. Jackson is an angel, but he is just a temporary fix."

"I know. But you've seen the types that showed up for interviews. I wouldn't let them take care of a dog."

"Neither would I, but we have to keep on looking. You deserve a life, Nathalie, a full one."

"I know, but I won't sacrifice my father in order to have one, I just can't."

Not even for Andrew.

Nathalie hoped it wouldn't be a deal-breaker for him, because if he left her over this, she would just die.

"I know, baby, and I'd never ask it of you. Hell, I would've been disappointed in you if you even considered it. I'm just trying to think outside the box. Perhaps we are going about it all wrong. There must be a better solution."

With a snort, she rolled off Andrew's chest and lay beside him. "I'm open to suggestions."

"I don't have anything yet, but I'm going to give it some serious thought."

"It's easier for those who have extended family, so they can take turns. But I have no one. It's just my dad and me."

Andrew made a face. "You have me, and I have an extended family. In fact, it's a pretty big one."

"Really? You've only mentioned one sister and your parents who are in Africa."

"True, but my sister is married to a guy who has a big extended family, so in a way they are mine as well."

"That's wonderful, and I would love to meet them, but it's not as if I can ask them to help."

"Maybe not, but I can ask for their advice. Or if they know someone who they could recommend as a caretaker for your father. After all, that's how you got Jackson."

She frowned. "What do you mean? Bhathian brought him."

Andrew shifted, and she had the impression that he'd said too much. "Bhathian is a cousin of my brother-in-law, and Jackson is the son of another cousin."

That didn't sound like something that should've been kept a secret, so why had no one mentioned it before? What exactly were Andrew and Bhathian up to?

Come to think of it, it was so strange how the two of them had shown up at her shop and how quickly they had ingrained themselves in her life. Bhathian was there almost every morning, drinking his coffee and sampling all of her pastries, complimenting her each time as if it was his first time tasting them. And Andrew, hitting on her full force from the first day.

Somehow, she doubted it was all a coincidence. Still, why would anyone bother to deceive her? She had nothing of value and was no one special.

Did it have something to do with her mother's disappearance?

After all, Eva could've been more than a simple drug enforcement agent, downplaying the kind of work she'd really done before retiring.

Suddenly, Nathalie saw it all clearly.

Eva hadn't retired voluntarily, she had been forced to leave and hide because she knew something that others wanted to either get their hands on, or silence her so it would never be found. And in that context, her mother's secretiveness and aloofness made perfect sense. Then six years ago they must've discovered her, and she'd had to run again. Not keeping contact with her daughter had been necessary to keep them both safe. Or… the option that Nathalie didn't want to consider—that those mysterious *they* had gotten to her mother.

Bhathian and Andrew were looking for Eva, and she'd been stupid enough to supply them with information. Luckily, there wasn't much that she really knew, and she was going to get rid of the box with her mother's stuff as soon as Andrew left.

God, am I just being paranoid? Please, oh please make it so.

To find out that Andrew was just pretending to care for her so he could get information about her mother was going to kill her.

Nathalie wouldn't survive a disappointment of this magnitude.

Hopefully, the whole mess was just in her head.

Yeah, like there isn't enough of it in there already.

But in case it wasn't sheer paranoia, to be on the safe side, she wasn't going to tell him anything else about Eva.

"What's wrong, sweetheart?" Andrew sounded so genuinely worried.

Damn, if her suspicions were true, then the guy deserved an Oscar. "Nothing, I'm just tired."

"You're crying because you are tired?"

Was she? Nathalie swiped a finger at the corner of her eye, and sure enough —it came away wet.

57

ANDREW

What was wrong with her? Why had Nathalie lied about the reason for her tears? She couldn't still be mad about him pulling out, could she?

Was it the talk about her father?

Probably.

He hugged her closer and caressed her arm. "Oh, sweetheart, you're so good and so brave. Such a wonderful daughter. Don't worry about your dad. We will find a solution that will make things better for him, not worse. I promise."

Nathalie nodded into his T-shirt. "I know."

"So what is it? Are you hearing voices again? Are they bothering you?"

Andrew suspected that she wasn't telling him about most of her ghostly visits. He'd often caught her making hand gestures as if she was having a conversation with someone—an internal one. But Nathalie was so uncomfortable talking about what she believed was a mental disorder that he hadn't pushed.

She snorted. "They are always bothersome, but it has been quiet in my head lately. Tut is basically gone, I haven't heard from him in days, but there is a new guy that calls himself Sage, who tends to pop up at the most inopportune moments."

"What do you mean?" Thinking about that ghost seeing her naked when she'd looked at herself in the mirror made Andrew see red.

Nathalie lifted her eyes to him, and a small smile bloomed on her beautiful face. "Are you jealous? Of a ghost?"

"You're damn right, I'm jealous. And the worst part is that if that ghostly pervert is sneaking up on you when you're nude in front of the mirror, I can't even beat him up."

Nathalie snorted.

Great, he was mad as hell, and she was laughing.

"You have nothing to worry about, Andrew. Sage, and I'm quoting him, is more interested in seeing you naked than me."

A gay ghost? Hell, that was something. Except, there was no reason to believe that all ghosts were straight. If the guy liked other guys when he was alive, there was no reason for his preferences to make a flip around just because he was dead.

But then, another disturbing thought occurred to him. He narrowed his eyes at Nathalie. "Don't tell me he actually got to see me naked…" because that would mean the pervert had watched them making love.

Nathalie rolled her eyes. "No, I wouldn't let him. And he is nice; when I tell him to go away he does. But he butted in a few times, giving me advice."

"About what?"

"You. He encouraged me to hurry and bang you because you're so hot. His words, not mine."

"Why? You don't think I'm hot?"

"I think you're smoldering hot, and you know it."

Yeah, he did. And now he couldn't be too mad at the ghost either. Apparently, Nathalie's forwardness was at least in part due to Sage's active encouragement.

And yet, Andrew found it strange that Nathalie's ghosts were all male. It would've bothered him less if they were female…

Was it possible that they were the product of her imagination after all? She'd been lonely, and craving male companionship. Her mind might have provided an illusion as a substitute. But now that she had a real boyfriend, the previous imaginary one was no longer needed, and she'd conjured another one who fit the role of the best friend she lacked—someone she could confide in, someone who would push her to do what she was afraid of.

Made perfect sense.

The problem with this scenario, though, was that it undermined his conviction that Nathalie was a Dormant.

Communicating with the dearly departed was a paranormal ability; making up imaginary friends at the age of thirty was a mental disability.

Damn, they really needed to find Eva.

Fast.

If Nathalie wasn't a Dormant, he would gladly spend his mortal life with her, helping her find a cure for her mental condition.

But if Nathalie was indeed a Dormant, he would have to go through the transition first in order to turn her.

And he wasn't getting any younger.

Tick, tock, tick tock… his time was running out.

DARK WARRIOR'S PROMISE

1

NATHALIE

"Damn it!" Nathalie slammed the oven door shut.

"What happened?" Jackson poked his head into the kitchen. "Need help?"

"No, get back to the register," she snapped at him.

He arched one blond brow before doing as he'd been told.

With a sigh, Nathalie braced her mitt-covered hands against her work table and let her head hang down from her neck.

She was short-tempered as hell this morning, and it wasn't only because she had slept less than three hours last night. Ever since Andrew's peculiar comment from yesterday, her mind had been churning with questions. She could no longer look at Jackson without wondering what his and Bhathian's agenda was, and by that, she meant what was Andrew's.

Why had none of them mentioned being related to each other before?

"Number two sandwich, mayo on the side," Jackson called out from the other room, instead of coming in or just sticking his head in to announce the new order. Her irritated response must've come out nastier than she'd intended, to scare off a guy who seemed to be afraid of nothing.

Good. Today, she really wasn't in the mood for seeing his pretty face and his fake charm.

Her father had had one of his episodes last night, waking her up sometime around two in the morning. He'd come into her room, saying that he couldn't sleep in his bed because there was some random guy already sleeping in it. No amount of arguing had managed to convince him otherwise. In the end, she'd given up and had moved his blanket and pillow to the couch in the den.

She'd been up since then.

You should have found him a place months ago.

Oh, hell, Tut. He was back.

What else could go wrong? Why couldn't she get one damn break in her stupid, miserable life?

She thought she'd found in Andrew the perfect guy to share her life with, only to discover that he'd been hiding things from her—like the fact that Bhathian and Jackson were part of his family. And she couldn't shake the suspicion that he'd gotten closer to her only to find out information about her missing mother.

She thought she'd found in Jackson the best helper for her shop, only to discover that the kid was part of the conspiracy.

She thought she'd found in Bhathian a great new friend, one who was selflessly helping her out of the goodness of his heart, but he was with them, and obviously had an ulterior motive.

But the last straw was Tut. After such a long stretch of silence, she thought she'd gotten rid of him. All that remained was to banish Sage as well. It would've meant that she was getting better. But her hopes had been shattered.

She was still as nutty as ever.

Damn it. Even if her suspicions about Andrew were nothing but paranoia, what kind of a future could someone as bat-shit crazy as her hope to have with a man like him?

Nutty Nattie would never have a normal life. She would never get married and would never have kids. She would grow old alone with only a bunch of cats for company.

Trouble was, she was allergic to them, and an old dog lady didn't work as well as an old cat lady.

With hot tears flooding her eyes and sliding down her cheeks, she fled the kitchen, afraid someone would come in and see her crying like a loon. And if the tears weren't bad enough, she was losing the battle against the sobs that were pushing up her throat.

Shit, she couldn't breathe.

The downstairs bathroom was the closest, but it served the coffee shop and didn't offer much privacy, especially since she was about to bawl her eyes out and sob uncontrollably. Which left only the second-floor bathroom. Dropping the mitts at the foot of the stairs, Nathalie ran up and locked herself in her cramped sanctuary.

Dramatic much? Tut's sarcastic tone was like a kick to the gut. Dirty, underhanded bastard, kicking her when she was already down on the floor.

"You're such an asshole." Nathalie dropped the toilet lid and sat down.

And you're overreacting because you're tired. It's happened before. You get depressed when you're sleep-deprived.

"Shut up. Just shut up. I can't deal with all this crazy right now." She dropped her head to her hands.

You're not crazy, you have a gift, he said softly.

"Says the crazy voice in my head."

What if I can prove it?

"How?"

Tell you something that no one else knows.

"Go ahead, I'm listening." Tut was so full of shit. For years he'd claimed that he could tell her nothing because it was against the rules.

Columbus didn't discover America.

Nathalie rolled her eyes. "Everyone knows that. Some Viking explorer got there first."

Tut chuckled. *The truth is that America had always been known, and various peoples had been crossing the Atlantic Ocean for thousands of years. It just wasn't known to the Europeans of Columbus's time.*

"Maybe yes, maybe no. It's not something I can use. There is no way to prove it. You need to give me something more concrete, something personal, not something anyone can dig out of obscure history books."

Sorry, I've been dead for far too long. All I have are anecdotes which are history to you.

"Bloody convenient excuse."

Ask the new guy, he's fresh.

"Sage?"

Whatever he calls himself. He's a newbie so there is a good chance that he died recently and can remember stuff to tell you that you can still verify. Except, time doesn't work the same on this side, so even though he might think he'd been alive only yesterday, he could've been dead for many years of your time.

This was more information than Tut had ever shared with her. "Why are you telling me this only now?"

I had no reason to tell you any of this before. But as I said, my time here is limited, and I don't want to leave you vulnerable.

"Fine. If Sage comes back, I'll ask him."

He will. You're like a beacon of light to those of us who cling to this existence for one reason or another. That's why you were bombarded with so many voices when you were little. I helped shield you, and as you got older, becoming more guarded and skeptical, that beacon of yours has dimmed. But some desperate souls will still find you, I have no doubt of that.

"Why? What do they want from me?"

Think about it. If there were only one person in the world who could hear you, wouldn't you fight for a chance to be heard?

He had a point. It must be awful to be all alone in the big void with no one to talk to. "Yeah, I guess I would."

Okay, now that we are clear on this subject, you need to get up, wash your face, and get back to work before they come looking for you.

For a change, Tut had sounded sincere and had actually made sense. If there really was an afterlife—and she tended to believe that there was, even though she wasn't religious like her father—communication with the dead must be very limited. Otherwise, instead of esoteric, it would be a commonplace occurrence. Perhaps she really was one of the *lucky* few who possessed this dubious talent.

But as disturbing as it was to accept that she was talking to actual ghosts, thinking of herself as psychic certainly beat thinking of herself as crazy. So why not adjust her belief system and change the story she was telling herself? How different would her life have been if she had been embracing her psychic ability instead of doubting her sanity all the time?

It was so simple—just a matter of a change in perspective, a change in attitude, a new storyboard. There would always be doubts; there was no way around it given the supernatural nature of the interactions, but she could choose to brush them off instead of letting them take over.

"You're right," she told Tut.

Invigorated by the shift in logic, Nathalie pulled down a long piece of toilet paper and dabbed her eyes dry before blowing her nose into it. Getting up, she lifted the lid and flushed the paper down the toilet. As she watched it get sucked down the small whirlpool, she hiccuped once, then turned around to examine the damage in the mirror.

God, she looked awful—blotchy nose, puffy eyes, the works. How on earth was she going to erase the signs of emotional meltdown from her face?

Makeup, and lots of it.

When she was done, her skin tone was flawless thanks to several coats of foundation. Her eyes were still red-rimmed, but the black eyeliner and mascara she'd applied liberally helped them look less puffy.

The downside was that she was painted like a hooker.

Whatever, it would have to do. She was going to spend most of her day in the kitchen anyway.

2

ANDREW

"Son of a bitch." Andrew slammed the phone down.

It was four in the afternoon, and he had to drag his ass all the way to the airport, in rush-hour traffic, to investigate a supposed prank. A baggage handler had shown up to work wearing a padded vest, which in itself wasn't all that unusual, but a coworker had noticed that the padding looked odd. That, combined with some troubling comments the handler had been spewing lately, prompted the coworker to approach security.

The guy had been detained, and his vest had been checked. It turned out that a bunch of empty matchboxes had been sewn into the padding, creating the square outlines his coworker had noticed.

Strange? You bet.

The excuse was that he'd been pulling a prank on his buddies.

Yeah, right. Andrew had a strong suspicion that it had been a test to see if the guy could get away with a dummy before attempting the real thing.

There were gaping holes in airport security that had to be plugged before something worse than 9/11 hit the United States. Problem was that the TSA and Homeland Security couldn't come up with a solution that didn't cost millions to implement, or create additional holdbacks. Airport personnel moved between secured and unsecured areas many times during their workday, and it wasn't feasible to screen them every time they re-entered the secured areas.

The only solution, in Andrew's opinion, was to screen everyone entering the airport.

Expensive? Sure. New checkpoints would have to be built at the entry points, and they would have to be numerous to facilitate fast processing of the inbound traffic.

Necessary? Absolutely. And if it meant that airfare would get even pricier to cover the additional costs, Andrew was willing to pay a few extra dollars for a ticket so he could fly safely and get rid of the anxiety even he felt every time he boarded a plane. And he was pretty sure that most travelers would gladly pay it as well.

Not that anyone had been paying attention to him or his suggestions at that fucking summit in Washington. No one listened to the field people. It was all about department politics and the bureaucrats covering their own pampered asses.

God, he hated politicians. Hell, he hated all bureaucrats.

They should each serve a few years in the armed forces before being allowed to run for office. Not that it was guaranteed to produce better judgment calls, but it would no doubt be an improvement. Fighting on the front lines and risking their own bloody lives would definitely make them rethink their priorities.

"Where to?" Kravitz asked as Andrew passed his desk on his way out.

"The fucking airport. I have a suspect to interrogate."

The agent glanced at the clock hanging on the wall behind him. "I don't envy you the drive. Traffic will be murder."

"Isn't it always?"

Kravitz nodded. "Can't argue with that. See you tomorrow, Spivak."

Andrew gave the agent a two-fingered salute. "Say hi to Lora for me."

Six months ago, Kravitz had married an intern from the accounting department and hadn't stopped smiling since. Evidently, marriage agreed with the guy.

"Will do."

Would he be as stupidly happy as Kravitz if he married Nathalie? Probably not. Even though he loved her passionately and saw himself spending the rest of his life with her, Andrew just wasn't the cheerful sort. All he could hope for was a measure of contentment, some peace for his restless soul.

He hated keeping things from her.

Hell, who was he kidding? Andrew was guilty of worse. He was plain out lying to her. But even if he disregarded the clan's directive of keeping its existence secret, it wasn't his place to tell her the truth—it was her real father's. Except, he just couldn't help thinking that the duplicity would blow up in his face at some point.

It had taken him a while to figure out why Nathalie had been upset last night, and why she'd lied about the reason for her tears. Clearly, she must've gotten suspicious after his stupid blurt about Bhathian and Jackson being related to each other and through his sister to him. The woman was far from stupid, and it didn't take a genius to figure out that he must've had a good reason not to mention this before.

God only knew what she was imagining. Women had a tendency to blow up every little thing into monstrous proportions even without having a good reason. And lying was a fucking big one.

Driving up the levels of the underground parking of his office building, Andrew waited until he cleared it before hitting Nathalie's number.

"Hi, Andrew," she answered in a flat tone.

Fuck, now he was sure he was screwed. "What's up, sweetheart, you sound off."

"I'm just dead tired. My dad had an episode last night, and I've hardly gotten any sleep."

She sounded truthful, but his gift wasn't as good when limited to audio clues. "Perhaps I should let you sleep and come over tomorrow. I'm on my way to the airport to interrogate a suspect, so I would be running late anyway."

Andrew held his breath as he waited for her response. If she agreed with him, he was screwed. But if she still wanted to see him tonight, it would mean that he hadn't screwed up as badly.

Or that the woman was a saint.

"No, I want you to come. I'll ask Jackson to stay a little longer and keep an eye on my dad while I take a nap. Wake me up when you get here."

Feeling the muscles in his jaw relax, Andrew let out the breath he'd been holding. "Are you sure?"

"Of course, I'm sure, you silly man. I miss you."

A big grin split Andrew's face. "Your wish is my command, sweetheart."

She giggled. "Duh, of course, it is."

Suddenly, the drive didn't seem as daunting, and as he hummed along to the tune of a popular love song on the radio, Andrew realized that he was still smiling.

Damn, he was turning into a fool just like Kravitz.

3

BRUNDAR

Pathetic.

Brundar rubbed his neck as he observed his students' clumsy attempts at toppling their opponents down to the mat. After two weeks' worth of intense drilling, he'd finally paired them up to see how well they had internalized what they'd learned.

Apparently, not very much.

And out of this bunch of losers, he was supposed to pick candidates for the advanced class. It was embarrassing to admit, but Michael, who had started training as a lowly human, had shown way more promise than this group of inept immortals. As of now, he was the only serious candidate they had for the Guardian training.

It had to do with attitude. Michael was an athlete who loved to challenge himself. On the other hand, most of these trainees had signed up just to learn basic survival skills. They loved their cerebral day jobs and had done nothing athletic in ages. Their motivation was marginal at best, and their attitudes sucked.

Surprisingly, the only one who had shown some aptitude was none other than Carol—the airhead with the drinking problem. Not that this was her only vice. On more than one occasion, he'd smelled weed on her. But she was trying, probably because she had no job to speak of and was most likely bored. Physically, she had a long way to go. Short and chubby, she lacked muscle tone, and her endurance was shit. But she was aggressive and had a decent aim with a handgun. In fact, she was the best shooter in his class—a dubious title considering who she was competing against.

He clapped his hands to get their attention. "Okay, people. That's enough."

Just as they'd been taught, his students lined up and bowed from the waist.

"When I call your name, you may leave."

"Yes, Master," was the response from the group of twenty-two immortals.

At least they had gotten this part down. Whipping some discipline and proper etiquette into the bunch of newbie civilians hadn't been easy, but it had been necessary. Their obedience and respect were the only things that made teaching the class bearable for him.

When those he'd called had departed, there were only four people left: Carol, her likewise unemployed buddies, George and Ben, and Roland.

Slim, slim pickings.

"You are the best in this class."

Smug looks and high-fives followed.

He grimaced. "That's not a great achievement. Being better than bad doesn't make you good."

The smug looks wilted.

"But I'm giving you a chance to get better. I've chosen the four of you for an advance class from which the best will be selected for the Guardian training program."

Carol and her buddies looked excited, Roland looked down at his bare feet.

"A problem, Roland?"

"I'm not interested in the Guardian program. I just want to learn self-defense."

"No problem. It's voluntary. Do you still want to join the advanced class?"

"If I don't have to join the Guardian training later? Then yes."

"The advanced class starts tomorrow at seven."

"Do we still need to come for the six o'clock beginner class too?" Carol asked.

Poor girl, not the sharpest tool in the shed. "No, Carol, just the seven o'clock."

"Yes, Master." She bowed her head, the mass of her strawberry blonde curls fanning around her cherubic face.

Lucky for her, Carol was beautiful—in that fragile sort of way that males found irresistible. They couldn't help but feel protective of her, and that perceived weakness was what drew them to her like moths to a flame. He wondered if she used it to her advantage, and her dumb act was just that —an act.

Still, even if she wanted to join the Guardian Force, he wasn't going to recommend her despite her talent with a gun. It wasn't about being a chauvinist. After all, he had no problem with Kri, but Carol was an irresponsible airhead, soft and weak. Definitely not Guardian material.

"Dismissed." He waited until they exited to turn off the lights.

Originally, the place had been designated as a classroom, but more space had been needed for training, and the room had been turned into a makeshift training area by removing the chairs and desks and covering the floor with rubber matting. There was another one just like it next door, and that was where he was heading next.

Bhathian was finishing up with his own class, and Brundar was curious to see how many students he'd chosen for the advanced training. Eleven left the room, and a few moments later five more headed out. Not bad. Together they had harvested nine.

"Are they any good?" he asked as he entered the classroom.

"Nah, not even one. If you ask me, it's a big waste of time. Basic self-defense is one thing, and training for the Guardian Force is another. Kian and Onegus are deluding themselves if they think these guys will amount to anything."

Brundar shook his head. "I don't remember it being like this when we were young."

Bhathian snorted as he turned off the lights. "Different times. Lads were stronger then, used to working with their hands. We carried a sword even before our voices changed, and learned how to use it even before we transitioned."

"We have to get our old friends to come back." Brundar followed Bhathian into the elevator.

"Talk to your brother."

"What for?"

Bhathian shrugged. "He has a way with people. Maybe he could convince some to reconsider. Kian is not having much success in luring them back, but then he's not the best guy to try and sell something to someone that doesn't want to buy. But Anandur, well, you know him, he is a charming bastard."

Not a bad idea. Anandur had always been the glue that had held the Guardians together. The fun guy, the prankster, the one everyone liked. Perhaps reminding the guys of the good old days would do the trick.

"I will. Listen, I want you to take over both of our beginner classes, and I'll take the advanced one. I don't want to waste any more of my time than I already have on this."

"No problem. How many of yours moved up and how many are left?"

"Out of the twenty-two, I chose four for the advanced course."

Bhathian rubbed his chin. "Your eighteen plus my eleven makes twenty-nine." He shrugged. "I'll manage."

"Good." Brundar nodded as the elevator stopped at the gym level. "I'm going to look for Anandur."

4

NATHALIE

"I made you a cappuccino." Jackson came into the kitchen with a peace offering.

Smart boy. He would do well in a relationship. Instinctively, he was trying to appease her even though he had no clue why she was angry. Nathalie wondered if he realized that he was partially responsible for her peeve and was trying to get back into her good graces.

Nah. Andrew had just blurted the newsflash of them being related yesterday, and she was pretty sure he hadn't informed Jackson yet.

"Thank you, I need it." Nathalie took it from him and sat down on the stool he'd brought for her from the front. It was hard to be mad at such a thoughtful guy. Jackson had noticed that she'd given up the only chair in the kitchen for her father to sit in and had nowhere to rest, so he brought her the stool.

"When you're done, I would like you to meet my friend Vlad."

God, not another one of his endless string of friends. She was grateful for the additional clientele Jackson was bringing in, and most days she enjoyed interacting with them, but today she was too tired for socializing. "Perhaps some other time. I'm barely keeping my eyes open, and I'm counting the minutes until closing time. As soon as I flip the sign to closed, I'm going upstairs and collapsing on my bed."

"But that's exactly why I want you to meet Vlad. You need help in the kitchen, and Vlad needs a job."

"That's very thoughtful of you, but even with the extra business you're bringing in, I can't afford another salary."

"I know, but he is willing to work for free until you can pay him."

"Why on earth would he want to do that?"

Jackson smirked. "Because I sold him on the idea that you'd teach him to bake."

"He wants to be a baker?" A highly unusual career choice for a teenager.

"Not necessarily, but he wants to make money."

Nathalie snorted. "Then he's choosing the wrong profession, that's for sure."

Jackson patted her shoulder as if she was a little slow. "Let's go sit down with Vlad and negotiate a deal. You're practically swaying on your feet."

"We can't take a break at the same time. What if someone orders something?"

"It's ten minutes to closing, and we can say that the kitchen is closed. You're done for today." He tugged on her apron strap.

Bossy kid. But whatever, he was right.

"Papi, are you okay here by yourself for a couple of minutes?" she asked her father.

When he nodded, she took the apron off, washed her hands in the sink, and followed Jackson out while drying them on a dish towel.

"Nathalie, this is Vlad."

She lifted her head to say hello to Jackson's friend and almost ran back to the kitchen. No wonder the kid was willing to work for free. Who in their right mind would want to employ him?

He'd scare the customers away.

Dressed all in black, with numerous chains and buckles for decorations, he was totally into the goth style. But that wasn't what was so disturbing. Vlad was very tall, probably close to six and a half feet, and so scrawny that she doubted he weighed more than her, probably less. Hunched over, with a face pale as a white sheet of paper and stick-straight black hair that fell over one eye, he looked like a cross between Dracula and his servant Igor.

The kid must've been wearing colored contacts because the blue of the one eye that was visible wasn't like any kind of blue Nathalie had ever seen before.

Her startled response had him hunching even further, and he dropped his head—the long swathe of hair covering most of his face.

"Hi, Miss Nathalie," he whispered from under the curtain of his glossy hair.

Shit, now she felt like a jerk. Poor kid. Being seventeen and looking like this must be hellish. She of all people should know.

"Hello, Vlad." She offered him her hand. "Is it short for Vladimir?"

After a moment of hesitation, he shook what she'd offered, holding her hand with gentle, slim fingers that were tipped with long nails.

"No, it's just Vlad." His murmur was barely audible.

"Come, let's sit over there." Jackson pointed to an empty booth.

"Okay, so here is the deal." Jackson addressed her as soon as they were seated. "I was thinking about your mode of operation and how you can make more money and work less."

Nathalie rolled her eyes. Kids and their dreams of money falling down from the sky. "Go on. I'm curious to hear what brilliant plan you've hatched."

Jackson smirked. "The coffee shop is already working at full capacity, so we can't expect to be making more money out of it. Your baked goods are in high demand, but you can't make more by yourself, and we can't sell more in this small shop."

"I'm not moving."

"That's not what I'm building up to. My idea is to sell directly to offices. I can have a bunch of my friends peddle your baked goods door to door, working on commission only. And as to production, we could start with Vlad, and if the thing takes off, we can hire additional helpers."

She had to hand it to Jackson, the boy was a natural entrepreneur, but he hadn't taken into account her kitchen's limited capacity. "First of all, I'm not set up for mass production. I don't have the right equipment or even space to put it in. Second, I have to wonder, what's in it for you?"

A big grin spread over Jackson's handsome face. "Money, of course. I manage and organize the door to door sales, and we split the profits from it. And as to your kitchen, we start with what we have, and when we outgrow it, we'll worry about the solution then."

Nathalie couldn't really find fault with Jackson's plan. On the face of it, his idea seemed good. But was she up to the extra hustle?

"I'll sleep on it. Right now I don't want to even think about extra work. And as for you, Vlad. Can you be here tomorrow at four in the morning?"

Vlad perked up, flipping his long hair back and away from his face. "Yes." He smiled a little, showing a pair of incisors long enough to be considered fangs. Was he wearing some kind of prosthetics? Nah, looked too real. But what was even more disconcerting were his eyes, which were both visible now—the eerie blue one and the glowing green one.

Fate had been cruel to the boy, more so than to her, and Nathalie was doubly glad that she'd offered him the job. It was on the tip of her tongue to tell him—welcome to the freak show—so he'd know she was a kindred spirit, but she managed to refrain. Vlad would've taken it the wrong way. Instead, she extended her hand to him with the biggest smile she could muster in her exhausted state. "Good. Come round the back and knock."

He shook on it vigorously. "I will. Thank you. You won't regret it, I promise."

"I know. Welcome aboard." On the inside she added, *Us freaks have to stick together, dude.*

To Jackson, she said, "I'm going up to sleep. Can you finish here and keep an eye on my dad until Andrew shows up?"

"Sure thing."

5

ANANDUR

*A*nandur grimaced as Brundar walked in with an expression more dour than usual on his pale face. Not bothering with pleasantries, like saying hello to his only brother, he headed straight for the fridge, pulled out a beer, and sat down on a stool next to the counter.

"Nice of you to show up, brother mine." Anandur couldn't help the sarcastic tone. Lately, Brundar had been gone most nights, turning up for work and a change of clothes and hightailing it right after.

They hadn't talked in days.

Not that Brundar was much of a conversationalist, but he was a good listener, and Anandur needed someone to talk to about the situation with Lana. Even if only to hear himself talk. He had stuff he wanted to get off his chest, and Brundar was better than a priest in a confessional at keeping things to himself.

Brundar swiveled the stool around to face Anandur. "What can I do for you?"

His brother knew him too well. "Nothing. I just feel like I'm living here alone. Should I start looking for a new flat mate?"

"Not yet."

What the hell was that supposed to mean?

"Are you serious? You're planning on moving out?"

Brundar raised his beer bottle in a salute. "Just messing with you."

Brundar? Joking? Not likely. The guy had no sense of humor whatsoever. But if he was set on keeping his plans to himself, there was no force known to man, mortal or immortal, that could pry it out of him.

Anandur wasn't going to even try. "So what's new with you?"

"The trainees suck."

"Oh, yeah?"

"Out of the twenty-two in my class, I barely scraped four for the advanced training, and one of them is Carol." Brundar's thin lips twisted in distaste. He lifted the bottle and took a long swig.

"That bad, eh?"

"You have to help Kian and call some of the old Guardians, using that famous charm of yours to persuade them to come back. We need them."

"Kian didn't ask for my help. He said he would handle this."

"Yeah, but I bet you'll have better results."

Anandur scratched at his beard. "Probably. I can start with Uisdean and Raibert. Last I talked with Raibert he was telling me about the construction company the two of them started. My impression was that they weren't doing that great."

"You should also give Niall a call. You guys used to be tight. You can pull on those old friendship heartstrings."

Not likely. Niall was happy with his successful antique dealership, wearing fancy suits and pretending to be related to royalty while shagging all the bored rich housewives who wandered into his showroom. Anandur doubted Niall would agree to leave his cushy lifestyle for that of a simple Guardian. Even if only temporarily.

Unless...

"I have a great idea. I can bait them—dangle Amanda's success with identifying Dormants. Tell them they'll be first in line for any females she finds."

Brundar gulped down what remained of his bottle. "That should work." He got up and pulled another one from the fridge.

Something was bothering the bastard, but asking him about it was futile. Brundar didn't share.

Anandur rubbed the back of his neck. "Anyway, I have this problem..."

Brundar reopened the fridge, pulled out another beer, and put both on the counter. "This one is for you." He pointed.

It was annoying, the way Brundar could read him like an open book while Anandur had no idea what was on the bastard's mind.

"It's about the Russian girl I'm supposed to seduce."

Brundar arched a brow. "And you need my advice? The self-declared chick magnet lost his touch? What happened?"

"It's not about the seduction part, you bastard. I don't need anyone's advice on that. My problem is that I don't want to thrall her. The scumbag Alex is screwing all of his crew, and he's probably thralled them numerous times. I'd hate to add to the damage. And anyway, you know me, I'm not all that good at thralling. If Lana has been subjected to it so many times, she might've built up a resistance. What if I fail to thrall her?"

Brundar shrugged. "Easy. Tie her up and blindfold her."

"And how is that supposed to help? It's not like she won't be able to feel my fangs sink into her neck, or ignore the euphoria that will follow."

Brundar sighed. "You've never engaged in BDSM, have you?"

Anandur cringed. "No, not my thing. And I'm sure it's not Lana's either."

Was it Brundar's? Or was he talking theoretically? And if it was, on what side of it did his brother play?

There was no point in asking. He wouldn't get an answer.

Brundar shrugged again. "Do whatever you want, but you asked my advice, and that's the only way you can bite a woman without having to thrall her afterward. Do you want me to tell you how to do it or not?"

If only to satisfy his curiosity, Anandur was eager to hear Brundar out. This was a rare opportunity to get some insight into the mystery that was his brother.

"Sure, why not. Tell me. I want to know. I'll decide if I want to try it or not after I hear what's involved." If Brundar brought up whips and chains, then it would be a definite no-no.

"First of all, you don't have to bite her neck. You can bite her inner thigh. The advantage being that it's less sensitive than the neck, and it will be less obvious what you're doing. Especially with your beard and mustache confusing the sensations. After all, once you remove her blindfold, and she takes a look, there will be no marks left. And if she happens to be really into it, she'll attribute the euphoria to subspace. But if it's only a game for her, then you have to make sure that she orgasms so many times that she can barely remember her own name."

Anandur smirked. "That I can do, no problem. But what is subspace?"

"It's very similar to the venom-induced euphoria. An intense scene can trigger the release of endorphins and other hormones that produce a morphine-like effect. It numbs the pain and creates an ecstatic floaty feeling."

Anandur cringed. Pain wasn't a word he liked to associate with sex. "Can it be achieved without hurting the girl, only with loads of pleasure?"

Brundar shook his head. "Not really. But again, if you exhaust her with plenty of orgasms, she can come close enough."

"Yeah, I think I'll stick to this. I'm not comfortable with what you call an intense scene."

A rare smile lifted the corners of Brundar's lips, and he clapped Anandur on the back. "I know, you're too soft." Then he got serious again, pinning Anandur with hard eyes. "A word of caution. If you decide that you want to play, there is much more to it that you need to learn. What goes up must come down, and the high always ends up in a low. The drop in endorphins and adrenaline produces symptoms similar to shock, and it's extremely important to help the sub come down gently. A warm blanket, a bottle of water, and something sweet to eat are a good start. Cuddling and reassuring, that's another part of it. Look it up before trying anything."

Damn, the guy was serious, and it was clear that he knew what he was talking about. But cuddling and reassuring? Brundar? Somehow Anandur couldn't picture his brother doing this for someone, or even being on the receiving end. Brundar didn't like to touch others or be touched. But then that was with males. He probably didn't mind it with women.

Anandur saluted with his beer. "Got it. And don't worry, I have no intention of playing this hard. I'm okay with pretend play, nothing more."

Brundar nodded, and then in a rare gesture of brotherly affection he squeezed Anandur's shoulder. "Good luck." He emptied his second beer and headed for the door.

"Where are you going?"

"Out."

"I figured that much. Where to?"

Brundar lifted a brow and opened the door, then closed it softly behind him.

Anandur sighed and brought the bottle to his lips. *I guess that was as much brotherly sharing as I'm ever going to get.*

6

NATHALIE

It was dark outside when Nathalie opened her eyes, the weak moonlight drawing a wavy pattern on her blanket. Damn, Andrew wasn't there. Could he still be stuck at the airport?

What time is it?

She turned on her bedside lamp and glanced at her watch. Nine twenty-two. He must've decided to go home.

How disappointing.

But then, as a sound of murmurs reached her, coming from the direction of the den, an excited flutter stirred in her belly. She couldn't tell for sure, but one of them sounded like Andrew's.

He'd come after all.

Nathalie got up and shuffled to the door. The voices became clearer as she opened it, and she recognized one as Andrew's and the other as Jackson's. For a moment, she contemplated standing out in the hallway and listening in. Perhaps she could catch them talking about whatever they were hiding from her. But then the name Vlad was mentioned, followed by Andrew's masculine laughter.

God, she loved to hear him laugh. He didn't do it often enough. She should make it her mission from now on. Perhaps she could subscribe to a website that delivered a daily dose of jokes. There must be something like that, and if there wasn't, there should be.

"Hi, guys," she said as she entered the den and walked over to the couch.

"Hi, sweetheart, what are you doing up?" Andrew asked as he opened his arms.

Gladly accepting the invitation, Nathalie sat on his lap.

She sighed as Andrew wrapped his arms around her, surrounding her with his warmth and his strength. It felt so good, and she wanted to stay like this forever. Closing her eyes, she rested her cheek on his hard chest.

Andrew kissed her forehead. "You should have stayed in bed. Jackson told me you were swaying on your feet from exhaustion, and that you almost fainted."

She turned her head and opened her eyes, casting Jackson a questioning look.

He shrugged. "I just tell it as I see it."

"It wasn't from exhaustion. It was because of Vlad."

That earned her another hearty laugh from Andrew, his big body shaking under her. "Jackson told me about him. Poor kid."

Nathalie felt a slight pang of guilt for using Vlad to amuse Andrew. "Yeah. What I don't get, though, is why he makes it even worse by dressing like a goth and growing his nails like that. Maybe if he wore jeans and a T-shirt like a typical teenager and cut those claws, he wouldn't be as scary. And that emo haircut isn't helping him either."

"Vlad is the guitarist of our band. The nails and the look are part of the gig."

"That explains a lot. But does he have to dress the part all of the time?"

Jackson sighed. "It's better to look as if he's doing it on purpose. Looking like an emo goth beats looking simply like the tall, thin, creepy kid."

"I guess you're right." Being a teenager sucked. Thank God she was no longer one.

Jackson pushed up to his feet. "I'm going. See you tomorrow, Nathalie. I hope Vlad will make himself useful."

"I'm going to make sure that he does."

"See ya, Andrew." He waved before disappearing into the dark hallway.

Nathalie listened to Jackson trot down the stairs, then open the front door and lock it behind him. It was amazing how quickly she'd trusted him with his own key and the code to the new alarm Andrew had had installed.

The kid had gotten under her skin, which was to be expected considering how helpful he was, especially with her father. And although she couldn't completely ignore the niggling suspicions as to his motives, she found it hard to believe that there could be something truly sinister hiding under that charming façade. He was just a kid on the cusp of manhood. With the enthusiasm and naïveté of youth, Jackson was looking for a way to prove himself as some big shot entrepreneur and to make money.

To Nathalie, he was a godsend. She should be grateful that he'd come into her life. And the dangerous vibe he emitted, the one that occasionally made her uncomfortable, must be due to his emerging masculinity. This one was going to grow into the ultimate alpha, but in a good way, hazardous only to the young girls' hearts he was going to break.

And Andrew? There was no way he could feel so good and so right while harboring some nefarious intentions toward her or her mother. It must've been all in her head.

Nathalie burrowed closer into Andrew's chest. "When I woke up, all alone in my room, I was afraid you decided not to come."

"I told you that I would be here. I would never dare disobey direct orders from my queen."

She loosened his tie and popped the first button on his shirt. "Your queen, eh? I like the sound of it."

He bowed his head. "I'm your humble servant, your majesty."

She was going to have fun with that. Andrew had no idea what he'd started.

"Kiss me," she commanded in a haughty tone.

He kissed her nose. "Like this?"

Nathalie giggled. "Nope, try again."

He kissed her forehead. "Like this?"

"Nope, a little lower."

Andrew smirked and planted one on her chin.

"I think you need a demonstration." She looped her arms around his neck and pulled him down.

With his palm cradling the back of her head, he took over and kissed her, his tongue slipping into her mouth and coaxing hers to join the dance.

When he drew back, his hooded eyes belied his smirk. "Like this?" he taunted.

"Exactly."

He closed his mouth over hers, his previous playfulness replaced by a hot, demanding hunger. With his shaft growing harder beneath her, Nathalie's hips moved as if they had a mind of their own, rubbing against it.

"You're driving me crazy," he groaned into her mouth.

"And you're wearing too many clothes."

"What do you want to do, love?"

"Let's go to my room."

"What about your father?"

"I'll lock the door, and if he wakes up, I'll stall for time while you duck into the closet."

Andrew shook his head. "Alright. I guess beggars can't be choosers." He pushed to his feet with her still in his arms.

"Ohh, you're so strong," she husked.

Andrew grinned, the smugness practically oozing from him.

Evidently, her guy wasn't immune to compliments.

"Go on..." he encouraged as he carried her down the hallway to her room.

"I like how you can lift me so effortlessly, as if I weigh practically nothing. I can feel your chest and arm muscles flexing against me, and I can't wait to have my hands all over that bare hardness."

"Woman, I'm gonna do such wicked things to you tonight," he said as he laid her down on her narrow bed.

"Lock the door."

"Yes, ma'am." He turned the key in the lock, already loosening his tie on the way back. "We'll have to be very quiet." He toed off his shoes and unzipped his slacks, pushing them down together with his boxers. "Which is going to be a problem since I'm going to drive you wild with pleasure." He shrugged off his shirt and sat on the bed to remove his socks. Foregoing the careful folding and draping he usually did, Andrew dropped his clothing in a messy pile on the floor.

Nice, she liked that he was impatient to get to her. She was impatient too.

Nathalie was still dressed when Andrew joined her in bed.

Stretching her arms over her head, she arched her back. "Could you help me out of my clothes? I'm still so tired," she teased.

"With pleasure." Andrew pushed her T-shirt up, stopping to cup her breasts for a moment before pulling it over her head. "Just checking that my beauties are still here."

She grinned. "I think you should make sure. Maybe those are imposters hiding under the bra."

He chuckled and snapped the front clasp, letting the cups fall sideways. "Nope, these are mine. But just so there are no doubts, I'll have to taste them."

Nathalie giggled as he caught one nipple between his lips, gave it a thorough licking, then repeated on the other. "Yep, the taste is unmistakable. These are mine."

"What do they taste like?"

His eyes were smoldering as he answered. "They taste like my woman and love."

Impatient with the game she started, Nathalie pushed down her stretchy jeans and kicked them off. A moment later, they were lying on their sides facing each other, skin to skin. It felt amazing. "I wish I could fall asleep naked in your arms every night, and wake up like this every morning."

Andrew ran a gentle hand down her back and cupped her ass. "Me too. This is my definition of bliss."

A beautiful dream, but for now an impossible one. There was no way Andrew could move in with her. Aside from the problem of Fernando's aversion to change, there was simply not enough room. And moving to a bigger place where the three of them could be comfortable wasn't feasible either. For Nathalie to work and take care of her dad at the same time, living above the shop was an absolute necessity.

Nathalie felt tears prickling the back of her eyes. "Make love to me, Andrew."

"Your majesty's wish is my command."

7

ANDREW

He'd promised Nathalie wicked things, but all Andrew wanted was to make slow and gentle love to her. To show her how much he cherished her with every touch, every kiss.

"I love you," he whispered as he palmed her face, looking into her tear-misted eyes. There was so much longing in her gaze. Andrew wished he could satisfy all of it, give her everything, solve all of her problems. But all he could manage for now was this suspended moment in time, a bubble of carefree pleasure that would provide her with a temporary distraction.

He kissed her, his tongue sliding into her welcoming mouth as his palm closed over her breast. Nathalie's eyelids slid shut, and he felt her body going soft in his arms. She was letting go of her stress, enjoying what he was doing to her.

Her hands brushed over his chest, caressing, following the contours of his muscles. "I love your body. You're so hard… all over."

"And you're so soft." One of her bra straps still clung to her shoulder, and Andrew pulled it off, touching the sexy lacy thing to his nose before throwing it down to the floor. He loved that she'd bought the front-closing bra especially for him, so he could get her naked faster.

His sweet Nathalie was a lustful woman. And he was one lucky bastard.

"You're so luscious." He plumped one breast before taking her nipple into his mouth.

Nathalie moaned softly and arched into him, her fingers digging into his hair as she held him to her. He licked and sucked until she pulled his head off and brought it to her other nipple.

Bossy ex-virgin.

When he lifted his head, he looked with satisfaction at her taut little peaks, reddened and pebbled from his attentions.

"You're so beautiful," he whispered.

She was still wearing a pair of lacy white panties that provided no cover whatsoever, and Andrew's shaft sprung to painful attention when he realized they had become transparent because they were soaked through.

Nathalie followed his gaze, and a soft blush colored her cheeks. "Take them off."

"Not yet, sweetheart." As he ran a finger over the gusset, Nathalie hissed in a breath. And as he pushed the fabric aside and slid his finger over her wet folds, her torso shot up, and she groaned.

"Shh, you need to stay quiet." He reminded Nathalie that her father was sleeping on the other side of the thin wall separating their bedrooms.

"Shit, I forgot," she whispered, and bit down on her lower lip.

"I'll tell you what." He drew lazy circles around her most sensitive spot. "For the next twenty minutes or so, I suggest you hold on to a pillow." He ran his finger down her slit. "Because you'll need it to muffle the screams." He winked and then dove between her legs.

With a giggle, she snatched a pillow. Spreading her thighs wide, she gave him better access to her center, where her little wet panties were wedged between her swollen lower lips. The view was sexy as hell, but Andrew doubted it was comfortable. God forbid this most sensitive area of her body would get chaffed.

Slowly, he pulled her lacy panties down her legs and threw them on the floor where they landed on top of the rest of the pile. Eyeing the mess, Andrew had the passing thought that he should push everything under the bed, or into the closet, to avoid a mad shuffle in case Fernando came knocking. Except, there was a naked beauty sprawled before him, her glistening sex too tempting to spare time on practicalities.

For a moment, Andrew just gazed, admiring the perfection and beauty of the female anatomy. Well, not any female's, his Nathalie's. He was still amazed at how quickly she'd taken to sex and how uninhibited she was. In fact, he was pretty sure that exposing herself to him like this was turning her on. Her hips were restless on the mattress, and she was teasing her own breasts, thrumming the nipples with her thumbs.

Fuck, he could explode just from watching Nathalie arouse herself. But she was getting impatient.

Lying on his belly, Andrew buried his face between her legs and inhaled deeply. Her fragrant womanhood was intoxicating. As he took his time luxuriating in her unique feminine musk, he rubbed his cheek on the soft flesh of her inner thigh, watching her arousal intensify.

Yeah, having his eyes on her most intimate flesh was definitely turning her on. It was like watching a flower bloom, the soft petals swelling to reveal the magic center where her dew was growing more copious by the second. With a groan, Andrew extended his tongue and lapped it up.

She hissed. "You're killing me."

He lifted his head. "With pleasure, I hope."

"I'm empty and needy, and you're taking too long."

Well, well. Gone was the shy virgin, replaced by an outspoken and demanding vixen.

And how hot was that?

Parting her soft pink petals with his thumbs, he pushed his tongue inside her, giving her what she wanted. Sort of. He knew she longed for a different part of his anatomy inside her, but if his goal was to give her multiple orgasms, he needed to start with his mouth.

Nathalie's fingers clawed at his head, holding him to her as if she feared he would stop. He had no intentions of leaving this heavenly place, not until he felt her falling apart and screaming into that pillow she'd dropped to hold on to his head.

Folding his tongue so it formed a spear, he kept thrusting it in and out of her at an ever-increasing speed, grunting with pleasure when he felt the walls of her channel start rippling around it.

It took no more than a minute of tongue fucking before she let go of his head to grab the pillow. Her pleasure cresting, Nathalie squeezed it hard over her face as she orgasmed violently, the sound of her screams muffled as her hips thrashed on the mattress.

And he hadn't even tongued her clit.

He should propose to her, like right now, because this woman was indeed a unicorn—one of a kind and magical.

Magically orgasmic, that is.

"Shit, I'm sorry," she mumbled into the pillow.

He stretched on top of her and tugged the thing away. "What for?"

Nathalie smiled shyly. "For coming too soon. It's supposed to be something guys worry about, right?"

He kissed her cute little nose. "Precisely. You, sweetheart, can climax as many times as you want. This was just a little one to whet the appetite."

"Oh, yeah? What have you planned next?"

"I wanted to spend some time with my ears squeezed between your thighs, eating you up, but now that I got you under me, I changed my mind." He nudged at her entrance.

She lifted her hips, and he gripped his shaft, guiding it inside her.

"Oh, God, Andrew, this is so good," she breathed as he glided inside her slick sheath. "I love the way you feel, so hard and yet so smooth and velvety. You fill me up so perfectly."

Did she have any idea how sexy she sounded? And how much he loved it?

Not dirty sex talk per se, it was nevertheless enough to make his cock rock-hard and ready to shoot. But he gritted his teeth and commanded the bad boy to behave himself.

After all, he was supposed to be the older, experienced man who was teaching the innocent girl about the art of sex. Not a young buck who suffered from premature ejaculation.

8

NATHALIE

*A*s Andrew made love to her slowly, tenderly, Nathalie cherished every second of it. It wasn't that she hadn't enjoyed their previous lovemaking, which had been more intense. She had—tremendously—even that first one, which had been quite painful. But this was special, because it felt like so much more than sex.

Her heart swelling with love, the powerful emotion was overwhelming, and tears—the happy kind—were stinging the back of her eyes. For Andrew's sake, though, she managed to hold them back. The experience would be ruined for him if he saw her tearing up, and it wasn't like she could explain things while he was thrusting in and out of her.

"I adore you," he whispered, the emotion reflected in his eyes.

Nathalie clutched him to her as if she was never letting go. "I love you and adore you too."

Andrew slanted his mouth over hers and kissed her long and hard. Soon, though, his shallow thrusts deepened, becoming more urgent, and he buried his face in her neck, groaning into her skin to muffle the sounds. She held on tight as the pounding became furious, and as her pleasure swelled and then exploded, she bit down on Andrew's shoulder to stifle her own desperate cries.

Breathing hard, Andrew remained sprawled on top of her. Nathalie ran her hands up and down his muscled back and tight buttocks, closing her eyes as she concentrated on the powerful beat of his heart and the heavy weight of his sweat-slicked body.

She was officially blissed out.

When he regained his breath, Andrew pulled out and rolled onto his back, pulling her with him to lie on top of him.

"Your father must be sleeping like a rock if he didn't wake up from the racket."

"What racket?" Nathalie thought they'd been good about keeping it quiet.

"Towards the end, the bed frame was banging against the wall so hard, I wouldn't be surprised if your neighbors across the alley heard us."

"Oh, God." Nathalie buried her face in Andrew's warm chest. "It's so embarrassing."

She felt Andrew's chuckle reverberate through her body. "Forget about the neighbors. As long as your dad slept through it, we are fine."

"I hope our luck extends to the shower." She slid off him and went to her closet for a robe. "I should get you one too." She was going to order Andrew a robe first thing in the morning. Why hadn't she thought of it before? She should've done so already. The poor guy was spending nearly every night at her place, leaving in the early hours of the morning to go shower and change at his house. The least she could do was get him a robe and maybe a few changes of underwear.

Damn, she was such a lousy girlfriend.

Andrew sighed as he swung his legs down the side of the bed and picked up his trousers. "It's a shame the bathroom is out in the hallway."

Nathalie felt her cheeks heat up. She wished her living conditions were better. An en-suite bathroom that she didn't have to share with her father seemed like the epitome of luxury to her. Andrew's big bathtub had been so nice. His home was just an average house in a middle-class neighborhood, and yet it was several steps above her own. All she had to offer was a builder's grade shallow tub and a small shower.

Later, when they came back from their quick wash up, she put on her nightgown, while Andrew had to dress back in his slacks and dress shirt, making her feel guilty as heck.

"Could you stay and cuddle a little?"

"Of course." He plopped down on the bed and pulled her down, wrapping an arm around her and holding her tight against his body.

She snuggled into him, laying her cheek on his chest. Poor guy, he deserved to sleep comfortably in a decent sized bed, not to mention a clean pair of boxers or conversely nothing at all. She wondered if Andrew slept in the nude. Yeah, he probably did.

"I hate it that you're so uncomfortable."

He dipped his head and kissed her forehead. "To be with you, I'll sleep on the floor. But eventually, we need to find a solution. I want to spend my nights with you and wake up with you in my arms."

Nathalie sighed. "The only thing that is even remotely possible is for you to move in with me. Which I know is a step down from the standard of living you're used to. You have such a nice and spacious house, with a yard and everything."

"Wouldn't it be better if you moved in with me? Other than the master suite, I have two more bedrooms with a Jack-and-Jill bathroom between them—perfect for your father and a caretaker."

God, this was so tempting. And so generous of Andrew to offer. But even if she were willing to subject her father to the turmoil of getting used to a new house—which he probably never would—she and Andrew were not married.

Nathalie believed their commitment to each other was solid, but it was not the same as marriage. Not that an official certificate was a guarantee for a lasting relationship, but still, to move into your boyfriend's house together with your mentally disabled father—and his caretaker—was a big no-no with a capital N.

Even though she was convinced they would end up together, this would be a mistake of monumental proportions.

"That's so sweet of you. But I can't. For many reasons."

His arm tightened around her as if to let her know he wasn't going anywhere until they got to the bottom of this. "Let's hear them. One at a time."

She shifted a little, trying to get some space. But there was nowhere to go on her small bed. "Moving my dad away from his familiar environment may send him into a downward spiral, and I can't take the risk of his condition deteriorating because of this."

Andrew had no intention of letting her slink away and pulled her back, holding her tight against his body. "We can try to do it gradually. I can come and pick you up after work, and the three of us will spend some time at my place. Then I'll drive you back home. This way, Fernando can get used to my place one little step at a time, and if he shows signs of distress, we retreat a little, then resume the offensive. But each time we gain some more ground, and before you know it, you'll realize that the objective has been achieved."

Nathalie chuckled. "You sound like you're strategizing for battle. You're such a military guy."

Andrew shrugged. "Same principles apply. If you want to achieve a difficult goal, you have to come up with a good and detailed plan."

"We can try a couple of times, but we both work hard, and this will soon become exhausting."

"Now that you have some help in the kitchen, I hope that you won't be as pooped at the end of the day."

"Let's not put the cart before the horse. Vlad is just starting tomorrow. I was incredibly lucky with Jackson, but I can't expect this new kid to be as good. And anyway, I probably need one more helper if I really want to take it easy. But I can't afford it, not unless Jackson's new scheme works."

Andrew frowned. "What scheme?"

"He wants to sell my baked goods door-to-door to offices, roping in a bunch of his friends to do it on a commission-only basis. That's why he brought Vlad. If I'm to produce more than I already do, I need help in the kitchen."

Andrew harrumphed. "This kid is something else, I have to hand it to him. But I think he's on to something here."

"What do you mean?"

"Think about it. Your baked goods are delicious, and I'm not just saying it because I love you. If you can scale up production without compromising quality while maintaining reasonable costs, you can have a profitable business. Instead of doing everything yourself, you can manage others."

This sounded like a dream come true, but that was all it was—a pipe dream.

"There are a lot of ifs in this scenario. And I'm not a risk taker, I can't afford to be. First of all, I don't have the money to invest in equipment for something that may or may not work, and second, I don't have the time or the energy to pursue this."

"That's why Jackson's idea is so brilliant. He is conducting a small-scale test that doesn't require extra expenditure or investment of time on your part. He and his friends are willing to do the work free of charge."

Nathalie shifted in Andrew's arms so she could look at him. "Okay, so let's assume that Jackson's idea is a success. How does it help with our problem?"

Andrew smiled and leaned to kiss her nose. "It solves the issue of you being exhausted all of the time. When your workdays are more manageable, you can bring your father over to my place for an hour or two a day to get him accustomed to it."

"Sounds like a plan to me." Especially since it didn't require any immediate action. First, Jackson had to execute his plan, then it had to be successful before the visits could commence. All of that would take a while, and even then there was no guarantee her father would respond well to the exercise.

Andrew yawned and pulled the comforter over them. "By the way, I spoke with my sister about the poor quality of caretakers we've been seeing, and she suggested we put an ad in the university's paper. As it's not going to be a full-time job, a student can be an inexpensive option. We might even get lucky with a psychology major."

As Nathalie's eyelids drooped and eventually collapsed over her eyes, she snuggled up closer, wrapping her arm around Andrew's middle. "Good idea, but can we talk about it tomorrow? That yawn of yours knocked me out."

He chuckled. "No problem, love. Goodnight."

9

ANANDUR

"Are you ready?' Anandur asked.

Shaking his head from side to side, Dalhu rubbed his neck. "As ready as I'll ever be."

"Okay. One, two, three!" Anandur let his pants drop.

He wasn't wearing underwear.

Dalhu groaned. "I don't know how you managed to talk me into it."

"Oh, don't be such a baby. I'm sure you've seen your share of naked men. I doubt there were private showers in the Doomers' camp. Though I bet none were as well-endowed as me."

"That's different. In the showers, men mind their own business and don't stare at each other's equipment. Just assume the pose and sit sideways on that stool, so I don't have to look at yours."

"Can you turn the portrait around? I don't remember the exact pose."

Carefully, holding it by the edges, Dalhu lifted the canvas off the easel and turned it so the front was facing Anandur.

"Got it." Anandur extended one leg to brace himself as he turned his torso to the right angle. "That's not the most comfortable position, just thought I should mention it."

"You wanted me to showcase your 'impressive musculature.' That's the best pose for it, so shut up and stop complaining."

"I'm not complaining, just stating a fact."

Dalhu rolled his eyes. "This must be punishment for my many sins. Never, like not in a thousand years, have I imagined myself drawing a naked man. And I've lived for nearly eight hundred already. So yeah."

"Not a man. A god."

Dalhu arched a brow but refrained from answering. Smart man. He was no match for Anandur who could carry on like this endlessly. Instead, the guy got busy with mixing oil paints on his palette.

Dalhu was getting better with those, and Anandur took credit for talking him into giving oils a try. At the start, the guy had been drawing exclusively with charcoal, refusing to touch oils—just because he'd been too big of a chicken to try. But then Anandur had bought him an Internet course on the subject and Dalhu had taken to the stuff like fish to water. He wasn't great at it, not yet, but Anandur had confidence in the guy.

"How is Annani's portrait progressing?" he asked, to banish the uncomfortable silence.

Done with the mixing, Dalhu paused, his gaze lingering on Anandur's thigh for a moment, before he touched his brush to the canvas. "I'm still working on it. Trying to get the right shades of red for her magnificent hair. But I'm afraid I'm not good enough to do justice to her ethereal beauty."

"I thought you said you're going to make hers in charcoal."

Dalhu paused with the brush in mid-air. "I started with black and white, but as hard as I tried, I couldn't get the results I wanted. It's impossible to express her magnificence without colors. But I'm just not good enough with them. Not yet."

"Maybe you should wait? Paint a few of the others before you tackle hers again."

"That is what I would like to do, but I'm afraid she'll be offended if I don't deliver her portrait soon."

Anandur smiled. Dalhu seemed to be still terrified of the goddess, in spite of all she had done to help Amanda and him. Without her help, the ex-Doomer would've probably been still rotting in a small cell down in the basement.

"Let me take a look. Maybe it's just in your head."

Dalhu put his palette on the counter and walked over to another easel, which held a canvas draped with what looked like a bed sheet.

Amanda must really love her Doomer to tolerate his mess and the destruction of her luxurious bed linens.

Despite her best efforts to keep it a surprise, the cat was out of the bag about the studio she was building for him. That kind of thing could've—maybe—worked on a human, but there was no fooling an immortal's sense of smell. Between the dust and the fresh paint he'd figured out that she was remodeling, and Amanda had given up on keeping it a secret—which in Anandur's opinion had been a foolish idea to begin with.

As Dalhu lifted the sheet off the painting, Anandur thought that he had never seen him looking more apprehensive. A whipping and an entombment hadn't fazed the dude as much as having his work critiqued.

"It's beautiful, but you're right, it still needs work." The image was true, and the lines were graceful. In fact, everything looked right, but it was just missing the something extra Anandur couldn't put his finger on. He wasn't an artist, so he couldn't even try to explain what it was. Maybe Dalhu was right, and it was impossible to capture Annani's beauty on canvas.

Dalhu's shoulders sagged, and he nodded. "I know. But what do I tell her when she asks about it?"

"The truth. Tell her you're not happy with how it's coming out, and that it needs more work. She'll understand."

Dalhu seemed doubtful. "She is a goddess," he said as if this fact explained everything.

"Yes, and she is a diva. But Annani is also kind and compassionate. She'll never throw a tantrum if there is a valid reason for her wishes not being met at the exact time and in the exact manner she would've liked them to. Don't worry about it; you will not fall out of favor with her because you're still struggling as an artist."

Dalhu closed his eyes momentarily and took a deep breath. "Thank you. For that alone, for the peace of mind you just gave me, your portrait is on the house. I'm not going to charge you for it, even though I deserve extra hazard pay for having to look at your naked ass."

Say what?

Anandur had never expected to pay for it in the first place. "Since when are you charging money for this?"

"Since Andrew has talked some sense into me. This is the only *job*—" he made air quotes—"I have right now, and I'd rather be embarrassed about charging for the pictures than about freeloading off Amanda. Who do you think pays for all the supplies? And now she builds a studio for me, which I'm sure is costing her a lot of money. I need to carry my own weight around here, and in my current situation, this is the only way I know how."

Well, Anandur couldn't argue with that. Dalhu's decision to charge money for his work was not only valid but necessary. It wasn't as if the guy was just passing the time during his recovery. For the foreseeable future, and probably indefinitely, this was going to be his only occupation, and therefore, his only source of income. He couldn't fault the guy for refusing to be a kept man.

"How much were you going to charge for it?"

Dalhu rubbed his neck, and Anandur could've sworn that there was a hint of blush in the guy's cheeks. "Five hundred?" he asked.

"Sounds reasonable enough. And when you get better, you could charge more. I'll tell you what. I'm going to drum up some business for you, spread the word about your talent." This was the least Anandur could do for getting his nude for free.

"I appreciate the offer, but don't, not yet. I'm in over my head with what I have. I'm putting the finishing touches on Syssi and Kian's wedding picture, I have yours and four other portraits, and I have Annani's. On top of that, tomorrow, I'm moving everything into my new studio, and I promised Amanda that I'd have the living room looking the same way I found it before I made it into my workspace."

"No problem, I'll wait a couple of weeks before I start harassing everyone and their mother to have their portrait done."

"That would be great."

For the next half an hour or so, Anandur shut his yap and let Dalhu paint. Because every time he engaged the guy in conversation, Dalhu would stop and hold the brush suspended in mid-air. Anandur wanted this session to be over sooner than later. His muscles were getting stiff from holding the unnatural pose.

Kian and Syssi's wedding portrait was right in his line of sight, and staring at it, he couldn't help thinking how happy Syssi had looked. Seeing her every day as he did, he hadn't noticed the change in her. But compared to her expression in that wedding portrait, he realized that lately she looked worried, preoccupied. It wasn't Kian; the guy still looked at his wife as if she was everything to him. Perhaps working for Amanda was stressing her out? Come to think of it, neither of them had mentioned discovering potential Dormants, and even Amanda's cheery disposition had been off lately. Yeah, that must be what was bothering the two.

The clunk of Dalhu's palette hitting the counter signaled the end of the session. "Okay, I think this is enough for today. Your face has started to look as if you're pushing out a load, so I assume you are cramping."

Thank you, sweet Fates in heaven.

Anandur pushed up to his feet and stretched, first up, and then side to side.

With a grimace, Dalhu turned his back to him and grabbed his brushes and palette off the counter, dumping them in the kitchen sink. "It's good that Amanda is at work. She would have a conniption seeing me doing this. I'm supposed to wash them in a bucket first," he said with his back still turned to Anandur.

It was hilarious to hear the ex-Doomer use the word conniption, just another indicator of how well he was acclimatizing. Anandur pulled on his pants and pushed his feet inside his boots, then joined Dalhu in the kitchen. He opened the fridge and grabbed a beer.

Dalhu arched a brow. "Isn't it too early for that?"

"Yeah, but you don't have a coke, and I hate drinking plain water."

Dalhu shrugged. "That reminds me, how is it going with your Russian?"

"Not too great, but I have to ask, what's the connection between my aversion to drinking plain water and my Russian friend?"

Dalhu rinsed out the brushes and put them on a stack of paper towels to dry. "The few Russians I've met didn't like drinking water either. But as to your investigation, is there anything I can do to help? Not that I can offer much more than advice."

Anandur grimaced. "No, thank you. I've already gotten all the advice I need from my brother."

10

BHATHIAN

"William, my man, you've outdone yourself." Bhathian put his hand on the guy's shoulder.

Less than a week ago, after he'd started training the advanced class, Bhathian had had the splendid idea of building a makeshift simulator for weapons training. They had a shooting range down in the underground complex, but aiming at a stationary target was easy and not all that practical for what they would be facing in the field. Because unless he wanted to train them to be sharpshooters, which, of course, they could choose to do later if they wished, he wanted to train his students for hitting a fast moving target while in pursuit—like in real life situations.

With only a vague idea of what he wanted and basically no clue how to go about building something like that, he'd approached William, asking him to come up with a solution.

As always, William delivered, quickly and brilliantly. First, he and his geek squad had roped off a large part of the clan's second parking level. Then they'd scattered around a bunch of big planters, which in addition to the plants they were housing had been outfitted with life-sized cardboard cutouts of random pedestrians; males, females, and children. But the real kicker was the large remote-controlled toy trucks, each rigged to carry a cutout of a big man. William had devised a computer program to move them at the pace of a fast runner, but he'd thrown in the mix a few that were slower and didn't look like Doomers.

William puffed out his chest. "Glad to help. Have fun with it." He handed Bhathian the tablet with the program to run the thing and turned around, heading toward the bank of elevators.

"When are you going to join a class?" Bhathian called after him.

William didn't even turn around when he waved a hand and called back, "Never!"

Bhathian chuckled. Frankly, there was no need. As far as he knew, William never left the keep. But he sure as hell could've used the physical exercise. On second thought, though, the guy's time was too valuable to spend on anything other than technology and computers, and as health wasn't a concern, William's excess weight and lack of movement was nobody's business but his own.

Pulling out his phone, Bhathian group texted the students to meet him in the parking garage.

Today, he had the perfect opportunity to put the simulator to the test with the advanced class, which was smaller, with only nine trainees. Brundar had asked him to teach it today, and in exchange, he was going to take over Bhathian's tomorrow.

Damn, he would've loved to try out the obstacle course himself—

Wait, this was actually a great idea. He could get the Guardians together, and they could have some fun with it. Man, they were going to love this. Besides, it would be interesting to see how the trainees compared to the pros.

A few minutes later, the elevator burped out the nine students he'd been waiting for. Carol and eight guys. The woman was an ace in the shooting range, and he was curious to see how well she'd do with the simulator.

"Gather around, people." He waited until they formed a semicircle and fell silent.

"Today, instead of the shooting range, we are going to try something new." He handed each one a laser gun. "These look like toys, but they are not." He hefted one in his palm, demonstrating that it was weightier than it seemed. "These are specifically made for training and are designed to act and feel like the real thing. They weigh as much as an average handgun, and the recoil is just as forceful. The laser is, of course, harmless, but the targets are wired to respond, so when you hit them, a light will go off at the exact point of impact as if it were a real bullet."

"That's so cool," Ben said, and a murmur of assent followed.

Carol was the only one who frowned. "Aren't we supposed to have our own weapons? Fitted specifically to each of us so we can take into account the heft and the recoil? Brundar said that it was crucial for us to train with our own weapon."

"This is true. But you are not there yet. When you're ready and we have the equipment, we will train with it, but for now, this will suffice. It's just too much work to replace all the targets after each of you makes the run and destroys them with real bullets. We will save it for the final stage."

Carol pouted. "I thought we were getting our own guns already."

"Next week, Brundar will decide what each of you gets, and you'll start training with it at the shooting range."

George aimed his gun at one of the stationary cutouts and fired.

Bhathian saw red. "If you ever fire a weapon again without permission you're out of the program, is that clear?"

"Yes, sir. But this is just a toy–" George shut his yap when Bhathian got in his face.

"Does this look like a game to you?"

Actually, it did, but George knew better than to say so.

"No, sir."

"Good." He turned to the rest of the class. "We follow the same safety protocol as in the shooting range, no matter what training instrument we use. It could be a wooden carving or a plastic toy. We treat it with the same respect we would if it were a live weapon. It needs to become an ingrained habit, second nature, not something you need to stop and think about. When the heat is on, an automatic response could mean the difference between life and death for a soldier. The split second slower response, the debilitating panic, all of those can be eliminated by falling back on the power of habit. Even a bunch of civilian newbies like yourselves should be aware of how crucial this is. Hell, a class of human fifth graders would've already understood this."

"I'm sorry, sir. Won't happen again."

Bhathian nodded, letting George off the hook. He had to remind himself that this wasn't military training, and that these people were civilians, most of whom had no aspiration towards joining the Guardian Force. Still, the same rules applied to self-defense, so he couldn't go easy on them just because they weren't going to become soldiers. He knew for a fact that proper training and ingrained responses could one day save their lives.

"Carol, you go first. Please stand right here." He pointed with his shoe to the X he'd drawn with chalk on the concrete floor.

"Yes, sir." She stepped on top of it, holding her gun down by her side.

He pointed toward the obstacle course. "The stationary cutouts are bystanders. You don't want to hit any of those. When I activate the simulator, a bunch of Doomer cutouts will start zooming around, but not all of the moving ones will be enemy targets. You need to focus and shoot only at those who look like Doomers and carry weapons. You need to hit the heart or to the head, anywhere else doesn't count for points. And any civilian hit will cost you points."

"Will they be shooting at me?"

Bhathian chuckled. "No, but that's a good point. Maybe I'll have William make modifications for next time."

"Like Laser Tag, we can wear vests and shoot at each other," Ben offered.

"That's also a great idea." Or maybe not. If it felt too much like a game, they wouldn't take it seriously. Bhathian hoped Brundar would have better luck than him at whipping these people into shape. As it was, after two weeks of basic training and one of advanced, the bunch still behaved like they were at summer camp. Trouble was, they also thought that they were battle ready.

Fools, they would get eaten alive by anyone with a shred of experience.

Bhathian still remembered his own training. Oleg had treated them like maggots, calling them names and making sure that they knew they were worthless. He'd hated the guy, but now he was starting to think that maybe Oleg had had it right. The worst thing for a trainee was to think he was better than he actually was and rush into danger unprepared. Better they underestimate their abilities than overestimate them. Perhaps he should adopt some of Oleg's attitude. Problem was, his students would just leave. They were here out of their own free will, and none of them felt bound by honor or some lofty aspirations to stay. The reality was that he needed to tread carefully if he didn't want them hightailing it out of his classroom and running to complain to Kian.

Bhathian shook his head. Things had definitely changed since he was a young man. And not all of them for the better.

"Okay, Carol, get ready, and go!" He pressed start on his tablet and Carol shot forward, her curls bouncing around her face as she jerked her head from side to side, following the erratically zooming toy cars.

Damn, he'd forgotten to tell her that she had three minutes until game over. Oh, well, she'd figure it out.

11

NATHALIE

"You look lovely today, my beautiful girl." Her father kissed her cheek before going back to his newspaper.

Nathalie couldn't remember the last time she had so much energy by the end of her workday. She felt like a whole new person, fantastic. Even Papi had noticed.

Problem was, now that Vlad had practically taken over the kitchen, and Jackson was manning the register, she was spending most of her time up front—either waiting tables or taking orders. Her father, however, had to remain in the kitchen because the place was always packed and she couldn't have him take up a booth. Surprisingly, he had no problem sharing space with Vlad. He simply ignored him as if he wasn't there.

From time to time, Fernando would have more lucid days, and Nathalie suspected that during those times, he was aware that not everyone he saw was real.

Perhaps he thought Vlad was one of his apparitions.

God knew the kid looked like a character from a vampire or a zombie movie. And earlier today, she'd discovered that he was also freakishly strong, which given his stick-like limbs was more than surprising. This morning, her earring had caught in her hair, and when she'd pulled to get it loose, it had fallen off. She'd watched it bounce off her work table and disappear behind the sheeter. But as she grabbed the broom to try and sweep it from under the thing, Vlad had lifted the two-hundred-pound machine with one hand, holding it up while reaching for her earring with the other. He hadn't uttered a grunt, hadn't broken a sweat, and once the retrieval had been accomplished, he'd lowered the machine slowly and carefully. The touchdown had been barely audible.

Though this incident had been the most notable, there was more. Vlad worked from six in the morning until eleven, took a break for three hours and then returned until closing. He never looked tired, and he never complained about his feet or his arms hurting, though they had to, at least at the beginning. After all, the only manual labor he had done before coming to work for her was playing the guitar.

Not that she was complaining. Vlad was the reason she could start her day at six in the morning instead of four. Now that he was in charge of preparing the dough for the next day, which he was doing every evening by the end of his shift, her morning routine had been cut in half. A huge improvement.

This new generation sure had better work habits than all of those that came before them. She'd never employed people as dedicated and hardworking as Jackson and Vlad. And judging by the cars they drove, it wasn't as if the teenagers were hurting for money.

Hell, how did she become so lucky?

Or was she?

"Hey, Nathalie, should I flip the sign to closed?" A tray piled with dirty dishes in his hands, Jackson passed her by on his way to the kitchen, flashing her that disarming smile of his that was charming the customers into leaving him big tips.

Shit, was it closing time already?

Her days sure seemed shorter and, preoccupied with her thoughts as she'd been, Nathalie hadn't noticed that it was done. Not that one could tell by looking at the booths—most were still occupied.

"I'll do it," she told him and hurried to the door. Nathalie hated when people came in and she had to tell them the coffee shop was closed.

Jackson was back with the empty tray, clearing another table. And as she watched him from her station next to the register, the insidious doubts started crawling around her brain again. There was something off about these guys, but she couldn't put her finger on it. And she still had her suspicions about Andrew and Bhathian's motives.

Funny how her doubts always flew out the window when she was with Andrew, only to return when he wasn't there. She glanced at her watch. What was holding him up? Was he stuck in traffic? He should've arrived by now. As worry squeezed her heart in a vice, she berated herself for imagining worst case scenarios—like his car mangled on the side of the road and paramedics loading him onto a gurney.

She hadn't been like that before meeting Andrew. With how deeply she used to be inside her own head, conversing with voices only she could hear, there hadn't been enough cerebral space left to imagine catastrophes. It hadn't happened immediately after she'd fallen in love with Andrew either. This was recent. A feeling of unease that wouldn't go away.

She lasted about a minute before pulling out her phone and calling him.

"Hi, sweetheart. I'm just parking the car. I'll be there in a moment."

"Okay." She clicked the call off and sagged against the counter. God, she was such a worrywart. How would she manage to be a mother and let her kids out the door? She'd have panic attacks on a daily basis. Or hourly. She really needed to work on this.

As Andrew burst through the door, Nathalie's face split into a big smile.

"Sorry that I'm late, love." He reached for her over the counter, pulling her toward him for a quick kiss.

"Traffic was that bad?" she asked.

"Nothing out of the ordinary, but I stopped by Syssi's place to pick up the resumes she collected for us. She says there are at least two she really liked, and she marked them with a red pen."

That's right, Andrew's sister had offered to post an ad in the university's newspaper, but Nathalie hadn't expected her to do it so promptly. And to interview the prospects as well.

"It's so nice of her to put so much effort into it. I would've thanked her in person, but you haven't introduced us yet." She made a face.

For some reason, Andrew was in no hurry for her to meet his family. So yeah, there were many extenuating factors, and arranging a meeting considering her limitations was difficult. And yet, if Andrew had really wanted them to meet he would've found a way.

With a sheepish expression on his handsome face, he walked around the counter and pulled her into his arms, fusing his mouth to hers in a smoldering kiss. His underhanded tactic worked, and as desire coursed through her, hot and molten, it robbed her of reason, and Nathalie forgot that she was supposed to be peeved at him.

When Andrew let go of her, she swayed on her feet a little, and he quickly wrapped his arm around her waist. "What's wrong, sweetheart? Are you feeling okay?"

She slapped his shoulder. "I'm perfectly fine. You just didn't let me breathe. Probably figured that asphyxiation will make me forget all about your stalling tactics. I don't understand why you haven't introduced us yet."

"Let's go upstairs and have this conversation there, shall we?"

"Fine." Nathalie turned toward Jackson. "You're okay closing up by yourself?" she asked.

He rolled his eyes. "It's the same answer I give you every evening when you ask; yes, I'm okay."

"No need to get snappy. Just don't forget to lock up."

"I won't."

In the kitchen, she said goodbye and thank you to Vlad, and then collected her father. "Come, Papi, your show starts in less than fifteen minutes. You don't want to miss the beginning."

Fernando folded his newspaper, put his coloring pencils away in their box, and followed her and Andrew upstairs. He ducked into his room to turn on the television, while she and Andrew continued into the den.

"What did you get?" She eyed the brown paper bag Andrew was holding.

"A bottle of wine."

"Did you stop by the supermarket as well?"

"No, this is a gift from Syssi's husband."

"Aha."

Andrew rubbed his neck before taking her hand and pulling her toward the couch where he insisted she sit on his lap.

"It's not that I don't want you to meet my sister. On the contrary, it's just that I don't know how to make it work. You'll feel awkward about having your father drag along, and telling Syssi to come see you at your shop doesn't sound like the right thing to do either. But now that you can take off earlier, leaving

Jackson and Vlad to take care of things, maybe we can invite Syssi to dinner at my house or at a restaurant, and then you won't feel weird about having your father there."

"What about her husband?"

Andrew grimaced. "I guess we have to invite him too."

"I was under the impression that you like the guy, so what gives?"

"I do like him, it's just that I'm not too thrilled about you meeting him."

"Why?"

"Because he is an incredibly handsome bastard, and if you start drooling all over him, I'll be tempted to make my sister a widow."

Nathalie giggled. "First of all, I'm sure he is not handsomer than you. He can't be, not to me. But in any case, I promise to save all my drooling for you."

12

ANANDUR

"Still nothing?" Anandur scratched his beard as he looked at William's computer screen. Not that he knew what he was looking at. A quick sidelong glance at Onegus reassured him that he wasn't the only one. His boss seemed just as dumbfounded by what the guy was showing them.

Good, so Anandur wasn't a complete moron for not getting it. Onegus was supposedly a smart guy, so he was in good company.

"Look at the patterns. Obviously, they have a device on board that interferes with transmissions." William pointed to the graph. "There is talking, but it's impossible to understand with the interference. I'm running it through one more program to see if I can filter it out."

"I don't get it. The boat must communicate with the shore, doesn't it?"

"They can either turn it off when they need the channel open or use cellular through a private satellite like we do. The bug is a radio transmitter."

"Damn. What about the detective monitoring the marina? His people must've seen something by now. Don't tell me that nothing suspicious happened before the boat left."

Onegus shook his head. "Nope. The captain and one other crew member went shopping for supplies and returned with a bunch of paper bags, nothing big enough to carry a person. Not unless they chopped him to pieces. And later Alex came on board carrying a briefcase. So as far as we know, there is no one other than Alex and his crew onboard. The only other possibility is that someone swam up to the boat and boarded it during the night. But that doesn't fit our scenario, so it's of no interest to us. If he smuggles drugs or criminals, I'm happy to leave it up to the human police to catch him."

"Fuck."

Lana had been gone for a week, and Anandur had hoped that the bug he'd planted would provide the information they needed. He was tired of keeping up the charade and wanted to end the thing with Lana. It wasn't that he didn't enjoy spending time with her—she was a hot piece of ass—but he was going nowhere with her. Getting Lana to talk about her boss, or talk at all, was like pulling teeth. Her poor English aside, the woman was more interested in screwing him than talking to him.

"How are you doing with your Russian?" Onegus asked.

"Getting nowhere."

"Keep pushing. As long as she doesn't get suspicious and dump your ass, there is no reason to stop."

"Yeah, I figured that much."

With a grimace, Anandur pulled out his phone and texted her. *Are you back?*

Lana had warned him not to call her while she was gone. Apparently, Alex had a strict policy about his crew fraternizing with other males. She was fine with breaking the rules—she just didn't want her boss to catch her.

The burner phone she used to communicate with Anandur had a shitty reception, so unless the Anna was back at the marina, the text wouldn't go through. But the excursion was supposed to be only a week long, so by now the boat should be sitting pretty in its dock.

He had to wait for a good ten minutes before she answered.

Come at 8. Dock.

Damn, he wasn't looking forward to another evening with the Russian. He was growing tired of her. With a sigh, Anandur pushed his phone back into his pocket. "I'm on for tonight."

"Good luck." Onegus clapped him on the back before leaving William's office, or lab, or whatever the guy wanted to call the cavernous room that was strewn with assorted desks and enough equipment to open a RadioShack.

Later, when Anandur got back to his apartment, he wasn't surprised to find it deserted. Damn, he hated how empty it felt. Not that Brundar was such great company when he was there, but still, it wasn't as lonely with him around. And besides, he needed the bastard to help clean the place. It was filthy, and Anandur had no intention of tackling the job by himself.

Okidu, who'd been keeping their place from turning into a pigsty, had stopped showing up lately. Probably Syssi's doing. She was treating the butler as if he were a real living breathing guy, making sure he wasn't taken advantage of or overworked.

Anandur loved the girl, he really did, but this was beyond nice and into the realm of stupid.

It was like worrying about the working conditions of a vacuum cleaner—one of those disk-shaped ones that were programmed to work on their own while the owners were gone. Actually, he should get one. Problem was, the thing couldn't pick up dirty clothes off the floor or swallow empty beer cans.

Oh well, it wasn't like his apartment needed to be presentable. After all, he never used the place for hookups. With a shrug, he headed to the bathroom and got in the shower. After he was done, he sprayed his face with cologne, even though he hadn't shaved, then sprayed a little more under his armpits and down his crotch. Smelling good all over never hurt.

The ladies loved it.

Looking over his modest clothes selection, Anandur chose an old pair of Levi's and a short-sleeved button-down that had seen better days. The thing had shrunk in the wash, and he couldn't even button it over his chest without it gaping in between the buttons. He left it partially open with his chest on full display.

As he examined his reflection in the mirror, Anandur had the passing thought that he was intentionally dressing up like a man-whore.

Did it bother him, though?

Nah, it was all good. Playing the gigolo was fun. After all, a guy had to have an awesome physique, well-polished charm, and impressive skills in the bedroom to be successful in that profession.

Anandur prided himself on all three.

Whistling to the tune of David Lee Roth's *I'm Just a Gigolo*, he grabbed the keys to the loaner truck and headed out to the marina.

13

SYSSI

"Lily, can you take a look at this? I need you to double check it." Syssi called the new postdoc Amanda had hired.

When she'd return to the lab, Syssi had been overjoyed to see the new face that had replaced David as their computational researcher. Lily was just as good, if not better, and Syssi no longer even bothered to try fixing things herself. At the first hint of a problem, it was Lily to the rescue.

"Let me see," Lily said as she took Syssi's seat.

Syssi left her to do her thing and walked over to Hanna's desk. "So, Hanna, you need to tell me your secret. How did you manage to lose so much weight while I was gone? Don't tell me the protein bars and the shakes were what did the trick."

Hanna smiled and pushed to her feet, then struck a pose, one leg forward and a hand on her hip. She must've gone down from a size eighteen to a size twelve since Syssi had last seen her. Pretty impressive.

"Wow, you look amazing."

"I do, right?" Hanna turned around in a slow circle, showing her backside. "Just look at this butt, I can wear jeans now. And I'm not done. I want to lose at least another ten pounds."

"So, how did you do it? Or is it a secret?"

As Hanna sat back down, her brows dipped low on her forehead. "Don't tell me you're thinking about going on a diet…"

Syssi chuckled. "I could lose a few pounds, but I figure it's not worth the effort. Though I'm still curious about how you did it."

Hanna sighed. "After I got so sick of the shakes that I couldn't stomach going one more day drinking that shit, I finally decided to shell out the money for a visit with a dietitian. I've already tried every diet on the planet, and nothing ever worked. The most I've managed to lose was five to ten pounds, and then I'd gain them back with interest. So my mom heard about this lady and made an appointment for me. And guess what was her brilliant advice?"

"What?"

"Eat less and move more. Like I didn't know that already. But she managed to drive it home that all those books and magazines with their fad diets of food combinations, food exclusions, supplements, timing and so on are just a huge money machine and that there are no tricks and no shortcuts. Her whole approach is eating small quantities of good unprocessed food, mainly plant-based, combined with daily physical activity."

"I'm sure there is more to it. If it were so simple, we wouldn't have an obesity epidemic in this country."

"You're right. The secret is planning, measuring, preparing, scheduling, and monitoring." Hanna reached behind her and lifted her purse off the back of her chair, then pulled out a medium-sized red journal. "You see this? This is my bible. In here, I write down my weekly plan. I do it every Sunday. It includes everything; a list of meals, recipes, grocery shopping list, an exercise schedule, and so on. I prepare and freeze all the meals that I can make ahead of time on the weekend, so I can just grab a container and go. On Fridays, I meet with the dietitian and she weighs me, checks my journal, making sure that I followed up on everything I wrote, and makes adjustments as needed to next week's plan."

"Don't tell me you don't cheat."

Hanna rolled her eyes. "Come on, I'm only human. But just a little."

"I'm so proud of you. I don't know if I could've been this disciplined. It requires so much focus. But thanks for telling me. I'll pass along your newfound wisdom."

"Please do. If I can do it, anyone can. And I hope that, in time, it will become a habit, so I won't need to weigh and measure and plan everything—just eyeball it and get it right."

"I'm sure you will."

Now that she understood how hard Hanna was working on this, Syssi felt bad about going out to lunch with Amanda and just ordering whatever she wanted. Out of solidarity, she should order a small salad and skip dessert.

But Gino's lasagna was so good…

Oh, boy, she was one lucky girl to get away with eating something as decadently delicious and fattening as that dish without worrying about gaining weight. Though on second thought, being immortal didn't guarantee a svelte figure, as evidenced by William.

That was it. Tonight, she was going to hit the treadmill down at the gym. Lately, her physical activity had been limited to sexcapades with Kian. Pleasurable, numerous, and often exhausting, they nonetheless weren't enough to keep her in shape.

"Are you ready, darling?" Amanda sauntered over and handed Syssi her purse. "I'm starving."

She slung it over her shoulder. "Yeah, me too. I was just thinking about Gino's lasagna."

"One of the best items on his menu." Amanda opened the door, and they headed down the corridor to the elevators.

As they passed by the heavy door leading to the emergency stairs, an involuntary tingle of anxiety rushed down Syssi's arms. It happened every time, reminding her of how it all started. She wondered how many times she would have to pass by this door before having no reaction to it. Except, the fear was puzzling. After all, despite the scary events surrounding her first encounter with Kian, it was still the best thing to ever happen to her.

The drive to Gino's was short, and when they arrived, Syssi was glad that they got there after the lunch hour rush was over, so a table was available out on the porch. It was a beautiful day, sunny but not too warm, the smell of freshly cut grass carried by a gentle breeze. The perfect weather for sitting outside.

Amanda accepted the menu from the waiter but didn't even open it. "Where is Gino?"

The waiter smiled. "Sitting at the hospital and waiting for his eleventh grandchild to arrive."

Amanda clapped her hands. "This is wonderful. Do you know if it's a boy or a girl? I want to buy a present."

The guy shook his head. "Sorry, I don't."

Amanda waved a dismissive hand. "Don't worry about it, I'll find something to buy for the baby that works for either gender."

"That's very nice of you, thank you."

They placed their orders, a lasagna and a big garden salad to share, and Amanda added a bottle of wine.

"What are we celebrating? Other than Gino's new grandkid, that is."

Amanda shrugged. "I don't know. I just need something for a pick-me-up."

"You too? I've been having a bad feeling lately, and I don't know why. Like something terrible is going to happen. It's not a vision or a foretelling, so I'm not freaking out, but I am worried."

"Maybe it's hormonal." Amanda smiled her wicked witch smile. "Maybe you're pregnant?"

Syssi snorted. "I wish. It's so embarrassing. When I didn't get my period on time, I was sure I was. Luckily, I didn't say anything to Kian before having Bridget check. Imagine how I felt when she explained that immortal females don't ovulate every month like humans. That it's a random, on demand kind of thing. You might have thought to mention it to me before I made a fool of myself."

"I'm sorry. It just didn't cross my mind. It's not something that I think about. But now you know."

Syssi sighed. "Yeah, now I know. I was a little bummed. But on the other hand, I'm not ready to be a mother. So what's your problem? Is it adjusting to living with Dalhu?"

Amanda waved a hand. "No, I love having him around, even with all his mess, which I tease him about mercilessly. It's not that. Have you noticed the lousy subjects we are getting lately? I haven't seen even one with as much as a hint of talent."

"I know. I even raised the hourly pay in our ad to lure more test subjects. Who knows, maybe that's why we are getting people without any talent. They come for the pay, not out of curiosity to see if there is anything special about them."

Deep in thought, Amanda tapped a manicured fingernail on the glass table. "We should venture outside the university," she finally said.

"Can we? Is it okay to recruit from the outside?"

"Sure it is. You can put an ad on Craig's List, or some other internet site where people look for odd jobs."

The friendly waiter showed up with a basket of Gino's famous fresh rolls, still steaming from the oven, and the wine.

Syssi waited until he was gone. "So let's do it. At the rate it's going now, we are never going to find new Dormants."

Amanda lifted the napkin covering the rolls to let the steam out. "Yeah. There are a couple of problems with that. First, we might get some unsavory characters we don't want to deal with. Second, with the scarcity of jobs that's going on now, we might get inundated with applications. We won't be able to handle it."

"Can we hire another assistant? If we have the budget for it, that is. Someone who will be in charge of only that. Screening the applicants, making sure to schedule only the most promising ones, handle the paperwork... God, I hate the paperwork. With the stacks of legal documents each one has to sign, you'd think we subject them to open brain surgery." If she could hand that to someone else her workday would be much more enjoyable. She liked conducting the testing and interviewing most of the applicants. In general, the people who applied were friendly and polite, but occasionally she would get someone who wasn't.

"Do you think we should hire one of ours for this?" Amanda poked one of the rolls to check if it was still hot.

Syssi considered it for a moment. "That's a good idea. But who would want an entry job like that? It's not as if any of you—sorry, us, I keep forgetting—needs to work for money. Those who work do it either because they want more than what their shares in the family business provide, or to do something they like doing. I can't imagine anyone getting excited over boring paperwork."

Amanda took a bite of the roll and chewed for a moment, her brows doing a little dance on her forehead in sync with her thoughts. On anyone else, it would've looked funny, but Amanda didn't have an expression that didn't look gorgeous. "Maybe one of the teenagers on summer break would want the job. They don't get their share until they reach twenty-five. Even though a high school student will be inexperienced, the upside is that we can tell her the truth about what we are looking for."

Syssi arched a brow. "Do we know exactly what to look for?'

Amanda sighed. "No, not really."

14

NATHALIE

"The dough for tomorrow is ready in the fridge, and I also pounded the butter inside the large Ziploc bags like you showed me." Vlad removed his apron and hung it on the peg with his name on it.

On a whim, while ordering extra aprons for the guys, Nathalie had also ordered three wooden pegs, each with its custom-carved name plaque. One for Vlad, one for Jackson, and one for herself. She'd chosen a spot by the back door on the small stretch of wall before the staircase began, and Andrew had done the drilling and hanging part.

It was official now. Jackson and Vlad were part of her team, and all was right with the world. Well, not really, but she couldn't help the buoyant mood. There was definitely something to be said for the extra shuteye she'd been getting lately. Since Vlad had arrived about a week ago and had taken over most of her kitchen chores, she was waking up later in the morning, and feeling more rested and energetic with each passing day. Heck, she didn't remember when was the last time she had felt so good. So happy.

Not that good sleep and hardworking teammates were the only reasons for her happiness. She had so much to be grateful for. Jackson already felt like part of her family, and once she'd gotten over Vlad's vampiric appearance, she had discovered that he was a sweet guy under his goth garb, and had adopted him too.

And then there was Andrew. Nathalie smiled. Today they were going to take her father to Andrew's house for the first time. Papi had been having a good day so far. There hadn't been much talking to people that weren't there, and he'd even said hello to Vlad. Which was a big improvement because up until today he'd been ignoring the kid—refusing to acknowledge his presence.

"Come on, Jackson; we are going to be late." Vlad called his friend who was still collecting dirty dishes from the tables.

"Go on, Jackson. I'll finish up. You guys need to get moving."

Finally, they had a gig lined up, opening for some heavy metal rock band that she'd never heard of but according to the guys was a big deal.

Jackson dropped the dishes in the sink, then took off his apron and hung it next to Vlad's. "I wish you could come see our performance."

"I wish it too. But unless you and your friends come play in my shop, I'm afraid it will have to wait." She couldn't take her dad to a rock concert. Come to think of it, even if they played right here in her shop, their music would probably upset him. Jackson had had her listen to a recording, and although she'd like it, Papi certainly wouldn't. He would call it noise.

Jackson stopped in his tracks. "That's a cool idea. I'll run it by them."

"Jackson!" Vlad held the door open.

"Coming! Bye, Nathalie, see you tomorrow."

"Break a leg!" she called after them.

"Thanks."

Nathalie finished washing the dishes and wiped clean the two tables Jackson hadn't gotten to before leaving. Done for the day, she took a satisfied look at her little café. Profits had been good lately, and she appreciated the added peace of mind of finally having enough money not only to cover her monthly bills but to start paying off some of her debt.

Thank you, God. She offered her gratitude to a God she'd been staunchly proclaiming not to believe in.

Aware of the irony, Nathalie shook her head as she flicked the lights off before climbing upstairs to join her father and Andrew in the den. Last she'd checked on them, they'd been sharing the couch and watching a game. It was nice to think that they were forming some kind of a connection, but the truth was that Papi didn't always remember who Andrew was, or even recognize him as someone he'd already met. Some days, he called him son; others he clasped his hand with a polite smile, looking up at him as if he were a stranger.

"Hi, guys, ready to go?"

"Go where?" her father asked.

Damn, he'd already forgotten. "We are going to Andrew's house."

As Fernando cast Andrew a sidelong glance, she was relieved that he at least remembered who Andrew was.

"Why?"

"He is inviting us to dinner. Remember? We talked about it this morning."

"Ah, Okay." He pushed to his feet, clearly having no recollection of the conversation but pretending that he did. "I'll just put my shoes on."

"We will wait here."

As Papi shuffled to his room, Andrew got up and pulled her into his arms. "One day at a time, sweetheart. It's going to be alright. After several visits, he'll remember it."

Trouble was, she knew he wouldn't. Most days, Fernando still believed that this wasn't his home and that for some reason she was keeping him away from his real one—the old house they'd sold years ago. So the chances of him remembering Andrew's home were nil. All she was hoping for was that he wouldn't freak out. This would be progress enough for her.

She lifted her face and kissed Andrew, just a little peck on the lips, saving her passionate kisses for later. "What did you make for dinner?"

Andrew chuckled. "Make? Me? Did I ever give you the impression that I can cook?"

"You've been a bachelor for so long; I would think that you'd know how to prepare something simple for yourself."

"Sorry to disappoint. But all I've learned is how to buy frozen meals and put them in a microwave. Dinner tonight is going to be the Chinese takeout I have in my car, reheated and served on nice porcelain dishes."

"Well, at least there is that. Though I'm surprised you have bothered to buy porcelain dinnerware."

"It was a gift from my grandma."

"Aha, that makes more sense. When was the last time you used them?"

Andrew looked a little embarrassed when he said, "This is going to be the first."

She was touched. Evidently, he'd never invited any of his other girlfriends to an elegantly served dinner at his house. But then another thought flashed through her mind as she imagined the heirloom china accumulating dust in some forgotten kitchen cabinet. "I hope you washed them."

"I may not be a great housekeeper, but I'm lucky enough to have one. Usually Milly comes only once a month, but I asked her to clean the house again yesterday, including the dishes."

"You never told me that you have a housekeeper." Nathalie put her hands on her hips and cast him a suspicious look. "Is she attractive?"

He nodded. "Milly is beautiful."

Was he messing with her? By the way his lips were twitching, he was. She was going to pay him back. With interest. "You'll have to fire her. I'm a jealous girlfriend, and the idea of you alone in your house with a beautiful woman infuriates me."

"That's why you need to move in with me. You'll keep an eye on me so I'm not tempted by Milly." The twitch turned into a big grin, and a chuckle escaped his throat. "Sorry, I can't keep it up. Milly is beautiful, for a sixty-something-year-old grandma, who's been happily married to her high school sweetheart for the past forty-something years."

"So why is she cleaning houses?"

Andrew shrugged. "I don't know. Maybe she's bored, or maybe their pension money is not enough. Not something you ask a person. All I know is that I can trust her with a key and that she gets the job done. I'm not a messy person, and I'm hardly ever home, so it's not like she has a lot to do."

Nathalie slapped his arm. "Did you have fun tormenting me like this?"

Andrew pulled her into a hug. "Yes, and I like that you're jealous. But you have nothing to worry about. You're the only one for me. And you know it."

Sweet man.

She might not be an expert on relationships, but a guy who was investing so much time and energy into making theirs work was a keeper. "I love you," she said and kissed him again.

Definitely husband material—

Except for the secrets that she was sure he was hiding from her, and all the other things he conveniently forgot to mention.

15

ANANDUR

"Come." Lana grabbed Anandur's hand and pulled him behind her.

"Where are you taking me?"

"It's a surprise."

"Should I close my eyes?"

"No need, we are here."

They were standing on the dock next to an old, rather small boat. Anandur cocked a brow. "So where is the surprise?"

She pointed at the yacht. "This is the surprise. The owner ask me to look at boat for the next five days when he go to New York. So it's all ours until he come back."

"Sweet." Anandur followed her inside.

The layout of the boat's interior was similar to that of a motorhome, compact and functional, and it seemed that Lana had been busy since she'd gotten back. Something smelled delicious. The table had been set with disposable plates and flatware, and the source of the smell was a big oval platter hosting a grilled chicken surrounded by baked potatoes. Other than the main course and a bottle of vodka, there was no other food or beverage on the table.

Anandur smirked. A typical Russian meal.

He pulled Lana into a hug. "You cooked for me. I'm touched." He kissed her plump lips.

"Not me. Renata cook."

Anandur lifted a brow. "You told her about us?"

She shrugged and took a seat. "It's okay. She say nothing to boss."

That was a good little nugget of information. The women were more loyal to each other than to Alex. It was an opening he might use to his advantage. "Thank you for arranging this, and give Renata my thanks for the food. It smells amazing."

Lana surprised him when she mumbled something under her breath that sounded a lot like grace. A hurried sign of the cross followed before she attacked the chicken with a pair of poultry scissors.

Interesting.

Anandur had heard her say *Jesu* several times, but he'd thought nothing of it. A lot of people did it without being religious in the slightest, but it seemed that Lana was.

"You want I put on your plate or take yourself?" Lana paused with half of the chicken skewered on a carving fork.

Anandur lifted his plastic plate with his palm, propping it from below, so it wouldn't collapse under the weight of the chicken. "Thank you."

She smiled and pushed the halved bird off the carving fork with her finger, dropping it on Anandur's plate. The thing held, even when she added a generous portion of potatoes. He wasn't a big fan of poultry, but the chicken was done perfectly, and as he chased his first bite with a chunk of potato, Anandur gave Lana the thumbs up and nodded his appreciation.

Satisfied, she poured vodka into the two plastic tumblers and handed him one. "Salute!"

"Salute!" he mumbled with a full mouth as he touched his tumbler to hers.

Lana was as much of a hearty eater as Anandur, and as he shoved the last tasty morsel into his mouth, she wasn't far behind.

"This was good." He rubbed his stomach, pretending to be full. A whole chicken wouldn't have filled him, but it wasn't as if he wanted to flaunt his excessive appetite. The more normal he managed to appear, the less suspicious the cagey Russian would be.

Damn, no matter how good his boy-next-door act was, she would be suspicious as hell if he tried the stuff Brundar had suggested. She'd probably kick him out. Unless she was into that kind of shit. Problem was, he couldn't think of a clever way to casually weave it into the conversation so he could observe her response.

"I'm happy you like. I'll tell Renata." She leaned to refill his tumbler.

The bottle was almost gone, and Lana wasn't showing any signs of loosening. He hoped she'd brought more than one.

She followed his gaze with a smirk. "Don't worry, I have more."

"Phew, I was worried for a minute." Anandur pretended to wipe away sweat from his brow.

Lana pushed to her feet, walked over to one of the wall cabinets, and pulled out a bottle. "Here," she said as she put it next to Anandur.

"Don't you think the owner would notice that his stash of vodka got smaller while he was away?"

Lana shrugged. "I buy him new bottles."

Without thinking, Anandur lifted up to pull his wallet out of his pocket. He took out a couple of twenties and handed them to Lana. "My contribution."

She shoved the two bills back. "No. You keep your money. You need it. I make more money than you."

Who could've known that the tough iron lady was hiding a heart of gold? Which made him feel even worse about his deception. *Just remember what's at stake, buddy. Women's lives are ruined forever with this one's help.*

"I may be a lowly deck boy, but I have my pride." He pushed the money back.

Lana took it, separated one bill and tucked it into her pocket, then handed him the other. "The vodka is cheap."

He could live with that. "So, I guess your boss is a nice guy if he pays you top dollar." Anandur returned the twenty to his wallet and stuffed it back in the pocket of his jeans.

Lana harrumphed. "Alexander is pretty, but not nice."

"Why? Because he doesn't allow you girls to bring guys onboard?"

"This too." Lana grabbed the plastic plates and tossed them into a paper bag. She took the empty platter to the sink and started washing it.

"So, tell me what other naughty things your boss does. Is he into kinky sex games? Does he tie you up and blindfold you?"

This was probably his best and only shot at the subject, and Anandur inhaled deeply to catch any changes in Lana's scent. But it seemed that kinky games were not her thing because there was no change in her level of arousal, which had been basically neutral throughout their meal.

So much for Brundar's brilliant plan.

Damn.

"He likes more than one woman in bed. Sometimes two, sometimes three, and sometimes more. Is that kinky?"

"No, that's living a dream."

Lana angled the spigot so the water spray hit Anandur in the face. "My mama say all men are pigs. She is right."

Anandur laughed as he wiped his face with a paper napkin. "Your mama is wise. Men are despicable creatures who think about nothing other than sex, but women are not always better, true?" He pinned her with a hard stare.

Lana seemed to shrink under his gaze, and her face twisted with guilt. She turned her back to him and continued washing the platter that was probably already clean.

For a moment, the silence hung heavy in the cramped space, and Anandur thought Lana had shut the door on that conversation, but then she said, "Some people so stupid and weak. They are like cows, and the bad wolves catch them. This is how the world is." She turned around to face him, drying the platter with a dishtowel. "I'm strong. I'm not a cow like the stupid American girls. I never fall into the trap of the pretty wolf."

"So there are cows, and there are wolves. Any other animals?"

She pursed her fleshy lips. "Snakes, people who see the wolf and hide from him but not say something to cows. Weasels help the wolf. And the lion who eat the wolf and the cow."

Anandur chuckled. Her analogy was spot on. "And what animal are you?"

Lana shrugged, but he could smell the stench of guilt coming from her. "I am weasel. I help the wolf because wolf keep me safe from lion."

"Aha, but here is the thing, baby. The wolf will gladly feed you to the lion to protect its own hide. You can never count on the son of a bitch not to betray you."

"I know." She put the tray into a clean paper bag. "And I watch wolf carefully, but I have no other way."

"How about helping the lion? That must be better than helping the wolf. And I don't think lions eat weasels."

She laughed, but it was a sad laugh. "I don't know any lions."

"Sure you do." With a roar, Anandur leaped out of the chair and pounced on her. He threw Lana over his shoulder and went searching for the bedroom.

16

CAROL

"Hey, guys, you want to go out tonight?"

The class was over, and Carol didn't have any plans, which sucked. Her bestie had bailed on her, using finals as an excuse. Why the hell had Sharon decided to learn accounting of all things? It was so boring, and it wasn't as if Sharon was starving for money. With her income from the clan's share, she could've managed just fine. Working was entirely optional for clan members, and Carol had no intention of seeking employment unless she found something really exciting to do. Unfortunately, the only occupation she'd ever found fulfilling was no longer available. And besides, being a courtesan had lost its appeal a couple of centuries ago, and she hadn't done it for the money anyway. Not that working for a living hadn't been a necessity back then, the clan hadn't been as wealthy as it was now, but she'd really enjoyed the lifestyle.

Nowadays, she could get sex almost anywhere, but without a girlfriend to accompany her on a club run, she was stuck with Ben and George. It wouldn't be the same with the guys, their presence might deter men from approaching her, but it was better than going alone.

Someone had to keep an eye on her so she wouldn't overdo it with the booze.

"I'm game," Ben said.

"Me too. Do you want to go home first and change, though? Personally, I'd rather shower and put on something decent." George was a clothes whore, so there was no way he was going to go as is.

"I'm with you. You can't expect me to go looking like this." She waved a hand over her training outfit.

Ben shrugged. "Where and when?"

"Eight, Harvee's," Carol offered.

"It's not safe. Harvee's is not a members club. Let's go to The Basement."

Easy for George to suggest, he was a member. Carol wasn't. It was too pricey. And as far as she knew, Ben wasn't a member either. "Don't be ridiculous, George. It's not like we are defenseless."

"Yeah, we are badasses." Ben pumped his fist.

He was right. The guys were getting pretty good at hand to hand combat. Unfortunately, Carol was still too out of shape to be any good. Per Brundar's instructions, she was supposed to hit the gym every morning and do an hour of cardio and another half an hour of weight training. She'd done it twice. Every evening for the past two weeks she'd been promising herself that the next morning she was going for sure. And every morning she'd pressed snooze on the alarm and had gone back to sleep. Fates, she couldn't understand people who actually enjoyed exercise. Weirdos, one and all.

Damn, Brundar would be furious, and he wasn't the kind of guy she wished to aggravate. But even though he scared the crap out of her, the fear wasn't a strong enough motivator.

Perhaps the problem was that at the back of her mind, she entertained a hope that he'd go easy on her because she was such a badass with the gun. Not everyone was meant to be an athlete, right? Trouble was, they didn't get to take their weapons home. She would've felt much safer carrying.

Still, living in fear was no way to live. She needed to get out and have fun, find a decent guy to screw, or she was going to go nuts.

She would never admit it to anyone because it was so damn embarrassing, but she even tried to look for hookups at Starbucks because it was supposedly safe. Except, she'd found out that the place was crawling with nerds. Carol loved simple guys, tall and heavily muscled, and didn't care much for intelligence. After all, she wasn't looking for a good conversation, was she?

"What are the chances of Doomers showing up at Harvee's out of all the clubs? We'll be fine," she said, feigning confidence.

An hour and a half later, showered and ready for conquest, Carol pulled up to the valet in front of Harvee's and left her Prius with the attendant.

Armed with killer four-inch spiky heels, a skirt that barely covered her ass, and a slightly sheer blouse that showcased her designer bra, Carol felt unstoppable. The bra had a matching thong, but only one lucky guy would get to see it tonight.

Naturally, heads turned as she wended her way between the tables to reach her friends—who apparently hadn't been waiting for her idly. Each already had a little hottie glued to his side. Good for them. But if she didn't want to feel like a fifth wheel, she'd better work fast.

"Hi, guys, want to introduce me to your new friends?"

"I'm Wendy." The one sitting on Ben's knee offered her hand.

"I'm Carol, nice to meet you."

"Monica," said the other one and waved.

Done with the introductions, Carol took a seat, crossed her legs, and began scanning the sparse crowd for the kind of guy she liked. It was still early, so there wasn't much of a selection, but the place was going to fill up in the next hour.

In the meantime, she ordered a drink, and another one, and another...

"What's your sign?" Monica tapped her shoulder.

"Capricorn, why? What's yours?" Carol loved talking about that shit. The first thing she read in the fashion magazines she subscribed to was the horoscope.

Monica's eyes sparkled with excitement. "So you're stubborn, determined, and loyal. It's a great sign, mostly for a guy. I'm a Libra, and I love Capricorns. Best boyfriend material. Have you had your astrological chart done yet?"

"No, I just read the horoscope."

Monica snorted. "Those are too general. If you really want to know your future and who is your perfect match, you need to have your chart done. But it's crucial to have the exact time of your birth. I can't make a chart without it."

Carol laughed. "I have no idea. I can call my mom and ask, but I doubt she remembers." It had been a couple of centuries…

"I'm sure she does. Call her up, and when you have it, I'll do your chart."

"Thanks. I will." She probably wouldn't, but there was no reason to be rude to the girl.

Monica twirled a lock of her dyed red hair around her finger. "Are you into tarot cards?"

"As in reading or being read?"

"Both, I guess."

"I don't know enough to read someone else's fortune, but I love to have mine read to me." Not that anyone today was as good at it as the gypsies of her youth.

The girl rummaged in her purse. "Shit, I forgot to bring them. I have a miniature pack I take with me everywhere I go. I must've left it at your place, Wendy."

"I'll check when I get home and call you."

"Thanks. But anyway, all is not lost. I also read palms. Give me your hand."

Carol finished her drink before offering Monica her palm.

The booth they were sitting in was dim, and Monica had to bring Carol's hand so close to her face that her nose was practically touching it. And still, it wasn't enough. Her brows riding low on her forehead, Monica traced the lines with a finger. "A big change is coming. There is a fork in the line that indicates a new path. It might be a new job, or a new boyfriend, or even marriage, but whatever it is it's going to be big."

For some reason, Monica's stupid foretelling, one that Carol was giving no credence to, sent chills down her spine. She yanked her hand out of the girl's grasp. "Thanks, but I don't really believe in any of it," Carol said with a tight smile.

Fates, she needed a drink. But there was scarcely anything left in her glass, and she waved the waitress over.

George covered her hand with his palm and leaned closer. "That was your fifth, you should stop."

Damn, six wouldn't get her drunk, but she'd told them to stop her after five. Fine, there were other ways to get rid of a bad humor.

She leaned into Ben and whispered into his ear, "Do you have any weed on you?"

"Plenty."

"Good. Let's go find a private spot."

On the sidewalk outside of Harvee's, several clubbers were enjoying a smoke —some of the tobacco variety, and some of the cannabis one. Carol went searching for somewhere secluded and dark. With a medical card in her wallet, she wasn't worried about getting arrested, but after years of smoking joints in hiding, she just couldn't derive pleasure from doing it in public.

The alley behind the parking lot looked secluded enough, but thanks to the floodlights that kept the lot illuminated it wasn't completely shrouded in darkness either.

Carol leaned against the block wall that separated the alley from the building on the other side, waiting for Ben to finish rolling the smoke. When he was done, he licked the paper to close it and pulled a lighter from his back pocket. "Do you want to light up? Or do you prefer for me to start?"

"You do it."

He nodded and lit the thing. After taking a big inhale, he handed it to her, keeping the smoke inside him for as long as he could.

Carol took a puff, then another, before handing it back to Ben. Already the tight feeling in her belly was starting to ebb, and as soon as Ben was done, she took it from him and took several more.

"We should be getting back," Ben said as she passed him the joint, and lifted his foot to extinguish the thing on the sole of his boot.

"No, not yet. Let me finish it."

Reluctantly, he gave it back, but his eyes darted from side to side, and he tucked his hands under his armpits as he shifted from leg to leg. "It's damn freezing out here. Be quick about it."

Carol frowned. What was he talking about? Ben was wearing jeans and a long-sleeved shirt, while she was in a miniskirt and a sleeveless top, and she wasn't cold. Was he coming down with something?

"Maybe you should go inside. I'll be done in a minute."

"No, I'll wait. I'm not leaving you alone out here."

She rolled her eyes. Even in her less than superb shape, Carol doubted an average human male could subdue her. But if they ganged up on her, well, that was a different story. With that in mind, she dropped what was left of the joint and put it out with her shoe. "Let's go."

As they crossed the alley and entered the well illuminated area of the parking lot, Ben released a relieved breath. A minivan rolled into one of the few remaining spots, and a moment later the side door slid open, which struck her as odd because she was expecting the valet to jump out from the driver seat then rush back to the front.

Instead, a tall, muscular guy got out, the kind that immediately caught her interest, and right behind him came two more, just as yummy.

My personal buffet.

As she started sauntering toward them, Ben grabbed her arm and yanked her back against his body. She was about to say something, but he twisted her around and clamped a hand over her mouth.

What the fuck?

"Walk slowly. Don't make any sudden moves. Pretend we are a couple," he whispered in her ear so quietly that even she had trouble hearing him. "Don't look back, and don't say a word when I remove my hand. Nod if you understand."

She did, even though she had no idea what had gotten into him. Yeah, those guys were built, but that didn't mean they were looking for trouble, right? But just in case Ben had seen something she'd missed, she followed his lead.

Listening to what was going on behind them, Carol waited breathlessly to hear the minivan's door slide shut, and then four sets of shoes hitting the concrete in the opposite way. Time stretched into infinity as she and Ben took one step and then another, waiting for those sounds so she could finally exhale. But those sounds never came. Instead, Carol heard them getting closer.

"Run!" Ben grabbed her hand and broke into a sprint, dragging her behind him. She did her best to run as fast as she could on her four-inch heels, but they never had a chance.

It all happened so fast that she barely registered what was going on. One moment she was holding Ben's hand, the next someone was grabbing her by the waist and lifting her up with a force that was clearly not human. As much as she flailed and fought she couldn't gain an inch. The arm wrapped around her felt like an iron band.

"What do we have here?" the Doomer holding her rasped in her ear. "A succulent little immortal female."

Carol fought harder, twisting and kicking, but it was no use. "Let me go!" she screamed.

He clamped a hand over her mouth. "Thank you, darling, for all that thrashing. It got my fangs primed and ready for this." She felt the excruciating burn of them sinking into the soft skin of her neck, but a moment later the pain subsided. With euphoria spreading through her brain and her body like a wildfire over parched brush, Carol sagged in her captor's arms.

Through her foggy brain, she forced herself to open her eyes and look for Ben. Did he manage to escape? Or did they get him too? But with the Doomer's fangs still embedded in her neck, and his hand holding her head immobilized, she could only see what was ahead of her, and Ben wasn't there.

As the Doomer's venom kept sliding into her vein, Carol had the passing thought that he was pumping her with too much and was going to finish her off.

Please, merciful Fates, make it so. Let death set me free.

17

SYSSI

"It's so nice to get out of the keep for a change of atmosphere. We should do it more often." Syssi stuffed another piece of an avocado egg roll into her mouth. "God, I missed these," she said as she cut off another piece and dipped it in the cilantro sauce that came with it.

Tonight, she had taken Kian out, choosing to revisit her favorite restaurant from her previous life as a human. Syssi felt as if decades had passed since that pivotal moment in Amanda's lab when she'd first met Kian. It had been the start of an incredible adventure, one that, hopefully, would last the rest of her very long life. Everything was perfect. She had an adoring husband, a warm extended family, and a job she loved. It should've felt idyllic, a fairytale, and yet she was restless.

Hopefully, this slice of normal would restore her equilibrium. It felt as if it had been ages since the last time she'd tasted her favorite appetizer, when in fact the actual time elapsed could be measured in months, not even years. Strange, how the perception of time didn't follow a linear path.

At first, Kian had felt ill at ease in the bustling restaurant, mainly because of the cramped seating arrangements that put him in close proximity to mortals, but little by little he was starting to relax. The ogling looks he was getting from females were kind of annoying, but he was either oblivious or chose to ignore them. Even the guys were paying more attention to Kian than to her.

Oh, well, this was a price she was willing to pay, especially since Kian had eyes only for her. While she was sitting across from him, the rest of the world might as well not exist as far as he was concerned.

But he was certainly paying attention to the egg rolls, picking them up with his fingers and stuffing them whole in his mouth. "You're right, these are good. And the tamales too, although I have to scrape off the sour cream. We should order another round."

Syssi chuckled. "Only if you plan on eating everything yourself. I'm done."

He glanced at the small appetizer plate she'd been using, then back up at her. "You must be kidding. We didn't even order the main course yet."

"I've had enough. These are very filling. When I used to come here before, I would often order just the appetizers. Their portions are huge. I swear, each one can feed a family of four."

Kian took the last egg roll off the platter and placed it on her plate. "Eat," he commanded.

So bossy, but in a good way. "Are you going to order more?"

"Yes."

Syssi nodded and cut a piece of the green delight, swearing it was her last. She hadn't hit the gym after work as she'd planned because her insatiable husband had had other ideas. Unfortunately, sex didn't count toward her goal of weekly exercise, which she'd set at minimum of half an hour a day.

"Tomorrow morning I'm coming with you to the gym. Don't let me stay in bed."

Kian arched a brow. Syssi wasn't a morning person, and while he started his day with a session at the gym—after their morning romp that is—she preferred to laze in bed with a cup of coffee or two, reading the news and some of the more interesting articles along with some mindless browsing on her tablet.

"What's going on, Syssi? Did you get it into your head that you need to lose weight? Because I assure you, you're perfect the way you are."

She dabbed at her mouth with a napkin. "Thank you, I appreciate the compliment. But I can't count on my super-duper genes to keep me looking great forever. You look the way you do for a reason." She waved a hand over his muscular upper body. "Your vegan diet and your dedication to a daily exercise routine keep you in shape. And conversely, William looks the way he does because he is eating indiscriminately and avoiding the gym like the fiery pits of hell."

Kian smiled and took her hand, bringing it up to his lips for a kiss. "I would love to have you join me in the gym every morning. I treasure every moment I get to spend with you. But I'm curious about the impetus for this resolution."

"You remember Hanna?"

"Sure, the postdoc at Amanda's lab."

"She managed to lose a lot of weight and looks amazing. She said it was all about eating less and moving more while being mindful of what and how much. It got me thinking that I need to be more disciplined with my eating habits and physical activity."

His eyes flared with the supernatural gleam she was so familiar with, and he hissed, "I can help keep you disciplined."

Syssi rolled her eyes. "Is everything about sex with you?"

"Obviously." He smiled, his fangs making an appearance.

She leaned forward. "Don't smile."

Kian's hand flew to cover his mouth.

"Want me to talk about disgusting things?"

He laughed from behind his hand. "Please don't. I don't want to hear about little kids puking all over themselves while I'm eating."

He remembered. How sweet.

"Fine, so I'll update you on the new plans Amanda and I have for the lab."

"That's better."

"I put an ad on Craig's List for subjects with paranormal abilities, offering to pay twenty an hour for their time."

"This will guarantee that you'll have a lot of people with no talent wasting your time."

"I know. That's why we decided to hire an assistant to do the initial screening. That way we will get to test only those with potential."

Kian shook his head. "I don't know. Doesn't seem to me like the best way to go about it, but I have nothing better to suggest."

"You want to hear some of the crazy ideas that I've played around with in my head?"

"Of course."

"Asking William to develop a computer or arcade game that will somehow test for abilities, and then lure the winners into some final competition for a big prize."

"That's actually not so crazy…"

"You must be kidding."

"Not at all. The game can be based on the random images program you use in the lab. It seems like a simple enough thing to do."

"Kian, you are a genius. I don't know why I haven't thought of it myself. It's so obvious."

"It would have never crossed my mind without you mentioning a computer game first. I wasn't thinking in that direction at all."

Syssi smiled and raised her hand. "High five for teamwork."

He slapped her hand, and then lowered it for a kiss. "This calls for a celebration. Champagne?"

She wasn't a fan of that particular bubbly. "How about a Mojito instead?"

"Mojito it is." He waved down a waiter and ordered two, together with another serving of avocado egg rolls.

Syssi leaned back in her chair and tapped her lower lip with the tip of her finger. "The trick will be to disguise it as a game and make it enjoyable for both young men and young women."

"I think you can leave this part to William and his 'Genius Squad'—that's how they asked to be called. They objected to us calling them the geek squad."

"Can't blame them. Though I thought it was kind of cute."

"Apparently not to teenagers."

The waiter came back with their Mojitos and Kian's egg rolls. "Are you ready for the main course?" he asked.

"Not for me, thank you," Syssi said.

Kian flipped the menu closed and handed it to the guy. "Please bring us the mango salad, without the chicken, and two plates. We're going to share."

"I told you I'm stuffed," she said as the waiter left with their order.

"Just in case you change your mind. If you don't want any, I have no problem eating everything by myself." He raised his tumbler. "To great minds working together!"

"To us!" She smiled and clinked his tall glass.

But as she brought it to her lips to take a sip, her hand began trembling, and her vision blurred, becoming a swirl of colors. Her head spinning, she felt herself slide down in her chair.

Oh, no, not now...

A vision was coming, and there was no stopping it.

"Syssi! What's wrong?" in a split second, Kian was out of his chair and on his knees beside her. The tumbler began sliding out of her hand, but he caught it in time and put it on the table, then clasped her hands. "Talk to me, sweet girl. You're scaring the shit out of me."

By now her whole body was trembling uncontrollably. "We need to go home. Now."

"Of course." Kian's beautiful face was pinched with worry as he pushed up to his feet and lifted her up. "Are you feeling sick?"

"No. It's not about me. Something bad is going to happen, and we should be home when it does. That's all I know for certain."

18

NATHALIE

"Some more orange chicken?" Andrew hovered with the serving bowl over Fernando's shoulder, ready to heap some more on her father's plate.

"Maybe just a few pieces. I'm full, but this is very tasty. Could you give me the recipe? I'm a baker, not a cook, but I know my way around a kitchen."

Andrew shot Nathalie a look that said, 'help!'

She patted her father's wrinkled hand. "You know, Papi, that we can't cook Chinese in the coffee shop. It will stink up the place. Customers want to smell coffee and baked goods when they come in, not something deep fried."

"Yes, you're right, of course. Can't cook Chinese in a coffee shop. What was I thinking? I'll tell you what I was thinking. That we have a perfectly good kitchen at home, where we can cook whatever we want, but you never let me go back there!"

"Papi, we've been over this before. We sold that home a long time ago. There is somebody else living there now."

"So you've been saying." He speared a piece of orange chicken with his fork and stuffed it into his mouth.

Nathalie sighed. She couldn't complain, it had been going well up until now. And as Fernando's tantrums went, this had been a mild one. Nevertheless, it was a sign that they should head home.

"Finish your dinner, Papi. We need to go."

"What's the hurry?" Andrew put the serving bowl on the table and sat down. "Let the man eat in peace, Nathalie. It's not healthy to rush a meal." He winked at her.

Fernando shot her a worried glance, checking to see if she'd gotten angry over Andrew's remark.

"It's okay, Papi. Andrew is right. There is no hurry. I want you to enjoy the meal."

Her father shook his head as if puzzled by something. "You can cook." He pointed his fork at Andrew, then at Nathalie. "And she listens to you and doesn't hold every word you say against you. I say it's a match made in heaven."

Andrew looked guilty, no doubt feeling bad about deceiving Fernando. But his little Chinese takeout deception aside, Nathalie wanted to jump on the opportunity and finally tell her father that she and Andrew were a couple. Problem was, in order to do so in a way that would be easiest for him to understand, she needed to twist the truth too.

"You are absolutely right, Papi. This is why Andrew and I decided to get engaged." She shot Andrew a glance, hoping he wouldn't look like a deer caught in the headlights of an oncoming truck. But the man was smiling from ear to ear as if he'd heard the best of news and couldn't be happier.

"Well, it's about time. I was wondering what was holding you kids back."

Nathalie glanced at Andrew, who was still smiling broadly as if all of their troubles were solved and all was good in their world. But she knew better. "How long have you known Andrew, Papi?"

Her father's brows dipped down as he concentrated. "Many years, I think. Didn't you kids start dating in high school?"

She wanted to correct his misconception, but Andrew put his hand over hers and shook his head imperceptibly. "It's time we settled down, don't you think, Fernando?"

"Absolutely. I want grandkids, and my Eva, she is going to be so happy."

God, how Nathalie hated moments like this. She was so angry at her mother. For leaving her father, for abandoning her and disappearing to God knew where. Such a selfish woman. And yet Fernando still loved her, still pined for her. It was so unfair.

"I'm sure she will," Andrew said. "Let's make a toast." He poured a little wine into each of their goblets. "To a happy marriage."

Fernando lifted his glass and clinked it with Nathalie's, then with Andrew's. "And fruitful," he added with a wink.

Andrew nodded solemnly. "And fruitful."

Later, when Andrew had driven them back home, Fernando clapped Andrew on the back and congratulated them again before retiring for the night.

Nathalie's shoulders sagged as soon as his door closed, and the fake smile she'd been fronting for his sake dissolved from her face. "God, this was so awkward."

Andrew pulled her into his arms. "I think it went well. In fact, it was better than I'd expected."

She pushed at his chest, and he let her go. "Oh, yeah? Which part? The one about us being engaged? Or the part about getting married and having kids? Or maybe the one about his long gone ex-wife he still thinks he is married to?"

Nathalie plopped on the couch and let her head drop back on the cushions, feeling exhausted and depressed. Damn, was she becoming bipolar in addition to her other abnormalities? This morning she'd been floating on a happy cloud, and now she couldn't muster one positive thought. What was wrong with her?

Andrew came to sit next to her and lifted her legs so her feet were nestled in his lap. "You're just tired, baby. This was a stressful evening for you." He started massaging her feet.

A ghost of a smile hovered over her lips as Andrew's expert fingers began working their magic on her toes. "You may be right. Though I hate lying to my father like this."

"You're not lying."

"Twisting the truth is the same thing as lying, Andrew."

"Look." He pressed his thumb to the arch of her foot, and she let out a moan. "We never set dates or made official proclamations, but I plan on spending the rest of my life with you. And, hopefully, you feel the same way about me. So, if these were our intentions all along, then we weren't lying to your father or misleading him in any way. True?"

She sighed. If there was one thing about Andrew that wasn't perfect, it was that he didn't have even one romantic bone in his body.

Nathalie regarded him with a mock sternness. "Andrew Spivak, this was the lamest proposal I've ever heard."

The poor guy looked so stricken that she just couldn't keep up the pretense. "But I loved it anyway." She leaned up and kissed his lips.

"I'm sorry. I should have planned this better."

"I'll tell you what. I still want you to propose on one knee or both, but I'm thinking along the lines of both of us naked while you do it."

"Woman, I like the way you think."

Andrew was up on his feet and lifting her up in his strong arms before even finishing his sentence. In several long strides, he closed the distance to her room and lowered her gently to the floor, then turned around and closed the door behind him, locking it.

Curious to find out what he was going to do next, Nathalie stood on the area rug next to her bed and waited for Andrew, a flurry of excited butterflies taking flight in her stomach.

With a predatory smirk, he sauntered up to her and knelt on the carpet. His hands reaching around to cup her ass, his nose was pointing at the junction of her thighs, almost touching.

"Let's get you naked, baby," he rasped as he tugged at the stretchy fabric of her pants and pulled them down without bothering with the button or the zipper. Next, he lowered her panties down her thighs, and she braced a hand on his shoulder to keep steady as she stepped out of them, one leg at a time.

Andrew got up to divest her of her blouse, pulling it over her head, then unsnapped her bra and let it fall down to the floor. Dropping back to his knees, he lowered all the way down to his haunches and looked up at her with a worshipful gaze.

"God, Nathalie, you're so beautiful that you take my breath away. My own, personal Aphrodite."

The love in Andrew's eyes, in his words, was shining so brightly that she felt tears stinging the back of her eyes, and a corresponding powerful wave of emotions burst out from her heart. She needed to touch him, to feel his strong body against hers. Nathalie went down to her knees in front of Andrew, and with a lurch flung herself into his arms, almost toppling them both.

She clung to Andrew as if her life depended on it, not caring if she was crushing him with her hug. "I love you so much," she whispered into his neck.

"I love you too, and you'll make me the happiest man alive if you agree to become my wife."

Her chuckle was accompanied by a sniffle. "I wanted both of us naked when you asked me."

"So is it a yes, or a no?" he teased.

Nathalie hesitated for a moment. Could she really agree to marry a man who was keeping secrets from her? It could've been absolutely perfect if not for her suspicions. But as she was well aware, life wasn't perfect, and neither was Andrew. Eventually, he'd have to trust her enough to tell her everything or there would be no marriage. But that didn't mean that she couldn't say yes to him now. They had plenty of time before any talk about a wedding was even possible, and, hopefully, by then all would be revealed.

"Of course it's a yes. But I hope you don't mind a very long engagement."

"I'm not getting any younger, you know. But there is no rush."

Nathalie let go and pushed back up to her feet. "I still want you naked as you kneel for me."

"Another fantasy?" He was teasing her for wanting to enact every item on the list of fantasies she'd collected over the years.

"Yes, but this is a new one."

"Now, this is exciting." He smirked as he started on the buttons of his shirt. "Is it a wicked one?" He shrugged the shirt off, exposing his mouthwatering muscular torso.

Nathalie shrugged, her lips twitching with the need to smile. "Maybe a little."

Andrew lifted up on his knees and unbuckled his belt, then pushed his pants down his legs. His boxer briefs went next, and then he was kneeling in front of her, fully erect, his shaft rising up from his groin like a flagpole.

With a slight incline of his head, he said, "I'm at your service, my queen. Awaiting your command."

Damn, she'd hoped he would guess what she wanted, and the wily man probably had, but he wanted to hear her say it.

"Pleasure me," she commanded.

"You need to be more specific than that."

Damn, he was pushing her to say things she was still too embarrassed to voice, which was kind of silly since she had no problem with the actual doing.

With one hand cupping a breast, she lowered the other to the juncture of her thighs, her finger hovering lightly over the seat of her pleasure. Andrew's breath intake was audible, but still, he hadn't made a move to touch her, waiting for her to tell him what to do.

"I want your tongue, right here." She tapped her finger lightly over the spot.

His smile was positively predatory, hungry, as if he was eyeing a tasty treat and was about to devour it.

"With pleasure, your majesty." Andrew's hands cupped her butt cheeks and pulled her closer, his tongue snaking out and flicking over that most sensitive bundle of nerves.

"Oh, yes..." she moaned and could swear he was smiling with satisfaction just from the way his tongue moved. The scene she had engineered was incredibly arousing, but a few moments into it, her legs started quivering, and she was having trouble staying upright.

19

KIAN

"Put me down, you're making a scene," Syssi hissed.

Reluctantly, Kian let her legs drop down but held her up with an arm wrapped around her waist. Bhathian, their designated bodyguard for this evening, had rushed ahead to get the car. He'd been sitting a few tables away to give them privacy. The idea was to provide Syssi with the illusion that they were just a normal couple going on a normal date. A bodyguard sitting right next to them would have spoiled the effect.

She'd seemed a little off lately, and Kian had hoped this outing would improve her mood. But apparently something more serious than missing her old life was causing her unease, and had been a prelude to the fucking vision that had hit her like an epileptic seizure. He'd never seen her like that, and it had scared the crap out of him. There was nothing more terrifying than watching the woman you love gripped by some mysterious force you were powerless to fight off.

It reminded him of how desperate and inept he'd felt during her transition, when he'd thought he was losing her. Not a good memory

As they pushed through the restaurant's door and stepped outside, the Lexus was parked right by the entry, thanks to the generous tip Kian slipped the valet so it could be quickly retrieved. With one glance at Bhathian's expression, the guy dropped the keys into the Guardian's palm.

As they got into the back seat of the SUV, Kian wrapped his hand around Syssi's shoulders. Her slight form trembled against his body as if she were cold. He rubbed her arm. "How are you feeling, sweet girl?"

"I'll be fine. You should call the keep and find out if anything happened."

He kissed the top of her head. "Someone would've called me already. Don't worry. Everything is going to be okay. Whatever it is, we'll deal with it."

"Call. I just want to make sure."

"I can do that." He pulled out the phone and selected Onegus's contact. "Anything going on?"

"No, why?"

"Syssi had a premonition that something bad is coming. Soon. And even though she doesn't know where or what, I suggest you put security on high alert."

"Will do."

Clicking the phone off, he glanced down at Syssi. The poor girl looked so shaken, clutching her purse in a white-knuckled grip and tapping her foot. He tucked her closer under his arm, holding her tight against his side and rubbing her arm until he felt her shoulders relax. Only then he asked, "What exactly have you seen?"

For a long moment, she just chewed on her lip, her brows pinched in concentration. "It's hard to describe. The input wasn't visual, or rather not visually clear. There was a darkness that started as a mere fog, evolved into a swirling mass of wispy dark tendrils, and then coalesced into a terrifying blackness. There were sounds. Again, nothing that I can make sense of. A cross between the roar of a turbulent wind and that of a pack of hyenas. But I felt a sense of urgency, of immediacy, as if there was something we needed to do to either prevent it or do something about it after it happened." She exhaled a breath. "I hate it. Hate that I get these premonitions of doom, but not enough information to do anything about them. What's the point of having them if all they accomplish is to make me miserable?"

Regrettably, she was right. For the first time, he had gotten a taste of what she'd been dealing with for most of her life, and it was absolutely infuriating. To wait impotently for the unknown disaster to strike, unable to do anything to prevent it or even prepare for it, was worse than having no forewarning at all.

He bent down and kissed her forehead. "It's damn frustrating, that's for sure. But when it comes we'll just have to deal with it, the same way we deal with any disaster that strikes. The only difference is that now both of us are stressed."

"I shouldn't have told you. It's bad enough that I'm burdened with these useless premonitions. You have enough real stuff to worry about without being bothered with this nonsense. In the absence of specifics, there is nothing you can do about it anyway. Shit happens all the time with or without my vague warnings."

"Don't be ridiculous. Of course, you have to tell me. Even if it's for the sole purpose of having someone to share it with. And don't even think about trying to hide it from me. We are a couple, a family, and we face shit together."

Syssi sighed and slumped in his grip, putting her cheek on his chest. Damn, even after all this time, it still got him every time she did something like this. The implied trust, the fact that she took solace in his arms and was willing to lean on him for support was precious to him.

"I love you, my sweet girl," he whispered and nuzzled her hair.

When Syssi didn't respond, Kian realized that she'd fallen asleep. Evidently, these damn premonitions were draining—emotionally and physically.

To keep it from disturbing her, he put his phone on silent and spent the rest of the drive staring at the screen, waiting anxiously for the bad news to arrive so he could get moving and do something about it. The wait and uncertainty were torturous.

As Bhathian eased the Lexus into its parking spot, Kian lifted Syssi into his lap and waited for the guy to open the door for him so he could slide out with his precious load.

She opened her eyes and smiled, then leaned up and kissed the underside of his jaw. "I can walk, you know."

"I do. But I like carrying you." He kissed her nose and gathered her closer.

With a sigh, she put her head on his chest and closed her eyes. "Did I tell you lately how much I love you?" she whispered into his neck.

He chuckled. "A couple of times. But not nearly enough."

"Really? My poor baby."

"Let's make a schedule. I think every five minutes will do fine. I just love hearing you say it to me."

"I love you."

"That's my girl."

When they got back into their penthouse, he lowered her to the couch. "I'm going to get myself a drink, and I suggest you have one too."

"Yeah, I need it. A simple gin and tonic, though easy on the gin."

He kissed her cheek. "Coming right up."

It had been good to joke around with Syssi for a bit, and during these lighthearted moments, he'd even managed to silence the countdown clock ticking in his head. But now the damn thing was back and louder than before.

Drinks in hand, Kian returned to the couch and sat next to Syssi. "Here, try it. Tell me if this is the way you like it." He handed her the tumbler.

She took a sip and nodded. "Perfect."

Taking a long one from his whiskey, he savored the burn in his throat, knowing that he'd be refilling his glass in short order. More than once. The fucking wait was killing him.

Kian got up, went to the kitchen, and grabbed a can of peanuts from the pantry. Syssi would have wanted him to pour them into a nice serving bowl, but he had no patience for that and brought the can to the living room, half expecting her to send him back for it. She said nothing, though, and as he offered her the container, she dipped her hand in it and pulled out a fistful.

A few moments later, his glass was empty, and he got up to refill it. "Would you like another one?" He glanced at Syssi's. She'd gone through half of it, but the melting ice cubes had probably further diluted the alcohol content that hadn't been much to begin with.

"No, thank you."

By the time he'd emptied his second serving of Macallan, Kian was ready to punch the walls—the prospect of Syssi's disapproval the only thing holding him back.

With a loud intake of breath and then a forceful puff through pursed lips, Syssi put down her glass and pushed to her feet. "This is nuts. I can't take it anymore. I'm going to fill up a bathtub and soak. You're welcome to join me."

As tempting as her invitation was, he knew he wouldn't be able to relax enough to enjoy it. "Go on. I'll stay by the phone and let you know as soon as I get any news."

Syssi grimaced. "What if nothing happens tonight? You can't stay up waiting for something that may or may not come."

He took her hand and kissed it. "We both know that there is no question whether it's going to happen; only when and where and what."

She nodded. "Let me know as soon as you hear anything."

"I will. Enjoy your soak."

With Syssi out of the room, the last of the façade he'd been keeping up for her sake had melted away. As he paced around his living room, Kian caught glimpses of himself every time he passed by the glass doors to the terrace, and the face staring back at him wasn't pretty, or even human. His fangs had punched down over his lower lip, and the swollen glands were distorting his features into something that looked savage, animalistic.

Time stretched into eternity, and when his phone finally vibrated in his hand, Kian was almost relieved to get the bad news he'd been waiting for. But as he lifted it up to answer, it wasn't Onegus's face that was displayed on the screen, it was Bridget's.

A medical emergency? Highly unlikely. But then, what other reason did the doctor have to call him this late?

He tapped the green button to answer. "Yes, Bridget. What's going on?"

"You'd better come down here. I have an unconscious Doomer-attack victim I need to take care of, and you'll want to talk to the friend who brought him in."

"On my way."

20

ANDREW

On his knees, pleasuring his woman, was exactly where Andrew wanted to be. But Nathalie's legs were trembling, and as much fun as holding her up with his hands under her sweet ass was, it was becoming difficult. Not for the first time, Andrew wondered how different it would be if he were immortal. Syssi had gotten stronger after her transition, and although he hadn't spoken with Michael about it, he was sure that the boy had gotten stronger too.

Even Vlad, with his spider arms, was most likely stronger than Andrew, and Jackson, well, the kid could probably finish him with one punch.

Ouch.

Transitioning was tempting, no doubt about it, but it was also scary as hell. Especially now that he had something to live for. Andrew wasn't a stranger to death. As a matter of fact, they were long time acquaintances, and he'd stared the fucker in the face many times before. He hadn't been afraid then because giving his life to save others was noble, and he'd been reconciled to the fact that one day his luck would run out.

But this was different.

To risk his life to gain something for himself felt frivolous to Andrew, even if that something was immortality. To borrow one of Kian's expressions, the Fates had been kind to him, keeping him alive when others in his unit hadn't been that lucky. He couldn't help the persistent thought that he'd been spared because of his willingness to sacrifice. But then, this line of thought was making him feel even guiltier for still breathing while his buddies were gone. Then again, it wasn't only his own immortality that was on the line. He had to consider that the love of his life had the same potential, and he was the one who should facilitate her transformation.

The irony of having these philosophical thoughts while his tongue was buried deep inside of Nathalie's cleft wasn't lost on him. Damn, he was a lousy lover. He'd better get his head back in the game before she noticed that his thoughts were miles away.

Redoubling his efforts, Andrew licked and sucked, holding on tight to Nathalie's ass while she gyrated her hips in sync with his tonguing. When her breath hitched, and she let out a guttural moan, he lifted her up and carried her to the bed, using the last of his strength to put her down gently and not let her drop.

Hopefully, she was too far gone to notice the quivering of his tired arm muscles. After all, a man had to preserve his damn pride, true?

"That was awesome," Nathalie rasped as she stretched her limbs, lying spread-eagled on her narrow bed.

Music to my ears. Andrew smirked. Even when his mind was distracted and he hadn't been focusing as he should, he'd given his woman a powerful orgasm.

"Scootch. Make room for me." He nudged her thigh with his knee.

"Nah, I'm not moving. You can cover me up with this incredibly handsome body of yours." She tapped her chest.

Okay, he could live with that. Andrew straddled Nathalie's legs, then lowered himself on top of her, bracing his forearms on both sides of her head.

Up close, her pleasure-suffused face was beyond beautiful and sexy as hell. And those pink, parted lips of hers were calling to him to take them. He dipped his head and kissed her, licking into her mouth with a tongue that still carried the taste of her juices. Nathalie moaned softly, her hips churning under him in invitation.

Andrew was tempted. In fact, his shaft had been throbbing painfully for far too long and denying it the pleasure of sinking into Nathalie's welcoming sheath was torturous. But he wanted to prolong her anticipation, driving her wild with need, so when he finally buried himself inside her, Nathalie's orgasm would catapult her into the stratosphere.

Andrew kept kissing her soft, fleshy lips and licking inside her mouth, his talented tongue dancing the mating dance with hers. Then he slid lower to pay homage to her perky little nipples, lavishing attention on each one until they were hard enough to poke a hole in a wall. But as he made a move to slide even lower, she caught his head and pulled him up by his hair.

"I want you inside me."

The lady knew what she wanted, when and how she wanted it, and he wasn't about to deny her. Whatever Nathalie wished for, Nathalie got, at least as far as it was in his power to oblige her wishes. Except, he was still going to push her a little, get her out of her comfort zone—because she loved it when he did that.

He positioned himself at her entry but didn't push. "Put me in," he instructed.

Nathalie reached between their bodies and took hold of his shaft, stroking it gently a few times before bearing down on it.

As he slowly sank into her wet heat, Andrew tried and failed to stifle a groan, but at least it came out somewhat muffled, and, hopefully, Fernando didn't hear a thing. Cupping Nathalie's cheeks, he held her gaze until he was fully seated inside her, and then he kissed her, deeply, passionately.

With her arms wrapped around him, Nathalie held on tight as she kissed him back, and for long moments Andrew didn't move inside her, enjoying the closeness, the connection, the joining of their bodies and their hearts. When he let go of her mouth, he touched his forehead to hers and whispered, "I love you, my Nathalie."

She brought her palm to his cheek, caressing it lightly. "I love you, my Andrew," she echoed, "But I need you to move."

And he did, unhurriedly, his thrusts shallow. Not only because anything more vigorous would've banged the headboard against the wall and they couldn't make noise, but because he wanted to prolong the pleasure as much as he could.

Except, if he had his sister's talent for predicting the future, he would've hurried up, because a moment later his phone went off with the ringtone he'd assigned to Kian, and he wished he hadn't taken his time. "Sorry, sweetheart, but I need to take it. They wouldn't call me this late if it weren't an emergency."

Her forehead wrinkled with worry. "Of course, go ahead."

Reluctantly, he abandoned the heaven of her wet embrace and rushed to retrieve the phone from the pocket of his pants.

"Yeah," he said.

"I need you to get here immediately. A female was captured by Doomers earlier tonight, and a male was savagely mauled."

Fuck, how the hell did that happen? Aren't immortal females supposed to be impossible to detect?

"I'm on my way." Andrew clicked the phone off and pulled on his pants without bothering to find his boxers.

"I have to go." When a quick glance produced only one sock, he decided to forgo those too and pushed his bare feet into his shoes.

"What happened?" Nathalie sat up in bed, clutching the comforter to her breasts.

He grabbed his shirt and shrugged it on while leaning to give her a quick kiss. "It's work related. I can't talk about it."

"Oh." She let out a relieved breath. "I thought something happened to someone in your family.

With a grimace, Andrew bent down to retrieve his jacket, electing not to respond and saving himself another unnecessary lie. Because in this case work and family were one and the same. He considered himself part of the clan—albeit not a fully-fledged member yet—and each of its members a relative.

21

SEBASTIAN

As Sebastian maneuvered his Explorer into a tight parking spot in the club's lot, his cellphone went off. Damn, he hoped it wasn't the attorney canceling their assignation for tonight. After a miserable week of whipping and fucking inferior specimens, he was all juiced up for her. He was looking forward to a satisfying session with his favorite sub.

But glancing at the display, he was relieved to see that it wasn't the attorney or the club's coordinator, but one of his men. Except, why the hell was the idiot calling him? The standard protocol was for the men to direct any and all inquiries to either Robert or Tom, and if they in turn deemed it important, one of them would call Sebastian.

The breach of protocol was highly unusual.

For a moment, he considered ignoring the call and letting it go to voicemail. After all, he had a dungeon room reserved for the next ninety minutes, and he hated to cut it short even by a few. Whatever the guy needed could probably wait until after the session was over.

Or maybe not. In any case, he'd better find out or spend the whole time wondering about it instead of enjoying this long awaited session.

He shifted the gear to park, but left the engine running to answer the call. "This better be good, Rupert," he barked. It might have been his agitation, but Sebastian couldn't help the passing thought that the name the guy had chosen for himself was ridiculous. Was anyone else born in the second half of the twentieth century still named Rupert?

"This is better than good, boss. We have a first class surprise for you." There was some snorting in the background, and from the sound of it Rupert and his comrades were calling from inside a moving vehicle.

"Just tell me what it is. I don't have time for games."

"We've snatched an immortal female, and we have her here in the car with us. We are on our way back to base."

I'll be damned.

His assignation all but forgotten, Sebastian threw the gearshift into reverse, backed out of the spot, and did a fast K-turn, sending the vehicle into a controlled skid that had its premium tires squalling. The huge SUV tilted precariously for a split second before righting itself, and Sebastian stomped on the accelerator, flying into the street of the commercial park that was mercifully deserted at this time of night.

"How?" Turning right to head back to base, he floored the gas pedal.

"She and a male were outside the club we were sent to scope. They were smoking pot in the parking lot." Rupert's snort was accompanied by others in the background.

"Do you have both?" Getting on the freeway, Sebastian forced himself to slow down to a lawful speed limit. The last thing he needed was to get pulled over by the cops for speeding.

"No, sir. There was a struggle, and the guy didn't make it. We left him there and took the female."

Morons.

Sebastian's grip on the steering wheel tightened. "Venom overdose?"

"Yes, sir. And there was not much left of his throat either. Sorry about that."

Well, he couldn't be too angry with the team that had brought him an immortal female. Hell, he couldn't believe they had actually done it. "Are you sure she is an immortal? It's not easy to tell."

"She fought like a wildcat, much stronger than a human female, and she is a soft and plump little thing—not some big muscular woman."

"Did you touch her?" He was going to kill any of them who'd dared. This one was his.

"No, sir. Only to subdue her and tranquilize her with venom."

"Good. Is she awake?"

"No, sir. She's still out."

Sebastian detected a note of worry in the guy's tone.

"Is she breathing?"

"Yes, sir."

"Then she is fine. How far away from base are you?"

"Another half an hour, sir."

"I'm on my way, but until I get there, lock her up in one of the rooms in the basement."

"Yes, sir."

He was about to click off when it occurred to him that the men expected to hear some praise, which they rightfully deserved. It was the first time since the cataclysm, as far as he knew, that an immortal female had been captured. "Excellent job, men. I'll see to it myself that you're all handsomely rewarded."

"Thank you, sir."

Sebastian ended the call and then dialed the club's coordinator. "Listen, something came up, and I can't make it tonight. Send my apologies to my partner and tell her that if she can find a substitute she is free to use the room I've reserved. I know you'll charge me for it anyway." He clicked off with a smile, feeling good about his magnanimous gesture. His attorney would be disappointed that he didn't show up, and as he had no problem with her playing with others, offering her the use of the room for free was his way of making it up to her.

Driving on the freeway that was still busy even at this late hour, Sebastian shook his head as he considered his good fortune. He still couldn't believe that there would be an immortal female waiting for him in his basement.

This was something every immortal male dreamed about and wished for. An immortal female represented a future, a chance of having immortal offspring, sons who would live as long as he did, sons he could train, sons he could impart his legacy to. The way Losham had done with him. In this, his uncle by blood and adoptive father was a superb example. If Sebastian did his job even half as well as his father had done, the sons he would raise would mature to be incredible men.

Frankly, though, this wasn't what had him excited. Sebastian had never dreamed of becoming a father, or of having a mate. But he did crave having an indestructible toy, which was exactly what an immortal female was. No matter what he did to her, no matter how severely he would beat her, she would heal, and she would heal fast. There would be no residual damage, no scarring, and by the next day she would be as good as new and ready for another session.

22

KIAN

"Tell me again what happened, George, slowly this time," Kian said as patiently as he could. The guy was so distraught that he was barely coherent, and yet he'd adamantly refused to leave his friend's side and have this done in another room. Watching Bridget working on Ben, who was hanging onto life by a thread, sure as hell wasn't helping to calm George down.

With a practically nonexistent heartbeat, it was a wonder George had realized that Ben was still alive when he'd found him. Though Kian suspected that the guy hadn't known that at the time and had brought Ben to Bridget because he'd had no idea what else to do.

With a shaky hand, George brought the cup of water Kian had handed him to his mouth and took a sip. Some of it trickled from the corners of his mouth, and he wiped it with the sleeve of his shirt as he put the glass away. Sucking in a ragged breath, he looked at Kian with eyes that were red-rimmed and misted with tears. "I need to go to the bathroom for a minute," he said.

Poor kid, probably needed some time to collect himself, time Kian couldn't allow him while the safety of the whole clan was on the line. Still, a couple of minutes wouldn't make a difference.

"Go ahead, but don't delay."

Damn, he should've brought Syssi with him. It wasn't that he lacked compassion for the guy, it was just that providing comfort wasn't something Kian did well, while Syssi found it as natural as breathing. On the other hand, seeing the damage that had been done to Ben would probably freak her out.

That was why Kian hadn't told her where he was going, just that he needed to check on something. She'd given him a suspicious look, but he'd played it cool, and she seemed to buy his nonchalant attitude. But now that Ben's torn neck was no longer gruesomely displayed, but neatly wrapped with bandages, he could have her join them.

Kian pulled out his phone and texted Syssi. *If you are done with your bath, come down to Bridget's clinic. I need your help.*

Hopefully, his short message conveyed urgency without causing anxiety. Perhaps he should've worded it differently...Not that it would have helped. Syssi was going to be mad at him for not telling her right away as he had promised. Damn, he had no doubt that someone like the smooth-talking Onegus would've known how to say this in a way that would've sounded perfectly reasonable to her. Kian, on the other hand, tended to offend people with his gruff delivery, and a determined expression that was often mistaken for impatience or even anger.

With a curse, Kian ran his fingers through his hair. There were big gaps in his education, the most glaring one being his deficient communication skills, the other being lack of emotional intelligence, or whatever they called the ability to provide solace and emotional support to another. In his defense, all this touchy-feely mumbo jumbo was the product of recent decades, while he was an ancient relic from a time where thinking like that would've gotten people killed.

But finding excuses for his shortcomings wasn't going to fix them. Problem was, at his advanced age, Kian doubted he had it in him to change or learn new skills. And really, as a leader, his job was to find people to perform tasks he was no good at instead of him trying to excel at everything. As hard as it was to admit, especially to someone with his enormous ego, it just wasn't possible. Onegus would've been a better choice to handle George's interrogation, but Kian had sent him to the crime scene to investigate. The only other Guardian available at the moment was Bhathian, whose grumpy attitude was the opposite of what was needed.

Kian's phone buzzed with Syssi's return message. *Getting dressed, be there in a minute.*

Regrettably, George came back at the same time Kian finished reading the text, which meant that until Syssi made it to the clinic, he would have to do his best with what little skills he had.

The guy glanced at his unconscious friend and sighed. With slumped shoulders, George shuffled to the chair he'd been sitting on before. Frankly, the sigh he'd let out had sounded more like a whimper, embarrassing for a grown man, and more so for an immortal who was training to become a Guardian. Obviously, the guy didn't have what it took.

Nevertheless, under the circumstances, he was doing his best.

Kian walked over to him and patted his shoulder awkwardly. "He is going to be okay, and he probably owes you his life."

George nodded, his back straightening a notch. "I guess you're right. But they took Carol, and I wasn't there to help her." He slumped again, dropping his head into his hands.

"Are you sure they've taken her? Maybe she escaped and is hiding?"

George shook his head. "I saw her purse on the ground. I didn't pick it up because I was desperate to save Ben. I tied my shirt around his neck to try and just keep everything together." He shuddered. "Fates, it looked as if his head was barely attached to what was left of his neck, and that at any moment that last piece would tear and he would be gone. The purse was the last thing on my mind as I carried him to the car while trying to keep his head immobile."

"How come you guys weren't together?"

George winced. "They went out to smoke, while I stayed inside. After more than twenty minutes passed and they didn't come back, I started to worry and went looking for them. When I couldn't find them, I checked to see if Carol's car was still there, thinking that maybe they'd ditched me. You know, played a nasty joke on me. Or perhaps they ran out of pot and went looking for more. I really started panicking when I found her Prius still parked at the lot. I started running around, hoping I'd find them hiding in some dark corner, sharing a joint. That's how I stumbled upon Ben. The block wall separating the parking lot from the house on the other side was casting shadows on the bushes growing next to it. I would've missed his body lying crumpled in those bushes if not for his white Converses. They reflected the little light coming from the floodlight attached to the back wall of the club."

A sob escaped George's throat, and he turned his face away. Kian patted his shoulder again. "You should get some rest. You can lie down on the cot in the other room and leave the door open. I don't think I have any more questions for you. If you happen to remember anything else, no matter how trivial, come find me in Bridget's office."

His face still turned the other way, George nodded.

Kian walked over to Bridget. "Let me know the moment Ben wakes up. And if you can do anything to hasten it, please do. I don't need to tell you what's at stake."

She regarded him with her smart eyes. "Are you going to order an evacuation?"

"I don't think I have a choice. I can't expect Carol to hold off for long."

"I need to stabilize him first."

"I know."

A gentle knock on the door announced Syssi, and Kian opened the way for her. She was trying to put on a brave face for him, but the strong scent of despair coming from her told him that Bhathian must've already updated her on what was going on.

"Is he going to make it?' she asked, her bottom lip quivering.

"Yes, he is. It's not easy to end the life of an immortal. As long as there is a tiniest of sparks, he'll live." Kian pulled Syssi into a hug and squeezed tight, grateful that she was safe, that he was holding her, and that no one was going to take her away from him. Fates. Until now, he hadn't really internalized the shockingly devastating turn of events.

A female had been captured by Doomers.

A female he knew personally, a female whose face he would be seeing every time he closed his eyes until he freed her. Because he knew that he would move heaven and earth to get her out of the Doomers' clutches.

But first, he had to safeguard the rest of the clan, which meant relocating everyone residing in the keep, as well as anyone who had ever been in contact with Carol.

Luckily, he was a paranoid bastard and had a contingency plan for something exactly like this happening.

23

ANDREW

*A*s Andrew arrived at the keep, he had no idea where he was supposed to go. Kian hadn't told him where he was holding the meeting. Not wanting to bother the boss, he dialed Bhathian's number instead. An emergency meeting would no doubt include every Guardian available.

"Yeah," Bhathian answered.

"I'm already in the building, but I don't know where the meeting is held."

"Bridget's office."

"I'm on my way."

So the male had been brought in, and Bridget was taking care of him. This could be the only reason for having the meeting in her office.

Crap, he wasn't ready to face her yet. This was going to be awkward.

Fuck, what was he doing? Worrying about facing his ex-non-girlfriend while the whole clan was in turmoil? A female had been abducted by the fucking Doomers, and this time not by someone like Dalhu who had treated Amanda with the utmost respect, but by males who would do horrific things to her.

Getting face to face with Bridget would be fine. They were both adults, and they'd already said their piece to each other over the phone. This couldn't be much worse. Unless, she still had feelings for him...

Nah, the whole thing had been nothing more than two lonely people scratching each other's itch. Problem was, the scratching had been quite intense. It would be tough to talk to Bridget and not picture her naked with her face soft and relaxed in a post orgasmic bliss.

Fuck, get a hold of yourself, Spivak. You're a grown man who is in love with an amazing woman and is about to get married. You can be friends with an ex-lover and not imagine her naked just because you know how she looks without clothes. You're going to show her the utmost respect even if it kills you.

Thank God, Bridget wasn't in her office when he got there, and the small room was bursting at the seams with the four large men—Kian and three of the

Guardians. If more were coming, they would have to move this meeting out to the hallway.

"Andrew." Kian waved him in. "I was just about to start the briefing. The victim is still unconscious, so all we have is George's report, which isn't much. Apparently, Carol and Ben went outside the club to smoke, and when they didn't return, George went out looking for them. He found Ben slumped in the alley behind the parking lot of the club, unconscious and with half of his throat torn out. All that was left of Carol was her purse, which he saw lying on the ground. I think it's a forgone conclusion that they were attacked by Doomers and that the fuckers took Carol."

"We need to evacuate," Yamanu said.

Bhathian crossed his arms over his chest and looked at Kian. "Question is to where and who needs to go?"

"For now, we get everyone through the tunnel to the other building, block off the access to the underground from here, and leave only the human security detail that has no idea the underground exists."

What the hell was Kian talking about? Andrew searched his memory for any mention of another location. "What other building?"

"The high rise across the street is ours as well. We can access it through a tunnel that goes under the road. We left the six top floors vacant just for a situation like this, and the apartments are furnished. We can have everybody out in a couple of hours."

"You want me to get on it, boss?" Bhathian asked.

"Yeah, you and Arwel. Unfortunately, the two of you are experienced in herding people out of their homes."

Yamanu pushed away from the counter he was leaning against. "I can thrall the security people to forget about all of us."

Kian nodded. "Wait until everyone is out before you do it."

"Naturally."

The three left, leaving him and his brother-in-law alone in Bridget's office.

"What do you want me to do?" Andrew asked. It seemed that Kian had summoned him and the Guardians not to brainstorm the situation but to assign tasks.

"A couple of things. First, I want you here when Ben wakes up. You've done this before and know what to ask. Then I want you to find the Doomers' fucking base. I'm going to call every male who has ever served as a Guardian—locals as well as those who live in Scotland—and even the few who reside with my mother in Alaska. I'm going to assemble an army and storm that motherfucking base of theirs as soon as you find it."

Damn, as if it were so easy. Andrew rubbed his neck.

As Kian walked over to him and put a hand on his shoulder, Andrew fought the instinct to back away. Kian's eyes were glowing with that eerie luminescence he got going whenever he was in a murderous state of mind, like the one he was in now, and his fangs were starting to show.

"I want you to go all out on this. In less than an hour, I'll have a bank account in your name ready, with a couple of million in it. Recruit as many people as you can. Spare no expense on informants. I don't care who you have to bribe, and I don't even care if the money goes to drug and arms dealers if they have information to sell. The only thing I care about is getting Carol out and eliminating the threat to my people. I want every fucking Doomer in this local unit dead. Hell, I want all of them wiped off the face of the earth, but for now I'll be satisfied with those who came here to hunt us."

Damn. When he'd been part of a rescue operation like this in the past, Andrew's job had been the actual retrieval. All the ground work of accumulating information had been done for him by people who were experts in doing just that. What Kian was tasking him with was to be the mastermind who orchestrated it all.

Flattering, that's for sure, and challenging, but could he pull it off?

Perhaps, if he had months instead of days, he could learn on the job. But Carol didn't have this kind of time, and the stakes were too high for him to use this as a learning experience. He had to bring in the best in the field, someone who had masterminded dozens of these kinds of operations.

Fuck, Andrew never thought a day would come when he would consider working with his fucking old boss again. Turner was a prick. Emotionless, demanding. A guy who'd never had one single good word to say to anyone. But he was brilliant, and the best strategist Andrew had ever met. Not that he had met that many. Nevertheless, as much as he hated the guy, he also admired him.

Turner had retired a year before Andrew, and he wondered whether the guy was still working in the same field or chilling on a tropical beach and enjoying his retirement. But knowing Turner, he'd probably joined some civilian operation and was making tons of dough, masterminding corporate espionage and takeovers. In Andrew's humble and unprofessional opinion, Turner was borderline sociopath, which meant the guy couldn't enjoy anything, let alone something like chilling on a beach.

Shaking his head, Andrew made the decision to seek his old boss out. God, he'd hoped never to see that SOB again, and now he was planning on recruiting him for this mission.

Kian eyed Andrew suspiciously. "Is there a problem? Am I asking too much of you? You need to tell me now."

"It is, but only because of the urgency. If I had more time, I could find the right people for the job, make a good plan, and eventually figure out how to coordinate everything. When I was involved with hostage retrieval, another department was in charge of gathering information, and yet another did the reconnaissance. My old boss, Turner, orchestrated the whole thing. He had done it so many times that he could do this sleepwalking. If I can get him to help us, there is no one better for this. He is perfect for the job. Turner retired a year before me, and I believe his contacts and informants are still active. Problem is, I have no idea how hard it will be to find him. But assuming I manage, there is the issue of telling him the truth about what we are dealing with. The bastard is good at keeping secrets, but I know you have a problem with involving humans."

Kian took a few moments to think it over, then shook his head. "I'm breaking all kinds of my own rules here, but I'm sick and tired of our old tactics. I don't want to cower and hide anymore, I don't want to wait anxiously for the Doomers to make their next move. This time, we bring the battle to them, and I don't care what it takes. Do it. Find that Turner guy and bring him here. Is he for sale?"

"I'm sure he is. And if not for the money, he'll do it for the fun of it. The guy was one hundred percent dedicated to the work. No other interests, no wife, no girlfriend, a complete loner. Turner lived the job. We used to joke that after being forced to retire, he probably jumped off the nearest bridge."

"Let's hope he didn't. We need him."

24

DALHU

"So, where are we moving to?" Dalhu asked Kian as he started wrapping Anandur's half done portrait in brown paper.

"Just across the street. But Carol doesn't know that we own it. In fact, we own half of the high rise buildings on this block, and I have vacant and furnished apartments in each of them."

"Smart. But what happens the next time your location is compromised? You can't keep evacuating your people like this. Where are you going to move them the next time?"

Instead of answering, Kian walked up to the bar, grimaced at the modest selection, and reached for the Chivas.

"Anyone want anything?"

"Can you fix me a gin and tonic?" Syssi joined him and wrapped her arm around his waist.

"Amanda? Anything for you?" Kian called.

From the moment she'd learned about the evacuation, Amanda had been busy packing her wardrobe, or rather supervising Onidu as he filled suitcase after suitcase with stuff she deemed absolutely necessary. Which was most of her closet.

"Gin and tonic sounds great!"

"Dalhu?"

"I'm good." He could drink later—after he was done packing the most important stuff, which were all of his creations. Not only were the paintings and drawings the only things of value he owned, but they all depicted clan members. In the event that the Doomers actually infiltrated the building, it would be a disaster if the portraits fell into their hands.

Kian handed Syssi her drink and the one he'd made for Amanda. She took the two tumblers and headed toward Amanda's closet.

DARK WARRIOR'S PROMISE

Drink in hand, Kian walked over to Dalhu. "If I play this right, there won't be a next time."

"What's the plan?" Dalhu wondered if Kian trusted him enough to share.

"A war. I'm sick of running, and I'm not about to let them keep Carol. No one deserves the hell they'll put her through."

With only seven Guardians, one of them a female, Kian was deluding himself if he thought he could take on such a large contingent of Doomers. The Guardians were good, but not that good.

"You're somewhat short on warriors for that. But if you're going to do it, you can count me in." Dalhu didn't expect Kian to take him up on his offer, but he could hope. A good fight would release some of the pressure that had been building up inside him. His gym sessions with Anandur were good for taking off the edge, but they were no substitute for the rush of battle.

Shockingly, Kian nodded. "I can definitely use you. You know them, their weaknesses, their strengths, their style of warfare. And as for the Guardians, I've already started calling all of those who have left the force. I haven't had much luck convincing them to come back yet. Those I've spoken to have gotten too comfortable in their civilian lives. But Carol's capture is a game changer. Any Guardian who refuses the call to save a female from Doomers will lose face."

"How many are there?"

"I have over a hundred and fifty names on the list. If I can get one third of them to come back, we are good."

Probably. The Guardians could take on a force twice as big as theirs, or even more, and come out on top.

"It will take time, Kian. Time Carol doesn't have."

The guy's face twisted into a grimace. "Tell me something I don't know."

"Regardless, you need to find a better solution for your keep."

"If you have some bright ideas, I'm open to suggestions."

"I hate to bring him up, but Navuh solved this problem beautifully. The Doomers don't know where the island is, and the human pilots are under powerful compulsion not to reveal the location. That way, if a Doomer is captured, he can't lead anyone back to base." Dalhu finished wrapping his fourth portrait and propped it against the two others he'd already put next to the front door.

Kian rubbed his neck. "Problem is, my people work in the city. How am I going to shuffle them to and from work every day? Windowless busses? Have them blindfolded and blast music in the transport, so they don't hear anything from the outside? It's much easier to do with a plane. Without visuals or a compass, it is nearly impossible to tell where it is going."

"Yeah, I guess you're right."

As Dalhu picked up another portrait to wrap, Amanda and Syssi entered the living room. He lifted his head to glance at his woman, prepared for the impact of her beauty that never failed to deliver a punch to his gut, a zap to his heart, and a hardening to his shaft. It hadn't diminished even an iota since the first time he'd seen her, and he was certain it never would.

"I have an idea," she said, bracing her elbow on her arm and swishing the ice cubes in her gin and tonic.

"About what?" Kian asked.

"How to solve the problem of the keep's location and the commute to work. It's not cheap, or easy, but it may work."

Kian chuckled. "As if any of your ideas are ever cheap, or easy."

"Ha, ha, ha." She rolled her eyes. "Remember the cabin Dalhu and I stayed in after he'd kidnapped me?"

"As if I could ever forget." Kian's face twisted in an angry scowl. Apparently, he still held a grudge over what had happened there. He was entitled, though. To protect Dalhu, Amanda had attacked her own brother, tearing out a chunk of Kian's hair while riding his back buck naked. Not a fond memory for the guy, that's for sure.

"Anyway, the location is perfect. With some grading work, the flat area can be significantly enlarged. The mountain it sits on isn't very steep. We can build a little city of bungalows, buy a few more helicopters, and shuttle whoever needs to get to work in the city to one of the rooftops we own."

Kian snorted. "And what? Have some thralled humans pilot the crafts? This is not something we do, Amanda."

"Of course not, silly. We can use the Odus—like Mother does."

Kian opened his mouth to say something, then closed it, then opened it again, frowned, and closed it again. "It might be doable. I'm just thinking aloud here, so you are all welcome to jump in and correct me, or offer better ideas. Let's say we build this base on the mountain. If we use cars to travel to and from the place, the extra traffic may attract attention, but the same is true if we use helicopters. Aircraft are monitored by humans, and unlike Annani and her people, who seldom leave her place, our people will need daily transport. On top of that, the place is too far away for ground transportation."

"How about a tunnel? Like on Passion Island? You land in one place, but then travel by car to another," Dalhu suggested.

Kian shook his head. "Too involved and time-consuming for daily commute."

"Could a decoy work?" Syssi asked.

"What do you mean?"

"I once saw a science fiction movie, where they had a huge camouflaged door leading into a side of a mountain, and the helicopters flew right in. We can have something like this, and build a fake landing pad and a helicopter hanger nearby as a decoy."

Kian raked his fingers through his hair. "It might work. We can have William design and install something that will introduce a momentary interference, like a short glitch, to hide the fact that the helicopter landed in a different place. But the problem with this whole idea is the insane cost. On top of those we already have, for that kind of money I can build several luxurious high rise buildings in downtown Los Angeles, with connecting tunnels to the crypt and the underground structure. The buildings are designed in a way that access to the underground can be closed off or even eliminated with no one any the wiser."

"In that case, why not relocate everything to the underground?" Dalhu asked. "It will eliminate the need to pack up and move every time there is a breach in security. All you'll need to do is change the entry point."

Syssi shuddered. "I don't want to live without windows. It's okay for a few days, but not all of the time."

Amanda wrapped her arm around Syssi's shoulders. "Yeah, me neither. I love the idea of living in the mountains, with fresh air and beautiful views, but Kian is right; too complicated and too expensive."

"Wonders never cease. Are you agreeing with me? Do you have a fever?"

"Well, apart from the costs, how are we going to hide the massive building project? And what about the workers and suppliers? When we build in downtown Los Angeles, there is nothing peculiar about it, just another developer building for profit. But out there? Too many questions will be asked."

"If this was the only problem, it could be solved. I can bring a big construction crew from China or Mexico to do the work, and then thrall all of them before sending them back home. And as to passersby, I can have Brandon produce a movie *on location* as a cover-up."

"So the only problem is money?" Amanda asked. "We have plenty."

"No, it's not only the money. It's the whole thing. Here, we are in the center of the city. If I need Andrew, I call him, and he comes over, and if I want to buy my wife a present, I don't need to plan an expedition, I just hop in my car and go. We can go to restaurants, movies, and so on. Mountain air and nice views sound good for a vacation, not a permanent living arrangement."

Dalhu shrugged. "It works on Passion Island. No one is complaining about the living conditions there."

Kian shook his head. "That's because there are so many people, and only some of them are coming and going on missions. Besides, between the Doomers, the hookers, and the service personnel, not to mention the tourists, the population probably numbers in the tens of thousands—mortals and immortals. We have only a few hundred immortals, that's it. Something like this can't work for us."

Amanda sighed. "I wish there was a third alternative. Something in between these two extremes."

"You can think about it while you pack. The sooner we are all out of here the better. Syssi and I are already done, and I suggest you hurry up, Amanda. You don't need to pack your whole wardrobe."

"But what if the Doomers come in and destroy it?"

"Then you buy a new one. When was the last time you wore the same outfit twice?"

"Fine." Amanda huffed and stormed out of the room.

Kian glanced at the remaining portraits, then at those that were already wrapped and ready to go. "Let me help you with these. It's taking you too long." He grabbed one of the canvases and headed toward the roll of brown paper.

"Thank you, I appreciate it," Dalhu helped him pull a large piece of paper and tore it off the roll.

"I'll go help Amanda," Syssi said, kissing her husband's cheek before heading toward the master closet.

If not for the dire circumstances, Dalhu could've enjoyed this. It almost felt like he was finally part of the family.

25

ANDREW

Alone in Bridget's office, Andrew paced around while waiting for Ben to wake the hell up, which could happen in the next couple of minutes, or the next day, or even longer. Trouble was, it was time he couldn't afford to waste.

If he had his laptop with him, he could dig into his old boss's file, or at least the parts his security clearance would allow to unlock. He had no doubt that the majority of Turner's file required the highest level of clearance, several degrees above Andrew's. Still, there was a slight chance that one of the old veterans, those who had served with Turner since the beginning of his career in the unit, had kept in touch with him over the years and would know where to find him.

Hopefully, the guy hadn't been such a fucking sociopath when he was younger and actually had made some friends.

Question was, whether Andrew's contact list included the phone numbers of the few old timers that had been still serving during his time. After being forced to retire, he hadn't called anyone other than Jack and Rodney, and he couldn't remember who he'd added to his phone's short list of contacts and who he had not.

Damn, as if he needed another reminder that his brain was aging along with his body. He used to have an impeccable memory.

With a curse, Andrew fished out his phone from the inside pocket of his jacket and started scrolling through the names.

The first one he recognized was Rafael's, or Rafi as they'd used to call him. But when he dialed the guy's number, all he got was the annoying notification that the number he had reached was no longer in service.

Damn.

The only other one on the list hadn't heard from Turner in more than ten years.

That left Andrew's buddies. He sent both of them a message. It was a long shot, but it was worth a try. Maybe they knew someone who knew someone who knew someone. It didn't hurt to cover all the bases.

With that done, Andrew couldn't think of anything else he could do while waiting, and decided it was time to grow a set and face Bridget. It had to be done sooner or later, and there was no better time than right now.

"Come in," she said when he knocked quietly on the door.

As he pushed it open, Andrew was impressed by the sophisticated equipment of the intensive care unit Bridget was keeping Ben in. Not that he knew anything about medical equipment, but he'd spent time in enough ICUs to recognize state of the art when he saw it.

"Hi, Bridget. How is your patient doing?"

"He'll live."

"With you as his doctor, I'm sure he will. But I need to know when to expect him to wake up. If it's in the next hour, I'll stay. Otherwise, my time can be better utilized doing other things."

She shrugged. "I know. And I wish I could give you a definite answer. But frankly, what do you expect to learn from him when he wakes up? With most of his throat missing, it will take Ben weeks of recovery until he'll be able to talk, and I doubt he'll be strong enough to write answers to your questions."

"Do you have a tablet here? Touching a finger to a screen doesn't require much effort if we hold it up for him."

"Yeah, I do."

"Good."

Bridget turned around, pretending to focus on the monitors tracking Ben's vitals whose output hadn't spiked or dropped even once.

Damn, this was awkward. What the hell was he supposed to say now?

That he was sorry? Maybe ask her about the guy she'd met at Julian's graduation?

She beat him to it. "This shouldn't be this awkward. I want us to be friends."

"I'd like that. But I can't help feeling guilty about ending it the way I did. You deserve better than a phone call."

Bridget tugged on her ponytail, readjusting the rubber band that held it secured at the top of her head. "You would've been right to feel like a heel if I wasn't guilty of even worse. You called me before you made your move." She smiled with just one side of her mouth. "I was already halfway there. When Daniel started flirting with me, I didn't do anything to discourage him, even though I felt like a slut for actually encouraging him. It's just that the chemistry between us was off the charts. I couldn't resist. Hell, I didn't want to."

Phew, this was a huge relief. He should be just as gracious. "I should write this Daniel a thank-you note. If not for him, I would've felt like a scumbag. Because I had a similar reaction to Nathalie. There was no way I could've waited for you to come back before putting the moves on her."

"Is she your one?" Bridget pinned him with a set of smart blue eyes.

He nodded. "Without a doubt."

"Do you want to tell me about her?"

"Are you sure you're up to it? Maybe you should tell me about Daniel first."

The smile that spread over her lovely face was as good an indicator as anything she might have said about her feelings for the guy. "He is the head intern at the hospital where Julian is about to start his internship. He is thirty-one years old, about your height, but not as strongly built, and he is absolutely brilliant. I think I fell for his intellect first, or maybe it was his macabre sense of humor. Probably both. Not that the physical attraction wasn't enough, but I've been powerfully attracted to guys before." She blushed and looked down at her hands.

"I was to you." Her whisper sounded like an apology. "With Daniel, though, I felt an affinity. It's hard to describe, but it kind of felt like I'd known him forever and had finally found my way back home. Strange, right?"

She chuckled, an embarrassed high-pitched sound. "It's fascinating, the power our hormones have over our lives. We think we are in control, and that we are making our own decisions, but we are not. We are ruled by powerful chemicals that regulate our moods, influence who we think we are in love with. Free will is an illusion."

Andrew shook his head. "You can't really believe this. I'm sure hormones are part of it, but we are more than the chemical interactions in our brain. Our thoughts and beliefs might be colored by them, but we retain at least some control over our reactions."

"Or do we?"

She still wasn't convinced.

"You said it yourself. You were attracted to Daniel physically, but that wasn't what caused you to fall for him. You fell for his sense of humor and quick mind. I'm not a scientist, but I don't think humor and intellect produce pheromones."

"Ha, but the joy of laughing at a joke and having an intelligent conversation might."

Andrew raised his hands in surrender. "I give up. You're incorrigible."

"Just messing with you. I'm not completely convinced it's only chemical reactions either." Bridget winked. "But this is a discussion for philosophers. I want to hear all about your woman. I told you about mine, now it's your turn to tell me about yours."

Where should he start? Did Bridget know about Nathalie being Bhathian's daughter? Kian and Syssi knew, and Bhathian hadn't asked them to keep it a secret, but should he assume that they told everyone?

Andrew pulled out his phone. "Can you give me a moment? I need to send a quick text first."

"Sure..." Bridget's brows formed an arch.

Fully aware of how peculiar his behavior must've seemed to her, Andrew turned around and texted Bhathian, asking if he could tell Bridget. It took only a few seconds for the guy's short reply text to arrive.

It's fine.

Turning around, he slipped the phone back into the inside pocket of his jacket. "Sorry about that, but I had to ask Bhathian's permission first."

Her brows arched even higher. "Bhathian?"

"It's a long story, but Nathalie is Bhathian's daughter. Her mother had told him she was pregnant and then disappeared. He's been searching for her for years, not sure if he had a child or not. When he heard about my connections, he asked for my help. That's how I met her."

"Wow, what a story. Does she know?"

Andrew shook his head. "She doesn't even know her adoptive father is not her real one. And she thinks Bhathian is just a friend. But what's an even bigger story than Bhathian having a daughter is that we suspect her mother is an immortal. Unfortunately, the woman pulled another disappearing act, so we can't know for sure. Not until we find her."

"How is it possible?"

"We don't know. But going by Nathalie's account and a fairly recent picture, the woman hasn't aged even a little in thirty years."

"So Nathalie might be a Dormant?"

"Yes."

"Are you going to try to activate her?"

"I can't."

"I know that. But someone else can do it."

"Over my dead body."

Bridget laughed. "How did I know you were going to say that?"

Andrew grimaced. "I have no idea."

She patted his shoulder. "Right. So I guess you'll be attempting the transition after all."

"It seems so. But I want to find her mother first. I don't want to take the risk unless I'm convinced Nathalie is a Dormant."

"Does she know you're searching for her mother?"

"Bhathian and I offered to help find her, and Nathalie is under the impression that we are working for some secret government agency."

"I wonder what gave her that impression?" Bridget said mockingly.

Andrew tugged on his tie to loosen it. "I hate the fucking lies. But for now, I have no choice."

Bridget sighed. "Yeah, I know what you mean. Daniel thinks I'm Julian's sister. I'm going to have a tough time explaining things if he decides to come visit me in Los Angeles."

It occurred to him then that Bridget's guy lived thousands of miles away, which was probably a good thing. "I was under the impression that you guys didn't do relationships. So I assumed that after you said your goodbyes you thralled him to forget you."

"Usually yes. But females have a little more leeway. It's not like I need to thrall him each time we have sex." She chuckled. "Aside from my stamina, there is nothing that suggests I'm anything other than a human female. I really like Daniel. I want to see him again."

"Well, I guess it's okay given the distance. It's not like you guys are going to get together often enough for him to notice anything."

Andrew knew there was more to the story when Bridget began fidgeting with her stethoscope.

"Daniel is applying for positions in hospitals over here. And with his excellent record and a stellar recommendation from his chief of staff, he'll have no trouble finding one. I just don't know what I'll do once he moves here. It's difficult to keep the lies going even when he is on the other side of the continent."

"Tell me about it. I'm not even an immortal, and I'm forced to lie to the woman I love. With my job, I should be used to this, but keeping secrets that have to do with national security is easy. What I hate are the lies I have to tell

Nathalie about my family. I had to come up with all kinds of contrived excuses as to why I haven't introduced her to my sister and her husband yet."

"Why didn't you? It's not like they have Immortal stamped on their foreheads. We interact with humans on a regular basis, and it's fine."

"I don't know. Syssi could pass for a human easily. After all, she was one until recently. But Kian is a different story. The dude is too good-looking for his own good."

Bridget laughed. "Are you jealous of your brother-in-law, Andrew?"

"I'm not. But I know Nathalie is going to gape at him like a fool. She will not be able to help it. And it's going to drive me crazy."

Bridget shook her head and patted his back. "You've got it bad, buddy."

"I know."

26

NATHALIE

"Good morning, Vlad." Nathalie opened the back door to let the guy in. She had gotten so used to him that most days his appearance no longer shocked her. But today, in addition to his usual all-black garb, the traces of black eyeliner around his eyes made his pale and gaunt face look more vampiric than ever.

"Good morning, Nathalie." He ducked his head as he entered, then closed the door behind him.

With a frown, she looked up at the top of his head. Had the boy grown a few inches since yesterday? Because as tall as he was, Vlad had never had a problem clearing the doorway before. But obviously, it was absurd, and the only reasonable explanation was that he was wearing heeled shoes. A glance at his feet confirmed her assumption. Vlad's black-leather boots reached midway to his calves, sported a row of metal buckles on their sides, and had platforms at least two inches high.

Good God, what was he thinking?

If any of the customers ventured into the kitchen and saw this cross between Dracula and Frankenstein's monster, they would run away screaming.

Damn, how was she going to tell the kid to tone down his style without offending him? Maybe she should just let it go and hope no one peeked into the kitchen.

Oh, Nathalie, you are so sweet.

"Sage?"

"Did you say something?" Vlad asked while tying the apron's belt around his narrow midriff.

She waved a hand. "Just ignore me. Sometimes I talk to myself." Heck, if she could tolerate a vampire lookalike in her kitchen, Vlad could live with a boss who talked to herself.

He shrugged. "Just let me know when you're talking to me."

"No problem. I'm going upstairs for a few minutes. You're okay here by yourself?"

"You know I am."

"Fine." Yes she did, but out of courtesy, she had to ask.

Taking the stairs up to her apartment, she whispered, "Where were you? I didn't hear from you for days. I thought you were gone."

Gone where?

"How the hell should I know? To the great beyond? Heaven? Hell?"

I'm sorry I had you worried. It's difficult for me to estimate the passage of time. It's not the same as it is for the living.

"I wasn't worried. More like relieved."

Oh...

He sounded offended.

"Don't get me wrong. I like you, Sage. You seem like a very nice guy. But hearing you in my head is not normal. I wish one day to be free of the voices. So every time a few days pass without intrusions, I get my hopes up."

I'm truly sorry.

Shit, Sage sounded as if he was on the verge of tears. "It's okay. It's not your fault. So what have you been up to?"

I was trying to figure out who I was before.

"Any luck?"

I must've done programming. I know how to do it. I can even ghost into a system and program it from the inside. I can influence electric pulses. If you want, I can type a message on your laptop's screen. But it has to be on.

Now he sounded excited, even proud. "Maybe later you can show me. But I have to get back to work."

I'll try to come back later today. But if I overshoot it will probably be tomorrow. And as to the kid, tell him he's got the rock star look nailed, but that it is not a look appropriate for a day job.

"You are good at this. You sure you were a programmer? Those guys' social skills are usually not that great."

I'm sure. Bye, Nathalie.

Sage was so nice and easygoing that she almost didn't mind his sporadic intrusions. After all, he always left when she asked him to, and his advice was actually useful.

When she returned to the kitchen, Nathalie leaned against the worktable where Vlad was busy cutting dough into little triangles and rolling them into croissants.

"Vlad, honey, I need to tell you something."

He paused, lifting his head to look at her with a worried expression on his face. "Did I do something wrong?"

"No, of course not. You're wonderful. And this outfit you are wearing is so cool, for a rock star, but not for a baker."

He glanced down at his boots. "I see."

"It's not just the boots. You have traces of makeup around your eyes. I know it's from last night's performance, but you need to take it off completely."

"I do?" He rubbed at his eyes. "I thought I got it all off."

She shook her head. "Go to the bathroom and see for yourself. You probably rubbed your eyes, and the little that was left got smeared all over. Happens to me every time I put eyeliner on."

Vlad rushed off and returned a few minutes later with an almost clean face. "I have a pair of sneakers in my car. I should go and put them on. The boots are cool, but they are not comfortable."

"Go, I'll finish this batch." Well, that went smoothly. *Thank you, Sage.*

You've never thanked me, even when I saved your little butt from getting in trouble.

Damn, she almost nicked her finger with the knife. What was it? The national ghost appreciation day or something?

"Tut, you bastard, you scared me. I thought you were gone for good."

First of all, I'm not a bastard. My parents were married when I was born, unfortunately, not happily. It was an arranged marriage. Not to say that all arranged marriages are doomed to fail, some work out beautifully, but I digress.

"Why are you still in my head?"

I wish I knew. Believe me, I want to go more than you want me gone. But it's like this single strand of hair tethers me to you, and it refuses to break. I think I'm supposed to teach you how to block the others before I'm allowed to leave.

She waved the hand holding the cutting knife as if he could see it. "Be my guest. I'd love to learn this trick."

Yeah, problem is, I'm not sure how you're supposed to do it. But I have a few suggestions that you may try.

Great, the blind leading the blind. "Shoot."

Imagine a door, one with heavy locks and a key that only you have. The next time Sage intrudes, imagine slamming the door in his face and locking it.

Nathalie winced. "That's terribly rude. Sage is nice. I'll feel awful about treating him like that."

Fine. I guess that's why you haven't been practicing blocking him like I've told you to do. If you like him so much, let him in on what you're trying to do. And if he is really so great, he'll help you figure it out.

"Oh yeah? How come you didn't offer yourself for me to practice on?"

You've got a point. Okay. I'm going to ghost out and then ghost back in. The moment you feel me coming, slam the door.

She frowned. "Most times I feel nothing until you start talking in my head. How am I supposed to slam the door when you're already inside?"

Good point.

"Can I imagine kicking you out with a giant boot to your ass?"

Whatever works, sweetheart. Let's try it.

Weird, now that she paid attention, she actually felt him ghosting out. So why hadn't she felt him ghosting in?

Focusing all of her attention on Tut's reentry, Nathalie tried to determine whether she could detect any peculiar sensation before he made his presence known by speaking to her inside her mind.

Well, I'm here. Kick me out.

She realized that there had been a slight pressure before he spoke, but to stop him would be like trying to close the door on a gust of wind—too late because it was already inside.

So all that was left was to try and boot him out. Or conversely, isolate him in a virtual soundproof booth. Nathalie closed her eyes and imagined that Tut was inside a special room in her brain, a glass isolation chamber with a trapdoor. She commanded the door to slide down shut, trapping him inside the chamber, then shrank the whole thing and put it on a shelf of an imaginary bookcase.

Waiting, she expected Tut's cackling laugh or snarky remark, but all she heard was silence.

No way. She couldn't have done it on her first try. "Say something!"

There was no response.

Ugh, having a ghost trapped in her imaginary isolation chamber, displayed like some trinket on her virtual bookcase, was even more freaky than hearing him talk to her. Nathalie closed her eyes and imagined the little glass box with a little shrunken Tut inside it expanding. When it was back to its original size, she commanded the trap door to lift. "Come on, Tut, get out and talk to me."

Don't ever do that again! The great Tut sounded shaky.

"So it worked?"

Yeah, it worked. But I don't think you want a bunch of trapped ghosts in your head. Even if you can keep them silent.

"What if I use this as a threat? I can tell uninvited intruders to either get out or stay trapped forever in a little glass box."

I'm positive that this would do the trick. It was the most terrifying experience of my existence—including the time I woke up dead.

"I'm sorry. I didn't know it would be so bad for you."

Oh, Nathalie. You are indeed way too nice.

God, even Tut's compliments sounded like insults. "Is it your way of saying that I'm a pushover?"

One last piece of advice in case I manage to finally get out of here for good. Stop putting everyone's welfare before your own. You come first. Everyone and everything else comes second.

"I don't think I can do it. But thanks for the advice."

Farewell, sweet Nathalie. Hope to never see you again.

"Same here."

27

CAROL

Crap, what am I doing here?

As Carol opened her eyes, she was convinced that she had woken up in her old cell at the keep. Except, Ingrid must've done some decorating, because the little box of a room had pictures hanging on the walls, and Carol was lying on an actual bed with a headboard and footboard and not on a mattress on the floor.

Fates, she felt so spaced out. She must've really overdone it with the alcohol and the pot, and that was probably why she'd landed back in prison. Kian had warned her to watch it.

On second thought, they must've put her in a different cell, because there were two doors. Her old cell had only one. The bathroom area had been separated only by a partition. A quick glance confirmed that there was none here.

Which was worse. Because it meant that she was going to spend way more than a few days in the slammer this time.

But what had she done?

Had she been telling stories again?

Her memory was fuzzy, and she wasn't sure what had really happened and what had been a dream. There was a dim memory of being thrown over some guy's shoulder and carried away.

Boy, had she done more than pot?

It had been a while since she'd snorted, and even longer since she'd injected. Hopefully, she hadn't fallen off the wagon as the drunkards called it. But if she had, it must've been because someone had slipped it to her. She'd been good lately. Or as good as she could be.

Carol reached for the glass of water that someone had thoughtfully left for her on the nightstand and emptied it on a oner. Still thirsty, she looked around, hoping to find a pitcher or a bottle. There wasn't any in sight. Never mind, she could use the faucet in the bathroom. And anyway, now that she was thinking of water, she felt an urgent need to empty her bladder.

With her head spinning, it was a struggle to get vertical, and as she trudged toward the door leading to what she hoped was a bathroom, Carol was thankful for the small size of the room. Much easier to use the furniture and the walls for support when everything was in arm's reach.

Surprisingly, she found the bathroom kitted out for a female, with hairbrushes and a hair dryer, and an assortment of lotions and fragrances. There was even a fluffy white robe hanging on a hook, and on the floor below it, a pair of white terry slippers were still in their original packaging.

Nice. She didn't know they had cells dedicated to females now. Or maybe it was all for her, since she was obviously going to spend a lot of time here.

With a sigh, she took care of business, then stepped into the shower. The water pressure wasn't as good as she remembered, which was the only downside of this new prison cell compared to her old one.

She spent a lot of time in the shower. After all, it wasn't as if she had anything else to do. When she was finally done, Carol used the dryer to dry her hair, which wasn't a complicated affair since she just waved it around her head and let her curls take shape naturally. Some lotion on her face and her hands, a little spritz of fragrance on her pulse points, and she felt like a new woman. There was no makeup, but then she had no one to get pretty for.

Lying in bed and watching TV, if there was one, or reading a book, was all she had to look forward to for the foreseeable future.

Pushing the door open, Carol frowned as an unfamiliar scent reached her nose. Was there a male in her room?

"Hello, darling. Did you have a pleasant time in the shower?"

A gasp escaped her throat, and she jumped back, slamming the bathroom door closed. Her heart pounding like a jackhammer, she backed away until her ass hit the wall.

The handle turned, and the male pushed the door open unhurriedly, smiling a blood-chilling smile. "Don't be afraid, little rabbit. I'm not going to hurt you. Yet. I just want to talk." He extended his arm in invitation.

There was nowhere to go, and instinctively she knew that making him wait was a really bad idea. Placing her shaking hand in his palm, she let the Doomer lead her back to the room.

Because yeah, this Dorothy was for sure not in Kansas anymore.

He had her sit on the bed while he took the only chair. "What's your name, darling?" he asked in a most pleasant tone that she didn't buy for a second.

"Carol." She managed a hoarse whisper.

"My poor darling, I see that you're parched. I'll call someone to bring you a drink of water. Would you care for something to eat? I'm afraid our culinary selection is limited at the moment, but I'm working on procuring a chef."

She shook her head. "I'm not hungry."

"Nonsense. You must eat, at least a little something." He pulled out his phone. "Tom, could you please bring a pitcher of water, a glass of orange juice, and some fruit and crackers for Carol?"

She heard the other guy respond with a 'coming right up.'

The weird thing was that the Doomer appeared genuine in his concern for her well-being. Except, it did nothing to assuage her fear of him. He wasn't a big male, no more than six feet tall, maybe even an inch or two shorter than that, and although trim and muscular, he wasn't buff. He had a handsome face and a pleasant voice, and yet he scared the crap out of her.

"By the way, I'm Sebastian, Sebastian Shar, but you can call me Master."

Carol swallowed. She wasn't a submissive. In fact, she had a very low tolerance for pain. But she'd played the game before with men who were more interested in dominating than hurting her. As a courtesan, she had met her share of guys with deviant appetites, and she hadn't turned any away as long as they hadn't requested to tie her up. One on one and with nothing to restrain her, if things got out of hand, she could overpower a human male quite easily. Trouble was, this guy was an immortal male, a lot stronger than her, and she had a feeling he didn't play by the rules, nor was he interested in a mild game of domination.

There would be no safe words for her, no way out. Just pain.

A tear sliding down her cheek, she whispered. "Yes, Master."

"Smart girl. I see that we are going to get along splendidly."

28

SEBASTIAN

"Come in!" Sebastian called.

He wasn't surprised that Tom fulfilled his order so expeditiously. The guy probably couldn't wait to lay his eyes on the immortal female. Last night Tom hadn't been at the base when she'd been brought in, and Robert had been the lucky bastard who had made all the necessary arrangements for her.

As Tom came in with the tray, Carol raised a pair of pleading big blue eyes to the guy. Silly girl, there was no one here who would raise a finger to help her. She was completely at Sebastian's mercy.

Not that he had any.

Placing the tray on the nightstand, Tom leaned toward Carol, using the excuse to get close to the woman and take a sniff. The growl that started deep in Sebastian's throat had him hastily backing away.

"Would there be anything else, sir?"

Sir? Sebastian regarded Tom with a frown. Since when had the insolent bastard become so courteous? Was he mocking him?

The pungent scents of fear and despair wafting off Carol masked Tom's more subtle one, but with a little effort, Sebastian managed to isolate it. The guy was scared.

Good. Fear would keep him from getting any smart ideas.

Carol belonged to Sebastian, exclusively.

"No, that will be all, Tom. You're excused."

"Yes, sir." Tom gave a slight bow and got out of the room as fast as his short legs could carry him.

Carol released a barely audible sigh and let her head drop. She hadn't touched anything on the tray, not even the water. The girl seemed frozen in her pose, barely breathing.

Obviously, she'd figured out Sebastian's intentions for her and was terrified. Which meant that even though she'd known the proper response, she wasn't a submissive. She had probably dabbled her dainty little feet in the game once or twice, and the little knowledge she had was more harmful than complete ignorance.

Sebastian realized that he needed to back off if he didn't want to break her. After all, it wasn't as if there was a chance in hell another immortal female would fall into his lap anytime in the near or far future. He was one lucky son of a bitch to snag this one.

Thank you, Mortdh.

He still toyed with the idea that Carol could be much more than an indestructible toy. He could get her pregnant, she could give him a son, an immortal whom he would raise and groom for greatness the same way Losham had done for him.

"Drink your juice, Carol."

She shook her head but didn't dare look up at him.

With a sigh, he got up and sat on the bed beside her. She scooted away, but he grabbed her chin, gently but firmly, and tilted her head, so she was forced to face him. Her big teary eyes and trembling lip had no effect on him, and it didn't matter to him if she was putting on a show or not.

"When I tell you to do something, I expect to be obeyed immediately. And by immediately I mean instantly. I will not tolerate even a split second delay. Is that clear?"

She nodded quickly, her little chin moving up and down as much as his fingers allowed, and her beautiful blonde curls bouncing enticingly around her elvish face.

The girl was not only adorable but seemed trainable. He smiled at her and gently cupped her cheek. "Now, was it so hard, darling? It's very simple. Obedience will be rewarded, and disobedience will be punished."

Carol seemed to relax a little.

Sebastian reached for the glass of juice and handed it to her. "I want to see you drink the whole thing. Take your time, I don't want you to choke on it, but I want this glass empty before you put it down."

She nodded.

"Tsk, tsk. I allowed a nod once, but I don't consider it a proper response."

She whispered, "Yes, Master."

"Much better. Now drink up."

29

ANDREW

"Rodney, my man, I owe you big time." Andrew scribbled the number Rodney had given him on a piece of paper. "How the hell did you find the old bastard?"

"Remember Chris?" Rodney asked.

"The new recruit? Sure, how could I forget a guy with a big tattoo of a naked woman on his back? He started training a few months before I left."

"Yup." Rodney chuckled. "Betty Boop but with no clothes. I remembered him mentioning that he went to a military academy with Turner's son."

"I'll be damned. Turner has a son? I didn't even know that the dude was married."

"He wasn't. Apparently, Turner knocked up the guy's mom during freshman year in college. I called him up; his name is Douglas by the way. He and his old man are not close, but he gets to meet Turner twice a year. His mom married another guy, but with Turner paying support all those years and then for the academy, she insisted that they stay in touch. Long story short, that's how I've gotten Turner's private number."

"Thanks, and I mean it, I owe you."

There was a moment of silence before Rodney replied. "How about you buy me a drink, and we call it even? We haven't gotten together in ages. What's up with that?"

Damn. Rodney was right. Ever since Andrew had gotten involved with the clan, he had neglected his friends. The last time he'd seen them had been on Amanda's rescue mission, which of course they remembered nothing of. As far as they were concerned, it had never happened. The hefty sum in their bank accounts had been explained as payment for a job so secret that they'd agreed to get hypnotized to forget. Pretty damn close to the truth. "You're absolutely right. How about Monday after work? We can call Jake."

"Why not tonight?"

"Sorry, I've already made other plans."
"You've got yourself a girlfriend, Spivak?"
"Yeah."
"About time. So have fun tonight with your girl, and we'll talk again on Monday."
"Good deal."

As he ended the call, Andrew stuffed the piece of paper with Turner's number in his pocket, collected his car keys and headed out. Most of the agents were already gone. People didn't do overtime on Friday unless it was absolutely necessary.

If not for Rodney's help, Andrew would've been one of the unlucky ones who had to stay behind, trying to dig out names he could hit for information. But now that he had Turner's number, he may be able to go home and take Nathalie out as he'd planned before the shit had hit the fan with Carol's abduction. He still had the tickets.

The big question was whether Turner would accept the mission and take this thing off Andrew's shoulders. He'd call the guy from the car, on the burner phone he kept for instances like this. Not that he was doing anything illegal, but he preferred to keep his call to Turner private. The office was outfitted with surveillance cameras that were monitoring everything, and his cellphone was probably monitored as well. There was no reception in the underground structure, so he would have to drive out and park on the street or find a strip mall's parking lot somewhere nearby.

Five o'clock in the afternoon in downtown Los Angeles was the worst time to drive around, but at least there were plenty of parking spots in front of the nearest Starbucks.

As he turned off the ignition and reached for the burner phone, a sudden craving for a tall iced cappuccino had him out of the car and standing in line to order one. In the back of his mind, though, Andrew was well aware that this was nothing but stalling. Calling his old boss was a task he would've gladly delegated to someone else, and what's more, asking the bastard for a favor was something he had never imagined doing, outside of hell that is.

His ice-cold drink in hand, Andrew went back to his car... and just sat there.

Damn, why was he fretting about a bloody phone call? The condescending prick had no power over him, not anymore.

It had been such a relief when the guy had retired. It wasn't that Andrew could prove that Turner had done anything wrong. It was more about the potential. The bastard was an emotionless sociopath and therefore extremely dangerous. If he believed that sacrificing a team would achieve his objective, Andrew had no doubt the guy wouldn't even blink before sending them out on a suicide mission. In fact, he was convinced that Turner had done it on more than one occasion.

No soldier wanted his superior to deem him expendable. Not even an adrenaline junkie like Andrew.

On the other hand, he had to admit that Turner's brilliant mind had come up with strategies that had probably saved many more lives than his ice-cold heart had allowed to perish. But it was of little solace when some of those lost lives had belonged to Andrew's friends.

Besides, the condescending prick and his goddamned superiority complex had rubbed Andrew the wrong way. The fucker was indeed brilliant, but that didn't give him the right to treat everyone around him as if they were dimwits.

Anger was always a strong motivator for Andrew, and thinking about Turner's callous and condescending attitude had been enough to rile him up. He pulled out the piece of paper with Turner's number from one pocket, the phone from another, and punched in the numbers.

"Turner here, and who the hell are you?"

"Andrew Spivak, sir." Damn, Andrew wanted to bang his head against the steering wheel. Why the hell had he tagged on the honorific? Turner was no longer his commander. They were both civilians for fuck's sake.

"Spivak, how the hell did you get this number?"

Andrew rolled his eyes. Nothing had changed over the couple of years since he'd seen Turner. The guy was as *charming* as always. "It doesn't matter how. I need to know if you're interested in a civilian job that pays big money."

"I'm listening." Turner's tone had changed from angry to curious in a heartbeat.

"It's a short-term assignment, but it's urgent. Are you free to come on board right away?"

"For the right amount, I can be free by tomorrow. There is something I'm wrapping up, but it's at a stage that I can have someone else tie the loose ends if need be. How much are we talking about?"

"I can arrange a meeting for tomorrow morning, and you can name your price. A family member was taken by an enemy and the guy is willing to do and pay whatever it takes."

Turner snorted. "That's what you're calling me about? You can't handle something this simple on your own?"

Andrew gritted his teeth, striving for a measured tone. "It's way bigger than what I've just told you. But I can't tell you more until we meet face to face with the client."

"Fine. Where and when?"

He almost gave Turner the keep's address, when he thought better of it. If things didn't work out, Kian would thrall the guy. But if Turner inputted the address in some database it may later trigger a memory. After all, thralling didn't work as well on those with sharp minds. Besides, Kian had moved everyone to the other building, and he probably didn't want to conduct the meeting in the underground complex.

"Let's meet at the Starbucks on South Grand and from there drive together to the meeting place. Ten o'clock good for you?"

Turner chuckled. "Afraid I'll get lost on the way, Spivak?"

"Aw shucks, you've got me. With old age comes confusion and memory loss, I didn't want an old timer like you driving in circles."

That earned him a snort. "See you tomorrow, Spivak. Ten sharp. Starbucks."

"Yes, sir." Damn, old habits died hard.

Andrew returned the burner phone to the glove compartment, turned on the ignition, did a K-turn, pulled into the snail-pace traffic, and called Nathalie on his regular cellphone.

"Hi, sweetheart. Are you getting ready for tonight?"

She sighed. "Not yet. It's a madhouse in here. I don't think I'll be able to leave Jackson alone until we close."

Andrew had had Jackson make himself available to babysit Fernando every Friday so he could take Nathalie out. He'd kept the concert tickets a surprise, and until his talk with Turner he'd thought they would go to waste. But now that it seemed Turner was on board, Andrew could finally tell her about them.

"It's okay, the concert starts at eight, but the *Infected Mushroom* will probably not go up on stage until nine."

He heard Nathalie's shriek even though she was holding the phone away from her mouth. "Guys, Andrew got tickets for the Infected Mushroom, can you believe it?" She shrieked again then brought the phone again to her mouth. "How did you do it? They were sold out weeks ago."

"I have my mysterious ways. But I've got only two, so you shouldn't go advertising the fact to everyone. I'll get mobbed when I get there. Their fans are lunatics."

"That's not true."

"Says the lady who a moment ago shrieked like a possessed Valkyrie. Are the shop's windows still intact? Or should I stop by a glass repair store on the way?"

She laughed. "Don't worry, I'll sneak you in from the back so you won't get mobbed. And thank you. The Infected Mushroom is my favorite band."

"I know, that's why I pulled some strings to get these tickets."

"You're so sweet. But, Andrew, you hate their music. "

"I don't hate it. It's just that some of it sounds like burps. I'm not a big fan of concerts in general, they are too loud. But I bought us two pairs of quality earplugs. Just in case you want to protect your ears as well."

Damn, this sounded a lot like something his mother would've said.

Andrew sighed. Getting old was a bitch. He wondered if he would still feel this way when and if he transitioned. Probably not. Age-wise, Kian was ancient, but he talked and acted more or less the age he looked. Though not when he was talking business. Exuding the authority his job demanded, Kian seemed at least a decade older.

It would be fun watching him with Turner. Andrew would bet that his old boss couldn't intimidate Kian no matter how hard he tried. And he would try, no doubt about it.

Which reminded him that he still needed to call Kian and let him know about the meeting tomorrow morning.

"Yeah," Kian answered on the first ring.

"I'm meeting Turner tomorrow at ten at a Starbucks. Where do you want to meet him? Should I bring him to the keep, or the new place?"

"Let me give you an address of an office in one of the other buildings we own. I'd rather keep the new location secure."

"I'm driving. Can you text it to me?"

"I'll do it right now."

"Thanks."

30

KIAN

"Come to bed." Syssi wrapped her arms around Kian's neck and pulled him down for a kiss.

For the first time, her soft curves and hungry lips didn't stir the beast inside him. He returned her kiss almost absentmindedly, his head a million miles away. Or more accurately, a little over five thousand, which was the distance between Los Angeles and Sari's keep in Scotland.

He pulled her hands away. "I have a few phone calls I need to make first. I'll join you later."

Damn, he should have said he was sorry, or told her that he loved her before turning down her sweet invitation. Was he ever going to learn? Kian expected to find a hurt expression as he glanced down at Syssi's beautiful face, but found a thoughtful and worried one instead.

"Are you going to call more of the retired Guardians?"

He sighed.

Unfortunately, almost all of the guys had chosen to remain in Scotland, and as inept as Kian was at charming people, he was even worse over the phone.

"I'm not having much luck. I've got two who said they would think about it, and only one who said he is coming on the next flight. I'm going to talk to Sari again and see if her results are better."

Syssi cupped his cheek. "I hope I'm not being presumptuous, offering you advice about dealing with people that you know so well, and I don't. But I think you're going about it all wrong."

"You're not being presumptuous, ever. You're my wife and my confidant. Who else is going to give me honest advice?"

Syssi chuckled. "Oh, I don't know... Amanda? Your mother? Sari?"

Yeah. He was surrounded by women who loved telling him what and how to do things. But in truth, Kian didn't mind. After all, he was only obligated to listen, and later decide if their advice was good or not, and whether to accept it or discard it.

"But I value yours the most." Kian meant it. Syssi seldom offered suggestions, but when she did, not only were they spot on, but he usually didn't think twice before implementing them.

"Okay. So here is the thing. I'm not surprised you're having trouble luring them back. You're asking these men to leave behind the life that they've built for themselves, and that they love. Instead, you should present it as an emergency situation for which their help is desperately needed, and once this crisis is over, they'll be free to return to their regular lives."

"But I want them to stay. Even after we get Carol back, I want to have a formidable force in place."

Syssi smirked and patted his cheek. "I know. But for now it is crucial to mobilize the men as quickly as possible. You don't have time to wait for them to reevaluate their lives and decide whether they are ready for a change or not. The old Guardians will find it very difficult to refuse a call to come save a female from Doomers, and once they are here and get a taste for the excitement and camaraderie, and whatever else men get out of serving together, some may elect to stay. As to the others, you can introduce a reserves program. They'll be called in for training now and then, and serve one month out of a year. Again, not an earth-shaking change, and, hopefully, one that they will find acceptable."

He picked her up and smashed her to him. "You're a genius, Syssi. This will work."

She kissed his cheek. "You've said it before, it's called teamwork."

As he looked into his wife's smiling eyes, Kian's heart swelled with love for her. She was such a blessing to him. "I'm so in love with you, sweet girl, that I can't imagine I could ever love you more, and yet I find that I do."

"Oh, you're such a romantic."

"Am not!"

"Yes, you are. Stop denying it." She wiggled out of his arms. "Go, make those phone calls already. I'm going to wait for you in bed." She winked before walking away, exaggerating the sashaying of her hips.

Fates, the woman had a sexy ass.

He forced himself to stick his itching palms into his pockets and head down the hallway to his makeshift office in the new apartment they'd moved to. It had been a while since he'd spanked her, and those swaying hips were her way to remind him that he'd been neglectful lately. It had been easier when they'd worked together—plenty of opportunities to find good excuses for playtime. But between their busy schedules and this latest crisis, he found it next to impossible to get into a playful mood.

With a sigh, Kian plopped down into his executive chair and picked up the receiver. It was mid-morning in Scotland, and Sari should be in her office.

"Kian, what's up? Any news about Carol?"

"No, still working on it. But I need those Guardians. Once we have the Doomers' location, I want to attack. Can't do it with six men. And no, I'm not taking Kri with us no matter how much she or you bitch about women's rights. I'm not going to risk another female falling into the Doomers' clutches." Damn, now he'd made himself furious.

"Calm down, Kian, I wasn't going to suggest that you do."

He sucked in a deep breath, then exhaled it forcefully. "Good."

Sari humphed. "I was hoping Syssi would manage to tame you. But I see that she hasn't. You still have a short fuse."

He snorted. "Oh, she tamed me alright. This is me tamed."

"If you say so. Okay, enough with the pleasantries, what do you need from me?"

Good old Sari—no nonsense and too busy for chitchat—just like him. "I told you. I need those Guardians. We have to stop pussyfooting around and get them on the plane by tomorrow. Carol's abduction changes everything. It's no longer a long-term plan of building a larger force. I need as many Guardians as we can mobilize, and I need them here as soon as possible."

Sari sighed. "I'm not having any more luck than you, and I'm summoning each one of them for a private conference. They still shake their heads and say they will think about it and never come back to me."

"I was afraid of that. But Syssi had a great idea. We tell them that this is an emergency, and we need them to get Carol back. After that they can go home. We can't afford to let anyone off the hook, and I'm not above shaming them into it."

"Me neither. You want to split the list in half? That way we can do it faster."

"I have a better idea. Summon them all together at once for a mandatory meeting, and I'll talk to them via video conferencing."

"What time do you want them?"

"Let's say in an hour and a half? I'm going to prepare a rallying speech." He might not be a charmer, and heart-to-heart talks one on one were not his forte, but he was an experienced commander and knew how to address his warriors.

"No problem. Can you wait on the line for a few minutes? I'm going to shoot a quick email to my assistant. Now that it's only a summons for a meeting, I don't need to make the calls myself."

"I'm here."

Damn, he'd promised Syssi he would come to bed after making the calls. But now that he had a speech to prepare and deliver, it wasn't going to happen. There was no way she would stay awake that long, and he would be an asshole if he asked her to. He'd have to make it up to her tomorrow morning.

"Okay, it's done. Beth is making the calls. The reason I asked you to wait is that I was wondering what are your plans for later, after this crisis is over. You'll be back to where you started at—no Guardian Force, and a keep that is easily compromised."

"I'm going to introduce a reserve program. A month of service every year and a few training sessions in between to keep everyone in shape. Hopefully, some will decide to stay. Besides, we are still working on training new Guardians. As for the keep, I don't know. And by the way, yours is not safer than mine. If one of your people gets captured, they can lead the enemy right to your front door. We've been safe as long as the Doomers didn't know where to start looking for us. You're still good; they have no idea where your keep is, but they know that mine is in Los Angeles. And now that they have Carol, the exact location is compromised. I had to move everyone into a new building. Thankfully, I have several in the area where I keep some of the floors vacant just for a situation like this. Otherwise, everyone would be staying at a hotel." He chuckled. "Who said that being paranoid is a bad thing?"

"What do you suggest we do? Not allow our people to come and go? We can't do that unless we abduct a bunch of humans and turn them into our sex slaves."

"Yeah, that is a problem. We've done a little brainstorming here, and we have a few ideas that are too crazy to mention, but I'm going to run them by William anyway. Maybe he can come up with something that is doable."

"You let me know when he does."

"I will."

31

ANDREW

Andrew kissed Nathalie's warm cheek and carefully untangled their limbs to get out of bed without waking her. It had been late when they'd gotten home last night. She'd had the time of her life at the concert, jumping up and down and singing along with the rest of the teenagers. Or rather screaming. He'd had fun watching her. The music had been atrocious, and he was thankful for the earplugs, but nevertheless, the next time the Infected Mushroom were in town, he was going to purchase tickets no matter the cost. To see Nathalie so carefree and joyous he was willing to spend the money and tolerate the noise.

Besides, it wasn't all about altruism. She'd been full of excited energy when they had gotten home, and had found a most pleasurable way to release it. The blowjob she'd given him was one for the books. Then, of course, he'd repaid in kind, giving her multiple orgasms and keeping her up until three in the morning. The poor girl had fallen asleep exhausted, but with a big smile on her face.

Andrew smirked. *Job well done, Spivak, well done indeed.*

Making as little noise as possible, Andrew got dressed and then tiptoed out holding his shoes. He stopped for a moment outside Fernando's room, listening to the old man's snoring.

Good. Hopefully, he wouldn't be waking anytime soon.

Nathalie needed her sleep, and letting Fernando roam the place unsupervised was not a good idea. The guy was surprisingly sneaky, and God forbid he found a way to get out. He would get lost in no time and might fall prey to some punks. The old man didn't carry a wallet, or even wear a watch, and the punks might beat him up just because he had nothing they wanted. Not that there was much chance that these kind of scumbags would be awake so early on a Saturday morning.

Nevertheless, before leaving, Andrew made sure everything was locked up tight and the alarm was on.

The traffic was light on the way to the designated Starbucks, and he made it there more than half an hour before ten. Plenty of time to go in and fuel up on a grande double-shot cappuccino. He thought about getting an espresso for Turner but decided against it. It would be cold by the time his old boss arrived, and the bastard wouldn't be happy. With Turner, gestures of goodwill counted for nothing. He just didn't get the concept. All he cared about were results. An espresso with a less than perfect temperature would just piss him off.

Cup in one hand and a paper bag with the sandwich he'd ordered in the other, Andrew went back to his car to have his breakfast while waiting for the old bastard to arrive. Fifteen minutes later, a brand new black Cadillac pulled into the parking lot. Its license plates still displayed the dealership's logo, and the driver's shiny bald head belonged unmistakably to Turner.

The guy cut the engine and got out. He hadn't changed much in the past two years. Turner was still the same short and muscular bastard with a face of an angry bulldog.

He headed straight for Andrew's car. "Hello, Spivak," he said as he opened the passenger door and let himself in.

"It's good to see you, Turner," Andrew offered his hand, and the guy shook it. In a way, he wasn't lying. He was glad to drop Carol's case in Turner's lap so he could focus on finding Eva.

"You too, Spivak."

"So, what have you been up to?" Andrew turned the ignition on and pulled out of the parking lot.

"Oh, a little bit of this, a little bit of that."

"Independent work?"

"Yeah. I didn't like what the guys upstairs had to offer."

"Why? It's not like you were giving up active duty, like me. Whatever they offered you was probably not all that much different from what you were doing before."

Turner nodded. "True, but the money was better outside. For a change, I wanted to get compensated according to my abilities, not some standard pay package dictated by my rank."

"And did you get it?"

"I'm working on it. You said this guy we are going to see will pay whatever I ask for."

Damn, had he actually said that? "What I meant was that he was looking for the best and was willing to pay accordingly. It still has to be reasonable. He is a savvy businessman."

"Of course. But I know what I'm worth."

"I'm not in a position to negotiate for him. I have no financial stake in this. I'm doing it purely as a favor. For both of you." And for himself, but Turner didn't need to know that.

Turner cast him a calculating glance but said nothing.

The address Kian had given Andrew was located one street over from the keep. It was a fancy high rise office building with a valet service, which Andrew decided to use.

The front desk was just that, not a security station, and no one stopped Turner and him as they headed for the elevators. They got out on the fifth floor and walked down the wide corridor until they reached suite number five hundred and four. There was no name plaque on the double doors, just the number, and as Andrew knocked before pushing it open, he wasn't sure what and who was waiting for them inside.

The front room was kitted out as a reception area, and Andrew was surprised to find Shai sitting behind a desk with a computer and a big stack of files. This was either an elaborate setup to impress Turner or Kian's new temporary office.

"Go right in. He is waiting for you." Shai waved a hand to one of the two inner doors.

"Thank you," Andrew said and led the way.

Turner hadn't said a thing since they'd arrived at the building, but his eyes were busy watching and recording everything.

Kian wasn't alone in the big executive office. Brundar and Bhathian were with him, and the three were sitting around an oblong conference table that took most of the floor space. As they rose up to greet him and Turner, his old boss didn't bat an eyelid at the three imposing men towering over him, even though each topped him by almost a full head.

Kian offered his hand. "Mr. Turner, I presume?"

Turner clasped the guy's big hand and smiled, but there was no warmth in it. Its purpose was to show that he was in no way intimidated by Kian and his bodyguards. "In the flesh. And you are?"

"Kian."

"Kian what?"

"Just Kian. Please, take a seat." He pointed to one of the chairs surrounding the table.

Turner sat down and looked at the other men. "Aren't you going to introduce me to your associates?"

Kian took his place at the head of the table. "My bad. This is Bhathian, and that is Brundar." Each nodded when Kian said his name.

"Scots?"

"Aye," Bhathian let his accent revert to its original brogue.

Brundar inclined his head in a nod.

"What a coincidence, I'm half a Scot on my mother's side."

Turner rubbed his hands together, and the first genuine smile spread across his face. "So, boys, what are we dealing with here." As always, the guy was all business.

Kian cast Andrew a quick glance as if asking him if it was okay to confide in Turner, but this wasn't for Andrew to decide. Kian was on his own. He shrugged.

"First, Mr. Turner, there are some rules we need to agree on."

"Shoot."

"Whatever my associates and I tell you, stays between us. The information we are sharing with you must be held in the utmost confidentiality. My attorney prepared this, and I would like you to read it and sign it before we begin." He pushed a legal-sized piece of paper toward Turner.

Turner smirked as he scanned the thing, which took him only a couple of seconds. And yet, Andrew had no doubt the guy had read every word. He pulled out a pen from his light jacket's inner pocket and scribbled his signature on the dotted line.

Pushing the thing across the table, he looked at Kian. "If I didn't know how to keep secrets, I wouldn't have been as successful as I am in this field. Heck, I would probably be dead. That's the number one rule in my line of work. Whatever I know goes with me to the grave. I tell the people who work for me only what they need to know, and I make sure that no one person needs to know too much. I can provide references if you want proof."

Kian looked pointedly at Andrew and lifted a brow.

Turner was boasting a little to impress Kian, but he wasn't lying. Problem was, one never knew with sociopaths. The lack of emotions made them the world's best liars, and Andrew wasn't sure his gift worked on them. On the other hand, he had no proof that Turner was indeed a sociopath. It was just his unprofessional and totally biased opinion.

Andrew nodded. Confirming that Turner hadn't been lying.

"Okay, so this is the situation. We are immortal and so are our enemies—" Kian dove right in without preamble.

Andrew watched Turner, waiting for an incredulous brow lift, or a smirk. He'd even been prepared to intervene in case the guy got up and told them to stop wasting his time. But Turner's face revealed nothing. Damn, he was good. If the guy ever got tired from the cloak and dagger game, he could play poker professionally and make a fortune.

"Since the Doomers' patriarch dropped that nuclear bomb that eliminated our ancestors, including him, his successor and disciples have been pursuing two objectives. To kill us off, and to destroy any progress we help humanity achieve. Almost every dark age, and there were many aside from those you learn about, was instigated by them. Problem is, they outnumber us by many multiples—"

As Kian continued to tell him the abbreviated version of the clan's history and the part they had played in shaping human civilization, Turner's expression didn't change throughout the bizarre tale. And when Kian was done, Turner nodded instead of walking out like most people would have done in his place.

But Turner wasn't most people.

"I've always believed that there were some mysterious forces at play. Things just didn't add up. And major events in history couldn't have happened for the reasons I've read about in books, but I couldn't deduce a better explanation. I'm an atheist, so the God and Devil thing didn't do it for me. The missing pieces of that puzzle were driving me crazy. Thank you for telling me what they were."

In the silence that followed, Kian's amazed expression echoed Andrew's. "I didn't expect you to just accept my tale so easily. I was prepared to make a demonstration."

Turner chuckled and waved his hand. "By all means, I would love to see what you can do."

Kian turned to his men. "Brundar, please show our guest one of your tricks."

Brundar shrugged and snapped his fingers. Immediately, the three immortals vanished. Then, with another finger snap, he brought them back.

Turner clapped his hands. "That was fantastic. Is the finger snapping necessary? Or is it just for show?"

"What do you think?" Brundar asked.

"I think you don't need it."

Brundar nodded. "You're right."

"Impressive." Turner looked at Kian. "Back to the business at hand. Let's recap what we know and what we don't."

"Would you like to write it down?" Kian suggested.

Turner smiled and pointed to his head. "It's all up here. I just want to make sure you didn't forget to tell me anything."

Smug bastard. Still acting all superior.

But Kian didn't seem to notice, or maybe he just didn't mind. "Good idea." He motioned for Turner to begin.

When all the details had been rehashed, Turner pushed to his feet, and the rest of them followed. He offered Kian his hand. "I have all I need for now. How do I contact you?"

"Through Andrew."

Interesting, so Kian still didn't trust Turner. Or maybe he was just being cautious. As it was, Turner was walking away with nothing but an unbelievable tale he had no way to prove. Having an address and contact information was more tangible.

"Good deal. I'll start working on it right away. I'll contact you as soon as I have anything. I expect to have it wrapped up in a few days."

"We didn't discuss your pay."

"I'm a reasonable man. I'll provide you with a detailed list of my expenses which, of course, I expect to be reimbursed for. And once I find your enemy's hideout, and you verify the information, I want a quarter of a million on top of that. But if you want me to plan and coordinate the attack and rescue, then the price doubles."

Kian nodded and shook Turner's hand. "It's a deal. Would you like to put it in writing?"

Turner snorted. "Contracts are worthless in our business. Trust and reputation are everything. Besides, if you fail to pay my fee, I'll find a way to collect it." He winked.

32

NATHALIE

Andrew was gone when Nathalie woke up, but the space where he'd been sleeping snuggled up to her was still warm, and his scent lingered on his pillow.

His pillow. In her bed. Nice.

Lifting it, she brought it to her face and took a good sniff. The effect was immediate—a feeling of languid contentment. She wondered if Andrew's trace scent carried pheromones. It made sense, though; otherwise, her physical response to an inanimate object was hard to explain. Or perhaps it was as simple as his smell reminding her of how much she loved her man.

Last night, he'd pleasured her for hours, and even though she was paying the price this morning, it had been well worth it.

Unfortunately, she couldn't go back to sleep, or spend half the morning thinking about how wonderful Andrew was. It was time to get up and see about Papi's breakfast. Hopefully, he was still in bed and hadn't tried to fend for himself. The man who'd run a busy café for most of his adult life was now a disaster in the kitchen. The muscle memory was still there, so he could prepare dough and make cookies and breads same as he had done for years. Problem was that he would forget the things in the oven and burn them to a crisp, or set the kitchen on fire by forgetting his omelet on the stove.

Just thinking about all the possible disasters her father could cause had her out of bed in a flash. Wrapping a robe around her, Nathalie opened her door and sniffed. Thank God. The hallway didn't smell of burned food.

Her weekend morning routine was the same as every other day, and Nathalie showered and got dressed quickly. When she was done, she went looking for her father, finding him sitting in the kitchen with an empty cereal bowl in front of him.

"Good morning, Papi." She leaned and kissed his cheek.

"Good morning to you too, sleepyhead." He tugged playfully on the bottom of her braid, the same way he'd used to do when she was a little girl.

"Would you like me to make you an omelet and some toast?" she asked.

"You know I do. Your omelets are delicious. You should make one for Andrew too."

Nathalie felt herself blush. "I don't know when he's coming. I'll make him one when he gets here."

Papi tilted his face up toward the ceiling but then shrugged. "I thought he stayed the night, but I must've been mistaken."

Avoiding his questioning eyes, she turned around and opened the fridge. "How many eggs do you want in your omelet?"

"Three will do."

With her back still turned to her father, Nathalie got busy chopping an onion and a red bell pepper for the filling. Hopefully, he'd drop the subject.

Shit, she should just come out and say it, and if her father threw a tantrum, so be it. When she was young, he would often trap her into admitting all kinds of wrongdoing by calmly implying that he'd already known about it, and then admonish her anyway. But she was a grown woman, and shouldn't fear her father's chiding.

The vegetables sizzling in the skillet must've masked the sound of the back door opening, and Andrew's hand on the small of her back startled her. "I didn't hear you come in."

He leaned and planted a soft kiss on her cheek. "Good morning, beautiful. It smells amazing in here. What are you making?"

"An omelet. Take a seat. I'll make you one too."

"Can I help?"

She chuckled. "No, not really."

Andrew grabbed the only other stool and sat down next to Fernando. "Good morning, sir."

"Good morning, young man. Would you like a section of my newspaper?" He lifted the carefully folded sections he was done with.

"Sure, thank you."

Andrew pretended to flip through the pages until Fernando got up, holding the few sections he hadn't read yet under his arm, and headed for the downstairs bathroom.

"How did your meeting go?" she asked.

"Very well. The powers that be dropped a big project in my lap that I didn't feel I was qualified for. So I contacted an old colleague who happens to be an expert in that particular field. I arranged a meeting, and, thankfully, it was agreed that he would be taking over for me. Which is great news, because this project is so big and complicated that it would've taken over my life for the foreseeable future. I would've hated not being able to see you every evening. Besides, I want to continue searching for your mother. That's my top priority right now."

Nathalie dropped the new batch of chopped vegetables into the frying pan and turned to face Andrew. "Why?"

"Why what?"

"Why is finding my mother top priority for you?"

She saw his Adam's apple bob as he swallowed, and for a fleeting moment an odd expression settled over his face. Nathalie wished she was better at reading facial cues because Andrew's didn't make sense. There was guilt, and longing, and hope. Strong feelings for a woman he'd never met before.

And just like that all of her suspicions came rushing back.

"Because it's important to you, of course," he said, looking her straight in the eyes as he lied. He was good, appearing so sincere and loving, but she knew he wasn't telling her the truth. Not all of it anyway.

The smell of burning vegetables forced her to release her gaze, and she quickly turned around to kill the burner, then turned back and stared him down. "What's going on, Andrew? Why are you so desperate to find my mother? A total stranger to you?" She pointed the spatula at him. "And don't you dare lie to me. I know there is more to it than helping me. There is something you need from her. Does it have to do with her work for the government? Some secrets you need to uncover?" She narrowed her eyes. "Or maybe secrets you want to make sure stay buried?"

"Whoa, whoa." Andrew raised both palms in the air. "You've got some imagination on you, girl. I swear to God that I'm not after any government secrets. This is purely personal."

"Personal how? And don't tell me it's all about me."

"But it is! I have to find her for your sake."

"You're driving me nuts, Andrew. I'm going to swat you over the head with this spatula if you don't start talking."

Andrew dropped his head and rubbed the back of his neck. "I can't tell you what it is exactly, not until I find her. But I can generalize. It has to do with genetics. Something she might have and had transferred to you."

"Oh, my God! What is it? Am I sick? Tell me the truth!"

Andrew got up and reached for her, pulling her into his arms. "You're not sick. But you might be very special." He chuckled. "Not that you're not special to me as you are, but you might be a rare possessor of a genetic mutation. It's not dangerous, and it's not life-threatening, on the contrary. But for reasons I'm not free to disclose, I'm not allowed to tell you unless I'm positive that you are indeed a carrier. And the only way to find out is to find your mother."

Damn, damn, damn. He sounded so sincere that she was inclined to believe him. But what did it mean? For some reason, she remembered how accepting he'd been when she'd told him about the voices. "Does it have anything to do with my ghosts?"

"In a way, yes. Special abilities are one of the indicators, but they are not proof positive."

"Special abilities or mental disabilities? Tell me the truth, Andrew." Maybe it was this rare genetic mutation that was causing her hallucinations?

"Definitely special abilities."

This was so frustrating. She needed to know more, but he was feeding her crumbs that were just whetting her appetite for more. "Does it have anything to do with the government?"

He shook his head. "No."

"So who is not allowing you to talk about it?"

"I can't tell you."

She pushed him away and punched his shoulder. "This is not going to work, Andrew. I love you, but I can't stand the secrets and the lies. Why haven't I met your sister yet? What are you hiding?"

"Fuck, Nathalie, this is the worst time possible for this. Syssi and her husband are going through something difficult right now, and I'll feel like a complete asshole if I demand that they drop everything and come meet you now."

Nathalie crossed her arms over her chest. "What happened?"

"Their building was compromised and they had to move."

"You're not making any sense. What does a compromised building mean? Water damage? Fire? Vermin? What?"

"Security. Kian's family has enemies, and it is crucial that their location is kept secret. Once it's compromised, it's no longer safe."

This was just great. Worst case scenario—Andrew's sister was married to the mob; best case scenario—Kian and his family were political refugees from somewhere. But whatever the case, Andrew was not going to tell her. He would just come up with another lame excuse.

"I'm sure they can take a break from whatever they are doing and meet us for dinner at a restaurant. They need to eat sometime. Right? So why not with us. We can pick a place that is close to where they are staying, and I'll ask Jackson to stay with my father."

"I'll see what I can do."

"You'd better…"

33

ANANDUR

I'm not going to clean another fucking thing for as long as I live.

Anandur dropped the scrubbing brush inside his bucket. The yacht he'd been cleaning this afternoon hadn't been washed in Fates knew how long, and he'd been going back and forth between the deck and the nearest sink to empty his bucket and get fresh sudsy water. It would've been so easy to just dump the contents overboard, but he had an audience.

He always had a fucking audience. Normally, he wouldn't have minded the females watching him, lounging on the decks of their respective yachts with drinks in hand and leering expressions on their faces. He liked to put on a good show. But this was not the time for this.

He'd been pussyfooting around Lana, being all noble and shit, and that's why he was still stuck doing this fucking pretend job while his time could've been better spent looking for Carol.

Trouble was, no one even knew where to start.

Good thing that Andrew's old boss from Special Ops, a guy named Turner, had taken over the investigation. Apparently, he had an extensive network of informants, snoops, and snitches. It was only a matter of time until information would start pouring in. For what Kian was willing to pay, the bloody snitches would clamor to deliver whatever they could.

He'd better wrap up this investigation quickly.

Kian was recruiting every Guardian who had ever served, and Anandur would be damned if he allowed the fun and games to start without him because he was stuck washing decks. Hell would freeze over before he would let an opportunity like this pass him by.

For the first time in the clan's history, they were going on the offensive. Storming a Doomers' stronghold.

If Lana didn't start talking tonight, he was going to thrall the hell out of her, and fuck the consequences. He could no longer afford to play nice.

Frustrated, Anandur dumped the contents of his bucket, flooding the top deck with soapy water, and grabbed a broom. As he put the thing to good use, he was dimly aware that he was working at an inhuman speed, and the gasps coming from the neighboring yachts confirmed it. But he was so done with this nonsense. After this, he was going to pitch the damn bucket into the nearest dumpster and never scrub anything again.

Catching sight of Lana heading his way, Anandur bowed to his admiring audience. The sounds of their enthusiastic clapping and whistling followed him as he jumped off to intercept her.

"What this?" She waved a hand toward the females.

"My audience of lusty wenches."

"He is wiz me!" She showed them her fist.

Anandur pulled her in for a scorching kiss that brought another round of catcalls and claps. "Baby, I'm all yours."

She tried to look dismissive, but he knew she liked him saying it, even though they both knew it for the lie it was.

"Come, I make dinner."

He wrapped an arm around her shoulders. "You're spoiling me, darling. What did you make?"

"Your favorite. Steak."

"Just one?"

"Five."

"That's my girl."

As they got closer to the yacht Lana was looking after, the smell of grilled meat was mouthwatering, and Anandur's stomach responded with a loud growl.

Lana patted his midsection. "Good, you hungry."

For some reason, the woman loved feeding him and delighted in watching him consume inordinate amounts of food. The more he ate, the bigger was her smile. Which was saying something, since the Russian seldom smiled. Not because she was unhappy, necessarily, but because she considered it a perceived weakness. An angry face was a tough face, and the message it sent was 'I'm not someone you want to mess with.'

As they sat down to eat the dinner she'd prepared, Lana poured them each vodka—to help the food go down. Anandur didn't disappoint, devouring all five steaks and guzzling most of the vodka. Lana had only two, but she heaped her plate with mashed potatoes, and as the level in the bottle dropped to dangerous levels, she opened another one.

"Thank you, baby, this was an excellent meal." Anandur popped the button on his shorts, giving his expanded stomach some room. The afternoon spent in the sun and the food were taking their toll, and he felt his eyelids droop.

Bad idea.

As soon as he did, Carol's face appeared behind his closed lids, and the wave of guilt that washed over him twisted his face into an ugly grimace.

"What's wrong?" He heard Lana's worried tone. "The food not good? You want more vodka? It's good for the stomach."

Anandur forced his eyes opened. "No, baby, it's not the food."

"So what is it?"

Eh, what the hell, he might as well tell her. "My cousin was kidnapped by some thugs from a parking lot of a club. I fear for her, but I don't know what to do or where to look for her. It's just eating me from the inside, this feeling of helplessness. And here I am, enjoying a great dinner with a great girl while my cousin is suffering at their hands. Or maybe even dead."

Damn, his venom glands were swelling, and his fangs were probably showing. With Lana watching, he shouldn't have allowed himself to think about Carol in the hands of Doomers. It would be best if he kept his mouth closed.

"You go to police?"

"Yes." Naturally, they hadn't, but explaining why would have complicated things. He didn't want to go into lengthy and elaborate lies. The short answer was better.

She harrumphed. "Police not good for this."

"I know. But who is?"

"Is she pretty? Your cousin?"

"Yes. Very."

"You need to find a Vor and ask help."

"Who or what is Vor?"

"Vor is a boss, criminal big boss. They know more what's going on than police. But you owe him if he help you."

"Oh, like a mafia boss?"

"Yes. Big, big criminal."

"Do you know someone like that?"

She shrugged. "Maybe I ask a friend. Maybe a friend of a friend know."

There was an opening here he could use to get more information out of her. This hadn't been his intention when he'd told Lana about Carol, simply because he hadn't thought one had anything to do with the other. There was no connection between Alex's nefarious activities and Carol's abduction. After all, Alex was kidnapping women to sell for sex slavery, and the Doomers catching Carol was just a stroke of really bad luck…

But wait a minute, there was a connection; the local unit who'd arrived to hunt for immortal males wasn't here to acquire women, but their headquarters was. It was entirely possible that the Doomers were using scumbags like Alex to do the dirty work for them—to procure new stocks of young females for their island.

He could use Carol's case to lure Lana into talking about it. "The mafia is not interested in random abductions perpetrated by rapists. They will know something only if the thugs that took her are sex traders who will try to sell her."

Lana looked into her vodka glass and swished the liquid in slow circles. "You said she is pretty. If she has red hair like you and white skin, they can sell her for lot of money."

"How would you know about this kind of trade?"

She shrugged. "It's not secret. Everyone know about it. I read in newspaper."

Anandur didn't need Andrew's lie-detector skills to know that she was lying. For an accomplice in one of the most heinous categories of crimes, Lana was a lousy liar.

"What did they say in the newspaper?" he asked, hoping to get her to talk some more under the pretense of reading about it in an article.

"They say girls are stolen from the streets and sold for sex. They take the easy ones. Girls who run away from home, girls that use drugs and are selling sex to get money for the drugs. Girls that no one will miss and report their disappearance to the police."

Anandur didn't need to pretend his outrage. "This is despicable. What kind of scum does things like that?"

Lana winced. "People do very bad things for money."

"Money is not everything."

"When you don't have it, sometimes it is."

Given the sheen of tears in her pale blue eyes, Lana wasn't indifferent to the fate of the women Alex was smuggling. In fact, it seemed that under the thin veneer of toughness, Lana felt guilty.

He took her hand and gave it a light squeeze. "Do you want to talk about it? Carrying it all inside is corrosive. You can share your burden with me."

She looked away and pulled her hand out of his grasp. "I don't know what you talk about. I'm just sad for the girls."

It was time to stop playing and get serious. He wasn't good at thralling. Hell, he absolutely sucked at it. The slightest resistance could block him. But Lana was in a vulnerable state, and her defenses were down. He could tell she wanted to unburden herself of the guilt she was carrying. All she needed was a little push—something even his weak thrall could accomplish.

"I know, baby, it is tragic. You can tell me everything, your secrets are safe with me."

34

ANDREW

"I'm going to get us a movie. Anything in particular that you're in the mood for?" Andrew asked as he parked the car.

They had taken Fernando on a little trip down to Santa Monica Pier and a long walk on the beach, then stopped for ice cream on their way home. Exhausted by the long day in the sun, Fernando had fallen asleep in the car and was snoring loudly.

"Whatever you bring is fine with me." Nathalie got out and opened the back door. "Papi, we are home. Time to wake up." She nudged his shoulder.

The snoring stopped with a snort. "I wasn't sleeping."

Nathalie laughed. "Of course not. You always snore while wide awake. Come on, let's go." She helped him get out of the car, her hand gripping his arm as he swayed—dangerously close to stumbling. Andrew wished it was the sleepiness that was affecting Fernando's balance, but Nathalie had explained that this was just another manifestation of her father's dementia. It wasn't bad, not yet, but the doctor's advice was to get Fernando a walking cane as soon as it got worse. At his age, a fall could be extremely dangerous. Old bones just didn't mend as well.

Andrew grimaced. He should remember this the next time he decided to play warrior.

"Don't take long." Nathalie waved as she opened the shop's door.

Renting a movie was just the excuse he'd needed to get some private time and call Syssi about that damned dinner get-together Nathalie was demanding. Fuck, she couldn't have picked a worse time for this. The last thing Syssi and Kian had the time or energy for was a meeting with their future sister-in-law.

Man, he still couldn't believe that he'd found the one, and that she agreed to marry him. But with the long engagement Nathalie wanted, there was always a chance she'd change her mind.

Especially if he didn't make this damn call.

"Hi, Andrew." Syssi answered her cellphone on the first ring.

"Hi, yourself. How is the new place?"

"Oh, it's fine. Not as luxurious as the penthouse, that's for sure, but I'll take safety over luxury any day and twice on Sunday."

"Amen to that. Listen, I know that this is probably the worst possible time for something like this, but Nathalie is giving me grief for not introducing her to my family yet and wants to meet you guys for dinner."

"She is absolutely right. And we would love to. How about tonight?"

"Are you sure? You should check with Kian."

"Here, talk to him yourself. I'm sure he's just as thrilled to finally meet Nathalie as I am."

Maybe so, but Andrew was sure that there was a shitload of things Kian had to attend to, most of which took precedence over meeting Andrew's fiancée.

"We can do dinner tonight. A quick one." Kian's no-nonsense attitude was a relief.

"Thanks, man. It means a lot to me. With all the shit you're dealing with, I know it's not easy to drop everything just to make my fiancée happy."

Kian chuckled. "Nonsense, family comes first. And anyway, I've taken care of everything I could for now, so this is actually a good time. As soon as Turner delivers, shit is going to hit the fan, and well… Fates know when we'll have time for anything fun again."

"Makes sense. Where and when?"

"It's five now, and I'm sure Syssi needs time to get ready, so let's aim for eight. And as to where? There is only one place I deem safe enough at the moment— By Invitation Only. I'll text you the address."

"Isn't this the fancy-schmancy restaurant where you proposed to Syssi?"

"It is."

"I thought you had to be a billionaire to get in."

Kian chuckled. "Or the brother-in-law of one of the owners."

"I hope Nathalie will not freak out when she sees the place."

"If she has anything of her father in her, she'll be fine as long as the food is good. And it is."

"About that. Remind Syssi that Nathalie still doesn't know anything about Bhathian being her father or any of the other stuff. She's aware that he is a relative of yours and so is Jackson. But that's it."

"Don't worry so much. See you later."

Yeah, as if he could. With a brother-in-law that looked like a statue of a Greek god, Andrew was worried about more than a simple slip of a tongue. He clicked off the call and started looking for a convenient place to make a U-turn. After all, he and Nathalie wouldn't be watching a movie tonight.

She was in the kitchen when he got in, making sandwiches for their dinner.

"Guess what." He circled her tiny waist with his hands.

She smiled. "What?"

Andrew pulled her into his arms. "I've talked to Syssi and Kian, and we are meeting them tonight for dinner at a fancy restaurant called By Invitation Only. It's a members-only place, and the food is supposed to be amazing."

"Oh, my God! Tonight? Why so soon? I have nothing to wear!" Nathalie dropped her apron on the work table in the kitchen and ran upstairs as if the place was on fire.

This hadn't been the response he'd been expecting. Go figure. He'd arranged exactly what she'd asked him to, and instead of being happy about it she was having an anxiety attack.

Were all women this confusing?

How the hell was a guy supposed to know how to please them if they themselves were so conflicted about what they wanted?

With a sigh, Andrew finished making the sandwiches Nathalie had started and then loaded them on a platter. After all, Fernando still needed to eat, and Jackson, who was coming to watch him, would want some too. God knew the kid had a healthy appetite.

"Andrew!" Nathalie hollered from the top of the stairs. "You don't have anything to wear either! Go home and change!"

She had a point. By Invitation Only was not a place he could show up wearing jeans and a T-shirt, not to mention sneakers that were covered in sand. Damn, did he even own a suit fancy enough for that place?

Probably not, and wearing the tux from Syssi's wedding wasn't going to cut it either. Suddenly, Nathalie's panic started to make sense to him.

Andrew glanced at his watch. It was only twenty minutes past five. Could they make a quick run to the nearest Macy's and get some decent clothes?

With a new idea brewing in his head, Andrew headed for Nathalie's room. He took the stairs two at a time, and what he saw when he got there cemented his idea. Looking like a woman possessed, Nathalie stood in front of the mirrored closet doors, wearing only her bra and her panties. But there was barely anything left hanging inside. Most of her clothes were strewn about the floor.

For a moment, he got distracted by her mouthwatering backside, but all carnal thoughts were forgotten when she turned to him with tears in her eyes.

"I can't go. Call and cancel. Tell your sister that I came down with a cold or something."

When he pulled her into his arms, she was stiff as a broom, but eventually, she slumped into him. "I'm so sorry. But I just can't. Not to a place like that," she murmured.

He stroked her shiny hair. "I have an idea. We shower, you put on your makeup and do your hair, we drive to the nearest Macy's, get clothes and shoes and whatever else we need, and looking great in our new stuff we drive to that fancy restaurant. But we need to hurry."

"What about my father? We can't leave him alone, and Jackson will not get here before seven."

"I'll call him and ask him to come over right now."

Nathalie stretched on her tiptoes and kissed Andrew's lips before looking up at him with a pair of smiling eyes. "Did I tell you lately how much I love you?"

35

NATHALIE

"Stop fretting. You look beautiful," Andrew said as Nathalie checked herself out in yet another mirror—one of the many they passed by on their way out of Macy's.

She couldn't help it. It had been ages since she'd worn anything that wasn't either jean color or black, and it was startling to catch her reflection in the red dress Andrew had chosen for her. She would've never even looked at it if it hadn't been for him, and not only because of the bright color. The dress clung to her curves, and the narrow belt that came with it emphasized her small waist, which was good, but it also made her big butt look positively enormous, which was really bad. And yet, Andrew had insisted that her big ass was beautiful, firm and shapely, and that it was a crime to hide something as sexy as that under too much fabric.

A pair of elegant, low-heeled black pumps completed the outfit. After showering, she hadn't had time to blow out her hair and had left it loose to air dry. The bottoms curled up a little and looked as if she had spent hours at a salon to achieve the effect. A little bit of eyeliner and mascara brought out her eyes, and she hadn't bothered with anything else. As it was, the red dress contrasting with her dark, almost black hair already felt like too much color.

Andrew looked dashing in his new charcoal suit and a cream colored dress shirt. The tie they'd selected was silk, burgundy with a charcoal pattern on it, and he'd even splurged on a fancy cologne for himself and a perfume by the same designer for her. It was so nice of him to pay for all of this stuff. Andrew wasn't rich, and from what she'd gleaned he was getting a decent salary that allowed for a comfortable living but not for frivolous splurging. Nathalie wasn't a big spender either, and not only because she never had the money to waste on luxuries. She certainly didn't expect Andrew to shower her with gifts. But it was nice to know that her future husband wasn't stingy.

She smiled at him. "I'm not fretting, just trying to get used to all this color. I haven't worn red since I was a little girl."

He opened the door for her, and they exited into the parking lot. "That's a shame. Red looks good on you."

For some reason, he sounded strange as he said it, and she cast him a sidelong glance. There was no reason for him to lie to her about it. After all, he could've chosen the same dress in a different color for her. But something about the color bothered him.

Whatever. She wasn't going to ask. There should be no secrets between them, but that didn't mean that they had to share every little thought. Some privacy and some mystery weren't necessarily a bad thing for a healthy relationship.

Nathalie hadn't shared with Andrew her latest ghostly communications, and it was fine. Unless it concerned him, she didn't feel the need to tell him about it every time it happened.

"Is there anything I should know about your sister and her husband?" she asked as the GPS indicated that they were nearing their destination. "Touchy subjects I should avoid? Like religion, politics, money?"

Andrew chuckled. "Those are better left alone no matter who you talk to. But Syssi and Kian are chill. Feel free to talk about whatever you want."

That was good to know. Her social skills were honed by years of dealing with customers, but it wasn't the same as spending a whole evening with people she didn't know. People she needed to impress so they would deem her worthy of Andrew.

Oh, God. What if they didn't?

She was a baker who didn't have a college degree, and her reading was limited to romance novels. So unless Andrew's sister was into those too, they would have little to talk about. Damn, she should've read today's newspaper to brush up on current affairs. If they started discussing topics that she had no clue about, she'd look like an idiot.

Damn it. Why the hell had she pestered Andrew about meeting his sister before thinking to prepare herself better?

Nathalie sighed, letting herself slide low in her seat.

Andrew put a hand on her knee. "What's the matter?"

"I'm a little nervous. What if they don't like me?"

"Don't be silly, they are going to love you."

"What if they think I'm dumb? What if we have nothing to talk about?"

"Don't worry. If you run out of topics, I'll cover for you. I have an arsenal of stories about Syssi's shenanigans as a little girl that would keep everyone entertained for hours."

God, she felt so lucky to have an incredible man like Andrew. A man who she knew would always have her back.

Nathalie grasped his hand and gave it a squeeze. "I love you so much."

"Ditto."

As Andrew turned into a parking lot and pulled up to the valet sign, Nathalie glanced around, but didn't see anything that indicated that there was a restaurant anywhere, or any other place that was open for business at this time for that matter. The house to the right had a sign that proclaimed it to be a dental office, and the one to the left said Dr. Chen, Chiropractor.

Two uniformed guys opened her and Andrew's doors at the same time. One took the keys and scribbled Andrew's name on a tag he attached to them; the other one said, "Welcome to By Invitation Only. Please, follow me."

He led them to the rear of the parking lot and punched a code into a keypad that was attached to a narrow iron gate in the tall block wall. A lush garden greeted them on the other side, and as they followed the valet down a stone walkway that wound between neatly trimmed mature trees, bushes, and flowerbeds, Nathalie had a feeling that she'd stepped into a different dimension.

The only illumination came from tiny LEDs embedded in the narrow walkway. But as they wended deeper into the garden, she saw more and more outdoor lights, bathing the greenery in a lambent light. They passed a few sitting areas with comfortable looking lounge furniture, but nobody was sitting in any of them.

Holding onto Andrew's hand, Nathalie wondered how much further they were going to have to walk. The path seemed to go on and on. She leaned into Andrew and whispered, "I'm glad I chose these shoes. I would've been miserable walking this far in high heels."

"Why are you whispering?"

She chuckled. "I don't know. It kind of looks like an enchanted forest, and I don't want to spook the magical creatures."

He wrapped his arm around her shoulders. "The only magic here is lots and lots of money."

The valet turned back with a smile. "We are almost there. Follow me and watch your step."

As they approached a stone staircase leading down a pretty steep slope, Nathalie was relieved to see a courtyard at the bottom that was set up with tables and chairs, some of which were occupied. Behind it was a one-story building that housed the restaurant.

"Aren't you required to have wheelchair access?" she asked the valet.

"Oh, but we do, Madame. Over there we have a lift." He pointed.

It was hard to see in the dark, but a few feet away there was something that looked like an ornate iron cage resembling an old fashioned elevator.

"Would you like to use it?" Andrew asked, glancing at her shoes.

"No, I'm fine. Just hold my hand as we go down these steps."

"My pleasure."

His arm was strong and steady as she leaned on it for support. Her heels were short but spiky, and if one caught in the grooves between the stones the stairs were paved with, she could twist her ankle and tumble all the way down.

This wasn't a good design for a fancy place like this, but she had to admit that it was beautiful and very private.

"If this is just the approach, I can't imagine what the inside of the restaurant is like," she whispered to Andrew.

"My thoughts exactly."

As the valet pushed the double doors open, a hostess with long legs and a perfect set of teeth welcomed them. "Ms. Vega, Mr. Spivak, welcome to By Invitation Only. Please, follow me."

Nice. It seemed that guests of this place were chaperoned from the moment they exited their vehicles until they returned to them. And the hostess was waiting for them because the other valet must've informed her that they had arrived and were on their way.

The interior was dimly illuminated, and soft music was playing in the background. But Nathalie was surprised to find the place not as large or as ostentatiously decorated as she'd been expecting.

Along the walls, a few semi-circled alcoves provided a more intimate seating, and the various sized round tables that took up most of the floor were generously spaced from each other. With the music playing in the background, hushed conversations could remain private while everyone still got to be seen.

Nathalie gasped as she recognized a famous movie star, digging her fingers into Andrew's arm while fighting the urge to run up to him and ask for his autograph. The guy was gorgeous on screen, but he was even better in person. Not surprisingly, the woman sitting at the table with him could have put the whole lineup of Victoria's Secret models to shame.

"Come on, stop staring." Andrew tugged on her hand, and she realized that the hostess was waiting for them a few feet away in front of one of the alcoves. It was more secluded than the others, tucked into a corner of walls, and the little candles that were glowing from each one of the other tables were extinguished.

Nathalie couldn't see the people sitting inside and wondered if it was intentional. But Andrew hadn't said anything about Syssi or her husband being famous, so there was no reason for them to hide in a shadowed corner.

Or was there…

Perhaps Andrew had been stalling the introduction for a reason. But she couldn't imagine what it might be.

As they caught up to the hostess, a tall man pushed to his feet and stepped out of the alcove… rendering Nathalie speechless.

The movie star had nothing on Syssi's husband. No wonder she was hiding him in a dark corner. Every woman in this place would've been drooling all over him if Syssi had allowed them to see him.

"Nathalie, it's a pleasure to finally meet you. I've heard so much about you." He offered his hand and after a moment she took it, only to get pulled into a chest that was made from granite. He was surprisingly gentle for a man this big, and she realized that he was being careful with her.

She heard a feminine giggle coming from behind Kian's back. "Kian, let go of Nathalie before Andrew explodes."

He released her immediately and stepped aside to let his wife come forward. Syssi's smile was genuine and friendly as she embraced Nathalie, and her body soft. But under the softness there was strength. Syssi must've been working out, a lot.

"Come, let's sit. I took the liberty of ordering appetizers for us. I'm starving. But, of course, you can order your own." Syssi slid into the booth, pulling Nathalie by the hand to sit next to her and leaving the guys no choice but to sit across from them. "The food here is amazing. Gerard is a genius, and he is also Kian's cousin. He catered our wedding, by the way. Well, part catered, because it was such a rush job that he couldn't do the whole thing. But he gave us the recipes to prepare the rest, and our household staff handled it beautifully. They are partners, Kian and Gerard, but Kian is a silent one. He just put the money up for this place. Everything else is Gerard. He'll probably come over later and introduce himself."

Nathalie smiled, feeling her shoulders relax. Evidently, she'd worried for nothing. Syssi was taking over the conversation, which was perfect. All Nathalie had to do was listen and nod.

"Oh, my. I don't know what happened to me. I'm usually not so chatty. It's just that I'm so excited to finally meet you, Nathalie." Syssi leaned into her and whispered in her ear, "You have no idea how worried I was about my picky brother. I was afraid he would remain a life-long bachelor. Can you imagine? It would've been such a loss. He is going to make a wonderful father. Ask me how I know." She nudged Nathalie's arm.

Nathalie barely stifled a chuckle. "Okay. How do you know?"

"Because he practically raised me. Our parents had Andrew and then for many years our mom couldn't conceive. So when I came along, and a year later Jacob, Andrew was already a teenager. He did a good job, and it's a big endorsement considering that it's coming from me."

All of this was news to her. Andrew had never talked about raising his siblings. Heck, she didn't even know that he had a brother. The only one he ever mentioned was Syssi. "Andrew is so tight-lipped. I didn't know any of this." She glanced at Andrew, who was watching her conversation with Syssi with an amused smile on his face. "How come you didn't tell me you have a brother?"

His smile melted away. "Had. I had a brother. Jacob was killed in a motorcycle accident."

Damn. Way to go ruining Andrew's mood. But how was she supposed to know?

Nathalie felt Syssi's hand on hers. "It happened a long time ago. It's hard for me to talk about it, so I'm sure it's hard for Andrew too. Let's talk about happier subjects." She smirked. "Like when are you two going to get married? I'm a pro after planning our wedding, and I'm offering my services. Because let me tell you, it is way more complicated than it seems. And the dress, oh my, wait until Kian's sister introduces you to her friend Joann. She has connections in all the big designer houses. Thanks to her my wedding dress was not only beautiful, but it was made in under two weeks. Can you believe it? Two weeks! Hold on, let me get my phone and show you some pictures—"

36

SEBASTIAN

"Please," Carol pleaded weakly.

She should've known by now that her pleas were not going to stop what Sebastian was doing to her. But she probably couldn't help it, which was fine by him.

He loved the sounds she was making. The screams, the begging, the sobbing, these were all music to his ears. The only thing he didn't allow was cursing, which she'd indulged in before learning the cost of such disrespect.

In a way, he was hoping she would slip and call him vile names again.

Too accustomed to fragile humans, he'd stopped choking her when she'd turned blue, letting go of her before she passed out. Only later, he'd realized his mistake. She couldn't die. He could choke her literally to death, and she'd resurrect. Save for decapitating her or cutting out her heart he couldn't kill her even if he tried. And how awesome was that? Next time he wasn't going to stop until he choked the life out of her. Temporarily that is.

Somewhere in the back of his mind, he pitied her... a little. After all, he wasn't completely heartless. Carol wasn't a masochist, not even a submissive, and derived no pleasure whatsoever from the torture he was inflicting on her.

But he was a master at this; he would mold her into whatever he wanted her to be.

As much as she hated herself for it, blaming it on her traitorous body, Carol was always wet when he entered her. But it wasn't her body that was betraying her, it was her mind.

The mind he played so masterfully.

After a session, he tended to her, cuddled her, told her she was a good girl, and it was impossible for her to resist the comfort he was offering because she had no one else to turn to.

Sebastian was having the time of his life, but not everyone in his abode was enjoying this. The other girls were terrified, except for Letty of course, who had gladly stepped aside to make room for his new whipping toy. Even some of his men were giving him the stink eye. Most didn't give a damn about what he was doing to the female, but some couldn't stomach it. He'd never gone that far with Letty.

His basement playroom needed soundproofing, but until this was done, he had a convenient excuse no one could argue with. After all, the female had to be tortured for information.

They didn't need to know that he'd already done that. Not that she had anything of any value to divulge. She had no idea where the headquarters were, she had never been invited. And when he'd asked her about Guardians, it was obvious she had no idea what he was talking about. Carol was a beautiful female, but she was dumb as a brick, a drunkard, and a pothead.

There was, naturally, a chance that she'd been lying, but he doubted it.

It was true that the stench of fear and pungent aroma of despair had been so overpowering that there was no way he could've scented any of Carol's other emotions. And lying produced a very subtle one. But she was a soft little female, enduring pain that would've made tough guys sing.

His problem was that the excuse he'd given his men had a very short expiration date. They wouldn't tolerate this for much longer, and Sebastian didn't want to lose their loyalty over this. Mortdh knew how long and how carefully he'd cultivated this bunch of warriors. But the funny thing about people was, mortals and immortals alike, that what they couldn't hear or see they could pretend wasn't happening even when they knew for a fact that it was.

He was counting on this phenomenon to solve his problem.

The room he had designated for his own use had already undergone a few modifications. First, he'd had to reinforce the restraints. The female was much stronger than the average human. The second thing he had done was to remove the carpet. After Carol's first whipping, the thing had gotten so soaked with her blood that it had been beyond salvaging. The concrete floor was much easier to hose down. The third thing he'd done was to install the big wooden X Carol was now strapped to.

Admiring his work, he deemed the pattern he'd painted on her slender back and her pert ass complete, and moved his strikes to the back of her thighs. The deep welts were bleeding profusely, and Carol was so exhausted she'd stopped screaming several strikes ago. The only reason she was still up and perfectly positioned for the whipping was the ingenious contraption she was secured to. Her wrists and her ankles were each chained to one of the X's arms, while a strong leather harness kept her middle tied to the center of the X. She had zero wiggle room.

He was so hard he could drill holes in that X with his shaft. But he couldn't fuck her yet.

First, he had to complete the design he was drawing with his whip on her flesh, then he needed to take her down, lay her on her stomach and tend to her wounds until the skin mended and the bleeding stopped.

He found it fascinating to watch her heal. In less than an hour, the skin wounds would close, and by tomorrow there would be no sign of the whipping she'd taken.

A new and unblemished canvas for him to paint on again.

37

ANDREW

Whistling as he walked into the office on Monday morning, Andrew earned himself a couple of raised brows. People weren't used to seeing him so joyful. He was more of a somber guy. But after a great weekend with Nathalie, he was in a good mood today.

Except, he couldn't shake the feeling of guilt casting shadows on his happiness like a dark, stormy cloud. He shouldn't be happy when poor Carol was suffering at the hands of Doomers.

But the thing was, he didn't know Carol, had never met her, and although he tried to feel more for her, to him she was just another case of misfortune. Of random cruelty. One of the many faceless victims he couldn't help no matter how much he wanted to.

In fact, he shouldn't feel guilty at all. He'd handed the job to Turner, putting aside his deep antipathy towards the man, not to mention his own pride, in order to increase her chances of being found. Turner was a much better choice for this particular job, mainly because of his network of snitches.

The brilliance was just a bonus.

And a pain in the ass.

That arrogant son of a bitch had always grated on Andrew's nerves. Andrew didn't begrudge the guy his brilliance, but he hated the way Turner liked to rub everyone's noses in it.

Damn, just thinking about the bastard had soured Andrew's good mood. But all he had to do to get it back was to remember Saturday night's get together with Syssi and Kian.

Throughout the evening, Syssi had chatted up a storm with Nathalie, while he and Kian had spent most of it just listening to the girls talk. And eating of course. Kian's cousin was a culinary genius. Andrew had sampled some of the appetizers the guy had made for Syssi's wedding, but those little tidbits of tasty couldn't compare to the five-course dinner he'd had last night. None of it tasted like anything he'd ever put in his mouth before. Naturally, Kian had taken care of the bill, not allowing Andrew even a peek, but he had no doubt that the amount had been astronomical. Perhaps not for Kian, the guy could probably eat at a place like that every day. But it was out of reach for someone of Andrew's means, even for a once a month visit.

When it had gotten late, pulling the girls apart had been no easy feat, and after exchanging phone numbers, the two had parted with hugs and kisses like the best of friends.

Kian wasn't a fool, and he'd wisely refrained from sharing his opinion about Nathalie with Andrew. But Andrew had had no trouble deciphering the guy's brief look over. The bastard was lucky that the looks he'd been casting Syssi, all throughout dinner, had been so full of love and lust that by comparison, the one he'd given Nathalie had been purely platonic.

"Morning, Spivak. You're in a good mood today. What happened, you got laid last night?" Andrew heard Tim's mocking tone from across the room.

Damn, he'd been so preoccupied with his inner musings that he hadn't noticed the extra desk that had been added to the place, or that fucking Tim had been sitting behind it.

"What the hell are you doing here?"

"The boss said I can park it here until they clean up the mess in my cubicle."

"What mess?"

Tim winced. "Some idiot pissed on the carpet."

Andrew chuckled. "Appropriate, I would say. You piss off people all of the time, and for once someone pissed back."

"Yeah, yeah. Blow me."

"You're not my type."

Andrew parked his ass in his chair and turned on his computer. It was good that Tim's desk was on the other side of the room. He had a shitload of work to do, and Tim liked to talk. For some inexplicable reason, Andrew was one of the few people the guy considered a friend. A dubious honor that meant that he wouldn't let him be. But Andrew had no time for that. Aside from his regular assignments, he had some private business to attend to. Eva's case was gnawing a hole in his gut, and he couldn't wait to sink his teeth into it.

Especially since he'd finally thought of a way to get into those fucking Swiss bank accounts. He needed a hacker.

One or more of the other departments in this building was for sure employing these types, but he didn't know which and wasn't sure who to ask. It wasn't as if the fact that the government was using hackers was made official. There were no offices with plaques that said 'So and So, Hacker.'

Hell, perhaps he could take advantage of the situation and start his inquiry with Tim. The guy was the only forensic artist on premises and had done work for many of the departments. He might know somebody who knew a hacker.

"Hey, Tim, you got a moment?"

"For you, always. But it comes at a price."

"How about coffee in the break room?"

"You're a stingy date, but fine. Go ahead, I'll join you when I'm done with this sketch. Two minutes tops."

It took him five.

"Here, I made it special for you." Andrew handed him the paper cup.

"I'm touched. So what do you need?"

"A hacker."

"What for?"

"I need someone who can follow money that is funneled through a Swiss bank account."

Tim took a sip of his coffee, then flipped open a donut box someone had left behind. The thing was empty save for a few leftover sprinkles. Tim grimaced and opened the fridge, searching for something edible he could pilfer. "You need a good one."

"You know someone?"

Tim smirked, pulling out a half-empty jar of salsa and an In-N-Out cardboard container with a few leftover fries. "I do, but he is hard to get to."

"How so?"

Dipping a fry in the salsa, Tim stuffed it in his mouth and chewed. "There is this kid, a fucking world class hacker, working for our cyber security department. When he was fifteen, he hacked into some top secret shit at the Pentagon and got caught. The kid was too young to be put under lock and key, but also too dangerous to be allowed to do more harm. So they put him under house arrest with twenty-four-seven supervision. The kid isn't allowed to take a piss without his handler's approval. But there is no other way. Supposedly, no monitoring equipment is safe from his hacking. He can break into anything."

"How do I get to him?"

"I've told you. He works for cyber security on the fifth floor."

"Does he still have a handler?"

"Yup. That's how I know him. I'm friends with one of them. There are several who are assigned to the boy genius, and they take turns."

"That must be tough for a kid. How old is he now?"

"I guess seventeen or eighteen. I'm not sure. Last I saw of him was before Christmas last year. Do you want to go up during lunch break? I'll introduce you."

It all sounded good, except how the hell was this kid supposed to do any private work if he was living under a microscope? And even if he could, why would he take a risk for a stranger?

But it wouldn't hurt to talk to him. Andrew could try to tempt the kid with money, and if this didn't work, he could ask him to recommend someone else. As far as he knew, the underground community of the cyber world was interconnected, and hackers knew of other hackers.

38

NATHALIE

"I met your cousin and his wife, Andrew's sister, on Saturday," Nathalie told Jackson as soon as the morning rush was over and they had a moment to breathe.

"Oh, yeah?" He didn't seem surprised.

"Yeah." She tried to stare him down, which was difficult since he was way taller than her. Had he been that tall when he'd started working for her? He seemed to be the same height as Andrew now, and Andrew was over six feet tall.

"How did it go?" Jackson's face revealed slight nervousness.

"Very well."

"I'm glad." He seemed relieved. So this was more about the impression his cousin and Syssi had left on her than anything else. Such a good kid—he was worried about her getting along with Andrew's sister and her husband.

"It was great. Syssi is a sweetheart, one of the nicest people I've ever met, and the food at that restaurant was out of this world. I've never eaten anything so fancy or so tasty. Syssi said that Gerard catered part of her and Kian's wedding so you must know how good it is."

Jackson snorted. "To tell you the truth, I didn't get to eat much at the reception."

"Too busy chasing girls?"

"I wish, but no. Me and my friends snagged a few bottles of alcohol and drank them in hiding. When we were done, they were collecting the dirty dishes."

"I bet you guys got in trouble for that."

"Yeah, we did. And I can't even say that it was worth it. Hangovers are a bitch."

"Well, at least you've learned your lesson."

"I certainly did." Jackson tugged on the bottom of his T-shirt and adjusted the apron he was wearing over it. "What did you think of Kian?" Again, he sounded a bit anxious.

"Besides being the most handsome man I've ever seen?"

Jackson smirked. "He is? I thought that was me."

She punched his bicep. "You're still a boy. But when you're all grown up, don't go asking the mirror who is the most handsome of them all because it might choose you and give Kian ideas. The guy is scary."

Jackson's teasing and smug expression evaporated, replaced by an offended one. In fact, she'd never seen him as angry as he looked now, and as he glared at her, she took a step back. This handsome, pleasant young man wasn't as harmless as he pretended to be. And even though she knew she was perfectly safe with Jackson, that dangerous quality that she'd sensed in him from the start frightened her.

"So that's what you think of him? That he is like that wicked queen in Snow White? You're so wrong. Kian is a tough and strong leader, but he is fair, and he works his butt off for the family." Jackson seemed to notice that she was backing away from him and took a deep breath, then continued in a much calmer tone. "You just need to get to know him better; that's all."

"I'm sure you're right. It's just that he didn't say much during dinner, and he seemed kind of brooding. On a positive note, though, for a guy that looks like a god, he is surprisingly not full of himself, and he gazes at his wife as if he can't wait to get her alone and have his way with her. Which is kind of sweet. He didn't look at any of the other women in the restaurant. And I can tell you, without exaggerating, that there were more than one or two who made all of the Victoria's Secret models look ordinary."

That brought back the smile to Jackson's face. "Damn, I wish I could go there."

She patted his arm. "I don't think you can afford it."

"One day I will." He shrugged, then added with a wink, "When I'm heading Nathalie's baked goods empire."

Nathalie made a face and waved a dismissive hand at him. The boy was such a dreamer. Her chances of heading a baked goods empire were the same as Jackson's band getting to perform at the Staples Center. Non-existent.

39

ANDREW

"Hey, Volaski, can we go talk to your boy genius?" Tim asked the agent sitting behind a desk, which was practically glued to the glass wall separating the hacker's lair from the larger one they were standing in. By the looks of it, this was the handler. His guard station looked like any of the other work tables in the room, but unlike the others, it was clear of anything aside from a mug of coffee and Volaski's phone.

As Andrew peered through the glass partition into the hacker's domain, all he could see was the back of an executive chair and an array of monitors that looked like NASA's ground control center.

"You mean the royal pain in the ass? Go ahead, be my guest," Volaski said, waving a hand toward the glass door... in the glass wall...

Poor kid, he was watched like a monkey in a zoo.

"Do you need to buzz us in?"

"It's open. The boss loosened the security on our prima-donna. He is free to go anywhere he wants as long as he doesn't leave the building."

"And when he goes home?"

Volaski shook his head. "As soon as Roni turned eighteen, which was three weeks ago, he moved out of his parents' house. Now he lives here."

"You're shitting me. I didn't know we have residential apartments."

"We do now. The seventh floor had some unused space, and they converted one of the larger offices into a studio apartment for his royal highness. Anything to keep him happy and working overtime. I'm telling you, pretty soon the whole place will get overrun by pimply kids with nimble fingers, and we will become obsolete. This is just the start. Mark my words, in a couple of years, this place will look like Google. With a barista serving cappuccinos and a sushi bar—anything to keep the geeks from going home."

Tim snorted. "Are you done?"

"Yeah, sorry about the rant. But that's the future, my friends. You just wait and see. I know what I'm talking about." Volaski waved a hand toward the glass door. "Just go."

As Tim pushed the door open, the big leather chair took a spin, bringing its occupant to face them. The infamous, almighty hacker, was indeed a pimply, scrawny teenager, sitting in a chair built for a much larger occupant. But Roni's confident smirk made one thing clear. The guy's size might have been on the scrawny side, but his ego sure wasn't.

"Roni, my man. How've you been?" Tim high-fived the guy.

Roni remained seated, his flip-flop clad feet resting on the chair's spider legs. "As well as can be expected for a prisoner." The deep baritone coming from that narrow chest was surprising. Without seeing the speaker, Andrew would've imagined a big fat guy, and definitely older.

"I heard that they are giving you some breathing room now."

"Not voluntarily. It happened only after some threats and promises were exchanged with the boss and then his bosses."

"I'm glad it all worked out for you."

Roni glanced around his glass cage. "Yeah, I'm so fucking happy. Who's your friend, Tim?"

"This is Andrew. He works in the anti-terrorism department."

"Nice to meet you, Roni." Andrew offered his hand as Tim introduced him, and the kid shook it with a hand that felt as delicate as a girl's.

"You too. What can I do for you, Andrew?"

All working spaces in the building were bugged, and this room probably doubly so. Which wouldn't have been a problem if what Andrew was asking for had to do with the file he was working on, not his private investigation. But whoever was monitoring the recordings wouldn't know that for a fact. Careful wording could make his request seem legit.

"There is a money trail I'm investigating that stops in Switzerland. I need someone who can pick up its scent, sniff it behind their protective walls, and find where it goes from there."

"What's in it for me?" the kid asked straight out.

No wonder he and Tim got along. "Isn't it your job?"

"Nope, I work for cyber security, and if I have time after I'm done with what my department tasks me with, I can take a look at it. But with my workload, it could be weeks before I can get to it, if ever. So if you want it done, it will take an expediting fee."

"Name it."

The smile on the kid's face looked like something he had not practiced in a while. "Let's start with a game of poker. I'm going out of my mind with boredom up in my fabulous, technology free apartment. I need someone to play with. If you win, I'll owe you a favor. If you lose, you'll owe me one. How about that?"

"Are you any good?" Andrew lifted a brow.

"No, not really. I'm still learning."

Yeah right. Roni's eyes shone with intelligence, and Andrew had no doubt that the kid's thought process was about ten times faster than his own. Roni knew he was going to win, and what's more he knew that Andrew was on to him.

"Fine, one game. When?"

Roni pushed his glasses up his nose and leaned toward one of the monitors to check the time. "I haven't had lunch yet, did you?"

"No. This is my lunch break."

Roni pushed up to his feet. "Perfect, then we can have something to eat at my place while we play. I can even make you coffee."

"Am I invited too? Tim asked.

"Sure, follow me."

Roni stopped by Volaski's desk and lifted his arms. "Do it fast, I'm taking my friends up to my place for lunch and a game of poker."

When Volaski pushed away from his desk, got up, and patted Roni down, Andrew understood what this was about.

"You're good to go." Volaski dropped back in his chair.

As they walked out into the corridor and stopped by the elevators, Andrew glanced at Roni. "Does he do it every time you leave?"

"That's the only way they agreed to leave my apartment bug free." He shrugged his narrow shoulders. "Even I can't imagine a way to smuggle equipment from the office to my place in my pockets." He patted his baggy jeans. "They are just paranoid. And stupid." He said the last words loudly and looked up at the surveillance cameras.

"Why would I try anything when I'm on probation?" he said as they stepped into the elevator. "I'm not an idiot. I don't want to go to a real jail. This is bad enough."

Tim snorted. "You're never going to be thrown in jail. You're too valuable, and you know it."

Roni shrugged. "I'm not the only hacker or even the best. There is probably a snotty twelve-year-old somewhere who can do what I do and better. These kids are getting younger and younger."

And that was coming from the mouth of an eighteen-year-old.

The door to his studio was unlocked, which made sense. No one who didn't belong could get inside this building. Roni's apartment was safer than if he was rooming in a bank vault.

On the inside, it looked like a college dorm and smelled just as bad. The small sink in what passed for a kitchen was overflowing with dirty dishes, and dirty clothes and socks were everywhere. In fact, it was impossible to make a step and touch down on a clear patch of carpet.

"What happened? The cleaning crew skipped your place?" Andrew asked.

"I don't let them in. They will just snoop around my stuff."

Tim chuckled. "Newsflash, you have nothing to hide here. And they can snoop as much as they want while you're working."

"They don't."

"Don't be naive, kid."

"Trust me, I'm not. I'd know if they did."

Andrew cleared a spot on the couch by throwing a bunch of stinky clothes on the floor. This was such an unpleasant flashback to his time in college. His roommates had been just as bad. And since he couldn't stand it, Andrew had ended up acting as their maid.

As Roni turned on a sound system, the music was mercifully tolerable. He pulled three beers out of his fridge and a big bag of nachos from one of the cabinets.

He handed Andrew and Tim their beers and snapped the bag of nachos open. "Lunch."

"They let you drink beer?"

"One of the perks I negotiated." Roni threw the rest of the stuff covering the couch on the floor and sat next to Andrew.

"Where are the cards, kid?"

Roni took a swig from the beer, then pinned Andrew with a pair of smart eyes. "Neither of you have a sporting chance against me. I have an eidetic memory and make calculations in my head faster than the machine."

Great, another jerk who was too full of himself. Except, in Roni's case, Andrew knew it wasn't empty boasting. He was just saying it as it was.

"The game was obviously a ruse. What do you really want?"

"I want to get laid." The kid dropped the bomb.

Andrew scooted away. "I don't swing that way, buddy, and neither does Tim. At least as far as I know. You approached the wrong guys."

Roni rolled his eyes. "With a girl! I want you to bring me a girl. Someone around my age, and pretty. Not some old hag."

Damn, talk about mission impossible.

"And how am I supposed to arrange that?"

First of all, he wasn't a pimp. But even if he miraculously found a girl who volunteered to help Roni change his status from virgin to gotten laid, how would Andrew manage to smuggle her into the highly secure building?

"That's your problem, dude. But I can promise you that if you do, I'll find that money trail for you even if it leads straight to hell. There is no firewall I can't get through. There is always a flaw in the system. Perfection doesn't exist."

"You sure there is nothing else you need? Cuban cigars? A rare whiskey?"

"Nope."

"A cushy bank account? I can pay you well."

Roni looked at Andrew with the same infuriatingly condescending look as Turner. "And what would I do with that money? What would I spend it on?"

Yeah, the kid had a point. And frankly, in the same situation, Andrew would've probably asked for the same thing. For an eighteen-year-old dude, there was nothing more important than finding out what sex was all about.

40

NATHALIE

In the kitchen, slicing bread for the sandwich she was putting together, Nathalie thought about what Jackson had told her about Kian. He'd called him a leader, but a leader of what? And what had he meant when he'd said that Kian was working hard for the family? Syssi and Kian were newlyweds and had no children, so Jackson must have been referring to the extended one. Some kind of a family business that needed strong leadership. She wondered what it might be. Andrew would surely know, she could ask him. Or Jackson, for that matter.

She liked the concept, though. All the cousins and probably also the aunts and uncles working together, watching each other's backs. Must be wonderful to have a security blanket like that.

And Jackson holding Kian in such high regard meant that they all appreciated it.

Nathalie glanced at her father. How different their life could've been if they were part of a tight-knit family.

So marry Andrew already and become part of it.

Before Sage had spoken, Nathalie had felt a slight pressure in her head and wondered if he'd done it on purpose, giving her a warning so she wouldn't startle and cut herself.

No, I wish I could take credit for being so thoughtful, but I had nothing to do with it.

Nathalie finished the sandwich, put it on a plate, and handed it to Vlad. "Could you take this order to Jackson for me? I'm going upstairs for a little break."

"No problem."

Vlad was okay with her talking to herself, but she preferred not to do it in front of anyone when it could be avoided. Still, it was nice to know that she was safe in case something slipped. After all, they all had secrets that needed protecting.

Nathalie took off her apron, hung it on its peg by the door and climbed the stairs. Sage must've understood that she wanted to talk to him somewhere private that wasn't in her head, and he waited patiently until she entered her bedroom and closed the door behind her.

"I need you to do something for me."

He chuckled, which sounded very weird coming from a ghost. *There isn't really much I can do unless you want me to spook someone.*

"Can you do it? Can you make anyone but me hear you?"

I don't think so. But I can send messages on their computers, that will freak anyone out.

She laughed. "I bet. But that's not what I need. Though I'm going to keep it in mind if I ever seek revenge on someone. But I digress. I want you to ghost out and then try to get back in. I want to see if I can block you."

I can try, but once I leave, it might take me a while to get back. Well not from my perspective, for me it will be a few seconds. But for you it might be the next day. I'm still struggling to understand the difference in the passage of time between our realms.

Shit. She needed to test Tut's advice in case other ghosts spotted her supposed beacon and came knocking on her cranium.

"Tut said that I'm like a shining light, a beacon for ghosts. Try to focus on that so you will not drift too far away—time wise, that is."

That's it. Now I get it. Four-dimensional existence. I should be able to travel back in time if I want. Time is just another dimension. Wow! For the first time I'm excited about being a ghost!

"Sage, please focus and do as I asked."

Okay. Ghosting out.

She felt the slight pressure lift, and a moment later it pushed back, seeking entrance. But she was ready for him and slammed her imaginary gate down.

Nathalie waited a moment longer for Sage to come back, wondering if she'd succeeded in blocking him or just imagined she had. After all, Sage might have just gotten lost again, and she hadn't blocked anything.

When another quiet moment passed, she closed her eyes and imagined lifting the gate.

Then waited. And waited some more.

Ten minutes later, she was ready to give up and get back to work when she felt the pressure again. This time, Nathalie didn't resist, allowing Sage entrance.

You were right. You are like a beacon of light. As long as I kept it in my sight, I managed to hang on and not drift away.

"Great, but did it work? Did I block you?"

Yeah, you did. It felt like a door or a gate slamming in my face.

"Sorry about that. I had to test Tut's theory. But I promise not to block you unless it's a really inconvenient time, like when I'm in the bathroom... Oh, God, don't tell me you ghosted in when I was sitting on the toilet or something..."

For some reason, she'd never considered the possibility. Tut had always been good about this, leaving her alone to do her business. Though come to think of it, he might have been just keeping quiet. Shit, she hoped he'd had the decency to ghost out during her bathroom visits. If he ever showed up again, she was going to ask him about it.

She felt the slight pressure lifting. "Damn it, Sage, don't you dare leave before answering my question."

No, of course not. I wouldn't. Never. I don't remember much about my past life, but I know I was a gentleman.

So why the hell did he sound so guilty?

"Sage, if I ever feel you ghosting in while I'm taking care of business, so to speak, I'm going to kill you all over again. Is that clear?"

Yes, ma'am.

41

ANDREW

Andrew banged his fist on the steering wheel. Damn that horny little prick and his crazy demands. He would need to find someone else to pick up Eva's trail. Someone who would do it for good old fashioned money.

Getting the kid a girl was just not going to happen. Even if Andrew knew one that was easy, he would never ever dare propose something like that.

Just for the hell of it, Andrew had asked Tim if he knew of a service he could call.

Not that it would've done him any good. Even if Tim delivered the girl himself, there was no way to get her into the building. And Roni wasn't allowed to go anywhere without his handler. For one crazy moment, Andrew even entertained the idea of inviting them both over and then distracting Volaski while Roni got it on in another room, but Tim said it would be a no go.

Even with an escort, the kid could only leave for doctor appointments, family events, and the like. For all intents and purposes, Roni was indeed a prisoner.

Perhaps he should call Turner. If anyone knew how to solve this conundrum, it would be him. Fuck, he hated the idea of asking the guy for a favor, even though Turner owed him for the extremely well-paying gig Andrew had brokered for him.

He was still fuming when he opened the door to Nathalie's shop, but luckily she wasn't there. It was hard to leave the day's frustrations at the doorstep so he could show his woman a smiling face and a good time.

God knew she had enough stress in her life without him adding his crap to the mix. But he was only human and needed a few moments to cool down before interacting with her the way she deserved.

It was a shame that Nathalie had nothing stronger than wine and beer. He needed something with a kick.

"What's up, Andrew?" Jackson greeted him.

"Not much." As if he could talk about it. "How are things here?"

"Couldn't be better. It's just Vlad and me. Nathalie and Fernando are not back from his doctor appointment yet. But we are managing just fine. She worries for nothing."

"Good job, guys. You're making life easier for her, and I appreciate that."

"Yeah, she deserves a break. How about you? Can I offer you a cappuccino? A sandwich?"

"Maybe later. Right now I'm in the mood for something with a high alcohol content." Andrew tugged on his tie to loosen it a bit. "You don't happen to have some by any chance? I won't tell if you do."

"Sorry, man. You know we don't have an alcohol license. Nathalie has a few bottles of beer in the fridge for her private consumption, but that's it. I can't even let you drink it in here. You'll have to take it upstairs."

"You know what? I'll do just that. Could you bring me a sandwich there? I didn't have a real lunch today, and I'm hungry."

"Sure. The usual?"

"You got it."

On his way up, Andrew grabbed two Stellas from the fridge and tucked them in his jacket pockets, then reached for a container of what looked like leftover spaghetti and a jar of pickles. A fork went into one pocket, joining the Stellas, and a napkin went into the other one.

Just something to tide him over until Jackson delivered the sandwich.

In the den, he unfolded one of the tray tables and set it in front of the couch. The Stella was a weak beer, but it was cold and refreshing, and the leftover spaghetti was pesto, which he liked. The pickles didn't really go with any of it, but Andrew was hungry, and he wasn't picky.

A few minutes later, he heard Jackson's light footsteps as the kid jogged up the stairs. He showed up with two plates heaped like small mountains.

"If you don't mind, I'm going to join you."

Andrew scooted to the side, making room on the couch, and put the empty container of pasta on the floor under the tray table.

The three hefty sandwiches Jackson had stacked on each plate were resting on top of generous portions of potato salad on one side and coleslaw on the other.

"That's a bit much, but thank you."

Jackson put the plates down and grabbed a bottle.

"Hey, you're underage, and I'm a federal agent. Give it back."

Reluctantly, Jackson put the beer down.

For a few moments, the only sounds they made were crunching and chewing. But as Jackson finished his second sandwich and wiped his mouth with a napkin, he turned to Andrew. "So, you want to talk about it?"

"Are you offering to play shrink? I don't think so."

"Whatever, dude." The kid picked up the fork and attacked the potato salad on his plate.

Now Andrew felt like an ass. There was no reason to snap at the kid just because he was tired and frustrated. "I'm sorry. I had a bad day. I had what I thought was a breakthrough idea in my investigation of Nathalie's mother, but it didn't pan out."

"What was it?"

"To find a hacker to get into that Swiss bank and follow the money trail. But the guy demanded a price that was a deal breaker. Now I have to look for someone else who is more reasonable. A shame really. Because Roni is the best there is."

"You know Kian will help with the money, right?"

Andrew winced. "Roni didn't want money."

Jackson lifted a blond brow. "Oh, yeah? What was it?"

"A girl."

"So get him a girl. That's not a problem."

"For you, maybe. But we are talking about a scrawny, pimply, eighteen-year-old virgin, who is living under a microscope because he is too dangerous to let loose. The guy broke into the Pentagon's database when he was fifteen."

Jackson whistled. "Impressive."

"Yeah, well. Unfortunately, this superior intelligence comes with an equally big ego and wrapped in an unattractive gift paper."

"So you pay someone."

"I'm not a pimp. And even if I stooped so low, there is no way to smuggle a girl into the building. So unless I find a female agent who is willing to do it and is young enough to meet the guy's demands, I'm out of options."

Jackson scrunched his forehead. "I have a solution for you, but it will not be cost-free."

Andrew could just imagine... well, not really, but he knew it would be creative... "I can't wait to hear it."

"I can talk to my cousin Sylvia. She is like twenty-seven, but she looks really young, and she is not very picky." Jackson smirked. "You know how we are, we need a steady supply of sex. But the neat thing about Sylvia is that she has a very unique ability. Besides thralling humans, she can cause glitches in computers and short out other electronic equipment. Kind of like a jinx, but on purpose."

"I don't think Kian would agree to pay one of his own to prostitute herself. And knowing Bhathian, he wouldn't do anything without getting Kian's approval either."

Jackson waved a hand. "Sylvia will not want money."

"You said that there will be costs. And why would your cousin Sylvia agree to help us if there is nothing in it for her? I understand not being picky, but no one would volunteer for this out of the goodness of their heart."

"I'll call her and see what it would take. Worst case scenario she'd say no."

42

ANDREW

"You sure you want to do this?" Andrew asked Sylvia for the umpteenth time.

She was nothing like he imagined she'd be. When Jackson had said she wasn't picky, Andrew had created an unflattering picture in his head. But Sylvia was pretty, and not an airhead either.

"As I've said before, I've got it. If he is gross or stinky or behaves like a jerk, I'm just going to thrall him to believe that we did it. But if he is okay, I'll gladly help the boy get rid of his virginity." She shrugged. "It's exciting. I've never had a virgin before."

Andrew still had trouble accepting the nonchalant attitude of immortals toward sex. But he understood. There was something special about being someone's first.

As far as gross or stinky, she had nothing to worry about, but the jerky remained to be seen. Roni had promised that everything would be spotless and fragrant, including himself, and to be on his best behavior. But the kid was full of himself and had been isolated from people his age for years, which meant that his social skills probably left a lot to be desired.

"Okay, let's do it." Andrew got out of the car and went to the other side to open the door for Sylvia.

"Thank you."

"Are you sure the cameras are out?"

She smiled. "Wherever I go, everything is going to glitch and then go back to normal once I'm a few feet away."

"I hope you're right."

"Worst case scenario, security will stop us, and we'll tell them the story we prepared. Don't worry; it's going to be fine." She patted his arm.

In case they were caught, the cover story was that Sylvia was with Andrew, and they stopped to retrieve something he'd forgotten in his office on the way to their date.

Not kosher, but not a huge offense either. The worst he'd get would be a slap on the hand.

But Sylvia's magic must've been working because no one stopped them on their way to the seventh floor.

Roni opened the door and blushed like the virgin he was, but just as he'd promised, he was freshly showered and shaved, and soft music was playing in the background.

Sylvia smiled a dazzling smile and reached her hand to his cheek, cupping it gently. "It's okay. No need to be shy, Roni. I'm Sylvia."

The kid didn't move, holding the door open but blocking the way.

Sylvia chuckled. "Aren't you going to let us in?"

He shook his head as if trying to clear it and stepped back. "Please, come in."

Andrew looked around the small living room in wonder. The place that just yesterday had looked and smelled like a filthy college dorm was spotless and smelled clean. It had probably taken an entire container of air freshener to achieve that.

The question was, what now? Should he wait in the other room? Out in the corridor?

Going down to his office was a no-no. Sylvia's magic didn't work long distance. He had to stay nearby until they were done.

His dilemma was solved when Sylvia took Roni by the hand and said, "Let's go to the other room." She winked at Andrew before closing the door to Roni's bedroom.

These immortals were unbelievable—in so many ways. Sylvia hadn't been embarrassed in the slightest.

Maybe they had it right. After all, consensual sex between adults shouldn't be something to be embarrassed about. Except, Roni barely qualified as one. He was just a kid... one who was old enough to serve in the army, carry a machine gun, and risk his life for his country.

So, yeah, Roni was old enough.

All that self-talk, however, didn't make hearing the sounds that started coming out of the bedroom any less awkward. He'd been secretly hoping that Sylvia would thrall the kid instead of actually having sex with him, but apparently Roni had passed her test, and she was taking care of him for real.

Thankfully, Andrew had come prepared. In his pocket, he still had the set of professional quality earplugs he'd bought for that awful music concert.

43

NATHALIE

After helping her father settle in for the night, making sure he took all his medications and had a fresh bottle of water on the nightstand, Nathalie came back to the den and sat next to Andrew. "You seem in a peculiar mood," she said, hoping he'd tell her what was bothering him.

Earlier today, Andrew had called to let her know he would be coming late, and that she shouldn't wait up for him. Not that she had any intentions of going to sleep without Andrew. Nathalie hated letting a day go by without seeing him. But he'd ended up showing up earlier than she'd anticipated. It was just a little past ten.

He wrapped his arm around her and pulled her in for a kiss. "I had a weird day today, at work, but now that I'm here, with you, it's all better."

She wondered what he'd meant by weird. Usually, when Andrew was tired or irritated or both, he would say that it had been a rough or tough day. Weird was a new expression for him. But she knew better than to ask him about it. He didn't like to talk about his work, or perhaps couldn't.

She wished he could talk to her, share his burdens with her the way she shared hers with him. That's what couples were supposed to do, weren't they? Would he still keep secrets from her when they were married?

"Will you always shut me out?" she asked.

Andrew frowned. "What are you talking about?"

"You never tell me anything about your day. Only that it was rough, or tough, or boring. And today it was weird. Is everything you do top secret?"

"No, not everything. But a lot of it is. And the rest is either boring, administrative stuff, or things that would ruin your mood."

Andrew's eyes shone with love as he stroked her hair. "Sharing is overrated. There is no benefit in dumping your crap on the person you love. You know what I imagine when I open the door to your place every evening?"

"What?"

"That I'm like a farmer who removes his muck-covered work boots and leaves them outside on the porch, then uses the hose to wash his dirty hands before he enters his home. That's me leaving all the crap where it belongs. When I come to you, I want us to talk about pleasant things, or better yet, make love." Waggling his brows, Andrew moved his hand up her inner thigh.

And just like that, Nathalie felt a trickle of moisture between her legs.

She slapped his shoulder. "Stop distracting me. We're having a serious conversation here."

"Okay, but make it short. I'm feeling frisky."

As if he ever felt differently.

"I want you to tell me more. If something is troubling you, talking about it may help. I know that it helps me. And I want to be there for you when you need to unburden yourself. But if you're not allowed to talk about the serious stuff, I'll settle for office gossip; like who sleeps with whom, who just had a baby, or who is getting a divorce. Things like that. It doesn't have to be the top secret stuff. Just trivia. And I'm sure there is plenty of that going on. People are the same everywhere, and they like to gossip. Federal agents included."

He smirked. "I've always frowned upon gossip and tried to ignore it. But if it'll make you happy, I'll make a point of collecting all the juicy bits for you."

"Ugh. You make it sound so bad. Just tell me things you talk about with your fellow agents. I'm sure not all of it is work related."

"Deal. Can I take you to bed now?"

"Yes."

As Andrew tightened his hold on her and pushed up and away from the couch, his abdominals strained against his dress shirt and his strong thigh muscles bunched under her butt. It never ceased to impress her, the way he lifted her so effortlessly—as if she weighed nothing.

He wasn't even winded when he lowered her to her bed.

"I love how strong you are." Nathalie cast Andrew a come hither look, batting her eyelashes.

His smile was all male pride. "You do? That makes all those hours in the gym worthwhile."

She snorted. "What gym? You haven't exercised in weeks."

"You're right. I used to go to the one in our office building after work, but now I come straight here. I guess I'm going to grow fat and flabby now that I'm no longer on the market."

Nathalie wanted to say something snarky in return, but forgot all about it as he took off his jacket and hung it over the back of her desk chair. She knew he'd go for the shirt next, and waiting for that reveal was all she could concentrate on.

Andrew had a magnificent body, even though he didn't think so. The silly man was bothered by his many scars and by skin that wasn't as smooth and pliable as that of a twenty-year-old. But to her he was perfect. So much so that she couldn't believe he was hers to keep.

Unbuttoning his shirt slowly, he was tormenting her on purpose, prolonging her anticipation. But Nathalie knew how to speed things up. Grabbing the hem of her T-shirt, she pulled it over her head and threw it on the floor, then unhooked her bra.

Andrew sucked in a breath, his fingers fumbling and missing the small buttons on his shirt.

As her pants and panties joined the rest of her clothes on the floor, Andrew stilled completely, the bulge in his pants growing bigger as he stared at her nude body with hungry eyes.

"Come here," she beckoned him with her finger. "I'll help you get out of your clothes. Fast."

"You are so beautiful, my Nathalie, you take my breath away."

She smiled, knowing that he meant every word. "You're not so bad yourself. I can't wait for you to get naked."

He chuckled. "I've noticed."

Switching from slow motion to fast forward, Andrew was out of his clothes in about a second and a half.

Yup, her man was magnificent.

As he climbed on top of the bed and covered her body with his, she spread her legs to cradle him between her thighs, then wrapped her arms around his neck and kissed him long and hard.

44

ANDREW

As Nathalie held Andrew tight, kissing him like she couldn't get enough, he thought how lucky he was to be loved by her. It was hard to believe that this sexually assertive woman had been a virgin up until recently, or that his little striptease had been enough to get her so aroused.

Nathalie was so wonderfully responsive.

Rubbing against her wet heat, he was more than ready to push inside her, and by the way her hips were gyrating under him, she was impatient for him to get on with it. Except, he didn't want to rush their love making.

First, he was going to worship her sweet nipples with his tongue, then he was going to slide down her body and pay homage to the little nub that was the seat of her pleasure.

"I want you inside me," she protested as he started his downward trek.

"Patience, my love. Let me enjoy your body at leisure."

With a sigh, she let go of his shoulders as if conceding to a big sacrifice. But as his hands cupped her breasts and his thumbs started thrumming her nipples, her breathy moan was all about pleasure.

He took his time, tonguing one nipple and then the other, relishing Nathalie's stifled moans and gasps. With Fernando sleeping in the next room, they had to be extra quiet, but Andrew had gotten used to that, and it no longer bothered him.

If this was the only way he could have her, he'd take it.

With his Nathalie, even stealthy, guerrilla sex was better than any sex he'd ever had with anyone else.

Was it love that made it so special? The metaphysical connection of their souls? The knowledge that from now on it would be only her for him and him for her? Or was it just an extraordinarily good pairing of compatible pheromones? Nature and chemistry, nothing more.

Before he had met Nathalie, he would have said that it was the latter, but on a visceral level, Andrew knew that it was more than that.

As he abandoned her lovely breasts to slide further down, Nathalie cupped his cheeks and lifted his head. "I love you, Andrew. So much. And even though I get impatient sometimes, I love that you're so gentle with me, so focused on my pleasure."

He kissed her belly. "That's because I love you and treasure you. You're my life, my everything."

A tear slid down her cheek, and she wiped it away. "Now look what you've done. You made me all mushy and emotional in the middle of sex."

Yeah, he had. Although she'd started it.

"I know how to get you back in the mood."

"I didn't mean that I lost it...I'm still wet and needy."

"I know." Andrew pushed back to his knees, straddling her legs. "Turn around," he commanded in a whisper.

"Oh, you naughty boy, I like how you think," she breathed and flipped onto her belly.

Gripping her hips, he pulled her back until her ample behind was up and perfectly positioned, while her front remained down on the bed with her head turned to the side and her cheek resting on her pillow.

He pushed into her slowly, even though she was wet enough for him to thrust all the way in effortlessly. But what was the fun in that? Andrew savored the sweet torture of delayed gratification. It made the climax even more explosive.

At first, Nathalie let Andrew dictate the slow penetration, but soon she began pushing back against him, taking as much of him as he allowed her to.

Greedy, little minx.

Bending over her, he whispered in her ear. "You want it all the way inside you, don't you?"

"Oh, yes, please..."

"Well, if you're asking so nicely..." He pushed in with one strong thrust.

"Oh, God, yes..." Her cry was muffled by the pillow she buried her face in.

With a strong grip on her hips, Andrew started pounding into her, his hips smacking her beautiful ass every time he pushed in.

Given her barely contained moans and whimpers, Nathalie was loving this, her copious juices easing the glide of his pistoning shaft and dripping down her inner thighs.

They were making a racket, but there was no helping it. He was not stopping this freight train until it got to the end of the line. Gritting his teeth, Andrew held on until he felt Nathalie's inner muscles contracting around him. Only then did he let go, shooting his seed inside her with a stifled groan.

For a moment, they stayed connected, their bodies rocked by the aftershocks of the powerful climax. Not willing to let go of her yet, Andrew held Nathalie glued to him with a strong grip on her hips. But even though she seemed content to fall asleep with him seated deep inside her, he reluctantly pulled out.

Nathalie remained in the same position, her sexy butt up in the air and her face still buried in the pillow she'd used to muffle her moans.

He patted one upturned butt cheek. "Come on, sweetheart, let's get you cleaned up."

"You go, I need a minute," she mumbled into the pillow.

He chuckled. "As you wish. Do you want me to bring you a washcloth?"

"Yes, please."

"Okay." He planted a soft kiss on that creamy cheek and grabbed his clothes off the chair he'd left them folded over. Opening the door, he peeked at the corridor first, checking that it was clear before making a dash for the bathroom, which was mercifully only a couple of steps away.

He took a quick shower, got dressed, and wetted two washcloths with warm water. Adding a dry towel from the linen closet, he returned to Nathalie's bedroom.

Andrew found her in exactly the same position he'd left her.

Well, it worked to his advantage. Everything was where he could easily reach it with the washcloth.

Nathalie moaned softly as the warm thing touched her sensitive flesh. Andrew was very careful to pat instead of rub, cleaning her as gently as he could and getting hard all over again. It was so sexy, the way she trusted him, the way she wasn't shy about anything with him.

He wished he could be as open with her. It wasn't that he didn't trust her, but he was too ashamed of what he'd done for Roni to tell her about it. And then he'd made it worse by pretending he couldn't talk about it because it was work related.

He hated the lies, and yet he kept piling them on.

45

BHATHIAN

"Sylvia? How did you persuade her to help?" Bhathian switched the phone to his other ear.

Sylvia was young, and he didn't know her well. But he knew her mother. Ruth was still keeping her grown daughter at home, refusing to let go of her only child.

Bhathian used to sneer at Ruth's dependence on Sylvia, but now that he'd found Nathalie, had become a parent, he understood her a little better. The only times he felt truly at peace were when he was near his Nathalie. For someone who had been resigned to spending his life alone, having a daughter of his own was priceless. Even if she had no idea that she was his.

"She wanted a trip to Hawaii."

That was odd. He didn't know that Ruth or Sylvia had financial troubles. "Did she say why she needed it? Why she couldn't afford it on her own?"

He heard Andrew chuckle. "Her problem isn't money; it's an overly clingy mother. The deal was that I'd arrange for her to *win* an organized trip to Hawaii so the mother wouldn't be able to join her. The girl is desperate for some time away from her. But given her special talent to render electronic devices useless, she could've asked for much more. The whole stunt wouldn't have worked without it."

"I had no idea she could do it." As far as Bhathian knew, no other clan member had this ability. Therefore it was extremely valuable. He should tell Kian and Onegus about Sylvia. The girl was much more useful in this capacity than as a seductress of a virgin hacker.

And yet, he was extremely grateful for her cooperation. If not for Sylvia, the hacker wouldn't have agreed to infiltrate the computers of the Swiss bank and find Eva's money trail.

"Interesting. You guys should keep track of these things. Who knows what other useful talents your people may have."

"You're absolutely right. I'm going to talk to Kian about it."

"While you're at it, you should ask him for some time off to go look for your Eva. Now that we have a tail of a trail, we should pounce on it right away."

Bhathian rubbed his hand on the back of his skull. "I can't do it. Not when we are gearing up for a major offensive. Kian needs me here."

True, many of the retired Guardians had already responded to the call, and more were arriving soon. Kian's latest count exceeded eighty, which was more than enough to storm the Doomers' stronghold. Problem was, the last time these old timers had seen battle was in some cases centuries ago. They needed training, and Kian needed each and every one of the active Guardians to help out with that.

At a time like this, Bhathian couldn't abandon Kian and the rest of his people to go chasing Eva's trail in South America. After more than thirty years, a few more days would not make a difference.

"I'll go talk to him. But I'm not even going to suggest leaving before Carol's rescue is over and she is safely back."

"I understand. You do what you have to do. In the meantime, I'll try to gather as much information as I can."

"Thank you. I don't know what I would've done without your help. I owe you big time."

"You owe me nothing, Bhathian. I'm doing this for Nathalie and for me. You know why it's crucial that we find Eva. I need to make sure that Nathalie is indeed a Dormant. Your feelings for Eva are just one part of this."

"Yeah, I know. Though to tell you the truth, I'm afraid for both you and Nathalie. Syssi was only twenty-five, and she barely made it. You are forty, and my Nathalie is thirty. As much as I hope and pray for her to be a Dormant so she could transition and stay with me forever, I'm afraid of losing her just when I've found her. And I'm afraid for you too."

There was a moment of silence on the line before Andrew sighed. "You of all people should know that life doesn't come with guarantees, and sometimes taking a risk is necessary. But time is a crucial element here. That's why I want you to go searching for Eva as soon as possible."

"I'm going to call Kian right now and discuss it with him." There was no chance Kian would let him go, but it was worth a try.

"Good luck."

46

SYSSI

The vision hit Syssi fast and hard, coming out of nowhere. Absent was the usual forewarning of the spinning, swirling sensation. One moment she was talking with her test subject and scribbling notes on her tablet, the next she was transported into the twilight zone.

The vision lasted only mere seconds and ended as abruptly as it had started. But the impact was profound.

Coming out of it, she heard someone's panicked voice. "Oh, my God, she is having a seizure! I don't know what to do! Help!"

Gasping, Syssi opened her eyes, the terrified test subject's face hovering mere inches in front of her.

"I'm okay," she croaked and gestured for the young woman to back away.

"Are you sure? You don't look good." The woman remained uncomfortably close, Amanda and Hanna's worried faces peering over her shoulders.

Syssi pushed up to her shaky feet and attempted a reassuring smile. "I'm fine. I just need some fresh air. We'll continue in a few minutes." She patted the woman's arm.

"Nonsense. I'll finish for you." Amanda waved a hand. "Get yourself a cup of coffee and a bite to eat. You need a break."

"Thank you." Syssi cast Amanda a grateful look.

"You're welcome. Now go." Amanda took Syssi's seat and flashed her blinding smile at the rattled test subject. "What's your name, dear?"

Syssi grabbed her purse and hurried to the kitchenette, which was the nearest place that offered a modicum of privacy.

Leaning against the counter, she pulled her phone out of her purse. Calling Andrew would've been more expedient, but texts were his preference when at work. Problem was, she was still shaken by the disturbing vision, and typing the simple message had taken several tries because the stupid autocorrect kept messing it up for her.

Call me as soon as you can.

Her phone rang a few minutes later.

"What happened?" By the sound of Andrew's labored breaths and that of his footfalls echoing from the walls, he was running with the phone in hand.

"Nothing yet. I had a vision."

"Damn it, Syssi; you almost gave me a stroke with that message. I thought you guys were under attack."

"I'm sorry. But I needed to tell you right away. It was about you."

"You could've said so in your text." Andrew's breathing had slowed down to normal, but then his voice sounded as if it was coming from an echo chamber.

"Are you in the bathroom?"

"Yeah. Where else in this building can I have a semi-private conversation with my psychic sister?"

"I'm not psychic. I'm a seer. The two are not the same."

"If you say so. Want to tell me about your vision?"

The mocking sound of his voice irked, especially given the gravity of what she needed to tell him.

"It wasn't good. There were ticking clocks and a funeral procession."

"What does it even mean?"

"It wasn't clear, but the feeling I got was that it would be you in that coffin if you don't act soon. You need to transition, Andrew. If you want to survive it, you can't delay this any longer."

"I don't think it makes much of a difference if I do it even a year from now. I'm already in the red danger zone. The chances of me making it are not good."

"You're wrong. First of all, there are the clocks. If the funeral were a done deal, there would've been no clocks. Second, what about my other vision? You still need to become a father."

He snorted. "I don't need to change to father a child."

"True. But what about the clocks?"

"Yeah. I don't know. But anyway, this is not a conversation for the phone. Can you meet me somewhere for lunch? Where are you now?"

"I'm at the lab. How about Gino's? Is it too far away for you?"

"No, it's fine. I can be there in fifteen minutes."

"See you there."

Syssi rubbed her chest. The talk with Andrew hadn't helped alleviate her anxiety. He was still unconvinced that he needed to act now. She'd have to do her best to persuade him over lunch. And if that didn't work, she would ask Kian to talk to her stubborn brother. Maybe a man to man talk would help push him in the right direction. And she wasn't above asking Kian to shame Andrew into it.

Her gut was telling her that he would survive the transition, but only if he acted now.

In the lab's main room, Syssi walked over to Amanda who was still busy testing the young woman she'd been working with when the vision had hit. "I have to go. I'm meeting Andrew at Gino's in fifteen minutes."

Shit, she hadn't taken into account that Amanda might feel offended that Syssi wasn't inviting her to join them. But she hadn't given her sister-in-law enough credit.

Amanda narrowed her eyes. "Was it about him?"

"Yes."

She nodded. "Are you coming back?"

"Of course."

"You can go home, you know. I can do the rest of the testing for you today."

It was tempting. The vision had taken a lot out of her, and Syssi wanted nothing more than to head home to Kian, have him wrap his arms around her and tell her that everything was going to be okay. After she'd done her best convincing Andrew to go for the transition, that is. Come to think of it, talking with Andrew would probably exhaust the last of her reserves.

"Perhaps I'll take you up on your offer. I'll call and let you know."

On the way to Gino's, Syssi rehearsed her arguments, feeling torn between wanting to convince Andrew to transition and being afraid he would actually listen to her. Despite what her gut was telling her loud and clear, she was still terrified that he might not make it. She would rather die than live with the knowledge that she was the one who had pushed Andrew to take this step, and it had led to his death.

Except, cowering on the sidelines was not an option, for either of them. The vision had made it clear that Andrew needed to do it, and the sooner, the better.

47

ANDREW

Walking into Gino's, Andrew searched for his sister's blonde head. Her blue BMW was already parked in the restaurant's parking when he'd got there.

"May I help you, sir?" the host smiled.

"I'm looking for my sister." Andrew peeked behind the guy's shoulders. "Never mind, I see her." He strode to where she was sitting.

The smile she gave him was strained, and as she pushed to her feet and hugged him, her embrace was bone-crushing.

"I love you too," he whispered in her ear. "But my ribs are about to crack."

She let go of him immediately. "Sorry, I keep forgetting." There were tears in her eyes, and she wiped them off hurriedly. "I ordered us wine. Hope it's okay with you."

Andrew was in the mood for a beer, but wine was fine. He was in the middle of his work day, and it would be better if he had none. But one glass of wine wasn't going to impair his thinking or his reflexes. He took the seat across from his sister and snatched one of the fragrant rolls from the basket.

Syssi seemed to be searching for what to say, or rather how to say it, and he was content to give her all the time she needed. She took a few sips of water, then put her glass down.

"Are you making any progress with finding Nathalie's mother?"

Andrew chuckled, tempted to tell her about the teenage hacker he'd bribed, but then reconsidered. Syssi might not approve. Better to skip the details. "We've picked up the money trail. Eva is still receiving her government pension every month, but the money is automatically transferred to a Swiss bank account. And those fuckers are nearly impossible to break into. But I finally managed to find someone who could. The money is rerouted to a bank in Rio, and there is activity there. Sparse, no more than once a month, but withdrawals are made, so we know Eva must be in the area."

Syssi's eyes sparkled. "Is Bhathian going after her?"

"As soon as Carol's situation is resolved."

Her face fell a little. "I see."

Andrew reached across the table for her hand. "Don't look so forlorn. Turner is getting closer. We'll have the location in a matter of days."

"I know. It's just that thinking about what Carol is going through…" Syssi shuddered. "There was no suspicious activity at the keep yet. So she is not giving in. I can't imagine how horrible it is for her, and I feel guilty as hell for sitting here with you at Gino's and enjoying lunch. But there is nothing I can do."

"I know, sweetheart. It's difficult just to sit and wait, but there is no way around it. We are doing everything in our power to rescue her. Kian is mobilizing all of the old Guardians and is planning the first attack the clan has ever launched against the Doomers."

She sighed. "And that worries me too. I know Guardians are nearly indestructible, but so are the Doomers."

Andrew gave her hand a little squeeze. "What is your intuition telling you?"

"In my gut, I know they will be successful. But success can be relative. They may win the battle but lose Carol, or rescue Carol and lose the battle. Guardians may be lost. It's like my foretelling about you. I know that to survive the transition you need to do it very soon. But that doesn't mean I'm not terrified for you."

"What if I never attempt it? Because if Nathalie is not a Dormant, I have no reason to do it. I'd rather spend my life with her, getting old together, than risk dying for the promise of immortality, or surviving but having to leave her because I don't age."

Syssi regarded him for a moment with questioning eyes. "What if it takes Bhathian months or even years to find Eva? And when he finds her, Eva proves to be an immortal, which she most likely is, but by then it will be too late for you to transition? Will you deny Nathalie her immortality because you can't join her?"

Damn, she was right. "I don't know what to do." Andrew ran his fingers through his short hair.

"You said that there are other indications that Nathalie is a Dormant. That she hears ghosts in her head."

"Yeah, but that is not conclusive either. She might have a mental disorder for all I know. The only definite proof is Eva. She is either an immortal or she is not."

"Unfortunately, Andrew, you don't have the luxury of waiting for her to be found. You'll have to take a leap of faith."

"Yeah, you might be right."

"You know I am."

48

NATHALIE

Something was troubling Andrew. Ever since he'd arrived after work today, he'd been broody, preoccupied. It was disconcerting. Nathalie had seen Andrew upset and frustrated about things at work before, but he'd always done his best to leave his troubles at the threshold, as he was fond of saying, and give her his undivided attention.

Not this evening, though. He was letting her do all the talking, and given that his responses were limited to an occasional grunt, she suspected that he wasn't really listening to anything she was saying.

Evidently, Scheherazade needed some fresh material if she wanted to capture her surly mate's attention. Her stories needed to be entertaining enough to take Andrew's mind off whatever was troubling him. Something funny and lighthearted to cheer him up and chase away the dark clouds he'd brought with him from work.

The trouble was, however, that nothing overly exciting had happened in the coffee shop during the day, and she doubted Andrew would be interested in anecdotes from the romance novel she read a few chapters from during her breaks… apart from the sex scenes, that is. Some of them were quite racy. That could be fun, reading him the juicy parts and watching him getting all turned on.

Maybe some other time… when they were alone in bed… but then there would be no need for it. They'd be making scenes of their own. And besides, she was still a little embarrassed to admit how much of her sexual inspiration had come from these books.

Oh, boy, was she really that boring? The woman who heard voices of dead people in her head had no stories to tell? Pathetic.

Well, even though she was still reluctant to talk about her ghosts, nothing else came to mind.

She really needed to broaden her interests. Trouble was, the little free time she had she was spending with Andrew. And during her short breaks, she wasn't in the mood for anything complicated. More demanding subjects would have to wait until she had more free time. Perhaps when she retired...

"So, the other day, I managed to block Sage."

"Uh-huh."

Obviously, Andrew wasn't listening.

"He saw me naked in the mirror, Tut too."

"Uh-huh... Wait, what?"

"Gotcha. I knew that would get your attention. Just joking, though. About the naked part, that is. But not the blocking. Do you want me to tell you about it? Or do you want to be left alone to brood? I don't mind, you know, if you want to." Yes, she did, but it sounded better. She wanted Andrew to feel that he was free to be himself, even when he was in a bad mood, and that she'd be understanding and give him his space.

He pulled her into his arms and kissed the top of her head. "I'm sorry, sweetheart. It was rude of me not to pay attention. Please tell me all about it."

Now that Andrew was hugging her, all was good with her world, and Nathalie felt a weariness that she hadn't been aware of evaporate from her system.

"I don't remember if I told you about it, but Tut suggested that I practice blocking Sage."

"No, you haven't."

"So, Tut is on his way out. He says that he has pulled away and that he wants me to learn how to block the onslaught of voices that he's been blocking for me. He suggested I practice on Sage."

"Go on."

Even though it wasn't the first time she'd mentioned the voices to him, Nathalie was still struck by how seriously Andrew took her ghost stories. Without even a hint of mocking or doubt in his tone, he responded as if she'd been recounting a conversation with a real person.

"Sage is nice, and he listens to me. If I ask him to leave, he does. He was more than willing to help me with that. I told him to ghost out and after a few minutes to try and ghost back in. But when he returned, I imagined a heavy gate slamming shut in front of him, not allowing him entrance."

"Did it work?"

"Yeah, it really did. But because he was so nice about it, I promised Sage that I'd never block him unless it was a really inconvenient time."

"I'm sure he was glad to hear that."

Again, she listened carefully for any signs of mocking or condescending, but there were none.

"I can't believe how open-minded you are. Anyone else would have had me committed for telling stories like these, or at least think that I'm totally insane. You're such a great guy for believing me, Andrew. I'm the luckiest girl in the world to have snagged you."

For some reason, he grimaced at the compliment. "I have to believe you, love."

Was that it? Did he believe her because he was in love with her? She'd take it. "Well, loving me doesn't necessitate believing. Sometimes I myself am not sure that these are not hallucinations, so I can't expect you to take my word for it."

He sighed. "Let's go upstairs. There are some things I need to tell you."

As she took Andrew's offered hand and followed him up to the den, Nathalie's heart was pounding a frantic beat against her ribcage. She'd known this was all too good to be true, and now Andrew was about to tell her something that was going to prove her right.

Sitting next to him on the couch, she was anxious to hear what Andrew had to say, but at the same time reluctant to listen to it. Perhaps they could hit the rewind button, and this conversation would never happen. But at least he was holding on to her hand, so maybe it wouldn't be as bad as she was afraid it would. She could handle almost anything, other than him telling her that he had to leave her for some reason. Andrew loved her; she had no doubt about that. But sometimes love wasn't enough. Andrew had secrets that he'd refused to share with her, and now she regretted ever pressing him to reveal them.

"The reason I believe you, is that no one can lie to me. I always know when people tell the truth or lie when I am face to face with them. I'm better than a lie detector. That's my special ability that can't be explained."

She was still waiting for him to drop the bad news on her, but it seemed that this was all he was going to say. "Your special ability can be explained by sensitivity to minute clues that are invisible to others. Mine, on the other hand, can be only explained as a mental disorder." Or the genetic mutation he'd told her about. Though, frankly, she was starting to think that it had been all a load of crap to get her off his back and stop asking too many questions.

"But both will be wrong. I know lies when I hear them, and you know ghosts when you hear them."

"How can you be so sure? Isn't there a saying that claims that the simplest explanation is the right one? Why look for a paranormal cause when a simple one can do?"

Andrew smiled. "There is another saying, by Einstein, that everything should be made as simple as possible but not simpler."

It seemed Andrew truly believed that there was something mystical about their abilities. "Okay, so maybe we are both crazy. I'm good with that. It certainly beats being crazy by myself. On the other hand, it kind of casts doubts on whether we should have children. That genetic mutation you alluded to would be doubly potent in them. Poor kids. We really shouldn't have any. It's a shame, though. I wanted a whole brood of them."

Andrew mussed her hair. "Don't be silly. They'll be double blessed. I consider our talents gifts, not curses. But I need you to define brood. How many are we talking about?"

"Oh, I don't know. Five? Maybe six? I hated being an only child. I want a large family."

He kissed her nose. "We'll see. Talk to me again after the first one. I have some experience with raising babies. And I can tell you that it's tough. And as for our respective talents, you're not crazy and neither am I. Mine was proven beyond a shadow of a doubt. And as for yours, all you need to do is to ask your ghosts to tell you something that can be proven."

"Don't you think I haven't done that already? Tut says he's been dead for too long to have something that isn't written somewhere proven, and Sage is still too confused about who he used to be."

"Hm..." was Andrew's response.

"Yeah, so as you can see, I don't have a way to prove or disprove my ghosts."

"Not true. There is something else I haven't told you. But if you thought me crazy before, this will cement your opinion."

"Oh, yeah?" What else could he tell her that was crazier than her ghosts and his lie-detecting? That he'd been abducted by aliens?

"Oh, yeah, and then some."

49

ANDREW

Syssi's vision had been just the push Andrew had needed to get him off the seesaw of indecision. His mind was made up. As soon as this latest crisis was over, he was going to ask Kian to assign him an initiator—the male immortal who would induce his transition.

The first who came to mind was Bhathian. Out of all the immortals, the guy was the one Andrew spent the most time with. But as Nathalie's father, it seemed somewhat inappropriate. His second choice was Kian. But as Regent, the guy might be precluded from becoming anyone's initiator.

Surprisingly, Andrew's third choice was Dalhu. As one outsider to another, offering Dalhu the honor of becoming his initiator seemed like the right thing to do. And besides, he kind of liked the guy. His old rival for Amanda's affections had become a friend. Come to think of it, if Andrew hadn't been spending every free moment with Nathalie, he would have been hanging out with the dude more often.

Still, the choice of initiator might not be up to the initiate.

One might be chosen for him.

Probably one of the Guardians. Damn, he wasn't going to last long against one of these males. All he could hope for was to lose with dignity and not look like a wimp. It would be humiliating enough to be subdued like that, with the guy's fangs embedded in his neck and delivering the right dose of venom to help him transition. Hopefully, successfully.

Syssi might think that he was using the upcoming battle as an excuse to postpone the inevitable, but this truly wasn't the time for ceremonies. Everyone was gearing up for a fight, and with the levels of aggression all these males were ramping up, the one nominated as his 'initiator' may get overexcited and overdose him accidentally. The process was dangerous enough without factoring in Guardians on a testosterone overload.

The thing was, Andrew couldn't do it without telling Nathalie. Putting his life in danger like that wasn't something he could keep from her. She deserved to know. And if he was breaking the rules by spilling it all, so be it. Anyway, there wasn't much Kian could do to him in retribution without upsetting Syssi, and luckily for Andrew, the guy cherished his wife's regard above all else. Rules included.

So yeah, it wasn't very noble of Andrew to rely on his sister's protection, but considering the alternative, this was the lesser evil.

He needed to tell Nathalie everything.

"So what was it that you wanted to tell me?" Nathalie sounded anxious.

"I think we should open a bottle of wine for this. Wait here. I'll get it."

She held on to his hand. "Just tell me if it's good or bad before you go. I can't stand the suspense."

Whether it was good or bad depended on the outcome, but Nathalie looked nervous, and Andrew had no problem with bending the truth a little to assuage her fears. He gave her hand a reassuring squeeze and leaned to kiss her cheek. "It's all good, love."

Nathalie released a breath and let go of his hand. "Okay. But hurry, I don't like waiting to hear news, good or bad."

So he hadn't fooled her.

A few moments later, he was back with a bottle of red wine and two glasses. When he was done pouring, Andrew handed one tall glass to Nathalie.

Looking at how much he'd given her, she lifted a shapely brow. "Now I know this is really serious. Are you planning on getting me drunk before or after you tell me?"

"It's up to you. But I think you'll probably want a hefty dose after I'm done."

She took a sip, then another one, and put the glass down on the foldout tray table. "I'm ready. Shoot."

Damn, where to start?

"I'll try to explain the same way my sister and her husband explained it to me."

"Your sister?"

"Yeah. She was the first one to fall down the rabbit hole. Syssi has an uncanny talent to predict all kinds of things, and while attending architecture school at the University, she volunteered for testing at a neuroscience lab researching paranormal abilities. The professor running it was impressed with her results and offered her a job as a lab assistant. It wasn't Syssi's field, and she had an architectural internship lined up, but the guy died unexpectedly, so she took the offer."

"You didn't tell me that your sister could make predictions, and that you're not the only one in the family with a special talent."

"There was a reason for my omission. It'll become clear once I finish my story."

"Sorry. Go on."

Andrew ran a hand over the back of his neck. "Yeah, from now on the story gets really unbelievable, but every last bit is true. Syssi found out that her boss, Professor Amanda Dokani, is a member of a small clan of immortals—the descendants of the mythological gods that turned out to be not so mythological. They were real, and they took human mates, just as it's written in the Bible, and mixed children were born of those unions. The half-human half-god children were immortal, but when those immortals took human mates, their offspring were born mortal. Those born to the immortal females carried the dormant immortal genes that could be activated, but those born to the males didn't. The unique genetics transfer from mother to both daughters and sons, but only the daughter can transfer it to her children—the heredity is matrilineal."

As Nathalie listened intently, her eyes were focused on Andrew's face. His serious expression must've convinced her that he wasn't joking or telling her tall tales. "You were right. I do need this." She picked up the wine glass and drank half of it in one shot.

She made a face and shook her head before putting it down. "Assuming that this is all real, what does this story have to do with the voices I hear?"

"It will all be clear in just a moment. It wasn't a coincidence that Dr. Dokani was conducting research on paranormal abilities. Her hypothesis was that dormant carriers of the immortal genes might be more likely to manifest these talents. Syssi was one of Amanda's strongest subjects, and she decided to test that hypothesis on my sister."

"How?"

"One of the unique physical attributes of the male immortals are fangs and specialized venom glands. Those glands produce venom in two situations; when aggressing on other males and during sex. A dose or two of this venom facilitates the transition in a Dormant. Amanda asked Kian, who is her brother, to attempt Syssi's activation. At first, he refused because he considered it immoral to do so without Syssi's consent, but all his reservations flew out the window when he met her. Long story short, Amanda was right, and Syssi turned."

Nathalie could no longer hide her incredulity. "You want to tell me that Kian and Syssi are immortals?"

"Yes. But that's not all. As Syssi's brother, I'm also a Dormant, and the only reason I didn't attempt the transition is that it might be dangerous for someone my age. Evidently, the older the body, the tougher the transition."

Her eyebrows riding high on her forehead, Nathalie snorted. "So let me get it straight. You need to have sex with an immortal to transition? A male immortal?"

He laughed. "No. I think this would've been a deal-breaker for me. All I have to do is fight one of them and lose, which is not a problem since they are freakishly strong. As I've mentioned before, they also produce venom when aggressing on other males. All I have to do is resist until the guy fighting me produces enough to dose me."

Nathalie crossed her arms over her chest. "Okay...As fantastic as all of this sounds, I still don't get how any of it is related to my ghosts."

He smiled. "Think about it for a moment. Dormants exhibit paranormal abilities. I can detect lies, Syssi can predict outcomes, and you can hear ghosts."

It was almost comical, the way Nathalie's eyes widened and her jaw dropped. "You can't be serious. You think I'm a Dormant? This was the genetic mutation you were talking about?"

"I'm almost positive. And I think that your mother is an immortal."

"Oh my God." Her hands dropped to her sides. "As crazy as all of this sounds, it kind of makes sense. My mom never really aged. And she tried to hide it by wearing baggy clothes and putting on makeup to make herself look older." Nathalie gasped. "Yeah, and probably that's why she felt she had to disappear. She was probably afraid she'd be discovered and then experimented on. But how could it be? Her parents weren't immortal, they are both dead…"

"The only explanation I have is that she encountered an immortal male, by some incredible coincidence, and had sex with him. The males bite during sex but then thrall their partners to forget it. He didn't know that she was a Dormant and that he facilitated her transition. Because if he did, he would've never let her go."

"Why?"

"Because until my sister, they've never found one. It's a long story and even longer explanation, but Kian's clan is small, and because they are all closely related they can't mate with each other. The disparity in lifespans and risk of exposure prevents any long-term relationships, so they are basically doomed to one night stands. The females can at least have immortal children by having sex with humans. The males cannot. Finding Dormants that they are not related to is their only chance of having a life partner."

"Wow, that's sad. So Kian and his clan are the only immortals left? What happened to all the gods and the other immortals?"

"There was a big war over succession. One of the gods was pissed that the daughter of the leading couple refused to marry him, killing his chances of becoming their next leader. In retribution, or maybe because he was bat-shit crazy, he dropped a nuclear bomb on their assembly, killing all the other gods. But he didn't take into account the nuclear wind that followed, killing him and most of the mortal and immortal population of the region. The only goddess who survived was Kian's mother, the one who refused to marry a god she didn't love. She started the clan by taking human lovers and having immortal children. Her daughters continued her mission, and their daughters after them. A small group of the murderer god's descendants also survived, and to this day they are bitter enemies of Kian and his clan."

"How come they survived, and the rest of the immortals didn't?"

"Mortdh's compound, that's the name of the rogue god, was located several hundred miles north of the impact site, and the nuclear wind flew east, where basically all of the others lived."

"How tragic."

"After I heard the story, I did a little reading and found a Sumerian lament that describes it in eerie detail. To us, who are familiar with the type of destruction a nuclear bomb produces, the descriptions make it blatantly obvious that this is what it's talking about. But imagine all of those who came before—they must've thought that the wind of death the poem described was the product of someone's imagination, a myth."

She looked up at him with sad eyes. "Could you show it to me sometime?"

"Sure. I have the book at home."

In the silence that followed, Andrew watched Nathalie processing the incredible things he'd told her.

She shook her head. "This is a lot to take in."

"I know. And you're taking it all really well."

Nathalie sighed. "For a long time, I suspected that your motive for getting close to me was finding my mother's whereabouts. Is that true?"

"No. It's true that I originally came to your shop because I was searching for Eva, but my attraction to you was immediate and completely unrelated to her."

"Why were you looking for her? Did you suspect that she was an immortal?"

"At first, I searched for her because Bhathian asked me to help him find his long-lost love."

Her eyes grew wide again. "Bhathian? He is…"

"Yes, of course, he's a member of Kian's clan. He met Eva a long time ago, when she was still single and worked for the drug enforcement agency. She left an impression on him, but he lost track of her. I work for the government and have access to information he didn't. I found her file quite easily."

"So you came here searching for her? Didn't you know that she was missing?"

"I did. But Bhathian also wanted to see you."

"Why?"

"That, unfortunately, is not my story to tell. It's his. I think we should call him and have him come over."

"Wait. So if Bhathian and Kian are immortals, then so is Jackson?"

Andrew nodded. "And Vlad, and Kri and Michael, and many of the others who Jackson has been inviting to come taste your creations."

She slumped back into the couch cushions. "Wow. Just wow. But you know what? I had my suspicions. I told you about Vlad, right? Picking up a heavy piece of equipment with one hand, and Jackson's hearing is definitely superhuman. Bhathian, though, other than his size, looks completely normal, and so does Syssi. But Kian is inhumanly handsome, and his eyes are strange. When we were having dinner with them, I thought I saw them glow, but then dismissed it. Contact lenses reflecting light seemed like a good enough explanation."

"They glow when he gets overexcited or is under a lot of pressure."

Nathalie remained quiet for a while, her expressive face reflecting her thoughts. "Why are you telling me all of this only now? Why not before?"

Smart girl.

Andrew clasped her hand. "I wanted to find Eva and confirm that she was an immortal, so I could be sure beyond a shadow of a doubt that you were a Dormant. But I don't have the luxury of time. At my age, attempting transition is an iffy proposition, and I'm not getting any younger. If you are a Dormant, I want to be the one who facilitates your transition, but to do so, I have to go through it first. But if you're not a Dormant, then I want to remain mortal and live out the rest of my life with you."

She squeezed his hand. "That's so sweet." Her voice sounded choked. "You would give up your chance of immortality for me?"

"In a heartbeat. I don't want to live a day without you. It's just not worth it."

There were tears in her eyes when she pounced on him and peppered his face with kisses. "I love you so much. Let's forget about this immortal thing and just be together. You said that it's risky. I don't want you to do it."

Her face was buried in his neck, and he stroked her hair gently. "I couldn't live with myself if you could gain immortality and didn't because of me. Not going to happen. And there is no chance in hell I'll let another immortal have sex with you. So that's settled."

Nathalie chuckled and then sniffled. "But why now?"

"Syssi had a vision. She said I needed to do it as soon as possible. My sister loves me. She would've never pushed me if she believed the risk to be too high. She thinks I'll be fine if I do it now. And just to reassure you, Syssi's visions are never wrong."

Andrew hadn't mentioned that the foretelling was vague. There was no need to worry Nathalie unnecessarily. After all, if the message was to hurry, it must've meant that he would survive the transition if he did. True?

50

NATHALIE

Curiosity was eating Nathalie alive. What was Bhathian's story? Why had Andrew insisted that it wasn't his to tell? With all the fantastic things he had told her, what more could Bhathian reveal?

But Andrew wouldn't budge, and Bhathian was on his way. She could survive a few more minutes.

"Please, could you at least give me a clue? I can't take the suspense."

"I'm sorry. I can't. But I can distract you while we wait." He waggled his brows.

She slapped his shoulder. "How can you think about sex at a time like this?"

"Sweetheart, I'm a man, sex is always on my mind."

Usually, that would have been enough to get her all hot and bothered. Nathalie wasn't one to say no to some hanky-panky. But she was too distraught. Andrew's revelations had been shocking, and she was anxious to hear what else Bhathian had to add to the story.

"Could you pour me some more wine?"

"Are you sure? You've had quite a lot."

"Yeah, and I want more." The nerve of the guy. Dumping an outrageous story like this on her and then expecting her to be all reasonable and drink in moderation. Right now, Nathalie wished she had something much stronger than wine.

"Fine. But don't you want to be sober to hear what Bhathian has to say?"

"No, not really. I need something to take the edge off the turmoil that's going on inside my head."

Andrew shook his head and poured, but only half a glass.

Agh. She loved him to distraction, but he was pissing her off. "All the way to the top."

Reluctantly, he did as she asked.

"Maybe I should go downstairs and make coffee." Andrew began pushing up to his feet.

She tugged on his hand and pulled him back down. "No, you're not leaving me here alone. You can keep telling me things while we wait. I'm sure there is a ton of stuff you haven't told me yet."

Andrew wrapped one arm around her shoulders, the other one under her knees, and pulled her onto his lap. "Better?"

Cocooned in his warmth, she felt the tightness in her belly ease. "When you hug me like this, it always is."

He kissed the top of her head. "I'm glad."

"So the goddess, Kian's mother, what happened to her?"

"She is still here. I've met her."

Nathalie turned to look up at him. "You did? What's she like?"

Andrew snorted. "She looks like a teenager. Tiny, maybe an inch over five feet, skinny, with long flaming red hair and an incredible presence. She has a way to tamp down her powers, but when she doesn't, it radiates. She glows in the dark."

"Really? Like fluorescent?"

"Something like that. But it's a gentle glow. She is stunning. The most beautiful woman I've ever seen. And that's saying a lot. Before I met Annani, I thought her daughter, Amanda, was the most beautiful."

"Now I'm jealous. Were you attracted to either of them?"

She felt Andrew's thigh muscles tighten under her. So the answer was yes. Would he fess up to it?

"Although friendly, Annani was too intimidating. But for a little while, I had a crush on Amanda."

"Oh yeah? What ended it?" Hopefully, it was over. If not, she would have to find the woman and scratch her pretty eyes out.

Andrew laughed, his strong body shaking. "First of all, she had her eye on someone else, which might have been part of the allure, since I'm a competitive bastard. But when I realized that I was more excited about going out on a mission than winning Amanda's heart, I had to admit to myself that what I felt for her wasn't real. I even became good friends with the guy she ended up with, my old rival."

Interesting, this was a facet of Andrew she was unfamiliar with. Was he a thrill seeker? A daredevil?

"How about me? Would you be more excited about going on some adventure than spending time with me?"

He hugged her closer. "Never. In fact, there is a big thing brewing right now, and Kian asked me to be in charge of it. But I gladly fobbed it off on someone else. Other than helping Bhathian look for your mother, all I want to do is spend time with you."

As if summoned by the mentioning of his name, Andrew's phone buzzed with a message.

"Bhathian is downstairs. I need to go open up for him." Andrew lifted Nathalie up and deposited her back on the couch. "I'll be right back." He kissed her cheek.

A moment later, two sets of footsteps and a hushed conversation sounded from the staircase.

Nathalie tensed.

But then, as Bhathian entered the den with a vulnerable expression on his rugged face, Nathalie felt her heart soften. Whatever he had to say, it wasn't easy for the big guy. She patted the spot next to her. "Come sit with me."

He cast a glance at Andrew, who nodded his encouragement.

With a sigh, Bhathian walked over and carefully lowered himself down as if afraid he might break the couch with his bulk.

"Do you want me to stay?" Andrew asked gently.

"Yeah, I do." Bhathian sounded insecure. Did Andrew tell him that she knew he was an immortal? That must've been what they had whispered about on their way up. She'd listened when Andrew called Bhathian, and he hadn't told him much. Just that it was time to tell Nathalie everything.

Bhathian lifted his head and looked at her with soft eyes. "How much did Andrew tell you?" he asked.

"That you're an immortal, about him and me being Dormants, the transition and how it works, the clan, the goddess. That you guys suspect my mother is an immortal, and that a long time ago you were in love with her."

He chuckled nervously. "Yeah, that about sums it up. But there is more."

"I figured. Do you want to tell me the rest?"

With a sigh, he nodded.

51

BHATHIAN

Bhathian had known that this day would come, but he hadn't expected it to come so soon. He wasn't ready.

Andrew should've given him a warning, time to prepare his story, to find the right words to tell Nathalie the truth gently. Damn, it wasn't going to be easy no matter how carefully he chose his words.

As she waited for him to start, looking at him so expectantly, there was no judgment in her expression, no apprehension, just kindness. Nathalie trusted him. Which made him even more anxious, and the words just wouldn't come.

Nathalie took his rough hand, sandwiching it between her small palms. "I can tell that this is difficult for you. You may find it easier if you start at the beginning."

Good advice.

He nodded. "I met Eva, or Patricia—the undercover name she used—over thirty years ago, at a bar frequented by pilots and flight attendants on layovers. She was stunning, the most beautiful, hottest woman I've ever met. And there had been plenty throughout my long life. We spent the night together, and the next day we said our goodbyes. I thought I would never see her again."

Keeping his eyes trained on Nathalie's face, he was relieved that she didn't seem to mind the hookup style encounter he had had with her mother. "I assume that Andrew told you about our lifestyle; the one night stands, the impossibility of lasting companionship."

When she nodded, he continued. "Until Eva, I never had a problem with that. It suited me just fine. But she was different. Saying goodbye to her hurt." He rubbed his chest. "I should've known that there was more to it than a simple attraction to a beautiful woman. The one glaring tell was that I couldn't thrall her. It's very rare to encounter resistance. Usually, human minds are easily manipulated. Luckily, though, I found out in time and refrained from biting her."

He paused his story and glanced at Andrew who was sitting on the other foldout table across from them. "Did Andrew tell you about the fangs?"

"Yeah, he did." She tipped her head, trying to look into his mouth. "Though to tell you the truth, I don't see how you can do anything with these—they are just slightly longer than normal incisors."

His lips twitched. "With the right stimulation, they become much longer."

"I see." Nathalie's cheeks reddened as his meaning sank in.

"A month later, I met Eva again at the same place, and she invited me to her hotel room." Bhathian dropped his head and rubbed his hand over the back of his neck. "I thought we were going to hook up again, which was fine with me, but she had another reason for seeking me out that night, and inviting me over."

Fuck, this was the toughest part, and Bhathian felt like a coward for avoiding Nathalie's eyes. Forcing himself to man up, he lifted his head and gazed at his daughter's beautiful face. "She told me that she was pregnant and that I was the father."

From her expression, it was clear that Nathalie hadn't connected the dots yet. Which was good. Bhathian preferred to tell her the rest of the story first.

"I'm ashamed to admit it, but I asked her to have an abortion. She refused, saying that the pregnancy was a miracle at her age, which was shockingly forty-five. She looked twenty years younger. I told her that I couldn't be a father to her child and offered to help her financially, which, frankly, was the only thing I could provide her with. It wasn't as if I could be with her, or even sign my name on the birth certificate."

"Did she end up aborting the pregnancy?" There was a slight tremor in Nathalie's voice. Was she starting to suspect?

"I don't think so. She told me she would think about it and get back to me. But she never did. In fact, she disappeared. I've searched for her for years, not knowing if I had a child or not, if Patricia, I'm sorry, Eva, was doing okay on her own or not. It's been eating me up for the past thirty years. But I'd hit a brick wall in my search and basically given up hope of ever finding out. Until Andrew joined the clan, that is."

He glanced at Andrew. "I owe this man more than I could ever repay him."

"We've been over this before. You owe me nothing," Andrew dismissed him.

Nathalie let go of his hand to cross her arms over her chest. "I guess she must've either aborted the baby or lost it because I'm her only child."

Bhathian shook his head. "No, she didn't."

Nathalie's eyes grew wide. "Oh my God, did she give it up for adoption? Do I have a half-brother or a sister somewhere?"

"No, sweetheart, Eva didn't give the baby up."

"I don't understand," she whispered with tears glistening in her eyes.

"I think you do. You are my daughter, Nathalie."

"No, I'm not. Papi is my father."

It hurt, but what had he expected? Nathalie loved her adoptive father. Fernando had been an amazing parent, probably better than most biological ones. Maybe he didn't know? Maybe Eva never told him that she was pregnant when they had met? And had fooled him into believing that Nathalie was his?

"Fernando is your father in all the ways that count, and he always will be. Because he loved you and raised you in the best possible way. I'm not even sure he knows you're not his. But I have no doubt that I'm your biological father. Just look in the mirror, Nathalie. Now that you know, you won't be able to deny the resemblance."

The tears sliding down her cheeks felt like daggers to his heart. The last thing he wanted was to make Nathalie cry. Damn, how was he going to make it better for her? What could he say to take away her pain?

Why was it so horrible for her to find out that he was her father?

With a resigned sigh, Bhathian dropped his head on his fists. This wasn't how he'd imagined it would go. In his fantasies, Nathalie would be surprised, even shocked a little, but then jump into his arms with happy tears in her eyes. Not sad ones that were tearing at his gut.

He wished he could take it back.

If finding out he was her father made Nathalie so miserable, then maybe it would've been better if she had never found out. For him, it sufficed that he knew.

But then, there was a way to press rewind, wasn't there? He could thrall the memory away, and everything would be back to normal.

"If you wish, I can make you forget this whole conversation," he whispered. "Hurting you was the last thing I wanted. I love you, and I'm so proud that you're my daughter. But it's enough for me that I know. You can go back to believing that Fernando is your biological dad. Just say the words and it'll be done."

"What? No!" Nathalie grabbed his hand. "I'm sorry." She wiped her eyes with her sleeve. "Poor Bhathian, I must've hurt your feelings so bad with my stupid tears. It's just that it's such a shock. I love my father, I mean my Papi. Oh, God, this is difficult. I love the man who's been my father for the past thirty years, and I always will, but I have room in my heart for you too." She lifted her hand and touched a finger to his brows. "The shape is the same, but mine are not as bushy."

Bhathian chuckled. "Thank the merciful Fates. Imagine the pain of plucking all of that on a regular basis."

Her laughter was like salve on the raw endings of his frazzled nerves.

"Be careful, Bhathian, I might be tempted to pluck out some of yours. I bet you'll look much less scary if I tame these a bit."

"So what are you saying? That I'm intimidating? Me? I'm nothing but a big teddy bear."

Andrew chuckled. "A teddy ogre is more like it."

"Hey, don't insult my father." Nathalie winked at Bhathian.

Her words melted his heart, and he couldn't help but pull her up and into an ogre hug. "That's the nicest thing anyone ever said to me."

Andrew tapped his shoulder. "Easy there, big guy, you are squishing my fiancée."

"Sorry." Reluctantly, Bhathian let go of Nathalie. If it was up to him, he would've cradled her in his arms like a baby, making up for lost time. But he was sure she wouldn't appreciate it. Nathalie was a grown woman, a beautiful, smart, accomplished woman, who was about to be married to a great guy that Bhathian felt privileged to call a friend.

Nathalie stretched up to her toes and kissed his cheek. "That's okay. You didn't squeeze too hard. But I think I'll have to keep calling you Bhathian. First of all, you look younger than me, and it will be beyond weird to call you daddy. People might get the wrong idea. And anyway, I can't do it as long as Papi is still around and still aware."

Even though he was disappointed, Bhathian couldn't argue with her logic.

Andrew must've noticed his crestfallen face. "Don't look so glum, my friend. When we find Eva, you guys can pick up from where you left off thirty years ago, and make a brother or sister for Nathalie. That way you'll have someone to call you daddy after all."

Bhathian felt his ears heat up. "First, I need to find her. And when I do, she might not want to have anything to do with me."

Wrapping his arm around Nathalie's waist, Andrew clasped Bhathian's shoulder. With the three of them standing clustered together, he said, "I promise you both. We are going to find Eva and make this family whole again."

52

ANDREW

It was after midnight when Bhathian hugged Nathalie one last time and said goodnight.

With a sigh, she dropped on the couch next to Andrew. "I'm exhausted, but I don't think I'll be able to sleep."

He lifted her up onto his lap. "I can sing you a lullaby."

"The obscene one that your grandpa taught you?"

"That's the only one I know."

"Maybe some other time."

"Deal." He kissed her forehead. "Are you okay?"

"Yeah, I am. It was a lot to take in, but at the same time, it clarified so many things. I no longer think I'm crazy, which is great. It's like a great weight has lifted off my chest. And I can understand why my mother felt like she needed to disappear. I've spent such a long time being angry at her, feeling abandoned, unloved. It's good to know that she didn't do it on a whim. That she had a very good reason for going into hiding. But what was even worse was imagining that something awful had happened to her. It made me feel guilty for being angry at her. Now I'm more hopeful that she is alive and well."

"She is. I've traced where her pension money goes. She has it routed to a Swiss account, and from there to a bank in Rio."

Nathalie perked up. "So we can find her?"

"Not we, Bhathian. He is going to Brazil as soon as this big thing I've told you about is over."

"Can you tell me more about it? Or is it a secret?"

"I no longer have a reason to keep anything from you. Other than anything related to my work and national security that I'm sworn not to reveal, that is. A female immortal has been captured by the clan's enemies, and they are planning a rescue. It's going to be an all-out assault on the enemy stronghold. Just as soon as we find where they are holding her."

Nathalie's face grew pale. "Are you going to take part in it?"

He chuckled. "No. As a human, I'll be more of an impediment than help. These guys are powerful."

"But Bhathian is going, right?"

He nodded. "Bhathian is a Guardian. One of only seven."

"What's a Guardian? Like a bodyguard?"

"Something like that. They used to be warriors, but during peacetime, they are more like an internal police force. Kian called in the reserves, all the old Guardians who left the force, but they need each one of the seven currently serving to train the others and make them battle ready."

He felt Nathalie shiver. "That's so scary. And I thought I had problems before. They seem so trivial compared to this."

"You have nothing to worry about. The Guardian Force is formidable. They'll overpower their enemies and rescue the female with ease." Well, there were no guarantees. But it was likely. Enough so Andrew could assuage Nathalie's fears with a clear conscience.

Chewing on her lower lip, she looked up at him with sad eyes. "It's not only Bhathian that I fear for. I fear for Kian. And I fear for Syssi who must be going crazy with anxiety as she thinks about her husband going into battle. But most of all I fear for you."

"Why? I told you I'm not taking part in this one."

"Yeah, I know. But you are going to attempt the transition, risking your life for pie in the sky. I don't want it. I'd rather have you with me for the span of our mortal lives than lose you over this. We can be so happy, Andrew. We could have children and grandchildren and age together, and it would be wonderful. Why risk it?"

He couldn't refute or dismiss her concerns. Echoing his own thoughts, Nathalie was right on every count. Except one. She had the chance of becoming immortal and he would be damned forever if she gave it up for him. "We can have all of this but for much longer. The kids and the grandkids and their grandkids. It will all work out. I promise. I'll transition just fine. A stubborn bastard like me is not going to give up on a life with a woman he loves. I'll fight for it with all I have, and I'll survive."

"How can you promise something that you can't control? You don't know how your body will react. You're strong and healthy, but don't tell me not to worry. I know that you do. Otherwise, you would've done it a long time ago, right after your sister's transition."

Again, she was spot on. "Look, Nathalie. I won't deny the risk, and I've waited till now because, frankly, I didn't have a strong enough reason to go for it. Not until I met you. You are everything to me. You are my reason for wanting to live for as long as possible, so I can spend as much time with you as I can. But I wanted to make sure that you're a Dormant before I went for it. That was the only precaution I cared about. But after Syssi's vision, I no longer want to wait. Besides, you being a Dormant is almost a certainty."

She cupped his cheek. "Don't you see, my love? If something happens to you, I don't want to go on without you. Especially since you are doing this for me. I wouldn't be able to live with myself."

"Oh, sweetheart." He gathered her closer and kissed her trembling lips.

"Sometimes we need to take a risk. Life doesn't come with guarantees, and if we let fear deter us from reaching for what we want, we would never achieve anything. The safest thing is to sit on the couch and watch the dumb box, but that's not living. And besides, there are risks involved even in that. Like muscle atrophy, getting fat, etc., etc."

She slapped his arm. "Don't make fun of it. This is serious. I'm not talking about complete inactivity. But you'd agree with me that there is a big difference between going for a walk and skydiving. One is a pleasant activity; the other is life-threatening."

He chuckled. "But much more fun."

Nathalie crossed her arms over her chest. "Not everything is about having fun."

"Oh, yeah? I thought it was. Don't knock it until you try it."

"What? Skydiving?"

"Yeah. It's a great rush."

"Never. Not in a million years."

Andrew bent his neck and rubbed his nose on Nathalie's. "How about in a million and one?"

Her lips twitched. "Stop it. I know what you're doing."

"I'm rubbing your cute little nose."

"You're trying to distract me."

"True. But you worry too much, my love. Everything is going to be alright."

"How can you say that? I have a feeling that I'm marrying an incorrigible thrill seeker."

"Yes, you are."

"So you're not even trying to deny it?"

"Why would I? It's the truth. I love adventure, I thrive on danger, always have."

"Oh, boy."

"But I promise always to be careful."

"You're full of promises tonight."

"I am. And I intend to deliver on each and every one."

DARK WARRIOR'S DESTINY

1

CAROL

*E*ndless suffering. A nightmare Carol was never going to wake from.
Like every other evening, the sadist had whipped her bloody, treated her wounds, comforted her, fucked her, then left her to heal overnight.

It was a vicious cycle.

Not that she cared one way or another, but it was impossible to tell the actual time of day in this basement, or underground, or whatever it was. There were no windows. Not in her room, and not in the torture chamber as she called what the sadist referred to as his 'playroom.' Those were the only places he'd taken her to.

There were girls in the adjoining cells. She'd heard them talking, and fucking, and even laughing. Evidently, the other Doomers were not as bad as Sebastian. And even though she had no doubt that the women were held against their will, they were at least treated better. They even got to get out and see the sunlight, something the sadist believed Carol, as an immortal, didn't need.

Once a day, she would hear the Doomer in charge of this place herd the women out.

Whatever. The whole place was silent now, so the others must be sleeping. Carol shifted, trying to get more comfortable. Lying face down for so long was becoming hard to endure, but she was afraid to turn around. Her wounds should be closed by now, but her entire back was still throbbing with pain.

Damn, she would do anything for a joint right now. Scratch that; she needed a morphine injection to numb the pain. Both physical and emotional. Though she would settle for a Percocet. Anything to take the edge off.

Fuck, if she hadn't been such a pothead, she would have never stepped outside to smoke that joint, would have never ended up as the whipping toy of a merciless sadist, and Ben would still be alive.

Dear Fates, the guilt was even worse than the physical pain.

Carol still harbored a smidgen of hope that Ben had managed to escape, or that George had found him in that alley and had rushed him to safety. But at the back of her mind, she feared the worst. There was no way he could've escaped. There had been too many of them. And if he'd been still alive, the Doomers would have loaded him into their minivan and brought him here.

Maybe they had.

She'd been out when they'd locked her in this cell, this hell. They might've brought Ben as well, and were holding him somewhere else. This was the worst possibility, though, worse than his death.

After all, as a female immortal, she was a rare and irreplaceable commodity, and the sadist would want to keep her alive. But he had no need for Ben. Sebastian would torture him for information, and after getting everything he could out of Ben, he would finish him.

An honorable end in battle would've been a mercy.

The one bright spot she clung to, her only victory in this losing battle, was that the sadist had bought her dumb act. Somehow, through the haze of pain, she'd managed to keep the façade of a stupid airhead who knew nothing about anything. Surprisingly, he'd believed her when she'd cried and sobbed, claiming that she had no idea where the keep was.

But if Sebastian had Ben—

Carol shivered. It didn't matter if Ben had told the sadist everything or nothing. Sebastian would've tortured her friend for the fun of it. Like a cat playing with a mouse, he would've given Ben an illusion of hope, just to kill him in the end.

Fates, please, please, I'm not asking anything for myself. But please save Ben. Let him be alive and well at the keep, or already dead. But not here, suffering at the hands of this monster.

Her sobs scraped over a dry throat that was still raw from her screams, and glancing at the nightstand, she eyed the water bottle her tormenter had left for her. She was so thirsty, but reaching for it meant stretching her arm and moving her bruised and knotted back muscles. Besides, her bladder was full, and any more liquid would force her to get up and shuffle to the bathroom. Something she was hoping to avoid for a couple more hours. If she managed to fall asleep, by the time it was morning, or the end of whatever the sleep cycle was here, the pain would be gone and going to the bathroom would not be the Herculean effort it would be now.

In the end, the thirst and the full bladder won. Moving as few muscles as possible, Carol shifted toward the edge of the bed and lifted an exhausted arm to grab the bottle. Enduring the pain had sucked out every last iota of energy from her, and every muscle in her body hurt, even those that weren't bruised.

Shit, she needed her other hand to twist the cap off.

Gritting her teeth, Carol pushed through the pain to get herself to a sitting position and opened the fucking thing.

Bliss. The water was still cold, and going down her throat, it felt like the life-giving liquid it was. Carol didn't stop until it was empty. With a grunt, she pushed to her feet and took the empty plastic container to the bathroom.

When she finally made it to the toilet, she had another moment of bliss as she sat down and emptied her bladder. Who would have thought that the simplest things would feel so good? Apparently, when deprived of everything else, a drink of water and a toilet seemed like the best life had to offer.

Perhaps she could muster enough strength to get into the shower. The sadist had cleaned her before tucking her in bed, but to stand under a stream of water without anyone watching her was another simple pleasure she craved to claim for herself. Fates knew there weren't many.

She was naked, so at least there was no need to take anything off. Carol stepped inside the tiny shower stall and turned the faucet to the maximum it had to offer. The pressure sucked, but the water was hot enough and seemed to be in endless supply. The temperature didn't vary for the entire hour or more she just stood under the weak stream, letting it soothe her bruised and abused body.

When she was done, Carol patted herself dry with a soft towel, then filled her bottle with tap water. She brushed her teeth, doing it in slow motion because it hurt even to move her arm, then rinsed her mouth with the bottle. It was a little gross, since she intended to drink from it later, but bending to reach the stream of water straight out of the faucet was a definite no go. She intended to do as little bending as possible.

As she got back to her bed, she took her time to lower herself gently to the bed, gingerly lying on her side. When the position proved tolerable, Carol sighed and closed her eyes.

Despite what her family thought of her, Carol's life hadn't always been easy, but nothing could've prepared her for this. The pain and the blood weren't even the worst of it. In fact, if there were an Olympic competition for misery, the pain would've gotten only the bronze, the guilt would've won the silver, while the shame would've taken the gold.

Fates, the shame.

Carol buried her face in the pillow. Her tormenter was playing with more than her body; he was manipulating her mind, breaking her and molding her into what he wanted her to become. And she was letting him because she was too weak to fight it, too needy to refuse the little comfort he was offering her. Worst of all, as impossible as it seemed, she was wet for him when he entered her.

It must have been his immortal pheromones working their magic on her body. There was no other explanation. She wasn't submissive, she didn't get off on pain, and she sure as hell found nothing attractive about the sadist. In fact, nothing would've given her greater pleasure than to cut the fucker's heart out, but only after she'd whipped him to within an inch of his life the same way he was doing to her. Over and over again, allowing him just enough time to heal, then doing it again.

The image brought a bitter smile to her face.

Sweet Carol, the one who'd been nice to everyone, was gone. The sadist had created a monster—a vicious, bloodthirsty woman who was bent on revenge.

2

NATHALIE

"Time to wake up, sleepyhead." Nathalie kissed Andrew's bare chest.

"What time is it?" he mumbled without opening his eyes, his warm hand caressing her back in a downward trek that she knew would end up on her butt.

Yup, and here it goes. He closed his palm over one cheek, kneading it lazily.

Nathalie chuckled. Andrew was definitely an ass man. He couldn't get enough of what she used to consider her worst feature. He loved it, constantly praising and fondling it at every opportunity. So much so that she could no longer hate her big butt. Pretty soon she'd be like the mammoth from *Ice Age*, the one voiced by Queen Latifah, asking if her butt looked big in this or that and saying thank you for an affirmative answer.

Unfortunately, with Vlad waiting for her in the kitchen, they had no time for a morning romp. Still, she couldn't help rubbing a little against Andrew's muscular thigh, the friction from his sparse leg hair providing a tingle of excitement.

"It's quarter to six, and you still need to go home to shower and change."

With a groan, Andrew cupped her butt cheeks with both hands and lifted her on top of him. "Kiss me," he commanded.

She gave his lips a light peck and tried to wiggle out from his embrace.

"Uh-uh-uh. A real kiss." Andrew abandoned one of her cheeks to cup the back of her head and kissed her long and hard.

As his talented tongue licked into her mouth and his hand traced the seam between her ass cheeks, it didn't take long for Nathalie to grow moist.

"Stop it!' She slapped his chest. "We have no time for this."

His face fell, and his disappointed pout made her laugh. He looked like a boy who didn't get the toy he wanted.

"What's funny?" Andrew reluctantly let her go.

"You. I promise your favorite toy will be waiting for you when you get home this evening."

"Who said it's my favorite?" he teased as he followed her out of bed and reached for his pants.

Nathalie assumed an akimbo pose and glared at him. "It's not only your favorite, but it's your only one. Are we clear?"

Andrew zipped up his pants and reached for her, pulling her into his strong arms. "Forever and ever, you're the only one for me. I love you, my Nathalie. You are my treasure."

"You'd better believe it." She pouted.

The corners of Andrew's lips twitched. "That's it? No, I-love-you-too-my-prince? Or, you-are-the-only-one-for-me?"

It was hard to keep her pretended peeve when he was being so sweet. She looked up into his blue, smiling eyes. "You know, I do. I adore you."

Andrew nodded, his harsh features turning soft. "It's good to hear. Really good. I don't think anyone ever said they adored me before."

"Didn't your mother tell you that?"

He chuckled. "When you meet her, you'll understand why something like that is unlikely ever to leave her lips."

"Is she strict?"

"No. And she is not cold either. Anita expresses her love for us freely, but in a reserved way. My dad is the opposite. But that's because he is a salesman, or maybe he is a salesman because he is so charming and affectionate."

She was dying to meet both. But according to Andrew, they had no plans to leave Africa and come back home anytime soon. As a doctor, providing crucial healthcare to the children of the war-devastated region, Andrew's mother believed that her work was more important than visiting her adult children. Not that anyone could argue with that.

Nathalie wondered, though, if Andrew's parents knew anything about the immortals, or that their children were part of this bizarre world.

She looked up at him. "Do they know? About Syssi? About you?"

He nodded. "They do. They came for Syssi and Kian's wedding, so it was unavoidable. Normally, Kian or one of the others would've thralled them to forget anything that had to do with immortals, but my mother asked to be allowed to keep the memories. The compromise was to place them under a strong compulsion to never talk about it with anyone outside the clan."

Thralling, compulsion, what else could these people do? But more importantly, had they used any of it on her? Without her consent? It was a disturbing thought.

Nathalie grabbed her robe and put it on, tying the belt a bit too snugly.

She narrowed her eyes. "Did anyone thrall me? Or place me under some compulsion without my knowledge?"

Andrew paused with his shirt dangling from his fingers. "No. There was no reason to. And besides, they have strong laws against it. It's permitted only when there is no other way to hide who they are." He shrugged the shirt on. "In fact, by telling you, I broke a promise to keep their existence secret, and so did Bhathian."

"Are you going to get in trouble for this?"

"Probably. But now is not the time to rock the boat. Kian has enough on his plate as it is. We are going to tell him after the battle. In the meantime, though, don't let Jackson and Vlad know that you're on to them. You'll need to watch how you act around them, or even think. Immortals have an extraordinary sense of smell, and each emotion produces a distinct scent."

"Great. So how am I supposed to hide my feelings?"

He smirked. "Ah, this is the essence of the art of deception. You can pretend that they are caused by something else. If you emit an anxious scent, they can't know why you feel that way, only that you do."

"Got it." She could pull it off. Immortal or human, the boys were only teenagers; still confused about women and their peculiar behaviors. Not that men got any smarter with age. Most never figured it out. Even the married ones spent their lives bewildered by their wives, trying to cope the best they could.

Like her poor Papi.

Even when his brain had been still functioning properly, Fernando had probably had trouble figuring out why her mother had left him. And what Andrew had suggested was too preposterous to believe. There was no way her father, adoptive that is, had cheated on her beautiful mother. There must've been another reason. Maybe it had to do with her mother discovering that she was immortal. Or maybe it was as simple as Fernando not getting Eva, not knowing how to please her, how to make her happy.

Nathalie had to admit, though, that Andrew was pretty good at reading her. Maybe because he had a younger sister who he'd watched growing up into a woman. Or maybe it was just the way he was. He didn't have to guess what she wanted or needed because he saw her and listened to her. Andrew paid attention. Like with the coffee. He'd noticed that she liked drinking cappuccinos during the day but preferred drip first thing in the morning. Once was enough for him to not only remember, but to make it for her whenever he'd slept over. Andrew always put her needs first.

After a quick visit to the bathroom, he left her to shower and dress in peace, the way he'd noticed she preferred, and trotted down the stairs to make coffee.

The man was absolutely perfect, and he was hers.

Nathalie was never going to let him go. Not into the arms of another woman, and not into the great beyond, or whatever people wanted to call the place where ghosts lived or existed. Because ghosts weren't technically alive, right?

She'd claw out the eyes of any floozy who even dared look at him for too long. Except, loose women were the least of her concerns. Nathalie's most fearsome adversary wasn't some horny cheapie with greedy hooks aimed at her man. Her real opponent carried a deadlier weapon—a scythe—and it had the potential of harvesting Andrew's soul. But even the Angel of Death would not win against her. Like the biblical Jacob, Nathalie would wrestle him for Andrew's life. And if she lost? That would mean that she was dead too and could follow him into that other realm. Hopefully, ghosts were allowed to have relationships.

No one was taking him away from her. Not even God. And if she was committing blasphemy by thinking like that, it was in the name of love, and therefore excusable. At least she hoped it was.

Damn, she wished Andrew had never found out about being a Dormant. Or that she might be one as well. Then he would not have been contemplating this transition that sounded like an ingrained invitation for that big guy with the scythe.

But then, they would have never met. The only reason she had Andrew in her life was that he'd been asked to search for her by Bhathian—her biological, immortal father.

3

ROBERT

I can't stand it anymore.

Robert clamped both hands over his ears. Listening to Carol's gut-wrenching sobs was tearing him apart. She'd been at it on and off for hours. It was almost as bad as the screams. The door to his 'office'—the pantry with his desk in it—was closed, which meant that if someone came in he would have a split second notice to assume his regular pose. A guy hunched over his laptop, with a bunch of ledgers and loose notes littering the rest of his desk.

In truth, he wasn't all that busy. It was good to appear as if he was, but there wasn't that much to do. Sebastian appreciated hard work.

Damn, Robert despised the sadistic son of a bitch with an unprecedented fervor.

He'd never liked Sebastian. But when the guy had handpicked him to be his assistant, Robert had been flattered. Sebastian was well known for treating his men well, or at least fairly, and the guy was smart. Robert had hoped to learn from him. Naturally, he'd been aware of the rumors—it wasn't as if Sebastian was trying to hide his sexual preferences. On the contrary, he flaunted them. But as long as Robert hadn't witnessed his commander's depravity, he could pretend it didn't bother him.

He could no longer do that.

It bothered him now. A lot.

Before Letty, Sebastian had been indulging in his kink away from the base, going to that private club where other monsters like him went to abuse women. The only difference was that the women were supposedly willing. Though Robert couldn't wrap his head around it. Who in their right mind would want to get whipped and fucked by a stranger? And as far as he knew, the women didn't even do it for money.

Insanity.

Poor Letty. Such a nice girl. Sebastian had been brutal with her, but that was nothing compared to what he was doing to Carol. When mortality was of no concern, Sebastian's cruelty knew no limits.

She was such a soft little thing. Looked so fragile. His heart was breaking every time he'd go into her cell to deliver her meals and see the state she was in.

Her immortal body was resilient, thank Mortdh for that. But at this rate, her mind was going to snap. No one could suffer what she was going through day after day and not lose their shit.

He had to help her.

Springing her free was impossible. But he might be able to ease her pain. The last time he'd been on club patrol he'd made some purchases. For Carol. Something to numb the pain.

Robert hoped that what he'd bought was legit. He was clueless as far as these things went. A straight arrow, he never drank, never smoked, and never used drugs. Using went against the code of conduct of a Doomer, but it wasn't strictly prohibited. The commanders allowed it as long as it was kept under wraps and no one lost their shit. It just didn't appeal to him. Why muddle his faculties when it was difficult enough to perform all that was required of him when operating on his full brain power? Robert wasn't the brightest guy, Tom could run circles around him, but he was the most hardworking and dedicated of each and every last soldier in this place.

At the end of the day, perseverance and grit counted for more than intelligence. Or at least Robert liked to think it did.

There was another advantage to his straight-arrow but not too bright reputation. Sebastian would never suspect him of anything. Even if Robert reeked of anxiety, there would be nothing new about it. He was always nervous around his commander.

Behind the charming smiles and the soft voice lurked a monster. Robert had seen it at work, and so had the other men handpicked by Sebastian to serve with him here. Carol's screams could be heard all over the building, and a hush would fall over the men until the screaming stopped; either because Sebastian was done or because Carol could scream no more. Some would joke about it, dismiss it as nothing, as the commander's due, but Robert had seen the resentment in the eyes of others.

None of the men were guilt free. They were all using the girls imprisoned down in the basement, himself included. But according to the teachings of Mortdh, that was what females were for. Still, there was a difference, a big one, between having gentle sex with a woman and ensuring that she enjoyed it, and what Sebastian had been doing to Letty and now to Carol. Or at least Robert liked to think that there was.

Robert thought of himself as a good man. He wasn't a monster like Sebastian, and he was going to do something about it even though he was terrified of the consequences. Sebastian would flay his skin off piece by piece if he ever found out, not leaving enough of him to bury.

So just make sure never to get caught.

Robert pushed up to his feet and stretched, reaching for the container of barley on the top shelf. He'd hidden his contraband inside the tin can, knowing no one was going give the barley a second glance. It wasn't something the men would think of cooking. So until Sebastian got that cook he'd been promising them, it was the safest place to hide the things.

But now he had a problem. He'd dropped the little white pills inside the grain and then shaken the container before putting it up on the shelf. Finding the two he needed for today was taking him too long.

What if someone walked in and saw him with his hand deep inside the barley? What excuse could he give? Anyone would know that he'd been up to something.

Damn, it had seemed such a good hiding place, but he would need to find a better one. Somewhere that was easily accessible and yet hidden, and not where anyone could walk in on him.

Later.

Sebastian had left with Tom that morning, and they wouldn't be back until after lunch. They were meeting some radio station owner who was looking into selling the thing.

This was the perfect time to give Carol her present and then find a new hiding place for her pills.

Putting the two he fished out of the barley in his pocket, Robert went out into the kitchen to prepare breakfast for the girls. He would start with the others and keep Carol for last so he could stay with her for a few minutes.

Breakfast was an easy affair; cereal, cut fruit, two pieces of toast and orange juice. But there were seventeen human girls in the basement, and one immortal, and each got her own tray.

Usually, he stayed a little in each room, chatting with the girls to find out if they were comfortable, and if they needed anything. But today he had no patience for it. Trouble was, to avoid suspicion he needed to behave exactly the same as he had every other day.

When he exited the last room, Robert wanted to sigh with relief but didn't. He could not allow himself any behavior that was out of the ordinary. Everything needed to seem the same.

Still, he'd taken extra care with Carol's tray, heaping it with more food and adding a thermos with coffee. But that was okay. She was the commander's toy and therefore deserved better. Besides, the poor thing needed the extra energy.

Balancing the tray on one hand, Robert knocked twice before entering, same way he did in front of every room, just to let the girls know that he was coming in.

Most greeted him with a hello, or a come in, but not Carol. As usual, she lay on her side, facing the wall, and didn't acknowledge his presence.

He needed her to look at him so he could sneak her the pills. There were surveillance cameras in all the rooms, recording sound as well as visual. Standing in a spot where he was blocking the only camera in this room with his back, Robert took care of the visual, but there was nothing he could do about the sound.

"I brought your breakfast. The strawberries are fresh and juicy, and so is the peach. Would you like me to pour you coffee?" It was more than he'd ever said to her before. He'd been too ashamed and guilt-ridden to try and strike up a conversation. Hopefully, she'd notice the difference and turn around.

When she didn't, he snuck his hand into his front pocket and then lifted a strawberry off the plate. "Here, I want you to taste it. I'm sure you've never had something as good before."

Talking to her like that, Robert was taking a risk, but he was running out of options, and he was already spending too long in her room.

Finally she responded, turning her head and pinning him with a pair of blue eyes that were big and round and so innocent that they cut straight into his heart. But she was looking at his face, not his hand.

"Look how big it is, and how red. I bet it will render you speechless." He shoved his hand in front of him, careful that it was still hidden by his body.

Carol's beautiful face revealed her puzzlement, but she glanced down at what he was holding in his hand, then jerked her head back up.

Don't say anything, just take them. They are for the pain, he mouthed.

She nodded imperceptibly and lifted her small hand to take his offering, closing her fingers around the strawberry and the two Percocet pills.

"Thank you," she whispered. "It's very kind of you to bring me such beautiful fruit."

He smiled. "You're welcome. And tomorrow I'll bring you more. If not strawberries, then another succulent fruit."

She nodded again, letting him know that she understood his meaning.

Take them right before. But you need to keep pretending it hurts the same, he mouthed.

She nodded again, her reddish-blonde curls bouncing around her small face.

"Thank you," she said aloud and turned around to face the wall again.

Smart girl.

Anything else would've been out of character for her.

4

NATHALIE

"Good morning, Papi, did you sleep well?" Nathalie asked when her father came down to the kitchen.

He sidled up to her and kissed her cheek. "As well as can be expected." Shuffling away, he sat at his designated spot in the kitchen, where his breakfast and his morning paper were waiting for him.

Nathalie frowned. That shuffle was getting worse. Not only that, but Papi also looked a little thinner. He was still overweight, just a little bit less. Fernando losing weight would have made her happy a few years back, but now it was a reason for concern. Just another sign of the dementia that was creeping up slowly but surely and destroying yet another piece of him.

With a sigh, Nathalie turned back to her work station and the sandwich she'd been making before Papi had come down.

Funny, all her life she'd been convinced that she looked more like her father than her mother, when in fact Fernando hadn't contributed any of the genes in her mix. Pausing with the piece of lettuce in hand, she glanced at him again.

The only real resemblance was their coloring, which her mother shared as well. His eyes were shaped differently than hers, and so was his nose. Only their lips were similar, not in shape but in thickness. They both had full lips.

Did he know? This was the question that bothered her most. Had he married her mother not knowing she was pregnant? Or had he known all along?

Problem was, she couldn't ask him. He might not remember. Besides, bringing up a subject like that would distress him. Her questions would have to wait for her mother to be found.

"Hey, Nathalie, is that sandwich ready?" Jackson came in and dropped a tray of dirty dishes into the sink.

Shit, this wasn't the time to think about things like that. She had work to do. "Give me another moment," she told Jackson as she heaped coleslaw and salad on the plate then decorated it with slices of cut pickle. "Here you go." She handed Jackson the plate. "Anything else?"

"No. That was the only sandwich. All the other orders were cappuccinos and baked goodies. You can take a break."

"Thank you, boss," she said.

Most of the time, Nathalie appreciated all that Jackson was doing for her and her business. Sometimes, though, when he behaved as if he owned the place and she was the one working for him and not the other way around, she was ready to kick him out.

Well, not really. She needed him.

"You're welcome." The kid smirked and headed out.

Ugh, Nathalie's hand itched to smack the arrogant immortal over the head. Now that she knew he and Vlad were immortals, some things became clear. Like Vlad's incredible strength, and Jackson's inexhaustible stamina.

Poor Vlad, no wonder he looked like a cross between a human, a snake, and a vampire. This was in a nutshell what he was. Still, Jackson came from the same family and he was movie-star gorgeous. Question was whether the guy was so full of himself because he belonged to a superior race of beings, or because he was so incredibly good looking?

Probably the good looks. He would've been just as cocky if he were a human. Getting too much female attention would've inflated any guy's ego.

Nathalie shrugged and took off her apron.

If Jackson wanted to play at being boss, she'd let him. Let him experience how hard it was to do everything by himself when the place filled up with people. Because that was what bosses did. They had to handle stuff others had the luxury of refusing to deal with.

"Papi, I'm going out on a short errand, but Vlad and Jackson are here if you need anything."

"Who is Vlad?"

"That would be me." Vlad paused from washing dishes and waved with a sudsy hand.

"Oh." Fernando pretended that he knew who Vlad was. "You can go, Nathalie. I'll just finish the paper and head upstairs for my show. It starts in a few minutes." He glanced at his watch. "Seven minutes to be exact."

Memory was a funny thing. Fernando couldn't remember who Vlad was even though the kid was there every day, but he had no problem remembering the schedules of all his shows.

Nathalie retrieved her purse from one of the kitchen cabinets and slung it over her shoulder. "Tell Jackson I went to the bank, okay?"

Vlad frowned and then nodded.

Damn, she had forgotten all about the immortals' enhanced senses. Vlad had smelled the lie on her. Whatever. She didn't need to tell him that she just needed to get away for a little while, find a quiet spot to sit, preferably somewhere that was green, like under a tree, and just think.

"I won't be gone for long." She got out through the back door and locked it behind her. Vlad had a key and so did Jackson.

Walking down the street by herself felt oddly liberating. It was mid-morning and no one besides her was taking a stroll. The traffic was sparse as well, which meant that it was quiet. A nice change from the busy clamor of the café.

The further away she got, the easier her breathing became. Nathalie felt relaxed. Hell, she hadn't been aware of being tense. Though come on, after the recent revelations she would've been crazy not to feel some sort of distress. Her destination, a public park, was another street over, and as she reached it she headed straight for her favorite spot. A bench shaded by a big oak tree. Usually, she came here with Papi. He liked to sit down and watch the moms and their babies playing in the sandbox. It was too early for that, and the park was deserted, same as the streets leading to it.

Nathalie sat down, closed her eyes, and took a deep breath.

Ah, the smell of fresh grass, such a nice change from the cooking and baking smells of the café, not to mention that she finally had some quiet time for herself.

It didn't last long, though. She felt the pressure a fraction of a moment before she heard the voice in her head.

I'm sorry to interrupt, but there is something I really need to tell you.

"What is it, Sage?"

I figured it out. I know why I'm still here.

"Oh, yeah?"

Someone I care about needs my forgiveness. I believe that once I tell her I'm not angry with her, and that I want her to have a good life with the one fate has chosen for her, I could finally cross over to the other side.

For some reason, the idea of Sage going away and never coming back made her sad. Perhaps he was wrong?

"Are you sure? The last time we talked you had no idea who you were. What jogged your memory?"

I apologize for eavesdropping, but as I listened to what Andrew and Bhathian were telling you last night, it all sounded oddly familiar to me. I wasn't surprised at all to learn about immortals. In fact, I realized that I was one.

"But you're dead, Sage. If you were an immortal you would be alive."

Actually, it's Mark. And, unfortunately, immortals can be killed in several ways. Decapitation or cutting out the heart are two, a deadly dose of venom is the other.

Nathalie's hand clapped over her mouth as bile rose up her throat. "Please tell me you didn't have your head cut off or your heart cut out."

No, I was murdered by a Doomer. That's what we call the followers of Mortdh. He pumped me with enough venom to stop my heart—permanently.

It sounded a bit less horrible than the first two options, but it must've taken a while for the poisonous venom to do its work. "You must've been terrified." Nathalie shivered.

Not really. The thing about our venom is that it has a euphoric side effect. Great for sex, by the way. When Andrew turns, you'll understand what I'm talking about.

Nathalie felt herself blush. It was good that he couldn't see her unless she was facing a mirror. The last thing she wanted was to talk about her sex life with Sage. *Mark*, she corrected herself. Having him in her head was intrusive enough, thank you very much. A change of subject was in order.

"You said something about telling someone you're not mad at her. Who is this woman that needs your forgiveness and why?"

It couldn't have been a rejected lover, not unless Mark hadn't been exclusively gay. Perhaps before admitting to himself that he preferred other men, Mark had a girlfriend? Someone he'd dumped for another guy?

Nathalie heard Mark's ghostly chuckle. Damn, she'd forgotten to shield her thoughts from him.

No, it's not an ex-girlfriend. I've always been gay. It's my cousin, Amanda.

"Kian's sister? What did she do to you?"

Nothing, and that's why I need to tell her that none of that was her fault and she shouldn't feel guilty. Her only crime was falling in love with the guy who'd ordered my murder.

Nathalie cringed. That was awful. The woman must've had some serious issues. There was no justification for getting entangled with your cousin's murderer. "It's not exactly trivial, you know. I don't think I would be so forgiving if I were in your shoes—figuratively speaking, of course. I don't suppose ghosts wear shoes, right?"

He laughed, and it felt like little bubbles inside her head.

I wear whatever I want. It's all conjured. And as to Amanda, when she fell for Dalhu, she didn't know the guy was the commander of the Doomer unit and, therefore, the one who'd ordered my death. Since then, he's repented in a big way and redeemed himself in Amanda's eyes as well as the rest of the clan. He is her fated mate.

"You're a nicer person than I am, Mark. Even with all the extenuating circumstances, I don't think I would've been able to forgive her."

Nathalie, Nathalie, Nathalie. What you fail to see is that forgiveness liberates not only the wrongdoer but also the one who was wronged. Without unburdening myself, how can I cross over to the place of eternal love and happiness? Knowing that Amanda is suffering needlessly, I'm not weightless and carefree as I need to be to go where I want to go.

"Is the other side really a place of love and happiness?" This was a question she'd posed to Tut many times over the years, but had never gotten an answer to.

I don't know for sure, but I can feel it; the warmth and the light are calling to me.

Nathalie nodded. "I get it. You need to do this for yourself just as much as for her."

Exactly.

"Did you try to reach her?"

I did. I tried her, I tried Syssi who is a seer, but neither has your unique talent. They can't hear me. You'll need to tell Amanda for me.

Oh, boy. As if her life wasn't complicated enough already. "If you listened to what was said last night, you must be aware that your relatives are not supposed to know that Andrew and Bhathian revealed their secrets to me. If I admit it to Amanda, which I don't see a way around if I want to tell her your side of the story, I'll get Andrew and Bhathian in trouble."

Mark snorted. *Girl, but that's the beauty of blaming the security leak on a ghost. What can they do to me? I'm already dead.*

True, but that would mean lying. Not the best way to start a relationship with her new family. Except, to keep Andrew and Bhathian out of trouble, perhaps she could phrase things in a way that would imply that Mark had spilled the beans without actually saying it.

Then again, pretending not to know was just another form of lying.

5

ANDREW

*A*s Andrew entered Nathalie's shop, her face lit up as if weeks had passed since she'd last seen him and not hours. She must've been thinking about the sex they hadn't had time for this morning.

It certainly had been on his mind, distracting him the entire day.

Andrew smirked as he walked behind the counter to take her into his arms. "Missed me much?"

"I did. What took you so long?"

Puzzled, he glanced at his watch. It was quarter to seven, which was more or less the same time he got there every day. "Ah... what do you mean?" Had he forgotten something? Was there a reason he needed to come home earlier?

"Never mind." Nathalie clasped his hand and pulled him behind her, heading for the stairs. "I have something very exciting to tell you."

Damn, he hated surprises. "What is it?"

"I'll tell you upstairs." She kept climbing.

When they reached the den, she took him over to the couch, holding his hands as they sat facing each other. God, he hoped she wasn't going to tell him she was pregnant. Someday, he wanted children with Nathalie, just not yet.

"I talked with Sage today." Nathalie squeezed Andrew's hand.

Okay, so this wasn't about her being pregnant. *Phew...*

"And?"

"He told me that his name isn't Sage, it's Mark. He remembered his past. He was one of them."

"One of whom?"

"The immortals. He is, was, Amanda's cousin, and he needs me to relay a message to her. He says that she feels guilty about falling for the guy that had ordered his murder, but Mark says that he is not angry. He wants her to have a good life."

Andrew's throat clogged. Nathalie had no way of knowing about Amanda and Dalhu. This was the proof he was waiting for. Other than finding Eva and confirming her immortality, this was the best he could hope for. Talking to ghosts was a real God-given paranormal talent.

He pulled her into his arms. "This is the best news you could've given me."

"It is? I thought you would be concerned about Amanda finding out that you told me everything. I'm trying to think of a way to talk to her without getting you in trouble."

Andrew waved his hand. "Don't worry about her. Amanda is a rule breaker herself. She will keep quiet about it."

Nathalie's frown eased only a little. 'I don't understand why Mark's revelation makes you so happy."

"Oh, sweetheart, because it proves so many important things. I know exactly what Mark is referring to, but you don't. You never heard the story. This proves that ghosts exist and that there is a continuation after death. But for me, what I'm happy about the most, is that now I'm a hundred percent sure you're a Dormant."

Nathalie narrowed her eyes at him. "I see. I thought you were already convinced. Talking about transitioning like you had everything figured out."

She'd got him there. "I was ninety-nine percent sure." Time to make a quick change of subject. "What I wonder, though, is if we should arrange a meeting with Amanda and Dalhu, or just Amanda."

"I think it would be awkward to talk in front of Dalhu. Mark said nothing about forgiving him, just Amanda."

It worked, she forgot about being mad at him. *Hallelujah.* "You've got a point. But if we want to talk to her separate from Dalhu, we need to invite her over here. Are you okay with that?"

"Sure. Except, you might want to arrange it for much later to make sure the boys are not here when she shows up."

True. Jackson and Vlad might wonder what Amanda was doing at Nathalie's place. It would be better if they didn't know.

Andrew fished his phone out of his pocket and texted Syssi. *Do you have Amanda's cell number?*

I'm not going to ask why you need it. I'm sending you the link.

Don't be stupid. I want her to meet Nathalie.

K. Say hi to Nathalie for me.

Will do.

"Syssi says hi." Andrew started punching the message to Amanda, but after writing and erasing it several times he gave up and called her instead.

"Hello?" she answered. He wasn't on her contact list, and his caller ID was blocked.

"It's Andrew. How are you doing?"

"Great. And you?"

"Good, good. Listen, can you come to Nathalie's coffee shop in about an hour, or an hour and a half?"

"Hurrah! I'm so glad you're finally going to introduce us. I would love to meet your girl. Let me just check with Kian if it's okay for Dalhu to come with me. I think it is, but I don't want to aggravate him needlessly. Lately, things have been going well between Dalhu and him. It would be stupid to ruin all this progress for an outing."

"Actually, you should come by yourself. We will have a couples date some other time."

"What's going on, Andrew? Are you in some kind of trouble?" Her tone changed from cheerful to worried.

"No, of course not. Nathalie wants to have a girl talk with you."

"Is it about you and me?" Amanda whispered.

Andrew chuckled. "There was no you and me, Amanda. It's about something else. A surprise." He rolled his eyes. If she kept asking he would just tell her the good news over the phone and be done with it. His patience was wearing thin.

"Okay, I'm coming."

"Thank you. I'll text you the address."

After sending Amanda the information, Andrew lifted his head and was confronted by a set of narrowed cat eyes.

"What 'you and me'?" Nathalie made air quotes.

"Come here, you jealous monster." He lifted her to sit in his lap. "She knows of my brief infatuation with her, that's all."

"Are you sure it's over?"

"Yes, sweetheart, a long time ago. I dated another immortal woman since, before I met you, that is."

Nathalie crossed her arms over her chest. "How come you never told me there was another one?"

"I'm nearly forty, Nathalie. There have been many. I'm sure you don't want to hear about each and every one. But my heart never belonged to any of them, not even temporarily. All along it waited for its true owner. You." He planted a kiss on her pouty lips.

She smiled and kissed him back. "Your birthday is coming up."

Andrew grimaced. "Don't remind me—the dreaded four zero. And please, don't make a big fuss about it. We can go out to a nice dinner or something. Maybe even to By Invitation Only. Would you like that?"

"It's your birthday. You should get what you want. Not what I want."

"Hm… In that case, my birthday wish is simple. You, in my bed, in my house, for the entire night and the next day. A full twenty-four hours of your undivided attention."

She slapped his arm playfully. "One-track mind. But you got yourself a deal. Am I supposed to be naked the entire time?"

"Naturally."

6

NATHALIE

Nathalie was arranging some of her leftover pastries on a platter, when a knock announced Amanda's arrival.

"I'll get it," Andrew said.

Holding her breath, Nathalie awaited her first glimpse of the woman Andrew used to have a crush on. After meeting Kian, she had no doubt that his sister would be one hell of a looker. The guy was jaw-droppingly handsome.

"Andrew, darling, it is so good to see you," she heard Amanda exclaim overdramatically.

Great. A freaking diva.

The snooty tone of voice was enough to make Nathalie dislike Amanda immediately, but when Andrew stepped aside, revealing the stunning woman, the dislike turned into deep resentment bordering on hate.

There was no way Andrew felt nothing for Amanda. She wasn't only beautiful, she oozed sex and confidence and charm as well. Any red-blooded man would get a hard-on for her. And as Nathalie knew first hand, Andrew's blood was deep crimson.

Elegant, even though she was wearing nothing fancy, just jeans and a T-shirt, Amanda was also really tall. Probably close to six feet. Her feet ensconced in a pair of flats, the top of her head was only a couple of inches below Andrew's.

An intimidating woman.

Amanda kissed his cheek before shifting her attention to Nathalie. "Oh, my, you are gorgeous!" Amanda rushed toward her and grabbed her hands. "Let me look at you." She leaned back to give Nathalie a once over. "No wonder Andrew fell in love with you at first sight. These big chocolate eyes, and this hair..." She ran her hand through Nathalie's long tresses. "Magnificent." She breathed as if awed. "So exotic."

Okay, so Amanda wasn't all that bad. "Thank you. But please, stop, you are making me blush."

Amanda smiled brightly. "I'm so happy to finally meet you, Nathalie. I've been so curious to see the woman who managed to steal Andrew's heart. His sister and I were afraid he'd end up an old bachelor."

"Ladies, I'm right here. Please stop talking about me like I can't hear you."

Amanda waved a hand. "Okay, darling, no need to get your panties in a wad."

Nathalie relaxed. It seemed that Amanda meant nothing by calling Andrew *darling*. It was just a figure of speech. "Let's sit down and have some coffee. I heard that you liked my pastries and prepared some for you to sample."

Amanda followed her to the front booth which Andrew had set up with three place settings. "Darling, they are divine. You could make a fortune mass-producing them. Though I guess it's not easy to replicate such perfection on a large scale."

Evidently, Amanda had more than looks going for her—she was smart as well—but after the barrage of compliments Nathalie could no longer feel animosity toward the woman, even if she was annoyingly perfect.

"Jackson, your cousin and my assistant, suggested the same thing. He is working on a plan to test the idea on a small scale first."

Amanda clapped her hands. "I love it when young people show initiative. I had no idea Jackson was so enterprising."

Nathalie pushed the platter toward Amanda. "Try some."

Andrew slid out of the booth. "I'd better get the coffee going. Cappuccino, anyone?"

Amanda grimaced. "Not for me, thank you. Syssi is giving me caffeine poisoning, if there is such a thing, forcing me to taste each new variation she tries with her wonder gadget. I'll have tea. Herbal, if you have it."

"Me too."

Andrew lifted a brow. "Since when do you drink herbal teas?"

Nathalie shrugged. "I also feel all coffeed out."

"Fine."

Amanda took a bite of a croissant and closed her eyes while chewing slowly. When she was done, she opened her eyes and gave Nathalie a thumbs up. "I had your croissants before, and this is just as good as I remembered. You're truly gifted."

"Thank you."

Andrew came back with three steaming mugs and an assortment of teabags. "Here you go, ladies."

With the introductions and pleasantries over, it was time to get down to business. Nathalie closed her eyes and concentrated, checking if Mark had already arrived. Although he was getting better, he still had trouble with managing the time differences between their worlds. *You'd better show up in the next five minutes or I'm starting without you*, Nathalie sent, hoping he would hear her. In the meantime, she could explain some of the background.

"There is something I need to tell you, but before I do I have to explain some stuff."

Amanda looked curious. "What is it?"

"I can hear ghosts."

Amanda's eyes widened in what looked more like excitement than surprise. "That's wonderful!"

Nathalie chuckled. "Not really. It's hard to have a normal life when you hear people talking in your head all the time. Anyway, I've had this ability since forever. At first, I thought everyone was like me. In time, though, I realized that talking to imaginary people wasn't commonplace. I didn't know if what I was hearing was real or imagined." Nathalie took Andrew's hand. "Andrew convinced me that I'm not crazy. He told me about his own special ability with detecting lies and about Syssi's foresight."

Understanding dawning, Amanda nodded. "He told you about us."

"Yes, and about the possibility of me being a Dormant. Thanks to him, I started to believe that the voices were real, and recently I was given proof."

Nathalie felt the slight pressure in her head, indicating that she had a visitor.

"How fascinating." Amanda's eyes shone with excitement. Not sparkled. Shone, like a pair of freaking flashlights.

Is it you? Nathalie asked to make sure it was Mark and not Tut, or God forbid someone new.

It's me.

"The proof has to do with you, Amanda. I had no prior knowledge about what I was told, but Andrew did, and he immediately validated it."

"What is it?" Amanda placed a hand over her chest.

"The message is from Mark."

Even though Amanda closed her eyes, Nathalie saw the tears gathering at the corners.

"Thank you, merciful Fates. I've been waiting for a sign from Mark for so long. I thought I was never going to get it."

Tell her I love her and want only the best for her.

"He says he loves you, and he wants only the best for you."

Amanda opened her eyes. "Can he hear me?"

"Yes. He can hear what I hear."

Amanda looked into Nathalie's eyes, but from her expression it was clear she was not seeing her, she was addressing Mark. "Can you ever forgive me, Mark?" Her upper lip trembled and more tears spilled from her eyes.

"He says there is nothing to forgive, that you've done nothing wrong."

The sorrow in Amanda's eyes didn't ease. She was still doubtful.

"Mark says that he is not angry, not even at Dalhu. He says that he knows it wasn't personal."

Amanda shook her head. "I find it hard to believe."

Mark sighed inside Nathalie's head. *I don't know what else to say. She doesn't believe me.*

Nathalie reached across the table and took hold of Amanda's hand. "You have to accept Mark's forgiveness, Amanda. You are tormenting him with your guilt. It puts a burden on him that prevents him from crossing over to the place of love and happiness. Stop blaming yourself. If you need to blame somebody, blame fate, or the Doomer high command. Imagine that your guilt is a sack of rotten tomatoes that you've been lugging around for far too long. Give it a good swing and hurl it to where it belongs. This will be your final gift to Mark— giving him the peace he deserves."

That was good. I couldn't have said it better myself. Thank you.

Amanda smiled through the tears, then pretended to swing a sack over her head and toss it. "Did it work?" she asked Nathalie.

"You tell me. Do you feel better?"

With a deep inhale, Amanda closed her eyes and then exhaled. "I do."

"Mark? How about you? Feeling lighter?"

I need to hear her say it.

Nathalie turned to Amanda. "You need to tell him that you accept his forgiveness and that you no longer feel guilty."

"I love you, Mark," Amanda said instead. "And I always will. No matter where you are, I hope you can remember that. It's so unfair that you've been taken away. You of all people, who were so kind and so gentle and so giving." She was sobbing in earnest now, the tears streaming down her cheeks in two dirty rivulets of dissolved mascara and eyeliner, falling on her white T-shirt and staining it. "And if you find Aiden on the other side, tell him Mommy loves him too, and misses him and always will. Would you do this for me? Please?"

Watching Amanda fall apart, Nathalie started crying as well, it was impossible not to. Poor woman. For a mother, there was no greater tragedy than losing her child. Crap, they should have invited Dalhu. Amanda could've used his love and support to get through this. But Nathalie hadn't expected things to become so emotional.

In her head, Mark sniffled. *Tell Amanda, of course. I'll do all I can to find Aiden and give him the message. Or perhaps he can find you and relay it through you?*

By all means. But I'm not going to tell her that. I don't want her waiting and wishing for it to happen and then it doesn't work out. We'll be doing her a great disservice.

You're right.

"Mark says that he will do everything he can to find Aiden and give him your message."

"Thank you." Amanda lifted a shaky hand to wipe away her tears.

"Scoot," Nathalie said, nudging Andrew to let her out. Someone needed to comfort Amanda.

She walked over to the other side of the booth and slid next to Amanda, wrapping her arm around her, "Shh… it's okay, Just let it all out."

Amanda collapsed into the embrace, sobbing on Nathalie's shoulder until she was all sobbed out. "I'm sorry," she said as she lifted her head.

Nathalie rubbed her back. "We all need a good cry from time to time."

Grabbing a napkin, Amanda wiped her eyes then used it to blow her nose. "Sorry again. I know it's gross."

"Will you stop? That's what girlfriends are for. Right?"

She nodded. "Thank you. And you too, Mark. I accept the gift of your forgiveness. I'm going to treasure it forever."

You're welcome. Goodbye, Amanda. See you on the other side. Hopefully, in a long, long time.

7

ANANDUR

Today was the day Lana was going to tell him everything. Anandur had been pushing, gently but doggedly, and he felt she was ready. One last shove would do the trick.

It must.

If he failed to get information out of her again, Anandur was going to drop her and this whole line of investigation. He had already wasted too much time on it, and he was getting sick of Lana, and of pretending to feel for her more than he did.

She was a fine piece of ass, but not fine enough to keep coming back for more.

Besides, the owners of the boat they had been using as their shag-pad were due back the next day. If nothing else, this was reason enough to end things tonight.

"Here you are," he greeted Lana as she finally showed up, pulling her into his arms, shopping bags and all. "Where have you been? I've been waiting here for over half an hour."

She lifted the paper bags. "I go buy food. Renata no cooking today. She go with Geneva."

That was a shame. Anandur had gotten used to Renata's superb cooking. She was a wizard with fish and not too bad with meat either. Except for the goulash—a disgusting dish that was more a soup than a stew and that the Russians loved. She might have been the best cook of it in the world and it would still be disgusting.

"What you got in there?" He peeked into one of the bags.

"The usual. Steaks, corn, and frozen chips to heat up."

"French fries, baby, not chips. Chips are the thin crispy things. If you want to become an American, you need to get your potatoes right."

She flipped him the bird and shoved past him into the tiny kitchen.

Someone is in a bad mood.

He followed her in and put his hands on her shoulders, kneading the kinks as she emptied the contents of the bags on the counter. "What's wrong, baby? You seem tense."

The muscles in her shoulders were as hard as stone. It must've hurt. "Talk to me, sweetheart." He leaned and kissed her neck.

She stopped what she was doing, and for a moment he thought she would start talking, but then she shook her head. "After we eat. I'm hungry."

"No problem. Anything I can do to help?"

"Start the coals in the barbecue."

"Yes, ma'am."

He stepped out onto the deck and fired up the barbecue. A few minutes later, Lana brought the steaks, seasoned and ready for the grill.

He took the plate out of her hands. "I'll take care of the meat. You prepare the French fries."

As he got busy flipping, the smell filling his nostrils was making him hungry. There was nothing better than a steak fresh off the grill. Kian was missing out on the good stuff with his healthy vegan diet. They were immortals for Fates' sakes, there was no need to obsess about eating healthy.

When the meat looked just the way he liked it, Anandur heaped the five steaks on the plate and stepped inside. Lana was just finishing setting up the table with the usual. Corn on the cob, French fries, and a bottle of vodka.

He dropped two of the steaks on her plate and the remaining three on his.

"Let's eat." Stuffing the fabric napkin in the open collar of his shirt, Anandur got ready to attack the meat—fork in one hand and the knife in the other—when Lana cast him a baleful glance. He paused with both suspended in the air. Dipping her head over her steepled hands, she mumbled a quick grace in Russian then crossed herself.

"Now we eat," she said.

The rest of the meal went by in silence. Perhaps because they were both hungry, or because Lana was nervous. Less so after chugging down most of the vodka, but still, he smelled the faint scent of her irritation.

Interesting. Lana seemed pissed about something but not fearful. Not a good sign as far as her spilling the beans went. Anandur assumed that if she were about to reveal her boss's secrets, she would've been terrified.

When both of their plates were empty, Lana leaned back in her chair and rubbed her stomach. "It was good, *da?*"

"Very good. Thank you for a lovely meal."

She reached for her shot glass and he refilled it for her. Shooting it back down her throat, she clanged the small glass on the table and pinned him with a pair of very pale blue eyes. "I want to ask you something."

"Ask away." He waved a hand.

"Did you find your cousin? The one that was taken?"

"No."

She crossed her arms over her chest. "You say you are lion. How come you not find her?"

He smiled even though he was sure it looked more menacing than reassuring. "I'm a small one. But two very powerful lions are working on finding her and punishing those who took her."

She nodded as if he told her something she wanted to hear. "These lions, are they willing to protect weasels from wolf?"

"How many weasels?"

"Six."

The whole crew.

"What could the weasels offer the lions in exchange for their protection?"

"Information. About the wolf and the bad things he does. But the weasels also want new papers. They want to be Americans and start a new life far away from the wolf."

"It's a deal." Anandur had no doubt Kian would approve. Arranging new identities for the crew and taking care of the women's legal status was easy, maybe a little costly, but Kian wouldn't even bat an eyelid before paying up. The information they could provide about Alex and what he was doing was well worth it.

"How do you know the lions say yes? You didn't ask."

"I don't need to. I know that they have the means to arrange for what you need and are willing to do it for information about your boss." The time for allegories from the animal kingdom was over.

Lana narrowed her eyes. "Are you detective?"

"No, I'm not."

"What are you? I know you're no deck boy."

If he wanted her to trust him, he needed to give her something. Apparently, Lana wasn't as dumb as she pretended to be.

"You are right, I am not a deck boy. I work for one of the guys that can help you girls out. He is concerned about Alex's illegal activity. I was sent to investigate. But I'm not a policeman or even a private detective."

"You have sex with me for information?"

Anandur shrugged. "Not that it was such a chore. You're a hot piece of ass, Lana. I enjoyed every moment of it."

That seemed to mollify her. "The man you work for, is he like a Vor?"

Anandur chuckled. Kian would have been affronted to be compared to a mafia boss, but what the hell, for Lana this would be a good enough explanation.

"In a way. He is the head of a big organization, but what we do is mostly legal."

Lana looked skeptical. Legal was not what she was after.

"Don't worry. We have no problem arranging fake papers. In fact, we can provide you with the best papers money can buy. Foolproof. I can also include some cash in the deal to give you girls a head start on your new lives."

She eyed him with a raised brow, her fleshy lips pursed. "What you want in exchange?"

"As I said, information. You practically already admitted to me that Alex is smuggling women and selling them to sex slavers. First, we want to know how he does it. Next, we want details about an upcoming transaction so we can find out who the buyers are."

"I want to see papers first."

Not surprisingly, Lana wasn't going to take him up on his word. The Russian needed to see concrete proof that he could deliver what he was promising."

"No problem. You girls get mug shots for the papers and tell me what names you want to use and I'll have the papers ready for you the next day, and I'll show you the cash. How much do you want? Just don't go crazy with the money, I still need to sell the deal to my boss."

"Twenty thousand each."

Chump change.

"That's reasonable."

"Good."

"Can you tell me at least how he does it?"

She considered for a moment. "They come for him. The girls. He promise them things. Alexander is handsome and rich. They like it. He drugs them and puts them behind the wall in his closet. They sleep all the way until he meets the buyer. Then he transfer them like cargo, and they keep sleeping."

8

CAROL

*L*ying on her side Carol faced the wall, the note she'd scribbled for Robert clutched in her hand.

Her unlikely savior.

Each morning, he would show up with her breakfast and the two little pills that were making her existence a little more tolerable. Actually, she took it back. There was nothing tolerable about getting whipped, healing overnight, and getting whipped all over again the next day. Her torment was still horrendous, just a tiny little bit less excruciating. A never-ending cycle of fear and pain and misery.

How long did the sadist think she could endure this until her mind snapped? Did he even care?

The fucker would have been a complete idiot not to. What were his chances of capturing another indestructible whipping-toy?

None.

Unless he didn't give a shit if she went raving mad or conversely catatonic.

Robert was her only ray of hope. Except, with the surveillance camera monitoring her room twenty-four-seven, there was little she could do to sway him to her side. He seemed a decent fellow, for a Doomer, that is, and he obviously didn't approve of his commander's sadistic treatment of her, but that didn't mean he would be willing to help her escape.

She had to try, though. No one was coming to her aid.

Having a male fall for her was something Carol was an expert at. Over the years, she'd perfected her seduction into a form of art. It was easy to seduce a guy's body, but seducing his heart and soul required real mastery. Except, it was of little use when she had a total of about five minutes daily with the guy, and couldn't say or do anything because of the fucking camera.

There was none in the bathroom, but it wasn't as if Robert could join her there for a rendezvous. Nothing in his behavior could change or his boss would be onto him and her supply of pills would be gone.

It was obvious Robert was terrified of Sebastian. With good reason.

The sadist was a soulless monster.

It hadn't been easy to come up with a sneaky way to write a note without arousing suspicion. Carol was pretty proud about the clever solution she'd come up with to fool whoever was watching the camera feed. They had seen her taking paper and pen into the bathroom, but they had also seen her emerging with a written page she'd pretended to hide in her closet. If anyone checked on it, they would discover a rambling journal entry describing her ordeal. She'd even gone one step further, writing shit Sebastian would find flattering. Perhaps he would go easier on her after reading it. What they wouldn't discover, however, was the little note she was going to slip to Robert when he came in with her breakfast.

She'd wracked her sluggish brains trying to write something that would cause a guy to fall in love with her. Carol wasn't a poet, or even a decent letter composer. Usually, her childlike innocent appearance combined with her sultry seduction technique was enough to fell the majority of men. She could count those who had resisted her charms on the fingers of one hand. The few men who had escaped her clutches had been already deeply in love with another woman, or just not interested in females in general.

Robert, obviously, didn't belong to either group.

Excitement over giving Robert the note was making her restless, and when the knock came, she had to force herself to remain still and face the wall. Any change in behavior would've looked suspicious.

She had to play it cool.

"Good morning, Carol," Robert said as he entered. "Today I have a special treat for you. A cold, fresh watermelon."

Turning around slowly, she checked to see that he was blocking the camera with his wide back. Robert was quite good looking, for a Doomer. And tall, the way she liked her men—despite being a shorty, or maybe because of it. Carol smiled at him sweetly. "Thank you. It's very kind of you." She reached for his hand and exchanged the note for the three white pills he was holding.

Robert gaped, first at her face, then down at his hand. He had never seen her smiling before. Out of her arsenal of seductive tools, it was the only one she could use under the circumstances.

Blushing like a schoolboy, Robert closed his hand over the note. "I'll come later to collect the tray."

She nodded, training her eyes meaningfully on his closed fist before turning back to the wall.

If Robert was indeed a good man, and she had a feeling that he was, he would at least answer her most pressing question. Was Ben here? And if not, did Robert know if he was dead or alive?

Of course, that hadn't been the only thing she'd written in her note. Carol had made damn sure that it was clear Ben was her cousin and not her boyfriend. She'd complimented Robert on his bravery and had expressed her gratitude for his help, including a few subtle clues about how attractive she found him, and how under different circumstances there could've been something between them.

Anyone with any common sense would've figured out what she was trying to do, but Carol hoped Robert would fall for it. Obviously, the guy liked her, and as an immortal male and a Doomer, he'd never been around women long enough to learn all the manipulative tricks they used.

He had no reason to be jaded, yet, and he might believe that she was genuine.

For real, though, it wasn't a complete lie. She wasn't attracted to him, not because he was lacking, but because she was in no state to feel anything other than rage. But if she had met him in a club and he were a human, she would've flirted with him for sure.

Anyway, if he ended up helping her, she was going to give the guy the best fucking of his life. Many times over. The trick would be to communicate the promise without sounding like the slut she was.

Carol knew men, and Robert was the kind of guy that would help her only if she kept up her sweet and innocent act.

There was no chance in hell he would risk his hide for a glorified ex-whore.

9

KIAN

Kian took his seat at the head of the conference table and laid a single printed sheet of paper on top of the glossy surface. The short list of items he'd composed last night had been emailed to each of the council members. In preparation for the brainstorming session he'd invited them to, Kian had asked them to look into possible solutions for a new location that would provide the clan with a secure keep.

The list was by no means complete.

Pushing up to his feet, he walked over to his desk, grabbed a notepad and his engraved Montblanc, then went back and sat down at the oblong table.

Just one more thing to peg him as an old timer, Kian thought while twirling the pen between his fingers. This current generation of millennials, or whatever they were called, no longer bothered with old-fashioned pen and paper—their quick fingers dancing over tablets and smartphones and laptops, typing up notes and memos at an enviable speed. Kian had given it a half-hearted try, only to go back to good old-fashioned handwritten notes. For some reason, his mind worked better when his hand penned the letters rather than tapped them.

The night before, Ben had woken up from his coma, but as Kian had anticipated, he had no information to add that was of any help to Carol. He remembered something about a van full of Doomers and running away while holding Carol's hand. After that it was all hazy. Kian hadn't pressed Ben for more. The guy couldn't talk yet, and had had to write his answers with a hand that was as weak as an infant's.

The more Kian had thought about it, the more he'd become convinced that they needed a new location that would be kept secret from civilians. Not the existence of the facility, necessarily, but its location. When needed, civilians could be brought in using windowless buses or something of that nature.

Dividing the page with a squiggly line down its middle, Kian dedicated the first half to what he wanted from the new location, and the other to the obstacles in the way of achieving his desired results. The list would provide a foundation for the meeting during which he hoped to hammer out an action plan with the help of his crew.

He hadn't included the Guardians, just the council members, not because he valued their input less, but because the meeting would have spiraled into too many directions. Even Bridget and Edna were somewhat superfluous to this particular discussion, but omitting them would've looked bad.

The clan was a family, not a corporation, so no one would've sued him for discrimination, but the last thing he needed was to be called a chauvinist. Which was bound to happen even though Amanda and Syssi would attend the meeting. Amanda was on the council, and he wanted Syssi to be there even though she wasn't officially a member. Kian wondered if there was a way to change it.

Replacing a council member was a no go, but maybe he could convince his mother to add another seat for Syssi.

After all, he valued her opinion the most.

As the double doors to his office opened soundlessly, Kian didn't need to look up to recognize the scent of Brandon's expensive cologne. But even without it, Brandon's unique smorgasbord of scents identified him just as well as his face. Arrogance, aggression, and impatience.

"Good morning, Brandon," he greeted his media expert. "I'm surprised that you're the first to arrive, usually you're the last."

Brandon pulled out a chair next to Kian and dropped his laptop case on the table. "Shorter commute. Instead of my posh Brentwood townhouse, I have the displeasure of inhabiting the tiny apartment I was assigned here."

"You'll survive. I still remember when you lived with the rest of us in a cold and drafty old castle with no toilets or running water."

Brandon shook his head. "Those days are long gone. Part of my job is to entertain my contacts, and I haven't been able to do it since I was forced to move in here. You need to let me go back to my place."

"First, we have to eradicate the Doomer nest of vipers. After that's done, I'll reconsider."

Brandon tapped his fingers on the table. "Fair enough. Any progress with that?"

"Turner says he is close. One of his informants heard something about a big shipment of weapons delivered locally. He is following up on that. His hunch is that the trail will lead him to the Doomers, and I'm inclined to agree. With the number of warriors they brought, they needed a lot of stuff to supply them with. It's not like they could've traveled halfway around the world with their gear in their suitcases."

"That's good to hear. Because of Carol, of course," Brandon added quickly.

Kian nodded. Brandon was selfish, but not heartless.

"Hello, gentleman." Edna walked in and took a seat, pulling a yellow legal pad out of her briefcase.

Apparently, she preferred handwritten notes as well. Another old timer.

Bridget walked in with William, who was holding his tablet to his chest as if it was precious. Onegus was next, with Amanda and Syssi trailing behind him.

"Good. Everyone is here so let's begin." If he'd let them, they'd spend the next hour on hellos and how'r'yas.

"Don't you need Shai to get here?" Amanda asked.

"No, I'm in command." He lifted the clicker Shai had given him to start the recording. "Shai is busy pretending to be me." His assistant was answering emails Kian had decided to delegate to him.

"Item one on the agenda. Location. I've been racking my brain trying to come up with a place that could be easily hidden but still within a reasonable driving distance to downtown. Any ideas on that front?"

Brandon raised his hand. "I have a solution you are going to love."

That should be good. Brandon was knowledgeable about lots of things, though Kian hadn't been aware that real estate was one of them. "Let's hear it."

"The mountain area above Malibu. Very sparsely populated, but close to everything. And what's even better, it's a location that is used often for movies. We can disguise the entire building project as a grandiose movie set." Brandon cast Kian a hopeful glance.

An interesting idea. "Sounds good so far."

Encouraged, Brandon pulled his laptop out of the case and flipped it open. "I prepared a rough action plan." He looked around to see that he had everyone's attention. "We buy a large parcel of land. I pull permits for building a movie set. Obviously, some bribing and thralling will be needed to hasten the approval process." He cast Kian a questioning glance.

Kian nodded. "In this case, it's justified and I'll allow it."

Brandon puffed out a breath. "Good. We build a tall chain-link fence around the project and cover it with pictures of greenery so it blends into the surrounding mountains. When we are done, we'll have Yamanu shroud the area in an illusion so it will look as if we are taking everything down, when in fact we would not."

Amanda frowned. "But shrouding doesn't work against other immortals. The whole point of this is to be able to keep the location secret from our people as well as the Doomers."

"I know. But all we need to do is hide it the same way humans hide things from other humans. We will need to build low and plant big mature trees all around and in between the buildings to hide them under the canopies. I know more is needed, but this is as far as my expertise goes. William can probably take it from here."

"I can, and I will." William tapped his tablet, probably to produce a list of his own. "Brandon's idea is a perfect foundation for what I have in mind. I worked on the how, but couldn't come up with the where." William saluted Brandon with two fingers. "Good job, buddy."

"Thank you."

"I'll expand on Brandon's suggestions. To hide the complex from immortals, we will need to employ tricks and technologies that can hide things from humans without the help of thralling. As Brandon said, we need to use the same methods humans employ to hide things from other humans. The roofs will have to be covered with mirrors that will reflect the greenery around the complex. The angles will have to be carefully designed for the desired effect. That would take care of the visuals. To avoid detection by electronic means, I can use a modified version of the device I built for Annani's sanctuary to deflect and distort the signal in a way that will seem natural."

It all sounded great in theory, but there was still one problem that needed to be solved. "What about the access to the compound? The entire thing will be useless if the road leading up to it is visible. Even if marked as private property, sooner or later someone will disregard the signage and hike up there."

That got everyone stumped, and for a few moments no one spoke.

"Hazardous waste," Bridget offered. "The sign could say access forbidden due to hazardous waste."

Brandon snorted. "In Malibu mountains? No one dumps anything there."

Bridget shook her head. "Not now, but what about fifty, sixty years ago? We can fabricate a report of whatever hazardous material we can think of that is buried there, thrall someone to put it in the system, and that's it. No one would ever look at it again. You know how bureaucracies work."

"What about bringing people in and out? And who will get to live there and who will not?" Syssi asked.

"Count me out." Brandon crossed his arms over his chest, his fitted jacket not lending itself to the pose. "As I told Kian before, I need to entertain my human business associates. I can't live in a reclusive compound."

"You can always keep your townhouse in Brentwood for this purpose. I'm sure you're not entertaining every day. But it's up to you." Kian wasn't going to force the issue, not now, anyway. "We will have to have some kind of shuttle service. But we can figure out the details later."

"I have an idea," Edna said. "I'm not sure if it's doable, and even if it is, it will probably cost a lot, but it could make everyone's lives easier in the long term."

Kian snorted. "This project is going to cost us a fortune either way. Let's hear what you have in mind."

"What if we build the compound on top of a hill that is inaccessible on foot? Then we build a mansion nearby, with a gated entry, of course, that will have a big underground garage that can house all of our cars. A tunnel will lead under the compound. An electrical motorcar will take passengers from the parking garage through the tunnel and up into the compound. We can make it go much slower for civilians, so they will think it is taking them further away than it actually does."

Not a bad idea at all. But he was going to take it one step further. "The mansion would be as far as civilians will go. We will build our training facility there, as well as some conference rooms and offices, so there will be no need for anyone that doesn't live in the compound to come up there. No one will even know that there is another location. They will assume that this is it. If that house is compromised, we abandon it and build another, but we will no longer need to evacuate our homes."

Brandon uncrossed his arms and leaned his elbows on the table. "So why go to all that trouble in the first place? We can stay in the city and separate the facilities."

Brandon had a point. But Kian was no longer comfortable with the weak defenses a downtown building could offer. It had been sufficient when the Doomers had no clue where on earth Annani's clan was hiding, but now that they'd discovered that Los Angeles was a central hub, they would keep coming. Especially after the elimination of the current force they had there.

Syssi raised a hand. "I think I have a solution that is easier to implement.

Even though the building we have lived in is compromised, we are still using the offices and training facilities in the basement because it has multiple entry points and can be accessed from several buildings. We can keep it as it is, and the civilians can be brought in from any of the other buildings that have access to it. If one entry point is compromised, we block it and use another. I'm just thinking about the catacombs. Do you really want to start moving around the dead and the undead?"

"Syssi is right," Bridget said. "It will save us a bundle. Besides, I love my medical facilities here."

Everyone turned their focus to Kian, waiting for him to decide.

"We do both. We keep these facilities and we build the new ones. I know the cost is going to be staggering, but my family's safety is worth it. Having several locations, while keeping everything on a strict need to know basis, will provide additional layers of security that will allow me to sleep better at night."

10

ROBERT

Peering over Carol's note, Robert scrubbed his hand over his face. Was he reading too much into what she was trying to say? Was she really interested in him?

He was aware that she might be saying these things about him because she was grateful, or because she wanted him to help her even more than he already had.

Did she hope he would help her escape?

Stuffing the note in his pocket, Robert walked outside to the courtyard and started pacing around. The fountain he had had installed was making noises that he'd found pleasing before, but now they were a distraction he could do without. Anyway, pacing like a caged animal would look suspicious to his fellow soldiers.

A run, however, was business as usual for him. Not in combat boots, but he doubted anyone would pay attention to his footwear.

Breaking into a jog, he headed down the trail circling the grounds. Not surprisingly, he wasn't the only one there. A group of five warriors was jogging the trail ahead of him. But this was as good as it got. Other than his room, or a bathroom, there was no private spot he could use to think.

"Hey, Robert, what's up, my man?" Another runner caught up to him.

"I'm good. Just stretching my legs." He offered what he hoped was an impassive expression.

"I'll leave you to it." The guy sprinted ahead, showing off.

Good riddance.

Back to Carol.

Beautiful, soft, sweet Carol.

He had to help her. Except, doing so would mean the end of his career as a Doomer. And that was if he got lucky and they both survived. Even if he succeeded, he still needed to figure out where to hide and what to do for money.

Manual labor was all he could hope for.

It would be worth it all if Carol remained with him, maybe even became his mate. But that was too much to hope for. The moment he sprung her free, she'd run as fast as she could back to her family, and he would be left with less than nothing.

What if she promised to stay with him?

Could he trust her word?

He knew nothing about her. Carol might be the most honest and trustworthy person on earth, or the most deceitful one. And yet, if she promised and lied, he would smell the lie. Or at least he hoped he would. He'd met immortals who had figured out how to mask their scents.

Would he keep her against her will?

No. If she didn't want to be with him then he didn't want her. Robert didn't need a female for sex—he'd had plenty, both paid for and free.

What he craved above all was to be loved and to love in return.

Robert stopped in his tracks. He'd never realized that he had such yearning lurking inside him. Maybe because it was so impossible that he'd never given it any thought?

He'd be a fool not to seize the opportunity and make this immortal female his.

He was a decent guy, and females found him attractive... that is until he opened his mouth.

Robert groaned. Any female who'd spent more than a few minutes with him had lost interest in anything other than his wallet. He was shy, awkward, clumsy, stomped around like a grizzly bear, and didn't have anything interesting to say.

Carol would lose interest as well.

And yet, the yearning couldn't be denied. Dear Mortdh, how he wished she would give him a chance.

Not only because she was so pretty and so cute, but because she needed him. He could be her knight in shining armor, and if nothing else maybe gratitude would compel her to stay with him. How the hell was he going to pull this off?

A mastermind of covert operations he was not.

Conveniently, Sebastian was leaving tomorrow for Phoenix Arizona, and as was his habit, he would be taking Tom with him and leaving Robert in charge. He was supposed to fly back the same afternoon, but if he succeeded in negotiating a good deal on the radio station, he and Tom were going to stay one more day to iron out the details.

That left the rest of the warriors to contend with.

It wasn't as if he could just take Carol and walk out without anyone trying to stop him, or calling Sebastian to let him know. He would need to do it at night, when most of them were patrolling the clubs.

But by then Sebastian might be back.

That meant that after Sebastian was done with Carol today, Robert would have to sneak her out and hide her in his car overnight. Which would be torture for her because she wouldn't have enough time to heal.

Tomorrow, after Sebastian and Tom left, he would come up with an excuse for going into town—some supply issue that couldn't wait for delivery—and drive off to never come back.

Perhaps he could give Carol an extra dose of painkillers for tonight. He wondered if it was safe to give her four pills. Or even five. He'd have to. If he had something stronger to knock her out with, it would have been even better…

Robert slapped his palm over his forehead. He was such an idiot. Of course he had something to knock her out with: his fangs and his venom! Nothing man-made was more powerful than that.

He'd better get going. There was a lot that needed to be done in preparation. Sebastian almost never left the base for more than a few hours at a time, and this absence was a rare opportunity. Mortdh knew when would be the next time.

Carol couldn't wait much longer.

Breaking into a sprint, Robert ran back full speed ahead, hoping the stench of his sweat would mask the stench of his fear; better yet, he should avoid Sebastian altogether.

It wasn't his lucky day.

Finding Sebastian waiting for him at his 'office' i.e. the pantry, Robert almost shit his pants.

Sebastian offered him a smile. "Good to see that you keep yourself in shape. A man can lose muscle tone sitting all day at his desk."

"Yes, sir." Damn. He was so stressed the 'sir' popped out involuntarily.

Sebastian sighed. "Robert, I know you're stressed about tomorrow, but Tom and I will be gone only one day, two at the most. You can handle being in charge. The men are used to answering to you. They will not give you any trouble."

Thank you, holy Mortdh. Robert wanted to sag in relief. Instead, he straightened to his full height and saluted. "I will do my best, Sebastian."

With a proud smile, Robert's commander clapped him on his shoulder. "You're a good man, Robert. You'll do fine. Bravery is not the lack of fear, but the ability to do your duty in spite of it."

"Yes, s…Sebastian."

A moment later, when he finally closed the door to the pantry behind his commander, Robert collapsed into his chair and sucked in a shaky breath.

Courage, man, you have a lot to do.

11

ANDREW

As Andrew strode down the hallway to Kian's office, excitement tinged with a dose of envy swirled in his gut. Excitement about the upcoming battle; envy for the warriors who would get to charge the Doomers' stronghold. Hopefully, Kian would allow him to join in some noncombat capacity. He could be the driver, or the water boy, or something like that.

An hour ago, Turner had called Andrew with the Doomers' location. The old monastery in Ojai was almost certainly the Doomers' base in California. There was, of course, a slight chance that it belonged to some other militant group, but it was highly unlikely.

Turner's source worked for a large weapons supplier who sold mostly abroad. That's why the large delivery to a local address was an anomaly he'd remembered.

Being the thorough and methodical SOB that he was, Turner had provided more than just the location. He'd researched when it had been purchased, included a map of the terrain, and even blueprints from fifteen years ago when the monks had pulled permits for renovating their twenties-era kitchen. The timing matched, and the place was perfect for a covert military base. Not only was it secluded with no other inhabitants for several miles around, but a tall block wall fence surrounded its perimeter.

Andrew had no doubt that surveillance cameras had been installed all over that fence, and probably along the road leading up to the monastery as well. Standard operating procedure to secure a facility against unwanted intruders and prying eyes.

That's what he would have done.

Soon, he would find out if Kian had succeeded in pulling off the impossible in the space of an hour—obtaining close-up satellite pictures of the place.

Good luck with that.

Then again, when enough money greased the wheels, they spun much faster.

The other option was to send out a drone. Problem was, it could potentially alert the Doomers to the fact that someone was on to them. Satellite was an invisible, undetectable eye in the sky.

When he got to Kian's office, it was already bursting at the seams with burly immortals. Pausing for a moment in front of the glass doors, Andrew scanned the room. Aside from the Guardians he knew, there were five more he hadn't met before.

The reserves.

Upon entering, Andrew clapped hands with Arwel, was pulled into a bro embrace by Anandur and then Bhathian, and then got introduced to the new guys—forgetting their names a moment later.

Not his fault that these Scots had strange, hard to pronounce names he'd never heard before.

A moment later, he was put to work rearranging the furniture. Arwel, Onegus and he each lifted two chairs, clearing one side of the conference table, while Anandur and Bhathian grabbed the heavy thing and pushed it all the way to the side. He helped the guys line up the chairs in three rows facing the big screen behind Kian's desk.

Kian turned on the big screen and after a few clicks on his desktop an aerial picture of the compound appeared. He leaned against his desk and waited for everyone to hush down.

"Good evening." Kian picked up a ruler and pointed at the screen. "The road leading up to the Doomers' compound is almost a mile long, and there are cameras installed every two hundred feet or so. Twenty-seven in total. They are stationary." He moved the ruler to the wall surrounding the grounds. "The wall, as you can see, is twelve to thirteen feet tall thanks to the barb wire added on top of it. Cameras are mounted in seventy-five foot intervals and they rotate. There are no blind spots in front of the wall."

Kian took hold of the computer mouse and zoomed the picture in, then pointed again with the ruler at a big metal box attached to the side of the building. "They have an emergency power generator large enough to supply their entire facility in case of a power outage, so that option is out. If we want an element of surprise, we will need to parachute into the place, which, admittedly, isn't the best way to go about it. First of all because as far as I know none of us has ever done it before. Second, if spotted, we will be easy and defenseless targets. They can just shoot the parachutes and have us splatter on the ground."

Anandur humphed. "We can take them even if they know we're coming. What do they have as far as weapons? Machine guns? We can bring portable rocket launchers to blow up their wall, launch smoke grenades to render them temporarily blind, and then charge ahead. Anyway, it's going to be hand to hand combat in the end, with or without the element of surprise."

He looked around seeking support for his plan, but encountered multiple raised brows instead.

"Where do you get ideas like that?" Arwel asked.

"What? I watch a lot of war movies."

One of the new Guardians snorted. "If they can see us coming from a mile away, they can just blow us up on approach. They might have rocket launchers of their own."

Anandur crossed his arms over his chest. "So we get armored vehicles. I've read somewhere that the Israelis developed a sophisticated shielding mechanism. They call it a wind jacket or coat or something like that."

Kian shook his head. "We might get our hands on rocket launchers, but armored vehicles? It would take weeks if not months to arrange a purchase and delivery of something like that. I want to attack tomorrow."

Murmurs of agreement sounded all around, the air thickening with tension.

Andrew wondered if testosterone could go airborne, and if it could, was there any way to test its levels in the air. If there were, this room full of warriors readying for battle would blow the top off the scale.

He could just imagine all these Scots charging ahead with a terrifying battle cry, brandishing swords and axes, their kilts flapping in the air... He chuckled.

"What's funny?" Onegus asked.

"Oh, it's nothing. I was just picturing all of you guys wearing kilts while attacking your enemies."

Onegus cocked a brow. "And that is funny because?"

Andrew knew he should shut up, but he just couldn't help it. "I heard that Scots wear nothing under those kilts. Everything must go flapping up and down and side to side as you run, and I'm not talking about the fabric." He demonstrated with his arm.

Kri chuckled, some of the guys grunted, and Bhathian cast Andrew one of his more formidable scowls.

Anandur shrugged. "No sweaty balls, my friend, ponder this. And after the battle, with the lasses, no need to take anything off."

He had a point.

Kian clapped his hands to get their attention. "People, this is not the time or place for horsing around. You're all grown men, and woman." He pointed his chin at Kri. "Not a bunch of horny teenagers. We are trying to plan an offensive that will hopefully result in as few casualties as possible for us and as many as possible for the enemy."

The mention of horny teenagers reminded Andrew that there was another way of disabling the Doomers' surveillance cameras. "May I offer an alternative?"

Kian grimaced. "Not to the kilts, I hope. We are kind of attached to them. They are like a good luck charm."

What the hell? He'd been only joking. Did they really plan on wearing skirts to battle?

A snort escaped Kian's throat, and the room erupted with laughter. "Got you." He pointed at Andrew. "You should've seen the expression on your face."

"I thought we were supposed to get serious."

"You're right. We are. I just couldn't miss an opportunity like that to mess with you." He waved his hand. "I'm sorry. Go ahead. You were saying?"

Sorry my ass.

"We can use Sylvia to disable the cameras."

Kian frowned. "Isn't her ability limited to only a few feet distance from the device?"

"It is. But that's actually better than fritzing them all at once. Less suspicious. Sylvia and one of the Guardians could pretend to be hikers and walk up that road, while we follow in a vehicle close behind. A short glitch in just one camera at a time might go unnoticed."

"I can improve on the plan," Anandur said. "We send a group of all female hikers. They'll spread out with about two hundred feet between them. The two or three up front will be hotties in short shorts, while Sylvia and perhaps Kri will drag behind and wear long pants. The Doomers in the control room will be watching the screen with the short shorts, and I bet they will not notice the other monitors glitch for a few seconds."

"Brilliant." Andrew high-fived Anandur.

Kian nodded. "I agree. It's a plan."

12

CAROL

Usually, Carol dreaded dinner.

Like clockwork, Sebastian would show up an hour and a half after her last meal, making sure she was done metabolizing her allotted calories for the day by the time he started her torture. For that reason, dinner never included meat or anything heavy.

The sadist didn't want her puking all over him.

Today, though, she couldn't wait for Robert to show up with her tray, and hopefully, a note with answers about Ben.

Fates, she was restless. Carol wished she could pace, or scribble nonsense in her notebook—anything to provide a distraction that would help pass the time. Except, that would've been out of character for her.

Like every day, she sat sideways on her bed with her back propped against the wall, gazing vacantly into space.

When the knock finally came, Carol gritted her teeth against the urge to jump up and... what? Kiss him? Hug him? Ask for the note?

Ask for the note. Definitely the note. Kissing and hugging belonged in the past. The old Carol used to love engaging in both, but not anymore. Now, she prayed to never be touched again. Not in cruelty and not in kindness. Her nerve endings were too raw and too frazzled to tolerate either.

"Good evening, Carol," Robert said as he entered, pushing the door closed with his foot.

She didn't answer, because she never did. But she looked up at him. She couldn't help it.

Robert gave her a tentative smile as he lowered the tray to place it on her nightstand. "Since you enjoyed the watermelon so much this morning, I brought you more." He lifted a wedge and extended his hand, angling his palm so she could see the three white pills and the folded note he had tucked under the fruit.

With a frown, she scooped his offering into her palm. He never brought her pills in the evening. He always did it in the morning, and she swallowed them after dinner. She still had the other two.

Did he know something she didn't? Was Sebastian going to be even more cruel to her this evening?

Robert must've sensed her distress. "I know that fruit in the evening is unusual, but I thought the vitamins in it will help you sleep better at night."

He was trying to tell her something, but she had no idea what. Lifting her eyes to his face, she searched his expression for clues.

Pointedly, he looked down at her hand. "When I come back to collect the tray, tell me if the fruit agreed with you. I heard that some people can't digest it more than once a day. It upsets their stomach."

Carol nodded and lifted the fist holding the pills and the note, pressing it against her heart. Robert should stop talking in riddles and making whoever listened suspicious. His note probably explained everything.

He got the message, thank the merciful Fates.

"Well, enjoy your meal. I'll see you later."

After he left, Carol took a few bites from the watermelon, nibbled on a piece of dry toast, then figured enough time had passed and it was safe to go to the bathroom. With an effort, she shuffled the way she always did, crossing the distance in what seemed to her like slow motion.

Closing the door behind her, she tucked the new pills inside her robe's pocket, sat down on the toilet, and unfolded Robert's note.

He had neat handwriting, and managed to cram a lot into a piece of paper no larger than three by five inches.

Your cousin is not here. I don't know if he lives, but he wasn't a confirmed kill either.

As she sagged in relief, Carol let her hand drop by her side. Ben might be alive. She lifted the crumpled piece of paper and kept on reading.

Your note suggests that you like me, but even though I suspect you are only saying it to get me to help you, I want to anyway. I can't do nothing while you're tortured. But if I help you escape, there is no going back for me. I'm a dead man. To make my sacrifice worthwhile, I want your promise to stay with me for at least three months. If you agree to my terms, we have to move tonight. Sebastian is leaving tomorrow but he is probably coming back the same afternoon. Our best chance is to hide you in my car overnight and tomorrow morning, after he leaves, I'll pretend to go for an errand in town and drive off. I know that when he is done with you you're in too much pain to move or spend the night in my car. That is what the additional pills are for. After Sebastian brings you back to your room, turn off the lights completely and put on loud music—something annoying so the guys in the monitoring room will turn down the volume. Put pillows under the blanket in the shape of your body, get dressed, and wait for me. I'll come in quietly and take your hand to lead you out in the dark. Don't make a sound. When I come back for the tray, all I need is a nod from you to let me know you agree to my terms and to my plan. When you're done reading, flush this note down the toilet.

Carol read over the thing three more times before she did as he asked, dropping the precious piece of paper into the toilet and watching it go down the drain. He could've asked for a year and she would've gladly agreed. Hell, a decade. And who knows? Maybe she would even like him enough to stay.

Later, when Robert came, she did more than nod. She grasped his hand and squeezed, mouthing a thank you.

His eyes were haunted as he nodded back.

Robert was terrified.

Even her limited sense of smell picked it up with no problem. Hell, she hoped the poor guy wouldn't get himself killed while trying to help her. This was totally out of his comfort zone.

What a brave man.

Obviously, Robert wasn't a commando. He was a mere assistant, a yes-man doing Sebastian's bidding. And yet, he showed incredible courage where it counted the most.

If they made it, she would make sure Robert never regretted his decision to help her. She was going to make him the happiest male alive.

13

ROBERT

Now that Robert had set things in motion, there was no turning back. Carol had agreed to his terms, and she would be waiting for him to deliver on his promise.

With a shaky hand, Robert poured himself a drink, cursing when more of it ended up on his desk than inside the glass. He took a sip and grimaced. Why the hell was he drinking this shit? His usual fare was beer, he rarely drank anything stronger than that, and this was really not the time to get drunk.

Problem was, the fear was paralyzing, and he was useless like this. There was no way Sebastian would believe this was anxiety over being left in charge for one day.

Robert groaned.

He was a warrior for Mortdh's sake, and he'd held his shit together in numerous battles, under heavy artillery fire, and even air strikes. He was a good soldier, well trained. Even when covered in the blood and viscera of his enemies as well as his comrades, he'd remained on task, had done his duty.

Closing his eyes, Robert reached deep inside of him to the cold place that had allowed him to function during those times. If he wanted this mission to succeed, he had to achieve that emotionless state again.

An automaton needed to be set in motion.

Damn, Robert had hoped that by joining Sebastian's crew he would never have to go there again. Sebastian was more of a covert operations guy, not a field commander. As his assistant, Robert had hoped that he would never again have to witness the atrocities of war, and that the soulless creature he'd been forced to become would be left behind for good.

He hated having to rely on that other persona of his, always afraid that this time he wouldn't be able to come back, and that the other side would take over permanently. It was becoming more and more difficult to shed that hard shell, and each time it was taking him longer.

A long time had passed since he'd last summoned that other side of himself, and yet he slipped into that persona with relative ease. In moments, the disassociation was complete. The Robert everyone here was familiar with was gone, and the Robert who his previous commander had relied on to do a superb job in the field was back.

His hands no longer shook as he took the half-full glass and emptied the whiskey in the sink, then wiped the counter clean.

He was ready.

The first part of his plan was to send as many of the guys as possible out on club patrols. Pulling the list of clubs up on his computer, he added four more locations to the roster by borrowing from tomorrow's list.

Keeping the illusion of business as usual, he left the door to his pantry office open, and when Sebastian passed by it on his way down to the basement, Robert blocked thoughts of Carol and what his commander was about to do to her.

To pull this off, he was going to follow his plan to the letter and disregard all else. The teams had to be dispatched while Sebastian was otherwise occupied, and there was no better time than while the sadist was torturing Carol. Sebastian would not interrupt a session for anything less than a level one emergency.

Robert had an entire hour at his disposal, and he was going to use it wisely.

Most nights, the men were assigned thirty clubs, which meant sixty warriors were out of the base while twelve remained. Two were assigned to the control room, and the other ten were sent out on patrols around the grounds. A waste of time since no one ever came up there. Especially not at night.

But patrols were standard operating procedure for a military base, and Sebastian had seen no reason to deviate from protocol. It seemed to Robert that Sebastian was more interested in buying studios and radio stations than chasing immortal males in clubs. It was part of the mission he'd been assigned, and he couldn't abandon it completely, but he wasn't putting any pressure on the men to deliver results.

By adding four clubs to the list, Robert would be sending eight out of the ten off the base. Only four would remain; two in the control room, and two on patrol.

If anyone noticed, he had an excuse ready. After all, Sebastian had said on more than one occasion that he was waiting for Robert to show more initiative. Adhering to the goals of their original mission, Robert would claim he'd decided that patrolling the clubs was more important than patrolling the base, and two men could handle a four-hour shift without requiring replacements.

Chances were good, though, that no one other than the two remaining patrolmen would notice. Worst case scenario, Robert would knock the two out. Aggression and violence weren't his dominant traits, but that didn't mean he couldn't summon them when needed.

His biggest worry was Sebastian, but after the sadist was done with Carol, he usually retired to his suite of rooms for the night. Tom, who was Robert's other worry, would be out trying to snatch more girls for the basement.

Calling the men and sending them out in two waves, Robert was pretty sure no one had noticed the four additional crews. Not unless someone counted the remaining cars. Luckily, there were two separate parking lots and he doubted anyone would check both.

Everything was going according to plan.

Almost.

When an hour later Sebastian emerged from the basement, stinking of sex and blood, a murderous rage threatened to destroy Robert's carefully thought out plan. The other him wasn't as meek and subservient as the one Sebastian and the others were familiar with.

Killing that evil son of a bitch would have been the most satisfying thing Robert had ever done in his life. It even crossed his mind that it would be easy to do with only four men on the premises. There would be no one to stop him, and Robert had no doubt that he could overpower Sebastian. The guy was a head shorter than him and probably weighed at least fifty pounds less.

He stifled the urge.

Saving Carol was more important than this momentary satisfaction. Killing Sebastian wasn't part of the plan, and Robert was not the kind of man who could come up with a new one on the spot.

Better stick to what he had planned so carefully, taking into account every obstacle no matter how small.

"Goodnight, Robert," Sebastian said as he passed him on his way up.

"Goodnight, Sebastian."

His commander stopped and turned around, casting him a curious glance. "Is there a problem, Robert?"

He was well aware that this other part of him sounded very different than what Sebastian was used to. Instead of fear, Robert was pretty sure he was radiating hatred and aggression. "No, sir. I just need to release some steam. A visit to one of the girls is in order."

Sebastian nodded in agreement. "You do that. Sexual frustration will diminish the quality of your performance."

"As soon as I'm done with tonight's duties, I will."

"Good." The sadist turned back and kept climbing.

Robert waited a few minutes, then climbed up to Sebastian's third-floor residence. Standing by the door, he listened for the sound of running water.

For the next twenty minutes, Sebastian would be taking a shower.

Going down the stairs to the second level, Robert headed toward the control room.

"How is it going? Anything worthy of notice?" he asked, looking around for the screen monitoring Carol's room. As instructed, it was completely dark. A few of the other girls were sleeping as well, so her light wasn't the only one off. The watchers had muted the sound on all of them. Again, Carol wasn't the only one listening to music, and some of the girls were watching movies in their rooms. The guys had no choice but to turn it down, otherwise the cacophony of sounds would've been unbearable.

Perfect.

"Nothing. It's just as peaceful and as boring as every other night."

"Good. No news is good news, right?"

"Absolutely."

"Do you guys need anything from the kitchen? I can send someone up." He knew they didn't. There was a fridge in the control room, and earlier he'd made sure that it was fully stocked with soft drinks and snacks.

The guys shook their head in unison.

"Goodnight, then. If you need me, I'll be downstairs in my office." He made a face. Everyone was making fun of his pantry workstation, and he played into it, feigning business as usual.

One of the guys chuckled.

With part one and part two accomplished, it was time for part three. Supplies.

His weapons, one change of clothes, and the little cash he had were rolled up in a blanket in his room. Dropping his comforter on the floor, he added two pillows, a few cans of soft drinks, and several protein bars, then tied everything together into one tightly packed bundle. With a quick glance out his window, he double-checked the location of the patrolmen. Satisfied that they were on the opposite side from where his minivan was parked, he dashed downstairs and loaded the weapons and cash in the trunk, folded up the third row and then spread out the comforter and the pillows in the back to make it as comfortable as he could for Carol.

Time for part four. The most difficult one that required the most careful calculation.

The patrolmen needed to be at the furthest possible point away from the building, and nowhere near the line of sight to both the front door and the lot where his car was parked.

Five minutes and twenty-three seconds later, Robert was down at the basement. His shoes discarded at the top of the stairs, he rushed in his stocking feet through a corridor completely devoid of light, counting his steps to make sure he arrived at the right room.

As he stopped in front of Carol's door, he forced his breaths to come out shallow and soundless. The music blasting from the inside was sure to drown out any noise, but he didn't want to take any chances. Inserting the key into the lock, he turned it gently and pushed the door open.

Counting his steps again, he arrived at Carol's bed and fumbled in the dark until he found her arm. Her bicep twitched, but she didn't utter a sound. He slid his palm down until he reached her hand and pulled gently. She resisted for a moment, giving the pillows a few pats before letting him help her up to her feet.

He pulled and she followed, waiting for him to re-lock her door. He could feel she was struggling to maintain her balance. Poor girl, between the beating and the drugs and the darkness, she was in a terrible state. Robert bent at the waist and wrapped an arm under her butt, hoisting her over his shoulder. As careful as he was not to touch any of the fresh welts, she couldn't suppress the groan that escaped her throat. It was okay, though, there were no listening devices in the corridor or the stairwell leading up.

"Hold on for just a little longer," he whispered in her ear, counting his steps all along until he reached the stairwell. Thank Mortdh, there were no cameras in the main living areas. Only the basement. Outside was a different matter, though. A few were mounted on the perimeter of the building, and many more were on top of the wall surrounding the compound.

Except, he knew where each and every one was and how to slip out unnoticed. Pushing his feet back into his shoes, he went out the front door that he'd left purposely wide open. Now, all he needed to do was creep close to the building's walls until he reached the side parking lot.

Easy. Carol's weight barely registered.

She was such a tiny thing, and yet tougher than most men.

With a press of a button, the back door to his minivan lifted open, and he lowered Carol gently to the little nest he'd prepared for her. It got cold out here at nights, and she wasn't in good shape. Given the strong coppery scent coming off her, her wounds were still fresh and bleeding, and now that he looked at her in the light of the pale moon, he could see that her shirt was soaked through with blood.

"I'm sorry," he whispered. "But you'll have to take the shirt off. You don't want the blood to crust and stick the fabric to your healing skin." He wanted to offer her the option of his bite, but it was too embarrassing. It was such an intimate act, and probably the last thing Carol wanted.

"Help me. I can't do it myself." She lifted a pair of red-rimmed, tear-misted eyes at him, breaking his heart into a thousand pieces. Until now, he'd only seen her after several hours had gone by and she was somewhat recuperated from her ordeal.

This was fresh.

"I could bite you to help with the pain..." He rubbed his hand over his neck. "But the problem is that I need to be... ah... you know... to produce venom..." He sounded like an idiot. But there was no way to say what needed to be said without sounding either like a pervert or a stuttering moron. Robert preferred the second option.

Carol smiled feebly. "It's okay. I'm actually relieved that you can't get aroused seeing me like this. Besides, I'm already drugged out of my mind with all the pills I took. I don't want to be completely knocked out."

Robert let out a breath.

Gently he lifted her T-shirt up and over her head, barely stopping a horrified gasp when he saw what the sadist had done to her back. Even the sight of her naked breasts stirred nothing in him.

He should have helped her escape days ago. "I'm so sorry," he whispered again, wiping her tear-streaked face with a corner of the comforter.

Gripping his hand, she brought it to her lips and kissed his palm. "Thank you. I swear that you'll never regret helping me. I'll make it my life mission to make you glad that you did it. You have my word."

As he lifted their joined hands and kissed hers, tears he hadn't shed since he was a little boy pricked the back of his eyes. "First, let's get you out of here in one piece. There are soda cans and power bars over there, and if you need to relieve yourself there is also a big plastic container with a lid. Stay down, don't lift your head. The windows are darkened but these are immortals you are hiding from. Sebastian leaves at six o'clock in the morning, and I have to deliver breakfast to the girls and then collect the trays. That way no one will realize that you're missing until lunch, and it will give us a few hours' head start. I'll try to be here around eight."

She nodded and lay on her side, her hands clasped in front of her. He tucked a pillow under her cheek. "Try to get some sleep."

"Thank you," she whispered as he closed the trunk.

14

NATHALIE

It was after midnight when Andrew returned from his meeting with Kian. She'd made him promise to come home to her at any hour of the night and tell her about it, or at least whatever he was allowed to.

The worst thing was not knowing what kind of danger her fiancé and her father would be facing. Andrew reassured her that he was probably staying behind on some noncombat duty, but that wasn't the case with Bhathian. He was going to be there in the midst of the fighting.

Was it going to be a commando operation? A full on assault? Something else? It wasn't as if she was versed in military terminology or strategies. All she knew was that no matter what they called the offensive, people always got hurt or died fighting.

"Why aren't you in bed?" Andrew asked as she opened the back door for him.

Nathalie had felt too restless to sleep and had passed the time while waiting for him by preparing dough and putting it in the freezer—an emergency supply she'd been meaning to make for weeks and hadn't gotten the time for before. "I was too nervous to sleep. Do you want some coffee?"

Andrew rubbed his temples with his thumb and forefinger. "Yeah, coffee would be just what the doctor ordered."

"Headache?"

"Yeah."

"Would you like a couple of Motrins?"

"No, not yet. Maybe the coffee will help."

Nathalie had brewed some ahead of time and kept it in a thermal carafe. She grabbed a tray and loaded it with two mugs, the carafe, and leftover pastries. "Let's have it upstairs."

"I'll take it." Andrew took the tray away from her and headed up.

A smile tugged at her lips despite the worry churning in her stomach. She loved that Andrew was such a gentleman. Even though he was well aware that she was schlepping trays all day long, he would never let her carry anything while he was around.

As they sat on the couch in the den, Nathalie poured the coffee into the two mugs, put sugar and cream in hers and handed Andrew his. Like the macho man he was, he liked it black with nothing added. "What parts can you tell me?" Nathalie asked without preamble.

"We deploy tomorrow afternoon."

That was unexpected. "During daylight?"

"Yeah, the plan involves 'hikers' who will go first and disable the surveillance cameras for us, one at a time, while we creep behind them."

"I see." Made sense. Hikers at night was not something one expected to see.

Suddenly, it dawned on her that he'd said 'we.' "I thought you were not taking part in this. Being a 'puny human' and all." She made air quotes.

"I'm not. I'm driving and helping whenever I'm needed, bringing up the rear."

As if that was supposed to put her at ease.

Nathalie crossed her arms over her chest and pinned Andrew with an angry stare. "I don't care. You shouldn't be there at all. You said so yourself. These immortals are faster, stronger, and better trained than any elite special-forces unit. You are no match for them, Andrew. If you feel you must participate, you should be handling communications or something like that, miles away from the actual fighting." Her voice was rising in volume and she was running out of breath as panic and anger began constricting her throat.

"I'm going to be fine." Andrew pulled her into his arms.

She shook her head, but then sagged into his warmth, letting the hot tears flow and soak his shirt.

"Look, I'm not going to be anywhere near the fighting. I'm just driving the bus with the warriors, and Kri is driving the other one. They wouldn't have allowed a female anywhere near the Doomers."

Was he telling her the truth? Or was he feeding her a modified version to prevent hysterics? Nathalie wished she had Andrew's gift of detecting lies.

Except, even if he wasn't twisting things around for her sake, it didn't mean she had no reason to worry about Andrew. Besides, Bhathian would be fighting, probably at the front line. She was getting nauseous just thinking about him getting hurt. Or worse.

He'd come into her life only recently, and she wanted more time with him. Much more time. They hadn't talked face to face ever since Bhathian had revealed to her that he was her father. He'd been so busy training for this mission that he hadn't had time for more than a phone call.

Nathalie had no idea how the families of servicemen could handle this. Every time their loved ones left the house there was a chance they would not be coming back. So yeah, to some extent it was true for everyone, but for a soldier the odds were higher by an order of magnitude.

"I can't help worrying. I worry that Bhathian might get hurt. I worry that the Doomers will circle around and attack the rear. You can't predict everything."

"You're right. Sometimes shit happens. But what is the alternative? Sit around and do nothing? Hope that someone else will do the job for us? Guess what? No one would. I'm capable and well trained. Even if I can't join the front line in this fight, I feel obligated to do all I can from the back. I'm sure you can understand this, true?"

Oh, hell. He was right, and she had no choice but to nod in agreement. A man like Andrew, who had spent most of his adult life saving and defending people, couldn't stand idly by, content to let others handle the job. It would have been devastating to his ego.

"What time do you need to be there?"

"We are meeting at nine in the morning to go over the details and leaving at three in the afternoon. It will get us there around five. The hope is that the Doomers will be busy with dinner, or at least part of them will. They are not expecting any attack at all, let alone one in broad daylight. The security will be lax."

Hearing him talk about the upcoming battle, it all sounded so reasonable, so mundane—as if he'd gone on missions like that so many times before that he was neither excited nor fearful at the prospect of yet another one.

"I wish I could just turn off this worry, but I can't. There is a tornado swirling inside my stomach, making me nauseous and short of breath. I hate feeling like that, and I don't know what to do about it."

Andrew waggled his brows. "I can think of something that will take your mind off of it."

"God, Andrew, is this the only thing you ever think about?"

"Pretty much. Yep. And especially now." He leaned and in one swift move lifted her onto his lap—the hard length beneath her butt proving that he hadn't been joking around.

"It's late. Aren't you supposed to be well rested before going out on a mission?"

"I don't need to wake up early tomorrow, and besides, with the jacked up level of testosterone in my system, I won't be able to sleep anyway. I'd rather make love to you than to my fist."

Nathalie chuckled. "As if I would let you cheat on me. Not even with your own hand."

He nipped her earlobe. "I love it when you get all jealous and possessive. Makes me feel like a stud."

"You are—my stud-muffin." She wiggled her ass on top of his shaft, the friction pulling a hiss out of his mouth.

"Baby, you have no idea." Andrew pushed to his feet, almost knocking over the folding tray table with their coffees as he rushed to the bedroom with her giggling in his arms.

Dropping her unceremoniously onto her bed, Andrew attacked her clothes, getting her naked in seconds. There had been no finesse to his moves, and it was a wonder none of her things had gotten torn as he'd jerked them off her body.

Maybe because she'd been helping him along, just as impatient.

Expecting Andrew to shuck his clothes next, she squeaked in surprise when he dove between her legs, spreading her thighs as far as they would go. Without a second delay, he began licking her in long drags from top to bottom and back again, groaning in pleasure as if she was his favorite flavor of ice cream.

With his hands clamped on her thighs, he held them spread and motionless as he speared his tongue and plunged it forcefully into her quivering sheath.

Nathalie couldn't remember Andrew ever being so aggressive with her, so dominant, and she loved every freaking moment of it. His fingers were going to leave bruises where they were digging into her flesh, and she couldn't care less. This was beyond hot. She was going to explode like a Fourth of July firecracker the moment his talented tongue made contact with her clit.

Problem was, Andrew knew how to push all of her buttons and drive her crazy.

Lifting his head, a wicked gleam sparkled in his eyes as he got ready to do exactly that. Her clit throbbing in anticipation, she watched Andrew lower his chin in infuriatingly tiny increments.

The moment he took it in between his lips, the fuse under the firecracker got lit.

Not yet, not yet, not yet... If it ignited right away, the rocket wouldn't reach as high. With a keening moan hissing out from between her gritted teeth, Nathalie tried to hold on for just a little longer.

But Andrew wasn't in a patient mood this time, and when he sucked on that most sensitive bundle of nerves, the rocket shot up into the stratosphere not like a firecracker, but like a lunar shuttle.

Long moments later, when she opened her eyes, Andrew's handsome face was poised above hers, his legs between her thighs, his weight pressing her into the bed.

"Hi," he said before dipping his head to take her lips. As his tongue invaded her welcoming mouth, she tasted herself on him, and there was something incredibly erotic about it. Her core contracted, feeling empty and needy.

"I want you inside me," she breathed and wrapped her arms around his muscular torso. Sliding her hands down to cup his tight ass, she jacked her hips up, seeking the tip of his shaft and pushing against it.

Andrew lifted his hips, and with one powerful thrust he joined them, his shaft so deep within her it was hitting her cervix.

Nathalie gasped, her sheath spasming around the hard length inside her. As he began pumping into her, Andrew's expression was almost scary. The gentle lover she was accustomed to was gone. His thrusting growing in urgency, Andrew groaned and grunted like a male animal in heat; aggressive, dominant, magnificent.

This wasn't making love, this was fucking, and she needed it just like that. Mindless, desperate, intense. Under the onslaught, there were no worries, no thoughts, just the brutal carnality that was hurtling her toward another orgasm.

Sweet, wonderful oblivion.

15

ANDREW

The gym, where Kian had assembled everyone for the mission briefing, was teeming with people when Andrew rushed in. He was late. No one had bothered to inform the human where the meeting was going to be held, and he'd run around the basement until it had occurred to him to check the gym.

At least that was the story that he was going to stick to if anyone asked.

The truth was that he had left Nathalie's place later than he intended to. She'd looked so anxious and worried that he'd decided to stay and take her mind off it in the only way he knew how—make love to her until she saw stars. Besides, after the rough fucking of last night, and there was nothing else it qualified as, Nathalie deserved some tender loving from him.

Besides, it didn't look as if anyone was in a hurry to start.

In preparation for the meeting, the gym had been outfitted with line after line of foldable chairs to accommodate the unprecedented number of people. The warriors took up most of the space, in numbers as well as their formidable presence. Sylvia and four other girls were huddled in a corner, talking excitedly, probably discussing their role in the mission. It wasn't as if an opportunity to be included in something like that presented itself often, or ever. For the civilians, it must have been both scary and thrilling.

The three girls who were supposed to be the decoy were indeed wearing khaki short shorts that barely covered their pert asses, and hiking boots that emphasized their long legs. Andrew wondered who'd been in charge of selecting the 'hikers.' His bet was on Anandur.

As the one who'd come up with the idea, Anandur wouldn't have left the selection to anybody else.

Bridget sat at the front, flanked by two other immortal females Andrew hadn't met before.

"Good morning," he said, offering his hand.

She shook it. "Let's hope it's going to be a good afternoon as well. Andrew, these are Gertrude and Hildegard. They are going to assist in taking care of the injured." She pointed to her companions.

"It's a pleasure to meet you." He shook hands with both, then scanned the room in search for other familiar faces. His eyes were drawn to the one bright island of color in the crowd of fatigues or khakis. William's Hawaiian shirt was hard to miss. Not just because it was so bright and so colorful, but because it was as big as a tent.

Heading toward the guy, Andrew weaved in between the chatting groups of people, stopping to nod quick hellos and shaking a few hands. Damn, he couldn't remember who he'd been already introduced to, and who he had not. Not that it made a difference when he couldn't for the life of him remember any of their names.

Old age sucked balls. Couldn't one of his special talents be eidetic memory?

"William, buddy, good to see you." He clapped hands with the guy. "Are you joining us on the mission? Or are you here to supply everyone with gadgets?"

William grinned. "Both. I had to pull some strings and jump through a few hoops, but I got everyone earpieces that respond to voice commands. No need to tap on and off or to leave the thing on continuously." He pulled one from the pocket of his shorts. "Here, put it in."

Andrew took the tiny bug and inserted it into his ear. The thing was rubbery and flexible, immediately molding itself to rest comfortably in place. "Good fit."

"Yeah, that is another advantage of these new ones. They adjust to fit everyone. You have to program it to recognize your voice and the word for on and off. You can choose your own. But I suggest you do it in a quiet place. It's too noisy in here and it can mess it up. You tap once to start recording, and it will guide you through the rest."

Ingenious little thing. "Good deal. If I have any problems, I'll come to you."

"That's what I'm here for. I'm also going to be out there with you guys in my tech-mobile, handling the communication and troubleshooting on the spot."

Andrew lifted a brow. "Who is going to be your driver?" As far as he knew, only Kri and he were assigned driving duties. Two yellow school buses would be the transportation mode for the warriors and Bridget and her crew. The idea being that even if the vehicles were spotted parking on the side of the road, they would not raise suspicion. Just kids on a school trip, nothing to worry about. After everything was over and it was time to collect the bodies, another truck was scheduled to drive straight up to the monastery, but it wasn't part of the initial contingent.

William puffed out his chest. "No one, I'm going to drive my baby myself. She's loaded with a king's ransom worth of equipment, some of it one of a kind instruments I've designed myself."

"I guess you'll be hanging back with Kri and me and the doctor."

William high-fived him. "I'll be in good company."

Andrew glanced at the group of pretty girls surrounding Sylvia. "You know any of the 'hikers'? I've only met Sylvia."

William followed Andrew's eyes. "The one wearing the long pants is Ruth, Sylvia's mother. The other three are Sylvia's friends. The short curvy one is Monica, the leggy brunette is Ashley, and the mousy looking one is Amber."

Andrew wouldn't call Amber mousy. She was skinny, true, but her ass filled her shorts very nicely. Ruth, Sylvia's mother, however, was a bit of a shocker. She looked the same age as her daughter. He shouldn't have been surprised, these were immortals after all, and he'd met Annani who looked younger than her children, but damn. Standing next to each other, mother and daughter looked like twins.

On some level it was disturbing.

Hell, he should get used to this. Pretty soon it was going to be him, standing next to a son that would look exactly like him, with Nathalie's big brown eyes and high cheekbones, but Andrew's height and build. And they would look about the same age...

Disturbing? You betcha. Nevertheless, bring it on. It was going to be one hell of a ride, and Andrew couldn't wait to take his foot off the brake and stomp on the accelerator.

He was ready.

Glancing at the rows of white chairs and the huge guys overflowing the narrow seats, Andrew was pleasantly surprised to find Dalhu among the warriors. Or rather at their fringes. He sat alone at the end of the last row, with two mostly empty lines of chairs separating him from the other guys.

Eventually, these rows would be filled as well, but while people were still mingling, Dalhu looked like the ostracized kid who no one wanted to play with.

Where was Anandur?

If there was one Guardian who'd accepted Dalhu without reservation it was him. Andrew spotted the guy schmoozing with two of his old pals.

It seemed that it was up to Andrew to keep Dalhu company. Actually, this wasn't a bad idea. Andrew was tired of coming up with ways to avoid using names he didn't remember.

Embarrassing.

Those who'd met him greeted him by name, while he responded with 'dude' or 'my man,' feeling like a delinquent.

Dalhu pushed to his feet as he saw Andrew coming his way. "I'm glad you're here," he said as they clapped hands.

"I can imagine. Where are the other Guardians? The only one I spotted was Anandur." Andrew pointed to where he saw the guy standing a moment ago, but he was gone.

"Kian pulled them out. He is probably briefing them first so they can help with the rest of us."

Andrew narrowed his eyes. "Are you here in an advisory capacity? Or is he letting you fight?"

Dalhu's smile was answer enough. The guy hadn't looked that happy since... Hell, Andrew couldn't remember him ever looking so joyful.

"I'm fighting. Kian has given me the best gift ever. Weapons. My own knives that he had retrieved from the cabin where Amanda and I stayed at, and one of his own swords. She is such an incredible beauty that I can't believe he is willing to part with her."

Andrew chuckled. The guy was talking about the sword with more reverence than he'd ever talked about Amanda. Not that anyone would ever doubt Dalhu's love and devotion for his mate, not after what he'd been put through for her. He must've missed his fighting days more than anyone had realized.

"Maybe she's just a loaner? And after the mission he expects you to give her back?"

"You think? It sounded as if he was gifting her to me."

Andrew found it hard to believe that Kian would let Dalhu keep deadly weapons at his disposal. Up until recently, Kian had detested everything about the guy and hadn't trusted a word he'd said. His attitude had changed for the better after Dalhu's redemption, but he'd remained reserved and careful around the guy. As far as Andrew knew, Dalhu still wasn't allowed to leave the keep. The new one, that is. The old one was waiting for its inhabitants to come back following the successful completion of this mission.

Kian had been clear about his objectives. No Doomer would be left alive. He hadn't demanded a final death, but chances were that in the heat of battle few would take the time to carefully calculate the amount of venom they were injecting into their enemies. Andrew didn't expect to bring many of the Doomers back to be entombed in the crypt.

It was going to be a vicious blood bath.

Kian had issued a gag order. No one was allowed to tell Annani a thing about the upcoming battle. She would've insisted on keeping as many Doomers as possible alive, or whatever the suspended state they kept them in was called.

The living dead?

Trouble was, that would've meant more casualties for the clan, which was unacceptable.

Andrew didn't envy Kian the hell his mother was going to give him once he confessed—after the fact.

In theory, she could remove him from his station. It was her prerogative, but it was highly unlikely she'd go that far. Kian would spend some time in the proverbial doghouse, but the truth was that she had no one to replace him.

Besides, Kian was an excellent leader and the good of his people was his first priority.

As it should be.

Annani, on the other hand, believed for some reason that the Doomers were her people as well. Delusional wishful thinking, at least in Andrew's opinion. At one time it might have been true, but these two factions had been at war for thousands of years, and other than some shared ancestral genes they had absolutely nothing in common.

16

CAROL

Carol woke up to the sound of a car door opening then slamming shut. Moments later another door opened and closed. Thank the merciful Fates it was further down the line of parked vehicles.

Still groggy from all the pills she'd consumed yesterday, Carol experienced the explosion of terror in her gut with a split second's delay. Quickly, she pulled the comforter over her head, huddling under it, afraid of the sound of her own panicked breaths.

What if someone saw her? Or heard her? Immortal males were the most dangerous predators on earth, with superior hearing and a sense of smell to rival that of dogs.

Was the stench of her fear strong enough to percolate through the slight crack in the window Robert had left open?

He'd insisted she needed some fresh air. Now she wished he hadn't done it.

If she got caught in his van, Robert's head would roll off his neck before he got a chance to come up with an excuse. She would live, but wish to join his fate. Not because she was in love with the guy and couldn't go on without him, but because Sebastian would make her life even more hellish than it had been up until now.

When the other car's engine was turned on, Carol clutched the comforter with trembling hands, waiting breathlessly until its wheels rolled over the parking lot's gravel. She relaxed only after the vehicle reached the black top. The small change in elevation had been enough to produce a squeak when the rear shock absorbers reacted to the bump.

Was it Sebastian who'd left in that car? She prayed it was.

Not that it meant she was safe. The escape plan would fail and the results would be the same if any of the other warriors found her hiding in Robert's car.

Carol shifted to her side and hugged Robert's pillow, bringing her knees up to her chin. It was freezing cold inside the van, even under the blanket. The early morning sun was still too weak to burn through the dark overcast and warm things up.

The goosebumps covering her chilled skin weren't her only problem. Carol needed to pee in the worst possible way. Eying the container Robert had provided for just that purpose, she was sorely tempted to use it. Problem was, she was well aware of what happened when someone tried to maneuver inside a parked car. She'd had her fair share of backseat action during the '60s. No matter how careful she would be, the van would wobble on its wheels.

Carol groaned. Holding it in would be one hell of a challenge. But she wasn't going to risk her one and only chance of escape because she couldn't handle a full bladder.

Her distress growing more acute by the minute, time slowed down to a standstill as she waited for Robert to show up. When he finally did, he didn't open the trunk or say a word to her. Instead, he pretended as if it was business as usual and there was no female hiding in the trunk of his van. Sliding into the driver's seat, he turned the engine on.

A smart move. They weren't safe until they put some distance between them and the compound.

Following his cue, she stayed huddled under the blanket and kept her mouth shut, with only her nose peeking from under the small tented opening she'd made with her hands.

Robert shifted into reverse and backed out from his parking spot straight onto the asphalt driveway. The small bump was surprisingly rough, and Carol barely stifled a groan as her back slammed against the hard grooves lining the van's floor. Unfortunately, the road Robert turned into was in obvious disrepair, and Carol felt every pothole as her body got bumped around.

A few minutes later, he finally abandoned the country road and turned into a highway that provided for a much smoother ride.

"Are you okay?" he asked, looking up at his rear-view mirror to catch a glance of her.

"I need to pee, like right now. Can you stop somewhere?"

"Why didn't you use the container I left for you?"

"I was afraid to shake the van." She snorted. "Heck, I was afraid to breathe."

He nodded. "You can use it now."

"You must be kidding. I'm not going to pee with you in the car."

"I want to put some distance between us and the compound before I stop. I promise not to look."

"But it's going to smell…"

"I'll open the windows. You have only two options. You either pee in the container or wait until we reach the town."

Fuck. Not only was she going to have to relieve herself inside a moving vehicle, hoping none of it splattered around, but she would need to do it half naked because she didn't have a shirt. Her old one was covered in crusted blood, stiff enough to stand on its own, and it was too much to hope that Robert had thought of bringing a change of clothes for her.

Humiliating. But whatever. It was worth it. To be free of that hell, she would've done it fully naked. In the middle of the mall. During the Christmas shopping craze.

True to his word, Robert kept his eyes on the road and didn't peek. She checked before letting go. The relief was incredible, and by the time she was done the container was full. Thank the merciful Fates, nothing had spilled, not on the hand holding the thing and not on the van's carpeted floor, but boy, did it stink. Carol hurried to fasten the lid, and put the container as far away from her as possible in the small space.

There was a lesson to be learned here.

Torture didn't have to be inflicted by a merciless sadist—a denial of a simple bodily function was almost as effective.

"Better?" Robert asked.

"Much. You don't have a change of clothes in here somewhere by any chance?"

"In fact, I do. I put on two T-shirts. One is for you."

What a thoughtful, considerate man.

Holding the steering wheel with his knees, Robert pulled one of his shirts over his head and tossed it to her.

As she put it on, Carol wanted to purr like a satisfied kitten. The shirt, although short-sleeved, was still warm from his body and felt like heaven over her chilled skin. It smelled like him too. A good, clean smell. Laundry detergent with a tiny bit of cologne and Robert's natural scent, which was quite pleasant. Masculine, but not overbearing.

She'd never attached much meaning to the different scents males produced, unless they were unwashed that is, and then she kept her distance from the brutes. And yet, sniffing Robert's shirt she couldn't help feeling as if his scent hinted at the kind of man he was. He smelled like honesty and dependability and hard work.

A good man.

Carol shook her head. Her gratitude to the man was playing tricks on her. Robert was good because he was helping her escape, but he was still a Doomer. There was no way he was as good as he smelled.

On the other hand, Dalhu had been a Doomer too, and yet Amanda had taken him on as her mate. Not officially, but they lived together with Kian's blessing. Or at least his grudging acquiescence. Everyone was talking about the great sacrifice Dalhu had made for Amanda, and how bravely and admirably he'd submitted to the ordeal Micah had demanded. But courage and strength didn't necessarily mean that he was a good guy. Except, Amanda had apparently deemed him good enough. And so did Kian, the council, and the Guardians.

The Guardians, right. She should let them know she was okay. Her instructors and her classmates must be worried out of their minds. Even if, Fates forbid, Ben hadn't survived to tell what had happened to her, George would have reported her missing.

She'd promised Robert she'd stay with him, and Carol was not going to go back on her word, but she needed to make that phone call.

Lifting up to her knees, she asked, "Can I come up front? Or is it still too dangerous?"

Robert glanced at her through the rear view mirror. "I don't want to take any chances. Stay in the back where no one can see you through the tinted windows."

Carol rearranged the comforter to make herself a little cushy seat, and sat down leaning her back carefully against the van's side wall. So far so good. Overnight, her wounds had healed completely, and all that was bothering her now were the knotted muscles that could use a good relaxing massage.

"Robert?"

"Yeah?"

"Thank you."

"You're welcome."

"I meant what I said last night. You are not going to regret this. I'm going to make you a very happy guy."

His face got so red that the flash of color was clearly visible in the small rear view mirror.

"You being with me will make me happy. You don't need to do anything more."

"I know. I want to return the favor in any way I can. And don't worry about money. I have plenty saved up. I'll probably need a few days to arrange for a new driver's license and a passport, credit cards and such."

The color on his cheeks turned from tomato red to deep crimson. "Keep your money. I'm going to find work and support us. I'm a healthy, hard-working male. And I'm certainly not going to rely on a woman for support."

Without meaning to, she'd offended him. But the same was true for him. His outrage at the idea that she'd support them was offensive to her. But what could she expect from a Doomer? Their views on females and their roles in a relationship belonged in the Stone Age.

Hell, not even then. Caveman had had better opinions about their female counterparts.

She had her work cut out for her. By the time she was done with him, Robert would think and act like a modern man. Not an ape. In the meantime, however, she should be mindful of his sensitivities.

Robert deserved her gratitude, not her derision.

"I didn't mean to imply you're incapable of earning an income. I'm sure you are. My offer is for the meantime, just until you find work."

He nodded, some of the redness on his cheeks receding.

When they reached the town, Carol climbed over the seats and joined Robert up front. "So where to? Any ideas?"

He shrugged. "Not really. I need to refuel if we want to keep going in this van. But I'm hoping to catch someone I can thrall easily into trading cars. I'll try to find someone at the gas station."

It seemed Robert wasn't very confident in his thralling abilities, but Carol hesitated to offer her help. His male ego might get hurt again. She'd wait and see how he was managing, and intervene only as a last resort.

As Robert pulled into an Arco, Carol eyed the gas station's mini-mart. "Do you have any money? I want to buy a burner phone."

He cast her a suspicious glance. "Why?"

"Because we need one. And if you have yours on you, you should dispose of it together with the car."

"Good point. Here." He pulled out a hundred from his wallet. "Is this enough?"

"I hope so. If not, I'll let you know." She took the money and headed for the mini mart. It was one of the larger ones, and she was glad to find a whole row of disposable phones in a wide range of prices. She chose one of the cheapest. After all, she only needed it for a short time to arrange access to her money. After that was done she could buy a full-featured smart phone like the one she'd had before.

The guy at the front desk helped her activate the device, and in no time she had a working phone in her hands.

What a great feeling. Having a phone felt almost as crucial as having a shirt on. She'd felt naked without either.

Through the window, she saw Robert approach a guy then shake his head and go back to the pump. She'd been right. Robert's thrall was weak.

Lifting the phone, she debated whether to tell him that she was going to call home to let everyone know she'd escaped, or just do it and tell him later.

Don't be a coward.

She needed to tell Robert first and then do it even if he was against it. A small confrontation was better than deceit, and it would set the right tone for their relationship from the start.

Sauntering up to him with a slightly exaggerated, sexy sway of her hips, Carol surprised herself with how easily she was slipping into her old self. Only last night, she'd been convinced she'd never attempt to seduce anyone again. Hell, any thought of sex had been repulsive to her. Still was, but she had a feeling that it wouldn't last long. Dimly, she was aware that there was nothing better to make her forget the sadist than making love with someone who cared.

Like Robert.

His eyes widened and his Adam's apple bobbed, as she leaned next to him against the van's flank and treated him to one of her sultry smiles.

"I have the phone." She lifted it to show him. "I'm going to call home and let them know I'm okay. They are probably going out of their minds with worry."

Robert straightened to his full height, looking quite imposing as he glared down at her. "Don't repay my kindness with betrayal. I didn't rescue you so you can tell your people where to find mine and annihilate them. I'm a deserter, and they are probably going to hunt me like a stray dog. But some of them are my friends, and I'm not going to hand their enemies their heads on a platter."

She put her hand on his arm. "I'm only going to tell my family I'm fine, and that you helped me escape. Nothing else. You can listen to the conversation if you want."

Her placating tone and big innocent eyes melted Robert's harsh glare away. Apparently, she still had it. The way he was gazing at her, she could ask for the moon and he'd try to get it for her.

"Wait until we are on the road. I didn't find anyone who was both easy to thrall and had the kind of car I wanted. We will drive this van into Santa Barbara and find something there."

"Okay." She stretched on her tiptoes and kissed his cheek. "Thank you."

Robert blushed again and got busy with the gas pump, replacing the nozzle and screwing the cap back on.

When they were seated and buckled, Carol lifted the phone. "Now is it okay?"

He nodded.

She'd already decided who she was going to call. Brundar. Other than her friends', his was the only phone number she had memorized, and he also had direct access to Kian.

"Who is it?" Brundar answered in a tone that was neither angry nor combative but sounded threatening nonetheless.

"It's Carol. I'm calling from a burner phone. Just wanted to let everyone know I'm okay."

"Do they still have you or did you get away?"

"I escaped."

"How?"

"I had help. One of the Doomers risked his life to help me."

"Does he want to return you to the keep?" Brundar's tone sounded venomous.

Carol rolled her eyes. How stupid did he think she was? Did he expect her to lead Doomers to the keep's front door?

"No. We are running away. I promised Robert I'd stay with him. I just wanted to let you guys know so you don't worry about me. I'm okay now. Their commander thought I could tell him things about the clan, and he tried to torture the information out of me, but I had nothing to tell. As if a pothead like me would know anything, right?" She chuckled nervously, hoping he caught her drift.

"That's good. But how do I know you're not being coerced?"

She smiled. "Remember telling me to get in shape and visit the gym every day? Well, I didn't. I lied about it."

"That sounds like you. I'm glad you escaped. Saves us the trouble of rescuing you. You caught us at the last minute before we put pressure on the police to search for you." Brundar was trying to tell her something. He was never this talkative. Besides, there was no way they would've called the police. Even if they did, the authorities would've done nothing. She would be just another girl gone missing. Were they planning an attack? Were they going to cancel it now that she was free?"

"I'm not the only girl who needs rescuing."

"I see. Do you know how many?"

Carol felt Robert tense at her side. "How should I know? There are always some damsels in need of rescuing, right?" She hoped Brundar would get what she was trying to say and why.

"Right. Well, good luck to you and your Doomer. Tell him that we owe him a debt of gratitude. He is welcomed to collect it at any time."

"I will. Goodbye, Brundar." Carol frowned. Was there a secret meaning in that last sentence too? Or had Brundar really meant it?

"Who was that guy, Brundar?" Robert asked.

How to answer that without lying but also without revealing Brundar's position? Robert would flip if he knew she'd called a Guardian.

"He is my cousin, of course. All members of our clan are related to each other. And he is also my fitness trainer. Or was, that is." She smiled innocently.

17

SEBASTIAN

"Where is Robert?" Sebastian asked the soldier coming up the stairs.

The man paused, shifting the stack of trays he was carrying to his other side. "He went to town on a supply run, sir."

"Who did he leave in charge?"

"It would be me, sir."

"Naturally." Sebastian grimaced.

He'd never thought to spell it out for the idiot, but with both Tom and him gone, Robert should have known not to leave base for any reason, let alone some missing supplies.

"Did he say when he'll be back?"

"After lunch, sir. He should be back shortly."

And when he did, Sebastian was going to have to teach him a lesson. In Robert's case, it was probably stupidity that had prompted him to do such an irresponsible thing, and not insubordination. The guy was a dedicated soldier who'd always performed his duties to the best of his abilities.

Nevertheless, this couldn't go unpunished.

Trouble was, Sebastian could think of no one who could replace Robert even for a few days. Tom's schedule was already full, and other than Tom the rest of the men were even more incompetent than Robert. They were simple fighters, good at only one thing.

There was no avoiding it, though.

Robert needed to spend a few days chilling his ass locked in solitary confinement and surviving on half rations. What a pity Sebastian couldn't just whip him and be done with it. True, it was his prerogative as a commander to do as he pleased with his men, but he was too smart and too experienced to use such crude methods. He needed his warriors loyal, and loyalty wasn't earned with the help of a whip.

Regrettably.

Besides, not only did he not derive as much enjoyment from whipping males, Sebastian preferred to keep his hobby separate from his job.

He could use a good whipping session, though.

The trip to Phoenix had been a waste of time. The redneck owner of the radio station refused to even deal with Sebastian on the grounds that he wasn't an American.

"What's wrong with an Australian?" Sebastian had asked.

The old redneck had replied with his own question. "Are you planning on becoming an American citizen, son?"

Sebastian should have said yes, but it just hadn't occurred to him that this would be a deal breaker.

Damn, he was tempted to blow the old hoot's precious station up. Stage a terrorist attack. Maybe he still would. No one should be allowed to treat Sebastian Shar with such disrespect and get away with it.

The meeting had been over before it had even begun, and Tom and he had been lucky to catch the last two remaining seats in an earlier flight. He should blow up the radio station just for having to fly coach. First class had been sold out.

It was still too early to pay a visit to Carol. She wasn't recovered yet from last evening's session. Perhaps he could use Letty for a change?

Nah, the human was a poor substitute for the immortal. Besides, accustomed to Carol's resilience, Sebastian would probably kill Letty before recalibrating the intensity for her fragile, human body.

Besides, with both Robert and him gone most of the morning, there were things Sebastian needed to do before indulging in his favorite pastime. He would check on the men and make a tour of the grounds, giving Carol another hour to recuperate before paying her a visit.

As he made the rounds, Sebastian's irritation with Robert subsided. Before he'd left, his assistant had assigned tasks and shifts, and everything seemed to be rolling like a well-oiled machine. Two sets of patrolmen were circling the grounds, a group of soldiers was training at hand to hand combat in the back while another was eating lunch, and the rest were off duty, either sleeping or visiting the girls down at the basement.

He joined the group in the dining room, spending some time talking with the men. All part of the job. Appearing friendly and approachable was crucial to keeping his men loyal. When he was done with that, he went up to his third-floor apartment and took a leisurely shower.

After all, subjecting Carol to offensive body odor wasn't one of his torture techniques. He even sprayed himself with his most luxurious cologne before heading down to her room.

He'd try to go easy on her.

Normally, she would have several more hours to recuperate before his nightly visit. The healing of the mind took longer than that of the body, and even though her wounds would be closed, emotionally she wouldn't be ready.

It was a delicate balance. Sebastian needed to tread carefully. He didn't want to break her beyond repair. If her mind snapped, she would be useless to him. Whipping a zombie was probably as much fun as whipping a wooden post.

As he pushed the door to her room open, he was surprised to find it completely dark. It seemed Carol was sleeping. She didn't even stir when the light from the corridor banished the darkness. On the nightstand, her lunch tray remained untouched.

Was she planning on starving herself to death? Stupid girl. Immortals couldn't die from starvation. She'd only go into stasis. But perhaps that was her goal. In stasis, she wouldn't feel a thing.

Two steps brought him to the side of her bed. He leaned down to shake her shoulder, realizing immediately that it wasn't Carol's body under the comforter. He tore it off, the pillows that had been arranged to resemble a female form tumbling to the floor.

"NO!"

His bellow of rage must've shaken the compound.

Naked warriors burst into the corridor from the adjoining rooms, and more came running down the basement steps.

"Is Robert back?" he hissed.

The men exchanged looks. "I haven't seen him," one dared to speak.

"Go up and find him. Now!" he ordered, knowing perfectly well that Robert wouldn't be found.

Not now and not later.

The traitor wasn't coming back. Obviously, he'd absconded with Carol. How had a simpleton like him managed to fool a mastermind like Sebastian?

He'd underestimated Robert, that's how. All that 'yes, sir,' the vacant expression when he'd failed to understand something the first time, and Sebastian had had to patiently explain it again. It had all been a great big act.

"He is not back yet, sir," the one he'd sent to look for Robert came back to report.

For a moment, he considered running upstairs and activating the tracker on Robert's van. Sebastian's head was evidently not working well when overheated, because it took another moment before he remembered that it had been Robert who'd attached the devices to the undercarriages of the cars. The guy was certainly not stupid enough to leave the thing on.

Apparently, Robert wasn't nearly as dumb as Sebastian had thought he was. He'd stolen Sebastian's most prized possession from under his nose.

As Tom appeared at the head of the stairs, his hair still wet from the shower he'd taken, Sebastian motioned for him to stay where he was.

There was no point in staying down in the basement.

He needed to organize a search party, even though their chances of locating Robert were slim. According to the soldier Robert had left in charge, he had left shortly after breakfast, which meant an almost six hours' head start. But if he was driving the van, and after removing the tracker he might, there were other ways of locating it even without the tracker. Sebastian could call up some favors and have the license plate searched.

After all, there were traffic cameras everywhere, and all it took to get access to them was either a fat bribe to the operator or legit payment to a good hacker.

In short, it would cost money.

18

KIAN

As Brundar relayed the news about Carol, Kian's fingers thrummed a staccato beat on his desk. "What do you think? Do you believe she wasn't coerced? Maybe they are on to the snitch accountant and know that we are coming. Or perhaps he took money from both sides."

The unlikely informant worked in the accounting department of the weapons supplier, and the large shipment delivered locally piqued his curiosity. When Turner's people had started asking questions, he'd taken the opportunity to make a quick buck. Or a whole sack of them as was the case.

According to Turner, pencil pushers were among the best informed personnel in an organization, and his first choice in snitches.

Brundar shook his head. "I know Carol. She sounded grateful to the guy who helped her. Aside from hinting about the other females, she didn't divulge information about the location. My impression was that the Doomer didn't allow it. What surprised me, though, is that she didn't reveal ours. I was sure they would torture it out of her."

"Indeed. It seems that we underestimated our Carol. She is a lot tougher than she looks." Kian pushed to his feet and began pacing the length of his office. "It changes nothing. The threat remains, and the next civilian they catch might talk. We need to eliminate them. But the women are a problem. Considering the possibility that the Doomers might slit their throats as soon as we attack, we need to adjust our battle plan."

"We don't know where they are holding them. And it's too late to make changes to the plan, unless you want to cancel. We can come up with a new strategy today and go to war tomorrow, or the day after. With Carol's situation resolved, there is no urgency."

Kian glared at Brundar's stoic face. If he wasn't as good-looking and blond, the guy could have played Spock or Data on *Star Trek*. He rarely spoke, and when he did, there was barely any inflection in his tone. Everything coming out of his mouth sounded emotionless—like computer speak.

"I'm not cancelling the mission. Even if I were inclined to, which I'm not, we would have a riot on our hands. The guys who answered the call and came here to help liberate Carol would not be happy to have their fun and games postponed. They are pumped on testosterone and psyched to go."

Brundar surprised him with an almost angry sounding retort. "What about the females? Are we going to forfeit their lives because our warriors thirst for Doomer blood?"

"Of course not. We need to find out where the fuckers are holding them. We will have to split the force into two groups, and while one keeps the Doomers busy, the other will free the women."

"How are you going to find out where they are holding them in the next hour?"

"We have the blueprints of the monastery. It shouldn't be too difficult to deduce where the Doomers would stash a bunch of abducted females." Kian fired up his desktop, and a moment later he had a blown-up layout of the building displayed on the big screen hanging above his credenza.

"As far as I know, the fuckers are not into orgies, so they would need individual holding cells for their victims to serve the men in private."

Kian counted the number of bedrooms. "There are forty-two rooms. Assuming they have about one hundred warriors, and they are sleeping two and three to a room, there are no bedrooms left for the girls. That only leaves the basement." He pointed to the large unfinished area.

"Or, they can sleep four men to a room, and put the girls in the remaining ones."

Brundar was right, logically it was possible. But Kian's gut was telling him that the women were held underground. From the Doomers' perspective, it made more sense to keep their sex slaves away from the warriors' main quarters. Order had to be maintained, visits needed to be scheduled and monitored.

"They are in the basement. Trust me on that."

Brundar nodded. "It's your call. Just in case, though, let's send Arwel with the rescue team. He might be able to sense the women and point us in the right direction."

"Agreed."

The gym, which had been basically converted into a war room, was bustling with activity when Kian and Brundar returned from their brief meeting. With the eighty-six Guardians who'd answered the call and his current six, and Dalhu, he had ninety-three warriors. Andrew, Kri, Bridget and her two assistants, William, and the five 'hikers' brought the number to one hundred and four participants.

He wondered if they needed a third bus for the women. Just in case it was needed, he should have one on standby.

Kian clapped his hands to get everyone's attention. "Please take your seats. I have an update." He waited until they did as he'd commanded and a hush fell over the cavernous room.

"Carol escaped. One of the Doomers helped her get away."

A murmur that had begun at one corner of the gym spread like wildfire throughout the ranks, and bodies shifting in the rickety foldable chairs amplified the sound of disquiet. As he'd expected, the men were glad for Carol, but disappointed at the prospect of the mission getting cancelled.

Kian raised his hand. "We are still going in." That got everyone's attention. "First of all, even though this is no longer about Carol's rescue, the fact remains that for us to sleep peacefully at night this viper nest of Doomers needs to be eradicated. Second, Carol said that there were other women held prisoner by the Doomers, and we all know what they need them for. We are going to rescue them."

"How many?" Anandur asked.

"She either didn't know or couldn't talk in front of the Doomer. But it doesn't matter. Two or twenty or two hundred, they need to be liberated. We are helpless to help those taken to the island, but we can and must help those in our own back yard."

He got back nods, murmurs of agreement, and even a few grunts.

"We need to split the force into two groups. One to keep the Doomers occupied, and the other to rescue the women. Thanks to your willingness to drop everything and come, we have more than enough warriors to do both."

Kian signaled to Shai who turned on the projector, displaying the layout of the Doomers' compound on the gym's back wall. With a ruler, he pointed at the stairs leading down to the basement.

"I suspect that they are holding them down here. But I'm sure that it no longer looks like that. My bet is that they divided it into individual rooms for the females. Still, these stairs are the only point of entry, which creates a bottleneck. Therefore, the rescue team will need to be limited to no more than a dozen men. In case I'm wrong and they are not there, Arwel will lead this team, using his telepathic ability to locate the women." He motioned for Arwel to join him in front of the warriors.

"I need eleven more. Who's volunteering?"

Bhathian got up but no one joined them.

Bhathian glared at the men. "I would've loved nothing better than to fight and kill Doomers with you, but these women need my help more than I need to kill Doomers. Their families must be frantic with worry over them. I would be if my daughter went missing. Who's with me?"

Anandur sighed and stood up.

"Come on, men. We need nine more." Kian scanned the room full of warriors. Suddenly the men got busy looking at the shoulder of the guy sitting next to them, or down at their shoes. But they couldn't hide from him their guilty expressions.

"Okay. You leave me no choice but to decide for you." Kian pointed at the first row. "Uisdean and Niall, you two."

The two warriors grunted their disapproval but joined the others up front. In the back, Alesteir grabbed the back of Muir's shirt and lifted him up. Muir shook his head but followed. Raibert was next, then Eoin.

"Thank you, gentleman." Kian shook each of their hands as they joined the group. "We need three more."

Morogh stood up and pushed his way through the line of warriors, tapping Nachton and Uarraig as he passed them by. The three completed the count.

Kian clapped each on his shoulder.

"Good. Now we are ready to roll out. In twenty minutes, I want everyone in the parking level. Shai made a list of who goes on which bus, so check with him before you board. Hikers, you are with me."

19

DALHU

"Dalhu, you're on the front bus." Shai checked off his name on the tablet he was holding.

Dalhu felt his shoulders relax. The seating arrangements for the rescue team had been reassigned so they would all ride on one bus, which happened to be the one Andrew was driving, and the one Dalhu hoped he'd be riding as well.

The only friends he had made since he was accepted into the clan were Anandur, Andrew, and to some degree Kian.

The guy who'd despised everything about Dalhu had reconciled himself to his sister's choice of mate. But it was more than that. A few days ago Kian had shocked him when he'd come to ask his advice.

Dalhu's opinion, the ex-Doomer who in Kian's eyes had been lower than the worst scum of the earth, suddenly carried weight.

It wouldn't have been so surprising if Kian had asked him about insight into the Doomers' fighting style, or weaknesses in their strategies. But it had been about something personal troubling him that he couldn't discuss with anyone else. One mated male to another.

Who would have thought?

Not Dalhu, that was for sure. He hoped that what he'd told Kian had helped. Syssi was not herself lately, and Kian couldn't get her to talk about what was troubling her. Dalhu's advice had been to give her space and wait until she was ready to share whatever it was. Not an easy task for a guy like Kian, who had an obsessive need to control everything and everyone around him.

At least the man didn't think of himself as a know-it-all and welcomed input from others. The final decision, though, was always his. Unless Annani overruled him. That was why everyone had been ordered to keep their mouths shut about this mission until it was over.

Kian would have hell to pay once his mother found out.

Was that why he was driving the 'hikers' and Brundar in his Lexus instead of joining the others on the bus? Some attempt at plausible deniability?

Or perhaps it had been something else. Maybe Kian believed that his SUV was a lucky charm or something. Dalhu had his own irrational beliefs. Like taking the fact that he'd been assigned to the same bus as his only two other friends as a good sign, because if the day started with a lucky break, there was a good chance it would continue that way.

Warriors were a superstitious bunch, especially before a battle. None would ever admit it, but they considered all kind of bullshit as signs, either lucky or unlucky, and he wasn't immune to the nonsense.

Apparently, there was truth in the saying that there are no atheists in a foxhole.

Anandur and Arwel had already boarded and were sitting directly behind Andrew. The bench across the aisle from them was unoccupied. His second lucky break for the day. Dalhu put his butt in it before anyone else had a chance to snatch it.

Bhathian taking the seat next to him was the third lucky break. The guy wasn't exactly a friend, but he didn't show exceptional animosity toward Dalhu either. Bhathian scowled and grunted at everyone. Though lately, the guy had been smiling more often. Still, even Bhathian's scowls were better than some of the looks Dalhu had been getting from the newcomers. More so now, when they saw the monstrous sword Kian had given him strapped to his side.

They didn't trust him. Not yet. He had to prove himself to them too.

In a couple of hours he would.

Dalhu was an exceptional fighter, even if he said so himself. The Guardians were superior warriors, but he was just as good if not better. The skill level was equivalent, but they weren't as vicious.

Dalhu had no qualms about dispatching each and every one of the Doomers. His world view was simple. Those who posed a threat to his mate and her family had to die.

"I'm hungry," Bhathian grunted.

"Why didn't you grab something to eat before we left?" Arwel asked.

Bhathian folded his arms across his chest. "There was no time."

Anandur leaned to smirk at Bhathian. "Don't worry, boys, I'm sure we'll get fed."

Dalhu doubted that they would stop at a drive-through on the way. Besides, fighting with a full stomach was a bad idea. He was about to share his opinion when Kian's butler climbed the stairs with two huge plastic bags in each hand, lowering them gently to the bus's floor next to Andrew's seat.

"Gentlemen, I brought provisions for the road." He lifted one bag and headed for the back of the bus, distributing neatly folded lunch bags.

"Need any help?" offered a warrior sitting behind Dalhu. Was that Uisdean? Dalhu thought so but wasn't sure. It would take some time before he learned all the newcomers' names.

Okidu turned around with an affronted expression on his broad face. "No, sir. I do not. If you wait patiently, your turn will come shortly."

The butler accentuated every word with a flawless British accent. It was hard to believe that he was basically a machine. Amanda's butler, Onidu, who was an almost exact replica of Okidu, looked and sounded so real that Dalhu had no problem following Amanda's example and treating her butler as if he were a person. Onidu was so good at mimicking emotions that Dalhu often caught himself thinking that the mechanical butler actually liked him.

Or, what was more likely, that he was imagining the affection because he needed it. Dalhu had lived for so long as an island, with no one to trust, no one to even share his thoughts with. Now that he'd gotten a taste for it, he wanted more. Amanda's love was wonderful, the best that life had to offer, but he craved more interactions with people.

Good interactions, with people who actually liked him.

When Okidu was done distributing the bags, he returned to the front, faced the bus full of warriors, and bowed at the waist. "Gentlemen, I wish you the best of luck on your mission. May you come back victorious and unharmed."

With another bow, he stepped down.

It had taken another ten minutes or so before Andrew turned on the engine and closed the bus's door. Shai had come up to take a tally, making sure everyone was accounted for and sitting on the right bus. William had performed a communication test, ensuring that everyone's earpieces were working fine, and Kian had given his version of a rally-the-troops speech. Short and to the point with not much fluff.

Dalhu's appreciation for the guy had gone up another notch.

When Kian had given him the sword this morning, Dalhu had assumed that as regent he wasn't going to join the assault, but was going to lead from the back like Dalhu's superiors had done. Not a bad strategy, in Dalhu's opinion. Kian was irreplaceable, the other warriors weren't. And yet, Kian had had a sword strapped to his side when he'd come to give his laconic speech.

He was going to fight, which meant Dalhu would have to watch the guy's back. Amanda would never forgive him if he let her brother get hurt.

Earlier, when he'd kissed her and said goodbye, she'd surprised him. The woman who'd cried buckets when he'd faced Micah's challenge smiled and wished him success.

Damn, he hoped that the reason was her confidence in him, not lack of caring. He was sure Syssi hadn't been as calm with Kian.

"What's the face for?" Bhathian asked. "Worried?"

The nerve of the guy. For someone who wore a perpetual scowl he had no right to make comments about Dalhu's facial expressions.

"No, you?"

Bhathian sighed. "Yeah, I am. All these females who might get hurt today... It's not the same as us warriors. We are trained, and we expect pain and blood and loss. What if the Doomers kill them before we get to them? Do you think they are capable of this? Hell, of course they are. But will they?"

Dalhu was embarrassed. He'd thought Bhathian had been teasing him, but apparently the guy was just looking for an opening to start a conversation.

"I don't think so. Not unless they are ordered to. If we take out their commander first, I doubt the rank and file soldiers will go out of their way to slaughter women. Not all of them are monsters."

Bhathian arched one of his formidable brows. "Just most, right?"

Dalhu shrugged. "It's impossible to tell who has some soul left in them and who doesn't. It's not like Doomers sit around a fire, sing kumbaya, and share their feelings."

Anandur snorted. "Now, that is a picture."

Bhathian opened the paper bag that had been sitting on his lap and pulled out a water bottle and a nicely wrapped sandwich. Not a bad idea. The ride to Ojai would take at least another forty minutes. Plenty of time to digest a light meal.

As with everything else in the clan's world, the sandwich tasted like something from a fancy restaurant, and the brownie dessert had Dalhu's eyes rolling back. He washed it down with the second water bottle, then wondered what to do with the trash.

Bhathian crumpled his into a ball and shot it into one of the plastic bags Onidu had left up front.

"Score!" he exclaimed when his paper bag made it in.

Someone in the back snorted. "Big deal. You're practically sitting on top of it."

A projectile flew over Dalhu's and Bhathian's head, landing inside the container.

"That's what I call a score," the shooter congratulated himself.

After that it rained crumpled paper bags as the rest of the guys joined the game. One of them missed, hitting Andrew in the head.

"Hey, watch it! A fragile human here!"

Dalhu smiled. Those who never went to war didn't realize how warriors handled the time just before the battle. No one would imagine them eating lunch, joking around, and regressing into boys.

In less than two hours, though, these same men would morph into killing machines. That part was easy. The hard part was morphing back. For some it would take days, for others months, and some would get stuck in that mode and never come back.

20

KIAN

"Let me fight, Kian, or at least join the rescue team. The kidnapped women will cooperate better with a female. Our guys will look no different to them than the Doomers, or maybe even scarier. Can you imagine the reaction they'll get given the gear they'll be wearing?" Kri had been arguing her case for the last five minutes, and Kian's resistance was faltering.

Considering the large number of Guardians going in with her, Kri would be safe. She might get injured, but the chances of Doomers somehow managing to take her captive were so slim that they were nearly nonexistent. He couldn't, not in good conscience, tell her that he still feared she'd fall into enemy hands. That he didn't want to see his young niece hurt was his problem, not hers. Kri was a fighter who'd been training for this for decades. To deny her would be wrong.

"Did you bring your body armor? I can't let you fight without it."

She smirked. "Of course I did. I'm an optimist."

Damn, she'd known he'd cave in. "Fine. But once you get the women out, you take them to the bus and stay there. I don't want to see you rejoining the fighting. Are we clear?"

Kri jumped on him and hugged him, very un-warrior like. "Thank you, Kian. Thank you, thank you, thank you."

Over her shoulder, Kian glared at the amused expression on the faces of the male Guardians. They were going to taunt her to destruction over this. He pushed her away. "Stop it, you're embarrassing yourself." She'd been so excited that she paid no attention to the snorting and chuckling behind her.

Kri turned around and flipped the guys off with both hands. "You watch and see, boys. I'm going to show you how it's done."

"Sure, lass. Don't get your panties in a wad." Niall patted her shoulder.

"Grrr. You guys are all cavemen. This is the twenty-first century!" She stomped her foot on the ground, then kicked a stone before marching back to the bus to get her gear.

Too big to pass through the trees and make it into the clearing, the buses were parked on the side of the road, about five hundred feet before the turn into the single lane leading up to the monastery.

Bearing the name *Trinity Christian High School*, the buses were supposed to imply teenagers on a field trip. Kian's Lexus and William's van were parked inside the clearing, hidden behind the line of trees. The van was an old beaten up VW, but that was the outside. On the inside, it had equipment to make the Blackbird spy plane jealous.

Hopefully, the yellow buses would be ignored by any Doomers going out or coming back. They hadn't been in the area long enough to know if school trips to the mountains around Ojai were a common occurrence or not.

Kian faced the large group of warriors. "Listen up. I want to go over the basics again. Stationary cameras are mounted at five-hundred-feet intervals all along the road leading up to the monastery. Which means that the four hundred remaining feet in between them are big ass blind spots." He motioned to the 'hikers' to join him up front.

"Monica, Ashley, and Amber are going first, with Sylvia and Ruth five hundred feet behind them, and everybody else another hundred feet behind Sylvia. When we reach about a hundred feet before the first camera, we stop. The three will continue. Once they pass the second camera, Sylvia will move forward and fritz out the first one. Everyone will follow and stop again a hundred feet before the next one. I don't have to remind you to keep the ranks tight. We can't spread out. Listen to your earpieces. William has everybody on a grid, and he will tell you when to move and when to stop."

Bridget and her crew of two medics were to his left, standing apart from the warriors. Kian turned to give them their instructions. "Small change in plans. Kri is joining the rescue team, which means that when the signal comes that the compound is secured, one of you will have to drive the second bus up there."

"No problem, I'll do it." Bridget waved her hand.

"Andrew, you know your assignment. Help William with the communications."

"Yes, sir." Andrew saluted.

Kian smirked. That was the first time Andrew had treated him as a commander and not a brother-in-law.

"Don't get used to that. It was just an old reflex. I haven't been out of the service long enough."

"We'll see. I like getting some respect from you for a change."

Andrew looked like he was itching to say something back, but, wisely refrained. Even though Kian wasn't flaunting any official titles, he was in charge. To disrespect him in front of the troops, even as a joke, would have been inappropriate.

"Let's move out, people. William, you got us?"

"Everyone's number is on my screen," William answered inside his earpiece.

The first group of 'hikers' started walking, and a few minutes later William told Sylvia and Ruth to move out. The rest of the troop followed a hundred feet behind. Kian led the group of warriors, Anandur and Brundar flanking him on each side. Dalhu was right behind him. The irony of an ex-Doomer guarding his back and him trusting said ex-Doomer to fight by his side wasn't lost on Kian.

How things had changed...

As instructed, no one in their group talked. The hikers were supposed to act naturally, and that included chitchat. A group of women walking in silence would've made even a Doomer suspicious.

It was a slow and annoying progression. The girls were keeping an easy pace, which seemed to Kian snail slow. The other warriors probably felt the same.

The good news was that the road was only about a mile long. They'd be at the monastery walls in no time. The cameras there didn't leave any blind spots, but that would no longer be a problem. Once Sylvia fritzed out the last of the stationary ones, William's drones would start dropping explosives at strategic points of the big wall, and Yamanu would shroud the entire area in a thick mental cloud. No mortal in a fifty mile radius would hear anything.

As they halted for the last time, Kian shrugged off the backpack he'd been carrying, and each of the warriors followed suit. Unlike humans, who couldn't fight in heavy armor, immortals were strong enough to do so covered head to toe in reinforced body armor and ballistic helmets. Bullets couldn't kill them directly, but a strategic hit could incapacitate an immortal long enough for an enemy to finish him off with either fangs or a sword. Given that the Doomers were armed with machine guns, the specially designed suiting was a necessary precaution.

The clan owned most of the patents and the only manufacturing facility that made them. It wasn't a for profit enterprise, not yet. Very few orders had been made since the rumors about the special armor began spreading. But even if none of the human governments would've ordered any, it was fine by Kian. For now it safeguarded his people. Later, when the lighter version they were trying to develop was ready, many more orders would come.

Once everyone was suited up, they marched the remaining three hundred feet, and Sylvia took care of the last camera. When the explosions started, the hikers turned around and started running back downhill, while the warriors charged ahead.

Anandur left Kian's side, joining the rescue group, and Dalhu took his place, guarding Kian's flank. With the masks on, it was hard to tell who was who, but Dalhu was easy to identify. His height and Kian's sword strapped to his side gave him away.

Surreal. Kian felt safer with the ex-Doomer by his side than even Anandur, his trusted bodyguard for close to a millennium. Dalhu was a force to be reckoned with, and what was even more unbelievable, Kian trusted him.

As they breached the shredded wall, Doomers started filing out the monastery's front door, some carrying swords but most carrying machine guns. Just as Kian had known they would. They started firing immediately, but the bullets could do Kian and his men no harm. Nothing save for a missile could penetrate their armor.

Which wasn't outside the realm of possibility.

According to the snitch, the weapons the Doomers had ordered included several portable missile launchers.

The Doomers realized pretty quickly that bullets were ineffective, and most retreated into the building. If not for the women, Kian would've blown the whole thing up, reducing it to dust. But that wasn't an option. The Guardians would have to fight inside the building. It was going to be a bitch.

As Kian ran full speed ahead, his heavy boots pounding the ground in sync with Dalhu's and Brundar's, he had the passing thought that to humans they must've looked like alien invaders. Their masks and their body armor were the stuff of a science fiction movie—their gear belonging on some futuristic soldiers.

Suddenly, there was an explosion behind him, missing him and his companions by only a few feet. As the force of it propelled them forward, Kian found himself sprawled on the ground, face down, with Dalhu's hulking body on top of him, and no air coming into his lungs.

Fuck, he hoped the guy wasn't hurt and was just playing hero. If the idiot had been injured, or Fates forbid killed, while shielding him, Kian would rather face fifty Doomers—alone with no backup—than come home to face Amanda with the news.

Experimentally, Kian bucked up, trying to get the heavy weight off him. It took several moments before Dalhu rolled away and Kian's ribcage could expand to take a breath.

He wanted to ask Dalhu what the hell he thought he was doing, but his earpiece wasn't functioning. Either that or his left ear had gone deaf. The piece must've gotten damaged from the explosion. In either case, he had to remove the headgear to be able to communicate.

Fuck.

21

SEBASTIAN

As Sebastian looked at the warriors surrounding him, he schooled his expression into a mask of calm and confidence. His tone was measured as he addressed the men. "Don't worry, the traitor will be brought to justice."

Years of practicing self-discipline helped him hide the shit storm going on in his head. Hopefully, nothing in his demeanor revealed the boiling hot anger that was threatening to consume him. A leader had to show a cool head at all times. Losing it in front of the men was out of the question, and experience had taught him that pretending was the first step in controlling the rage.

Fronting calm helped.

Besides, he didn't have time to vent. Time was of the essence, and phone calls had to be made.

Leaving the warriors down in the basement, Sebastian climbed up to his third-floor apartment, focusing on keeping his limbs loose and his steps measured and unhurried. A perfect performance intended to impress upon his men that their leader was always in control.

Hell, he was impressing himself.

Sebastian had managed to keep the same measured and calm tone throughout all of the fifteen phone calls he'd made. When his objective had been achieved, he hung up the phone, put the handset back on its cradle, and leaned back in his chair.

He hadn't expected to spend so much time on what he'd perceived as a simple request, but in the end he had gotten what he'd wanted. One of his contacts had a guy who specialized in hacking into traffic cameras' databases, and then running the information through a specialized program to identify a specific car model in a specific area.

Sebastian had been under the impression that traffic cameras worked nonstop, taking pictures of license plates, but he'd learned that it wasn't so. Those that could read plates were activated only when a car crossed a red light, and those that videotaped regular traffic had resolution that was often too low to read something as small as letters and digits on a plate. Problem was, Robert's minivan was a popular model, and Sebastian doubted the guy would be crossing any red lights. Still, he hoped to get lucky, and that the hacker would find something useful. All Sebastian needed was the direction in which Robert and Carol were going.

He'd reserved a private plane, and it was on standby ready and fueled. Once he knew where they were heading, Sebastian and a couple of his men would fly to the next town and intercept them.

A shaky plan, but it was the best he'd come up with.

Capturing Robert and Carol was not optional. His men would never respect him again if he failed to bring the traitor and the escapee back and make an example out of them.

While the men watched, Sebastian would make sure that Robert's death was slow and painful. He was going to delight in punishing the traitor, but it was a shame he would have to do the same to Carol. Punishing her was what she deserved, but he didn't want to kill her. After all, immortal females weren't exactly dropping into his lap every day. He might never find another one.

Regrettably, she'd forced his hand in this.

Left with nothing to do other than wait for the phone call, Sebastian was tempted to pay Letty a visit. Except, it was a bad idea to engage with the female while in the enraged state he was in. He should try and calm down first.

Killing her would only make him angrier. He couldn't afford to lose both of his playmates before he secured a new one.

Pushing up to his feet, Sebastian paced the length of his study, then stepped outside onto his balcony for a breath of fresh air. A buzzing sound attracted his attention and he looked up with a frown. A toy plane was zipping toward the wall surrounding the monastery.

Curious, he appraised it. The toy was impressive, not one of those tiny models sold in stores. This one was big, and quite fast...

As the thing got closer, it dawned on him that what he was looking at wasn't a toy at all. This was a military grade drone.

Someone was spying on them.

The rage must've melted the gears in his brain because it took him another moment to connect the dots. Robert had not only absconded with Carol, but had betrayed them to the enemy.

The drone was probably sent by the Guardians and was taking shots of the compound, or videotaping it.

The clan was planning an attack.

He needed to shoot the drone down and raise the alarm. His assault rifle was in the closet, and Sebastian ran to retrieve it. Loading it with ammunition on his way back, he was about to burst out onto the balcony when the explosions started.

Son of a bitch. They were under attack.

The sight that greeted him chilled him to the bone. The drone was joined by three more, and the little suckers were dropping explosives on the compound's wall. But that wasn't the worst of it; through the newly created entry points, an army of invading robots was pouring in. Because these couldn't have been

Guardians. The clan didn't have that many. They must've used their technological knowhow to create the mechanical fighters.

Ingenious fuckers.

Machine guns in hand, his men were running out of the building and shooting at the invaders that kept advancing as if they were being pelted with hail and not bullets.

Robots, definitely.

"Get back inside," he shouted at his men to retreat. They were going to get slaughtered by these monsters. Someone with initiative launched a missile, but the idiot overshot and the thing missed three of the machines by a couple of feet. The blast lifted them in the air and propelled them several feet forward despite how heavy the robots looked. For a moment, he thought they would stay down. But no, they were on their feet and one of them removed his headgear, shaking out his longish, sweat-saturated hair.

Not a robot. A male. Immortal. In a very fancy body armor.

Sebastian marched back to his closet, returned the rifle to its stand and grabbed a sword. He pulled it out of its scabbard, flung the leather sheath at the wall and marched out.

The body armor protected the Guardians from bullets, but a sword thrust with enough force would cut through. This wasn't going to be a gentlemanly fencing duel. Sebastian was going to aim at the most vulnerable spot; the exposed seam between helmet and suit.

The quickest way to dispatch an immortal was to chop off his head.

Running down the stairs to the second floor, he leaped over the railing down to the first, landed on his feet, and shouted orders as he bolted for the front door to help the men barricade it. "Drop the rifles and get rocket launchers and swords. These are immortals in body armor."

The heavy wooden door wasn't going to hold for long, but hopefully the few extra moments would give his men time to arm themselves with the right weapons.

"Bring the dining table and make a shield," he shouted as he helped push the heavy sideboard against the door.

Two men upended the large wooden table, then Sebastian and the warriors who'd armed themselves already got behind it. The Guardians had protective gear, but his men didn't. He hadn't seen the invaders carrying anything other than swords, but if they had rifles as well, the table would shield him and his men from bullets.

Two more men leaped over the railing and joined him behind the table, one of them holding an RPG.

Thank Mortdh.

With the invaders about to break the front door, Sebastian was glad to hear several pairs of boots pounding down the stairs. Once the Guardians broke in, he would need as many men as possible to hold them off.

Suddenly, the pounding noises stopped. It seemed that for now the Guardians had given up on breaking the door. Sebastian didn't doubt for a moment that they would resume their effort soon. Focusing on the front, Sebastian was startled by the sound of shattering glass. The dining room window imploded, and the next second several immortals jumped through.

The guy with the RPG panicked, aiming the missile at the few men coming through the window and firing before Sebastian had a chance to shout, "No!"

Their only strategic advantage had just gotten wasted. Unless more of his men armed themselves with RPGs, it was down to swords.

The armor was protecting the Guardians from bullets, but it was encumbering their movements, making them more vulnerable to swords and knives and giving Sebastian and his men an advantage.

He just hoped it would be enough.

22

DALHU

*D*amn, nothing was working according to plan.
Kian's earpiece had malfunctioned big time, rendering him temporarily deaf at least in that one ear. He removed his helmet and was shouting orders, not because the Guardians had trouble hearing him, but because he couldn't hear himself.

Dalhu removed his as well.

There was no point in having them on anyway. The Doomers were no longer shooting. That missile had been the only one so far, but he expected more.

Out in the courtyard, the Guardians were exposed.

Dalhu glanced up, expecting rifles and RPGs pointed at them. Curiously, he could see no one in the second- and third-floor windows.

For now.

The Doomers had been taken by surprise, and it would take them a few minutes to get organized. In addition to assigning men to the upstairs windows, they were most likely creating another barricade on the first floor, with missiles aimed at the front door.

Kian must've reached the same conclusion because he shouted at Bhathian and Anandur to stop trying to break it down.

It was one big cluster-fuck.

Kian had been expecting a big courtyard fight, with Guardians engaging most of the Doomers, and the rescue team going inside and taking care of the few who had remained to guard the women. Instead, the Doomers surprised them all by making a hasty retreat the moment they realized their bullets were ineffective. They barricaded the front door before the rescue team had a chance to get inside.

Since when did Doomers run from a fight?

For nearly eight hundred years it had been drilled into his head that Doomers fight to the death.

Retreat?

They would've been executed by their own commanders.

Things couldn't have changed so drastically over the few months since he'd left. Which meant that the commanding officer of this unit had trained them differently.

To some extent, Dalhu had been familiar with all of the commanders, and as those rarely got replaced, he probably knew this one as well.

Which one could it be?

He must be one of the higher ups to be allowed to deviate from the standard training. That limited the list of possibilities, but also precluded Dalhu from guessing which one it was.

Dalhu had commanded a small field unit and could testify to the style of his own superior and the other unit commanders under him, but none of the others.

Except, there was one top commander who everyone had known was different. The one who treated his soldiers exceptionally well, but tortured women. The sadist, as everyone called Sharim behind his back. But there was no chance in hell he was here. Losham would never send his son on a mission like this. It didn't fit his status. Sharim was almost on the same footing as Navuh's sons.

Unless, Losham's golden child had failed at something, falling from grace, and this was his punishment.

Dalhu should be so lucky.

If there was one man he'd been dreaming of killing for years it was this one. Dalhu had seen first-hand what the sadistic bastard had been doing to the girls. The brothel's manager had been keeping Sharim's victims off the roster until they healed, and no one had been supposed to see the amount of damage they had suffered. Dalhu's visit had been a fluke. He'd promised the girl to bring her a gift from her homeland, and returning from a stint in Russia he'd thought nothing of visiting her in her room to deliver it even though she'd been reported sick and out of commission.

When he'd seen what that son of a bitch had done to her, Dalhu had wanted to get his hands on Sharim's neck and just rip it off so badly, he'd almost gone insane from the need. Lucky for Dalhu, Sharim had left for an overseas trip and hadn't come back for several months. By then Dalhu had calmed down enough to realize that he would gain nothing by attacking the sadist. He would most certainly lose his head to the nearest guy with a sword. Sharim's warriors were loyal to him.

"Dalhu, snap out of it. This is not the time for daydreaming!" Kian snapped his fingers in front of Dalhu's face.

"Sorry. You were saying?"

It seemed that Kian's hearing was back to normal because he was no longer shouting. Several Guardians were huddled around them, and Dalhu felt like an idiot for being so deep in his own head that he hadn't noticed them coming.

Damn, he'd spent too much time playing at being an artist and had forgotten how to be a soldier. This inattention could've gotten him killed.

Kian glared at him and continued without repeating what he'd said before.

"We can't remove the body armor, and after we are done here, I want you to put your helmets back on. They can shoot at us from the windows on the upper floors. We need to stay close to the walls so they will not be able to launch rockets at us."

"What about grenades?" Brundar asked.

"Yeah, then we are screwed. But with the suits the damage won't be as extensive."

Bhathian shifted from foot to foot like he had an itch inside his pants he couldn't reach, which was entirely possible with the damned armor. It wasn't easy to put on or take off. "What about the women?"

Kian pinned him with a hard stare. "Nothing we can do until we take the Doomers out."

Bhathian grimaced. But what other answer could he have expected?

Kian seemed pissed, and for a good reason. Bhathian should've known better. "New plan. Onegus, we need to blast that door with explosives. The Doomers probably shoved all their furniture behind it. We need enough of a blast to not only clear the way but hopefully incapacitate anyone who is lying in wait behind it."

"I'm on it."

"Team commanders. You all remember the layout, right? On the lower level there are two windows in the front, one on the east wall, and four facing the back. I'm talking only about the big ones." He glanced around making sure they were clear on that.

"Bhathian, you take your team to the one in the kitchen. It's the closest to the staircase leading to the basement. Oideche, you and your guys take the dining room..." Kian continued until there were only a few men who hadn't gotten assigned an entry point, including Dalhu and Brundar. It seemed that Kian wanted them to stay with him.

No problem. Dalhu's first priority was to ensure Kian's safety.

"Onegus, your team charges the front. Brundar, Dalhu and I are with you."

"Welcome aboard, sir." Onegus saluted with a smile.

Kian's lip twitched but that was the extent of his amusement. "Brundar, check with William if he heard everything I said?"

"He did."

"Onegus, how long do you need to plant the explosives?"

"Five minutes tops."

"Good. It's five fifty-six now. At ten past six William will say go. No one moves until then. I want a synchronized attack. If any of you encounter a problem and can't make it on time, let everyone know when and if you can make it. If it's a few minutes, I'll delay the go signal. Otherwise we go without you. Everyone clear?" He waited a split second to see if anyone had any questions. "Okay. Move out, people."

As Onegus crept up to the front door, their group stayed behind. He was going to set the explosives to go off at the same time as the other teams broke through the windows, which meant that theirs would do it with a slight delay. They had to wait a safe distance away and only then rush for the opening the explosion would create.

Hopefully, any RPGs aimed at the front would get discharged before their team got there. Getting hit with one was nasty and the damage was so extensive that it took weeks to heal. Especially if a limb had to be regenerated. In some rare cases it was deadly even to an immortal. There was a limit to how much damage their bodies could repair at the same time. In most cases, though, the body just went into stasis while repairing itself. The problem with that was the vulnerability—easy to kill by someone who knew what needed to be done.

Like an enemy immortal.

"Go!" William's voice sounded in Dalhu's earpiece at the same time Onegus's bomb went off, and their group charged ahead leaping over the debris to get inside.

The sight that greeted them was one that Dalhu would never forget.

The other teams were already inside and fighting. Immortals brandishing swords and going at each other with grim determination was a vision to behold. The power, the deadly intent—in a way it was beautiful. This was a clash of titans, and no other battle he'd fought in before could compare.

Except, the moment his eyes landed on Sharim and recognition set in, the beauty of battle faded away, replaced by a haze of red-hot rage.

The fury he hadn't experienced in months hit him with a vengeance. As far as he was concerned, no other opponent existed other than the sadist. The son of a bitch was his to kill.

Dalhu pulled out his sword and took off his helmet at the same time, flinging the headgear aside. With a laser-like focus, he advanced toward his target, swatting away Doomers as if they were annoying flies. Dimly, he was aware that Kian and Brundar were fighting by his side, dispatching those who he'd flung aside.

Finally Sharim noticed him, and a split second later Dalhu saw recognition settle in the sadist's eyes. His first response was surprise, but then he smiled with a mouthful of fangs and started advancing toward Dalhu while his soldiers kept Guardians off his back.

"Look who's here. The biggest traitor of them all. Supposedly dead but not. Well, not for long." Sharim swung his sword in an arc.

23

KIAN

Kian watched Dalhu zero in on one of the Doomers, advancing toward the guy as if there were no other fighters in the room. Like a force of nature, or perhaps a fighting machine, he plowed through the warriors, swatting them aside as if they were puny humans.

Damn.

Kian was reminded of *The Terminator*, one of the few movies Anandur and Brundar had succeeded in convincing him to watch with them.

Dalhu looked more formidable than the character in that movie.

Brundar and Kian had no choice but to fight those Dalhu was flinging aside. Embarrassing. As if they were his squires and not his superiors.

Except, it seemed that Dalhu had a good reason for his razor-like focus on that one Doomer. When the bastard recognized him, he smiled as if Dalhu wasn't the most terrifying warrior in the room. This was no doubt the leader, and he was either overconfident in his fighting skills or an idiot. Dalhu was a head taller and fearless. But there was no fear in his opponent's eyes either.

"Look who's here. The biggest traitor of them all. Supposedly dead but not. Well, not for long." The guy advanced on Dalhu.

"I've been waiting a long time for this day, Sharim, you sadistic son of a bitch."

"Tsk-tsk. So rude. But also so true. I am a sadist, proud of it, and my dear mother was a bitch and a whore, just like yours."

Sharim was goading Dalhu, waiting for him to make a stupid move. As fearless as the guy was in the face of Dalhu's superior size and strength, he must've believed himself a master swordsman, and observing the way he was handling his sword, Kian suspected that his confidence was merited.

Damn, if something happened to Dalhu, Amanda would blame Kian for not watching his back.

Except, all he could do at this point was ensure that the duel remained between Dalhu and Sharim and none of the other Doomers jumped in to defend their leader.

There was some kind of personal vendetta going on here, and to interfere was to rob Dalhu of something he evidently had been wanting to do for years.

Dalhu would never forgive Kian if he took this kill away from him.

A conundrum. He was damned if he did and damned if he did not.

As the two started circling each other, Kian, Brundar, and the rest of the team engaged the other Doomers.

The fighting was vicious, and Kian was sure their casualties would have been much greater if not for Brundar—a true master swordsman. In short order he had a pile of Doomers at his feet, but it didn't seem as if he was intending on finishing them off. He just kept dispatching the warriors, skewering one after the other on his sword like pieces of shish-kebab, then casting their limp bodies aside as he went for the next one.

Kian and the other Guardians weren't having it so easy. A deep thigh wound was impacting Kian's balance, and most of the other guys had bleeding cuts all over. Brundar not only didn't have a scratch on him, but not one of his long blond hairs had gotten loose from the ponytail he had pulled it into before the battle.

The guy was indeed a killing machine. Except, he wasn't the one doing the actual killing. He was leaving the final kill to the others and only preparing the bodies for them.

Damned Brundar, he should've cut off their heads and been done with it. Now Kian couldn't justify a final kill. The Doomers were already down.

It didn't take long for the sounds of battle to start dying out, and in the end the only ones still going at each other were Dalhu and his opponent.

Brundar wiped his sword on a Doomers' shirt, returned it to its scabbard, and picked up one of the upended chairs. Putting it down so it faced the duel, he sat down, crossed his feet at the ankles, his arms over his chest, and settled down to watch.

Kian shook his head. At least the arrogant bastard could've gotten him a chair as well. His thigh was killing him.

"Onegus, grab me a chair, will you?"

"Sure, boss."

His chief Guardian picked up one with his uninjured arm and brought it over.

"Much obliged."

"You're welcome."

Sitting down, Kian sighed with relief as the weight shifted off his leg. The Doomer must've hit the femoral artery. It not only hurt like a motherfucker, but it bled like a faucet had been opened in his leg.

With gritted teeth, he put a hand over the cut and compressed it, then turned his head to look at Onegus. "Check on the others." Kian would've done it himself if his earpiece was working, but without it he was dependent on others.

Note to self. Never go out on a mission without a spare one.

"Activate wide channel," Onegus commanded his device.

"Team one report." He listened and nodded. "Good job, guys."

With a light tap he closed the channel and turned to Kian. "The rescue team has the basement secured and they are breaking down one door at a time to free the women. What do you want to be done with them?"

"Keep them there until we clean up the mess. Tell the other teams to search every room and the grounds for stray Doomers. Some might be hiding."

As Onegus checked with the other teams and relayed his instruction, Kian watched the fight. It was good that Brundar was available if intervention was needed. Kian would take Dalhu's anger at the interference over Amanda's grief of losing her mate any day.

Surprisingly, Dalhu and Sharim turned out to be equally matched. What Dalhu lacked in skill he compensated for in size and strength, and the opposite was true for Sharim. The guy was almost as good as Brundar, maybe even just as good.

They were both tiring.

Dalhu was cut in several places, while Sharim was scratch-free, but it was obvious that his sword arm was weakening while Dalhu's was just as strong and as steady as it had been at the start of the duel.

"The men are asking what to do with the Doomers. Those who still have their heads attached to their bodies and those who do not."

"Body bags for the dead, and venom to the brink for the others."

Onegus cocked a brow. "I thought you didn't want to take any more to the crypt."

Kian sighed. "If they didn't kill them during battle, I can't justify an execution. I can stretch the limits but I can't cross them completely. Their punishment for disobeying my directive will be to put their fangs in those Doomers' necks. Have them do it now before any of the fuckers start reviving."

"What about Brundar's pile?"

"Let him watch the duel. Have the others take care of it for him. I haven't seen the guy enjoy himself this much since... well, ever."

Onegus chuckled. "You're right. Should I tell Bridget and Andrew to get up here?"

"Yeah. But first call Rick. I want to get rid of the bodies before we bring the women up from the basement. No need to traumatize them any more than they already are."

Richard and the extra large truck they had rented to transport the bodies had been waiting at a nearby gas station for the okay to drive up.

"We need Bridget here."

"Yeah, you're right. Tell Andrew he can drive up as well. They can park outside the wall until the truck leaves. There's not enough parking space in the front yard for the truck and the two buses."

As Onegus got busy relaying his instructions, Kian turned his full attention back to the duel.

Sharim was covered in sweat, but so was Dalhu, and Dalhu was bleeding from several deep cuts. On the other hand, Sharim was starting to realize that he'd already lost. His men were dead or being put in stasis, and he was the last one standing. If he surrendered, Kian would be forced to offer him the option of stasis as well.

He hoped like hell the guy would fight to the death.

Sharim's death, that is, not Dalhu's.

It hit him then that his concern for Dalhu wasn't entirely about Amanda and keeping her mate safe. It was a big part of it, but Kian had to admit that he'd actually started to like the guy and didn't want to lose a friend.

The Fates must've been cackling with glee over this one.

From the corner of his eye, Kian noticed Brundar abandon his relaxed position and sit up straight. A sure sign that the fight was reaching a pinnacle.

Kian leaned to get closer to Brundar. "What's going on?" he whispered.

"It's about to end."

"How?"

"We'll know in a moment."

24

DALHU

The smugness was slowly melting off Sharim's arrogant face. He knew he was losing. The sounds of battle had been dwindling steadily until the only grunts and clangs of clashing swords belonged to the two of them.

There was no doubt who had emerged victorious. Sharim's force was destroyed and he was the last one standing.

Not for long, though.

Dalhu's many wounds should've been slowing him down, draining out his energy, but the hot furnace of rage burning in his gut had been replenishing his reserves with what he thought of as dark energy.

Dark as in evil, not the invisible dark force physicists were theorizing about.

Or maybe it was.

Just as light was the source of life and represented good, or the God humans believed in, dark was the opposite force and it represented the devil humans feared.

Or maybe darkness was no more than the absence of light, and evil was just the absence of good, but not a force of its own.

The destructive power of a vacuum.

As Dalhu slid into the zone—a strange and surreal sort of awareness he'd been able to attain only a handful of times before—his body became fluid, his responses automatic. He found himself reacting to Sharim's moves a split second before they happened, reading Sharim's intent as if he was broadcasting it. Dalhu didn't even need to focus anymore. In fact, as his conscious mind was contemplating all these philosophical questions, his subconscious was controlling his arms and his legs.

His body was doing the fighting as if set on autopilot.

Except, this semi-awareness was sufficient for defending, not attacking. The strategy Dalhu had adopted, as soon as he'd realized Sharim was the better swordsman, had achieved its objective. The sadist was slowing down, his sword arm was getting fatigued.

It was time to end this.

The question was how.

Somewhere in the calm and quiet of the zone, Dalhu had lost his rage, and as he readied to finish Sharim off, decisions he'd never expected to ponder started flitting through his mind.

Should he kill Sharim or just incapacitate him and put him in stasis?

What was the right thing to do?

Who was he to decide what was right and what was wrong?

Would Annani have wanted a male like that to be given another chance?

Would the world be a better place without Sharim?

Yes. The man was evil and had inflicted untold cruelties upon countless women over the centuries. He shouldn't be allowed to ever live again and hurt more women, which he theoretically could if Dalhu put him in stasis instead of delivering final death.

Would someone mourn Sharim's passing?

Losham, his adoptive father would. Perhaps some of Sharim's warriors would as well.

Which way did the scale tip?

Put this way, the answer was obvious.

Dalhu decided on a slight compromise. If someone was going to mourn Sharim's demise, it meant that there were a few spots of light on the sadist's black soul, and Dalhu would grant the sadist a swift death. A mercy Sharim hadn't shown his victims, but so be it. The end result was what was important, not Dalhu's need to avenge Sharim's victims. He would rid the earth of an evildoer who delighted in the torment of others.

With clarity of purpose, Dalhu's mind left the quiet contemplative place behind, funneling all of its focus toward finishing off his opponent. The opening he was looking for came within seconds, and he put all of his muscle power behind the blow.

A swift death. Slicing through Sharim's neck with surprising ease, Dalhu severed his head from his body.

He had done what he'd set out to do; he'd delivered a final death to the sadist. And yet he didn't feel gloriously victorious, or even satisfied, just numb.

With gruesome fascination, Dalhu watched Sharim's head land on the floor and roll until coming to a full stop at Kian's feet.

Someone started clapping, soon to be joined by others. Dalhu lifted his eyes to look at the Guardians and frowned.

Had they all lost their minds?

Their grinning faces annoyed him even more than their deafening thunder of applause.

"Please stop." His voice was barely above a whisper, and yet they heard him, and the room suddenly went quiet.

Brundar got up and put a hand on Dalhu's shoulder. "We are not applauding the kill, Dalhu. We are applauding the skill. You defeated a master swordsman."

Dalhu closed his eyes. Brundar's words would mean something to him later, but not now. He couldn't handle the Guardians' eyes on him. "I need to get out of here."

Brundar clapped him on the back. "The buses are parked outside the wall."

The scent of blood was overwhelming, and through the blasted door the clean air outside was calling to him. Dalhu wanted to get out as fast as his legs could carry him, but he was a warrior and Kian was his commander. Permission had to be granted.

As he stopped by Kian, he was relieved that Sharim's head was no longer there. Someone must've picked it up. Either that or Kian kicked it away.

"Can I leave, or do you need me for something?"

"I need you to help carry the bodies to the truck. I want it done quickly so we can bring up the women. I don't want them to see this bloodbath. But you can go outside and take a breather, have Bridget look at your wounds."

Dalhu nodded. "I'll only take a few minutes." He started walking.

"Dalhu," Kian called after him.

"Yeah?"

"You did well. I'm glad that the other guy is going into a body bag and not you. Can you imagine the hell Amanda would have given me if anything happened to you?"

That wrested a chuckle out of him. "Yeah, I can. If I were you, I would've booked a one-way flight to Timbuktu."

"Glad I don't have to."

Kian offered his hand, and as Dalhu shook it, his eyes were drawn to the wound in Kian's thigh.

"I'll send Bridget over. You need stitches."

Kian grimaced. "I'm not the only one."

On his way out, Dalhu realized that some of the thick fog that had descended upon him after the kill had dissipated, thanks to Kian no doubt. He shook his head as he strode toward the opening, thinking about his uncharacteristic reaction to this latest one. He'd killed many over his lifetime, and none more deserving than Sharim. So why had it affected him like that? Was he growing soft?

Yeah, he was.

Life had been good recently. He had won the heart of the woman he loved, had been accepted into the clan, and had discovered that he had a talent other than killing. No wonder he'd gone soft. But the realization didn't bring about the sense of shame he'd been expecting. Instead, he felt as if he'd been given the most precious of gifts.

He no longer needed to numb himself in order to carry on, going through life dead on the inside. He was allowed to feel. And even if not all of these new feelings were positive, it was better than having none at all.

It was okay to feel bad about taking a life, even if the killing had been justified. Dalhu had become softer but not weaker. He had still done what had been required of him, and would do so again. He was a strong, skilled warrior, and it was his duty to defend those who needed defending. It wasn't the same as before.

He was no longer an assassin. He was a defender.

A big difference.

25

ANDREW

Not taking an active part in the mission hadn't been as bad as Andrew had expected. Between the earpiece and sitting in William's control center, he'd felt as if he'd been there with the Guardians—stressing when things hadn't worked out according to plan, cheering when the objective had been achieved despite the last minute changes.

Except, he regretted missing Dalhu's epic duel. Was there a chance someone had videotaped it? Andrew would've loved to have been there to watch the guy defeat a master swordsman. Not that he was an expert on sword fighting, but still.

Speaking of the devil.

Coming out one of the holes in the ruined fence, Dalhu looked like shit. His body armor was stained with blood, either his adversary's or his own, and his stride lacked the purposeful energy it usually implied. In fact, he was shuffling his feet. It looked like Dalhu's victory hadn't been easy, and his injuries were taking their toll. That, or the guy's spirits were low for some reason. Given his triumph, Dalhu should've been pumped, not deflated.

Bridget and her two helpers came down the steps of her bus. Gertrude and Hildegard headed out, each carrying a large first aid kit. The doctor waved Dalhu over.

With a quick glance at the two retreating medics, Dalhu turned to Bridget. "Kian's leg is badly wounded. Maybe you should go to him instead."

"Don't worry. Either of them knows what to do. Come on up." She gestured for him to follow her into the bus.

As Andrew walked up to Dalhu, he intended to offer his hand for a handshake and congratulate him, but the guy's grim expression gave him pause. Dalhu didn't look as if he'd be receptive to praise. Perhaps his wounds were more serious than they seemed and he was in a lot of pain.

"Hey, big guy, need help?"

Dalhu cast him a puzzled glance. "With what?"

"You look like you've taken a beating. I thought maybe you needed assistance getting on the bus."

Dalhu snorted. "These scratches? They are nothing."

"Let me be the judge of that." Bridget took Dalhu's elbow and steered him up the stairs of her bus where there was a makeshift sickbay in the back.

Andrew followed them inside.

Bridget showed Dalhu to a seat and then knelt on the floor at his feet, getting busy removing his boots. "Andrew, I could use your help getting the body armor off him."

Andrew stifled a chuckle. This was the first time he'd ever seen Dalhu blush.

The guy put a hand on the doctor's shoulder. "Please, get up. I can do it myself."

Bridget gave him one of her no nonsense I'm-the-doctor-and-you'll-do-as-I-say looks, and he sighed in defeat.

"As you wish."

"That's a good boy." Bridget patted his knee, which was about the only place on his big body that wasn't cut and bleeding.

"How do you want to do it?" Andrew asked, kneeling beside her and easing off Dalhu's other boot.

"You grab one pant leg and I'll grab the other. Dalhu, can you unbuckle the pants and lift up?"

"Sure, but why don't you just cut them off?"

She shrugged. "It would be a waste. Besides, I need a cast saw to cut through the layers, and I don't have one here."

Dalhu fumbled with the closing that was hidden under a protective flap that extended from his vest.

"Ready?" Bridget asked Andrew when he was done.

"On three. One, two, three."

As Dalhu lifted his butt, they pulled at the same time. The reinforced pants slid off Dalhu's fatigues, landing with a heavy thump on the bus's floor.

"Now, these, I'm going to cut away. I hope you have underwear on."

Dalhu chuckled. "Would it have stopped you if I didn't?"

"Nope. You've got nothing I haven't seen before."

Damn, Andrew felt heat engulf his ears. He remembered Bridget saying these exact words to him, but under very different circumstances.

She must've remembered it too and cast him a sheepish sidelong glance. "I use that line a lot, don't I?" She got busy with the scissors to hide her embarrassment.

"Given the bunch of macho guys you need to take care of, I'm not surprised." He pretended this wasn't personal.

Watching Bridget clean Dalhu's wounds, Andrew wondered what kind of medical care an immortal would need.

She leaned back on her haunches and looked up at Dalhu. "These two are the worst." She pointed. "I would like to put stitches in them. If I don't, and you go back to help the others, these deep cuts will not only hurt, but will take longer to heal."

"Do your thing, doctor. You know best."

Bridget beamed. "You're my kind of patient."

While Bridget worked, Andrew debated whether he should join Dalhu and go help the guys with the cleanup. Trouble was, compared to the immortals he had the strength of a child, not a man, which would prove to be damned embarrassing. He could just imagine those guys striding with a bounce in their step while carrying a body bag over each shoulder, and him staggering under the weight of one.

The Guardians didn't need him for anything that demanded brute strength.

The rescued women, however, could probably use his help. God knew they would be scared, traumatized, and confused.

Who would ease their fears? Make them feel safe?

Kri wasn't exactly the nurturing type, and all the Guardians he'd met were tough guys who knew nothing about women. Bridget and her two assistants might be more up to the task, but they would have their hands full patching up the guys.

Even though no one had thought to assign Andrew to the job, it looked like it was up to him. His experience in hostage retrieval would be helpful. Except, he'd never had to deal with a large number of rescued people. One traumatized, hysterical woman was a handful, a group would be a nightmare.

"Dalhu, how many girls were freed? Do you know?"

"No. The rescue team is keeping them down in the basement. You can ask Anandur."

"Never mind. It's not important." The exact number didn't matter. Anything over two would be difficult.

Bridget finished the stitching, wiped Dalhu's legs clean and handed him a plastic bag with a new pair of nylon pants in it. "XXL, right?"

"Perfect. Thank you." He ripped the plastic, shook the pants out, and pulled them over his legs. "Let's go." He turned to Andrew and attempted to stand up.

"Not so fast." Bridget stopped Dalhu. "Take off everything on top and let me see what's going on up there."

"No need. I'm fine. They are all superficial."

"Sit!" Bridget barked, and both Dalhu and Andrew dropped their butts onto their seats.

The tiny redhead smiled sweetly. "Thank you. Now strip. Not you, Andrew, just Dalhu."

Dalhu's big body began shaking, and it took Andrew a moment to realize that the guy was trying to stifle laughter. He couldn't hold it in for long, though, and erupted in a strange sounding guffaw. Or perhaps it only sounded weird in Andrew's ears because he'd never heard the guy laugh.

"Ow, I shouldn't be laughing." Dalhu held onto his stomach where a nasty cut was threatening to reopen.

Bridget didn't find it funny. "Stay still, you big oaf, and let me clean this mess."

Andrew, on the other hand, found it hilarious even though the joke was on him. Besides, there was no better way of releasing stress than a good laugh, and Dalhu seemed like he needed it.

26

NATHALIE

"Is everyone okay?" When Andrew's call finally came, Nathalie answered on the first ring. Holding the phone in her hand ever since he'd gotten in the driver seat of that bus, she'd even took it with her to the bathroom. Heck, relieving herself would've been impossible if she were stressing over missing his call.

When she moved it to her other hand, there was a rectangular indentation in the shape of the device left on her palm.

Andrew had called her once when they'd arrived at the location, and one more time to tell her that he and Bhathian were fine and that none of the Guardians had been lost.

Thank God.

That had been hours ago. She'd been sorely tempted to ring him, but she'd promised him she wouldn't. Apparently, communicating with significant others while on a mission was a big no-no, and Andrew would have been embarrassed if his fiancee were the only one who called.

"Yeah. Some injuries, but nothing that won't heal in a day or two."

"And the women?"

When Andrew didn't answer right away, Nathalie started to worry.

"We got them all out."

There was something Andrew wanted to tell her but didn't know how.

"I'm glad. Now tell me whatever it is you think is going to freak me out. It won't."

Andrew chuckled. "You know me so well it's scary. Okay. Are you sitting down?"

"Just spit it out, Andrew!"

"Your Tiffany was one of the abductees."

With her knees turning to jello, Nathalie plopped onto the couch. "You're shitting me."

"No. I thought you'd be glad."

"I am. I'm so relieved my legs gave out. It's just such an unbelievable coincidence."

"Not really. The Doomers were grabbing pretty girls that no one was going to miss, and Tiffany fit the bill."

Hardly. Nathalie remembered feeling sorry for the girl. She wasn't ugly, but she wasn't attractive either. "I don't know about that. Tiffany isn't a great beauty. She's kind of plain."

Andrew chuckled. "Well, well. Apparently getting abducted by Doomers agreed with her. Your little Tiff must've gone through quite a transformation, because she's a looker."

Nathalie's eyes narrowed even though Andrew couldn't see her. The guy was skating on thin ice. "Watch it, Andrew, or I'll call my father to keep an eye on you."

Andrew laughed. "My gorgeous, jealous monster. I love you. Poor little Tiffany together with all the other girls can't hold a candle to you."

That was better. "I love you too. A good save, by the way. You're such a smooth talker."

"That's the God's honest truth. To me, you're the most beautiful woman in the world."

"Yeah, yeah. What have you guys done with the girls?"

"Bridget took them to one of Kian's buildings. They need help on so many levels we don't even know where to start."

"Can I help?"

"I wish you could. But we still didn't tell Kian that you know about immortals, and now is, again, not a good time."

Ugh, so frustrating. It seemed like it was never a good time.

"You know what? To hell with it. Tell me the address, and I'll tell Kian myself. It doesn't matter if he finds out today or tomorrow. You were supposed to tell him after the mission. And guess what? It's after the mission."

"No, Nathalie, you can't."

"Watch me. If you won't tell me where to go, I'm going to ask Jackson."

"You're one hell of a stubborn woman. Fine. But I'm driving and Kian is hurt. Give me a couple of hours. I need to catch him at a good moment. I'll call you back."

"Okay, but if I don't hear from you by then, I'm going to wring it out of Jackson."

He chuckled. "Yes, ma'am. Two hours or less."

"You better believe it." Nathalie clicked off the call and took a deep breath.

She'd been too hard on Andrew, and now that her anger had evaporated, it left behind a residue of guilt. He didn't deserve her talking to him like that, issuing an ultimatum. It must've been the stress of waiting with the phone in hand and fearing bad news. Still, she shouldn't have unloaded it on the man she loved.

Should she call him and apologize?

The mission was over and Andrew and the rest of the guys were on their way to one of the clan's secure buildings. Phone silence was no longer required.

Except, she didn't want to apologize. It hadn't been done in the most delicate fashion, but her goal was achieved. Andrew was finally going to talk to Kian, and Nathalie couldn't wait for all the stupid secrecy to be over.

Every day, so many questions about the immortals were popping in and out of her head, and it would've been wonderful to corner either Vlad or Jackson in the kitchen and just ask away, having them answered right then and there.

Nathalie had two hours to kill, and instead of spending them idly, overthinking things, she should get busy preparing the list of supplies she needed to order. Business was booming, and she routinely underestimated the quantities needed, ending up sending Jackson to the nearest supermarket to get stuff to tide them over until the next delivery. This time she was determined to do it right, and it involved pulling out the calculator and actually using math.

Nathalie's phone rang sooner than she'd expected, and suddenly she didn't feel so brave. What if Kian was furious? What if he kicked Bhathian off the force for the breach in security?

What if he denied Andrew his transformation?

Wait, the last one would actually be good news. Nathalie would have loved for Andrew to forget about immortality and just live a normal life with her. She wasn't the type to reach for pie in the sky. Having a loving husband and a few kids was all she ever wanted.

It was greedy to wish for more.

Still, if Bhathian got in trouble because of her that would be bad. Fearing the answer, Nathalie asked in a hesitant tone, "Are you okay? How did it go?"

"What happened? My tigress turned into a scaredy pussycat?" Andrew's taunting must've meant that it went well. He wouldn't have been joking otherwise.

"I assume Kian didn't make a big stink out of it."

"How did you know?"

"Oh, come on, Andrew. Just tell me what Kian said."

"I cornered him with Syssi present, so he had to be nice. But as it turned out, it hadn't been necessary. I told them I decided to go for the transition as soon as possible, and they were both so happy to hear that I've finally made up my mind that when I told them you were coming over to help with the girls, Kian didn't even notice that there was something out of the ordinary with it."

She should be happy, right? The cat was out of the bag, so to speak, but talking about the transition always made her gut roil.

"Wonderful. Text me the address and I'll be there as soon as I can. I have to talk to Jackson and see if he can come over to watch over my father."

"Love you, sweetheart. I'll see you here."

As she punched in Jackson's number, Nathalie debated whether she should tell him that he and Vlad no longer had to pretend around her, hiding who and what they were. More to the point, though, she wanted to stop pretending she didn't know.

Nah, better to leave it for tomorrow.

She was in a hurry, and telling him the full story would take time she didn't want to waste.

"Nathalie, what's up?"

"I need a favor. Could you come and watch over Fernando for a few hours? I need to go out."

"Sure. I can use the extra dough, and I don't mean the kind you keep in the freezer."

She shouldn't ask, but heck, she was too curious about what he needed it for. Jackson had more cash than most any guy his age. He was making good money, mainly from tips, and Nathalie paid him double for the evenings and sometimes nights he'd stayed with her father. Jackson's mom was covering his car payments and insurance, so other than spending some of his earnings on gas and on dates, he was saving up all the rest. What did he need more money for?

"I know it's none of my business, but what do you want to buy that is so expensive?"

"The love of my life has just gone on sale. And she ain't cheap."

It took a moment, but then she laughed. "I'm guessing you're talking about a guitar." Jackson had several, all of them famous brand names. Not that she was familiar with any of them. Nathalie knew about guitars about as much as Jackson knew about the different kinds of yeast. Still, the way Vlad's expression turned wistful whenever Jackson talked about his 'girls,' she had to assume they were costly. Vlad wasn't a poor kid either.

"You guessed right. A PRS Hollowbody."

"I have no idea what you're talking about. But if you need an advance, let me know. When can you be here?"

"Less than half an hour. And thanks for the advance. I'll take you up on your offer."

"Sure thing. I'll see you later."

27

ANDREW

Bridget's crew, which included Kri, the girls, and the worst injured Guardians, had arrived at the keep more than an hour before Andrew and the rest of the guys. A lot of work had still needed to be done.

Given the severity of his injury, Kian should've been on that first bus, but of course the stubborn ox had refused. He'd had to stay behind and personally supervise the torching of the monastery. As if it could not have been done without him.

The guy had serious control issues. Hell, Andrew had spent enough time with Kian to know that his brother-in-law was a control freak, but on this mission he'd realized that he'd underestimated Kian's obsessiveness. The guy concerned himself with every detail, no matter how minute, and was compelled to check and double check that his instructions were being carried out exactly.

When they got back, Kian wanted to go check on the injured Guardians, and Andrew had to blackmail him to go straight up to his apartment instead, threatening him with a call to Syssi.

How did she tolerate this? Living with someone like Kian would've driven Andrew nuts.

"Is he in bed?" he asked her when she came back into the living room.

With a sigh, she flopped next to him on the couch. "I managed to get him into the shower and tucked him in bed, but he is far from resting. The laptop is sitting open, balancing on his uninjured thigh, the phone is glued to his ear, and he is barking commands left and right."

Sounded like Kian.

"You're a saint. The guy is an overbearing piece of work."

Syssi slapped his shoulder. "Watch it. This is my husband you're talking about."

He kissed her cheek. "I love the guy, and respect the hell out of him, but he needs to chill."

"I know. I'm working on it. But enough about Kian. I'm curious to hear what made up your mind. Except..." She scrunched her nose. "You stink from ash and fire. Do you want to grab a shower first?"

"I don't have a change of clothes. I'll have to borrow something from Kian. But first, I want to know what was done with the girls." When he'd gone out to call Nathalie, he'd heard her telling Kian that she needed to leave soon and help Amanda settle them in their rooms.

"Amanda has it covered. She and Vanessa took them to one of the larger apartments on the forty-eighth floor, and Vanessa is talking with them, assessing the damage. When she's done, I'll help with getting them settled and see if anyone needs anything. Like pajamas, or some other items they might be missing. There is a twenty-four hour Walmart in South Gate. I can probably get everything there."

"Vanessa is Jackson's mom, right? The therapist?'

"Yes."

Twenty-two women had been rescued, and they weren't in as bad a shape as Andrew had expected they would be. At least physically.

"You know, I was surprised at how well Kri handled the situation. When I got down to the basement, I was expecting a bunch of hysterical women. Instead, I found a well-organized group, waiting patiently for the okay to come up. No thralling or even influence involved. I asked her later."

"How did she manage it?"

Andrew shrugged. "It seems that Kri's no-nonsense attitude was exactly what they needed. She had the girls busy collecting their belongings and stuffing them into pillowcases because they had no bags to put their things in. Then she had them line up in twos along the corridor leading to the staircase, while keeping the male Guardians in the back and out of their line of sight."

"How about you? Weren't they scared of you?"

"I guess without the body armor, I didn't look as big or as intimidating as the Guardians. The girls were fine with me and Kri herding them up the stairs and into the waiting bus."

Syssi grabbed a throw pillow and started playing with the fringe. "When I didn't see you coming off the first bus, I was disappointed. Why did you stay behind? Was it because Kian was hurt?"

She'd been worried but didn't want to admit it. Except, she'd forgotten who she was dealing with. He knew her too well. There was nothing his sister could hide from him.

"First of all, I was the driver of that second bus. And besides, I wanted to see them torch the place."

After Bridget had left with the girls, the second part of the mission had been set in motion—covering the evidence by having the compound burned to the ground.

They had staged it as a gas explosion, so it would be assumed that nothing but ashes had remained of whoever had been inside. No one believed that it would fool the Doomers' high command for long, but at least there would be no hard evidence to be found.

Kian had ordered everyone out and away from the structure, while Arwel had let his senses probe, making sure no human or immortal had been left inside. Next, the armory had been cleared of ammunition.

Syssi leaned into Andrew and put her head on his shoulder. "I was worried about that part. Even with Yamanu's shrouding, the fire must've been enormous and someone might have seen it. How did you prevent it from spreading? Or hurting someone unintentionally?"

Aha, so that had been the cause of her concern.

Andrew wrapped his arm around Syssi. "Onegus ignited the fuse only after every precaution was taken, and Yamanu cast the area in a thick mental fog to let the fire do its work without the fire department arriving to put it out. He stayed behind with William when we left. I'm sure Kian is on the phone with him and William, checking what's going on."

Syssi lifted her head. "I'll go and ask him. It's bothering me. In the meantime, get in the shower. I'll get you clean clothes."

"Thank you."

As Andrew pushed up and stretched, it occurred to him that he'd been careless and had probably stunk up Syssi and Kian's couch. He should've showered first. The good news was: one; the couch was leather, probably easier to clean than fabric; and two, Okidu would get on it, not Syssi or Kian, so Andrew could feel less guilty about creating a mess for someone to clean.

The spare room in Kian and Syssi's temporary apartment wasn't as nicely appointed as the guest suite in Kian's penthouse, but it had a bathroom with a shower and a clean towel hanging from the towel bar. In short, everything Andrew needed. For now.

Later, he might get Nathalie into the nice queen-sized bed and have his way with her.

According to her text message, Jackson was glad to babysit because he needed money for some fancy guitar he had his eye on, so he wouldn't mind staying the night, and Andrew could really use a comfortable sleep for a change.

Nathalie's small bed was great for cuddling, and other things, but Andrew had been waking up with a sore back for far too long. It was a price he gladly paid to spend his nights with his love, but that didn't mean he would pass up an opportunity to spend a restful night in a roomy bed with a good mattress.

28

NATHALIE

Driving around downtown Los Angeles at night wasn't on Nathalie's list of favorite things to do. The streets were deserted, and she was a little scared. Worse, though, she was lost. Her car was an old model not equipped with a GPS, and the one on her phone was dangerous to use while driving. It could've been helpful if she knew how to activate the phone's voice navigation, but of course she didn't because it had been ages since she'd been someplace new.

Still, if she'd been paying better attention she might've been fine. The thing was, her mind had been preoccupied with stressing over the kind of reception she should expect from Kian. He didn't impress her as an easygoing guy. Andrew was deluding himself if he thought Kian would let insubordination go unpunished. Someone was going to pay for her impatience, and frankly she hoped it would be her rather than Andrew or Bhathian. It didn't mean, though, that she was looking forward to it. Kian might be as handsome as a god, but he was also intimidating as hell.

Shit, she should call Andrew, but then she'd have to admit that she was lost. He was probably wondering what was taking her so long, worrying while waiting for her on the street with that sticker or sensor she needed to get into the clan's parking level.

Trouble was, even if she called him, his instructions would be meaningless to her. She didn't know the street names, or what to look for. Quite ridiculous considering that she lived and worked no more than thirty minutes' drive away. The tall buildings, the wide boulevards, this felt like a foreign country to her—most of Los Angeles didn't look like that.

With a curse, she slowed down and parked on the side of the road. Zooming in to see the names of the streets on the tiny screen of her phone, she checked the location of the blue dot representing her car in relation to the red arrow pointing to where she was supposed to be.

Of course, she'd passed it.

Great, now she needed to make a U-turn somewhere. If she were a braver soul, she would have done it right there, in the middle of the six-lane-wide road. Except, she wasn't feeling particularly brave, not tonight, and especially not behind the steering wheel. With few opportunities to drive, uncommon in a city that had no public transportation to speak of, Nathalie wasn't a confident driver.

She put the transmission in drive and eased out onto the street. Continuing to the next intersection, she turned left, then another left, and was now heading the other way—the right way.

A few minutes later, she saw him, her handsome Andrew, waiting for her with his hands tucked into the pockets of a pair of jeans that were a few inches too long, and a loose hoodie. Obviously, he'd borrowed someone else's clothes, either Bhathian's or Kian's.

The question was why? Had his own been covered in blood? Because he'd been fighting? He'd promised her he'd be nowhere near the action.

No, he wouldn't have lied to her about this. He'd been helping transport the wounded. That must've been the source of the blood. It hadn't been his. Besides, perhaps it hadn't been blood at all. Maybe he'd been sweating, or digging...A shiver shook Nathalie's body. Andrew had said there had been no casualties on their side, but the other one must've suffered plenty.

Had he been digging graves?

How horrible. She hoped not. And yet, it was the most likely explanation.

Easing up to the sidewalk, she popped the locks, and Andrew jerked the door open. In one fluid move, he got inside and reached for her neck, his hand traveling up to cup her head and pull her to him for a kiss.

God, she'd missed him.

As his tongue pushed past her lips and entered her mouth, he groaned as if he'd been starving for this moment. She slid her arms around the back of his neck, holding him in a tight grip that must've left her finger imprints on his skin.

Andrew's groan turned into a soft growl, and he nipped her bottom lip, then sucked it into his mouth.

Holy hell, one hot kiss and her panties were soaked through.

Andrew eased up on his assault, his lips turning soft and gentle as he smoothed them over her cheek, down her jawline, and then latched onto her neck.

She giggled. "Stop it. You're giving me a hickey."

"Mm-hmm..." He kept on sucking and nipping the sensitive skin, making her squirm.

Well, if he was going to be like that.

Nathalie cupped Andrew's cheeks and pulled his head away from her neck. He looked disappointed, until she started showering him with small kisses. "I love you. But if I have to walk into the immortals' den with a huge, ugly hickey on my neck, you're gonna sleep on the floor tonight."

With a worried look on his face, Andrew leaned back and examined the damage. "It's just a little one. You can hide it behind your hair." He pushed his hands into her long strands, his forehead furrowing as he tried to play hairdresser and arrange them to cover his work. Poor guy. He'd taken her empty threat seriously.

Nathalie giggled. "It's okay, Andrew, I was just joking."

He heaved a relieved sigh. "Good, because I have plans for you tonight, my dear."

She lifted a brow in mock innocence. "Oh, yeah? And what kind of plans are those?"

He cupped the back of her head and kissed her again. "Syssi and Kian have a nice spare bedroom with a queen-sized bed. I intend to make good use of it tonight."

Heat flared in Nathalie's cheeks. "I can't. Not in their apartment. They are going to hear us with those bat ears of theirs."

Andrew chuckled. "One thing you're going to discover about these immortals is that they are not shy. They are highly sexed creatures. Besides, if I don't care that my sister hears us, neither should you."

"We'll see about that. I'm going to be as quiet as a mouse."

Andrew snorted. "Not likely, I'm going to make sure you won't."

She shook her head. He was probably right. She couldn't keep quiet with her father sleeping on the other side of the wall from her bedroom. But there was always the option of taping her mouth shut with some duct tape. Which reminded her. "Do you have the sticker?"

He pulled it out of the pocket of his baggy jeans. "Maybe we should switch places and I'll drive."

"Why?"

"No reason. It's just that I know this place well. The drive down is steep, and the turning circles are tight."

Typical macho man. Two things alpha males had trouble relinquishing control of the most: the television remote and the steering wheel. But whatever. Frankly, she didn't mind.

Smart decision. The circles were indeed tight and it seemed they were going on forever. The clan's private parking level was, naturally, the last one, and it was closed off by a commercially-sized garage door. As they waited for the heavy door to open, she wondered how deep in the ground they were.

"How many parking levels are there?" she asked Andrew.

"Twelve, excluding this one."

"That's really deep."

Andrew chuckled. "It doesn't end here. There is a whole underground below it. Several floors of it."

Uncomfortable. She didn't like thinking of the many layers above them. It made her feel claustrophobic. And the underground Andrew was talking about was even more daunting.

"Are we going down there?"

As the garage door retreated, Andrew eased her car inside and parked at one of the empty spots. "We are. But we are just passing through. We are going to use one of the underground tunnels to get to another building. Safety precautions."

He turned off the engine, got out of the car, and went around to open the door for her.

Nathalie frowned. "I thought that after the threat was eliminated, things would be back to normal."

Ugh, she really hated that expression. It was a euphemism for something ugly, even if necessary. The reality was that a lot of people had lost their lives today, and hiding behind big words didn't make it any less horrible.

"There was no time to make changes to the protocol. For now everything stays as it is." Andrew led her to a bank of elevators and pressed his thumb to a scanner.

These guys took security seriously.

"Are those Kian's clothes you are wearing?"

"Aha." He held the door open for her.

"You look funny. They are too long."

Andrew shrugged and pulled up his pants. "They are clean. That's all that matters to me."

The elevator took them three floors down, and they exited into a wide, drab corridor, with doors on both sides leading to what she assumed were offices, or maybe storage units. Andrew punched a few numbers into a keypad on one of the doors, and it opened into another, narrower corridor, lined only with industrial light fixtures.

"Is this the tunnel?"

"Yeah."

"How long is it?"

"It goes under the street to the other side and then the building is a few minutes' walk to the south."

Nathalie chuckled. "It fits. I feel like I'm stepping into another world, another reality, and walking down an underground tunnel with our voice echoing off the walls is creepily appropriate. I'm just glad I don't have to do it by myself."

Andrew wrapped his arms around her waist, bringing her closer to him, and kissed the top of her head. "Never, sweetheart. I'll always be there for you."

And just like that, he'd turned her into a puddle of goo—stupid tears and all.

Andrew frowned. "Why are you crying?"

"Happy tears, Andrew. These are happy tears."

"Oh..."

29

ANDREW

"It looks so normal up here," Nathalie said as they exited on Syssi and Kian's floor.

The tunnel had taken them almost fifteen minutes to traverse, and Andrew suspected it had made Nathalie uncomfortable. She had said very little until they got into the elevator that took them up to the fifty second-floor. A perfect indication that she hadn't been feeling like herself. Nathalie wasn't a blabbermouth, but she was usually more talkative.

"What did you expect? Batman's cave?"

"Kind of."

"Then you'll be pleasantly surprised. This apartment is not as fancy as their penthouse in the keep, but it's still several steps above what regular folks like us are accustomed to."

On the remote chance that Kian had actually fallen asleep, Andrew rapped his knuckles on the door gently. Highly unlikely, though. His brother-in-law was probably still on the phone.

Syssi opened the door with a bright grin spread over her face. "Nathalie, I'm so happy that you're here." The two embraced like they hadn't seen each other in weeks.

"How is Kian doing?" Andrew asked as Syssi led them inside and pointed them toward the sofa.

She grimaced. "Do you need to ask? He is still on the phone. I persuaded him to take some painkillers, because frankly I couldn't stand his grouchiness anymore, and I hoped they would make him drowsy. But no. He is so hyped up I don't think he is going to sleep at all."

"I'm not." Kian hobbled into the living room, holding his laptop under his arm and his phone in his hand.

Syssi rushed to him and wrapped her arm around him, propping him up. "Bridget said you shouldn't put any pressure on that leg until tomorrow!"

"I can't stay in bed anymore. And anyway, I'm hungry."

She helped him to one of the overstuffed chairs and pushed over an ottoman for him to put his leg up. "This is just an excuse. I could've brought you something to eat in bed."

Kian waggled his brows and pulled her down for a kiss. "There is only one thing I like to eat in bed, sweet girl, and that's you."

Syssi's ears turned red.

In his previous life, Andrew would have been embarrassed to hear this kind of an exchange between his sister and her husband, but he'd grown numb to it. He leaned toward Nathalie, who was trying very hard not to gape. "I told you…" he whispered in her ear.

"You told her what?" Kian asked.

Bloody immortals and their supernatural hearing.

"I told her that you guys were a horny, oversexed bunch."

Kian made an air toast. "I'll drink to that. Syssi, could you pour me a shot?"

Standing with her hands on her hips, Syssi glared at her husband. "You know perfectly well that alcohol and painkillers do not mix. Especially the stuff Bridget gave you. She said it would knock a horse out. Apparently, though, it doesn't work on stubborn mules."

The look he gave her was wicked. "I think someone is getting herself into trouble."

Syssi's ears turned crimson. "Fine. But I'm telling Bridget." She turned around and marched up to the bar.

Andrew pinned Kian with a hard stare. What the hell was that all about? Was the guy threatening Syssi?

Kian smirked. "Down, Andrew. It's not what you think."

"Oh, yeah?"

"Trust me on that. And if you don't, you can ask Syssi. Though I'm afraid her hair will catch fire if her ears get any redder."

Okay, if Kian was hinting that this was some sex game they were playing, then Andrew really didn't want to know.

Nathalie stifled a giggle behind the palm of her hand. "You're right. They are terrible," she whispered in his ear.

Kian chuckled. "What, this? That's nothing. You haven't met Anandur yet. Prepare to be shocked."

A cute little snort escaped Nathalie's throat. "I think I'm all shocked out. If Martians landed on the White House lawn today, I would probably shrug and say, 'welcome to the United States and have a nice day'."

"I know exactly how you feel." Syssi came back with a tray loaded with a pitcher of ice tea, glasses, pieces of cut fruit, nuts, and crackers. She handed out small plates, loading Kian's for him. "When I was first sucked into this world, I felt like Alice in Wonderland. The falling down the rabbit hole part."

"Thank you." He took it from her hands, popped a grape in his mouth, then pinned Nathalie with one of his intense stares.

Andrew smiled. The guy had no idea who he was dealing with. If he thought he could intimidate Nathalie, he had another think coming.

"You're a unique case, Nathalie. The reason we keep knowledge of our existence secret from humans is not because we are paranoid, but because it would have catastrophic consequences for us. If you were just any girl that Andrew fell in love with, even a potential Dormant, I would have immediately thralled you to forget all about us. After I ripped Andrew a new one, that is. But you're Bhathian's daughter. This is a situation I've never encountered before; therefore, there is no protocol for it. So I'm going to ask you. Are you sure you can keep this secret airtight? Or would you rather I thrall the memory away? It's a big responsibility to carry this knowledge with you."

Throughout his entire speech, Nathalie didn't back down from Kian's intense eyes. Andrew felt his chest swell with pride. The woman was brave—a true fighter even if she didn't think of herself as one.

"You have nothing to worry about, Kian. I'm an expert at keeping secrets. I've been hearing dead people talk in my head since I was a little girl, and the moment I realized it wasn't something everyone experienced, I never mentioned it to anyone again. The first one I told was Andrew. Even my parents heard nothing from me about it for years and years. The last time I mentioned my voices to them, I was a kid, and they assumed I was playing with imaginary friends."

Kian held her eyes for a moment longer, then grinned. "Oh, boy. I can just imagine my mother's response when she hears about this. I don't think we've ever had anyone with this particular talent. I need to ask her if any of the other gods could do this. Can you summon the ghosts at will?"

Nathalie harrumphed and crossed her arms over her chest. "I've never tried. Why would I, when I was doing all I could to keep the uninvited intruders out of my head? Can you imagine sharing your brain with another entity? The lack of privacy? The constant distractions? I'm surprised I managed to retain my sanity."

Perching on the arm of Kian's chair, Syssi cast Nathalie a pitying look. "Good God, that must've been terrible."

"Yeah, well, I got used to it." She pushed to her feet. "Shouldn't we get busy? As lovely as the company is, I didn't come here to socialize, I came to help."

Poor Nathalie, her feathers had gotten ruffled.

"Actually." Syssi lifted her palm. "We are waiting to hear from Amanda. She promised to let me know as soon as Vanessa was done talking to the women, and she hasn't yet. So I assume they are not done. Vanessa is a psychologist."

"Jackson's mom, I know." Nathalie sat back down.

"I'm still waiting for my drink." Kian patted Syssi's behind.

With a huff, she abandoned her perch and headed for the bar. "Ugh, you're the worst kind of patient, playing the invalid just so you can boss me around."

Kian lowered his injured leg to the carpet. "I can get it myself."

"No!" Syssi was back by his side in a blur. "Please, sit down. I'm sorry. It just annoys me that you insist on drinking when you shouldn't. It's irresponsible."

Kian rolled his eyes and took her hand in his. "You forget how old I am, sweet girl, and where I grew up. That's what a Scot does when he's hurting. Besides, with my constitution, one drink will do nothing, so stop fretting." He kissed her hand, the little gesture so gentle and full of love that it made Andrew uncomfortable. For some reason, this felt more intimate than their previous sexual banter had been.

But the man had a point, and Syssi wasn't the type who stuck to her convictions even when the argument against them was indisputable. "You're right. Andrew? Nathalie? What can I get you?"

"I'll have a beer," Andrew said.

"I'll share it with you, if it's okay?" Nathalie's voice had a little quiver to it, and she put her hand on Andrew's knee. So he hadn't been the only one affected by the tender display of love.

Covering her hand with his, he gave it a little squeeze. "Of course, my love."

30

NATHALIE

Nathalie hadn't heard a knock, but there must've been one because the door to Kian and Syssi's place burst open, and Amanda entered followed by a woman who looked like Jackson's sister.

Amanda's brows lifted in surprise. "Nathalie, what are you doing here?"

"I came to help."

"I see." Amanda's eyes darted from Kian to Syssi to Andrew. "Actually, I don't. What's going on?"

Syssi got up and gave Amanda a hug. "Andrew told Nathalie everything." She embraced the woman who was obviously Jackson's mom. "Nathalie, Andrew, this is Vanessa. Vanessa, this is my brother Andrew and his fiancée Nathalie."

Vanessa smiled. "Finally, I get to meet Jackson's boss. He doesn't stop talking about you. He worships you. I think he has a little crush."

Nathalie blushed. "I assure you he doesn't. But half of my clientele has a crush on him."

Vanessa waved a dismissive hand. "He's just a big show-off."

It was amazing how clueless parents could be about their kids.

Syssi pointed Vanessa toward the other overstuffed chair, next to Kian. "Come, take a seat and tell us how the girls are doing."

As Vanessa got comfortable in the chair, Amanda flopped on the couch on Nathalie's other side.

Stretching her long legs in front of her, Amanda pushed off her shoes and wiggled her toes. Like everything about the woman, even these were perfect, complete with glossy blood-red nail polish. "After some reshuffling of roommates, everyone is settled in. I have a huge list of things they need, though. Shoes, slippers, flip flops, comfortable underwear, nightgowns, T-shirts, jeans. The Doomers supplied them mostly with sexy lingerie and bikinis." Amanda grimaced.

"How is Tiffany holding up?" Nathalie asked. "She used to work for me, and one day she just disappeared. I was worried and asked Andrew to look for her, but of course he only found her today."

Vanessa heaved a sigh. "The weird part is that she is fine, all of them are. Except Letty, that is, but her case is different. They were thralled to believe that they were working in a high-end brothel, voluntarily, and were making loads of money. One of the Doomers must've possessed a very powerful thralling ability. They don't even remember being bitten. I have to assume that they were either being thralled nightly, or that the initial thrall programmed them to ignore that particular experience—have it slide into the subconscious without registering in their conscious memory."

Kian shifted so he could look at Vanessa. "That must've been their leader. Dalhu recognized him. Apparently, he was Navuh's direct grandson. Sharim. His mother was Navuh's daughter, who had never been activated. Her father let her die a Dormant. One of Navuh's other sons had adopted Sharim. The only one who was allowed to have a son."

Vanessa nodded. "That would explain the ability."

"I didn't know it was possible to thrall a memory before it happened." Syssi got up and headed for the kitchen. "Can I offer you ladies something to drink?"

"Water for me," Vanessa said.

Amanda pushed to her feet and followed Syssi. "I'm going to play with your cappuccino machine and make myself some. Anyone want coffee?"

There were no jumpers on the offer.

Kian ran his fingers through his disheveled long hair. "I don't know if even I can do something like that. I've never tried. If it were easily done, it would've solved a lot of problems for us. The only one I know that can do it is Annani."

Vanessa shrugged. "As I said, it is possible that the women were being thralled nightly. I will know more tomorrow, after I speak with each one individually and assess their cognition."

Kian didn't look happy with that. "I was planning on thralling them to forget the entire experience and sending them away as soon as possible. I don't want a bunch of humans hanging around here. Too risky."

Nathalie released a puff of air and got a little closer to Andrew. Was Kian bundling her together with the unwanted humans? Did he want her gone?

Vanessa shook her head. "Not yet. How can I explain it in layman's terms?" She closed her eyes and let her head drop back for a moment. "Thralling doesn't dispose of the memory, it only sweeps it under the rug. The dirt is still there, just not acknowledged. Before you or anyone else thralls them, I need to do some cleaning first. Otherwise, the dirt would eventually corrupt everything. Do you get what I'm saying?"

Kian grimaced. "How long do you need?"

"Give me at least a few days. Though, frankly, this is something that requires years of therapy."

"You have three days."

Vanessa pinned Kian with a pair of pleading eyes. "What are you going to do with them? It's not like we can dump them somewhere with no money, no identification documents. They have nothing."

"That's what I've been working on for the past several hours. I think I've got most of it figured out, but there are still some loose ends I need to tie up."

That should be interesting. Nathalie couldn't imagine a solution for this problem. She lifted the beer out of Andrew's loose grip and took a swig as she waited for Kian to elaborate.

Amanda waved an impatient hand at her brother. "Let's hear it."

Kian handed Syssi his empty glass, and by the look on his face he would've loved another, but when she shook her head in an adamant no, he sighed. "Could I at least have a beer?"

"Just one." She lifted one finger to emphasize before heading to the kitchen.

"So here is the plan," Kian began as she returned with his bottle and sat on the ottoman he had his leg propped on. "We own a large hotel on the big island of Hawaii, and we are just completing a new tower. It will be ready next month. Naturally, we need to hire additional service personnel, from housekeeping to receptionists and everyone else. So I thought, these are jobs that don't require much work experience or training, and we can fill some of the positions by offering them to the girls we rescued. We fly them out there, put them up in the hotel, and stage a training seminar they all supposedly signed up for in order to get the job. That will help explain the missing chunk of time in their lives. For the past month and a half, or however long they've been held by the Doomers, we'll make them believe they've been taking part in this training. As to why they didn't call their families or friends the entire time, the excuse would be that they were supposed to interact only with the other participants to create a bond that would help them work better as a team. Or something like that. If anyone has a better idea, I'm open to suggestions."

The guy was a genius. Not only would this plan provide a plausible explanation, it would give these girls jobs and friends and a new start.

Vanessa seemed to agree. "This is an excellent plan. I can go with them and continue my work under the guise of a seminar leader. Only problem is what to do with my current patients. I'll have to talk to a few of my colleagues and see if they can take over for me for a couple of weeks."

"What about paper work? Credit cards? Cell phones?" Nathalie asked.

Andrew patted her knee. "Don't worry about that. This is small and insignificant stuff. But what Kian is suggesting will change the trajectory of these girls' lives for the better. From what I understand, none of them was doing all that well before getting captured."

"Speaking of new beginnings." Amanda lifted her cappuccino cup and finished it with one long gulp as if it were a glass of water. "We need to go shopping. Syssi? Are you coming with me?"

"Of course."

Nathalie did some quick thinking and decided she wanted to join them. Tiffany and the other girls were probably exhausted after the eventful day and were getting ready to sleep. None of them would be in a mood to meet new people. The best way for her to help was to contribute another pair of hands and feet to the shopping expedition. "Can I come with you?"

Syssi smiled. "Sure. If we split the shopping list into three, it will go faster."

"Brundar is going with you. It's late and I don't want you going alone." Kian's voice carried a tone of command no one was about to argue with.

Amanda shrugged. "Fine. I need to take your Lexus. We need a large trunk, and showing up with a limousine at Walmart is the epitome of douchiness."

"I'm heading home." Vanessa got to her feet. "The ladies have my phone number, and I told them to call me anytime if something bothers them, even in the middle of the night. I'm afraid that as the thrall they've been under dissipates, they'll begin to remember things differently."

Nathalie kissed Andrew's cheek. "Are you staying here?"

"Yeah, I'll keep Kian company while I wait for you." He leaned to whisper in her ear. "Remember what I told you before? We are staying here tonight."

Nathalie wrapped her arms around his neck. "It's a date. Just don't fall asleep on me."

"If I do, I expect you to wake me up."

Nathalie had a pretty good idea what Andrew had in mind. Stifling a smile, she saluted. "Yes, sir!"

She was going to have fun with that.

31

ANDREW

Andrew kissed Nathalie goodbye, then waited until the girls got in the elevator before closing the door. Taking the armchair Vanessa had vacated, he asked Kian, "How is your leg doing?"

"It's healing." Kian pushed up on his good leg and hobbled his way to the bar.

"I'm surprised it's taking you this long. I still remember the demonstration you gave me when we met. The cut you made on your forearm closed in seconds."

Kian grabbed a bottle of whiskey and a tall glass. "Yeah, but this is not a simple cut. The fucking Doomer carved a piece of flesh out of my thigh. It takes time to regrow muscle tissue."

"Ouch…"

Kian filled his glass all the way to the top and gulped a third of it on a oner.

Andrew chuckled. "When the cat's away the mice will play, eh?" He reached for an empty shot glass and held it up for Kian to fill up.

"Are you calling me a mouse?" Kian asked as he poured, his brows dipping in pretend offense.

"Yeah, but I'm no different. We are both pussy-whipped. Here, lean on me." He offered Kian his shoulder and took the glass from his hand. "If you don't want incriminating evidence splashing on your hardwood floor, I'd better carry this for you."

With a muffled grunt, Kian put his hand on Andrew's shoulder, grudgingly accepting the help. "I prefer to look at it as choosing my battles."

Andrew lifted his glass in a salute. "Well said. I'll drink to this."

They sipped their drinks in companionable silence, with Andrew checking his emails and Kian punching at his laptop with the fingers of one hand while holding his glass in the other. It could've been a nice, peaceful time if not for Kian's intermittent cursing when he kept mistyping the words.

An hour later, Andrew was done going through his messages and reading the few new emails on his phone. His eyelids began drooping and he yawned. "I'd better get in bed before I fall asleep in this chair. Do you need help getting back to your bedroom?"

"No thanks. I'll manage."

Andrew stretched his aching muscles, then headed to the kitchen to rinse out his empty glass. He stopped by Kian on his way back. "It went well today," he said.

Lifting his head, Kian nodded. "Yeah, it did. We've been lucky. With everything that went wrong it could've all gone to shit."

True that. "I'm glad it didn't. Goodnight, Kian."

As he lay in the dark bedroom, staring at the moonbeams dancing on the ceiling, Andrew fought the temptation of sleep and the oblivion it promised, refusing to close his eyes and let himself drift away.

Today's excitement had both tired him out and made him horny as hell, and it was becoming difficult to choose between the two contradicting needs.

Perhaps he could just let it happen. He could get a little shuteye, hoping Nathalie would make good on her promise and wake him up when she returned.

As he let his eyelids drop over his eyes, Andrew conjured the image of Nathalie's lush lips closing around his cock. He was naked under the thin comforter, so there was nothing to keep it folded against his belly, and the bad boy made like a pole, popping a small tent.

Correction, big tent.

Small and his cock didn't belong in the same sentence.

Palming his erection, Andrew remembered another night, not so long ago, in Kian and Syssi's guest bedroom, when he'd tried to masturbate thinking of Amanda. Thankfully, it hadn't been a successful attempt since Dalhu's face had ruined the fantasy.

Man, Andrew was infinitely grateful that his stupid crush on the woman hadn't been reciprocated. It would've messed up both of their lives. For a guy who'd never believed in fate, Andrew had become a true convert. There was no doubt in his mind that Dalhu was Amanda's destined mate, or that Nathalie was his.

The Fates had smiled upon him. Only the lucky few were ever granted such blessing. But there was a flip side to the joy. He hated to be separated from her, even for a short time. Nathalie's absence felt like a gaping hole in his heart, especially in quiet moments like this. When he was busy, he could tolerate it for a time, but he wasn't busy now.

Jerking off didn't count.

Besides, his hand was a poor substitute for Nathalie's lips.

Reaching for his phone, Andrew texted. *When are you coming back?*

A few seconds later she replied. *We are on our way. Brundar says ten minutes.*

Andrew smirked. *Good. I'm already in bed, waiting impatiently. My cocky yet upstanding associate says hi.*

Ha ha she texted back.

Twenty-five long minutes later, he heard the front door open, and then a couple more minutes passed as the girls whispered their goodnights.

Who did they think was sleeping?

Nathalie knew he was waiting for her, and Kian was most likely still awake. The guy wasn't the type to relax and close his eyes while his wife was out in the middle of the night—the bodyguard keeping her safe notwithstanding.

Not that there was anything wrong with that. Any self-respecting man would've done the same.

Come to think of it, Andrew should've joined the shopping expedition. He wasn't injured like Kian, and being tired was not a good enough excuse. Trouble was, none of the girls would've agreed to that. Taking Brundar along was different. The guy's presence was as unobtrusive as that of a container of pepper spray.

A moment later the door to his room cracked open, the faint light from the corridor illuminating Nathalie's silhouette.

"Hi there," he said quietly.

"Hi," she whispered back and closed the door behind her, plunging the room back into darkness. "I'll be right back." She ducked into the bathroom.

She hadn't closed the door all the way, and like a horny teenager, Andrew tried to peek through the small crack and see her undressing. He'd seen Nathalie naked plenty of times, but there was something thrilling about watching her unveiling unawares. Catching only a partial, occasional glimpse, he relied on his imagination as he listened to her undress, brush her teeth, and take a quick shower.

A few moments later, she pushed the bathroom door open and got out, wearing a long T-shirt. There was some design on the front, but with the light behind her, it was impossible to see more than a general shape, or even the color of the shirt. Not that it mattered. He would've preferred her with nothing on at all.

Her small, bare feet making a pattering sound on the hardwood floor, Nathalie crossed the short distance to the bed and ducked under the blanket he'd lifted for her in invitation.

"You're so warm." She snuggled up to him as he wrapped his arm around her.

He tugged on the shirt from behind. "What's that?"

"I bought it at Walmart. It's just too cute. I also got panties and some other necessities for the night. You told me you wanted to stay only after I got here, I needed stuff."

"Like what? All you need is me."

He felt her teeth on his earlobe and squirmed a little as she nipped it. "True, but I thought you'd appreciate the lotion. I smoothed it all over my body so my skin is all soft and fragrant for you."

His cock twitched, getting even harder. "Next time, let me do it. I'll make sure to get every nook and cranny covered, and I'll throw in an erotic massage."

He felt her butt cheek contract under his palm.

"Sounds lovely, but tonight there is something I fantasized about doing ever since you told me to wake you up. " She whispered in his ear, "Thinking about it got me so wet that I had to buy a change of underwear."

Andrew puffed out a groan. "God, woman, you got me so hard I can hammer nails with this thing." He lifted the blanket to show her.

Nathalie took a peek and chuckled. "Houston, we have a problem. There is a rocket in here and it's ready to go."

"What are you going to do to address this potentially explosive situation?" He played along.

Nathalie slid down and gently palmed his throbbing erection. "I think I need to put out the fire." She licked the crown and Andrew's butt shot up, thrusting his cock deeper into her mouth.

"Oooh, the problem is more acute than I thought. I believe total immersion is in order." She closed her lips around his shaft, then slowly lowered her mouth, taking as much of it as she could all the way to the back of her throat.

As Andrew's eyes rolled back in his head, he let out a pained groan. Heaven. He'd died and gone to heaven. Nathalie was deep-throating him like a pro—the woman, who was a complete novice in everything to do with sex, was giving him the best blow job of his life.

Mercy...

Up and down her head bobbed as she sucked and pumped, giving it all she had. At this rate she was going to suck the seed straight up out of his balls.

"Oh, baby, keep it up for five more seconds and I'm going to—" Before he could finish his sentence, Andrew felt his balls draw tight and a second later his seed shot straight up into Nathalie's mouth.

She clamped her lips tight around him, swallowing everything like it wasn't one of the biggest loads he'd ever released, then finished him off with a few gentle licks.

Leaning up on her elbow, she watched him with a satisfied little smirk as he tried to catch his breath.

When he could move, Andrew lifted his arm and wrapped it around her, pulling her on top of him. He kissed her swollen lips then sighed. "I officially declare you the queen of blowjobs. That was out of this world."

"Thank you." Nathalie closed her eyes and rested her cheek on his chest. "I love you," she mumbled sleepily.

"I love you too. But I'm not letting you doze off. It's my turn." He flipped them over and dove between her legs. "You can sleep if you want."

Nathalie giggled, then pretended to snore as he pulled her panties down.

With a few strategically placed swipes of his tongue, Andrew made sure that sleeping was the furthest thing from her mind.

32

NATHALIE

"Are you crazy? I'm not coming to your drunken party," Amanda huffed.

With a frown, Kian turned to Syssi. "What about you?"

"I'm with Amanda on this. The idea of me, and maybe two other females, hanging around a rowdy bunch of drunken Guardians is not appealing. Besides, I know you guys. You'll start talking about your glorious gory battles and gross me out with the details. I'll pass."

Kian raked his fingers through his hair. "That's what I get for trying to be progressive. A resounding no-thank-you."

Nathalie felt bad for him. The guy was trying to do the right thing and include the women in what had traditionally been a male only party.

Well, not exclusively. In days past prostitutes provided the female companionship.

Yuck.

Most of these guys had been around during those times. Not a pretty picture. She'd rather celebrate with the girls...

"Guys," she interrupted the ongoing argument. "We need to throw a party for the rescued women. Naturally, it needs to be a girls only party. So while you guys have your rowdy warrior celebration, we'll have a separate one with the girls."

Syssi clapped her hands. "That's a lovely idea. How about a pajama party?"

"I love it." Amanda turned her back to Kian and grabbed both Nathalie and Syssi's hands. "Let's adjourn to the dining room and make a list of party supplies."

As Nathalie let Amanda drag her along, she cranked her neck around to cast Andrew an apologetic glance. Syssi had insisted that they stay for breakfast, and then had invited Amanda and Dalhu as well.

With a smile, he blew her a kiss, while Kian shook his head. Dalhu stared at Amanda's retreating butt.

"I can't stay long. I need to get back to the shop," Nathalie said as they sat down around the dining room table and Amanda pulled out a tablet.

She'd left Jackson in charge of her father and the shop. Shouldering all of her responsibilities, the kid must've been exhausted, mentally if not physically. After he'd worked a full day, she'd called him to come babysit her father for a few hours, which had turned into an entire night and half of this morning.

It wasn't fair to him.

Doing her a favor from time to time was one thing; taking on the job of a caregiver was another. Even though he wanted the extra money, Jackson was young. He needed to hang out with his friends and chase girls. Not babysit a mentally-challenged old man. Problem was, other than Nathalie, Jackson was the only person her father trusted enough to be left alone with.

"Don't you want to go say hi to your former employee?" Syssi asked.

Tiffany, that's right.

"I would love to, but I can't. I really need to get back and relieve Jackson. I've already overburdened his young shoulders."

Using a stylus, Amanda scribbled something on her tablet. "You can stop by her room on your way out."

Nathalie shook her head. "I don't want to just pop my head in and say hi and goodbye. I want to talk to her without the clock ticking over my head like a bomb."

Lifting her head, Amanda quirked a smile. "You have a point. Besides, we are having the party tomorrow, and you can hang with her then."

Nathalie fidgeted with the strap of her purse. "I'm not sure I can come. I can't leave my father with anyone other than Jackson, and I've already imposed on him too much. He has a life outside the shop."

Amanda waved a hand. "Nonsense. You must come. Pay the kid double and promise him a day off or something."

She hadn't thought of that, but a day or two of paid vacation would be a nice thank-you gesture Jackson would, hopefully, appreciate.

As it turned out, Jackson was more than happy to babysit again.

"Go and have fun at your pajama party." He patted her shoulder, took another look at what she was wearing, and burst out laughing. Again. Vlad giggled like a girl. "I just can't help it. It's adorable…"

Last year, she'd bought the fuzzy-bunny onesie as a costume to entertain the little trick-or-treaters on Halloween. It was pink in the back, with a little flap that closed with two large buttons, a white, fuzzy tummy, and a hoodie with fluffy ears.

The girls were going to love it.

She rolled her eyes, kissed her father's leathery cheek, and waved goodbye to Jackson.

As Vlad followed her with a pile of cardboard boxes filled with fresh pastries, Nathalie wondered if Andrew's reaction would be the same as that of her two helpers.

Coming straight from work, he was waiting outside to pick her up. They were going in one car so she could drive him home in case he got drunk tonight.

She shouldn't have been surprised at his reaction. It was typical Andrew.

"Well hello, my sexy bunny, this outfit gives me such wicked ideas." He waggled his brows as he leaned to kiss her, ignoring Vlad's giggling.

"I can wear a potato sack and it will give you ideas." She laughed as he opened the car door for her.

After loading the boxes into the trunk, Vlad said goodbye and hopped like a rabbit back to the shop. She couldn't help the laughter bubbling up. The kid looked more like a kangaroo than a rabbit.

A very skinny, very tall, chain-wearing, goth looking, kangaroo.

When they reached the keep, Andrew helped Nathalie carry the boxes up to the forty-eighth floor. He put them down by the door, and they parted ways, but not before he showed her exactly what he had in mind for later.

Leaving her to catch her breath before facing the loud crowd inside, Andrew got into the elevator heading down to the catacombs. As a somber reminder that their victory hadn't been without bloodshed, Kian was holding a ceremony for the fallen enemy before the party.

Nathalie rang the bell, and as Amanda opened the door, her lips lifted in a big smile. "Is it Easter? And what treats did the bunny get us?"

"Check it out yourself."

Amanda winked. "Oh, you bet I will." She bent her knees and lifted the pile of boxes all by herself. "Come on, hop inside."

Enviable. It wasn't that the boxes were extremely heavy, but there were a lot of them. Amanda was not only incredibly strong, but her arms were really long compared to Nathalie's. She was also half a foot taller, several pounds thinner, and definitely prettier.

Oh, well.

Nathalie scanned the packed living room for Tiffany. Between the humans and immortals, there must've been about forty females crowded inside, with some mingling in the kitchen. They were all wearing some type of sleepwear, most of which Nathalie recognized as things she'd picked up for them last night.

It took her two more rounds before she found Tiffany, and that was only because one of the others called her name. The girl looked nothing like what she used to when she'd worked for Nathalie.

At least ten pounds heavier, which filled out her curves and eliminated the gaunt, hollow look her face used to have, she looked beautiful. Her hair was highlighted and cut in fashionable layers, but most notably, it was clean and not oily.

A wave of guilt washed over Nathalie. The supposedly evil Doomers had taken better care of the girl than she had. Instead of buying Tiffany's story about watching her weight, she should've insisted that the girl ate. Looking at her now, it was obvious to Nathalie that Tiff refused the food out of some misplaced sense of pride and not because she thought stick-thin was a good look for her.

If Papi's faculties had been intact, he would've noticed and would've fed the girl. But Nathalie lacked her father's natural charm and his talent for getting people to open up to him. She was always too rushed, too busy, and, until recently, too tired.

God, she missed the man her father used to be.

Wending her way toward Tiffany, Nathalie forced her eyes to stop tearing and put a big smile on her face.

The costume must've confused the girl, or perhaps the thralling she'd been subjected to had messed with her memory, because even though she was looking straight at Nathalie, there was no sign of recognition in her eyes.

Nathalie pushed the hoodie down. "Hi, Tiffany, remember me?"

Tiffany's eyes widened. "Nathalie? What are you doing here?" She jumped up and hugged her.

As Nathalie held on to the girl, tears started cascading down her cheeks. "I'm so happy you're okay. I was so worried."

Tiffany lifted her head, a puzzled expression on her face. "Why?"

Nathalie was about to answer when she noticed Amanda shaking her head and mouthing no.

What the hell had they been telling these girls about their captivity? Had they already thralled them with the story they'd prepared?

She should've asked Amanda, but it just hadn't crossed her mind that there was a need. "Hmm, I don't know. I just haven't heard from you and didn't know how you were doing."

Tiffany tilted her head. "So why are you crying?"

Because you're alive and going to be okay thanks to these kind immortals.

"I just missed you, that's all."

33

KIAN

"Why the hell do you want us to assemble in the catacombs?" Anandur grimaced. "I had enough of that depressing place yesterday, going back and forth with the bagged Doomers. It gives me the creeps, thinking how many undead we have in storage. I don't want to be there for even a minute longer than absolutely necessary."

Neither did Kian, but it had to be done.

Last night, when he'd planned today's celebration, he'd realized that he couldn't do it in good conscience without performing a service for the fucking Doomers first.

Kian shook his head. Annani and her bleeding-heart rhetoric must've rubbed off on him.

His mother was a bad influence.

First, it had been Syssi, all sad and teary because of the lives that had been lost, regardless of the fact that these lives belonged to scum that had wanted her dead. Then, her response had gotten him thinking about his mother, and how furious Annani was going to be when she found out that they had gone out on a mission without telling her. There would be hell to pay and it would come out of Kian's hide.

As it turned out, though, the carnage hadn't been as bad as he'd hoped it would be, and most of the Doomers were undead rather than dead for good, which would no doubt make Annani happy.

And yet here he was, adamant about giving a prayer for the few that had died because it was the decent thing to do. And he was a decent guy, goddamn it. Even if sometimes he didn't feel like one.

Kian raked his fingers through his hair. "I'm not ecstatic about it either. But it feels wrong to celebrate without sending off the dead on their final journey with a few words first."

Anandur let his head drop and shook it from side to side. "You never cease to surprise me, Kian. A couple of months ago, you would've chewed the head off anyone who dared suggest it. What happened to you? Is it Syssi? Is she turning you into a pussy?"

Kian flicked the back of Anandur's head. "Watch it! What did I tell you about referring to her with anything other than the utmost respect?"

"Sorry. I love her—" He winced when Kian lifted his hand again. "Like a sister, you moron. She is wonderful and kind and sweet. But you have to admit that she is making you soft."

It irked, but Anandur was right.

Except, Kian was tired of the anger and of using it as both a shield and a weapon. Syssi was like a balm on his frayed nerves, rounding his hard edges, filing away some of the abrasiveness.

Lately, Kian had been able to summon compassion where there had been none before, and even patience on occasion, but that was a good thing. He liked himself just a tad better this way.

"Is it so bad, Andu? Frankly, I'm tired of being a monumental asshole."

Anandur chuckled. "Part of the job, buddy. You're not the head of a reading club. You're the commander in chief of the clan. You're supposed to be a giant prick."

Brundar made a sound that resembled a snort, but Kian couldn't be sure. When he glanced at him, the guy's expression was as somber as always. Anandur, on the other hand, seemed all too satisfied with himself.

Kian slapped Anandur's back hard enough to send the big oaf tumbling forward. "Thank you. I don't know what I would've done without your pep talks."

"You're welcome," Anandur gritted out.

Kian and the brothers were the last to arrive at the big central chamber of the catacombs. Everyone was waiting for them, and by the Guardians' expressions most of them shared Anandur's sentiment. They seemed eager for Kian to be done with what they must've considered an unnecessary hurdle on their way to party time, i.e. getting shit-faced drunk.

Shai made a little podium for himself from two wooden crates, and was ready with a camera mounted on a tripod to film the ceremony.

Anandur put two fingers between his lips and whistled, bringing everyone's attention to Kian. When the rowdy bunch hushed down, he bowed to him. "The stage is yours, Regent."

Kian's finger twitched to flip Anandur off, but this was a somber occasion and he was here in an official capacity. "We are here to pray for the souls of the dead and those who remain in a suspended state until such time in the future when they are deemed salvageable."

A wave of murmurs swept through the crowd of Guardians, some agreeing and some sneering. Kian ignored both.

Having only a dim idea of what he was going to say, Kian hadn't prepared a speech. He needed to say something positive about a hated enemy, and it wasn't easy. What good can be said about monsters?

For starters, he had two examples of Doomers who weren't pure evil. Dalhu and the guy who'd helped Carol. This meant that not all of them had lost their souls, which meant that once upon a time, before Navuh's machine had ground them to dust in order to reshape them into what he wanted them to be, Doomers' souls had been the same as everyone else's; some good, some not so good, and most somewhere in the middle.

"These Doomers weren't born evil, because all children are born pure. In some rare cases, faulty brain chemistry turns these pure souls into monsters; in others, like in the Doomers' case, it's hateful, relentless brainwashing. I pray that in the afterlife their souls will shed the layer of evil that has been forced onto them and reclaim their original purity."

Anandur was the first one to pound his chest with his fist, then Brundar, then Bhathian, and soon the chamber exploded with the sounds of fists pounding on burly chests, the noise magnified and amplified by the echoing stone walls.

Kian waited until the chamber quieted. "Okay, people, time to celebrate! Follow me!"

As the noise level rose all over again, this time with cheers and hoots, Kian winced, wishing he'd thought to equip himself with earplugs.

It had been a long time since he had that many Guardians with him. Come to think of it, he'd never had that many. People had joined and people had left, but this was the first time the majority of all Guardians had come out of retirement to help rescue a female who had ended up rescuing herself.

Actually, that wasn't entirely true. She'd been helped by a Doomer. Kian couldn't believe he was thinking it, but he regretted the guy's decision not to cross over to the clan. He would've loved for Vanessa to analyze both Dalhu and Robert to see what made them different. How they had managed to resist the brainwashing and retain some decency.

Amanda claimed that Dalhu was different because he'd been raised by a loving mother until he'd been taken away. She believed that the memory of that love was what kept his soul from shriveling.

Did Carol's rescuer share the same story?

It would've been interesting to investigate this theory.

As they reached the gym, Kian set aside his musings for later.

It was time to celebrate the clan's victory with shitloads of Snake's Venom and whisky. He'd had Okidu and Onidu whip up a feast, which they managed beautifully on such short notice. Syssi had helped, arranging the rental and delivery of folding tables and chairs to accommodate all the Guardians.

The tables were covered with white tablecloths and set with disposable plates, glasses, cutlery, and everything else. Shai had brought a microphone and a karaoke machine loaded with old Scottish songs. Kian wondered where he'd found music that was several hundred years old, and if he could download it for him to listen to later. It would be fun singing along, but not in public.

Perhaps in the shower...

Tomorrow, most of the Guardians were leaving. Only five had decided to stay and join the force. A shame, really, he'd hoped more would stay. But at least the rest had agreed to the reserves program. It felt good to know that he had an army at his disposal in case he needed one. Those returning to Scotland had promised to keep up their training, and the few who lived in Los Angeles would be coming to train at the keep.

"Hey! Anandur!" Arwel called, lifting his bottle of Snake's Venom in a sloppy salute, his words already slurring. "Are you going to do a striptease for us tonight?"

Onegus slapped him over the head. "You bloody drunkard. You had to remind him? Once was enough for a lifetime."

Arwel ducked a safe distance away from Onegus and climbed on a chair. "Who wants to see Anandur strip? Say, aye!"

Between chuckles and hoots some shouted, "Aye!"

Anandur shook his head. "I'm only stripping for bachelor parties. So if you guys want to see the show, you'll have to come back for Andrew's." He grabbed Andrew and pushed him in front of him like a shield.

Someone started a chant. "Strip! Strip! Strip!"

Anandur shouted back. "Not going to happen!" Snatching a bun from the bread basket, he chucked it at Raibert, who'd been the one who had started it, hitting him smack in the face. Raibert picked it up from where it landed on the floor and chucked it back. The chanting immediately switched from "Strip! Strip! Strip!" To "Food fight! Food fight! Food fight!"

Kian rolled his eyes. *Here goes the party...*

34

ANDREW

"Tell me again why Syssi invited us tonight?" Andrew really wasn't up for socializing, not even with his sister. He was still hungover from last night's celebration. Nursing a pounding headache throughout his workday, he'd been dreaming of the moment he could get to Nathalie's and fall asleep on her couch. Not very romantic, true, but he was exhausted.

Between the stress of the mission and the crazy party the following night, he hadn't had time to recuperate.

This experience had really driven home the difference between him and the immortals. Without even taking an active part in the fighting, Andrew still felt like the walking dead, while Kian, who'd had to regrow a chunk of missing flesh, was back in full operational mode.

"Just a little get-together. Amanda and Dalhu, Bhathian, maybe a few others. I don't know."

Nathalie was such a bad liar that he would've known she was lying even without his gift. What puzzled him, though, was why she kept at it even though she knew perfectly well that it was futile.

Whatever, he'd play along. The less talking he did, the less his head hurt. He'd show up, stay for half an hour, then excuse himself and take Nathalie home.

She cast him a worried glance. Unfortunately, though, her eyes showed no guilt about forcing him to go. "Maybe you should take some Motrin. You look like you're suffering."

He rubbed his temples with his thumbs. "Good idea. Though I took some this morning and they didn't do shit for my headache."

"Get in the shower, and I'll make you a fresh cup of coffee for when you're done."

Bossy woman.

Still, a shower might help.

Standing under a scalding stream, he let it pound his head until the hot water ran out, and when he was done, Nathalie handed him a big cup of black coffee together with four Motrins.

Twenty minutes later, Andrew felt a little better about getting in the car and driving to the keep.

"I can't wait to see their penthouse," Nathalie said as he parked the car in the same spot he had parked it the other day. Except, this time they were going straight up, instead of down and through the tunnel to the other building. A good thing, since Nathalie was wearing a pair of killer heels.

When they got into the elevator, he glanced at her feet again. "Why are you wearing these shoes? They look like torture devices."

She smirked. "Because they make my legs and my butt look awesome." She turned around to show him.

The woman was playing with fire. Naturally, he had to grab that amazing ass and squeeze.

Nathalie surprised him when she leaned into his hands, letting him play a little longer. "Remember the epic blow job I gave you the other night?"

He looked at her through the mirror, leering like the dirty old man he was. "Baby, that was unforgettable."

She winked and pursed her fleshy lips. "Tonight, I'm going to give you one that's going to be even better."

Andrew groaned. He was wearing slacks, which meant that he was about to enter Syssi and Kian's place with a huge tent in his pants. "I'm going to hold you to your promise. But for now, please, no more talk about blowjobs or anything sexy. I have a problem down here."

Nathalie glanced behind her with a devilish smile on her face. "You should button up your jacket to hide this flag pole."

Yeah, like he hadn't thought of this brilliant solution himself.

The door swished open, and they exited into the penthouse level's vestibule. The vase on top of the round stone table had a fresh flower arrangement, and Andrew wondered who had gotten it there so quickly, and how. They had just moved back.

"Andrew, this is beautiful." Nathalie turned in a circle, taking in the mosaic on the floor, the domed ceiling with the mural painted on it, the two ten foot high, carved double doors. "You weren't kidding about this."

Andrew huffed. "Wait until you see the inside. They have a swimming pool on their terrace."

"Unbelievable."

As Andrew knocked, Nathalie walked over to the flower arrangement and leaned to smell it.

Syssi opened the door with a big smile on her face, but for some reason the light was off in her living room. Had Nathalie confused the time and they were early?

"Come on in, Andrew," Syssi said, and as he followed her inside, someone flipped on the lights.

Multiple voices shouted, "Happy birthday!"

Andrew was speechless.

The big banner hanging over the flat screen said *Happy 40th Birthday Andrew*.

Several helium balloons with the same dreaded number on them were floating near the ceiling.

Syssi pulled him into a bone-crushing hug. "Happy birthday, Andrew." Next, he had his ribs compressed by Kian, then Anandur, then Bhathian, and next was Dalhu. Even Brundar shook his hand. Arwel and Onegus each clapped him on the back, Amanda kissed him on both cheeks, and so it went.

"My birthday is next week, people." He laughed.

Nathalie smiled and wrapped her arms around his neck. "It wouldn't have been much of a surprise if we did it exactly on your birthday, now would it? Happy birthday, my love." She kissed him.

"I knew there was something you weren't telling me. Should have guessed what you were up to."

The smile started sliding off her face, and he realized that he should be thanking her instead of scolding. "Thank you, baby." He kissed her forehead.

Nathalie peered up at him, still not sure whether he was happy or mad about this. "You should also thank Syssi, this was her idea."

His sister should've known better. Andrew hated surprises, they made him uncomfortable, especially when everyone's attention was on him.

Syssi looked away when he tried to pin her with a stare. "Come on, guys, grab a drink and take a load off," Syssi pointed them toward the bar where Kian was waiting with two empty glasses.

Just the thought of alcohol made Andrew nauseous, but he wasn't about to fess up and provide the guy with ammunition for more teasing. "Nathalie, you go ahead. I'll have some later."

She gave him a knowing little smile, but didn't say anything.

Andrew walked over to Michael who'd been waiting patiently for his turn to congratulate him. "Just the guy I wanted to see." He shook hands with the kid.

"Happy birthday, Andrew. Forty, wow, that's... awesome."

Andrew smiled. "You meant to say old. It's okay, next to you I feel ancient. I wanted to talk to you about the transition." He steered Michael toward the kitchen where they could have some privacy.

Michael took a swig from his bottle of Snake Venom, then asked, "What do you want to know?"

"Whatever you can tell me. I'm planning on doing it as soon as I can, and I want to know what to expect."

Michael took another swig and furrowed his forehead. "There isn't really much to tell. I didn't feel anything until my gums started to hurt. I thought I had teeth problems and wanted to go see a dentist. Yamanu figured right away what was going on and took me to Bridget. It was hell growing these things—" He pointed at his small fangs. "The venom glands weren't easy either. It felt as if my throat was on fire. Then my bones started hurting, which was the weirdest thing because I didn't know bones could hurt. The worst was over in about three days, but it's still happening. I'm still getting random aches and pains, and my fangs are useless because the venom glands are not active yet. Bridget says it will take another month or two until these babies will be functional."

Michael's transition didn't seem all that harsh, but Andrew didn't expect his to go as smoothly.

"Andrew, what are you doing hiding in the kitchen?" Syssi grabbed his elbow and pulled him back into the living room. "Go, mingle, talk to people." She shoved him toward William.

Mingling and socializing wasn't his thing, but he could do that, spend a few minutes talking to his mission partner. Well, partner was a gross exaggeration. Andrew had been no more than a lowly apprentice in William's tech-mobile, and his help had been quite unnecessary. Still, after spending several hours with the tech genius, Andrew now considered him a friend as opposed to a casual acquaintance.

"Hey, William, my man. How are you doing?" Andrew offered his hand.

William grasped what he was offered, but not before transferring the pastry he'd been holding to his left hand, then wiping his right on a napkin. "I'm in heaven. Your fiancée makes the most delicious Danish."

"Those are Nathalie's?"

"That's what I've been told."

She must've been planning this right under his nose days before the mission. Come to think of it, Vlad had been casting him weird smiles over the last several days. But the kid was such a strange bird that Andrew had thought nothing of it —just another oddity.

Andrew grabbed a croissant from a tray Okidu was passing around and headed to where Nathalie was chatting with Dalhu.

Interesting. What the hell could she be talking about with the guy?

He hadn't told her that he was planning on asking Dalhu to be his initiator. First, before he told anyone, including Dalhu himself, Andrew had to clear it with Kian.

"Andrew." Nathalie turned to him with a big smile on her face. "I've just commissioned Dalhu to paint your portrait. I wanted something special for your birthday, and this seems like a really unique gift. Dalhu is such a talented artist. But you need to make an appointment."

Dalhu grinned, looking happier about this than he should. "And your birthday present from me is the fifty percent discount I'm giving your fiancée."

Damn.

Andrew wrapped his arm around her narrow waist and pulled her close against his side. "I'll make you a deal. If you really want to make this a special birthday present, you'll come to pose with me. I want a portrait of the two of us together."

Given her bright smile, Nathalie wasn't going to object. "That's a wonderful idea, Andrew, I would love to."

35

KIAN

It was getting late, and half of the people had already left when Andrew approached Kian.

"I want to talk to you about my transition."

Kian had been expecting it. "When do you want to do it?"

Andrew rubbed his hand over the back of his neck. "I want to say tomorrow, but if I don't get rid of this fucking headache first, I'll need to push it up a day."

The guy seemed anxious and with good reason.

Hell, just thinking about the possible consequences, Kian's gut clenched with worry. If Andrew didn't survive, it would devastate Syssi beyond repair. And frankly, Kian would miss the stubborn bastard as well. Andrew had become not only a brother-in-law and a friend, but also a valuable asset to the clan.

"We need to choose your initiator." Obviously, Kian was going to do it, and the choosing would be symbolic, for tradition's sake.

"I want it to be Dalhu."

"What? Why him?" Kian felt as if Andrew had just spat in his face.

Andrew rubbed his neck again. "I thought it through. Bhathian was my first choice, but he is Nathalie's father, and it didn't seem appropriate. So it was either Anandur or Dalhu. I decided on Dalhu because, in a way, we are both outsiders. We started as rivals and ended up as friends, and I figured Dalhu could use the honor of being chosen. At least I hope it's an honor."

As Andrew recounted his reasoning, it dawned on Kian that his brother-in-law hadn't considered him because he might feel weird about getting activated by the same guy who had activated his sister.

Nevertheless, he asked, "What about me?"

Andrew lifted his head with a genuinely surprised expression on his face. "Are you allowed? I mean you're the regent. I assumed you are above such mundane tasks."

"There is nothing mundane about your transformation. I don't know if

Amanda is right about it, but she says my venom is the most potent because I'm a direct descendent of the gods. I will not trust your life to anyone else."

Andrew looked down, scratched his chin, then sighed. "I appreciate your concern, and I'm not ungrateful, but you are also my sister's husband. And her initiator. This would be even weirder than with Bhathian."

He could see Andrew's point, but it was an unimportant one. "I get it, Andrew. It may seem as something intimate to you, but it's not. Changing a male is a completely different experience. You'll be fighting me, man to man, nothing even remotely sexual or intimate about it. We've just done it to a bunch of Doomers. You think any of us would've been able to do it if it involved emotions or intimacy?"

"No, I guess not. But I still feel weird about it being you."

Kian's patience was wearing thin. "What's more important? Enduring something that is a little weird or off putting, or surviving the transition? Your sister would never recover if you don't make it. And what about Nathalie? Who is going to activate her? Would she even agree to go for it without you? Personally, I doubt it."

If Kian's tirade didn't convince Andrew, nothing would.

In the meantime, everyone stopped talking, and all eyes were focused on Andrew.

Bridget walked up to Andrew and put a hand on his bicep. "You have to let Kian do it. He is your best chance of surviving this, and I'm saying it as a doctor and as your friend."

Andrew was stubborn but not stupid. "You're right. I accept Kian as my initiator. Is that how it goes? Or is there some kind of ceremony?"

Kian expelled a breath and clapped Andrew on his shoulder. "Of course there is a ceremony, but we have a big enough forum here to proceed. That way, we can start the actual process as soon as you feel up to it."

"Okay. So what do I do next?"

"Nothing, for now. But we need wine. Okidu, could you please open a new bottle of ceremonial wine and give everyone a glass?"

"Of course, master." Okidu rushed to the kitchen.

Kian turned to look at the small assembled group. Everyone was smiling, except for Nathalie, who was crying and trying to cover it up. He'd had first-hand experience of what she was going through, and yet had no words of comfort for her. Andrew's life was on the line, and he was not going to offer the girl meaningless reassurances.

Kian was relieved, though, to see Syssi embrace Nathalie and whisper something in her ear. If anyone could ease the woman's fears, it was Syssi—the seer with the foreknowledge.

When Okidu was done distributing the small wine glasses, Kian cleared his throat and waited for everyone to hush down. "We are gathered here to present this fine not-so-young man to his elders. Andrew is ready to attempt his transformation. Who is vouching for him?"

Kian raised his hand, as did all the other Guardians present.

"I volunteer to initiate Andrew into his immortality."

"Andrew, do you accept me as your initiator? As your mentor and protector, to honor me with your friendship, your respect, and your loyalty from now on?"

For a moment, Kian was afraid Andrew would come back with something snarky. But his brother-in-law gave the ceremony its due respect and answered with a solemn "I do."

"Does anyone have any objections to Andrew becoming my protégé?"

When no one did, Kian raised his wine glass. "As everyone here agrees it's a good match, let's seal it with a toast."

After the cheers quieted down, Kian pulled Andrew into a bro hug, holding on tight until Syssi pulled her brother away for a quick embrace, then transferred him into Nathalie's waiting arms.

Damn. It had all sounded good and logical when he'd been convincing Andrew, but now, watching the emotional display, Kian's gut started roiling with worry again.

He had to ensure Andrew's survival, and the only way he could guarantee it was with the help of Annani's blood.

Except, his mother was all the way up in Alaska, and going there and back to collect an ampule of her life-giving blood would take most of tomorrow. He would have to postpone Andrew's initiation until he had the means to keep the guy alive.

Trouble was, Kian couldn't tell anyone why he needed the extra day. Coming up with a convincing excuse that would satisfy the others was easy. The problem was Andrew—the human lie detector.

As Kian saw it, there were two ways to go about it. He could call or text Andrew with the excuse, because the guy wasn't as good at detecting lies when he wasn't facing the liar. Or, he could use Shai to deliver the news, with the caveat that Shai and everyone else would believe the lie.

Yeah, that was how he needed to play it: Invent some emergency meeting with his mother—perhaps a summoning to discuss the mission no one had told her about. That was actually an excellent excuse. No one would question his need to obey Annani's summons. And whoever told Andrew would not be lying because they would believe Kian's lie.

Perfect.

There was one thing that bothered him about this plan, though. He would also have to lie to Syssi.

36

KIAN

"Shai, please email me today's agenda. I'm going to work on the plane ride." Kian stuffed the pile of files Shai had left on his desk into an old briefcase that he hadn't used in at least twenty years.

"I don't get why you're going up there. A phone call or even a video conference would have achieved the same objective without all the wasted time."

Kian pinned him with one of his intimidating stares. "You know Annani. She is furious. Showing up in person at her place, I may have a chance of her listening to my excuses. She's been after me to come visit her for a long time."

With an exaggerated eye roll, Shai handed him another file. Apparently, Kian's intimidating looks were not as effective as he hoped. Either that or Shai had developed an immunity. "Here, you wanted to go over the profitability analysis on the Marriott."

"Thank you." Kian added the folder to the others and closed his briefcase by pushing hard on the top. Hopefully, the thing was sturdy enough not to burst open.

The Marriott group was selling the Hawaiian hotel complex because the property was underperforming, but Kian believed it could be turned around. Except, he would need to see what the professionals had to say before making an offer. Most of the time the accountants and analysts confirmed his gut feeling, Kian had a knack for seeing potential where others did not, but even if they agreed with every one of his hunches, he would still keep asking their advice. A smart man should always seek the counsel of experts before making big decisions.

It was the first file he pulled out on the way to the airstrip, and by the time Okidu parked the limo next to Annani's private jet, he'd finished reading it from cover to cover.

Kian closed his briefcase, texted Shai the broad terms of the offer he was willing to make on the property, and then boarded the plane.

"Good morning, Oridu," he greeted Annani's butler who was piloting her jet.

To get to her place, Kian had no choice but to use one of Annani's pilots. No one aside from them knew exactly where in Alaska her hidden compound was. Implementing this safety precaution had been his own idea, and it was a good one, but it meant that there could be no surprise visits to Annani. Kian had called his mother last night, and she'd sent the jet to pick him up.

Oridu bowed. "Good morning, master. May I offer you breakfast before we take off?"

"No, thank you, I've already eaten." Kian sat in one of the two reclining chairs and pressed the release mechanism on the retracting table top. Pulling the stack of files out of his briefcase, he placed them on one side, his laptop went in the middle, and a yellow pad and pen went on its other side.

A perfectly adequate setup for a productive workday.

Between phone call appointments, emails, and going through five of the nine reports, Kian had barely felt the hours fly by.

"We are landing, master. Would you be so kind as to fasten your seatbelt?"

"How soon?" Kian asked as he returned everything to the briefcase and clicked it closed. He pushed the table back into its compartment and buckled up.

"Fifteen minutes, master."

Once the plane touched down, he pulled out his phone and texted Syssi. *Just landed.*

She'd made him promise to let her know as soon as he landed that he'd arrived safely.

The plane continued its forward momentum, sliding on its skis almost up to the hatch leading inside the dome. The hatch opened, and a pushback tractor emerged, hooked a tow-bar to the plane and got it inside.

When the hatch closed, Oridu lowered the stairs and Kian got out, half expecting his mother to be waiting for him in the hangar.

Puffing out a breath, he watched it fog in the freezing air and wondered why the hell no one thought to keep the place warm. People were being shuffled in and out of the dome on a daily basis. There was no need for them to freeze while getting on and off. In addition to the small jet he'd arrived on, the hangar housed two medium-sized passenger planes, one cargo plane, and another executive jet. The small group of immortals who called this dome their home didn't lack transportation options. Was it too much to ask for heating as well?

He needed to have a talk with whoever his mother had put in charge of this.

"This way, master." Oridu bowed again and waved his hand toward the double sets of sliding glass doors separating the cold hangar from the warm interior.

His mother wasn't there either.

Damn, she was probably waiting for him in her 'reception' room—the one reserved for formal audiences with clan members that needed to be reprimanded.

Now, it seemed that his turn had come. So be it. Kian was prepared to take his mother's wrath, but he hoped no one saw him on his walk of shame.

The Fates showed him mercy.

He hadn't encountered a single person, and Oridu led him directly to his mother's private quarters instead of her reception room.

This was definitely good news. If his mother was receiving him in her living room, it meant that she wasn't as furious as he'd expected her to be.

Oridu knocked twice and pushed the door open. "The Clan Mother is expecting you, master." He bowed, letting Kian enter ahead of him, then backed away and closed the door behind him.

Kian scanned the room in search of his mother. Where was she?

"Mother?"

"Over here!" A slender arm waved him over from behind the tall back of an armchair facing the outside.

With a muffled sigh, Kian lowered his briefcase to the floor and headed toward Annani. There was some groveling in his near future, and he wasn't looking forward to it.

Stepping around the throne-like armchair, Kian went down to his knees in front of Annani, took her hand and kissed it.

A string of gentle laughter left her lips as she patted his head. "You were always so cute when you were apologizing."

She must've remembered it wrong. He'd never been 'cute,' and he hardly ever apologized.

"I didn't come to apologize. I came to explain and to ask for a favor."

Her eyes sparkled. "What kind of favor?"

"You don't want me to explain first?"

Tilting her head to the side, she shrugged, a mass of her long, fiery curls spilling over her delicate shoulders. Annani seemed so fragile, and even though Kian knew better, he couldn't help the fierce protectiveness he always felt toward his tiny mother. It was impossible to reconcile the exterior of a young, blindingly beautiful girl with an interior that housed the oldest and most powerful creature on earth.

"There is nothing more you need to explain, Kian. Your phone call was enough. Carol was held by Doomers and you had to organize a rescue. Then she rescued herself but she told you there were other females the Doomers were holding captive, and you felt obligated to save them as well. I understand. What I do not understand is why you felt the need to hide it from me. Did you think for a second that I would forbid it? I do not condone unnecessary carnage, but I am all for taking care of our own." She narrowed her eyes at him. "Or did you think I would seize the occasion for an adventure and insist on coming along?"

The possibility had never even crossed his mind. And yet, it would've been so easy to tell her yes, but that would've been a lie, and he wanted to come clean.

"I wish my reasons were as noble as that." He threaded his fingers through his hair, pushing it back and away from his face. "The ugly truth is that I wanted to kill all these Doomers, and I knew you wouldn't allow it."

The smile vanished from her face, and fire blazed in her ancient eyes. "Did you?" There was power in her voice, and he felt it all the way down to his gut.

Kian shook his head. "No. I couldn't bring myself to order their execution. Those who were killed in battle were one thing, but those who were incapacitated but alive, I ordered to be put in stasis. I even said a short prayer for their souls."

Annani's face brightened again, and she smiled one of her I-knew-it smiles. "You are a good man, my son, despite your conviction to the contrary." Her eyes returned to their normal emerald glow.

Kian lifted up and sat in the other armchair. "I don't know, Mother. There is a lot of darkness in me."

She nodded. "Yes, this is true, but there is also light. No one is all dark or all light. It is a question of balance. I know that you have much more light in you than dark."

There was no point in arguing with her about it. As a mother, Annani was biased. Instead, he ended it with a, "Thank you."

Happy with his acquiescence, Annani leaned back in the big chair and put her hands on the armrests. "You still did not tell me about the favor you require."

There was no point in dancing around the issue, and Kian told her the simple facts. "Andrew, Syssi's brother, is going to attempt the transition. He is forty years old and I fear for him. Syssi will never recover if he doesn't survive it. I came to ask you for an ampule of your blood."

Annani lifted a brow and pursed her lips.

Damn, she was going to refuse. It had been bold of him to ask, but Annani had a big heart and he had hoped that she would agree.

"Kian, you surprise me. I would expect a man of your position and mantle of responsibility to think things through more thoroughly."

Fuck, he'd never expected her to say no. What the hell was he going to do now?

He was going to beg, that's what. Kian would never plead for himself, but for Andrew he would.

"Please, Mother, you have nothing to fear. I'll administer the shot myself, and no one will know—the same way as we did it with Syssi. Would you please reconsider?"

When Annani regarded him with a haughty expression, Kian's desperation morphed into anger, but before he had a chance to respond she lifted a small palm to shush him.

"You thought I was about to refuse saving the life of the brother of your mate? My own family? Shame on you, Kian." She puffed out a breath.

"What I was trying to say before you interrupted me, was that it is too risky to transport an ampule of my blood, even in that specially designed medical container, and not administer it directly while it has its full potency. What if the thing that provides miraculous healing dies when my blood is too long out of my veins? You would take the chance? And then it would be too late to do anything about it? The long and the short of it is that I am coming with you." She folded her arms across her chest.

In a blur, Kian was back on his knees in front of Annani. "Thank you. I'm so sorry I doubted you. Would you forgive me?"

"I will ponder it on the way to your keep."

37

NATHALIE

*Y*esterday, when Shai had called to let Andrew know Kian would be available only the following day, Nathalie had felt as if she'd been given a gift, a reprieve. One more day to get ready. Not that she felt ready now.

Even if given months of preparation, she wouldn't have been ready for Andrew putting his life in jeopardy. His survival was her biggest worry but it wasn't the only one. What if the transition changed him? What if he emerged on the other side a different man?

Would he still love her?

All that talk about fated mates worried her. As a human, Andrew believed she was his one; as an immortal, he might feel differently.

She'd been so distraught that Andrew had taken an extra day off work to be with her, and they had spent all of yesterday and today together.

Nathalie had wanted this time to be perfect, trying to fake it and put on a brave face, but she hadn't been strong enough. Desperately clinging to Andrew, touching him and holding him constantly, she hadn't been fooling anyone. Even her father had noticed, asking what was wrong.

Now the dreaded moment had arrived.

Standing next to the sparring mat, Nathalie resented the wide, happy grins on the faces of the clan members who'd come to witness the ceremony.

Nathalie couldn't understand their optimism. She felt so faint she was swaying on her feet.

The only other exception was Syssi, who was trying to hide her anxiety and put a smile on her face for Nathalie's sake. She wrapped her arm around Nathalie's shoulders and whispered into her ear, "It's going to be okay. You'll see. I had a premonition."

So why the hell had her voice quivered? What wasn't Syssi telling her?

Even with Syssi's arm around her, Nathalie felt so alone she wished for Mark to pop into her head. Hell, she would've welcomed Tut. Except, it seemed Tut was gone for good. It had been weeks since the last time he had spoken to her.

Mark! Can you hear me?

When there was no answer, Nathalie tried his other name.

Sage?

Nothing.

She was grateful when Anandur brought two chairs and pushed her into one. Next to her, Syssi plopped onto the other chair. They were the only ones seated. The Guardians all stood around the mat, as did the doctor and another woman Nathalie didn't know—a stern matron type that looked a little like Nathalie's old school librarian.

They were all waiting for Kian to show up.

Nathalie didn't know Andrew's brother-in-law well, but he didn't strike her like a tardy kind of guy. There must've been a good reason for why he wasn't there yet, and Nathalie prayed that whatever it was, it would keep him from getting to the gym altogether.

Another day of grace would be a blessing.

Her eyes trained on Andrew as she willed him to look her way, seeking the connection, desperate to hold on to it for as long as she could.

Except he was watching the door, waiting for Kian, probably waging war with his own doubts.

Suddenly, she saw him straighten up, his eyes growing wide. The others followed his gaze, turning toward the gym doors behind her.

As silence fell over the big room, Nathalie shifted in her chair and cranked her neck around to glance at what or who everyone was gaping at.

A gasp escaped her throat.

Kian and Amanda walked in with a petite girl between them. Except, this was no girl. Nathalie didn't need anyone to tell her who she was.

The power emanating from the Goddess was a physical presence, and it swept through the gymnasium in a wave, engulfing everyone in it and binding them to her.

She was blindingly beautiful, and her skin glowed like one of those glow-in-the-dark toys, except softer.

The Goddess glided up to Andrew who stood glued to the spot, looking stunned, and took his hands in her own tiny ones. "Andrew, my dear boy." The beautiful voice coming out of that small ribcage rung like church bells throughout the big room. "I would not miss your transition for anything. I came to give you my blessing."

A surprised murmur rose among the clan members. Apparently, the Goddess didn't make an appearance often.

"May your transition into immortality be blessed by the Fates and run its course smoothly and without undue discomfort." She stretched on her tiptoes and kissed him on both cheeks.

Andrew finally found his voice. "Thank you, Clan Mother, I'm deeply moved and honored that you came to witness my initiation ceremony."

She patted his arm indulgently, which looked kind of ridiculous since the Goddess looked like she was half Andrew's age. Not if anyone looked closer, though. Her eyes shone with ancient wisdom.

Annani turned toward the audience and clapped her hands. "Let the ceremony begin."

When Anandur brought another chair and put it down on Nathalie's other side, she stopped breathing. The Goddess was gliding her way, and the chair was no doubt for her.

Nathalie was going to die from... well, everything.

It was just too much.

As she took her seat, Annani smiled and leaned sideways to plant a kiss on Nathalie's cheek. "Welcome, child. I understand that you are next."

Nathalie wanted to open her mouth and say something, but nothing came out.

The Goddess laughed, and it was the most beautiful sound Nathalie had ever heard. "I do not bite, you know. Not girls, that is." She winked. "You are safe with me."

Had the Goddess just told a joke?

Syssi laughed, so yeah, apparently she had. How could Andrew's sister act so comfortable with the Goddess sitting no more than three feet away?

But wait, Annani was Syssi's mother-in-law. Oh, God. That must've been tough to handle. She hoped the two got along, otherwise Syssi was going straight to hell.

A goddess for a mother-in-law...

Nathalie shook her head. She'd been dreading meeting Andrew's mother because the woman was a doctor while Nathalie hadn't even finished college. Now she was grateful his mother was just an ordinary human.

Nathalie cast Syssi a sidelong glance.

Syssi smiled and squeezed her hand. "This is wonderful. Now I know for sure that everything is going to be alright. Annani said a blessing for me when I was transitioning, and from that moment on everything went well."

Annani nodded. "Indeed." She lifted her palm. "Now, girls, hush and watch."

Kian joined Andrew on the mat and the two embraced, clapped each other on the back, then assumed fighting stances.

Reassured by the Goddess's presence, Nathalie's anxiety ebbed. Someone as powerful as Annani could probably do anything, and she cared enough about Andrew to come all the way from wherever she lived to witness his ceremony.

The guys were still circling each other as if not sure how to go about this. Kian was taller, and as an immortal obviously stronger, but Andrew was a little stockier, sturdier. She knew both had extensive combat training, but Kian had been at it for much longer than Andrew. On the other hand, Andrew had been trained in new fighting styles, which might give him a small edge.

Suddenly, Andrew lunged at Kian, grabbed him by the middle, and toppled him to the mat.

Yay for Andrew! She cheered inside her head.

It took Kian only a split second to shake Andrew off, and their roles reversed, with Kian pinning Andrew to the mat. Andrew struggled, his grunts filling the otherwise silent gym and echoing from the walls, but Kian held on tight. Quite effortlessly.

Her heart sank for Andrew. They both had known he was going to lose, there was no question about it, but he'd hoped to last a little longer against Kian.

Annani startled her, gripping her hand and squeezing. "Brace yourself, child," she whispered and squeezed again.

A moment later, Kian opened his mouth, and Nathalie gasped, Annani's warning suddenly making sense. The handsome guy she had gotten to know and even like, had just turned into a monster; lips pulled back, two wicked looking fangs gleaming white and dripping venom, and his eyes... the glow she'd glimpsed at the restaurant had been nothing compared to how otherworldly and terrifying they looked now.

Kian hissed, and quick like a snake bit down, sinking his fangs into Andrew's neck. Holding Andrew's head he kept them imbedded, pumping his life- or death-giving venom into her man.

Annani squeezed harder. Syssi grasped Nathalie's other hand and squeezed it too.

Andrew stopped struggling, and when a few moments later Kian retracted his fangs and licked the puncture wounds closed, Syssi and Annani let go of her hands.

Syssi sighed and slumped in her chair. Her relieved expression must've meant that Andrew was going to be okay.

"Is it over?" Nathalie asked.

"Yes. And the good news is that Kian managed not to hurt Andrew. He'll have no bruises."

"Should I go to him?"

Syssi shook her head. "In a few minutes he is going to wake up, and because he is not bruised, he won't need aftercare. Knowing Andrew, he would prefer to walk out of here on his own."

Syssi was right.

While Nathalie had been worried sick about the transition, all Andrew could think about was losing with dignity to Kian. It had bothered him to no end that the result of this fight was inevitable.

No one talked as they waited for Andrew to open his eyes. Kian was crouching next to him, watching his face intently.

Thank God, the guy's fangs had shrunk back to their normal size and he no longer looked like a monster. Nathalie shivered as she imagined how painful being bitten by those fangs must've been.

How could immortal women find this pleasurable?

She had no idea. It was damn scary and not at all sexy. Shit, she hadn't considered it before, but when Andrew transitioned, she was going to be on the receiving end of this. He was going to bite her not only to facilitate her change, but as an integral part of sex.

Gross.

Except, she would need to learn to tolerate it. Fangs or no fangs, she was going to stick with Andrew. They'd work something out.

Finally, Andrew opened his eyes, and as Kian helped him into a sitting position, everyone started clapping, and some of the guys started shouting cheers.

Nathalie looked at Syssi for guidance about what to do next. Following her example, she pushed to her feet and joined the applause.

With Kian's help, Andrew got up, the two embraced once more, and then

Andrew was passed from Guardian to Guardian until Bhathian got him and pushed the others away.

"Move, you mongrels, let the man go to his woman. Nathalie has been waiting long enough."

She mouthed thank you to her father and got into a three-way embrace between him and Andrew.

"How are you feeling?" Nathalie asked.

Andrew's eyes were a little unfocused as he gave her a lopsided grin. "A little woozy, like after drinking a lot, sans the headache."

"You ready to go home?"

"Oh yeah, take me home, baby." He winked with a leer.

Okay, he was drunk, or high. Sober, Andrew would've never behaved like this in front of her father.

She wrapped her arm around Andrew's middle and started leading him outside when Kian stopped them.

"I think he should stay in the keep tonight. I want Bridget to keep an eye on him."

Syssi came over and hugged her brother. "Why don't you both stay here overnight?"

Andrew made a face. "I want to go home."

If her man wanted to go home she was taking him home. "It's okay, Kian. If he feels even a little funny, I'll call you right away."

"Hold on. I'm going to ask Bridget. If she agrees to let Andrew go, then it's fine with me."

As Kian left to find the doctor, Nathalie steered Andrew toward the exit, but they were stopped every couple of feet by another person wishing to congratulate Andrew.

Kian returned before they made it anywhere near the exit. "Bridget needs to take more blood samples. After that you can go home."

Reluctantly, they turned around and Nathalie helped Andrew get into a chair. Bridget was quick with her needles and her ampules. "All done." She taped the little puncture she'd made, then looked up at Nathalie. "Call me or Kian the moment he starts feeling warm. Syssi's transition started with a fever."

38

ANDREW

Andrew woke up feeling great. No back pains, no leg cramps. He stretched, surprised that his feet didn't bump against the footboard. Had Nathalie taken him to his house last night? He cracked one eye open and was greeted by the familiar painting of a sunset that hung across from Nathalie's bed.

What the hell? Had he shrunk overnight?

No one had told him that the venom could have such a side effect.

Don't be ridiculous.

Over a lifespan, a person might get shorter because of the atrophy of disks between the vertebrae. But no one shrunk over the course of one night.

Once the morning brain fog dissipated, Andrew found the explanation was much simpler; the footboard was gone. Another glance revealed that the headboard was gone as well. Damn, now it became obvious why he felt so well rested; the mattress was new and it was bigger.

Sometime after they had left yesterday afternoon and before they had come back last night, Nathalie had gotten rid of her old bed, replacing it with a larger mattress and a box spring but forgoing a frame so it would still fit into her small room.

Last night, Andrew must've been too dopey to notice.

What time was it anyway?

And where was his sweet Nathalie?

As he flung his legs over the side of the mattress and pushed to his feet, he didn't feel any different. Walking to the bathroom, he paid attention to how his body felt, but again could detect no new sensations aside from the lack of back pain.

He peed for what seemed like ten minutes straight, but that too was nothing unusual for him in the morning. Having showered last night before getting in bed, his morning routine was down to brushing his teeth and shaving.

When he got out, Nathalie was leaning against the wall next to the bathroom.

"How are you feeling?" She reached for him, not to kiss him, regrettably, but to put her palm on his forehead.

"I'm feeling great." He snaked his arms around her and grabbed her ass, bringing her flush against his body. Her lips were so wonderfully soft as he pressed on them with a gentle kiss.

Nathalie palmed his smooth cheek, caressing it lightly, and he was glad he'd shaved. "Anything feel different?" she asked.

"Nope. Except my backache is gone. Thank you for the bed." He lifted her up and stepped back into her bedroom, closing the door with his foot. "I need to check it out with you in it."

Nathalie let out a little squeak as Andrew dropped her the last couple of inches, then hopped on top of her.

"Very comfortable," he teased, resting his cheek on her breast. "And so soft."

With a giggle, she smoothed her hand over his hair. "I see a bigger bed was not needed after all. Maybe I should send it back."

He lifted his head. "Don't you dare. I love it. When did you do it? And how?"

"You can thank Jackson and Vlad. I gave Vlad money and told him where to go to buy it. He borrowed a truck, loaded the new mattress, and together with Jackson they muscled the old bed out and the new mattress in."

"These guys are worth their weight in gold." Andrew chuckled. "Especially Vlad. The guy probably weighs a hundred pounds, boots included."

Nathalie's lips twitched, but she refused to smile. "I'm sure he weighs more than that. I love those boys. They feel like family to me, not employees. I know I can count on them for whatever, and they know they can count on me."

"Soon the whole clan is going to be your family."

"That's a bit overwhelming to think about. It's a great feeling, though, to finally have a family. It has been just my father and me for such a long time. I felt so alone." She whispered the last sentence.

Damn, now she was sad. He had to change the subject quick. "I don't know how Jackson and Vlad managed to get it in here. The stairwell is so narrow."

"I took measurements before I chose the mattress. I knew there was no space left for a frame and the only way a queen size would fit was if it was pushed all the way against the wall. Even the nightstand had to go."

He hadn't noticed it before, but instead of the three-drawer cabinet, a tiny round stool served as the new nightstand.

Andrew wondered what Nathalie had done with the lingerie she'd kept in there. There was no room in her small closet for any additional items. That was one of the reasons he went home every morning to shower and change before work. There was nowhere to put any of his clothes except for a pair or two of underwear and socks.

They should really move into his house or even the keep. Now that he was about to become an immortal, and Nathalie soon thereafter, there was no reason why they couldn't.

He wasn't going to talk about it now, though, not after she'd gone to all that trouble to make him comfortable. Which reminded him that while he was doing all this thinking, he was squashing Nathalie under his weight. With a sigh, he rolled off her and lay on his back.

Nathalie pulled the comforter up and cuddled up to him, resting her head on his pectoral. Her hand snaked under the lapel of his robe and she started playing with his chest hair. "All this extra space and I'm still crowding you." She chuckled.

Andrew took hold of her heavy braid and brought it forward, putting it on his stomach. "You're not. I love having you close to me like this. If I were wearing pants, I could tie your hair to a belt loop and make sure you don't go anywhere."

A smile tugged at the corners of her lips. "Kinky."

Was it? Nah, just him being a possessive bastard. Fortunately, or unfortunately, his tastes in sex were of the vanilla variety. Unless a booty obsession counted as kinky. Then yes, sign him up. Not just any booty, though, Nathalie's.

He palmed a cheek and kneaded. "Do you need to get back to work? Or can you spare a few minutes?"

Nathalie's hand abandoned his chest and traveled south, turning his cock from semi hard to rock even before she touched it.

"I definitely have time for this. I've been horny ever since last night. Watching you fight Kian was so hot. You were so sexy. My warrior." She collected the bead of pre-cum that had formed on his tip, lubricating her up and down strokes.

Andrew snorted. "Piss-poor warrior. I lost before it even began. I'm surprised Kian managed to get aggressive enough to produce venom." It had been quite humiliating, the ease with which Kian had had him subdued.

"Oh, I don't know. You got him down to the mat first. I thought it was very impressive."

Her hand kept stroking, and his brain was losing the ability to think about anything other than getting her naked and pushing inside her.

"Let's get this off you." He tugged the hem of her shirt up, and she did the rest, tossing it to the floor.

Andrew unclasped her bra and latched onto a nipple before she even shrugged the thing off, his hand going inside her pants straight to her slick core.

As he put a finger in her, Nathalie gasped, pausing in the middle of pushing her pants down and letting her hands fall by her sides.

"Oh, God, Andrew, I love it when you're like that," she breathed.

"Like what?" He added another finger.

Nathalie licked her lips. "Impatient, aggressive, going all alpha on me."

Andrew chuckled. "You read too many of those shifter romance novels. I'm not an alpha, or a beta, or any such nonsense. I'm a man, not an animal."

He growled as he took her other nipple between his lips and pretended to chew on it.

Nathalie giggled. "Are you sure about it?"

"Grrr…" he growled again, lifting his head and letting his tongue loll from the corner of his mouth.

"You dog," she teased.

That gave him an idea.

Nathalie on all fours, her gorgeous, heart-shaped ass up in the air and him going at her from behind—doggie style.

Oh, yeah. That was exactly what he wanted.

Andrew reared back to his knees and discarded his robe. Nathalie looked disappointed to lose his thrusting digits, but not for long. He flipped her over, pulled her ass up, her pants down, and pushed inside her all the way in until his balls slapped against her butt.

Holding on to a pillow, Nathalie stifled a moan and lifted her ass higher to meet his thrusts.

Sexy Nathalie loved doggie style, and she'd just admitted that she loved him impatient and aggressive.

Andrew was going to give her exactly what she wanted.

Holding on to her hips, he started with a few slow thrusts, letting her stretch to accommodate his intrusion, then pounded into her without holding anything back.

With no bed frame to bang against the wall—Andrew biting his lips hard enough to draw blood and Nathalie drowning her moans inside the pillow—the smacking of his balls against her sweet, upturned ass were the only sounds in the room.

Dimly, Andrew was aware that he was being selfish, that gripping Nathalie like that would bruise her skin, and that the punishing force and tempo of his thrusts wasn't as fun for her as it was for him.

When she gasped and convulsed, her powerful climax took him by surprise, her spasming inner muscles squeezing so tight that he had no choice but to follow in an explosive rush. Smashing his mouth on her shoulder, he kissed and sucked on her skin to keep himself from biting down. With no fangs and no healing venom, he would've only brought her pain.

But hell, he craved it.

39

ANANDUR

"Good to hear you're feeling okay. Call me if there is any change. I mean it, Andrew. The smallest, most insignificant thing and you haul your ass over here. " Kian clicked off the call and put his phone down on the desk.

Kian's expression was severe on good days; now the added lines on his forehead made it thunderous. He was worried, and so was Anandur. Syssi's transition was still fresh in his mind. It had been a fucking nightmare.

Anandur scratched at his beard. "I gather that Andrew is feeling fine."

Kian's fingers started thrumming a beat on the surface of his desk. "Yeah, but so did Syssi at the beginning."

"Michael's went smoothly."

Kian sighed. "He is also half Andrew's age. I don't think I'll be getting any sleep until this is over."

He wasn't the only one. Anandur's gut was sending him distress messages ever since Andrew had announced his intent.

"How is Syssi doing? She must be going crazy."

As always, with the mention of his wife, Kian's expression softened. Well, not always. Not if the bastard misconstrued something as disrespectful towards her.

"She is worried, but surprisingly she is taking it better than me. She puts a lot of faith in her premonitions about Andrew."

"Maybe you should too."

"You know me. I'm an old skeptic. It is what it is. What did you want to talk to me about?"

Anandur was happy to change subjects. "Lana. She is willing to spill in exchange for protection for her and the rest of the crew. New names, new identification, and most importantly, American citizenship. Money is optional, but I promised her we will give them something to tide them over until they can get jobs and support themselves."

Kian snorted. "We can add them to the Hawaii group. They can manage the hotel's dinner cruises."

Anandur's eyes brightened. "This is perfect. It's their ultimate dream come true. Geneva is going to love it."

Kian's fingers increased their tempo. Had he been joking about it?

Fuck! Probably.

"I don't know if you're serious or not."

"Oh, I'm serious. But all I can give them are fake identification cards. I can't give them a real American citizenship, you know that."

Kian couldn't, but perhaps Anandur could. He wasn't above using a thrall here and there to get what he needed.

"But do I have the okay to offer them all the rest? Including the dinner cruiser in Hawaii?"

"It would depend on the information they provide. If they give us enough to catch Alex and charge him with human trafficking, then yes."

An offer this good would be too tempting for them to refuse, even without the coveted citizenship.

"I'll go talk to Lana and get back to you. But I know they'll take it. You're offering them all they've ever wanted."

As soon as he was out of Kian's office, Anandur texted Lana, but the message didn't go through. Perhaps she'd turned her phone off because Alex was onboard. Which would make it tricky to talk to her. He would have to send someone with a note to her, telling her to get in touch with him.

The old truck he'd been using for his undercover work was still parked next to his baby, and Anandur smoothed his hand over the Thunderbird's flank before getting inside the clunker.

This would probably be his last day driving the thing, and he couldn't say that he would be sorry to part with it.

He parked outside the marina, stuck a baseball cap on top of his mop and a pair of sunglasses on top of his nose, and headed toward the *Anna*. Not that Alex would have trouble recognizing him behind the impromptu disguise, if he saw him. With Anandur's uncommon height and coloring, it wasn't as if he could easily get mistaken for someone else.

Keeping his nose down, Anandur walked over to the old boat Lana had been looking after while its owners had been away. Two boats down from it there was a spot where he could get an unobstructed glimpse at Alex's yacht.

Damn, it wasn't there.

Anandur's gut clenched with worry. Lana would've left him a message if they were heading out. Something was up. Perhaps the real sleuths could tell him what was going on.

Anandur dialed the number and after a few rings the guy answered. "Melvin here, what can I do for you?"

"What's going on? When did the boat leave?"

There was a moment of silence. "How the hell should I know? Your boss told us to pack it."

Fuck. Alex was on to them.

"When?"

"Two days ago, and I'm still waiting for my final payment and the bonus he promised us."

"Did he call you? Or did he show up in person?"

"Was right here. Walked up to the van and shook hands with me. Told me it was all a big misunderstanding and that he'll settle the bill and add a twenty percent bonus."

"And it didn't seem odd to you that he approached you like that? How did you know it was him? It could've been anyone."

"I'm not some bloody rookie, I asked for the case number. He recited the whole thing."

Yeah, right. Alex had either pulled it right from the guy's head or just thralled him to believe that he had. Either way it wasn't the guy's fault.

"I'll talk to you later." Anandur hung up and dialed Kian.

"What's up?"

"Alex is on to us and the *Anna* together with her Russian crew is gone. He approached the private eye, pretending to be you and told him to go home. It was two days ago."

"Fuck." Anandur heard something hit the wall. "We've been so busy with everything else that I didn't even think to check with them. I'll try to get a satellite location on him. In the meantime, I'm sending Guardians to his club and to his estate."

Anandur would bet his left nut that Alex wouldn't be in either of those places. The guy had realized he was under investigation and hightailed it out of town to who knew where.

"You should put a freeze on his clan account. Not that it would do much good given the money he is making off his trade, but it would make me and you feel better."

"I'll have Shai do it right away." Kian clicked off.

Fuck, fuck, fuck. Why hadn't he put things in motion sooner? Who knew what Alex had done to the crew, or was going to do? Anandur's only consolation was that the girls were tough as nails and would put up a fight. The seven of them together might have a chance against one guy, even an immortal one. If they got to him before he thralled the hell out of them, that is. Then again, the women were naturally suspicious and even more so lately. It would be difficult for Alex to thrall someone who was actively resisting.

Did Alex possess a strong thralling ability? Anandur had no idea, but he hoped the scumbag didn't. That would give Lana and her friends a chance.

He walked over to the old yacht that had served as Lana's and his love nest for a while. One of the owners was sitting outside on a folding chair, reading the *Los Angeles Times*. Anandur put on a charming smile. "Hey, dude."

The guy lifted his head. "Lana's guy. How can I help you?"

"I've been away for a couple of days and now I see that the *Anna* is gone. Any idea where? And when they are coming back?"

The guy shook his head. "Sorry. I wasn't here when they left."

"When you see Lana, could you tell her I was looking for her?"

"Sure will."

"Thank you. Tell her to call me, would you?"

Fat chance of that, but he wasn't going to leave any stone unturned.

The guy nodded and went back to reading his newspaper.

When Anandur got back to the keep, he headed straight to Kian's office. Given the grim look on his face, the news wasn't good.

Anandur flopped into a chair across from Kian's desk. "Lay it on me."

"Alex basically went poof. His club was sold a week ago and is under new management, and his estate wasn't his at all. It was leased, and apparently he hasn't been making payments for the last couple of months. It seems our boy was planning his exit even before we started our investigation."

"What about the satellite?"

"Still waiting. But that's a long shot. My only hope is that he will stop to refuel somewhere. We are lucky to have someone like Turner we can turn to for help. He has snitches everywhere and they'll be looking for the boat."

Good. That gave Anandur hope. At this point he didn't care about catching Alex. Bringing one scumbag to justice would only mean another one taking advantage of the vacancy. Nothing in the grand scheme of things would change.

His only concern was for the fate of the boat's crew.

40

NATHALIE

"Yeah, no, still nothing." Andrew held the phone to his ear. "Yeah, I will. No worries, Kian."

It was the third day after the ceremony and still nothing. Kian had been calling every day at least twice a day, despite Syssi's hourly update texts.

Bhathian had called twice.

The good part was that Andrew was still off work, so they'd been spending their days together, having fun. The bad news was that he was going to run out of his vacation days and there would be none left when the transition finally began.

On one hand, Nathalie was glad nothing was happening; on the other, she hated the prolonged torture of uncertainty, and her fears being dragged out.

Andrew pretended he wasn't worried, but she knew he was.

"Anyone hungry?" she asked.

They'd taken her father to the park for a walk, and the plan was to go grab something to eat and then head to the movies. Provided Papi was up to it. Lately, he'd been tiring pretty quickly, and they had limited their walks to no more than fifteen-minute stretches at a snail's pace.

"I could use a bite." Papi perked up. One thing that hadn't been affected by his disease was his appetite. A very encouraging sign since the loss of interest in food usually signaled that the end was near.

She wrapped her arm around his shoulders. "What would you like?"

He didn't hesitate. "Chinese."

"Chinese it is," Andrew said.

Taking Papi for Chinese, especially an all-you-can-eat buffet, wasn't the best idea, and she should've said something, but her mind had been busy with other things.

Like, what would she do when Andrew's symptoms started to show? Would she even know what to look for? Syssi had said she had flu-like symptoms, but Bridget had said that Andrew might react differently.

What if Andrew needed a repeat round with Kian?

Shit, she couldn't deal with another tournament.

Papi stuffed himself until he could barely breathe and they had to take him back. The movie would either have to wait for some other day, or they could leave Fernando to nap at home and go out by themselves.

He fell asleep as soon as Andrew turned on the ignition.

"Jackson is bringing another guy over," she said as Andrew eased into traffic.

"Who is it? Do I know him?'

"You may. According to Jackson, I've met Gordon a couple of times, but with the constant parade of his many friends coming and going, I don't remember who is who."

Andrew tapped the wheel with his finger. "You have to admit that the kid is good for business."

"Jackson? He is good period. I offer a prayer of gratitude every morning for him. If we ever have a son, I hope he'll turn out like Jackson."

Andrew snorted.

"What? Is there something I should know about him?"

Andrew looked like he was about to say something, but then he shook his head. "No, you're right. I would be very proud if my daughter or son turned out like Jackson. Entrepreneurship is probably the most important forward driving force of humankind, or immortal kind. That's one of the reasons I have such huge respect for you."

At the compliment, Nathalie felt her cheeks warming.

Oh, the sweet man. What a nice thing to say. "I wouldn't call my little bakery-café an entrepreneurial achievement."

Andrew turned his head towards her, his gaze intense. "Modesty is not always a virtue, Nathalie. Pride in your hard work and accomplishments is good. It's motivating."

"Whatever you say." She pointed ahead. "Just look at the road and not at me. We are not immortal yet, and neither is Papi."

Andrew did as she said, but he wasn't done with her. "I want to hear you say it."

"What?"

"That you are proud of all you have accomplished."

Stubborn man.

There wasn't anything special about what she did. Like most people, she worked hard to pay the bills and take care of her family. There was nothing heroic about it.

"Okay. So I'm proud that I managed to keep a roof over my dad's head and pay the bills. Happy?"

"Not even close. How about the care you provide him with? How many children do you think would have dedicated their lives to the care of an ailing parent?"

"More than you think. There are everyday, unsung heroes all around you, Andrew, and they don't expect any medals for their hard work."

That shut him up, but not for long.

"I agree. No one is going to give them medals for their hard work and sacrifices, but at least they should allow themselves to feel proud."

Nathalie chuckled. "Why are we fighting?"

"We are not fighting."

"Aha."

Andrew sighed. "It must be the stress. I want this thing over and done with. It drives me crazy that nothing is happening, and anticipating symptoms starting at any moment drives me even crazier. Especially since I have no idea what the symptoms might be. For all I know, it can start with an itch in my big toe."

"Not the pinky?"

"I'm serious."

She sighed. "I know, baby."

As much as she hated to even think about it, Andrew had to go for another round or just forget all about it. Trouble was, he would never be happy with the second option because he'd gotten it into his head that he had to make her immortal.

Before that was on the table, he'd been undecided.

Should she try and push him to reconsider?

Nathalie had never expected to get another chance at talking him out of it, but here it was, and if she didn't take it and Andrew died in the process, she would never forgive herself for chickening out. Bringing it up again wouldn't earn her any points with him, that's for sure. But in the grand scheme of things, one more little spat was nothing.

"I know you are going to be mad at me for saying it, but this might be a sign that you need to reconsider. Fate is giving you another chance to back out. And just to make things clear, I'm all for forgetting about immortality and living the life we have."

Andrew sighed and reached for her hand. "I know, sweetheart. You're afraid for me, that's all. But be honest with yourself for a moment. If I was already immortal when you met me, would you think twice about wanting to become immortal as well?"

"Of course not. I would want to share your life, and getting old while you didn't wouldn't have worked."

"Okay, how about if you only met Bhathian, without me, and he arranged for some random male to be your initiator? Would you have refused?"

The answer was easy, she would not have.

Discovering she had an immortal father she hadn't known about, Nathalie would've wanted more time with him regardless of Andrew. And with the strong possibility that her mother was an immortal as well, it was a no brainer. Nathalie had been alone for so long, craving a family, a connection, she would've jumped at the chance of having one in a heartbeat.

"I would have accepted. To get to know Bhathian, to have another chance with my mother once he finds her, to have a big extended family. All of that is worth risking the remainder of my life for. But I can't tolerate the risk of losing you."

He brought her hand to his lips and kissed it. "You won't. Even without

Syssi's foretelling, I know I'm doing the right thing. But now there is something that bothers me."

Nathalie wiped the tears from the corners of her eyes before turning to look at Andrew. "What is it?"

"You would let some random immortal male have sex with you, your first time, and bite you?"

Pretending to ponder, she tapped her lips with her forefinger. "Well, no, of course not."

Andrew cast her a sidelong glance. "Really?"

It was so hard to keep a straight face. "Not just any random immortal. I would've lined them up and chosen the best looking one."

41

ANDREW

Nathalie had only been teasing, he knew that, and yet Andrew couldn't help the sharp spike of jealousy. Even hypothetically, the idea of her choosing one of the immortals to facilitate her transformation was enough to have his mood plummet into the dangerous zone of murderous rage. Because unless he transitioned, the hypothetical would become practical.

What if he was immune? What if he hadn't inherited the immortal genes like Syssi?

It had never crossed his mind that his transition might fail not because his body wouldn't survive the change, but because it was incapable of it. The clan had never tried it with someone his age. Syssi was the oldest Dormant they had ever activated, so they assumed that her difficult transition was what should be expected with older Dormants. They never considered that a Dormant's ability to transition might expire after a certain age.

It was strange how something you weren't even sure you wanted became so crucial and so desperately coveted once you realized you couldn't have it.

Andrew was reminded of what Susanna had once shared with him. For as long as he'd known her, his sparring partner and occasional friend-with-benefits had never wanted to get married or have children. Until the day her doctor had informed her that she couldn't. Susanna had been devastated. At the time, Andrew had believed that her illogical response had to do with infertility making her feel like less of a woman, her body betraying her in some way. Now he realized that it might have been one of the reasons but not the only one. The forever closed door, the irreversibility, that had been a big part if it too. If not the biggest.

There was nothing like walking a mile in someone's shoes to understand them better. The possibility that it was never going to happen for him terrified Andrew.

In small part because he'd already imagined himself as an immortal, living a charmed life with Nathalie by his side. Mostly, though, the panic had to do with the thought of losing her.

He could never accept Nathalie refusing immortality on his account. She might think she didn't want it now, but she would regret it later.

Damn, his hands shook with the need to pull out his phone and call Kian right away to schedule another round.

Patience.

First, he needed to help Nathalie get her father inside.

"Papi, wake up, we are here." She nudged her father's shoulder.

His eyes popped open and he smiled up at her. "I had the nicest dream. I dreamt about you when you were little, playing with your mother. My beautiful girls." He took her hand and let her help him out of the car.

Andrew stayed close in case the old man lost his balance, which happened to him a lot upon waking. Fernando was a heavy guy, and Nathalie might not be able to hold him up.

As soon as Fernando's feet touched the sidewalk, Nathalie wrapped her arms around his thick waist and heaved him up, holding on to him until he was steady.

A few minutes later, they had the guy settled on the couch in the den, watching one of his shows.

"I'm going to call Kian," Andrew told Nathalie.

She wrapped a blanket around her father's legs. "Wait," she asked, tucking the corners under Fernando's thighs.

As they stepped out into the corridor, her palm shot to his forehead. "What's going on, Andrew? Are you experiencing symptoms? I've never seen you looking so anxious."

He snorted. "I wish. I'm calling to schedule another round. And this time I want him to pump me as full of venom as he can without killing me."

Nathalie frowned. "What changed between now and fifteen minutes ago? I thought you wanted to wait a little longer."

"Come with me." Andrew took Nathalie's hand and led her to the bedroom.

Closing the door behind him, he sat on the bed and pulled her onto his lap. He was going to do something he had never done with anyone before—share his fears.

"I'm terrified, Nathalie. What if I'm too old for the transition to even begin? What if I missed my chance? I have to find out. I'll go one more round with Kian, and if this time around it doesn't work either, we'll keep on trying."

"For how long?"

Andrew rubbed his neck. "Until he gives up or I do."

Nathalie cupped his cheeks. "I love you so much." She kissed him softly on the lips. "If this is what you want, I'll be there for you each and every time, cheering you on. But if it doesn't work, then it wasn't meant to be. We will still have each other and our entire mortal lives ahead of us to enjoy, making babies and grandchildren like everyone else."

Andrew closed his eyes. He was being greedy. Already, he had more than most people ever hoped for—an amazing woman who loved him unconditionally, and a supportive, caring family numbering in the hundreds. A whole clan of powerful immortals who considered him one of their own regardless of him transitioning or not.

Immortality was just a cherry on top.

Except, by staying human he was going to lose the first and most important part of his happy equation.

Nathalie had admitted that if it weren't for him, she would've wanted to become immortal. Even though it was tempting to accept her sacrifice, it would be incredibly selfish of him, and he just couldn't stoop so low.

So what were his options?

Let her go? Keep her but convince her to have sex with some random immortal so she could transition?

Damn, those were two really bad choices.

As impossible as it was for him to even think about it, he would rather Nathalie had sex with another guy than let go of her completely. Except, he would have to ask Bridget to put him in an induced coma. That was the only way he could survive this without popping a vein in his brain and dying of an aneurism, or committing suicide by attacking the immortal male before he had a chance to do the honors.

"Penny for your thoughts," Nathalie murmured.

He kissed her forehead. "Nothing good. Just running circles inside my head, thinking of worst case scenarios. I'd better call Kian."

"Do you want me to leave? Give you privacy?"

Andrew tightened his arms around her. "Stay. There is nothing I can't say in front of you."

Nathalie sighed, resting her head on his chest while he pulled his phone out of his pocket and called Kian.

"What's up?" Kian answered before the phone even rang. He must've been on another call.

"Can you talk? I can call later."

"No. I mean yes, I can talk. Please tell me you feel something different."

"No, I don't. We need to go for another round."

"I was afraid of this. Tomorrow?"

"What time?"

"Six."

"I'll be there."

"We'll see. Maybe you'll get lucky and your transition will start tonight."

Andrew chuckled. "Didn't peg you as an optimist."

"You're right. See you tomorrow." Kian terminated the call.

Nathalie snaked a hand under Andrew's T-shirt and began caressing his abs. "What are we going to do in the meantime?"

Sweet, sexy Nathalie.

"Oh, I don't know, play chess?"

She wrapped a few of his chest hairs around her finger. "How about strip poker?"

"Do you have cards?"

"Nope."

"So I guess it would be a game of strip without the poker."
"You got it."
"Woman, I like the way you think."

42

SYSSI

"I can't believe Andrew has to do this again," Amanda said as she and Syssi stepped inside the penthouse's elevator on their way down to the gym. "The only cases where another dose was needed were when the boys were underdeveloped for their age."

Well, that certainly wasn't the case here. Maybe the level of difficulty increased on either side of the spectrum. Syssi wasn't a scientist, but she was starting to think that there was a limited window of time for the transition to happen. Making it difficult for those either too young or too old. Maybe even prohibitive.

God, she hoped it was the first. The thought of Andrew not transitioning at all was just unacceptable.

Kian and Dalhu had gone ahead of them, with Kian murmuring something about getting ready. Syssi had no idea what he could've meant by that. It wasn't as if any preparations were required, and why the hell had he needed Dalhu for that?

She hadn't asked. Kian had been so distraught since Andrew had called asking for another round, she'd figured she'd leave him alone. He didn't look like he wanted to talk about it. Heck, they hadn't even had sex. Not last night and not this morning.

"I know. I'm worried. Mostly because Kian is freaking out. Seriously, I've seen him going through some tough shit, dealing with one crisis after another, and he was always so cool and collected."

Leaning against the mirrored wall, Amanda folded her arms across her chest and frowned. "What do you mean by freaking out? What exactly is he doing?"

Syssi grimaced. "It's more about what he is not doing."

It took Amanda a moment. "Oh, I see. Yeah, that's bad. How long has it been going on?"

Even in this roundabout way, talking with her sister-in-law about her sex life was making Syssi uncomfortable. She looked away, examining the intricate carvings on the elevator's wall paneling. "Not long. Just last night and this morning. I know it doesn't sound like much, but it's unusual for Kian. That's why I'm so worried. Is there something you guys are not telling me? I'd rather know than guess the worst."

Amanda pulled her into a hug. "As I said, it doesn't always work the first time. Two times is not uncommon, three is rare. But it is in no way an indicator of trouble. The boys transition the same way whether they've gotten only one dose or three."

"So why is Kian freaking out?"

Amanda shrugged. "I have no idea. Except—"

"Yeah?"

The elevator doors swished open, and Amanda let go of Syssi. "Maybe he wanted to keep his venom glands rested. You know, like a guy who wants to get his wife pregnant so he abstains for a few days to increase his seed's potency."

Syssi cast Amanda a disgusted sidelong glance. "That's gross, Amanda. A really bad analogy. These are my brother and my husband you're talking about."

Amanda slapped Syssi's back. "Don't be silly. You know what I mean. And that would also explain what he needed Dalhu for. To get him primed before the fight. Andrew is not much of a challenge for Kian, and he might have thought that he didn't get aggressive enough last time to produce the amount and potency of venom required to facilitate the transition."

Syssi had to admit that Amanda's hypothesis made sense. Even if Kian was totally off about this, and it didn't matter at all if he used his venom glands the night before or not, he might've believed it did.

Kian cared about Andrew, a lot, and she had no doubt that his concern for her brother was at the root of his peculiar behavior. He was obsessing about giving it his best shot, and he might have gotten it into his head that refraining from sex was going to help.

When they reached the gym, Syssi took a quick glance around.

Nathalie was sitting on one of the three chairs positioned in front of the mat, biting her nails, her eyes not straying from Andrew. Next to the mat Kian was talking with Andrew and Bhathian. Only a few of the other guardians were present, and Syssi wondered if Kian had purposefully limited the audience this time. She would've found it odd if the others had just decided Andrew's second ceremony wasn't interesting enough.

Surreptitiously, she looked Kian over, checking for bruises, and then did the same with Dalhu. If they had sparred before everyone had arrived, they hadn't gone at each other too hard. There was nothing to indicate either of them had been fighting, other than a slight sheen of sweat on Kian's forehead that might have been the result of something else. Probably stress.

"Poor Nathalie, this must be really hard on her," Amanda whispered in her ear.

"I know. Let's go and cheer her up."

"I don't think it's possible."

Syssi sat next to Nathalie and clasped her hand. "How are you holding up?"

Nathalie turned a pair of wild eyes on her. "I'm not."

"Oh, sweetie." Amanda grabbed the third chair and put it down on Nathalie's other side. "Everything is going to be alright."

Her face pinched in an angry expression, Nathalie pinned Amanda with a hard stare. "How can you say that? Do you have a crystal ball or something?" Her voice quivered on the last word.

Amanda patted her knee. "I don't, but Syssi does. And her foretelling predicted that you and Andrew are going to have a future together. Therefore, he is going to survive his transition and everything is going to be okay."

It was Syssi's turn to get the look. "You did? Tell me about it."

Shit. Amanda and her big mouth. True, the little girl in her vision had looked a lot like Nathalie, but that wasn't a guarantee that Nathalie would indeed be the girl's mother. Maybe there was another dark-haired beauty in Andrew's future. Not likely, but still, Syssi wasn't going to tell her about it. Not exactly, anyway.

"I had a vision of Andrew playing with a child."

Nathalie waited for her to continue. "And?"

"That's it. My impression was that the child was his. Therefore, he has to survive to father it."

"You don't know if the child was ours, though."

Smart girl.

"No."

"What if he got one of his many previous girlfriends pregnant? And he is not aware of having a child? Some women decide to go it on their own without telling the father."

"He still has to survive to play with his child, right?"

That seemed to mollify her. "Right."

When Andrew and Kian got on the mat and shook hands, the room turned deathly quiet and all eyes turned to them.

They embraced, and after holding onto Andrew for what seemed like a few seconds too long, Kian clapped him on the back and they separated, each retreating to the opposite side of the mat.

As Andrew assumed a fighting stance, Syssi wondered if he was going to last longer this time. For his sake she hoped so. Losing didn't come easy to Andrew. He wasn't used to it, especially not so quickly. It must've been humiliating for him to be brought down in seconds, even though it shouldn't have been. He was facing off with a much more powerful opponent.

Kian was the first to move, his fangs already showing as he advanced on Andrew.

Well, what do you know. The abstinence actually helped. It was too early in the fight for him to be already pumped up enough with aggression for his fangs to lengthen.

Andrew surprised him with a roundhouse kick, sending Kian staggering backwards. Now Syssi had a problem. Who was she going to cheer for? Her brother or her husband?

Amanda solved her dilemma. "Give us a good show, boys!" she called out. "The best immortal against the best human!"

It sounded silly, but it was better than choosing sides or not cheering at all.

Andrew backed away, experience teaching him that pinning Kian down wasn't going to work.

Kian flipped himself back up and resumed a fighting stance, waiting for Andrew to make the next move.

"Come on, Kian, what are you waiting for?" Andrew stood his ground.

Kian smiled, but given his protruding fangs it looked more scary than friendly. "For you to show me what you got."

Why was Kian goading Andrew? His fangs were ready, his venom glands primed, he should get on with it and finish it.

Andrew came at him pretending to kick, but punched Kian in the face instead, then quickly jumped back before Kian could grab a hold of him.

Kian wiped his bleeding nose with the back of his hand and shot forward with a punch of his own.

Andrew's reflexes were excellent, and he turned in time to avoid getting his nose busted, absorbing the punch on the side of his face instead.

This time Kian didn't wait for Andrew to regain his balance, following the punch with a kick to the gut.

Andrew flew a couple of feet backwards, but managed not to fall on his ass. He was doing much better than last time. He'd figured out that to avoid getting grabbed was his number one priority. He just wasn't strong enough to get Kian off him or wiggle free.

The thing was, holding on for more than a few seconds might have been good for Andrew's ego, but not so good for his face. A big purple blotch was spreading over his cheek, and Nathalie's distress was growing with it.

Kian should end it already.

He must've reached the same conclusion because a split second later he grabbed Andrew and slammed him down to the mat.

Ouch. That must've hurt. Kian wasn't as careful with Andrew this time, and her brother would be bruised as hell after this was over.

Not a big deal, the venom would take care of it, and in a few hours he would be as good as new. A tear landed on Syssi's hand, the one that was clasping Nathalie's. Syssi gave it a little squeeze. She wanted to offer the girl a few words of comfort, but there was no time. Kian followed Andrew down, pinned his shoulders and arms to the mat, and bit down with a loud hiss that would've curdled her blood if she wasn't so used to it by now.

Nathalie whimpered.

Syssi leaned and whispered in her ear, "It's okay. In a second, he will feel no more pain. Watch his face."

Together with everyone else present, they watched as Kian kept pumping Andrew with venom for what seemed like minutes instead of seconds. The longer he was at it, the faster Syssi's heartbeat was getting.

Wanting to do it right this time, Kian might kill her brother.

"That's enough," she whispered, hoping he heard her.

Kian retracted his fangs and licked Andrew's wounds closed, then sat down on the mat next to him, watching his face and listening to his heartbeat.

Syssi's focus was on Andrew, but it was hard to ignore Nathalie trembling like a leaf beside her. "Breathe," Syssi commanded in a whisper. "You don't want to faint and miss him waking up."

Nathalie pulled in a shuddering breath and straightened her shoulders.

That's my girl.

It took forever, or at least it seemed like it, until Andrew's eyelids lifted. The sigh of relief was shared by everyone in the room including Kian. In fact, he looked like he was about to pass out himself.

Syssi pushed up to her feet and pulled Nathalie with her. "You can go to him now."

Nathalie ran and dropped to her knees in front of Andrew, pulling his head into her lap, crying and smiling at the same time.

Syssi gave Kian a hand up, and as soon as he was on his feet he wrapped his arms around her and crushed her to him, burying his face in her neck.

She stroked his head and murmured, "Shh, it's okay. You did well and everything is fine. Andrew is going to make it."

43

ANDREW

"Do you need help getting to the car?" Syssi's forehead was furrowed. Andrew had his arm wrapped around Nathalie's shoulders, and he was leaning on her only slightly to steady himself.

He was fine.

"I can walk. I'm just a little wobbly, no worse than after a night of boozing. Your hubby double-dosed me this time." Andrew didn't remember much, but according to Nathalie he'd woken up mere minutes after Kian had retracted his fangs. The venom-induced euphoria kept him down for much longer, though, and half an hour had passed until he could lift his head and stand up with Kian's help. The guy had practically carried him to a chair.

While he'd sat in that thing feeling like a very happy zombie, Amanda had brought him a bottle of water to drink and a cold compress to put on his cheek. In the meantime, Bridget had gone through her standard routine before clearing him as okay to go—checking his vitals and taking another blood sample to add to her growing collection.

Syssi shook her head. "Don't be a stubborn fool, Andrew. If your knees buckle, you're going to drag Nathalie down with you. She can't hold you up."

That managed to penetrate his foggy brain and he nodded. "Fine. You want to do the honors?" Syssi was strong enough to carry him over her shoulder if she wanted.

"I'll walk you to the car." She leaned to whisper in his ear. "I think Bhathian is feeling left out and is too shy to approach either of you. Let him help you."

Nathalie cast her father a sidelong glance. "You're right. Tell him we need his help."

"Gladly."

Syssi walked over to where Bhathian was talking with Kian, put a hand on his bulging bicep, and said something while pointing at Andrew.

Perking up, the big guy looked their way, then he turned back to Kian and the two clapped hands. As he came over, Bhathian shook Andrew's hand. "Good job. You didn't make it easy for Kian." He lifted Andrew's other arm and brought it around his massive shoulders. "You can let go, Nathalie, I got him."

Reluctantly, she did.

Andrew leaned his weight on Bhathian but held on to her hand. "I might have learned a thing or two, like not letting him grab me, but he could've ended it in seconds. He chose not to."

Bhathian shook his head. "Just take the compliment and shut up, how about that?"

Andrew chuckled. "Whatever you say, big guy. I'm not going to argue with you."

The walk to the elevators took twice as long as it should have because Andrew was shuffling his legs like a drunk who was about to pass out. When they got to Nathalie's car, Bhathian helped him into the passenger seat. "I'm going to follow behind. I want to make sure you can get up that flight of stairs."

Nathalie turned on the ignition. "Jackson is there. If needed, he can help Andrew."

Bhathian grimaced. "Are you telling me I'm not invited?"

Nathalie blushed. "Of course not, you're always welcome. I just didn't want to inconvenience you."

"I'll see you there." He shut Andrew's door closed.

Letting his head drop back on the headrest, Andrew closed his eyes and the world began spinning. "Your eyes are red-rimmed," he said.

"I know. I lost it there for a little while."

Andrew put a hand on her thigh. "What happened? It wasn't much different than the last time. Just a couple of minutes longer. You were fine then."

She shrugged. "I don't know. Maybe I was all worn out by the stress of waiting for the transition to happen, dreading it, then hoping for it. I felt as if I had no reserves left."

"I'm so sorry you had to go through this again, baby."

She cast him a glance. "It's not your fault. Besides, I'm starting to suspect that the other time Annani had something to do with my calm, and this time I was freaking out because she wasn't there. Do you think she did something to me? Some small thrall of relaxation?"

Andrew wouldn't put it past the mischievous goddess. He had a feeling Annani did whatever Annani pleased, and the rules by which her children lived did not apply to her.

Who would hold her accountable?

It was a scary thought that one person had so much power, and what she did with it was dependent only on her goodwill. Luckily, Annani was all heart and kindness.

When Nathalie parked her car in the alley behind her shop, Bhathian was already waiting. He opened Andrew's door and helped him out and up the stairs.

Jackson jumped off the couch to make room for Andrew. "What's going on, are you okay? Why is Bhathian helping you? Oh, that's a nasty bruise you got there."

Andrew let out a chuckle. "I'm fine, kid. You're stressing like you're my mother. Relax, it's just the side effect of all the venom Kian pumped me with. I think I'm slightly overdosed."

"Good, I hope this will do it." Jackson turned to Nathalie. "Is there anything else you need me for?"

"How is my dad doing? Did he give you any trouble?"

Jackson waved a hand. "Not at all. We watched porn and then I tucked him in for the night."

Nathalie huffed. "No you didn't."

"Yes I did. He's sleeping like a baby."

Obviously, the thing about the porn wasn't true—even in his impaired state Andrew heard the lie loud and clear—but how on earth was Jackson managing a straight face?

Nathalie shook her head. "I swear, I never know if you're joking or not. Could you make us some coffee?"

"With pleasure."

Bhathian rubbed his chest. "I'll go down to bring up a couple of chairs."

"Come here." Lying on his side and propping his head on his elbow, Andrew tucked himself against the back of the couch and patted the space he made.

Nathalie sat down, and he pulled her closer, so her glorious ass was pressed against his stomach.

She leaned sideways and kissed his lips softly, careful not to touch the bruised side of his face.

"It doesn't hurt anymore. The venom also acts as an anesthetic."

Her eyes sad, Nathalie smoothed a finger over the bruise. "It looks bad. The purple is turning yellow."

"That means it's healing."

Bhathian's heavy footfalls on the stairs were no doubt intentional, but Andrew wasn't going to let Nathalie move even an inch away from him. "Stay," he told her as she tried to scoot forward.

She sighed. "Yeah, you're right. I keep forgetting that Bhathian is not like Fernando. Different attitude toward intimacy."

A chair in each hand, Bhathian entered the den and positioned both across from the couch. He then unfolded one of the table trays for the coffee Jackson was bringing and sat down.

The kid got there a few moments later, poured coffee for everyone and planted his ass in the other chair.

"You feel anything?" he asked Andrew.

Andrew rolled his eyes. "Would you guys please stop asking me that? I promise I'll tell you as soon as there is something to tell."

Jackson pouted. "Sheesh, I'm just making polite conversation. No need to chew my head off."

Bhathian dropped two little cubes of sugar into his coffee and stirred. "I want to fly out to Rio as soon as you come out on the other side of your transition. I just wanted to make sure that I have all the information and that there is nothing more you can tell me."

Andrew shook his head. "I sent you everything I had."

Bhathian put the spoon away and took a sip. "Basically, all I have is the bank name, location, and Eva's account number. That's not much to go by."

As Nathalie handed Andrew his coffee, he pushed up into a sitting position, leaning against the couch's armrest. "It might be enough. There was no address listed with her account, but she must be nearby to make withdrawals. You'll need to stake out the place. But you don't have to do it all by yourself. Make a few copies of the picture Nathalie gave us and hire a few local kids to take turns watching out for Eva. It won't take long."

"How often does she make them?"

"Once or twice a month."

"If your hacker can find out when was the last time she took money out, it could be a great help."

"Good point. I'll call Tim tomorrow and ask him to talk with the kid. I'll call you as soon as I know anything."

"I can come with you and help you out," Jackson offered, his eyes sparkling with excitement.

Bhathian lifted a brow. "To Rio?"

"Yeah. You'll need help and I'm more than willing."

Bhathian patted Jackson's shoulder. "I know. But I need you to stay here and help Nathalie. She needs your help more than I do."

Jackson's shoulders sagged. "I guess."

"Besides, I doubt your mom would allow you to go."

"No, she wouldn't. Next time?" Jackson offered his hand.

Bhathian shook it. "Sure, but first you need to get some training. Let's talk about it when I come back. Now, we should leave and let Andrew rest."

The polite thing to do was to tell them to stay, that he was fine, but frankly, Andrew wanted them gone so he could take Nathalie to bed. He suppressed a smirk when she didn't say anything either.

Apparently, the lady was thinking along the same lines.

44

NATHALIE

The venom must've done something to Andrew's system because he'd been an animal last night. Perhaps it was the aphrodisiac component of it. Or maybe it had been the post-fight elevated testosterone level.

The last time Nathalie had been so sore was when she'd lost her virginity. Still, it had been well worth it, and nothing a long soak in a bathtub wouldn't cure. But that required getting out of bed.

Cuddling up to Andrew, Nathalie sighed like a satisfied kitten. He was so warm, it was like hugging a heated blanket.

Wait a minute, was he too warm?

Her hand shot to his forehead.

Andrew was burning up.

"Andrew, wake up, baby." Nathalie tapped his bare chest. "You have a fever. We need to call Bridget and ask her what to do."

"Andrew?" She shook his shoulder.

"Oh my God. He is not responding. What do I do?" Nathalie bolted out of bed and grabbed Andrew's robe just because it was the first item of clothing her hand landed on.

Running out barefoot, she tightened the belt while sprinting down the stairs. "Jackson! Call Kian! Andrew is unconscious!"

"I'm on it."

Nathalie ignored Papi's panicked expression and sprinted back, taking two steps at a time, all along fighting a wave of nausea. When she reached the landing, it got so bad that she could no longer ignore it and burst into the bathroom, reaching the toilet just in time to barf out the entire contents of her digestive system inside it.

What a miserable timing to get a stomach flu.

When there was nothing left to purge, she got up on shaky legs, flushed the toilet, and rinsed out her mouth in the sink.

There was a knock on the door. "Nathalie? Are you in there? Kian wanted me to tell you that he is on his way with Bridget."

She opened the door.

Wrinkling his nose, Jackson took a step back. "Are you sick?"

"It must be the stress. I just threw up in there. I need your help."

"Sure. Can I bring you crackers? Perhaps a cola? I heard it helps with nausea."

"That would be wonderful. But I need you to help me dress Andrew. I don't want him taken out of here in the nude." She could manage a pair of underwear, but with how badly her hands were shaking and the overall weakness from her prior rendezvous with the toilet, she doubted she was capable of much more than that.

Socks. She could deal with socks.

When Jackson came up with the crackers and a cold can of cola, she was ready to kiss him. Not that it would've been all that pleasant for him given the nasty smell of vomit that still clung to her.

"Thank you, you're a life saver." She took the bag of crackers and the cold can, and pointed at the bed. "I got his boxer shorts and his socks on. I left the rest for you."

"I got him. You go get dressed."

"I love you, Jackson. I mean it," Nathalie said as she pulled the few items of clothing she needed from the closet.

He chuckled. "I love you too."

She cast him a small smile before ducking out and into the bathroom. Stepping inside the shower, she started shampooing her hair even before the water warmed up. There was no time, but there was no way she could skip it. She had to wash the stink out.

Less than five minutes later, Nathalie was out. Quickly, she towel dried her hair, combed out the knots while trying to ignore the clumps she was pulling out, then braided her wet trusses in a tight braid.

All in all, she managed to be done and back in the bedroom just as Jackson was tying Andrew's shoes.

"Do you want me to carry him down?" he asked.

"No. Let's wait for the cavalry to arrive. Can you call them and ask that they park in the alley? I don't want to scare the customers."

"No problem. Though Vlad has it under control. You weren't exactly discreet when you called for me, and people started to get up. Vlad panicked and threw a thrall over them."

"What do you mean by threw a thrall?"

"Yeah, I didn't know he could do it either. Hell, I'm not sure he knew himself. Very few of us can thrall more than one person at a time. But regardless of how many people are thralled, it works basically the same way. Vlad just covered up the tiny memory of you shouting that Andrew is unconscious."

"I see." She'd been listening without really paying attention, and if he had asked her to repeat what he'd said she would've drawn a blank. Understanding the inner workings of thralling could wait for another time.

Jackson delivered her instructions and terminated the call. "Get ready. They are five minutes away."

Casting a glance at Andrew, Nathalie observed the rhythmic up and down movement of his chest. Reassured that he was still breathing, she tore the top off the bag of crackers and stuffed a few in her mouth, washing them down with the coke.

"I should open the back door for them," Jackson offered.

"Good idea."

As she sat on the bed beside Andrew, chewing on crackers, Nathalie felt guilty. It seemed so mundane, so out of place, to eat and drink while her man lay unconscious next to her. Except, she had to keep her nausea under control. After all, barfing all over Andrew was not going to help anyone.

A little later, she heard the back door open, and several people trotted up the stairs.

Kian was first, with Bridget and her doctor's bag by his side, followed closely by Anandur and Brundar. Jackson closed the procession.

Her tiny bedroom couldn't accommodate more than two people at a time, that is aside from Andrew who was sprawled on top of the bed. Kian and the others waited out in the hallway while Bridget stepped in, put her black bag on the new round table serving as a nightstand and popped it open.

"Could we switch places, please?"

Feeling like an idiot for not offering to do it first, Nathalie jumped up. "Of course, I'm sorry. Please do."

Bridget patted her arm. "It's okay. We all get a little confused when we are worried about a loved one."

Nathalie decided she liked the woman. Nevertheless, even though Andrew was unconscious, she wasn't going to leave the sexy petite doctor alone with him.

Better safe than sorry.

All those romances she'd read about soldiers falling in love with their care givers were onto something. Especially when the doctor looked like that.

Bridget checked his pulse, his heart rate, his blood pressure, his breathing and measured his temperature, noting the results on a tablet and comparing them to the ones she'd taken before.

"Exactly the same symptoms as Syssi. Fever and slightly elevated blood pressure. Everything else is working exactly as it did before."

Nathalie let out a relieved breath. "So he is okay? This is normal?"

Bridget shrugged. "As normal as Syssi's transition was. Two specimens do not make a norm, though." She packed her bag and got up. "Okay, boys, you can take him now."

She stepped out, making room for Anandur and Brundar.

"Hi, Nathalie," Anandur said, walking over to Andrew. Brundar bowed his head a little.

"The staircase is too narrow to bring up a stretcher. I'm just going to carry him out." Anandur bent and lifted Andrew fireman style. "Make room, people."

Brundar followed after his brother, which left Bridget and Kian out in the hallway. Kian reached for Nathalie's hand. "How are you holding up?"

"Having you guys here makes me feel better. It's good to know Andrew is being taken care of."

"Do you want to come with us in the limo? There is room for one more."

"Thanks, but I prefer to take my own car. I'll come in a few minutes. I need to talk to Jackson. Leave instructions."

"Of course. If you need anything, call me. You have my number, right?"

"Yes, I do."

"Good."

When Nathalie turned to Jackson after closing the door behind Kian and Bridget, he looked somber. Not a big surprise since he probably suspected what she was going to ask of him and it was a lot.

"I don't know what to do, Jackson. I need to be with Andrew, but I can't leave you here alone to manage the shop and take care of my father."

He shook his head. "Yes you can. Vlad has taken over all the baking, Gordon is waiting tables, and I man the register and make coffee. If Vlad needs help in the kitchen, I can call up another friend. Anyone can learn how to make sandwiches."

"What about my father?"

"I promise to call you if he asks for you. Go, you need to be with Andrew."

Nathalie reached for the boy and hugged him tight. "Thank you. I'll never forget this, Jackson, never. I owe you so much."

He patted her back awkwardly. "We are family, Nathalie. And this is what family does for one another."

45

KIAN

Looking at Andrew lying unconscious on the hospital bed and listening to the monitoring equipment, Kian felt like he was watching a replay of Syssi's transition. Same movie with a different actor in the starring role.

Not a pleasant déjà vu.

The big difference, however, was that this time around Kian was neither helpless nor hopeless. Andrew's vitals were stable, and Annani was on her way. She was due to arrive in less than an hour. The moment Andrew got infused with her blood, Kian would have nothing more to worry about.

Maybe he could even catch some sleep.

After all, Andrew had both Syssi and Nathalie to watch over him.

The poor girl. Kian could hear her throwing up all the way from the bathroom in the other room. The stress was killing her.

Perhaps Bridget could ease her suffering with some relaxant or an anti-nausea medication. Kian left Andrew's room and stepped into her office. "Can't you give her something for the stress?"

"I offered. She refused. Doesn't want anything to muddle her brain."

Kian chuckled. "These two are a match made in heaven. I don't know who's more stubborn, Andrew or Nathalie, but my money is on her."

Oh damn, he'd forgotten that Bridget had a history with Andrew. Perhaps she was uncomfortable talking about him and his new woman. He should ask Syssi, she would know. But until then, just to be on the safe side, he should avoid the topic altogether.

"So, how are Andrew's vitals, any change?"

Bridget cast a quick glance at her monitors and shook her head. "He is stable. Even his blood pressure remains the same. A little elevated but not climbing."

"And the fever?"

Bridget shrugged one shoulder. "Nothing life-threatening."

"Good." He hoped it was so. "I'm going up to eat lunch. Call me if there is any change."

"No problem."

On his way out, he bumped into Gertrude, who had left something like half an hour ago to get lunch for Bridget and her.

"What you got there?" He peeked into the brown bag.

"Two sandwiches from the deli across the street. They are quite good, you should try them sometime."

"I will. *Bon appétit.*"

"Thanks."

After the mission, Bridget hired Gertrude to come work in the clinic part time. Kian had no idea why Bridget had waited so long to get someone to help her. The clinic's budget included a nurse's salary. True, most of the time there was no need, but whenever there was a patient who required overnight stay, Bridget had to sleep on the couch in her office because other than her there was no one to look after them.

Up in the penthouse, he found Syssi cutting vegetables for a salad. He kissed her cheek and parked his butt on a stool. "Where is Okidu?"

"Readying the fanciest guest room for your mother."

Annani had informed Kian that she was staying the night, and since she'd stayed with Amanda the other time, it was Syssi and his turn. He was happy to accommodate her, and so was Syssi. Luckily, his wife was no longer intimidated by Annani's otherworldliness and was comfortable with her. For that, Kian was thankful to his mother. She was doing everything she could to make Syssi feel loved and accepted.

The thing was, the guest rooms were spotless, just the same as the rest of the penthouse, and Kian wondered what else there was for Okidu to do.

"What's to prepare?"

She smirked. "Exactly. I swear your Okidu is turning human. He looks so excited, running around, changing the bedding, dusting and polishing. He even ordered four different fresh flower arrangements so he could choose the one that worked best with the color scheme of the guest room."

Syssi put the salad bowl on the counter and handed Kian a plate with a sandwich on it. "I'm afraid it's not as good or as pretty as Okidu's."

"I'll be the judge of that." Kian waited for Syssi to sit down and pick up her sandwich before taking a bite out of his. "It's delicious."

Syssi lifted a doubtful brow but didn't press him to say anything more. "How is Andrew? Any change?"

"Nope."

She sighed. "I want to say good, but I'm not sure it is."

"He is going to be fine. The thing that worried me the most was that he wasn't transitioning. But now that he is, and that my mother is on her way, all is under control."

Syssi regarded him with a tilt of her head. "You put a lot of faith in your mother's blessings, dragging her here for the second time to say it over Andrew. That's so unlike you."

She had him there. But this was the best excuse Annani and he had. There were advantages to his mother's diva reputation. She got away with doing all kinds of weird things in the name of her eccentricity. After all, no one was going to argue with the Goddess when she decided she wanted to say a blessing.

"You know my mother. Her decisions have very little to do with logic and everything to do with heart. She believes her blessing will help Andrew pull through, so she is coming. End of story."

Hoping he'd satisfied her with his answer, Kian loaded his plate with the salad she'd made and dug in.

Wrong.

"That's Annani's side of the story. But you must believe in it too. Yesterday you were freaking out and today you are calm and confident in the success of Andrew's transition. What gives?"

"Nothing. Yesterday I was afraid Andrew was incapable of transitioning. But today I'm not." He pinned her with a hard stare. "And I wasn't freaking out. I was worried."

"You were and then some. You just can't—"

"He lifted a finger to her lips. "Shh, listen."

"What?"

"Can't you hear it? It's the chopper. It's getting near. I'd better go up to the roof to greet my mother. Do you want to come with me?"

"I would've loved to, but I promised Nathalie I'd bring her a sandwich. I have it ready, but I also want to put some of the salad in a container for her and make a fresh carafe of coffee."

Wiping his mouth and hands with a napkin, Kian got up and kissed Syssi's cheek. "Good luck with feeding that girl. She can't keep anything down."

"Poor thing. She is so stressed. I would be too if not for my vision. It reassures me that Andrew will be okay. Regrettably, Nathalie can't bring herself to trust my foretelling the way I do."

"There is nothing more you can do for her other than hold her hand." Kian pulled her in for a quick hug.

"Is Annani coming straight to see Andrew? If not, then I should come up and say hi to her."

"I'm sure she will want to go to him right away, but I'll let you know." He kissed the top of her head.

46

NATHALIE

As Nathalie sat down on the clinic's sturdy chair, Syssi pushed the rolling table to her. "Thank you," she said.

"My pleasure."

Andrew's sister was so nice, bringing her lunch and staying to make sure she ate. The least Nathalie could do was to pretend she was going to eat and take a couple of bites from the sandwich.

Had she ever experienced stress like this before?

Nathalie didn't remember barfing when her parents had gotten divorced, or when Fernando had gotten diagnosed with dementia. Was her love for Andrew more powerful than what she felt for her parents? Different? Was this the reason his condition was affecting her like that?

Over and over the bile rose up from her stomach and into her throat, sending her scrambling for the nearest toilet. Excess adrenaline was wreaking havoc on her body, and she seemed incapable of bringing it down to manageable levels.

"You should hurry and finish it. Annani is probably on the roof already and she is coming straight here. You don't want her to catch you with food in your mouth." Syssi snorted. "Imagine trying to say 'welcome Clan Mother' with cheeks stuffed full of sandwich."

"Or puking all over her dress." Nathalie regarded her plate again, then pushed it away. "I'll eat later."

Syssi looked crestfallen. "Me and my big mouth. I shouldn't have said anything. At least take a couple more bites. You must be hungry."

She was, but she was also nauseous. "I wish I had some saltine crackers. Right now I'm craving them like there is no tomorrow."

A grin splitting her face, Syssi lifted her hand. "Say no more. I know where I can get some. I'll be right back, don't go anywhere." She bounded out.

As if Nathalie would go exploring while Andrew lay in a hospital bed, unconscious, his future unclear.

He looked peaceful, though, content.

It made her feel a little better to think that she'd been the one who'd put that relaxed expression on his face. He'd fallen asleep looking like that after they'd made love, and the relaxed expression stayed because he hadn't woken up since.

She poured herself some coffee from the thermal carafe and took a tentative sip. It tasted amazing, going down without causing more nausea. Thank God.

She should ask Syssi what brand it was. Perhaps she could serve it in the café. If it wasn't too pricey. Though, like everything in the clan's keep, it probably was.

Nathalie counted their affluence as a blessing, grateful for the clan's plentiful resources that provided the clinic with the best medical equipment to monitor Andrew. Even to her untrained eyes it looked impressive.

Pushing away the cart, she stood up and went over to Andrew. "You are so handsome, my love," she whispered, smoothing her palm over his forehead, his cheeks, then bending down to kiss his lips. They were dry, and she reached for her tote and pulled out the little tube of Vaseline she used whenever her lips got chapped. One drop was enough, and she rubbed it in.

Kian's voice percolated from the corridor outside, giving her a moment's warning that Andrew's distinguished visitor was almost there. Quickly, she pulled out one of the perfume samples she carried with her for emergencies like this one. Not that she'd ever dreamed she was going to meet a goddess. Nathalie chuckled. But it was nice to have something to cover up the traces of puke clinging to her. It gave the illusion of feeling refreshed.

Annani glided into the room just as Nathalie dropped the sample back into her tote.

"Come, child." She opened her arms in invitation.

Damn, the last thing Nathalie wanted was to walk into those arms. The perfume could do only so much, and up close there was no chance Annani wouldn't smell something. But one didn't refuse a goddess.

Annani held her close and kissed her cheeks one at a time. "Wipe your tears, Nathalie. You are stronger than that." She let go and looked up into Nathalie's eyes. "You are going to have a long and fruitful life with Andrew."

Nathalie nodded. One didn't argue with a goddess either.

"Now I need you to leave. The special blessing I am going to say over Andrew requires complete privacy."

Strange. But whatever. Annani wasn't going to harm Andrew, that was for sure, and if she wanted to perform some weird, secret ritual over him, she was welcome to it. At this point, Nathalie would've accepted the help of witch doctors and voodoo priests. A real honest to goodness goddess was a step up from those.

"Thank you again for coming and doing this for Andrew, Clan Mother." Nathalie bowed a little. "I'll be outside."

The Goddess seemed impressed by Nathalie's good manners and nodded imperially.

With one last glance at Andrew, Nathalie stepped out of the room and closed the door behind her. Kian, who'd been standing outside with Bridget and Syssi, leaned his back against the door and crossed his arms over his chest.

Given the perplexed expression on Syssi's face, Nathalie wasn't the only one who thought this was strange. But the one who spoke up was Bridget.

"I don't think Annani is in any danger down here, Kian."

The sheepish look on his face was proof that the guy was hiding something, and not particularly well. Kian was not a good actor or liar. "My mother asked not to be disturbed until she is done. I'm making sure her wishes are obeyed."

Syssi waved a hand. "Fine. You stay and guard the door. Nathalie, I have a big box of saltines for you. Let's go eat them in the kitchen, shall we? You're coming, Bridget?"

"Count me in."

The kitchen was about a hundred feet away down the corridor, and it wasn't the small thing Nathalie had been expecting. The place was a cook's dream. Or with a few modifications, a baker's. Huge, it had a center island that was at least forty feet long, and brand new, top-quality commercial appliances that her fingers itched to explore.

She walked in and started touching everything like a kid on her first visit to Disneyland. "This is amazing. Who is cooking in here? And what?"

Syssi joined her on her walkabout. "Mostly it is used for storing food supplies. Our butler keeps a few cooked things in the fridge for the Guardians, and the rest are bottles of beer and sodas. I think the first time this kitchen was utilized to its full potential was for our wedding."

"What a waste," Nathalie blurted.

"Yeah, it is. Isn't it? Maybe if we had someone that was interested in the culinary arts we could put it to good use…" Syssi winked.

Nathalie shook her hands and raised her palms. "Don't look at me. I'm a baker, not a chef. This kitchen is set up for a restaurant or a banquet hall."

Syssi shrugged. "It was just a thought. Now how about those saltines?"

"Yes, please."

47

SYSSI

The second day since the start of Andrew's transition had come and gone and he was still unconscious.

Everyone's mood was somber.

The only glimmer of hope Syssi had was that his vitals hadn't fluctuated, remaining within a normal range, and Bridget reassured them that his life was in no immediate danger. What the doctor hadn't said, though, but what everybody was thinking, was that the lack of change also meant Andrew wasn't transitioning.

Nathalie was going out of her mind. And with good reason. Between worrying about Andrew's unchanging condition and having to rely on a couple of teenagers to run her shop and take care of her father, she was nearing her breaking point. Not being able to keep any food down wasn't helping either.

The woman looked like a ghost.

They needed to help her in any way they could. Peeking through the glass doors to Kian's office, Syssi checked to see that he wasn't in a meeting before going in. Shai was there, but what she needed to talk to Kian about didn't require privacy.

"Hi, guys," she said as she entered. "Kian, do you have a moment?" She sat in one of the chairs facing his desk.

"For you, always." He closed his laptop and moved it aside.

"Nathalie is in really bad shape. We need to help her."

Kian grimaced. "What can we do? Bridget said she wouldn't accept any medication."

Syssi shook her head. "She is stressing not only about Andrew but about being away from her father. You know he has dementia, right?"

"Yes."

"Do you know who is taking care of him and running her shop while she is gone?"

"No."

"Jackson, a teenage boy. And Vlad, another teenager, is helping him."

Kian's features darkened. "Why didn't you tell me earlier? We can send a caretaker to look after her father. Hell, I'll get the best money can buy."

Syssi shook her head. Not everything could be solved by throwing money at it. "Nathalie told me that her father doesn't trust strangers, and aside from her, the only person he is comfortable with is Jackson. She and Andrew interviewed several caretakers and none were a good fit."

Kian thrummed his fingers on the desk. "So what do you want me to do?"

"I want you to allow him in here. The man has dementia and wouldn't remember any of it. And besides, even if he gets a glimpse of fangs and later talks about it, you think anyone is going to believe him? Nathalie says he has hallucinations and talks to people who aren't there. So if he claims that he met vampires, it's not a big deal."

That got him to smile. "You're right. But if Jackson is the only one Nathalie's father trusts, and the kid is running her shop, who is going to look after the old guy here?"

"Nathalie says he doesn't really need much. He can still take care of basic stuff himself. Her biggest concern is him wandering away. Apparently, he is an escape artist, looking for any opportunity to sneak out, and then he gets lost. Down here, he can't get away. Not without a thumbprint access to the elevators. We can slap a locator cuff on him, so he doesn't get lost in the corridors. As to company, we can ask Michael or even William to spend some time with him. And Nathalie would be around in case he needs her."

Kian's fingers stilled for a moment, and then he tapped the desk with his entire palm. "Fine. Ask Bridget if he can stay in one of her patient rooms."

"Already did."

Kian grinned. "You knew I was going to agree."

Duh.

"You're a reasonable guy, and you're also compassionate, of course you were going to say yes."

"Yeah, yeah. I love you too."

Ignoring Shai, Syssi pushed to her feet, went around Kian's enormous desk, and kissed him long and good. "Thank you."

As she made her way to Andrew's room, Syssi was happy to have a piece of good news for Nathalie. It wasn't much, but something was better than nothing.

"Hey, girl, how are you doing?" Syssi asked even though there was no need. Nathalie looked as bad as she felt.

Saying nothing, she just lifted a pair of tired eyes.

"I've got good news for you. Kian agreed to your father staying here. We can send for him right away."

Nathalie perked up a little, but then slumped back in her chair. "I don't know if it's wise. He'll see me looking like shit and will get worried. Besides, where would he stay? What would he do?"

Syssi dragged a chair over to Nathalie and clasped both her hands. "Bridget is letting him use one of her recovery rooms, and those are outfitted just like a regular bedroom. There are plenty of people here who can take turns keeping your father busy. And as to you looking like shit? You are right. He can't see you like this. So how about you go take a shower, change into fresh clothes and go for a little walk? Sitting here and staring at the monitoring equipment would drive anyone insane."

Nathalie shook her head. "I can't. I don't want to leave Andrew alone."

Poor Nathalie. After years of shouldering everything on her own, she didn't know how to ask for or accept assistance.

"He is not alone, and neither are you. There is a whole clan of people ready and willing to help. Take it, use it. I'll stay with Andrew while you go catch a breather."

For a split moment, it looked as if Nathalie was going to argue, but then she closed her eyes and took a deep breath. "Thank you. I need to get out of here, stretch my legs and move a little, or I'll start screaming. Just a walk up and down the corridor a few times. Ten minutes. That's all I need."

Syssi shook her head. "First, go shower and change. Then take your walk. If you want to go out to street level, I'll ask someone to take you."

"No, I want to stay close. Shower, clothes, a little walk. That's it."

48

NATHALIE

Fifth day and still nothing.
Not even after the Goddess had given Andrew another blessing. On the third day, as she'd said her goodbyes before going back to her sanctuary, a somber expression dimmed the luminosity of her beautiful face.

Everyone was doing whatever they could to help, and Nathalie was grateful to each and every one of them.

The clan was wonderful.

At first, Fernando had been confused and anxious, clinging to her and casting worried glances at Andrew. All of that had changed when Amanda had taken him to William. Now it was hard to drag him away from the computer lab. Aside from the simple computer games William had her father playing, the guy was also a chatterbox who kept up a constant stream of conversation—much to Fernando's delight.

Michael and Kri came to take him on walks, and even Bhathian had spent some time with him. His trip to Rio had been postponed until Andrew woke up.

Jackson had stopped by with her checkbook, and she'd signed a bunch of blank checks so he could pay for supplies. He was managing just fine without her. According to him, the shop was working like a well-oiled machine with the help of Vlad, Gordon, and another of Jackson's friends, a guy named Chase. When her regulars asked about her, Jackson told them that she was visiting a sick friend.

Everything was under control, except the most important part.

Andrew was still out.

Nathalie closed the door. Careful not to dislodge any of the tubes and wires, she climbed on top of the tall hospital bed. Andrew was a big guy, and she barely managed to squeeze in, lying on her side. She rested her cheek on his chest and wrapped her arm around his middle.

He was warm, and as she felt his chest go up and down, Nathalie could pretend he was merely sleeping. A tear slid down her cheek and made a little wet spot on his hospital johnny.

There was nothing left to do but pray. And she did, repeating the same thing over and over again.

God, please let Andrew wake up.

Repeating it like a mantra, she dozed off, but in her dream she was still praying and Andrew was still unconscious. The sound of fingers clicking against glass didn't belong, and she opened her eyes to see Bridget typing away on her tablet.

Nathalie sat up. "I'm sorry. Let me get off."

Bridget's expression was soft and compassionate as she put her hand on Nathalie's forearm. "Stay if you want. Just be careful around the tubes and the wires."

Andrew was hooked up to an intravenous drip, a catheter, and a bunch of wires that were attached with little sticky pads to miscellaneous places on his body.

Nathalie lay back, propping her head on her elbow.

"Do you want me to bring you a pillow?"

Bridget was so nice.

"Could you? I feel less nauseous when I'm not lying flat."

Bridget put her tablet down on the rolling table. "I'll be right back." She ducked out from the room and returned with two pillows.

"Sit up," she commanded, stuffing the pillows under Nathalie. "I can raise the bed a little." She stepped on the pedal that was under the bed, and the motor wheezed into action, lifting the head part a few inches up. "Better?"

"Much. I never had stress affect me like this. Though there is one good thing about not being able to keep anything down. I'm probably losing weight."

Bridget's lips lifted in a small smile. "You have a beautiful figure, Nathalie. You don't need to lose anything."

Nathalie snorted. "You're very kind, but I wouldn't mind to see my butt shrink a little."

"Why?"

"It's huge, that's why."

Bridget laughed. "Not true. I have a nonexistent bottom, and I envy yours. No one is happy with what they got."

"True. I envy your boobs. Mine are small." The doctor wasn't wearing her white coat for a change, and the neckline of her red sweater revealed an impressive cleavage. Bridget had the type of body Nathalie always wished she had.

Not fair.

On top of being a doctor, one of the most respected professions, Bridget was also hot. Had Andrew been attracted to her? Or worse, had she been the other immortal woman Andrew had mentioned?

For some reason, the idea of Andrew with Bridget had Nathalie's jealousy flare hotter than for him pining after Amanda. Kian's sister was so stunning that she didn't look real—just as Andrew's feelings for her hadn't been real. But Bridget was a different story. She was pretty and approachable, and she was single. Add to that the immortals' promiscuity, and it almost seemed like there was no way Andrew and Bridget hadn't hooked up. It must've been her.

Oh, shit.

Nathalie felt the bile rise up her throat. She made a shooing motion for Bridget to clear the way as she bolted out of bed and ran for the toilet.

When she came back, Bridget was still there, waiting for her. "I would like to give you something for the nausea. This is going on for far too long."

Nathalie shook her head. "I'd rather not. The saltines are helping." She pulled a few out of the box and stuffed one in her mouth. The act of swallowing helped calm her stomach, stopping the dry heaves.

Bridget put her hands on her hips and pinned Nathalie with her smart eyes. "Is it possible that you're pregnant?"

"What? No! I'm on the pill. And I didn't miss my period." Frankly, the thought had crossed her mind, but it was impossible. Except, there had been that one night she'd forgotten to take the pill before going to sleep, but she'd remembered the following morning. No way the extra six hours made a difference.

"The pill is not one hundred percent effective. Women occasionally get pregnant while on the pill even when they take it exactly as directed. Did you miss a dose this month?"

"Well, once, but I took it six hours later. Can such a short time delay make a difference?"

"It shouldn't. But just in case, you should take a pregnancy test."

Nathalie snorted. "I'm not pregnant. It's just stress or something I ate. Andrew and I dined out a lot in the days between the first and the second ceremony."

Bridget didn't seem convinced. "If you change your mind, tell me. We can do either a blood test or a urine test, whatever you're more comfortable with."

Neither.

She wasn't pregnant. She couldn't be.

49

ANDREW

*H*ospital.
The beeping and hissing of medical equipment was so familiar that it was almost soothing. It meant that he'd survived and was being taken care of. Usually, the first thing Andrew did upon waking up in an intensive care unit was to check that none of his limbs were missing, but this time he didn't need to. The intolerable pain radiating from every part of his body confirmed that all of his parts were still there.

Andrew stifled a groan. He was badly injured, that was an indisputable fact, but he couldn't remember the mission he'd gone on or who'd gone with him.

Had any of the others survived?

He must've gotten hit multiple times to hurt this much. Or perhaps he'd been careless and had stepped on a landmine. That would explain the shattered bones, but not the burn in his throat. A bullet or shrapnel must've been responsible for that.

Why the hell hadn't the doctors given him something for the pain?

He could feel the IV needle stuck to the back of his hand, providing fluids but evidently no morphine. On the other end of him a bloody catheter was getting them out. He hated the shit, but prior experience had taught him not to try and pull it out himself.

"Nurse!" Andrew tried to call, but all that came out was an incoherent croak.

Damn, there should be a call button around here somewhere. Andrew patted the mattress. Why the hell did they keep his room in complete darkness? There was always light in hospital rooms.

Wait a minute...

Panic seized him as he realized he could hear the monitoring equipment, but couldn't see the blinking lights that usually went with it. Was he fucking blind?

His hand shook when he lifted it to his face and patted around. Thank God, his eyes weren't bandaged. But his eyelids were closed, something gooey and sticky preventing them from lifting. No wonder everything was dark. He was tempted to rub his eyes and force them open, but perhaps there was a good reason for the sticky residue gluing them shut. Maybe they'd smeared ointment over his eyes and he wasn't supposed to rub it off.

"Nurse!" Another croak.

Abruptly, the door banged open, and through the thin membrane of his closed eyelids he could see that the place was flooded with light.

"Andrew, can you hear me?"

The voice sounded familiar, but he couldn't bring up a face to go with it. Had he suffered a memory loss? Fucking PTSD. Sometimes soldiers couldn't recall any details from their last battle, but it had never happened to him before.

He moved his lips to say yes, but the sound he made wasn't even close. Fuck, it was so frustrating. He wanted to bang his fist against the mattress but only managed a thump. Would someone stick some morphine into the IV bag?

"Gertrude! I need twenty-five milligrams of morphine!"

Thank God. Just the promise of relief was already helping.

Back to the memory problem.

What was the last thing he remembered?

"Andrew, it's Nathalie. Can you hear me?"

Such a beautiful voice. He'd heard it before, melodic, deep for a woman, and husky. Perhaps he'd dreamt it?

Someone smoothed a few drops of water over his lips and he licked at them eagerly. Then there were a few more.

An image popped behind his closed lids to go with the voice. Long, dark brown braid, big chocolate-colored eyes, and lush, full lips.

Beautiful. His dream woman.

"Bridget, why is he in so much pain?" the girl asked, her beautiful voice quivering. She was crying. Why was she crying?

"I don't know," the doctor answered. Doctor Bridget. Funny. Bridget was a name of a starlet, not a doctor.

The gentle fingers that had wetted his lips were now holding a warm washcloth to his face, wiping away the sticky goo from his eyelashes.

"Thank you, Gertrude," Doctor Bridget said.

Suddenly, the pain just winked out of existence like it had never been there. The doctor must've put the morphine into his drip. Andrew was familiar with that effect. He'd experienced it many times before.

"Can I give him something to drink?"

"A little water is fine."

He felt a straw brush against his lips. "Can you open your mouth a little?" Nathalie asked.

He obeyed, and she pushed the straw past his lips. He couldn't figure out what to do with it. He was supposed to suck, but his facial muscles refused to cooperate.

Damn, what was wrong with him?

Nathalie must've squeezed the bottle because a little squirt of cool water landed on his tongue. She squirted a little more, and he drank some more, a few drops at a time. He was so grateful to her. His Nathalie.

Was she his? Why couldn't he remember?

"Oh, Andrew, baby, don't cry." He wasn't crying, was he?

The washcloth returned to wipe around his eyes again.

"Everything is going to be alright. The important thing is that you're awake. I've been worried sick about you. You were out for five days. Syssi's transition didn't take that long…"

Syssi was his sister, he remembered that. Another image flashed behind his lids, this one of his sister, she was young, maybe sixteen. But he knew that this was an old memory, she no longer looked like that. Syssi was all grown up; a married woman. Another image of her popped up, this time in a wedding dress, smiling happily with a pair of little fangs sticking out of her mouth. That's right, she had fangs now because she'd married an immortal, and he had turned her. Kian, that was his name—

Son of a bitch.

Andrew felt as if someone flipped on a switch inside his head, and the haze that had muddled his memory was gone in an instant.

"Nathalie," he managed a whisper.

"I'm here, my love." She took his hand, the one that was free of an IV drip, and held it between both of hers.

"I love you," he whispered.

50

NATHALIE

"Two double-double burgers and a triple order of French fries." Anandur handed Andrew a paper bag.

"You're the best." His eyes sparkling with excitement, Andrew snatched it out of Anandur's hand. "Nathalie, quick, close the door." He waved at her to hurry.

Anandur leaned his butt against the sink and shook the other, much larger, bag. "You can still change your mind, Nathalie, you can have one of mine. I got four, just in case."

Like the big guy wasn't capable of inhaling four double-doubles on his own. She'd seen what he'd eaten for breakfast.

"No, thank you." Nathalie crossed her arms over her chest and glared at the two idiots. Burgers and fries were not on Bridget's approved list of foods, and Anandur was sneaking them in behind her back.

"You're gonna get sick, Andrew. You're still on a morphine drip and Bridget said you are going to feel nauseous if you eat solids."

Anandur pushed the tray table over to the bed, and Andrew put the bag down. Pulling out one of the hamburgers, he gazed at the thing with such intensity that it made Nathalie jealous.

That hungry look should've been directed at her.

Since he'd woken up, Andrew wasn't the same. He was different with her, a little remote. She missed their sexually charged banter, and she missed feeling sexy and wanted.

"I'm so hungry I can eat a truckload of these." Andrew took a huge bite out of the burger, moaning in ecstasy and letting his eyes roll back in his head.

Nathalie pointed a finger at the monstrosity he was holding. "Bridget is going to come back and smell this the moment she steps out of the elevator. You're gonna get in so much trouble."

Anandur patted her shoulder. "Let the man eat, Nathalie. If he keeps it down and doesn't puke, Bridget will let him eat normal food." He waved a hand at

Andrew. "Just look at him, he looks like a scarecrow. Before being allowed on the streets, the guy needs to fill up or he'll scare little children and old ladies away."

Nathalie let out a puff of air and uncrossed her arms, letting them drop by her sides. Andrew indeed looked different, but even though he'd lost a lot of weight over the five days he'd been out, and the transition had drained him even further, he was still a handsome guy. In fact, he was even more handsome now than before the transition.

He looked bigger.

She kept nagging Bridget to measure Andrew's height, but the doctor had scoffed at the idea that he'd gotten taller. Michael had gained an inch since his transition, but that was because he was only twenty and his body was still growing. Andrew was supposedly too old for that. Still, Nathalie was convinced that he'd gained at least an inch if not more.

She was so familiar with his body and how it felt against her that there was no way she could miss even the slightest change, and there were many.

Not all of them exterior.

For starters, he kept sniffing her and saying that she smelled strange. Nathalie had showered and changed clothes four times since he'd woken up, just to get rid of what must've been the lingering scent of puke.

Which reminded her that she was out of clean clothes and would have to call Jackson and have him pack another bag for her. Bhathian could pick it up.

Problem was, it was embarrassing to have the kid handle her underwear. Perhaps she could manage without.

Ever since Andrew had pulled through, the puking had stopped, which reaffirmed her conviction that the nausea had been the result of stress. Andrew was doing well. She could wait until he fell asleep again, then drive home, pick up a few things and be back in less than an hour. Andrew wouldn't even know she'd been gone.

Still, it was possible that what he'd been smelling had nothing to do with her puking. Perhaps his new and enhanced sense of smell could detect things he couldn't before, and she'd always smelled this way.

"This is so good," Andrew mumbled with a full mouth and unwrapped the second hamburger. "Nathalie, come take a bite of this. You're gonna love it." He lifted the burger and extended his hand toward her.

Oh, no.

She'd celebrated too soon. Just the thought of putting the greasy meat in her mouth brought on an intense wave of nausea.

Anandur's forehead furrowed with worry. "Are you okay? You kind of turned gray."

Nathalie slapped a hand over her mouth and blurted from behind her fingers, "I'll be fine." Running out of the room, she kept going until the smell of meat faded completely. Leaning against the wall, she took a couple of deep breaths, then continued all the way to the kitchen for a new box of saltines.

She was so sick of those, but the salty little squares were all her stomach could tolerate, other than coffee and cola that is. Not a healthy diet by anyone's standards.

She tore into the box and removed the top two, took a bite and chewed.

Going down, the saltines helped relax her gag reflex and she let out a relieved sigh. With her stomach finally relaxed, Nathalie glanced at the two partially eaten crackers in her hand and chuckled. Her own version of a double decker.

A cold can of cola and half a pack of saltines later, Nathalie returned to Andrew's room in a better mood. Except, the door to his room was closed, and Anandur was out in the hallway, leaning against the wall and checking his Twitter feed or whatever other social media immortals favored.

"What's going on? Why is the door closed? Did anything happen? Did he barf?"

Anandur smirked. "Bridget caught him eating the burger. She kicked me out because she is removing the catheter and the IV drip."

Ugh, the hot doctor shouldn't be alone in the room with Andrew while handling his equipment, even if it was in a purely professional manner. Whenever Nathalie visited a male doctor, a female nurse was always present for the physical exam. She'd assumed that it was the proper standard protocol when dealing with a patient of the opposite sex.

She was about to go knock on the door when Bridget opened it. "You can come in now."

A wide grin stretching his face, Andrew was sitting on the side of the bed with his bare legs dangling from under the hospital gown. "I'm cleared to leave this room and to eat whatever I want as much as I want."

This was amazing news.

Forgetting that he had nothing on under that gown, Nathalie got in between Andrew's spread legs and the thing bunched up, but she covered him from view with her body and wrapped her arms around him.

Andrew was definitely bigger, and she wasn't talking about his height. His ribcage must've expanded because he felt much wider in her arms. "You've gotten bigger, Andrew." She turned to Bridget. "You have to take his measurements."

Bridget tapped her tablet. "I was just about to do that. First, let's get you on the scales, Andrew. I need to know how much weight you've lost."

"Can we stay?" Nathalie asked.

"If Andrew doesn't mind, then I don't."

Andrew smirked. "On one condition." He lifted a finger then pointed it at Anandur. "Stop staring at my sexy legs." He moved the finger to point at Nathalie. "You, sweetheart, can stare."

She grinned, her heart giving a little flutter of happiness. This was more like the old Andrew. Then when he sauntered behind Bridget, letting his gown part at the back, the grin turned into a giggle.

"Okay, big boy. Step up here." Bridget pointed to the scales. Andrew stepped up and she recorded his weight on her tablet. "Two hundred and five. Which is a twelve-pound drop. Not as bad as I thought. You can step down and go stand over there under the meter. Back straight, please." She adjusted the lever up, and Nathalie squinted to see the measurement.

"Six feet and three inches," Bridget announced. "Congratulations, Andrew, you grew an inch and a half."

"I knew it!" Nathalie exclaimed.

"I'll be damned." Andrew shook his head. "Didn't expect this to happen."

"Neither did I." Bridget pulled a measuring tape out of one of the drawers. "Let's see about the rest."

For the next fifteen minutes or so, Nathalie watched Bridget taking every measurement possible; the size of Andrew's ribcage, the circumference of his head, the length of his forearm, his torso, even his fingers got measured one at a time.

"So what's the verdict?" Andrew asked when the doctor finally folded her tape and put it in her pocket.

"You grew both in height and in girth. The surprising part is that it's not muscles that make you wider, since you've lost some of the muscle mass you had before during your convalescence, which means that your bone structure has gotten larger. That would explain both the prolonged unconsciousness and the intense pain you've suffered. Your body was rebuilding itself rapidly."

Andrew frowned. "How come it didn't happen with Michael?"

"Michael is still growing and changing, but that is not unusual for someone his age, and it's a gradual process. I don't understand why your transition was so different. I'll have to devote some time to examining the results and do some research before I can offer a reasonable hypothesis."

Andrew nodded. "Understood. What's next, Doc?"

"Next I'm going to take lots of blood. Then Syssi will bring you a change of clothes so you don't flash innocents on your way up to Kian and Syssi's penthouse."

Nathalie didn't like this idea at all. "I want to take Andrew home."

Bridget cast her an apologetic glance. "Sorry, Nathalie, not yet. Kian left explicit instructions regarding that. Besides, I want to keep an eye on Andrew for the next forty-eight hours, and I'll need to draw blood samples several times a day."

Crap.

Andrew reached for Nathalie's hand and pulled her into his arms. "We have a very nice room with a very nice bed at their place," he whispered in her ear.

That was true. But they had a comfortable bed at home as well.

51

ANDREW

"What about my father?" Nathalie asked.

Andrew leaned back to look at her. "What about him?"

"I can't leave him here by himself."

"He is here? Since when?"

Nathalie rolled her eyes. "I forgot you were out until last night. Kian allowed me to bring my father. Bridget let him sleep in one of her recovery rooms."

"And Fernando is okay with it? He didn't throw a tantrum and try to escape?"

Nathalie smiled. "At first, but now he seems to like it here."

This was good news. "I'm sure Syssi wouldn't mind."

His sister poked her head into the room. "I wouldn't mind what?"

"Having Nathalie's father stay with you until Bridget lets me go? She wants me to stay in the keep for the next forty-eight hours."

Syssi dropped a paper bag with clothes on the bed next to Andrew and kissed his cheek. "Of course he can come. Where is he? I want to extend the invitation myself."

Nathalie blushed. "It would be better if I talk to him. He is not so good with new people, and he might not understand why you're inviting him."

Anandur chuckled. "If you ask me, you underestimate your dad. He looks happy as can be. He loves hanging out with William."

Andrew lifted a brow. "What is he doing with William?"

Nathalie pulled a pair of jeans out of the bag and looked them over. "Listening to William chatter, occasionally talking, playing video games. Are these Kian's?"

Syssi nodded. "Bridget told me Andrew's clothes wouldn't fit him because he's gotten taller. So I got him some of Kian's."

Thank God his underwear still fit fine; he would've hated going commando, and borrowing someone else's underwear grossed him out. Except, maybe he shouldn't be thankful for that. It troubled him to think that this most important part was still the same size. If all of him had gotten bigger, wouldn't it look smaller in comparison?

Damn, he needed some time alone in front of a full-length mirror.

"Can I have the pants, please? It's way too drafty down here." He flapped the hem of his gown.

"Here you go." Nathalie handed him the pants and then pulled out a T-shirt.

Syssi came closer and peered at Andrew's feet. "How about shoes? Can you still fit in your old ones?"

Good question. Bridget hadn't said anything about them, but then she hadn't announced each of the many measurements she'd taken.

"One way to find out." Andrew pulled the T-shirt on and got busy with the socks. "Let's see." He pushed his foot inside a shoe. It was a tight fit, but he would manage until he could buy new ones or have these stretched out. He pushed his foot into the other one and tied the laces.

It was good to feel like a human being again, not a patient. Except, he wasn't really a human being anymore, he was an immortal.

Did it feel any different?

Yes and no.

The first few hours after waking up, the onslaught of sensations had been overwhelming, distracting. His vastly improved eyesight, hearing, and sense of smell provided too much information. It had taken his brain some time to get used to that. He wondered how much worse it could have been without the pain medications Bridget had been pumping him with. Without their numbing effect, he would've probably gone nuts.

Which reminded him. "Bridget, are you going to give me painkillers to take with me upstairs?' Andrew had no intention of suffering through his transition like Michael had insisted on doing.

The kid must be a bloody masochist.

The pain was no longer as excruciating as before, and his body no longer felt as if it had been smashed with a sledgehammer and put together again, but his throat and his gums still hurt like hell, and his muscles felt as if they were being stretched over a skeleton that was too big for them. Which was exactly what was happening.

Bridget handed him a plastic container. "The instructions are written on the label. Follow them exactly. If you need more, call me, don't just take another dose."

He saluted. "Yes, ma'am."

Bridget blushed and looked away.

The response hadn't gone unnoticed by Nathalie. She frowned, her lips pursing in a pout. He would have to tell her. There was no reason not to, but he wasn't looking forward to it. Nathalie had a jealous streak the size of the Grand Canyon.

She pivoted on her heel. "I'm going to get my father. I'll meet you upstairs."

Yep, she was mad. "I'll wait for you here and we'll go up together," he called after her.

"Fine."

Now that Nathalie was gone, Andrew planned to ask Bridget a few questions in private.

He kissed his sister on the cheek. "Thank you for inviting us, and for inviting Nathalie's old man as well."

She waved a hand. "No thanks needed."

"Well, needed or not, you have them. Listen, I have a couple of things I need to clarify with Bridget and there is no reason for you to wait for me. I know the way."

"Yeah, I'd better go and let Okidu know he needs to prepare another room." She pulled him in for a quick hug. "I'm so happy, Andrew, so relieved."

He patted her back. "I know. Sorry for giving all of you such a scare."

Syssi sniffled and wiped her eyes. "It's over. That is what's important. I'll see you in a bit?"

"You bet."

Anandur was smart enough to get a clue and offered to escort Syssi to the elevators.

Bridget closed the door. "Ask away."

He went straight down to business, asking the most important question first. "How soon can I initiate Nathalie?"

"As soon as your venom glands start producing venom."

"And that would take how long?"

She shrugged. "Two months at the minimum, six at the max."

Damn, he hated the idea of Nathalie being vulnerable for so long. Except, the only other option was to let someone else do the honors and he couldn't bring himself to even consider it.

His next question was embarrassing as hell, but he needed to know. "What about the biting. Will I have the urge even without the venom?"

He was expecting Bridget to blush—as a true redhead she did it a lot—but not this time. Apparently, when in doctor's mode she was able to control it. "Yes, but it will not be overwhelming. You'll be able to control it and you should. Without the venom's healing and euphoric properties, your bite will hurt and on a human it will leave bruises. Your saliva, however, will carry some healing properties in a matter of days. So if you do happen to bite, make sure to give the area a thorough licking."

Bridget's delivery was clinical and impersonal. She'd managed to do it without a hint of redness on her fair skin. Andrew, on the other hand, felt his ears catch fire.

Damn, Kian's longish hairstyle would've saved him further embarrassment. Either that or a hat.

He offered her his hand. "Thank you, Doctor Bridget. You're awesome."

She lifted a brow at the formal address. "You're not so bad yourself, Agent Spivak." She shook it.

52

NATHALIE

Nathalie's cheeks were hurting from being stretched in a perpetual smile. All throughout the afternoon, people had been coming and going in and out of Syssi and Kian's penthouse. Everyone wanted to congratulate Andrew, and he had graciously suffered through it all. As had Syssi and Okidu who'd been running around with trays of drinks and food, catering to the guests as if this was a party.

Thank God Kian had put an end to it, telling the last remaining few to get moving because Andrew needed to rest.

The guy still intimidated the hell out of her, but Nathalie was starting to appreciate her future brother-in-law. Kian was the type who did what had to be done with little or no consideration for manners or people's hurt feelings. She liked it about him.

The guy deserved her thanks, and not only for kicking everyone out.

She walked up to him. "Can I give you a hug?"

His response was almost comical. The tough, no nonsense leader looked confused, glancing at his wife for guidance. Only when Syssi smiled and nodded her encouragement, did he relax a little. "Sure."

Leaning down, he brought his arms around Nathalie as if he was hugging breakable glass, barely touching her. When she hugged him back, he cleared his throat and stepped away as soon as she let go.

"Thank you, for everything," she said.

His face softened. "You're welcome. I'm just glad it's behind us. Now it's your turn."

Nathalie laughed. "Not yet. Let me catch my breath first. I'm not ready for another trauma."

Andrew rested his palm on her shoulder. "Don't worry. Bridget says it will take between two to six months for my venom glands to start working."

"Phew, that's a relief."

To say she wasn't ready was the understatement of the year. Nathalie was exhausted, physically and mentally. Sleeping on a cot next to Andrew's bed hadn't been restful even when she'd managed to get a few hours of sleep.

Nathalie needed a long and relaxing vacation. But as that was not on the horizon for her, she would settle for a long relaxing soak in a nice bathtub. The one that came with the guest room Andrew and she were staying in was perfect.

"I need to get back to work," Kian excused himself and headed down the corridor to his home office.

Nathalie glanced around, checking out the mess. The butler was doing an admirable job of cleaning up, but it wasn't fair to leave him to do it alone.

"Let me help you." She grabbed a couple of plates, almost dropping them hastily when he gave her a look that was part offense and part outrage.

"Madam will do no such thing. Madam will take the master to the bedroom and make sure that he rests."

Andrew chuckled. "You heard the man, Nathalie. Your job is to take me to the bedroom."

Syssi shooed them away. "Go, before Okidu has a conniption. He is already mad at me for trying to help."

It seemed she had no choice. Good, she had no energy left. But there was one last thing she needed to do before ducking into the bedroom with Andrew and not getting out until tomorrow morning.

"You go ahead, Andrew. I'll just check on my father real quick."

When she entered the bedroom Okidu had prepared for Papi, Nathalie felt like giving the butler a hug as well. The BarcaLounger her father was sitting in and watching his show hadn't been in this guest room before. The color didn't match the perfectly put together theme of the room. Okidu must've dragged it from God knew where especially for her father.

Papi had his feet up, a cup of tea in the cup holder, and an expression of bliss on his face.

"Are you having fun, Papi?"

"Oh, yes," he answered without turning his head away from the screen. "I don't know how you can afford a five-star hotel, but thank you for the wonderful vacation, my sweet Nathalie."

Stifling a chuckle, she kissed his cheek. "You're welcome. Andrew and I are going to sleep. But if you need us we are two doors down from you."

He waved her away. "Yes, yes. I know. You told me. But if I need anything I'm going to call room service. They bring me whatever I ask for. Really, even new slippers." He wiggled his feet, showing her the slippers she'd gotten him last year.

The room service must've been Okidu. She really was going to hug the guy. "Goodnight, Papi. I'll see you tomorrow morning."

"Goodnight."

Closing the door behind her, Nathalie let out a relieved sigh. Fernando's mind creating a plausible scenario for the unexpected changes in his routine was a blessing.

Andrew wasn't in their room when she opened the door, and she was about to go looking for him when he cracked open the bathroom door. "I'm in here."

"How did you know I was looking for you?" she said without thinking. "Never mind. I know. Your superhuman hearing."

"Yep."

She walked over to the tub and cranked both knobs all the way to the end. "I've been dreaming about this tub the entire afternoon. I couldn't wait for everyone to leave."

"Yeah, me too. I'm still tired."

Translation. I'm in pain.

"Did you take the pills Bridget gave you?"

He lifted the small container off the counter and shook it. "I'm following her instructions to the letter."

It was on the tip of her tongue to ask Andrew if there had ever been anything between him and Bridget. But this was not the time. He needed his rest and so did she.

"Do you want to join me in the tub?"

The grin that split his face was all Andrew. Her lascivious, always ready for action fiancée. "Yes, I do." He was out of his clothes in seconds, dipping his toes to check the water.

"A little too hot." He adjusted the water temperature until he got it right.

In the meantime, Nathalie dropped her last clean outfit on the floor. Tomorrow, she would get up early and find the laundry room before the butler was up. She had a feeling that he would try to stop her from laundering her own clothes.

Andrew got inside the tub and made room for her, spreading his legs. She got in, leaned her back against his chest, and closed her eyes. "I missed this. Feeling your skin against mine."

He smoothed his palms over her arms, then moved her braid over her shoulder, exposing her neck.

Nathalie tensed. But instead of teeth, it was the gentle brush of his lips that feathered the delicate skin of her neck.

"What's wrong?" Andrew asked, his voice laced with concern.

Should she tell him?

Admit her fears?

Of course she should. It was hard, but she wasn't a chicken. Problem was, once she opened her mouth, things just tumbled out, one after the other, and she couldn't stop herself until she was done. "I'm scared of the fangs. I don't find it sexy, maybe other women do, but I don't. I watched the fight and it was okay until Kian opened his mouth and these monstrously long fangs protruded over his lower lip, dripping venom." She turned her head so Andrew could see her peeling her lips away from her gums and demonstrating with her fingers how long these fangs were.

"He looked like a monster, and I thought that if I didn't know he was a good guy, I would've run away screaming as fast and as far as I could. And then I thought that you were going to become just like him and it terrified me. Because you'll want it, need it, the biting will become part of sex for you. What if I can't stand it? What will happen to our relationship? It's like one partner not liking sex while the other does. It can't work. I will do all I can to learn to like it. But I'm terrified of failing."

She had gotten herself so worked up that tears were running in rivulets down her cheeks and splashing into the bath water.

"Oh, sweetheart." Andrew tightened his arms around her and kissed the top of her head. "It can't be too bad if the immortal females crave it so much. The venom is supposed to act as an aphrodisiac and a euphoric."

"I know all that. I just can't get past the biting part. The pain must be horrible, like two little knives stabbing into your flesh at once."

He was quiet for a few seconds. "I'm not going to lie to you. When Kian bit me it hurt, but the venom chased the pain away in less than a second, and then I was hit with such powerful euphoria that I was practically paralyzed. Somewhere in the back of my mind it scared me, the inability to move or say anything, but it was hard to care about anything." He chuckled. "At least when they kill their opponents this way, it's a merciful death."

Nathalie shivered. "I don't like talking about war and death. Especially since it is no longer them. It's us, for you that is."

"Us." Andrew let out a puff of air. "I'm still adjusting to the idea that I'm no longer what I used to be."

And that was the problem. How much of the old Andrew remained and how much had changed, and was enough of the man she'd fallen in love with still there? "I'm scared, Andrew. I don't want to lose what we had. It was perfect."

"I understand that you fear the unknown, it's natural. Perhaps you need to talk to Amanda, ask her how it feels to be bitten."

Nathalie harrumphed. "She is an immortal. Her body doesn't react the same as a human's. And she heals faster."

Andrew sighed. "So talk to Syssi. She was still a human when Kian and she got together."

The way he'd phrased it made it obvious that Andrew hated talking about his sister's sex life. But he was doing it for Nathalie, to ease her fears. Besides, it was a good idea. Syssi had experienced the entire gamut of sensations, being bitten as a human and as an immortal female. She could also tell Nathalie what she remembered from her transition.

"I'll do that. If anyone can assuage my fears it is her."

"I can do that too." Andrew sounded a little offended. "I can promise you that we will take it slow. I can control the urge to bite, at least until the venom glands start working, and I could probably refrain even then. I'm not sure I'm buying this crap about uncontrollable urges. I can stop myself from ejaculating almost until the last moment. I don't see how biting would be much different."

He sounded so sincere, so willing to sacrifice his own needs for her. On the inside, Andrew hadn't changed. He was still the same amazing guy who always put her needs before his own without even giving it a second thought. To him, that was the way it should always be.

He deserved nothing less from her.

Nathalie turned in Andrew's arms and cupped his cheeks. "I love you, Andrew Spivak. You are a sweet, wonderful man—as a human and as an immortal. And if to be with you I'll need to learn to love love-bites, then by God I will."

"I love you so much, my courageous Nathalie." Andrew crushed her to him, squeezing the air out of her lungs, then immediately easing off. "I'm so sorry. I'm still adjusting to this new body."

Nathalie rested her cheek on his chest, listening to the steady beat of his big heart. Everything was going to work out, for the simple reason that it had to.

"Love conquers all," she murmured.

Andrew smoothed his hand over her back, caressing it in slow gentle strokes. "You bet it does. All these obstacles that fate throws in our path will only help us come out even stronger on the other side. We are meant to be, Nathalie, you are my destiny."

DARK WARRIOR'S LEGACY

1

NATHALIE

"Where are you going?" Andrew murmured when Nathalie kissed his cheek, checking once more that he was indeed sleeping and not unconscious. Ever since his transition had started with him lying unconscious in bed, she'd been having mini panic attacks every time she opened her eyes to see his closed.

Relieved, she kissed him again. "Go back to sleep. I'll be right back."

Hoping to do her laundry while avoiding the butler, Nathalie had crawled out of bed at five in the morning. Funny. For years, she'd been waking up when it was still dark outside, and this would've been considered late for her. Getting used to good things was easy, and not having to wake up before the sun came up was definitely at the top of her list of good.

A bundle of dirty clothes under her arm, she tiptoed to the kitchen in search of the laundry room. Opening each one of its three doors, she discovered that one led to a secondary elevator, another to the dining room, and the third one to a large pantry.

"Figures," Nathalie muttered. Kian and Syssi probably used a service, and there was no laundry facility in the penthouse.

Unless one of the doors off the main hallway was hiding what she was looking for. On the remote chance that it did, Nathalie tried the one directly across from the guest suite.

Damn, it was the butler's, and he wasn't sleeping. He was sitting in a Barca-Lounger, not much different from the one he'd brought for her father, and watching some British show on the tube. His bed looked like it hadn't been slept in at all, but that was probably because he'd made it as soon as he'd woken up. Perfectly, like a display in a department store.

Well, he was the butler; of course, his bed would look like that.

"Can I help you, madam?"

Shit, if she asked him where the washer and dryer were, he would insist on doing her laundry himself. It was better not to mention it at all and avoid an argument.

"No, thank you. My mistake. I'm sorry to disturb you. Good day." She quickly closed the door before he had a chance to answer.

Well, not a big deal.

She was going home to check on the boys and could drop her dirty stuff there, change, and pack a bag with fresh things for the next day or two. The only problem with that plan was that, in the meantime, she was stuck wearing her clothes from yesterday.

"Good morning, Nathalie. What are you doing up so early?" Kian's voice startled her.

How the hell did he walk without making a sound?

With a hand over her chest, she turned around and plastered a smile on her face. "I was looking for the laundry room," she blurted before thinking it through. Not that she had a better explanation for the evidence under her arm.

Kian wouldn't offer to do her laundry for her, but he might suggest his butler.

As if reading her thoughts, Kian chuckled. "I'm sorry to disappoint you, but the entrance to the laundry facility is through Okidu's room, and he wouldn't let anyone set foot in there. If you're out of clothes and you don't want anyone doing your laundry, I suggest you borrow some of Syssi's."

That was awfully perceptive of him, not a trait men in general were known for and especially not Kian's type. She put her hands on her hips and narrowed her eyes at him. "Are you reading my thoughts?"

He shook his head, then winked. "I would never do so without your permission."

"So how did you know?"

A soft smile tugged at the corners of his lips. "Syssi had the same problem. She didn't like the idea of anyone handling her intimates. But she soon realized that resistance was futile."

Nathalie grimaced. "Ugh. I don't know how she does it. I can't even think of anyone touching my intimates, as you said so politely."

Kian dipped his head. "Thank you. My mother would've loved to hear it. She tried her best to teach me manners but had limited success. Come to the kitchen, and I'll tell you how Syssi solved the problem. I need my morning coffee."

She did too. "Thank you."

After dropping her bundle back in her room, Nathalie joined Kian in the kitchen and sat on one of the counter stools, watching him pull out the thermal carafe from the coffeemaker and pour its contents into three cups.

"I have it set on a timer, so the coffee is ready when we wake up," he explained.

Apparently, Kian wasn't the only early bird in the house. Syssi was too. "Do you guys always wake up so early?"

Kian pulled the creamer out of the fridge. "I used to get up even earlier and go to the gym, but Syssi doesn't allow me to get out of bed before her. She'll be here in a moment." He handed Nathalie the cup, then put the creamer and a small plate with sugar cubes on the counter.

"Thank you." Nathalie dropped two cubes into her coffee and poured a little creamer. From the first sip, she recognized it as the same brand of coffee Syssi had made for her before. It was so good that Nathalie was considering trying it in her café even if it was on the pricey side. The coffee might be well worth the added cost if she gained a few more regulars thanks to it. People would come back for coffee that good.

Kian rounded the counter and sat next to her, took a couple of sips from his cup, then put it down. "I apologize for not offering breakfast. We usually eat after our morning exercise."

Was it her imagination, or did Kian just wrinkle his nose?

"Okidu will make some later." He shook his head and reached for his cup, dipping low as he took another sip.

Oh, shit. He must've smelled her dirty clothes.

Mortified beyond words, Nathalie stayed seated by sheer force of will when everything in her demanded that she bolt out of there. After only one day of wear in an air-conditioned environment, her clothes should've been still good today, but evidently she'd been wrong. Kian was smelling something unpleasant, and it wasn't the coffee.

She took a few quick sips, burning her tongue in the process, and put the cup down. "I should get going. I need to go home and check on how things are going over at the shop." She got up and took a few steps back. "I hope to be back before my father wakes up, but if I'm not, could you please tell Okidu to serve him breakfast? Otherwise, he might try to cook it himself and set the kitchen on fire."

"Don't you want to hear how Syssi solved the laundry problem? It may save you the trip."

Hell no.

She wanted to be out of there as soon as possible and not come back until she was showered and wearing fresh clothes. There was nothing more embarrassing than an offensive body odor.

"I would love to hear all about it, but maybe some other time. I really need to check on the boys and see if they need anything. I've been gone for too long."

Kian shrugged. "I'll wait for you here until you're ready to go. The elevators are controlled by a thumbprint, and you'll need one of us to escort you down to your car."

Great. Now she was going to be stuck with him inside a small, enclosed space.

Can this day get any worse?

Shut up, Nathalie. Of course it can get worse.

She was stupid. It wasn't her fault that she didn't have clean things, and Kian wouldn't judge her because of it. He would understand. And anyway, wasn't he supposed to be ancient? He'd lived in an era when people rarely bathed. A little body odor shouldn't be a big deal to him.

Back in the guest suite, first thing she did was to check on Andrew. Poor guy. She'd woken him several times during the night just to check that he was responding. No wonder he didn't even twitch when she sat on the bed. He was exhausted. Lifting his limp hand, she kissed the back of it. His eyes popped open, shining with an eerie blue glow—the kind she'd seen in Kian's.

Scary and yet beautiful.

"Your eyes are glowing," she whispered.

Andrew smiled, and she was relieved to note that his canines still looked normal. After everything they'd been through recently, she couldn't handle more than one thing at a time. The extent of physical change Andrew had already undergone was staggering, and she hadn't been prepared for so much in such a short time. Thankfully, on the inside he was still the same old Andrew.

A wonderful, devoted, caring man.

"I'll be damned. I can see the light shining on your face. A useful trick in case of a power outage." He chuckled. "No need to go searching for a flashlight."

"Aren't they supposed to do that only when you're horny or stressed?"

"And your point is?"

She laughed. "You're right. You're always horny. I guess flashlights are no longer needed in our household."

He pulled her on top of him. "Only when I'm near you, my sexy lady." Reaching for the back of her head, he brought her down for a kiss, and a moment later she found herself pinned under him. Thank God he hadn't gained weight along with his other changes because he would've crushed her.

"Not now, Andrew. I need to go home, change, and pack a few clothes. I'm out of everything, and I'm wearing what I had on yesterday. I stink."

He sniffed her neck. "You don't stink, sweetheart. You smell great, like a ripe peach."

That was a relief. "Are you sure? Kian wrinkled his nose at me."

Andrew sniffed again. "I'm sure. But you do smell different. I told you that before. Have you gotten your period? That could explain it."

A wave of anxiety swept through her, and for a moment Nathalie couldn't breathe.

Kian had obviously smelled something that had caused him to react like that. And since he hadn't gone through any changes during their short acquaintance, it meant that she was the one emitting a different scent from before.

That, together with the nausea and Bridget's suspicions, all pointed to only one possible conclusion.

Damn. If it were true, she was so screwed.

Or rather the other way around. A snarky little voice whispered in her head that she had the cause and effect in reverse. After all, the screwing had to come first.

2

ANDREW

*A*s soon as Nathalie had left, Andrew jumped out of bed. Ever since Bridget had taken his measurements, he'd been itching to check himself out in the mirror. He'd grown bigger all over, which was great. The question was whether everything got bigger proportionally. Not the kind of thing he wanted to do in front of his fiancée. As much as he loved her, some things were too embarrassing to share.

Hell, he was embarrassing himself.

Only a delinquent attached so much importance to the size of his dick.

When he'd made love to her, Nathalie hadn't had any complaints, and that should've been enough. But damn his stupid ego, it wasn't. He had to know, and now that she was gone and wouldn't be back for at least an hour, he could finally do a thorough inspection without fear of getting caught doing something so juvenile.

Last night, before Nathalie had come into the bathroom, he'd managed to get a quick peek in the small mirror over the vanity. But if he wanted to see more, he had to do it inside the walk-in closet. The only full-sized mirror in the entire damn guest suite was in there.

Padding to the door, Andrew locked it before embarking on his mission—exploration of his new and improved body. A precaution in case Nathalie came back early, or one of the others decided to pay him a visit.

In the closet, he turned on the light, closed the door, and then stood in front of the mirror.

"Not bad," he told his reflection.

The two small scars on his face had faded completely, and the only evidence they were ever there was the missing hair in his brow and in the scruff over his upper lip. He had no doubt that in a few days the hair would grow and cover the small lines bisecting his upper lip and his brow.

Stretched over his frame, his skin was taut like a young man's. Hopefully, it would stay like that after adjusting to his larger frame. He needed to fill out more, though. Some of the muscle tone he'd had before going through the transition had been lost.

One of the things he'd hated most about his aging body had been the slight sag of his skin. All the iron pumping he'd done hadn't helped fill it up.

Did it feel as smooth as it looked? He ran his hand over his chest and his abs.

Nice. Everywhere he touched was taut, and what's more his old scars, even the big ones, were barely visible. In a day or two, they would probably be gone completely.

The ping of sorrow that followed surprised him. The old stab wounds and bullet holes told a history. So yeah, it was a history of battles, of losses and victories, of blood and sweat, but it was his, and he owned it. To see it disappear felt like erasing the memory.

With a jolt, he moved sideways to bring his tattoo in front of the mirror.

"Fuck!" It had faded so much that only the outline was still visible.

He should snap a photo before it vanished so he could have it redone once his body stopped changing. Except, he couldn't remember seeing tattoos on any of the Guardians.

Andrew frowned. Perhaps it was impossible for immortals to mark their bodies—the self-healing mechanism preventing any lasting changes. He hadn't seen any of them with piercings either.

The thought of losing the tat spoiled his good mood.

As long as he carried the monument to his fallen friends on his flesh, Andrew felt as if he was carrying on their legacy. In a small way, it made the guilt of surviving while they hadn't tolerable.

And now it was fading.

With his shoulders slumped, he shuffled back to the bed and sat down. What the hell was he going to do if tattoos were a no-go for an immortal?

He must've brooded a long time because he was still sitting on that bed when he heard Nathalie trying to open the door.

"Andrew?" she said quietly with a note of worry in her voice.

Still in the buff, he padded to the door and stood behind it as he opened it for Nathalie, closing and relocking it after she'd stepped in.

She dropped two overstuffed plastic bags on the floor and turned to look at him. "I see you've been waiting for me." A smile curved her lips, but after a quick once-over, it was replaced with a frown. "Not excitedly, though."

He'd better spit it out quick before she started thinking some nonsense like she wasn't turning him on anymore. "My tattoo is fading away."

"Let me see." Nathalie grabbed his elbow and turned him sideways. "It is. Do you know if you can get a new one?"

She hadn't forgotten its significance.

He'd told her about it almost at the start of their relationship, which had been as good an indicator as any that she was his one. Andrew didn't like to explain it to people. It was private. But there was nothing he wanted to keep secret from Nathalie if he didn't have to. It was enough that he worked for the government and couldn't tell her anything about his work. The least he could do was tell her everything else.

"I don't know. I suspect my body will keep repairing my skin and erasing it."

Nathalie looked at it closer. "We should take a picture before it is gone completely. I can still see the outline." She let his arm drop and reached inside her purse to pull out her phone. Snapping a few from different angles, she checked after each one to make sure it had come out all right. "What do you think?" She handed him the phone.

It was a relief to see that the white phoenix was clear enough for an artist to recreate, if not on his skin then on something else. Question was, on what?

"It's good. I can take it to a tattoo place, and they can use it to make a new one. I need to dedicate a budget for redoing it every few days."

"It doesn't have to be on your skin."

As if a picture on the wall could serve as a memorial. Maybe for someone else; not for him. "You know what it means to me. I need it on my body, always. That's how I keep them in here." He put his hand over his heart.

Her forehead furrowed, she closed her eyes to think.

Sweet Nathalie. That was what she always did when pondering a difficult problem.

"I have a solution." She lifted her hand in the air. "A pendant. We can have a jeweler create a replica in white gold, or silver, but gold is better because it doesn't tarnish. You can wear it without ever taking it off."

The woman was brilliant. He pulled her into his arms and swung her around. "My Nathalie is sexy." He kissed her. "And beautiful." He kissed her again. "And smart." Another kiss.

She laughed. "Put me down before you pull a muscle."

He did. "Can immortals pull muscles? I don't think so."

"Asked and answered yourself." She lifted one of the bags off the floor. "I stopped by your house and brought you your own clothes."

"Thank you. I hate to keep borrowing from Kian."

"I know. Now get in the shower and get dressed. Syssi is making us cappuccinos, and Okidu has his famous waffles in the warming drawer for you. Supposedly, they're heavenly."

Andrew took the bag. "I feel bad. I know Syssi has important work to do, but instead she hangs around here to watch over me."

Nathalie made a shooing motion with her hand. "After breakfast, she plans to go to the lab. So don't keep her waiting and hurry up."

"Yes, ma'am!" He saluted.

Ten minutes later, Andrew emerged from the bathroom and gingerly headed for the kitchen to join Nathalie and the rest of the gang. Everything he was wearing was too tight, too short, and pinched in various places.

Clothes shopping had just gotten pushed to the top of the list of things he needed to do once he was cleared to go. Shoes too. His feet must've grown overnight because the shoes that had barely fit yesterday didn't fit at all today.

"Oh, my God, Andrew!" Syssi exclaimed. "How much did you grow?" She turned to Nathalie. "Am I imagining it? Or did he get even bigger overnight?"

Nathalie giggled. "I don't think so. It's just his old clothes. They look ridiculous on him."

Syssi pressed a button on her cappuccino machine, and the thing started huffing and puffing. "Wait here. I'm going to bring you more of Kian's." She snorted. "You look uncomfortable."

"I am, but I don't want to take any more of his stuff. At this rate, he is going to run out of clothes."

Syssi let out a puff of air. "Don't worry about that. When Shai was in charge of buying Kian's wardrobe, he filled his closet with stuff Kian wouldn't have a chance of wearing before it went out of style. I was thinking of packing some of it up and donating it to the old people's home I used to volunteer at, but then I realized that his things wouldn't fit anyone there. He's too big."

"Well, in that case, I'll be happy to take some off his hands. What's his shoe size?"

Syssi and Nathalie both glanced at his socked feet.

"Fourteen," Syssi said. "I can bring you a new pair of flip-flops he doesn't like."

Andrew nodded. "It would be greatly appreciated."

"You know what they say about men with big feet," Nathalie said when they were alone.

Andrew quirked a brow, then glanced down at his straining jeans. "I don't know. Tell me."

She stifled a giggle. "Big socks."

"Ha, ha. Very funny."

She put her hands on her hips. "Come on, it *is* funny. I know you were expecting me to say something else."

"Of course I was, woman. I have a fragile ego that needs constant reassurances." His tone was joking, but he wasn't.

Nathalie sauntered up to him and wrapped her arms around his neck. "Andrew, my love, you're a perfect fit for me."

Damn, this wasn't the answer he wanted. "So what are you saying? I need to know. Did I get bigger all over, or not? It's not about vanity, but I don't want to look disproportionate."

It's very much about vanity.

A sexy smirk on her gorgeous face, Nathalie caressed his cheek. "You take my breath away, Andrew. You were always handsome, but now..." She fanned herself with her hand. "If you thought I was jealous before, you've seen nothing yet. I'm not going to let you out of my sight."

Good enough.

3

CAROL

Poor Robert.
   Hell, poor Carol.
   They were both miserable.
   The moment he'd come back from yet another unsuccessful job search, Robert had locked himself in the bathroom.
   Gazing out the window at the *scenic view* of the hotel's parking lot, Carol wondered when he was going to give up. No one would hire a guy who couldn't produce proof that he was allowed to work in the States. All he had was a fake Australian passport. It was as good as having nothing at all.
   Robert was growing desperate, and so was she.
   But for different reasons.
   Living in a hotel in Vegas would have been fun if she could've splurged on one of the big names. A fancy one with a nice suite like the Venetian would have been great. But her modest share in the clan's profits wasn't enough for living in style. She could barely afford a cheap room in the MGM. It wasn't crappy, but it wasn't great either.
   Not exactly the type of casino high rollers frequented.
   Which meant that she had no prospects of making the extra money she needed. Settling for some average Joe Schmo who could part with no more than two Benjamins wasn't going to happen. Besides, getting away from Robert wasn't happening either. Not for long enough to score with the type of client who could afford her.
   The dude still believed that she was his destined mate.
   Poor, delusional Robert.
   He bored her to death, but she wasn't going to go back on her promise. No matter what. Two weeks down and ten more to go. She would try her best to make the schmuck happy.
   The one bright spot was the sex. What an immortal male could do for her, no

other man could. It was mind blowing. Not that Robert was all that great—the guy was just as boring in bed as he was everywhere else—it was mostly about the venom's aphrodisiac and euphoric effect, and the incredible stamina. The guy could go for hours.

Carol sighed and plopped onto the hotel's uncomfortable chair. "Robert! Are you done yet? I'm hungry." That should get him out of there.

He was a good man; always mindful of her, making sure she was comfortable, well fed, and sexually satiated. She would've been ecstatic if things had worked out better between them. Robert could have made a great mate and maybe even a father.

But when it wasn't meant to be, it wasn't meant to be. Round pegs didn't fit into square holes, and there was no point in trying to force them.

Robert could make some other immortal female happy, just not Carol. She needed excitement, adventure, a variety of partners…

That alone was proof that this wasn't it. Carol had heard that after Amanda had hooked up with Dalhu, she no longer craved other dudes and was annoyed even when other men leered at her. Maybe that was what happened when an immortal female found her true love mate.

Obviously, Robert wasn't Carol's.

She could hook him up with someone else. Her bestie Sharon would be a good candidate. If the girl found accounting interesting, she might find Robert fascinating.

Nah. Not even Sharon would think that. The only type of woman who could tolerate Robert was someone who didn't mind a guy who had absolutely nothing to say.

"Come on, Robert! I don't want to be stuck in the long line to the buffet."

Finally, the door cracked open, and Robert came out showered and shaved and wearing a fresh T-shirt.

After George had FedExed her credit cards and her driver's license to the cheap motel they had stayed at the first night, she'd taken Robert shopping. They had found all they needed at the north side outlet. It was cheap crap, but at least there was enough of it so she didn't need to send him to the laundromat too often.

Slapping a smile on her face, she got up and kissed his cheek. "Let's go. You must be just as hungry as I am."

Robert nodded and followed her out of the room.

The line to the buffet wasn't too bad; she estimated about a half an hour wait. Carol had discovered early on that feeding Robert in regular restaurants was too costly. The quantities he consumed were huge, making an all-you-can-eat buffet a real bargain for her.

While they waited, Carol did all the talking—as usual. She told him about the latest Hollywood gossip, what happened on her favorite television series, and so on until she ran out of things to talk about. His responses were limited to an occasional nod, but she knew he listened. Or maybe he just liked the sound of her voice.

When they were finally seated, he insisted she go and load her plate first, while he waited for the waiter to take their drink orders.

Such a nice guy. Why, oh why, couldn't she fall in love with him?

When Carol came back with a plate full of various foods that had no culinary association whatsoever, Robert gave it an approving glance and got up. From experience, she knew that was only his first round and that he would be going for a second and a third and a fourth. Not including dessert.

Returning with a plate full of ribs, he stuffed a napkin into his shirt collar and went to work.

"Robert, I need to talk to you about something. Are you listening?"

He grunted.

"I would like you to reconsider coming home with me. I can't afford both the mortgage payments on my house and the extended hotel stay, and you can't find a job without proper papers. All of that will be solved if you just come with me. I can get you fake documents that would pass scrutiny, we will be living in my comfy house, and I can ask around if someone has work for you."

Robert finished chewing on the rib he was holding, put down the cleansed bone, and wiped his hands and mouth with a napkin.

"How do I know it's not a trap?"

"Do you think I would betray you like that? By now you should know that I keep my promises."

"I'm not questioning you. But what about them? Your clansmen?"

"I've been told that you're invited, but I can check again and ask to talk with someone in charge."

"They can lie to you."

Carol rolled her eyes. "You wouldn't be the first Doomer to cross over. There is a very positive precedent. A wonderful love story. She fought hard to get him accepted, and he went through hell for it, but there is a happy ending. They are together."

Robert frowned. "How did they meet?"

"I'm not sure. But there were rumors that he kidnaped her off the street. Personally, I don't believe that this is how it happened, but maybe."

"Let me think about it."

"Sure." A start. He was considering going home with her. She wouldn't mention hooking him up with someone else, not yet. It might spook him.

One step at a time.

4

ANDREW

One big happy family.

Sitting at the counter and stuffing himself full of waffles topped with strawberries, Andrew listened to Syssi and Nathalie chatter about this and that. He wasn't paying attention to the words being said, just enjoying the soothing sound of their soft voices and occasional chuckles. Next to him, grumpy as usual, Kian had his nose buried in the morning paper, grunting from time to time about something in the stock market and shaking the paper.

It was fucking great.

His family. His fiancée, his sister and her husband, and an entire clan of immortals who had accepted him as one of their own.

A man could spend half his life imagining a future, building different scenarios in his head, and get it all wrong. His life could take a detour into a completely different territory, one that would make him happier than he'd ever imagined he could be. And the opposite was also true. Fate wasn't kind to everyone. He was as lucky as a man got to be.

"Andrew." Nathalie nudged him.

"Yeah?"

"Do you want to go shopping? William is keeping my dad busy, so we have a good couple of hours to ourselves."

"Sure." Not his favorite activity, but any time spent with Nathalie was good. Besides, he really needed new clothes that fit.

Syssi shook her head. "I don't think it's a good idea. Bridget said you should stay put for forty-eight hours."

"No, she said she would like to keep an eye on me for forty-eight hours. But she is not monitoring me every moment of every hour. True?"

"I guess. Let's call her to make sure."

"No!" Nathalie and he exclaimed at the same time.

Kian chuckled from behind the newspaper.

Syssi crossed her arms over her chest. Never a good sign. "What if you collapse in some store? Nathalie can't pick you up. People will call 911, and the paramedics will show up."

What a role reversal. Andrew used to be the worrywart, the older, overprotective brother. He'd never understood why Syssi had been mad at him for butting into her life. He'd only wanted to steer her in the right direction. Now that the shoe was on the other foot, he realized what a pain in the ass he'd been. Hiding his amusement, he took a sip of coffee and let Nathalie handle it.

"My father can come along. I mean Bhathian, not Papi. He is certainly strong enough to carry Andrew if needed," Nathalie said with a clear note of pride in her tone. Calling Bhathian Father hadn't always been easy for Nathalie.

Discovering at the age of thirty that the man who'd raised her wasn't her biological father had been difficult for her. She loved Fernando dearly, and he loved her back. Even his dementia hadn't diminished his feelings for her.

Both Nathalie and Andrew wondered if Fernando knew she wasn't his. After all, her mother had married him at the early stages of her pregnancy. She might've deceived him. They wouldn't know until they found the elusive and mysterious Eva. Trouble was, the woman didn't want to be found and was very good at dropping off the face of the earth. She'd already done it twice.

Kian closed the newspaper and folded it into a neat rectangle. "Bhathian is teaching a class this morning. But if you can do your shopping fast, I could spare Anandur for an hour."

Andrew cast Kian a grateful look. "That would be great, thank you."

Kian nodded. "I'll send him up." He pushed to his feet and put his hand on Syssi's shoulder. "Ready to go?"

"Yeah. It's about time I got back to work." She leaned in to kiss Andrew's cheek. "Behave, and don't overexert yourself. I'm so profoundly relieved that you made it through the transition, but after all that stress, I can't help worrying about you."

Andrew pulled Syssi into his arms. "I'm fine. I'm better than fine. I'm spectacular, indestructible, and handsome as the devil himself. Nothing to worry about."

Syssi chuckled and punched his shoulder. "Careful, Andrew. By the possessive look on Nathalie's face, she is going to put you on a very short leash."

He cast a sidelong glance at his fiancée, confirming that the monster of jealousy had indeed risen to the surface. "I don't mind a leash as long as you're the one holding it, baby."

That got him a smile.

Fifteen minutes later, they were sitting in Nathalie's car with Anandur complaining about the cramped backseat.

"We should've taken my car."

Andrew turned to the Guardian. "As if the Thunderbird has more legroom in the back than this old clunker."

Nathalie needed a new car, and he was going to take care of it as soon as he could. It wasn't about being a snob and wanting to show off that his girl was driving something fancy, it was about safety. His Nathalie was still a fragile human, and this older model didn't have all the safety features the newer cars had. It was not safe enough for his treasure. He turned to her. "You need a new car, baby. First thing after we get home, we are going to get you a decent vehicle. This old thing is a safety hazard."

Nathalie shook her head. "Don't be ridiculous. It's old, but it has very low mileage. The car runs perfectly."

"I agree that it runs well, but is it built to the newest standards? Does it have airbags everywhere?"

"No, but neither does Anandur's Thunderbird. Isn't she vintage?"

"She sure is," Anandur said.

"Yeah, but he is an immortal, and you are not. Not yet. And until you are, I'm going to wrap you in Bubble Wrap every time you leave the house."

Damn. It was such a scary thought. Anything could happen to her. She could get into an accident, get sick...

Andrew's gut clenched. What if she was already sick? What if that new scent she was emitting was caused by disease? The immortals wouldn't know what it was because they were immune to all human diseases, and he doubted they bothered to familiarize themselves with all the different scents mortals produced.

Andrew was still getting used to the barrage of sensations assaulting him; the smells and the sounds, the sharpness of the visuals, it was all so overwhelming it was giving him a headache. The other immortals must've learned to block it.

Nathalie rolled her eyes. "Did the transition affect your brain, turning you into a mother hen?"

"I can't wait to turn you." Andrew rubbed the back of his neck. "I don't know why, but I feel like every moment that you're still human, you're in danger."

Nathalie's features softened, and she took one of her hands off the steering wheel to clasp Andrew's. "I know how you feel. I was going out of my mind waiting for you to go through your transition and praying for you to come out okay on the other side."

Anandur cleared his throat. "If you kids want to make out, just drop me off on the sidewalk."

Andrew ignored the peanut gallery. "I know my anxiety is irrational, but there is a nagging thought at the back of my mind that I've been too lucky and that my luck is not going to hold forever. I've survived missions that most of my friends didn't, and each time I asked God why? Why them? Why not me? Don't get me wrong; it wasn't as if I wanted to get killed. I was grateful for being spared. I just wondered why. I wasn't a better man. I didn't deserve to survive more than any of the others."

Nathalie brought his hand to her lips and kissed it. "God saved you for me, so one day you'd come into my coffee shop and fall in love with me."

A sniffle sounded from the backseat. "It's so romantic. I'm tearing up."

Andrew smiled. "You're an angel, my Nathalie, but if God wanted to reward you for your good heart and your sacrifices, he should've arranged for a more worthy man than me. I sure as hell didn't do anything to deserve you."

"Oh stop it, you two. Now you'll start a pissing contest of who is less deserving and who loves who more."

Anandur was right. They were sliding into soppy greeting cards territory.

Andrew took a deep breath and put Nathalie's hand back on the steering wheel. "Safety first, baby, both hands on the wheel."

"Yes, sir!" She winked.

"Anandur, I wanted to ask you something." Andrew turned to look at the Guardian.

"What?"

"Can immortals get tattoos?"

The guy shook his head. "Not permanent ones. Our body considers it a wound and heals it. But if you really want one you can get a henna tat, though personally, I think they're girly and they don't last long."

Henna wasn't going to solve Andrew's problem. "I'll pass."

"That's what I thought."

5

NATHALIE

"It seems we have the place all to ourselves," Andrew said as he removed the sticky note pasted to the door of Kian and Syssi's penthouse.

"What does it say?" Nathalie asked.

"It's from Okidu. He's gone grocery shopping, and we are to let ourselves in. The door isn't locked."

Handing her the note, he pushed the door open and motioned for her to go in, even though he was schlepping several large shopping bags that must've weighed a ton.

Always the gentleman, her Andrew.

She waited for him to get in and closed the door behind them. "Let's put these in the closet. I suggest we leave everything in the bags. Doesn't make sense to take it all out, only to put it back in when we go home tomorrow."

"Good idea. But I want you to try on the new dress and put on that *Angel* perfume. I love the smell."

Nathalie felt her face warm up. Was he hinting at something? Should she take another shower? Probably. She'd sweated a little. Trying to keep up with Andrew and Anandur's long strides, she'd been running around the mall and not strolling leisurely as she would've if she'd been there alone. Shopping with two impatient guys hadn't been fun. Andrew hadn't even tried on any of the clothes they'd bought. The sales lady took his measurements and handed him stuff in his size and that was it. At least he'd tried on the shoes, but only after Nathalie threatened not to leave the store until he'd made sure they fit.

"I'm going to grab a quick shower. I don't want to try on a new dress on a sweaty skin."

Andrew dropped their shopping bags in the master closet. "But you showered this morning," he said as he walked out.

"I know, but I had one hell of a workout running after you and Anandur. I feel icky, and I don't want to stink up a new outfit."

"You can never stink." He pulled her into his arms, lifting her easily for a kiss. "You always smell sexy. In fact, I want a better sniff." Still holding her up, he walked over to the bed and sat down with her on his lap.

Did he mean it? Only one way to find out.

Nathalie relaxed in Andrew's arms, snuggling up to him. "What exactly did you have in mind?"

He chuckled. "You know what I want, woman."

She had a clue, but she wanted to hear him say it. "I don't. Tell me."

With a wicked smile on his handsome face, he pulled her shirt up over her head and unclasped her bra before she even had a chance to blink. "How about I show you instead?" He started working on her zipper.

Apparently, the man had meant every word. Andrew's voice was husky with desire, and she knew he wasn't faking it. He prided himself on being a good liar when needed, but he couldn't fool her.

Nathalie was so attuned to him, knew him so well, that there was nothing he could hide from her.

"Andrew, this is gross. Let me shower first."

"No." Lifting her up a little, he pulled her pants and panties off with one hand. He was so strong now, holding her up on one palm as if she was a small child and not a healthy woman who wasn't exactly thin. Nevertheless, the size of his muscles didn't give him the right to boss her around.

"No?" She lifted a brow.

"You're clean, baby, and you smell fantastic to me. If you shower, your natural aroma will be replaced by artificial soap smell. I would much rather smell you."

"Are you sure? Does the smell of soap bother you now?"

He shook his head. "Only if it's a strong scent."

"Fine. I'll rinse myself without using soap, but that's all I'm willing to compromise on."

Andrew pinched her butt. "Stubborn woman. Have it your way. I'm coming in with you."

She could live with that.

Andrew picked her up and carried her into the shower. The thing was the size of a small carwash.

"It's cold," she complained as he laid her down on the curved bench.

"It will warm up in a moment."

While Andrew fiddled with the water temperature dial, Nathalie gathered her long hair in a tight bun, securing it by tucking the ends inside it. As the shower filled with steam, he got rid of his clothes and stepped in.

The man took her breath away; all six feet and three inches of him and his beautifully sculpted lean muscles. Or perhaps it was the steam. Nah, it was the man. Her body warmed up from the inside, and the moisture between her legs had nothing to do with the overhead spray.

Andrew's nostrils flared. "Oh, baby, spread those lovely legs of yours and let me get a lungful."

Nathalie's knees parted of their own accord, and Andrew's erection sprang to attention. He sat on the bench beside her, and she reached for him, gently rubbing the hard length. Was he bigger than before? She didn't think so. In fact, she hoped nothing changed in this part of his anatomy. The fit had been perfect before, and thankfully it was still perfect after his transition.

Andrew ran a finger between her folds. "So wet," he groaned.

The sensation was electrifying, and her hips jerked up. "Put it in," she whispered.

He did, and the moan that escaped her throat was loud. For a change, there was no need to keep things quiet, and Nathalie loved the freedom of making as much noise as she wanted and saying whatever she wanted. There was no one else in the apartment. "Make love to me, Andrew. I need you inside me."

He smirked. "I will. But first, I want a taste of that sweet pussy of yours. Spread wide for me, baby."

Oh. That was so naughty.

Andrew got between her legs and lifted them over his shoulders, exposing her even further, then dipped his head and gave her slit a long lick. "Delicious."

Nathalie closed her eyes and let pleasure overtake her. It was a bit selfish to lie on her back and let Andrew take care of her, but she had every intention of returning the favor later. For now, she would take everything he offered and enjoy every little bit of pleasure guilt free.

He was going slow, letting her simmer, licking at her folds and lapping at her juices but avoiding her clit. Impatient, Nathalie craved his fingers inside her and his lips on that most sensitive spot, but he was in no rush.

Her breasts heavy and full, her nipples stiff and in need of a good pinch, she ached for Andrew's hands on them, but unfortunately he had only two and they were busy elsewhere. Unbidden, Jackson's tentacle porn popped into her mind.

Oh, the possibilities. Nathalie chuckled softly.

In the real world, however, Andrew wasn't about to sprout extra appendages, but she had her own two hands. Nathalie cupped her breasts, thrumming her nipples with her thumbs.

Not the same as Andrew's rugged hands. Not even close.

Closing her eyes, she imagined Andrew's long fingers on her achy nipples, pinching, first lightly, than a little harder... "Ouch!" It hurt, and she hadn't applied much pressure at all.

"What's the matter, baby?" Andrew lifted his head. "Did I hurt you?"

She shook her head. "No, I did it to myself. My nipples are so damn sensitive."

"I told you. You're about to get your period. Your breasts are always tender a couple of days before you're due."

"Yeah, you're right, that must be it. Now go back to what you were doing." She pointed at the junction of her legs.

Andrew chuckled. "Your wish is my command."

6

ANDREW

Andrew would never admit it to Nathalie or anyone else, but he liked it when she got all bossy with him. Other than Bridget, his ex-girlfriends had been guarded around him. He'd known that he intimidated them, not intentionally, but between the scars and the secrets and his less than cheerful demeanor, women had trodden carefully around him.

It had been fine for the short-lived relationships he'd had—the distance hadn't bothered him. In fact, it had had its advantages. Fewer questions asked, fewer demands on his time, fewer opportunities for friction.

Nathalie was possessive, jealous, and bossy. If anyone had told him that he would love it, Andrew would've laughed in their faces.

The thing was, Nathalie was possessive and jealous because she loved him as much as he loved her. And the bossy part? It meant that she was comfortable with him and that he didn't intimidate her.

"Come on, Andrew, stop teasing. I'm so close." She rubbed her core against his mouth.

He lifted his head. "Do you want me to make you come? Or do you want me to take you to bed?"

She smiled with hooded eyes. "Take me to bed, big guy, and fuck me long and hard."

Damn, Nathalie talking dirty was hot. They really needed to get their own place so she could always let go like she was doing now.

"Give me ten seconds." Andrew jumped up and turned the water off, then grabbed one of the big towels stacked inside a big niche by the tub. He lifted Nathalie off the bench and wrapped her in the towel, all in one smooth move, then carried her to the bedroom.

"I love it that you carry me all the time," she said into his chest.

"Only when I want sex. It's a bribe." He deposited her on the bed and used the towel she'd been wrapped in to dry himself off. The thing was still wet, but it was good enough. Going back for another one would've taken too long.

Nathalie lifted up on her elbows. "Do I look like a woman who needs to be bribed?"

Andrew got on top of her and nuzzled her neck. "You don't, baby. It just makes me feel manly. Admit it; it's a turn-on."

Nathalie wrapped her arms around his neck. "Yes, it is. But everything about you turns me on. You're a very sexy man." She narrowed her eyes. "My sexy guy."

"Only yours. And you are mine. Only mine." For some reason, the statement carried a different meaning for him now. Before, it was a declaration of love; now, it was possession, and he felt it with every molecule of his new body.

It seemed that these immortal genes were advanced in some ways and primitive in others. On the one hand, the longevity and mental abilities were light years ahead of human evolution, but the urges and instincts were almost animalistic in nature. Not to mention the intensity. Compared to this, on a scale of one to ten—with what he was feeling now being ten—his pre-immortal human urges were at a two.

Nathalie was his mate, she belonged to him, and he knew without a shadow of a doubt that he would kill anyone who threatened to take her away from him. Tear the perpetrator to pieces with his bare hands…

Andrew shook his head. It was insanity. He had to control those animalistic urges before he became a mindless savage. How the hell did the other immortal males handle the intensity of their emotions? Was he having trouble because he was new to this?

After all, he hadn't grown up among them. The severe punishments imposed on the young immortals for breaching the clan's code of conduct made sense to him now. As their powers emerged following their transition, and puberty hit them full force with its avalanche of hormones, there was no other way to keep them in check.

Human teenage boys were hard enough to control; young immortals, who were just getting into their powers, were probably a nightmare. Between the insatiable sex drive and the predatory instincts, they could easily turn into monsters.

Jackson and Vlad seemed like well-adjusted, reasonable guys, but then restraint had been drilled into their heads for years, and the threat of a whipping was a formidable deterrent.

Maybe sating his sexual need would calm the other urges. He needed to be inside his woman. "Are you ready for me, baby?" He kissed her neck, fighting the urge to sink his teeth into the softness.

"Why don't you check for yourself?"

She was soaking, but he made himself go slow, prepping her with his fingers first. It had been a tight fit even before his transition, and if his cock had indeed grown bigger, he might hurt her.

When all three fingers slid in and out of her with ease, he deemed her ready and poised his shaft at her entrance.

Nathalie panted in anticipation. "Now, Andrew…"

He surged into her.

"Yes…" she groaned.

Andrew pulled out and pushed back again. "Like that?"

"Aha…don't stop." Her arms wrapped around him, holding him tight, Nathalie closed her eyes and let the pleasure take her.

God, he loved this woman. Loved the way she trusted him completely.

Love, he realized, that soft, tender feeling was the antidote to the madness. It allowed him to slow down and take his time pleasuring his sweet Nathalie.

Problem was, in no time at all lust overpowered love, and the savage need returned full force.

Nathalie took it all, meeting his pounding thrusts and spiraling out of control along with him. Her climax erupted, detonating his seed, together with an overwhelming urge to bite—a primitive need to mark her as his own.

Clinging desperately to his sanity, to his humanity, Andrew forced his teeth away from Nathalie's neck, licking and sucking the spot he'd nipped until his cock finally stopped shooting into Nathalie's spasming sheath.

It felt like he'd emptied a gallon of his essence into her. Good that she was on the pill. Otherwise, he would've gotten her pregnant for sure.

Except, right now, still surrounded by her welcoming heat, connected to her body and soul, he wished he could've put a child inside her.

Given their respective ages, there was no reason to wait.

I'm an idiot.

Of course there was reason to wait. Nathalie hadn't transitioned yet, and giving birth was dangerous even in today's world. He would not risk her life for anything.

Andrew lifted his head and winced. He'd made a mess. Teeth marks marred Nathalie's neck, clearly visible under the purple bruise of the hickey he'd left.

"I'm sorry, baby." He smoothed his finger over the bruise. "Does it hurt?"

Nathalie's expression was one of bliss, not pain, but it might have been the post orgasmic endorphins numbing the pain.

"Nah, just a little and it was worth it." She smiled. "And to think I was so afraid of the bite. It's really not so bad, it adds to the excitement."

Should he tell her the truth? Yeah, he should.

"I don't want to scare you, but this was more of a nip than a bite. My fangs didn't come out yet, and my glands are not producing venom, but the urge to bite is strong. I tried to be as gentle as I could because I can't give you pleasure this way. Not until I produce venom. The bite on its own is no fun."

"Well, I liked it. It was kinky."

Andrew felt his cock swell up again. Being immortal had its advantages, but he had to remember that Nathalie was still human. He didn't want her to get sore. Gently, he started to withdraw.

Nathalie grabbed his ass. "Where are you going?"

"Back to the shower?"

"Nah-ah. We are not done here."

"We aren't?"

"Nope."

7

ROBERT

It was humiliating.

Just like the other illegal workers standing next to him on the corner of a building supplies warehouse and baking in the Las Vegas heat, Robert waited for some random jackass with a pickup truck to stop and offer him a job for the day.

A day's worth of manual labor; that was all he could hope for. That was his future. That was what he'd abandoned the Brotherhood and the only home he'd ever known for.

It all would have been worth it for the right female, but he was coming to the sad realization that Carol wasn't the one.

He'd betrayed his brothers for a slut.

She'd fooled him with her big innocent eyes and her soft blond curls and her beautiful, angelic face. He'd made a bad bargain and was getting no more and no less than he'd asked for.

Carol's slutty disposition didn't mean she was without honor, though. She was going to stick to the deal she'd made with him, giving him the three months he'd asked for but not a day more.

After that, he would have absolutely nothing to show for his sacrifice.

A brief gust of hot desert wind ruffled his shirt, providing a little relief by drying some of the sweat dripping down his back.

Robert glanced at the group of men standing a few feet away from him. They kept their distance, sensing that he was different, dangerous, and not only because he topped the tallest of them by a full head.

The men knew he didn't belong with them. Except, his situation was the same as theirs—short on money and desperate for work.

He pulled out his wallet and counted what little was left of his cash; a couple of twenties, a five, two singles and some change. Carol offered to give him pocket money, but he would rather starve than take it. Her paying for all their expenses was shameful enough.

He would've loved a cold Coke, but water would have to do. The warehouse people had been kind enough to leave a cooler for the day laborers. Robert grabbed a paper cup, filled it with cold water, emptied it on a oner, then repeated two more times before crumpling the cup and throwing it into the trash bin.

A pickup rolled to a stop. The driver eyed the group of men, then pointed at Robert. "You, tall guy, ever installed sprinklers?"

Robert nodded. He knew what they looked like. That should be good enough. He'd figure it out on the job. It wasn't as if he could afford to turn down an offer.

"Then come on, get in."

Robert didn't even ask how much the guy was willing to pay. At that point, he would've accepted anything. He walked over to the passenger side of the truck and got in.

"Robert." He offered his hand.

The guy's eyes widened in surprise as he shook what was offered. "Don, but my friends call me Donny. I never expected to find an American here. Mostly it's illegal workers." He put the stick into drive, and the truck lurched forward. "I don't usually hire guys off the street, but two of my boys didn't show up this morning. The bums called in sick, but it was just a lame excuse. They were probably hungover." He winked at Robert.

Robert returned a tight-lipped smile. "I'm actually Australian." Interacting with humans wasn't something he was good at. Hell, he sucked at interacting with immortals and mortals alike. Lucky for him, the guy was a talker.

"Down under, huh?" Don imitated Robert's fake Australian accent. "What brings you here?"

"A woman." It was partially true.

The guy nodded with an expression of compassionate understanding. "A man would do all kinds of stupid things for the right woman; follow her half around the world if need be. I hope she is worth it."

Robert rubbed a hand over his sweaty neck. "I don't know."

"Is she trouble?" Don asked, looking eager. It seemed Don loved listening to gossip.

"Not really. She just isn't the kind of woman I thought she was."

"So you didn't meet her before traveling all the way to the States? Was it an Internet romance?"

"Yes, exactly." Robert liked the way the guy asked a question and immediately offered an answer. Coming up with lies on the spot wasn't one of his strong suits.

Don shook his head. "My friend's wife left him for a guy she met on the Internet; an Australian like you. Three kids and twelve years of marriage didn't mean shit to her. She gave it all up for a guy she chatted with on the Internet. He came here and they got married and everything. Two years later, she divorced that dude as well. But at least he got a Green Card out of it."

"What's a Green Card?"

Don regarded Robert as if he was missing a couple of screws. "How can you be in the States and not know what's a Green Card?"

Robert shrugged. It hadn't been part of his briefing.

"It's a piece of paper that says you are a legal resident of the United States. It means you get treated almost like a citizen. You can work legally, pay your taxes, stuff like that." Don drifted off as they arrived at the construction site.

This Green Card was exactly what Robert needed, but there was something he was missing in this story.

"I don't understand. How did he get a Green Card out of the divorce?"

Don rolled his eyes. "Not from the divorce, from the marriage. You marry an American woman, and you get a Green Card." He enunciated each word as if he was talking to someone who had trouble understanding English.

"Yes, of course. It makes perfect sense. I guess standing in the sun all day fried my brain." Robert attempted a smile.

That seemed to appease Don, and he clapped him on his shoulder. "The Vegas sun would do that. Lucky for you, we are installing sprinklers in the basement today. Compared to the outdoors, it is nice and cool there."

As the crew supervisor explained what needed to be done, Robert understood why Don had picked him out of all the guys who had been waiting at the warehouse. The sprinkler system was being installed up on the ceiling of the basement, and Robert's height was an advantage. The added benefit Don hadn't anticipated was Robert's strength and endurance. He was fast, efficient, and untiring. It didn't take long for the crew to realize that he could do the work of three men with ease.

An hour later, the supervisor stopped by Robert's ladder and looked up. "If you want the job, it's yours, son. It pays well."

That got Robert's interest. "How much?"

"Twenty-five an hour."

He had no idea what was considered good pay for this kind of work and didn't really care. He would've happily shoveled manure for half of that. Problem was, his lack of papers.

Robert wiped the sweat off his forehead and frowned.

The supervisor put his hand on the third rung and leaned in closer. "Don't worry about the paperwork. Don will make it happen for a guy like you."

"Thank you."

Glancing at all the work Robert had managed to do in the past hour, the guy smiled. "No, thank you!"

After a while the repetitious work became automatic, and Robert's mind was freed to mull over the important information he had gleaned today. If Carol agreed to marry him, he would get that coveted Green Card. It seemed that fate had brought him to the right place at the right time.

Las Vegas was, supposedly, the best place for a quick marriage.

Ever since Carol and he had made their residence in the MGM, he had seen many couples dressed in fancy attire walking through the lobby and the casino. Carol had explained that they were wearing traditional bride and groom outfits. She'd also explained the benefits of getting married in Las Vegas.

The problem would be convincing her to do it. She didn't love him, and

Robert had lost hope that she ever would. Still, she could do it as a favor. After all, it wasn't as if her true fated mate was going to show up anytime soon.

They could get a quick Vegas wedding and then go their separate ways.

Robert let the hand holding the heavy wrench drop by his side. Saying goodbye to Carol was going to be tough. He didn't love her, but he'd gotten used to having her around.

Was caring for a person not good enough?

They liked each other and the sex was like nothing he'd ever experienced with a mortal woman. Carol admitted the same. It wasn't perfect, they weren't each other's one true love, but what they had was better than going through life alone.

Much better.

Tonight, after he got back from work, he was going to have a talk with Carol.

Robert groaned. It wasn't going to be easy. By now he had a pretty good idea who Carol was and what she was all about. Even if she agreed, he knew what her conditions would be.

After his three months were up, she would demand the freedom to screw whoever she wanted, whenever, wherever, and he had a big problem with that.

8

NATHALIE

"I'm hungry." Nathalie stretched lazily. Exhausted after their marathon sex session, she had fallen asleep in Andrew's arms while he carried her from the shower back to their room.

Andrew propped himself on his elbow and leaned, dipping his head to plant a soft kiss on her lips. "I'm starving, but we need to get dressed before venturing out to the kitchen. Syssi and Kian are back."

Impossible.

They'd gotten back from their shopping trip shortly after lunch. Kian and Syssi should've been still at work. "How long was I asleep?"

"Over three hours." There was a very satisfied smirk on his face. "I tired you out, didn't I?"

"You're insatiable. If I didn't pass out, you would've kept going."

A frown replaced his smirk. "I'm such a selfish prick. I was curious to see how many times I can go and forgot that I needed to be mindful of you."

Nathalie punched his forearm. "I'm not fragile. And I could've stopped you at any time, but I didn't want to. I was curious too."

"Aren't you sore?"

"Yeah, but I didn't feel it before."

"The endorphins."

Nathalie smiled sheepishly. "It was worth it. I lost count of how many times I orgasmed."

That erased the frown from Andrew's face, but only for a moment. "Do you want me to bring you Advil or Tylenol?"

"Don't be silly." Nathalie swung her legs over the side of the bed and got up. "I'm fine." She rubbed her belly. "But I need to put something in here."

Andrew arched a brow.

The scoundrel.

Nathalie shook her head and pointed a finger at him. "I meant food. God, you've such a one-track mind."

"I'm a man, sweetheart," Andrew said as he padded to the closet. He leaned over the shopping bags and pulled out a new pair of jeans and a pack of boxer shorts.

She followed him inside. "That's your answer to everything?"

Andrew tore open the pack and pulled out one. "No, just anything that has to do with sex."

"What kind of sex?" He'd better not fantasize about other women.

He winked at her as he pulled the boxer shorts over his muscled thighs and covered his tight ass. "All the things I could do to you, where, when, and how."

Good answer.

Nathalie leaned against the doorjamb and watched Andrew's beautiful body move with the same elegant fluidity she'd noticed about the other immortals.

It was fun teasing him about his dirty mind, but that didn't mean she wanted him to stop. Nathalie loved that Andrew was always hungry for her. He made her feel desired, beautiful.

"I love you," she said.

His jeans halfway zipped, Andrew paused and reached for her. Nathalie went into his arms, placing her palms on the taut skin of his pectorals. He was still shirtless, and she was still naked, and the skin to skin felt incredibly good.

"I love you too." He kissed her lips softly, an almost chaste kiss. "If you want to eat, you need to get dressed, baby. Seeing you naked makes me forget I have any needs other than being inside you."

Reluctantly, she left the shelter of his arms. "You want me to try on that dress?" Another red number he'd claimed would look fantastic on her. If it were up to Andrew, she would be wearing nothing but red. Correction, she would be wearing nothing at all. Which was fine by her. Problem was, they seldom had the privacy to indulge in prolonged nudity.

Nathalie sighed. They needed to find a solution that would allow them to live as a couple and still provide for her father's needs.

"You don't have to wear the dress if you don't want to." Andrew misinterpreted her sigh.

"It's not about the dress." She pulled on a pair of black undies. "I was just thinking that we need to find a way to live as a couple; to have the privacy to be intimate with each other outside the bedroom, or walk around naked if we want to."

"Where there is a will, there is a way. We'll find a solution."

As Nathalie finished dressing, she thought about Andrew's reassurance. It was the same as saying everything would be fine. There was no way to predict with surety that indeed all would be well. No one could promise that. They needed to brainstorm solutions, maybe even get Kian and Syssi to brainstorm with them, and come up with a plan.

That's how things got done.

When they finally made it to the living room, they were met by three pairs of amused eyes. Kian sat on the armchair he favored, his laptop resting on his knees, while Bridget sat across from him on the sofa, her doctor bag on the coffee table.

Syssi closed the book she'd been reading and smiled. "Hi, you two. You slept through dinner. Your plates are in the warming drawer." She pointed toward the kitchen. "Okidu is not here, so help yourselves."

"How did you know we were sleeping?" Andrew asked as he walked over to where she pointed.

Nathalie's snort was echoed by Kian's.

"This is one thing your transition didn't cure. You still snore like a jackhammer," his brother-in-law said without lifting his head.

Andrew flipped him off, but Kian's eyes were glued to the screen of his laptop, and he didn't see it. Or pretended not too.

After Nathalie had helped Andrew with the silverware and the napkins, they sat down to eat at the kitchen counter.

"When you are done eating, I want to do a check up on you," Bridget said.

Andrew nodded with a full mouth. He was shoving food into it as if someone might take it away from him. Good thing that the plates Okidu had prepared for them were the size of platters and piled with enough to feed a family of ten. Humans, that is. Immortal males? Maybe one and a half.

When they were done, cleanup and all, they joined the others in the living room.

Bridget checked Andrew's vitals and took a blood sample. She also took a few measurements to see if he was still growing, making notes of everything on her tablet.

"Stand up, I want to check your height." Bridget took him by the elbow and walked him over to the nearest wall.

Nathalie smiled sadly. She remembered her mother checking her height and marking it on the kitchen wall. Eva had not allowed that wall to be repainted. Ever. There was no doubt in Nathalie's mind that her mother loved her, and yet she had left, never to be heard from again. The home they had shared, along with all those happy moments embedded in its walls and its floorboards, had to be sold, the memories of growing up with two adoring parents gone with it.

She couldn't understand how her mother could've done it. Even if she was on the run, she could've sent a postcard, or called from a public phone and let Nathalie know she was still alive. Didn't she know how devastating it was for her daughter, not knowing if her mother was dead or alive?

Hopefully, Bhathian would find Eva, and Nathalie would get the answers she desperately needed.

Bridget retracted the measuring tape and put it back in her pocket. "If there was any growth, it's minimal. Tomorrow, stop by the clinic so I can take accurate measurements."

"Yes, ma'am."

"How are you feeling, any pains, aches, discomfort?"

Andrew chuckled. "I wouldn't know. The pain meds you gave me are great. I feel the swelling in my gums, but it's like uncomfortable pressure, not pain."

Bridget patted his arm. "Smart man, following doctor's orders. Anything else?"

Andrew scratched his head. "The sharpened senses are very disturbing. I'm sure that without the meds I would've had a bitch of a headache. Sometimes it's so bad that I feel nauseated."

Bridget turned to Nathalie. "I forgot to ask, but are you still getting nauseous?"

Nathalie shook her head. "I'm fine. It was the stress."

Bridget nodded and turned back to Andrew. "I'm sorry, Andrew. You were saying?"

"That's about it." He scratched his head again. "I don't know if it's worth mentioning, but Nathalie smells differently to me now."

Nathalie felt her cheeks heat up. What was wrong with him? Why was he bringing it up?

He cast her an apologetic glance. "Don't get me wrong; she still smells amazing, just different. I don't know if it's me, or perhaps it's something else. Could she..." He hesitated and cast her another glance. "Could it be an illness?"

Bridget smiled, which was weird considering Andrew's obvious worry. "I think Nathalie is perfectly healthy, but I'll run a few tests. In fact—" She turned to Nathalie. "Why don't you come with me to the clinic now?"

"I feel fine, and I need to go get my father. William probably can't wait to be free of him."

Bridget lifted her doctor's bag and motioned for Nathalie to follow. "We can stop by William's on the way to the clinic and see what's the status there. If they're fine, we can continue to my examination room and run a few tests. If not, you can pick your dad up, and we will meet tomorrow."

As usual, Bridget was the definition of no-nonsense.

"Sounds like a plan. Let's go." Nathalie followed Bridget.

"I'm coming too," Andrew said.

Bridget halted him with a hand on his chest. "No, there is no need for you to be there. Let the girl breathe, she'll be perfectly fine without you hovering over her."

Andrew looked a little miffed and lifted a questioning brow at Nathalie. "Do you want me to come with you?"

From behind his back, Bridget shook her head.

"I'll be fine. I think you've had enough of that clinic. Right?"

By Andrew's frown, he wasn't happy about her leaving his side, but for some reason, Bridget didn't want him to come.

"Text me if you want me to join you. Okay?"

"I will." She kissed his cheek.

As they waited for the elevator, Nathalie didn't dare risk asking Bridget anything. If Andrew's hearing had become as good as Jackson's, he would hear them even out in the vestibule. She waited for the elevator doors to close behind them and then for the lift to start its descent. "What was that all about?"

Bridget smiled and clasped Nathalie's hand. "I'm almost sure you are pregnant. I didn't know if you wanted Andrew to be there when we found out the results or not, and I couldn't ask you in front of him. He provided the perfect excuse, and I seized it. Now you can decide if you want to find out first and then tell him, or if you want him to be there for the test results. If you do, you can text him to come down and join you before we start."

Nathalie pulled her hand out of Bridget's and crossed her arms over her chest. "I'm not pregnant. The nausea is gone, and besides, I'm not late. I'm due in a couple of days." Her breasts were full, and her nipples were sensitive—same as every month before menstruating.

"You smell pregnant. I didn't recognize it at first because pregnant immortal females emit a different scent, and I don't interact with human females enough to be familiar with it."

"So how can you be so sure if you don't know how a pregnant human smells?"

"I stood next to one in the sandwich shop across the street and then it hit me. I knew you were pregnant."

Oh, dear God, she couldn't be. No way. It wasn't part of the plan.

Bridget was smiling broadly as if she'd delivered the best of news.

"I can't be pregnant," Nathalie whispered, tears prickling the back of her eyes.

Bridget looked puzzled. "You don't want to be? Why the hell not? You're not a teenager, you're not destitute, and you have a wonderful man to raise this child with. Pregnancy is wonderful. It's a miracle. You're going to have a baby with the man you love! What could be better than that?"

With a ping, the elevator came to a stop, and the door slid open. Bridget pulled Nathalie out and practically dragged her to the clinic. Once there, she pushed her into a chair and handed her a box of orange juice.

"Drink. You look pale as a ghost. Though I can't understand why."

Bridget seemed angry, as if for some reason Nathalie's freak-out over the pregnancy was offending her on a personal level.

A few sips from the juice helped, and Nathalie took a deep breath. She didn't owe Bridget an explanation but she needed to voice her fears. "It's not that I don't want a baby, I do, just not yet. I'm stuck in a situation that I see no solution to. I have a tiny apartment above my coffee shop, which is perfect for keeping an eye on my father at all times, but too small for the three of us to live there together, or for Andrew and me to have any measure of privacy."

Bridget shrugged. "So you need to move to a bigger place. I don't see how this is an insurmountable problem."

Easy for her to say.

But the truth was that things had changed a lot since Andrew and Bhathian walked into Nathalie's life, bringing Jackson, who brought Vlad and now another kid. It was no longer just her father and her without any support whatsoever.

Furthermore, moving her father from his familiar environment hadn't resulted in the meltdown she'd anticipated. Fernando was fine away from the shop. Never mind that he thought they were on vacation in a luxury hotel. As long as he was happy, Papi could believe whatever he wanted.

Perhaps she could just keep telling him that they were on a vacation—a very long one.

Nathalie lifted her chin. "You're absolutely right. I'm no longer alone with no one to lend a shoulder when I need it. The boys are practically running the shop, William is keeping my dad busy for a few hours every day, and I have Andrew."

Bridget crouched in front of Nathalie. "And you have all of us and our not too shabby resources at your disposal. An entire clan is eager to help you in any way we can."

Choking on emotion, Nathalie nodded. "I still didn't internalize it. After managing on my own for so long, it's hard to expect and accept help."

"Understandable." Bridget pushed up to stand. "So, what will it be? Do you want Andrew to come down and wait with you for the results, or do you want to tell him after you know for sure?"

A tough decision.

On the one hand, she could've used the support; on the other hand, she wanted to spare Andrew the anxiety and stress. He'd been through enough. Besides, there was still a small chance that Bridget was wrong and Nathalie wasn't pregnant. Why make a big fuss for no good reason?

"Let's do the tests first. I don't want to tell Andrew and then discover that it was a false alarm."

Bridget cast her a disapproving look, but Nathalie didn't care if the doctor approved of her decision or not. It wasn't Bridget's call.

"Here, fill it at least halfway." Bridget handed her a plastic container.

In the bathroom, Nathalie did her best to aim straight into the cup, but it was easier said than done. Just another advantage guys had over girls. Mission accomplished, she closed the lid on the container, wiped it carefully with a paper towel, and returned to the exam room.

Embarrassed, she handed it to Bridget. It wasn't the same as depositing a pee container through a window in the lab's bathroom and having an anonymous lab technician pick it up long after she was gone.

Bridget took it with a gloved hand and walked to the other room. Nathalie frowned when she returned after a minute. No way she had the results already.

"I want to wait five to ten minutes to make sure. But it might be too early for a urine test to detect pregnancy. If it comes up negative, I'll do a blood test." The doctor handed her a magazine. "To pass the time."

As if.

She flipped through the pages while Bridget got busy with her laptop. After five minutes Nathalie could wait no more. "Could you go check?"

Bridget looked at her with an indulgent smile. "Sure."

The next few seconds were the most nerve-wracking moments of Nathalie's life.

When Bridget returned, the wide grin on her face announced the test's results, but Nathalie needed verbal confirmation.

"Congratulations, you and Andrew are going to become Mommy and Daddy."

Oh, my God!

Nathalie didn't know whether to laugh and clap her hands or cry. Mostly, she was terrified.

"Do you want me to call Andrew and tell him to come down here?"

Nathalie shook her head. "I don't want to tell him over the phone, and if you call him, he'll freak out. He already thinks I'm carrying a disease."

Bridget nodded. "Do you want me to come up with you?"

"No. I'll be fine, but you can do me a big favor if you'd check on my father and bring him up. I'm sure William is tired of his company."

"I will. Now, chin up, and a big smile. You don't want Andrew to think you're upset about carrying his baby."

Nathalie grimaced. "I'll practice in front of the mirror in the elevator." She turned to leave then stopped. "I don't want you to think I'm not happy. I'm just scared."

Bridget pulled her into a gentle hug. "I know. It's going to be okay. In fact, it's going to be wonderful, and I'm saying it as a mother and as your friend, not your doctor."

Nathalie wiped a tear when Bridget let go of her. "Thank you."

"You're welcome. You can't understand it now, but you will when you hold your child in your arms for the first time. Nothing in your life experience can prepare you for that magical moment."

9

CAROL

I found a job. I'll be back at 6, said the text from Robert.
Carol texted back. *I'm so happy for you. What kind of job?*
Installing sprinklers.
That's great. See you in the evening.

Carol dropped her phone on the bed and did a little victory dance. Not because she was happy that Robert had gotten a job, but because she was finally free of his constant supervision. Until now, even when he'd left the hotel room, she'd never known when he'd be back and hadn't dared visit one of the fancy casinos in search of a loaded high roller.

Freedom felt so sweet after being denied it for so long. Carol had spent her entire adult life doing as she pleased and answering to no one. Being shackled to a guy wasn't fun. Especially a guy like Robert. Spending time with him was as fascinating as watching paint dry.

She was sincerely glad for him; depending on her for money was making the guy miserable, and she didn't like seeing him moping around, getting more and more depressed with each passing day. He deserved better, and Carol desperately wanted to give it to him, but without sacrificing herself and her freedom.

Moving back to Los Angeles and arranging a job for him, maybe even hooking him up with one of her friends, was as far as she was willing to go to make him happy. She could also keep indulging him with fabulous sex, beyond the three months she'd promised, at least until she found him a substitute.

Not a bad deal if she said so herself.

He would be an idiot to turn it down.

Except, he had a job now.

Carol shrugged as she pulled her best dress off the hanger. Installing sprinklers wasn't the kind of job that would make him happy. A guy who'd been the second in command for the sadist wouldn't be satisfied with manual labor.

She pulled on the clingy black dress she'd bought in one of the hotel's stores and examined herself in the mirror, smoothing her hands over the stretchy fabric covering her feminine curves. She looked sexy, round in all the right places without crossing the line into overweight. Well, maybe a little, but this was exactly what men found attractive.

Guys didn't like sticks. They liked a woman who was soft and didn't poke them with her protruding ribs or wrap bony arms and legs around them. Those tall, skinny models looked great in clothes, but not so great in the nude.

A pink lipstick and some black mascara were all she needed as far as makeup. Pushing her feet into high-heeled stilettos, she glanced at the mirror one last time before stepping outside.

As she walked through the crowded lobby, her hips sashaying and her blond curls bouncing, Carol felt the eyes of every male, regardless of age or ethnicity, follow her.

She let out a breath, feeling like herself for the first time since her abduction. This was her gig. A sexy-childlike seductress was what she did best. She was irresistible.

"The Wynn Hotel, please," she told the cabbie.

The drive was short, and as she entered the high-class casino, Carol felt giddy like a teenage girl in a shoe store. She approached one of the tables and started her usual act.

It took less than an hour of schmoozing with the rich guys for her to realize that she couldn't do it with any of them.

None were attractive. In fact, she found most of them repulsive.

Strange.

Powerful, successful men were attractive even if their physical attributes left a lot to be desired, and she usually found the high rollers sexy because of their personalities and their wallets. That being said, she had some minimum standards in that regard.

What she didn't tolerate was vulgarity or rudeness.

Yes, she expected to be paid, but she also needed to feel desired and appreciated. It was an integral part of the deal.

"It's been fun," Carol said as she squeezed her target's shoulder, keeping her ass out of his reach. His pinching fingers had no doubt left bruises on her soft derrière.

He caught her hand. "Where are you going? You're my lucky charm."

"I have to go home and feed my five kids." Usually that line worked like a charm.

"You can go home later, after I've fucked you good and long."

Right.

She doubted the jerk knew how to make it good for a woman. Flashing him one of her saccharine-sweet smiles, she patted his cheek. "Oh, baby, I was looking forward to a tumble with you, but it's getting late for me, and I don't want to interrupt your winning streak." She tried to pull her hand out of his grasp while using no more force than a human female would.

Evidently, the asshat wasn't getting her elephant-sized hints. He pulled on her hand with such force that she landed in his lap. "Give me five minutes to wrap this up."

This was getting sticky. She couldn't get off him without using her strength, and if she did, it would cause a scene.

Carol didn't want to do it, but the idiot was asking for it. Pretending she wanted to kiss him, she held his fat cheeks in her hands and looked into his eyes.

Feh. It was ugly inside his head. Really ugly. The guy was a cheating, lying, abusive jerk. She was lucky she'd changed her mind and hadn't gone up to his hotel room.

With a wicked smile, Carol reached inside his mind and implanted something that was going to ruin his way of life but make it better for everyone else. From now on, whenever he considered cheating, lying, or being nasty to his family or anyone else, the guy was going to get severe stomach cramps.

His face twisting in a grimace, he pushed her off his lap. "Excuse me. Nature calls."

She smiled and patted his flabby arm. "Of course, sweetie."

As Carol sashayed away on her spiky heels, she wondered what else she could do with her time. Shopping with the killer heels on was out. Maybe she could watch a movie. But going to the theater by herself was just sad. If she were home, she would've pulled a new gourmet recipe off the Internet, whipped up a meal and invited a few friends for dinner. But there was no kitchen in the hotel room.

On the way back, she stopped at the giftshop and bought a bunch of new magazines and the latest Nora hardcover. Which was silly, since she read mostly on her phone. It was a bit of nostalgia, a throwback to simpler times.

She missed the feeling of holding a real book in her hands.

In the hotel room, Carol grabbed another shower even though she'd showered this morning, scrubbing herself all over and soaping twice. Just in case some of the jerk's scent had rubbed off on her when he'd pulled her onto his lap. If Robert smelled another man on her, he would go ballistic.

Carol snorted. For Robert, ballistic probably meant a frown and a grunt. She couldn't picture him raising his voice to her, or anyone else for that matter. He was so mellow it was hard to believe he'd had the courage to help her escape.

Still, one never knew. Immortal males were volatile and aggressive, even the more timid among them. Poked too hard, this gentle tiger might bite.

That was why she hadn't told Robert what had happened to those he'd left behind in the monastery. She knew he'd hated Sebastian, but it seemed he'd been on good terms with the others. Learning that they were either dead or semi-dead and buried in the catacombs in indefinite stasis, he might lose his temper.

Not something she was going to risk.

A little after six, she recognized his heavy footfalls coming down the long corridor, and a moment later his keycard opened the door.

The man who entered was not the same man who'd left the room this morning. It wasn't only the toothy smile he greeted her with; it was his loose posture, relaxed facial muscles, and fluid moves. She'd known his employment or rather unemployment status had been bothering him, but she hadn't realized to what extent.

"Hi." Carol laid the book she'd been reading on the nightstand and sat up cross-legged on the bed. "How was your day?"

Robert crossed the small room in two long strides and hauled her up, lifting her into his strong arms and twirling her around. "I got paid," he said when he finally let her slide down his body and stand on her own two feet.

Reaching for his back pocket, he pulled out a folded piece of paper. "Here, this is for you." He handed it to her.

Taking it, Carol lifted a brow. Had he written her a letter? That was awfully nice of him. She loved getting love notes, especially when they sang her praise. But when she looked at what was in her hand, she realized it wasn't a piece of paper but a folded check: Two hundred dollars written out to Carol with no last name.

"I don't understand." She lifted her eyes and took in the look of pride on his face.

"I didn't know your last name so I told Don, that's my new boss, to write my paycheck to Carol. You can add your last name." He pulled another piece of paper from his other pocket. "Don came up with a great solution to my legal status. He is going to write the checks to you, as if you are the one working for his construction company. And since you are a citizen it solves his accounting problem. But you need to fill in this form." He handed her the other paper.

That could work...

But wait, she didn't want it to work. She wanted to go back to Los Angeles, to her home and her friends and her old life.

Robert, like every typical male, was oblivious to her less than ecstatic reaction. "I'll shower quickly, and we'll go out to celebrate."

Carol managed a smile. "Sure, honey, and in the meantime think about where you'd like to go."

Hopefully, he wouldn't choose the buffet. She was getting sick of the greasy, mediocre fare.

He dipped his head and stole a brief kiss from her lips before heading to the adjacent bathroom.

Hmm, the smell of a man after a day of hard work was sexy as hell and it got her all hot and bothered. When he got out, she was going to start the celebration with an hour or two of wild sex.

Dinner can wait.

10

NATHALIE

Nathalie paused in front of the penthouse door, took a deep breath, schooled her expression the way she'd practiced in the elevator, and knocked.

Syssi opened the door. "You don't need to knock. Just come in."

Nathalie nodded even though she had no intention of barging into anyone's home without knocking. But that argument would have to wait for another day. Now she had a single task on her mind, and it was gargantuan.

"Hi, sweetheart." Andrew took her hand. "Is everything okay?"

"Yeah, I'm fine. Healthy as can be."

His facial muscles relaxed. "Good." He walked her over to the kitchen counter. "You have to try this cake."

Nathalie glanced at the small porcelain plate with a slice of chocolate cake on top of it and felt her stomach roil. Evidently, the pregnancy alone hadn't been the cause of her bouts of nausea, only when combined with extreme stress.

"Maybe later. I need to use the bathroom."

"I'm not sure it will still be here when you come back. I had to guard this last slice with my life."

"Then bring it to our room." Andrew had just given her the perfect excuse for taking him with her.

"Yes, ma'am." Not letting go of her hand, he grabbed the plate and let her pull him along.

In their bedroom, Nathalie closed the door, then led Andrew to the bathroom and closed that one as well.

"Missed me so much that you couldn't wait another moment?" With a smirk, Andrew put the cake on the counter and reached for her.

She batted his hands away and opened the faucets at both sinks, then dragged him into the shower and closed that door as well.

Andrew laughed and started unbuttoning his shirt. "I see that we are going to be very clean today."

And the guy was supposed to be an undercover agent? Really?

"I just don't want them to hear us," she whispered.

"I know. Good thinking with the faucets."

So he understood what she was trying to do, just not the why. "Talking. I don't want them to hear us talking."

The worried expression was back. "Why? What's going on?"

Nathalie grabbed the end of her braid and twirled it between her fingers. "I suggest you take a seat." She pointed to the shower bench.

Andrew didn't move. "Just tell me. I can take whatever you throw at me."

Sheesh, what was he imagining that she was going to tell him that he had gotten so defensive?

"It's not something bad, I hope. I want you to sit, so I don't have to stretch my neck while talking to you." The truth was that she wanted to see every nuance of Andrew's expression as she told him.

"Oh." Andrew backed into the bench and sat down, pulling Nathalie to stand between his spread thighs. "Now you can talk."

Seeing no point in prolonging the inevitable with a lengthy introduction, she leaned into him and whispered, "I'm pregnant."

Andrew's eyes popped wide, and he stopped breathing. Like a fish out of water, his mouth opened and closed a couple of times, but nothing came out or went in.

Nathalie patted his cheek. "Breathe, Andrew."

When he didn't respond, she patted him a little harder. "Come on, don't choke on me here. I'm freaking out enough as it is."

Instead of saying anything, Andrew pulled her into his arms in a crushing embrace. That was a good sign, right?

"How?" he mumbled into her neck.

Her strong, unflappable man was shaking like a leaf, and for some irrational reason, it amused her. "You know—peg A goes into slot B," she demonstrated with her fingers.

"You are on the pill. I see you take it every morning."

"The pill is not a hundred percent effective. Bridget said so herself. And anyway, the how doesn't matter. Fact is that we are going to have a baby."

"We are going to have a baby," he parroted quietly, then louder, "We are going to have a baby!" He pushed up to his feet and lifted her up. Twirling her around, he repeated, "We are going to have a baby!"

Lucky for her, the shower was so big that her airborne feet didn't hit anything.

She slapped his back. "Shh... they are going to hear you."

Andrew lowered Nathalie until her feet were back on the floor, but he didn't let go and sat on the bench, cradling her in his lap. "Do you want to keep it a secret?"

"No, of course not. I just wanted you to hear it before anyone else. And I don't want my father to hear it from Kian or Syssi either. I don't know how he is going to react. He's very traditional, and he's not going to be happy about his only daughter having a baby out of wedlock."

"So we get married. We can fly to Vegas today and be married by tomorrow."

Nathalie shook her head. "I don't want a crappy Vegas wedding."

"You're right. We have this huge family now. They won't be happy if we elope."

"No, they won't. Syssi said that she'd arranged her wedding in the span of two weeks. We can wait this long to tell my father." It would be awful to keep it a secret from him even for such a short time, but it was better than shocking him.

Andrew kissed her forehead. "No, sweetheart, we need to tell him right away. You can never know what will happen tomorrow. Your father is not well. If, God forbid, something happens to him between now and then, you'd never forgive yourself for not telling him in time."

She grimaced. "Way to spoil the mood, but you have a point. Besides, he already thinks we are married."

Andrew arched a brow. "Did he say something?"

"No, but he calls you son and doesn't make a fuss about us sleeping together. He would have if he thought we're living in sin."

"I think you are underestimating your dad. He married your mother while she was pregnant with you."

"I'm not sure she'd told him." Fernando had been a wonderful father to her. Still was, even in his impaired condition. His love for her was unconditional. Would it have been different if he'd known she wasn't his?

It was a question that would have to remain unanswered until her mother was found.

Andrew rocked her in his arms. "Tell me, baby, what kind of wedding do you want?"

She shrugged. "A big fancy white dress, preferably before I start showing, flowers, dinner, dancing, my father walking with me down the aisle..." She looked at Andrew. "Which one, though?"

"Neither. Syssi and Kian's was the first clan wedding and therefore created new traditions. The couple enters the ballroom together and walks up to the podium with Annani officiating over the ceremony. The whole "father giving away the bride" is so outdated, and besides, the clan females have no real fathers; they have sperm donors."

"Right. It makes sense for them, but I have a father; two of them."

"So does Syssi, one, that is. And the other thing that was out was the veil. Another outdated custom."

Nathalie snorted. "Look at us, planning a wedding inside a shower. We should go out and tell Syssi and Kian. And my father if Bridget brought him up already."

"About Bridget..."

"What about her?"

"I need to tell you something."

Here it goes. Nausea hit her fast and hard.

"We had a short fling before I met you."

"I knew it was her. I just knew it."

Bridget had seemed genuinely happy for her. There hadn't been even a hint of jealousy in her demeanor, but she'd gotten mad about Nathalie's lack of initial enthusiasm.

She must've at least still liked Andrew if not loved him.

Narrowing her eyes, Nathalie asked the one thing she needed to know. "Do you still have feelings for her?" Not that she was expecting an honest answer. Even if he felt something for his ex-girlfriend, he would never admit it.

"Of course I do."

Nathalie's mouth gaped open, but nothing came out. She closed it again and swallowed, wetting her suddenly dried out throat. "What?"

Andrew shook his head. "Not love. Not any romantic feelings, but we are friends. If she ever needs my help with anything, I'll do whatever I can for her. We parted on good terms."

She frowned. "Did you break up because of me?"

Andrew rubbed the back of his neck. "Yeah. I kind of dumped her over the phone."

Nathalie sat up straight. "Andrew Spivak, that was a horrible thing to do. How could you?"

Andrew patted her knee. "Don't judge me until you hear the whole story."

"I'm listening."

"I came into your coffee shop as a favor to Bhathian. The poor guy was afraid to even talk to you. I'd seen your picture, and I knew you were beautiful, but I didn't expect you to enthrall me with one smile. I knew I was going to pursue you with everything I had and not stop until you were mine, but I didn't want to do it while still officially seeing Bridget. Problem was, she was out of town, attending her son's graduation from medical school in Baltimore. I couldn't wait. Lucky for me, while there, she also met someone and was relieved I called to let her off the hook. So it all ended well."

Nathalie raked her fingers through Andrew's sparse chest hair. "It must be awkward for you since she is your doctor now and takes care of you." It was quite disturbing to think that Bridget had seen him naked. Worse, she'd fondled his cock to put a catheter in and then remove it.

Ugh!

"Hey," Andrew grabbed her chin and made her look him in the eyes. "Don't go all jealous Godzilla on me. I'll admit that there were a few awkward moments, but most of the time it was easy to just slip into a friendly, professional mode. You have to understand, we never loved each other or even pretended to. Our so-called relationship was nothing more than several hookups."

Andrew was telling the truth, and Nathalie couldn't fault him for any of it. She couldn't fault Bridget either. The doctor hadn't shown any signs of jealousy or resentment toward her for stealing Andrew away from her. She obviously didn't feel that way.

So why was it so hard? Why did the prospect of interaction with Bridget feel so uncomfortable?

"You're okay?" Andrew asked.

"Yeah. Any other revelations before we get out of here?"

"No, that's it. I just didn't want you to hear about it from someone else and get the wrong idea."

It had taken him a while to come clean about Bridget and himself, not that there was much to tell, but he should've told her earlier.

"Am I that scary?"

Andrew's brows dipped low. "You? Scary? Why would you think that?"

"You were obviously hesitant about telling me because you were afraid of my reaction. I might be jealous and possessive, but I'm not unreasonable."

"And that's one of the many reasons I love you. I didn't tell you because it never seemed like the right time and, anyway, there wasn't much to tell. But now that we are rushing into a wedding, I wanted you to know. I don't want any secrets between us, other than the classified government stuff that I can't talk about."

Nathalie reached up and planted a wet kiss on his lips. "You are the best, Andrew, and I love you."

His big grin was her reward. She liked to see Andrew smile.

"How about you? Any last minute confessions?" Andrew asked.

She shook her head. "None."

As Nathalie's belly rumbled, she realized that the nausea was gone and that she was craving something sweet. Other than the sweet man holding her, that is.

"Let's go. I'm ready for that chocolate cake now."

11

ROBERT

*C*arol was sprawled naked on the bed when Robert got out of the shower. His cock swelled, and his stomach rumbled at the same time. He hadn't eaten lunch and had been fantasizing about hitting the buffet, but when given a choice between sex and food—sex won.

Robert let the towel drop.

"Come here, big boy, and give me that magnificent cock of yours," Carol husked.

He hated when she talked like that, her true nature coming through loud and clear. But his cock begged to differ. The bastard loved her dirty talk.

Obligingly, he climbed on the bed and sat back on his haunches. His cock twitched as Carol seized it in her small, soft hand.

"Glad to see me?" She pushed up on her elbow and without preamble closed her sweet lips around the head.

With a groan, Robert pushed in. Not all the way, although he knew she could take him, just a little further into the moist haven of her mouth. Even a slut like her needed some time to get ready before accomplishing such a feat.

Wrapping one of her soft, blond curls around his finger, Robert marveled at the silky texture. Everything about Carol was soft and silky smooth. He loved touching her all over, running his hands over every inch of her. As incredible as her mouth and tongue felt on his shaft, he wanted to touch her too.

Swiftly, he pulled out and lifted her, sprawling on the bed and positioning her on top of him, with her sweet-smelling slit right where he wanted it, and his cock poised within easy reach of her mouth.

She cranked her head around and gave him a sultry smile. "I love it, how exciting."

Yeah, he knew what she was really saying; finally, something different.

He'd never been the type who'd liked to experiment with sexual positions. The one he loved most was the one the humans called missionary. In his opinion, nothing compared to face-to-face experience. It was intimate, and the closest he ever got to a woman emotionally. Even a hooker's face showed her pleasure and contorted in sweet agony when climax overtook her. For those few precious moments, she was giving herself to him.

As he gripped her ass cheeks, Carol moaned around his cock, and when he tongued her slit, she arched her back and pushed back like a cat in heat. Unlike human females, she was completely hairless there, and not because she shaved or waxed or did whatever else females did to get rid of pubic hair. Evidently, immortal females didn't have any.

She was even softer and silkier down there.

It didn't take long for her to reach her first orgasm, and in turn trigger his. By the time they lay exhausted on the bed, he'd lost count of how many he'd given her.

"Wow," Carol breathed. "You must've been in a really good mood. You've never fucked me like this before."

Leave it to Carol to spoil a compliment with insinuations of inadequate prior performance and vulgar language. If she'd said made love, instead of fuck, he would've been fine with the rest. Problem was, she regarded their coupling as fucking, while he regarded it as something more. Not love, he didn't love Carol, but he cared for her and liked her.

If only she weren't a slut.

If only she cared for him just a little.

She turned sideways and propped herself on her elbow. "Why the sad face? I gave you a compliment."

He was in no mood to discuss it with her. Besides, it was what it was. All the ifs were irrelevant.

"I'm hungry. Let's get dressed and go out."

Half an hour later, they were sitting in one of MGM's fancier restaurants. Carol refused to celebrate in the buffet and had chosen Italian cuisine. It was reasonably priced, so maybe they wouldn't end up paying more. He ordered a steak and asked for a basket of bread. One steak wasn't going to fill him up, but he wasn't going to order more while Carol was paying.

"You should've ordered an appetizer. This is not enough food for you."

"I ordered bread."

"It's complimentary."

"Exactly."

Carol sighed dramatically. "You know, all of this could've been a non-issue if you'd agreed to come home with me. I'm a great cook."

His mouth watered. That proposition was more tempting than all of her other ones. She hadn't told him she knew her way around the kitchen, and as someone who had never eaten a home-cooked meal, he was curious. Hell, he was salivating.

But that was his hunger talking.

Besides, he was employed now, and they might be able to rent a small apartment in town. One with a kitchen Carol could put to good use.

"We're here to celebrate my new job, one that has taken me forever to find, and you want me to give it up?"

"I'm tired of living in a hotel. I want my old life back."

Selfish woman. "So do I, but the difference is that I can't go back. My old life is dead."

Carol cringed. "I know, honey. I'm sorry. But I can give you a new life if you just agree to take the risk and come home with me. No one is going to harm you. The danger exists only in your head."

Their waiter arrived with the wine, and another one brought the bread.

Robert waited for them to depart before grabbing a slice of bread and stuffing it in his mouth. He chewed it quickly and helped it go down with a drink of water. "Even if I'm willing to take the chance, I'm not willing to sit around your house and do nothing. I'm a healthy male, and I need to work."

"You can do better than sprinklers."

"Like what?"

"I don't know. What have you done before?"

"I was second in command."

Carol shivered. "I don't know how you could've worked for that monster."

He shrugged. "We all do what we have to in order to survive."

They hadn't talked about her ordeal, not even once since they'd arrived at Vegas. Robert didn't know what to say, except that he was sorry, and she'd never brought it up—for which he was grateful.

In fact, he was impressed with her.

She was one hell of a tough woman. Anyone who had gone through the kind of torture she had, even a hardened soldier, would have had nightmares. But Carol acted as if it had never happened.

Instead of being angry at the world for dealing her such a blow, she was cheerful. Instead of crying at night like she'd done in captivity, she was sleeping like a baby, snuggling up to him with her angelic face peaceful and content.

Damn, if only she weren't such a slut.

Who was he kidding, Carol was more than a slut; she was a whore.

He'd been around enough of them to recognize the calculating glances she cast at men who seemed wealthy, and it didn't matter if they were sixty and older, had more bald spots than hair, or flabby bodies and fat bellies.

He chuckled. A whore and an ex-Doomer. A match made in heaven.

"What's funny?"

"Nothing. I was just thinking..." He had to come up with something.

She made a hand motion for him to continue.

What were they talking about? Oh, yeah, his ruined military career.

"For Sebastian, a second in command meant a glorified secretary. I was supervising deliveries, ordering materials, bringing meals to the girls. Basically whatever he told me to do. But I was good at it. Things got done on time, and it kept me off the battlefield."

She reached for his hand. "Not every man can be a fighter."

Hell, that wasn't the impression he wanted her to have of him. He pulled his hand away. "I was a fighter, and as Mortdh is my witness, I was good. I just hated every fucking moment of it. The whole fucking senseless carnage." He grabbed the wine bottle and filled his glass to the brim, then gulped it all down. It wasn't going to do shit for him; no amount of wine could affect an immortal. His body would process it too quickly. Something much stronger was needed to do the trick.

Carol looked at him with a pair of big sad eyes. "I'm glad you hated it. It means you're a good man."

No, he wasn't.

He'd been part of an organization that wasn't doing anyone any good, apart from itself, that is, and he'd had no problem with it. As long as someone else took care of the killing, he'd been content to be part of the Brotherhood. If not for Carol, he wouldn't have left. He'd despised Sebastian, that's all.

The most he would've done was request a transfer to another unit.

"If you say so."

"I know so. You saved me, risking your own life. If not for you, I would be as good as dead by now. Catatonic. My mind would've snapped."

He didn't know what to say to that and grabbed another piece of bread, then chewed it slowly to buy himself time to think.

"Come home with me, Robert. I owe you, and I don't mean the three months I promised. You saved my life by sacrificing yours, and I need to give it back to you. I'll find you a good job, and you can live with me for as long as you need."

Live with her... as if he was a mere roommate, then as soon as he had a job and earned enough to rent a place of his own, he was supposed to vacate the premises and get out of her life.

He would be all alone in the world.

If he thought he could go back to the Brotherhood without getting executed on the spot, he would've been on his way already.

Or the moment after he finished his damn meal.

An angry growl escaped his throat. "Where the hell is our food? Waiter!" He waved the guy over. "We've been waiting here for over half an hour."

The guy bowed politely, his voice trembling a little. "I'm sure it's coming out any moment now, sir. I'll go check."

"You do that, and if you're not back with our orders within the next five minutes, we are out of here." Robert saw himself fisting the guy's shirt and lifting him up—just to drive the point home. But he didn't. His self-control won.

"What's gotten into you?" Carol hissed when the waiter scurried in the kitchen's direction.

"I'm hungry." He took another piece of bread and shoved it in his mouth.

She crossed her arms over her chest and pushed her chin out. "If you don't want to tell me, that's fine. But don't lie to me."

With a grunt, he grabbed another piece of bread and then did some thinking while chewing and swallowing until the last piece in the basket was gone.

If she wanted him to come with her to Los Angeles so badly, he could use it to his advantage.

"Fine. I'll tell you what. I'll come home with you on two conditions."

"I'm listening."

He lifted a finger. "One, you marry me." He watched her eyes peel wide open. "Two, you tell me the name of the Doomer who supposedly crossed over and was accepted by your clan."

Carol swallowed visibly, then leaned toward him and whispered, "Why on earth would you want to marry me? We don't follow human customs, and you don't love me."

"If I marry you, an American citizen, I get a Green Card, and I can work legally at whatever job I'm qualified for."

Carol's expression relaxed, and she slumped in her chair. "I see." She leaned toward him again. "I can get you papers that are scrutiny-proof. The best money can buy."

"I want the real thing."

She narrowed her eyes at him. "You know that it's not enough to get a marriage certificate. For at least two years, we actually need to live together, have a joint bank account, and whatever else married people do."

Robert smiled. "I know, Don told me."

"Shit," was all she said.

"You said that you owe me and that you're going to give me a new life. Were those empty words?"

"Sir, I apologize for the wait, but here are your orders." The waiter put the plates down. "Would there be anything else?"

"No!" Robert motioned for him to get lost, picked up his knife and fork, and attacked his steak.

The fish on Carol's plate remained untouched.

"Aren't you going to eat?"

"I lost my appetite."

Ouch. "Is being married to me so disgusting that you cannot eat?"

"No, it's not you, it's me."

Right.

He arched a brow and cut another big chunk of the steak. She was killing him, but unlike her, he found solace in good food.

"Don't give me that hurt look. I mean it, Robert. I like you, you're a good man, but both you and I know that we are not each other's destined mates." She glanced at the neighboring table to check if anyone was listening in on their conversation.

Pushing her plate to the side, she leaned closer to him. "Eventually, I will want to hook up with other men, and I know it's not going to work while I'm married to you and we are sharing a house."

No, it was not going to work.

As long as they were together, they would remain monogamous. What reason did they have not to? It wasn't as if she had a lineup of immortal males to choose from, and even though he wasn't the world's greatest lover, he was sure as hell better than any puny, weak human.

Did she need the extra income? Was that it? Didn't the clan provide for its members? The rumors were that they were filthy rich, but as with everything else, the Brotherhood's propaganda might have been misleading.

Spearing another piece of steak with his fork, he leaned toward her. "Is this about money? Do you need to whore yourself out to cover expenses?"

Carol pushed back as if he'd punched her in the face, and then went redder than the wine in her glass. "Why— why would you say something like that? What made you think that I—" she stuttered.

He shrugged. "I figured it out as soon as we arrived at the first casino. You were eyeing rich men like juicy steaks, or in your case fat wallets, regardless of the attractiveness of their physiques. I've been around enough hookers to recognize that look." He shoved another piece of steak into his mouth.

She closed her eyes, breathed in and then out. Looking calmer, she asked, "And you don't mind?"

Robert finished chewing and wiped his mouth with a napkin. "As I said, we all do what we need to in order to survive. And if this is what helped you pay your bills, I'm not going to judge. But as long as we are together there will be none of that. I'll get work and pay for the household expenses. You don't need to go whoring while I'm around."

"I wish you didn't use that word. It's demeaning."

She was right. He'd done it purposefully. If she hadn't made him so mad, he would've thought of something that sounded better. "What word would you like me to use?"

"Courtesan. That was what it was called when I still did it to support myself."

That was a peculiar way to put it. "What do you mean? So you don't need to courtesan anymore?"

She smiled. "You can't use it as a verb. It was a title. But to answer your question, when I held that title, the clan wasn't doing as well as it does today, and each of us needed to work. I like sex as well as the next immortal, so why not get paid for it, right?" She ignored his grimace. "In time, however, the title lost its glamor, and I lost the taste for it. I managed to accumulate some wealth and lived off it until the clan's finances improved. Now I do it only when it's an emergency, or for fun."

"For fun? How can money be fun enough to compensate for having sex with an ugly motherfucker?" Robert gritted through clenched teeth.

"Not all men who pay for sex are unattractive. Some are busy businessmen who have no time to go looking for it; others prefer the honesty and lack of expectation. After all, paying for it upfront is often cheaper than falling into the clutches of a cunning gold digger. And some just get a kick out of it. For me, I do it because there is a thrill in getting paid. It means that I'm beautiful and desirable enough for guys to spend a small fortune on."

Astonishingly, he could understand her motives, but it didn't mean he could tolerate her fucking other men while she was with him.

Carol waited for him to respond, but he took his time. She watched him finish the last of his tiny, grilled potatoes, pour the rest of the wine into their glasses, and lean back in his chair.

"Here is my deal. If you can guarantee my safety in Los Angeles, we will get married in a human ceremony, which I guess is not valid under your clan's law. We will live together as husband and wife for a minimum of two years, and during this time you will not fuck anyone else. All the money I earn from whatever job I get will be yours and should be enough to cover the extra income you were making."

She arched a brow. "How about you? Are you going to stay true to me as well?"

He didn't miss the mocking undertone but chose to ignore it. "Of course. Why would I want inferior human females, when I have an exquisite immortal one? It doesn't make any sense. And why would you want to screw rotten humans when you have an immortal male who can satisfy you like they never could? I get it that I'm not the best lover in the world, but I'm the best you are going to get. Unless I'm mistaken, and I'm not the only immortal male you can fuck."

Carol chuckled, but it wasn't with mirth. "No, I don't have any other immortal males to choose from. I find it funny, though, that the most I ever heard you talk was when you were berating me. I don't think this is going to work. I will not invite into my home and into my life a man who doesn't treat me with respect. My gratitude is not infinite."

Damn it all to hell, he'd blown it.

There were tears in her big blue eyes, and he had put them there. Robert reached for her hand, and surprisingly she let him clasp it. "I apologize. Can we go somewhere and start this over? I know we can make it work."

She wiped a tear from her cheek. "Because I owe you, I'm willing to listen, but I don't promise anything."

Thank you, almighty Mortdh. Not all was lost.

12

ANDREW

Nathalie licked the last crumbs of cake off her lips, but a little smudge on her chin remained out of her tongue's reach. "It was good. No wonder you had to fight over it."

Andrew pulled her into his arms and licked the smudge for her. "Now your face is clean. How about I look for other spots that need a tongue bath." He waggled his brows.

Nathalie shook her head. "You're incorrigible. Let's get out of here. That little piece of cake just whetted my appetite. I want more chocolaty goodness. Maybe some strawberries too."

"Of course. I'm neglecting my obligations. Before I can feast on your delectable body, I need to make sure that you and the baby are properly fed so she can grow big and strong."

Nathalie arched a brow. "What makes you think we are having a girl? It's too early to know."

Andrew wrapped his arm around her waist, which was still as small as it was before, and walked her out of the room. "Remember Syssi's vision? She saw me playing with a beautiful girl who had long, luxurious, dark hair; like her mommy." He kissed the top of her head.

"Yeah, but maybe she would be our second or third child? The fact that Syssi didn't see anyone else in the vision doesn't mean there wasn't anyone."

"Hmm, I hadn't considered that." Andrew had been imagining his daughter for so long that it was impossible for him to think about the baby as anyone other than the girl in Syssi's vision.

When they entered the living room, Andrew was expecting to find Syssi and Kian, and perhaps Fernando. But Nathalie's adoptive father wasn't there. Instead, Bhathian was sitting on the large overstuffed chair across from Kian, and Bridget was sharing the sofa with Syssi.

"Here you are," Syssi said, "We thought you guys went for another nap."

Bridget smiled. "I'm glad you are taking naps. The body makes most of its repair work during sleep."

"Well, if it's under doctor's orders... Any cake left? Nathalie wants more."

"It will be ready in fifteen minutes. Okidu put another one in the oven. Would you like a cappuccino? And I can offer you some chocolate chip cookies while you wait for the cake." Syssi got up and walked over to her cappuccino machine.

"I would love some; the coffee and the cookies." Nathalie took Syssi's spot on the sofa. "Is my father still with William?" she asked Bridget.

"They are watching a show in the theater."

"I can't believe how wonderful William is with my dad. I need to bake him something special to thank him. In fact, I owe you all at least a year's supply of my best pastries, for all you've done for my dad and me, not to mention for Andrew."

Bridget patted her knee. "You don't need to get us anything."

"Speak for yourself." Kian winked at Nathalie. "I'm all for it; preferably fresh and still warm from the oven."

Bridget cast him one of her doctor looks; the one that said "I know things that you don't." "Aren't you supposed to be vegan?"

"I don't eat the cheese Danishes."

"And what do you think the other pastries are made of?"

Even before spending time in Nathalie's kitchen, Andrew had known what went into dough, and a lot of it wasn't plant based.

Kian closed his laptop and looked at Bridget. "From your mocking expression, I guess something I'm not supposed to eat."

Bridget chuckled. "Tell him, Nathalie."

"Butter, lots and lots of butter. And the better quality the butter, the better the pastries."

Kian didn't seem fazed by the newsflash. "In this case, I'm willing to make an exception for your pastries. They are worth the transgression."

Nathalie grinned. "I'm flattered."

Listening to Nathalie as she kept the chitchat going, Andrew rubbed a hand over his jaw. It didn't seem as if she was in a rush to make the announcement. They hadn't discussed who was going to deliver the news, and perhaps she was waiting for him to do it. Or she was planning on doing it herself but was waiting for the right moment. He'd give her a few more minutes. "I'll get the cookies if you tell me where they are."

"The pantry." Syssi pointed.

This was Andrew's first venture into the pantry, which he imagined would be the size of a small walk-in closet. The place was as big as his entire kitchen at home. The good news was that Okidu had it flawlessly organized and everything was clearly labeled. Finding the jar full of cookies was not a problem. In fact, it wasn't the only one; four more jars contained other kinds of cookies, and each was labeled with a name. He took two, the chocolate chip and the macadamia.

"Here you go, sweetheart." He placed the two jars on the coffee table in front of Nathalie.

Syssi gasped. "Oh, Andrew, you should have brought serving plates. You can't just drop storage containers on the table." She got up and rushed to the kitchen.

Women. Who cared about stuff like that? It wasn't as if he put a paper bag on the table. Not that there was anything wrong with that.

"It's fine," Andrew and Kian said in unison.

"Leave the jars, Syssi." Bhathian added his voice.

"You guys." She shook her head but abandoned her quest for fancy serving platters. "I swear, if not for us women, you would've still lived in caves."

Andrew couldn't argue with that. Kian and Bhathian seemed to agree, and no one said a thing.

"How are you feeling?" Bhathian asked. "All good?"

Damn, he was so sick of people asking him that. "As well as can be expected."

Bhathian nodded. "Growing pains, huh?"

"Yeah, that, and the enhanced senses. Too much input."

"You'll get used to that. In time, you'll learn to ignore it." Bhathian clapped his palms on his thighs. "Well, now that you're out of the woods, it's time for me to book that flight to Rio. I'm heading out on the first available seat I can find."

"Ahem," Nathalie cleared her throat. "I think you should wait a little longer."

Bhathian's bushy brows drew tight. "Why?"

She glanced at Andrew and smiled. "We are expecting."

The brows drew even tighter. "Expecting what?"

Bridget snorted. Syssi slapped a hand over her mouth. Kian looked just as puzzled as Bhathian.

"We are expecting a baby. You're going to be a grandpa."

Syssi erupted with a, "Yay! I'm so happy!" She pulled Nathalie to her feet, hugging her gently as if she was made from eggshells. "I need to be extra careful with you now." She patted Nathalie's flat belly.

"Congratulations." Kian pushed to his feet and offered Andrew his hand. They shook and then bro-hugged.

Through it all, Bhathian didn't respond. Not moving a muscle, he looked paralyzed.

Nathalie frowned and walked over to him. Crouching, she took his hand. "What's the matter? This is good news. Why aren't you happy?"

"I'm terrified," he admitted. "I don't want to lose you. I just found you, Nathalie. How could you do this to me?"

Talk about the wrong thing to say. Any other woman would have gotten offended and turned her back on him, but not Nathalie. "Why would you lose me, Bhathian? What nonsense have you gotten into your head?"

"You're not immortal. And you can't transition while pregnant. Women die in childbirth, even in this day and age and with the best type of care." He turned to Bridget. "Am I wrong? Doctor?"

She shook her head. "It happens. Not a lot, but it still does. Last I read, one in every five to six thousand births ends with the mother's death, either during childbirth or shortly after."

Damn, that was way more than Andrew would've guessed, and it scared the crap out of him. And then there was the realization that Bhathian was right about Nathalie's transition. He didn't need Bridget's education to know that it couldn't be attempted while she was carrying a child. Now they would have to wait until after the delivery, and God knew what might happen during those nine months and then the birth itself.

"Nathalie is strong and healthy, Bhathian. You're panicking for nothing," Bridget said with complete conviction, which eased the tight vice squeezing Andrew's heart.

"And there is my vision," Syssi added. "I saw Andrew playing with his healthy, beautiful daughter. They looked so happy."

Bhathian pushed to his feet, his large body swelling with aggression as he got in Syssi's face. "Did you see my Nathalie in your vision?"

Kian was there in a flash. His hand on Bhathian's shoulder, he pulled him back. "Easy there. Syssi is not the enemy."

Bhathian hung his head. "I'm sorry, Syssi. I'm just so fucking worried... forgive my language, ladies... But I still have to ask, did you see Nathalie in your vision?"

"No, I didn't," she admitted, then quickly added. "But that doesn't mean anything. Andrew and the girl were playing in the park. Nathalie could've been sitting on a bench nearby, or stayed at home, or gone shopping."

He nodded. "I know. But I also know that the next nine months are going to be torturous for me."

"You should talk." Nathalie snorted. "Typical male. I'm the one that will get to be the size of an elephant, and you are complaining about how difficult it's going to be for you?"

"You're right. Come here." He opened his arms and Nathalie went to him. Putting her cheek on his chest, she sighed. He closed his arms around her with infinite care. "Whatever you need, I'm here for you. And you—" He pointed at Andrew. "—are a dead man should anything happen to her. Understood?"

"Yes, sir."

Nathalie let Bhathian get his fill, then pushed against his chest. Reluctantly, he let her go. "So what's the plan? Are you kids getting married or what?"

"We are, and the sooner, the better. I don't want to walk down the aisle with a big protruding belly." Nathalie glanced at Syssi who took the hint in an instant.

"Give me three weeks. With Amanda's help, we can have it done, including the most gorgeous custom-made wedding dress you can dream up."

"Six," Kian said.

"Why six? I did ours in two."

"Because we can't hold the wedding here. The enemy knows where we are, and they will be sending new troops. Probably already have. I'm not going to risk bringing the entire clan here for the wedding. I propose we hold the reception at our Scottish stronghold."

Syssi's eyes sparkled, and she reached for Nathalie's hands. "Oh, Nathalie, it's going to be so beautiful. I'm already jealous. What Kian calls a stronghold is an old, majestic castle. You are going to have a real princess wedding."

Kian smiled. "It's not a done deal yet. I have to call Sari, get her okay, and see that she can have everything ready in six weeks."

"I feel uncomfortable about it," Bridget said quietly.

For a moment, Andrew thought she was going to say something about their prior involvement.

Nah, it wasn't Bridget's style.

"What do you mean?" Kian asked.

"All of us going to the wedding and leaving the keep unprotected. We've never done something like that before, and we don't have the procedures in place."

Kian waved a hand. "Don't worry about it. We will have it locked down and well guarded by our human security. Sari faced the same concern when she had to leave their castle behind and come to our wedding. Worse, they had to leave it exposed without the perpetual shroud they keep over their stronghold because everyone came here."

"Yeah, you're right. But we will need to keep it short."

"Naturally. Three days tops, that's all I can afford. If some of the others opt to stay longer, that's fine."

"Andrew and I will stay. A honeymoon in Scotland sounds amazing. Right, Andrew?"

As if he was going to deny her anything. "Sure, baby, whatever you want is fine by me. I just hope that I don't get fired for taking so many vacation days."

A hopeful expression on his face, Kian squeezed his shoulder. "You can always come work for the clan."

"It would be great if I can find Eva in time for the wedding," Bhathian said to no one in particular.

Nathalie turned around to face him and took his hand. "I don't want you to go crazy about it and take unnecessary risks. If you find her, great, if not, then not." She chuckled, but there was a sad undertone to it. "Instead of a mother and a father, I'll have two fathers at my wedding."

Andrew shook his head. "You know how it sounds...two fathers."

"Yeah, well, whatever." Nathalie suddenly looked bothered.

"What's the matter, baby?" Andrew picked up her hand and brought it to his lips for a kiss.

"I still want Fernando to walk me down the aisle. I know you have a different tradition, but this is something I always dreamt about, and I'm sure so did he." She glanced at Bhathian. "I hope you don't mind..."

"Not at all. It's important to you and Fernando, and it's your wedding day. You get to choose what you want to do. Right, guys?" He swept his eyes over everyone present, his stern gaze daring anyone to object.

"Yes, of course," Syssi hurried to agree.

Kian shrugged. "For all I care, you can get married on a beach in Hawaii, wearing swim trunks and a bikini. And I don't even care who will wear what. Though I have to admit that I'm not looking forward to seeing Andrew in a bikini."

Andrew rubbed his chin. "That's not a bad idea. I love it. We can have a luau, with hula dancers and fire eaters..."

Three pairs of irate female eyes speared him.

"It was just a thought..." Andrew mumbled, looking at Kian for support.

With a smirk, the traitor shook his head.

13

CAROL

Screw her promise. She should dump Robert now before he managed to soften her resolve.

Even after all he'd said, or rather the way he'd said it, she was letting him hold her hand as they made their way back to their room.

Carol, you are a soft-hearted fool.

In her defense, holding hands with a guy was a novelty, and it felt surprisingly good.

Her lovers from her courtesan days had never acknowledged her in public, and her modern-times hookups were of the *badabing badaboom* kind. No hand-holding or leisurely strolls involved.

In his other hand, Robert was carrying a shopping bag with the fruit-flavored vodka they'd bought at the gift shop. He'd wanted the plain stuff, but she'd told him that she hated it, and they'd compromised on a brand with a fruity flavor.

Carol smirked. If Robert thought to get her buzzed so she'd agree to his terms, he was underestimating her the same way most males did. She might've not been educated or highly intelligent, but she was a pro at the art of negotiation.

Back in their room Carol took the only armchair, while Robert opened the fruit-flavored vodka and poured a glass for each of them. He handed her one, then lifted the chair from behind the desk and brought it next to her.

Carol took a sip, waiting for Robert to start his spiel.

"You know what I want. Tell me what you want," he started.

Not bad for a beginner. She had to give him points for tactics. Letting the other side state their demands first lowered their defenses. Except, she was so ahead of the game she could run circles around him.

"I'll start with something simple. You never ever use that offensive W word, or the P word either. In fact, I don't want you to mention my old occupation at all."

Robert raised his glass. "Deal."

She smiled sweetly. "Your turn."

"I've already told you the big items, but it seems you want to discuss the small ones first, so let's hear them all."

Carol scrunched her forehead as she thought what else she wanted from Robert. She couldn't ask him to change his dry and boring personality. That was who he was, and no amount of effort on his part would turn him into charming and worldly. These qualities were innate, not learned. Other than that she had no complaints. He was a good-looking guy, clean, respectful—most of the time, not selfish, not arrogant, and seemed to be a hard worker.

Fates, if only he weren't such a bore.

She shrugged. "That's all. Up until today you treated me with respect and never got angry or raised your voice at me. I liked that about you, and I want you to continue treating me like that."

"I'm sorry I blew up before. Usually it takes a lot more to get me so angry, but, without meaning to, you dealt me a harsh blow."

What was he talking about? "How so?"

Robert sighed and emptied the contents of his glass down his throat. "In so many words, you made it clear that once I can support myself, you want me out of your home. Out of your life too. I don't have a home anymore, Carol. I can't go back to the Brotherhood because I'd be executed on the spot. And if you cut your ties with me, I'll be all alone in the world. Doesn't seem like a fair reward for my good deed."

Poor guy, he'd misunderstood what she had planned for him. "Robert, I would never dump you like that. What I had in mind was to introduce you to some of my friends, my cousins, as it happens. Maybe one of them would turn out to be your true love mate? Huh?"

Robert was taken by surprise. "You would do that for me?"

"Sure. I don't want you to be lonely."

"What about you? Aren't you lonely?"

With a sigh, she put her glass down on the table. "As you said before, there are no immortal males I can pick and choose from. But I have a big and caring family, and some of them are close friends who I love hanging out with."

"It's not enough."

She snorted. "You're telling me? But what are my options?"

"Easy. Me."

"We like each other, Robert, but you don't love me, and I don't love you. Each of us has a true love mate somewhere out there in the world. If we stay together, we might miss the chance of finding that special someone."

For a few moments he didn't respond, sitting with his elbows on his knees, the empty glass clutched in his hands, and his head bowed. She didn't press. Robert wasn't a fast thinker; he needed time to figure things out. A good quality, since he didn't rush into things the way she often did.

Less chance of getting in trouble.

When he lifted his eyes to her, she was hit by the intense emotion she saw in them and braced herself for whatever conclusion he'd arrived at.

"You don't know for a fact that there is someone out there for each of us. We can spend our entire long lives searching for them and never find them. We have something here, Carol. It isn't the all-consuming love of a true mate, it's not a perfect match, but I suspect that this is as good as it's going to get. Let's not squander this opportunity for companionship. It must be better than having no one."

Damn, he had a point. But...

"It may be true for me, but you're giving up on an opportunity most immortal males would kill for. I just offered to introduce you to a bunch of immortal females who would love to get their hands on a handsome guy like you. One of them might be your true love match."

That shut him up. Not that she wanted him to stop talking. They were finally having a real conversation.

After a moment or two, he looked up at her with such a stubborn expression on his face that she knew what he was going to say before he said it.

"I'd rather hang on to what I have than give it up for a dream. I don't need perfection. You're a beautiful, sexy female. You're nice to everyone. You have a good heart, and you're trustworthy. Doesn't get better than that. Not for me."

Carol couldn't help a smile. It was so sweet of him, but he was so misguided. Regrettably, she needed to shatter his illusions.

"Robert, sweetie, it's not going to work. I can't promise you fidelity, and I know you won't be able to compromise on that."

He looked so hurt that her heart ached for him.

"Why? What's so special about these humans that you would choose them over me? I know I'm not perfect, but I'm decent enough."

She sighed. "You might be, but I'm not. I'm just not the type of female who can settle down with one male. I need the variety, the excitement of the chase, of new partners. Every morning when I wake up, do you know what I think about first?"

"What?"

"Where I'm going to go prowling for hookups, and what I'm in the mood to cook. That's it. Occasionally, I invite my friends to dinner, and once or twice a week we go clubbing. That's my life. I have no other interests. I'm shallow, and I'm a pot head, which means I like to smoke pot in case you didn't know." Curiously, though, she hadn't had the urge to smoke or vape lately.

"I know what a pot head is." Robert got up and started pacing. "Are you satisfied with that? Isn't there anything else you would've liked to do?"

"Nope. I like my life the way it is."

He raked his fingers through his short, thick hair. "Fine, I see there is no changing your mind. After my three exclusive months are up, I move to a spare bedroom in your house, and you can do whatever you want with whomever you want. We will remain friends and roommates: nothing more. But the same holds true for me. If any of your friends want to hook up with me, are you going to be fine if I take them to my room?"

"Sure," she said without much conviction. "Roommates with benefits."

"What do you mean?"

"We can still have sex." She winked.

Robert shook his head. "I don't know. We will have to wait and see how it goes. But are you okay with the rest of the deal? The fake marriage and everything?"

Why not? It wasn't as if she was going to find her true love anytime soon. Two years were a blink of an eye in the lifetime of an immortal. "Yeah, I guess, unless I can get you legit papers some other way."

"You think you could?"

"I'm not sure. I'll have to call and make arrangements for your arrival. I want to get an okay and a guarantee that you will be treated like a hero and not an enemy."

14

ANANDUR

"Would you accept charges for a collect call from Mexico, sir?" The operator asked.

Anandur frowned. He didn't know anyone there and wasn't aware of any clan member vacationing south of the border. Not that he'd checked the register lately. Perhaps one of the young ones had gone for a short visit to Mexico. Maybe he or she lost a wallet, or it might have been stolen. But why would they be calling his number?

"Who's calling?"

"She wouldn't give her name. She says she's your girlfriend."

Anandur's breath caught. "Put her through." The only one who considered herself his girlfriend was Lana.

"Anandur?"

The sound of her voice was such a tremendous relief that he had to sit down.

"You there? Anandur?"

"Yes, I'm here. Where are you? I've been worried sick about you."

"You miss me. I knew you liked me for me and not the information I give."

Yeah, he did, a little. "What's going on, Lana, is everyone okay? I have been imagining the worst. I was afraid that Alex found out about me contacting you and did something horrible to you and the others."

"He found out something, but we don't know what. He thinks the FBI is after him."

Anandur chuckled. "They might be."

"Are you FBI?"

"No, I'm not."

"So why you afraid Alex find out about you?" As usual, Lana was suspicious as hell.

"He knows me. We used to hang out in the same circles. Not the criminal ones, just socially. If he found out about me snooping around his business, he would have known my people are after him. And believe me, he is much more afraid of us than he is afraid of the FBI."

"Hmm, more than the FBI you say?"

"Definitely. By the way, I'm glad you're calling me from a public phone. He has listening devices all over that ship, and now that he is ultra-paranoid, even your burner phone is not safe."

"I know. He is very suspicious. We do everything to look normal for him. I went to buy supplies, and I call you. Did you talk to your boss?"

"Yes and he had a sweet deal for you, but you were gone before I could tell you about it."

"What deal?"

"How would you girls like to own and operate a dinner cruise in Hawaii? Affiliated with a high-end hotel?"

"You joke?"

"No joke. Serious offer."

"Let me think." Lana was quiet for a few moments. "You help us start new? Papers and everything?"

He considered saying yes but ended up sticking to the truth. "I'm not sure we can get you real papers, but I can promise you that the fake ones will be top notch. I think it's not a big deal given everything else my boss is offering. You'll never get a better deal than that."

"I'm not complaining. It's a good deal, too good…"

Suspicious Russian.

"Why would I lie to you, Lana? To get away from Alex, you would've been happy with any help my boss offered. Am I right?"

"That's why it smells like fish. Why would your boss offer more? No one gives things for nothing."

She was right. But Kian was a businessman, and he saw opportunities where others didn't.

"You girls are an experienced crew and highly motivated to succeed. My boss is opening a new hotel in Hawaii, and when I told him about you, he saw an opportunity. You get what you want, and he gets a profitable side business for the hotel. Win-win."

"So the profit goes to him?"

"Part of it. Do you really want to negotiate the details now? You haven't escaped Alex yet."

"*Da*, I know. I will speak with others, and we make a plan. I'll call you from our next stop."

"You do that. And, Lana?"

"Yes?"

"Be careful. Super careful. Don't talk about any of it on the boat or even near it. Check your pockets and your clothes for listening devices. I don't want anything to happen to you."

"I knew you like me. Tell me, don't be shy."

Hell, why not, he could make the woman happy. "I like you, Lana. Stay safe."

"I will. And I like you too."

Anandur rubbed his beard-covered chin. Alex had taken the boat to Mexico, which presented a problem. He had no idea how to plan a rescue and an extraction operation on foreign soil. Hell, he didn't know the first thing about it, especially since it involved a boat the size of a cruise liner.

This was a job for Andrew.

Question was whether the guy was operational. He'd just emerged from his transition and was still adjusting to his new body. For a fee, however, they could always turn to Turner, Andrew's ex-boss and commander.

A creepy fellow, but extremely effective at what he did.

15

KIAN

"Do you have a moment?" Brundar walked into Kian's office and sat down on the chair facing Kian's desk.

"What's up?"

"Carol called. She wants to bring her Doomer home with her."

Kian had been expecting this. She couldn't keep living in a hotel in Las Vegas indefinitely. As someone who didn't hold a job in any of the clan's organizations, her share in the clan's profits was small. And as far as he knew, she didn't work outside the clan either. She had enough income to lead a comfortable life but not an extravagant one.

"What do you think?"

Brundar shrugged. "We don't know anything about the guy except that he saved Carol. It might have been a setup. Let her go free so she could lead him to us. On the other hand, Carol claims he still doesn't know we cleaned up his home base, which means he didn't try to contact them."

Kian rapped his fingers on the glass top covering his table. "I don't want him anywhere near here, not unless he is under lock and key or monitored twenty-four-seven. Can we ensure Carol's cooperation?"

Brundar shrugged. "She didn't spill under torture."

True, and it was quite remarkable, but in her home, surrounded by her friends, she might let her guard down and blurt something. Besides, she would have friends visit who were even less careful.

"I'm not comfortable with it. The only way I may consider it is if we bring him here and keep him guarded the way we did with Dalhu. Slap on the guy one of William's new locator cuffs, the kind that interferes with the cellular signal."

"Carol wants to bring him to her home."

"Can't allow it. If she wants to be with him, she will have to move into the keep."

Brundar leaned forward and snatched a notepad and a pen from Kian's desk, then scribbled something on it.

"Here is Carol's number. Call her." He pushed the notepad back toward Kian.

"Do I really need to deal with that myself?"

"You're dealing with it one way or another. It will be done faster without using me as a go between."

Good point.

Kian picked up the handset of his landline and dialed the number.

Carol answered on the second ring. "Hello? Who is it?"

"Kian. Are you alone?"

"Yes, Robert is at work."

"Good. You can't take him to your home."

"I can't keep living in a hotel in Vegas either, and I promised him I'd give him three months. And even after those are up, I need to make sure he is taken care of. The guy has nowhere to go. No identity, no papers, and no people to call his own. I owe him for what he sacrificed for me. I know I'm not an important member of the clan, and you don't have to help me, but I'm asking anyway. It's the decent thing to do."

Kian sighed. "I know, Carol, and I'm not turning my back on you or that Doomer. But we need to take precautions. If he comes here, I need him monitored around the clock, and that means he needs to stay here at the keep. He'll have to wear a locator cuff. If you want to be with him, you're welcome to move into the keep too. I want everyone to do so eventually, so it will only mean hastening the process for you."

"What about my house?"

"You can rent it. Make a few bucks."

"I'll run it by Robert, but I don't think he will go for it. He wants real papers, he wants a good job, and he wants a new life. That's not what you're offering him."

True. But what else could he do? It wasn't fair. If the guy was legit, then he deserved all that he'd asked for. Problem was, they had to make sure before they allowed him in.

"I'll give him something to do until we can be sure he is not still working on behalf of the Brotherhood. I'll have Edna probe him."

"Can I call you back?" Carol didn't sound happy.

Not that he blamed her. He wished there was more he could offer Carol. After what this poor girl had gone through, he would've loved to shower her with kindness. But safety always came first.

"Yeah, here is my cell number." He recited the digits. Kian never gave it away to anyone other than the Guardians, council members, and his mother and sisters. But he was making an exception for Carol.

It was the least he could do.

"Thanks."

It sounded more like thanks for nothing. But there wasn't much Kian could do about it.

Life wasn't fair.

16

LOSHAM

Losham stared at the scorched earth of what used to be his son's base. Were Sharim's ashes scattered on the ground? Was he inadvertently stepping on his son's remains?

The fire department had concluded that it had been an accident; the gas tank catching fire and exploding for some reason. It had been an old building, they'd claimed, and someone had renovated it without pulling permits. The work didn't comply with current safety codes.

Bullshit.

Losham knew who was responsible for his son's death, and he was going to make them pay. Dearly.

He wasn't a violent man, and the use of force had never appealed to him. Losham's sharp mind was much more formidable than any weapon or military force. Like an invisible puppeteer, he could cause damage on an unimaginable scale just by pulling the right strings. But that was before it had become personal. Now he would've given anything for the military acumen and training of his brothers so he could hunt and kill each and every one of those responsible for Sharim's demise.

Careless of his Salvatore Ferragamo loafers, he kicked a stone. The shoes were ruined anyway, covered with ash and scuffed from the broken debris strewn about.

The remains of what used to be a fountain stood in stark relief against the canvas of the desolate landscape, showing remarkably little damage compared to the utter destruction of the rest of the compound.

Like a sad monument to Sharim's memory.

But there would be no other. No mourning was allowed in the Devout Order of Mortdh Brotherhood, no tributes to the dead, no memorials to friends lost.

Death was celebrated, not mourned.

Losham had never believed in any of the crap the Brotherhood's propaganda spewed. In fact, some of the ideas had been his. For him, it was a game of wits. Could he outsmart everyone, from leaders of countries to simple garbage collectors, leading them to believe in whatever the hell he wanted them to? Could he move the chess pieces with his ghostly hand and deal Annani, her clan, and humanity a checkmate?

It used to satisfy him like no mindless bloodshed ever could. But now he craved his enemies' blood. When he'd sent Sharim over, the hunt for Annani's immortals hadn't been a priority for Losham. It had been all about gaining influence and playing the game. He'd left the "how" of the hunt up to his son.

It had been a mistake that had cost Sharim's life. Losham had trained him well, and his son had been a smart man. But no one could plan and plot like Losham. He should've given it more thought.

Annani and her tiny clan of average intelligence immortals stood no chance against Losham's brilliance. Once he devised a plan and put it in motion, they would be dropping like flies into his elaborate spider web.

He could've eradicated them from the face of the earth a long time ago, and the only reason he hadn't was his love of the game and his pride. With the clan gone, there would be no worthy opponent for him to outsmart.

"Sir, forgive me for interrupting your investigation, but we need to go. Your aircraft is ready." His assistant waved a hand toward the limousine parked outside the crumbled wall surrounding what used to be the monastery.

"Yes, of course." Losham's lips lifted in his well-practiced smile.

Sadly, he had to lie to Navuh about the purpose of the trip. Showing grief for his son would've been viewed as a sign of weakness and lack of devotion to the cause. Navuh would've never allowed Losham to visit the site. The stated purpose of his trip was a vacation in Las Vegas. For the sake of appearances, he'd reserved the penthouse of one of Sin City's most luxurious hotels, and purchased the services of several pretty girls from the best escort service in town.

In secret, he'd chartered a private flight to Santa Barbara, planning to be back before anyone noticed he hadn't been sleeping off a night of debauchery in his room.

The only one Losham trusted with his secrets was his assistant, Rami, and that was because Rami had a secret of his own that only Losham was privy to. A secret that if found out would get him tortured and killed. The Brotherhood had absolutely no tolerance for gay men. Not even as guards for the harem.

17

NATHALIE

Bridget put down her tea on the counter and crossed her arms over her chest. "How did your father take the news?"

Nathalie stirred sugar into her coffee, then added cream. "I didn't tell him yet."

Syssi had called for an emergency breakfast meeting to discuss wedding plans, inviting Bridget and Amanda. They had about an hour before Amanda and Syssi had to leave for work. With no patients waiting for her, Bridget wasn't in a hurry, and Nathalie could basically show up at the coffee shop whenever she pleased.

It was beyond wonderful, but old habits still had her waking up with a feeling of urgency every morning. She had to remind herself that everything was taken care of and she could take her time.

Bridget frowned. "Why not?"

"Last night, when William brought my father back to the penthouse, he was so tired that I decided to save the wonderful news for today and tucked him in bed instead. He is still sleeping."

Cappuccino cup in one hand, her other arm crossed over her chest, Amanda asked, "Before we start throwing ideas around, do you have any preferences?"

Nathalie finished chewing a piece of toast and washed it down with orange juice. "As I told Bridget and Syssi yesterday, all I want is a beautiful white dress and my father walking me down the aisle. My girly fantasies never carried me past that point."

Amanda tapped her fingers on her bicep. "If you don't want to feel like a guest at your own wedding, you need to put some more thought into it. When you walk down the aisle, what do you see?"

Nathalie closed her eyes and tried to visualize. It wouldn't be in a small, community church as she had always assumed, so she imagined the dining hall of a medieval castle. Too big. She could almost hear the organ music reverberating from the stone walls.

"What's the frown about?" Syssi asked.

"I'm imagining the castle in Scotland, and all I can see is a huge dining hall that feels awfully empty, with every little sound echoing from the walls."

Amanda snorted. "Don't worry about it. The place is going to be packed, bursting at the seams with people. I don't know about the echo, but I can ask Sari to check the acoustics."

Nathalie's eyes widened. "How many guests are we talking about?"

Bridget grinned. "Everyone is going to come to your wedding; around five hundred and fifty people."

"Why? I don't know every person in the clan, and I'm sure Andrew doesn't know that many either."

Syssi patted her knee. "Yeah, it was a big surprise for me too. I hate big parties, and I freaked out when Kian told me he was inviting every member of the clan. But then he explained the significance of it, and I realized I had no choice. I couldn't be selfish about it and have my way. I had to bite the bullet. It turned out to be beautiful, though, and I didn't feel overwhelmed at all. I even managed to enjoy myself. You are an outgoing girl, not an introvert like me, you're going to love it."

"It makes sense in your case since Kian is Annani's son and one of the most important people in the clan. But why would everyone drop everything to come to Andrew and my wedding? They don't know us. We are not important."

Amanda smiled indulgently. "I see Andrew and Bhathian did a shitty job explaining the history and dynamics of the clan to you. I'll have to rectify the situation, but not now. Maybe I'll come back in the evening. The one thing you should understand is that every new Dormant female who is not a descendant of Annani represents a new hope for the clan. A new bloodline. So you are a very important member of the clan. Also, yours is going to be only the second wedding in the clan's history and therefore a huge deal."

"So why didn't you and Dalhu get married yet?" Nathalie blurted before thinking it through. "I'm sorry. It's none of my business."

Amanda harrumphed. "The thing about large, tight-knit families is that everything is everyone's business. No privacy whatsoever. Get used to it."

It didn't escape Nathalie's notice that Amanda hadn't answered her question, but she didn't want to push. Instead, she turned to Syssi. "Over five hundred people, huh?"

Syssi nodded.

Nathalie closed her eyes again. With the number of guests dictating the visual, the one that popped behind her closed lids was the scene from Hogwarts' dining hall in the *Harry Potter* movie.

The rest of the pieces fell into place. "If the castle's banquet hall is big enough, we can have long tables on both sides of the room with a big center aisle between them, and an altar on a podium at the far end so everyone can see the ceremony. I don't want big flower arrangements because they interfere with socializing. Food can be whatever as long as there is enough of it and it's tasty. As to the booze, given your Scottish heritage, we need a lot."

Amanda nodded approvingly and offered her hand to Nathalie for a handshake. "It's a pleasure doing business with you, Nathalie. Decisiveness is an admirable quality."

"Well, it's a quality that emerged out of necessity. Running a business basically by myself, with no time for anything, decisions had to be made quickly. I didn't have the luxury of thinking things over."

"Nevertheless, it's admirable." Syssi filled a tall glass with orange juice and handed it to Nathalie. "Drink! Vitamin C is important for a pregnant lady."

Nathalie took a sip. "Thank you for the compliment, but it's misplaced. You forget that I also had no one to answer to. If I screwed up and made the wrong decision, I might have had trouble paying my bills, but no one was going to berate me, other than me, that is."

Amanda shook her head. "You really need to learn to take a compliment, Nathalie. The right answer is thank you, nothing more."

"That's what I keep telling her, but she never listens to her Papi."

Nathalie turned around and smiled. "Good morning, Daddy. Did you sleep well?"

"I slept like a baby. The beds in this hotel are top of the line. We should buy the same kind of mattress for our home. Your mother always complains how lumpy ours is."

And just like that Nathalie's good mood flew out the window. When Fernando didn't remember his wife was gone, it was a sign he was going to have a bad day.

Should she wait with her news?

"Would you like toast with your eggs for breakfast, Papi?"

"Yes, I would. Thank you. Good morning to you, lovely ladies. Are you my Nathalie's friends?"

Damn, he'd forgotten who they were. Definitely a bad day.

"Yes, we are. I'm Amanda." She offered her hand and dazzled him with her gorgeous smile.

Fernando shook it. "Such a beautiful lady. You look familiar, have I seen you in a movie? Or maybe one of those Victoria's Secret commercials?"

Her father was such a flirt.

"No, sir. I wish. Regrettably, I'm not voluptuous enough for Victoria's Secret." Amanda winked.

Fernando actually blushed.

Bridget saved him by offering her hand. "I'm Doctor Bridget."

"Yes, yes. I remember you. I don't know from where, but I do. You're also a very pretty lady." He glanced down at Bridget's impressive cleavage but refrained from making a comment. Good. It meant that his brain was still functioning. Never mind that he was probably faking remembering her.

"And I'm Syssi."

He shook Syssi's hand. "Another beautiful lady."

"Stop flirting, Papi, and sit down to eat." Nathalie put a plate on the counter for him.

"Thank you." Fernando paused his flirting to dig into his food.

"Has he always been such a charmer?" Syssi whispered in Nathalie's ear.

"Yes. When he was still running the shop, most of our clientele were ladies. Come to think of it, Jackson is a chick magnet as well. I swear, ever since he started working for me the female clientele has doubled, and not only the teenage girls. He charms grandmas just as well."

"Some guys just can't help themselves. They love women, and it shows. It's not necessarily a bad thing, though. I'll take a women lover over a women hater every day and twice on Sunday." Bridget took her coffee and headed for the living room.

"Yeah, unless you're the jealous type, and you're married to one," Nathalie said quietly. Her mother hadn't appreciated Fernando's innocent flirting.

Syssi and Amanda followed Bridget to the living room, leaving her alone with her father. She waited for him to finish his breakfast.

"Would you like some coffee, Papi?"

"Yes, please."

She poured him a cup. "There is something I need to tell you."

"What is it, precious?" Worry suffused his words.

"It's a good thing, Papi, a wonderful thing. Andrew and I are expecting a baby."

The bright smile that flitted through his face was immediately replaced by a frown. "Who is Andrew?"

Damn, most days he knew who Andrew was. She considered lying and saying he was her husband, but the lie couldn't pass through her lips. "My fiancé, daddy. We are getting married in six weeks."

He smiled and pulled her into a hug. "I'm so happy for you, my girl." He let her go with a mischievous grin on his face. "I'm happy for me too. I can't wait to hold my grandchild in my arms. But I'm not sure your mother will be thrilled about being called Grandma." He winked.

The best thing was not to correct him and just go with it. "She'll get used to the idea."

"Question is, will I? After all, I'll be going to bed with a grandma."

Unfortunately, only in your dreams, Daddy.

18

AMANDA

*A*manda glanced at her schedule for the day and sighed. It was going to be a rat race. There was so much she still needed to do in the two days before her scheduled trip to Hawaii.

They were taking the clan's largest jet to shuttle the girls and their escorts, Vanessa, Amanda, and Gertrude. Overkill on all accounts. The plane belonged to Annani's sanctuary and had to be flown from Alaska. Annani's people, who needed it on an almost daily basis, would have to manage without. Three escorts for a group of twenty-two kids made sense, but not for a same sized group of adult women. But the psychologist warned that the women's submerged memories might reemerge at any moment, and they might panic. According to Vanessa, a group that large required a minimum of three immortals with decent thralling ability.

"Is the next one here?" she asked Syssi.

Syssi glanced at the list of interviewees. "She is ten minutes late. I don't think she's coming."

"Good, I need a break. Join me for coffee?"

Syssi got up to her feet and stretched. "Sure." She turned to Hannah. "If someone named Mona shows up, come get us. We are in the kitchen."

Without lifting her head up from the monitor, Hannah gave her the thumbs-up.

In the kitchenette, Syssi put a fresh packet into the coffeemaker and leaned against the counter. "I can't believe how flaky these young ones are. Having a guaranteed source of income is spoiling them rotten."

Amanda nodded. "One didn't want to work full time, the other one expected an executive's pay, and this one made an appointment and didn't show up." She leaned closer to Syssi's ear and whispered. "I think we need to forget about hiring an immortal and settle for a mortal or two to handle the interviews."

Syssi pulled out two cups from the cabinet above the sink. "Not a bad idea. The questionnaire is vague enough. Paranormal abilities are strange, so it shouldn't come as a big surprise that some of the questions are a little out there." Amanda took a cup and held it out for Syssi to fill. "William is coming later today to show us his video game. If it's as good as he claims, we might not need to hire additional staff."

"Even if it's that good, it's not a substitute for a face to face interview. Besides, it only tests precognition and remote viewing. It can't test telepathy or any of the other paranormal phenomena."

Regrettably, Syssi was right. "We keep on looking then, but there are not that many unemployed immortals left. Shortly we will run out of names."

"I have an idea." Syssi put her cup down. "If I remember right, we have five high-school students and two local college students. Three of them are working for Nathalie, but we can offer the others part time jobs. Kids are always looking for an independent source of income, and they don't get their share in clan profits until they either graduate college or reach twenty-five years of age."

"Brilliant idea. I'll call Onegus and get their names and numbers."

"Yo! Amanda, Syssi, there is someone here to see you!" Hannah called from the other room.

Syssi lifted her cup. "Good. Ms. Mona decided to show up."

They headed back to the lab.

It wasn't Mona. It was William, and he was blushing like a red tomato.

Hannah cast him an indulgent smile. "So you're Amanda's cousin?"

"Unbelievable, huh? Look at her and look at me." He waved a hand over his rotund physique.

Hannah cocked her head. "I can see the family resemblance."

"You can?" Amanda and William said at the same time.

"Yes, of course. Don't you see it, Syssi? The blue eyes, the high cheekbones, the height."

Syssi glanced from Amanda to William and back, then nodded. "You're right. I didn't notice the eye color because of William's glasses, but it's the same shade of blue. Yeah, and you're right about the rest too."

What Syssi hadn't said was that William's cheekbones were not as pronounced because of his padding, and although he was only an inch or two shorter than Kian, his width made him look shorter. What Amanda couldn't understand, though, was why he was wearing glasses. Maybe it had something to do with filtering the glare from the monitors he was staring at all day.

William beamed. "Thank you. I'm flattered, especially since the compliment comes from such a beautiful woman."

Used to compliments, Hannah accepted William's graciously. Even before she'd lost weight, her pretty face, her confidence, and her witty sense of humor made her a very popular girl. Hannah never suffered from a shortage of suitors.

Which, unfortunately, didn't bode well for William. And anyway, there could never be anything more than a hookup between them.

"William, darling, you can come back and flirt with Hannah after you show us your game."

"Yes, right." He shifted the box he was holding under his left arm and offered his right hand to Hannah. "It was a pleasure to make your acquaintance, Hannah."

With a sly grin, she shook it. "Mine too. Come see me after you're done with these two."

The girl had just made William's day. Hell, she'd probably made his year.

"I certainly will," he said.

Amanda shook her head. She'd better have a little chat with Hannah before the post-doc had a chance to toy with William. He was too sweet and naive, and she could easily shatter his fragile ego.

"Are you coming?" Syssi asked.

"In a moment. Help William set up the console in my office."

Syssi cast her a perplexed look. She knew perfectly well that William didn't need anyone's help with anything that had to do with electronics.

Amanda made a shooing motion with her hand. Syssi might be a seer, but unfortunately, she was no mind reader. "And close the door behind you."

Finally, understanding dawned on Syssi's face, and she winked, then did what Amanda had asked.

Amanda braced her hands against Hannah's desk and leaned, so her face was only a few inches away from the postdoc. "Hannah, sweetheart, you're an awesome girl, and if you really like William, I have no problem with some innocent flirting. But if you're just toying with him, don't. He is a sweet man, and I love him dearly. I would hate to see him hurt."

With an offended expression on her face, Hannah crossed her arms over her chest. "I never toy with guys. Have you ever seen me encourage someone I wasn't interested in?"

"Darling, I don't follow your love life that closely."

"I like William. He looks smart and kind, and he is very handsome."

Amanda rolled her eyes. *Yeah, right.*

Hannah narrowed hers. "You're lucky you're my boss, so I'm not going to say what's really on my mind. But just so you know, William has a gorgeous face. You just don't see it. You focus on everything that is less than perfect."

Ouch. Amanda could practically feel the slap on her cheek. She leaned back, getting out of Hannah's personal space. "You got me, and I'm sorry. But he is my cousin, and I don't really look at him that way; as a woman admiring a man, that is. Anyway, I'll leave you to your work."

Hannah's face softened. "I'm sorry too. I shouldn't have exploded like that. It's just that for years I had people look at me and see a fat girl and nothing else. My mother included. I can't stand it when it's done to others."

"I totally understand." Amanda turned on her heel and marched toward her office. She knew all there was to know about being objectified but, in her case, it was her beauty that was getting noticed. Hannah would not appreciate the comparison. People viewed Amanda's looks as a gift, an advantage, and in some ways they were, but not if you wanted to get noticed for who you were on the inside.

In her office, William was already done hooking up his game system to her monitor. "Ready for a demonstration, ladies?"

Amanda waved a hand. "Wow us."

"It looks like any other game. The objective of the spy is to reach a destination while overcoming obstacles on the way. He needs to survive the assassination attempts; planes rigged with bombs, cars that are coming at him, and so on." He started the game and showed them a few moves.

"Someone with precognition or remote-viewing talent will be able to avoid the traps and choose the safe route. He or she will dodge a knife when it's thrown at them, not board a plane that has a bomb on it, and so on. Now, in most games, the players become familiar with the obstacles, and after playing it several times, they know what to expect. This game generates new scenarios all the time. A player will not encounter the same obstacle at the same spot in the game twice. It's always random. The only people who will do exceptionally well are those who have the paranormal ability to predict what will happen next."

Amanda put a hand on William's shoulder. "Excellent. It's violent and bloody enough to be rated M so, hopefully, we won't get kids. After all, we can only approach adults. Though we can take the kids' information to be used later when they reach legal age. The only problem is that we will get only guys. I don't see women playing a game like this."

Syssi nodded. "Is there a way to make the game attractive to females?"

William shrugged. "I wouldn't know. You need to tell me."

"We can have a choice of spy avatars and include female options," Syssi suggested.

Amanda had a few ideas of her own. "Get her a hunky counterpart. A hot British spy, or maybe a frenemy; a Russian spy."

William pulled his tablet from the box and started taking notes. "Got it. A female spy, and a hot counterpart. What else?"

Syssi smirked. "Get her a choice of disguises. Wigs, fashionable outfits, shoes. Girls like to dress up."

She was on to something. "Also a choice of flashy cars, and a condo to decorate, things like that."

William looked confused. "I'll need help. I know nothing about fashion or interior decorating..." His eyes widened. "Ingrid can help. Right?"

Amanda agreed. The interior decorator had a fabulous fashion sense. "Then it's a plan. What do we do once the game is ready?"

William shrugged as if it was too obvious to explain. "We sell it and rent it like any other game. To play, the gamers will have to be online, so we can collect the data. I'll have the software produce a daily list of top performers. With a certain threshold, naturally."

"Perfect." Amanda leaned and kissed his cheek. "You're a genius, William."

He pushed his glasses up his nose. "I know."

"And so modest too," Syssi teased.

They waited for William to pack away his equipment, then exited Amanda's office.

Once in the main lab William hesitated, casting a quick glance at the door and then at Hannah. When she smiled at him in invitation, he made up his mind and approached her.

"I was thinking," he started. "It's almost lunch time. Would you care to join me for a hamburger?" When he didn't get the response he was hoping for, William continued. "Or something else? What are you in the mood for?"

Hannah lifted a small cooler she had stashed under her desk. "I don't eat out unless I absolutely have to. I plan all my meals according to the guidelines of my diet and prepare them myself, so I know exactly what goes into them."

For a moment, William looked deflated but then remembered he was supposed to flirt. "You don't need a diet, you're perfect the way you are."

"Thank you. That's very nice of you to say. But this is the result of the diet. I've lost over sixty pounds. I could lose another thirty, but I'm happy where I am at. For now, I just want to maintain this weight."

"Good for you." He hefted his cardboard box. "Until next time, then." He turned to leave.

"Wait! I still want to have lunch with you. We can go out and sit on the grass, picnic style. You can share mine. I'm a great cook."

Turning back, William looked like she'd given him the best of gifts. "Thank you, but I can't eat your lunch. I'll just take a bite to taste your cooking."

"Don't worry. I packed double in case I needed to stay overtime and eat dinner here. I have enough, and it seems I'm going home on time today."

"In that case, I'll be delighted. Thank you."

Hannah lifted her purse off the back of her chair. "You can stash your box under my desk and get it when we come back."

Amanda shook her head. The game was too valuable to be lying around for anyone to snatch. "I'll take it and lock it in my office."

William handed it to her. "Thank you, that would be better."

Hannah threaded her arm in his and walked him out. "So tell me, William, what do you like to do?"

"Isn't it obvious? I like to eat."

"And I like to cook. We match perfectly."

19

ANDREW

"Did you check the bathroom?" Nathalie called from the walk-in closet.

Just to make sure, Andrew made another round of opening every drawer and even peeked into the shower to make sure he'd collected Nathalie's shampoo and conditioner. "It's clear. I stuffed everything into two Ziploc bags. Where do you want me to put them?"

Between the bags of clothes Nathalie had brought over several trips, and his recently purchased new wardrobe, they ended up with a lot of stuff to take home with them, but no luggage to carry it all in.

"Just put it in one of the shopping bags."

Ziplocs in hand, Andrew crossed the bedroom into the closet. "I think we should ask Syssi to loan us a couple of suitcases. We can bring them back tomorrow."

From her crouching position on the floor, Nathalie pushed up to her feet and examined the array of plastic bags. "We can manage. Several trips to the car and we will be done. As it is, I feel like we've imposed on your sister and her husband enough."

Andrew pulled her into his arms. "Sweetheart, you still cling to your old ways, when you had no one to rely on other than yourself. This is no longer the case, and you need to internalize that it's okay to ask family for things. They are happy to help. Not only that, you're making them feel uncomfortable by trying to do without. You have a whole clan of relatives now who've got your back. Get used to it."

In response, she lifted her head and offered him her sweet lips for a kiss. Not an offer Andrew could refuse. He kissed her, only a light peck at first, but as her tongue darted out and sneaked between his lips, he was lost in her. Cupping the back of her head, Andrew deepened the kiss, and when she moaned into his mouth, he couldn't help but push his hand under her T-shirt and gently caress her breast through her bra. Her nipples were very sensitive because of the pregnancy, so no pinching or tugging. It would have to wait probably until the baby was born—or even longer if she decided to breastfeed.

For some reason, the image of Nathalie nursing their infant daughter got him horny as hell, not that he wasn't a moment ago, but that was like dousing fire with gasoline. He lifted her shirt and knelt in front of her.

"What are you doing?" She tried to pull him back up.

A moment later, when he pulled her bra cups down and under her breasts then licked around one stiff peak, her question was answered.

"Andrew!" Nathalie whispered loudly. "They are all waiting for us in the living room. You can't do it now. Wait until we get home."

He palmed her wet nipple. "Just a little more. I can't leave the twin bereft; wouldn't be fair." He licked her other nipple, then rearranged the bra cups and pulled her T-shirt down.

A smile on her beautiful face, Nathalie smoothed her palm over his short hair. "I love you, Andrew."

"Because of this talented guy?" He pointed at his tongue and waggled it at her.

She laughed. "Among other things. Now, get up and start hauling bags."

"Yes, ma'am." Andrew pushed to his feet and grabbed a couple of bags in each hand.

"Need help?" Kian asked as Andrew crossed the living room and deposited the bags near the entry door. "I'm good for now. But later I'd appreciate help getting everything into the car."

Kian nodded. "Bridget asked that you come see her before you go home."

"Why? She already gave me the green light to go."

Kian shrugged. "Do you have all the pain meds you need?"

Nope, he only had enough for two more days. "I don't. I'd better go down to the clinic and get a big supply. I hope Bridget has enough on hand and doesn't give me a prescription to fill. I'm going back to work tomorrow, and God knows what's waiting on my desk. I'll probably have no time to go to a pharmacy."

Kian waved a hand. "Don't worry about it. I'll ask Shai to arrange a delivery for you."

"First, let me see if Bridget has some for now." Andrew turned to Nathalie. "Don't you dare lift any of these bags. I'll be back in a few minutes, and Kian or Okidu can help me down to the car."

By her guilty smile, he'd guessed right, and the stubborn woman had been planning to do just that. He pointed a warning finger at her, then turned to Syssi. "Make sure she doesn't do anything stupid."

As Syssi nodded, her lip quivered a little. At first, he thought she was stifling a laugh, but then he saw a tear sliding down her cheek.

"What's wrong?" He bent his knees so he could look into her eyes.

"I don't want you guys to go. It was so much fun to have you as flat-mates. The breakfasts. The dinners. It's going to be lonely with just Kian and me."

A snort sounded from Kian's direction. "A tiny hint, and you'll have the entire Guardian force descending on us for every meal."

Syssi laughed through her tears. "I know."

Andrew pulled her into a quick hug. "We live twenty minutes away, not on the other side of the globe. We will see plenty of each other."

With a soft sniffle, Syssi wiped at her eyes. "For some reason, I'm getting overly emotional."

"Oh, oh..." Nathalie cast Syssi an appraising look. "Maybe you're pregnant? As soon as I got pregnant, and I'm talking like right the next day, I started crying at the drop of a hat."

Andrew let go of Syssi and gave her a look-over of his own, not that he had a clue what he was looking for.

"I wish," Syssi said in a sad tone. "But no, I'm not pregnant. Is it so hard to believe that I don't want to see you guys go?"

Nathalie wrapped her arm around his sister's shoulders and walked her over to the sofa. "Come, let's talk wedding plans. It will cheer you up."

It did, and a moment later the two were discussing the color of the dress; whether it should be pure white, off white, or cream-colored.

Andrew couldn't care less, but he was happy to see Syssi smiling again as he left.

Bridget's office door was open, and he rapped his fingers on the jamb before walking in. "Good evening, Doctor. You wanted to see me?"

She lifted her head from her tablet and smiled at him. "Take a seat, Andrew. There are a few things I need to discuss with you."

Full on doctor mode. Good.

Every time Andrew was alone with Bridget, he had an anxious moment, not sure which Bridget he was about to encounter, the doctor or the ex-lover. The thought of her bringing up their brief past together was disturbing.

Andrew planted his butt in the metal chair Bridget tortured her patients with, wondering if she did it on purpose to get them to leave as quickly as possible. "What's up, Doc?"

"I'm not one to beat around the bush, so I'll get straight to it. Nathalie's pregnancy is complicating things. She can't transition while she is carrying a child."

Did she think him an idiot? "I know that."

"I know you do, but did you realize the impact it will have on your marriage?"

Andrew frowned. "What do you mean?"

Bridget looked like she was gathering patience to explain the facts of life to a simpleton. "In a few months, your venom glands will become active, and your fangs will reach their full length. The urge to bite your mate will be overpowering. But you can't. A bite may facilitate Nathalie's transition. Do you see the problem now?"

"I'm not an animal. If I can stop myself during sex, for any reason and at any time, I don't see why I can't do the same with biting. I'm sure it's not going to be easy, but there is no other way. Under no circumstances would I allow anything or anyone, myself included, to do anything that will endanger my girls."

Bridget's smile was sad. "You're a good man, Andrew, and I know you believe that you'll be able to abstain, but I'm telling you that you won't. You're not human anymore. I'm sure it didn't escape your notice that in some ways your new physiology is far more advanced than your old one; in others, it's more primitive. The instinctive urges will be undeniable. Not only the sexual ones either. You're more aggressive now and easier to provoke. You need to plan ahead and decide what to do when you feel like killing the next driver that cuts you off. It might be counting from one to ten, or taking several deep breaths, or whatever else works for you. You need to be careful and watch out for triggers."

Damn. He'd thought it was temporary and that the insane urges would calm down in a few days. But according to Bridget, he was stuck like that. He'd turned into a predatory animal, and the only thing he could do was to learn to control it.

Andrew rubbed his brows between his thumb and forefinger. "What am I going to do when the time comes? And how long do I have?"

"If you're lucky, it will take your glands six months to become active, so you'll only have to contend with Nathalie's final trimester. But it can happen sooner. As to what to do, I don't have good news for you. You either use a substitute or ask Kian to put you in stasis until after the baby is born. I don't see any other options."

Fuck it all to hell.

"Even hypothetically, the suggestion of having sex with a substitute is offensive to me."

Bridget raised her palms. "I know, I know. But it's my obligation to put it out there. It's up to you to decide what you do with it."

"I'd rather be put away like the rabid dog I am now."

"I'm sorry. I wish I had better news for you."

Bridget made it sound like it was the end of the world. It wasn't. After all, something wonderful had happened. Nathalie was pregnant with their child. And after suffering through some pain and misery—hers delivering the baby, and his rotting away in stasis—things would get to be wonderful again.

He and Nathalie would become parents.

"We still have time, and maybe some other solution will present itself. What worries me much more than my ability or inability to refrain from biting is that Nathalie must remain human until after the delivery, and in the meantime she is as fragile and vulnerable as any other mortal."

Bridget smoothed a finger over the tablet's glossy surface. "Nathalie is a healthy young woman. The chances of something going wrong are really minimal. You shouldn't lose any sleep over it."

Easy for Bridget to say, she wasn't in love with a mortal. Her entire life didn't depend on that one, perfect mortal's survival.

"Logically, I hear what you're saying, but it doesn't make it any easier for me, or give me the peace of mind to sleep well at night. I have a feeling that the only time I will relax between now and the delivery will be when Kian puts me in stasis."

20

ANANDUR

Twenty-eight hours had passed since Lana's call, and Anandur's phone hadn't left his palm the entire time. He'd even slept with it tucked under his pillow.

Damn, he hoped the girls were okay. The surly Russians had grown on him during his short affair with Lana, and he prayed to the merciful Fates that Alex hadn't discovered their plot. A guy who sold women into slavery for money would have no problem killing the entire crew if he'd gotten a whiff of their mutiny.

As he walked down the hallway to Kian's office, Anandur wondered what could have possessed Alex to sink so deep into the darkness. He was a relatively young immortal, just a little older than Amanda, which meant that he'd grown up when the clan had already accumulated enough resources to ensure a good life for all of its members.

It hadn't always been like that, and during most of their history everyone had to work to support their family. But other than the few who for some reason had gone crazy, like the infamous Vlad, Anandur couldn't remember any of them doing something so vile. There had been quite a few instances of clan members abusing their powers for personal gain, and some internal scuffles when tempers flared and men fought over this or that, but that was about it.

Since the beginning, Annani's teaching had drilled the sanctity of life, human and immortal, into their heads. The other thing she was unrelenting about was the importance of consent.

Alex was violating both in the most despicable way.

"Come in," Kian called when Anandur rapped his knuckles on the glass door. Ever since Syssi had come into his life, the guy was obsessing about everyone having to knock before entering.

"Good evening, gentlemen," Anandur said before taking a seat next to Onegus.

Kian cocked a brow. "Did you hear from them again?"

"No."

"I asked Onegus to join us for this because Andrew has enough on his plate right now. We can either make a plan ourselves or outsource it to Turner."

Anandur scratched his beard. "I vote for Turner, but I want to be there with the rescue team."

"The problem with Turner is that he doesn't work with anyone other than his own people or subcontractors he's thoroughly vetted. We need to apprehend Alex and bring him to trial. Humans can't do it."

Getting his hands on the scumbag was incredibly appealing, but Anandur was more concerned with Lana and the other girls. "My first priority is the crew," he said.

Onegus nodded. "Of course. They come first. But we don't want Alex to slip away and start the same disgusting operation somewhere else."

"Do you have an idea for a plan?" Kian asked.

Usually, Kian was the strategist and Onegus the implementer, but the head Guardian had no doubt learned something from his boss over the many years he'd served under him.

"We need to take the boat at sea. We will cause an international incident if we attack while it's moored in a Mexican harbor. Given enough time and resources, we could've arranged a cooperation with the Mexican authorities, but we have a narrow window of opportunity here, and we can't afford the delay."

Kian pushed up to his feet and began pacing, which he claimed helped him think. "All we need from Lana is the boat's location or that of their next stop. We can launch a drone to follow the yacht, so we'll know when it's in the optimal position for a takeover."

"We will need a fast boat," Anandur stated the obvious. "And, naturally, we need to get it there."

"Not a problem. You and another Guardian take one of the larger jets and fly to the nearest port city. I'll arrange for a boat to wait for you there. You use the boat to board the yacht, take Alex into custody, and put him under if needed. The crew gets the yacht to the nearest harbor. I'll have a local crew ready to take it back to Marina Del Rey. From there, all of you fly to our airstrip, where someone will take Alex off your hands. You refuel and continue with the girls to Hawaii. Case closed."

"Not a bad plan. One problem, I don't know how to drive a yacht or use its navigation systems. The last time I took a boat out, we were still navigating by the stars."

Kian stopped and glared at Onegus. "Add it to the list of skills your guys need to know. We will have to bring along a civilian. And if we can't find one who knows what he's doing, I'll have to come with you."

"You know how to drive a boat?"

"And I also know how to fly a plane or a helicopter, drive a tank and any other vehicle. And I know how to operate a submarine."

Anandur caught Onegus smirking down at his boots. So he'd known all along that Mr. Control-freak had learned how to operate all possible vehicles.

"A real life 007, aren't you? What I want to know is when and how did you manage to learn all of this without Brundar and me knowing about it? You're not supposed to go anywhere without us or another pair of bodyguards at your side."

Some of the arrogance leached out from Kian's expression. "On a simulator."

That was an interesting piece of information. "We have a simulator somewhere in here, and I don't know about it?"

"Not that kind of simulator—just the software without all the bells and whistles of the real thing. William designed it for me."

Anandur had known Kian for almost a millennium, and it had somehow escaped his notice that the guy was certifiable. "And you think that's good enough? Are you nuts?"

"You've flown with me. Did you notice anything lacking in my piloting skills?"

By then, Onegus was laughing so hard that his eyes were tearing up.

Fuck. Anandur slapped his palm on his forehead; he was such an idiot. He'd never given it a second thought. He should've wondered when and where Kian had acquired his pilot license. But the guy always exuded such an air of command and confidence that no one ever thought to question him.

"I'm not flying with you ever again. Not until you get a real license."

Kian shrugged. "Suit yourself."

21

NATHALIE

"Home, sweet home," Nathalie said as Andrew switched the lights on in the shop.

She'd thought getting back home would feel good; instead, it was depressing. At night, without the hustle and bustle of customers, her shop, her pride and joy, looked dingy, outdated, and small. Especially in comparison to the elegant opulence of Kian and Syssi's penthouse as well as the rest of the clan's keep.

"Where are we?" Fernando asked.

"We are home, Papi."

"Oh. I thought it looked familiar."

Did he? Or was it one of his attempts to hide his confusion?

"Let's go upstairs. I think one of your shows is about to start." Perhaps his room would remind him that this was where he lived. She took her father's elbow and led him to the staircase, then glanced back at Andrew. "You're okay with the shopping bags?"

"Pfft, do you have to ask?" He waved her on. "Get your dad comfortable, and I'll haul everything upstairs."

"Thanks." She cast him a sad smile. The real challenge would be to find a place for all their stuff. She had a feeling most of it would have to stay in the bags because there was no more storage space to be found. For a moment, she considered checking the big commercial freezer in the kitchen. It was never completely full, and maybe she could store some of their things there. Problem was, a health inspector would not find her solution amusing. Not in the least.

Nathalie cringed as she opened the door to her father's room. His old La-Z-Boy armchair was a poor substitute for the luxurious BarcaLounger Okidu had provided for him at Syssi's. The fabric had faded from its original blue to a dirty bluish gray, and the armrests had so many stains on them that they'd turned yellow and brown. The thing was disgusting.

Even Papi thought so. He didn't say a thing, just sighed heavily and trudged over to the chair.

Nathalie picked up the remote from the top of the television and turned it on. After the large flat screen television her father had enjoyed in his room at Kian's, this big square box with its pitifully small screen must've been another letdown.

She flipped the channels until she found the one broadcasting his show—something about truckers in Alaska. She had no idea why he found the subject so fascinating. Maybe it was all that snow.

"Are you comfortable, Papi? Would you like a blanket? A cup of tea?"

"Yes, please." He didn't smile at her as he usually did when she offered to do something nice for him.

"What's wrong, Papi?"

He shrugged. "I liked our vacation. It was nice there."

"Would you like to go back?"

"I wish we could afford to live in a hotel. But it doesn't matter. As long as we have each other, we should thank the Lord we have a roof over our head and food on our table."

Nathalie leaned and kissed his cheek. "I'll get you the blanket."

When she stepped out into the corridor, she had to plaster herself against the wall to let Andrew pass with the loads of bags he was carrying.

"That's the last of it," he said. "Do you want me to start putting it away?"

She shook her head. "Leave it on the floor. I don't think anything will fit in the closet."

"We really need a bigger place."

She rolled her eyes. "Tell me about it. I'm going downstairs to make tea for my father. Would you like some?"

"Sure. And can I bother you for a sandwich? I'm starving."

She slapped his shoulder. "It's no bother, you big goof."

Ever since his transition, Andrew's appetite had become ferocious, and not only for food. But she wasn't complaining, on the contrary. His appetite suited her just fine.

Going through the fridge, she was glad to see that everything was neat and organized. Jackson's friend, Gordon, was keeping things in the same order she used to, and using her labeled containers. Made life easier when several orders came in at the same time. To stop and read the labels on the packages of cheeses and cold cuts in the fridge would've slowed things down.

As she made the sandwich for Andrew, her hands did the job without engaging her brain. Muscle memory, she supposed. Years of doing the same thing would have this effect. She scooped some potato salad onto the plate, then laid the roast beef on rye bread next to it.

Wondering who prepared the salad and if it was as good as hers, she dropped another scoop on a different plate and grabbed a fork. It was good. Leaning against the counter, she ate it all.

"My sandwich ready?" Andrew poked his head into the kitchen.

"Yeah, I'll bring it out to you." She finished the last forkful of salad and lifted Andrew's plate.

"The potato salad is great. I think it's even better than mine." She put the plate down in front of Andrew. He'd already poured them both tea, but by the steam rising from the mugs, it was still too hot to drink. Too bad since the salad had made her thirsty.

"Do you want me to bring you an ice cube?" Andrew asked.

Such a sweet man. He knew her so well, was so attuned to her. She smiled at him, hoping it expressed her love and gratitude. "Thank you."

Andrew was up and back with the ice in seconds. "Here you go." He dropped two cubes into her tea.

A moment later, it was just the right temperature to drink, and she took several long sips. "I should call Jackson and ask him to come over. I owe him a big, fat check. Besides, he promised to go over the accounting with me. I have no idea where I stand financially."

Andrew swallowed a mouthful of sandwich and wiped a drop of mayo from his chin. "Can't it wait until tomorrow?"

Talking about appetite, Nathalie knew what was on his mind. "I don't need the extra stress. The shop is too busy in the morning for Jackson and me to exchange more than a few words."

"The last thing I want is for you to get stressed over anything. I was just thinking that Jackson might be out on a date or something like that."

She hadn't considered that, but if he was, he would tell her he couldn't come. Jackson wasn't shy or timid. Besides, the promise of a fat check would be too alluring for him to say no to.

Nathalie made the call.

"I'm coming over," he said before she had a chance to mention the check.

Andrew was chewing the last bite of the second sandwich she'd made for him when the back door opened and Jackson walked in.

"Andrew, my man, so good to see you on the other side." He offered Andrew his hand. When Andrew took it, Jackson pulled him up into a bro hug, complete with the backslapping. It sounded painful. Men were such weird creatures, expressing feelings of friendship by hitting each other on the back.

"It's good to be here," Andrew smiled.

"I'll bet. How are you doing, Nathalie?" The boy finally turned his attention to her. She'd forgive his lack of manners this time. After all, there were extenuating circumstances.

"I'm great. Are you hungry? Can I offer you a sandwich?"

Jackson shook his head and planted his butt next to Andrew. "This place is killing my appetite. Being around food all day is tough on the senses."

Andrew nodded in understanding. "The smells get to you, huh?"

"They do."

Now that he was so close, she noticed that Jackson looked a little skinnier, less fit. This job was taking a toll on him.

"So, tell me, Jackson, anything I should know about?"

Jackson leaned back into the Naugahyde upholstered bench. "Everything is going great, as you have seen during your short visits…" He cast her an accusing look. "The place is packed all the time. Your breakfast regulars were asking about you. They were worried that something happened to your dad, but I told them that you were taking him for some special treatment. Feel free to invent what it was. Gordon and Vlad and I have a good system in place, but we all need a break. This place is a slave camp."

Guilt squeezed at Nathalie's heart. It hadn't been fair to the boys, expecting them to shoulder grownup responsibilities basically on their own. She knew exactly how all-consuming and exhausting running the café was.

"I'm so sorry I dumped it all on you guys, and I'm so grateful to you." She pulled out the check she'd prepared for him from her pocket. "Here, a small token of gratitude. I'll write two more for Vlad and Gordon." She handed it to Jackson.

His eyes peeled wide as he unfolded it. "A thousand bucks? Are you nuts? That's too much! I can't take it." He pushed it back to her.

Nathalie put her finger on it and slid it over toward Jackson. "Don't argue, and take it. Did you buy that guitar of yours already?"

He glanced at the check. "I've put down a deposit, and the store owner is holding it for me."

"Including this check, how much more do you need?"

"Just this week's wages."

"Then take another advance and go get your beauty."

That was an offer Jackson couldn't refuse. With a sigh he palmed the check, pulled out his wallet, and carefully slid it inside. "Thank you, Nathalie. You're the best boss ever."

"And you're the best employee anyone could ever hope to find. You're one of a kind."

Andrew cleared his throat. "Are you guys done with that? Because I need to talk to you both."

Nathalie lifted a brow. "About what?"

"Your work schedule from now on. You can't put in twelve-hour workdays anymore, Nathalie. In fact, I don't want you on your feet for more than four."

Jackson's eyes darted from her to Andrew and then back. "Are you sick, Nathalie? What's going on?"

She smiled and patted his hand. "I'm not sick. I'm pregnant."

He gasped. "Get out of here...when did that happen?"

Andrew cleared his throat again. "I want Nathalie to take it easy."

"No problem. The guys will understand why a vacation is out for now."

Guilt assailed her again. "Maybe we should hire another one of your friends. So you guys can take time off in turns."

"It will have to be a mortal. All my immortal buddies are here."

"Is it a problem?"

He shrugged. "Not really. We need to keep up appearances for the sake of the customers anyway."

"Then it's agreed."

They shook on it.

Jackson pushed up from the bench. "Check your email, Nathalie. I forwarded to you the profit and loss figures for last month. I'm sure you'll be happy to see how well the shop has done."

Once again, the kid was exceeding her expectations. She hadn't known he could do accounting. "Thank you, I will."

The best part about Jackson organizing the numbers ahead of time was that it solved the problem of going over them while Andrew had other plans.

When Jackson left, she smiled sheepishly. "Well, I guess we have time now. I can look at what Jackson emailed me tomorrow."

Andrew leaned and reached for her hand. "Are you looking forward to getting back to work?"

Was she?

"I am. It wasn't exactly a vacation we were on. It was the most stressful time of my life. My old routine, mingling with my regulars, it will give me a sense of normalcy. I miss it."

"How about being home? Are you happy to be back?"

"Frankly? Not as much as I thought I'd be. We were very comfortable at your sister's penthouse. In comparison, this place feels more cramped and dingy than ever. And the upstairs smells like a bakery. I guess it takes being away for a while to notice it." She shook her head. "Not pleasant, not at all."

In the brief silence that followed, Andrew looked like he was choosing his words carefully, which wasn't like him. Normally, he preferred the direct approach and didn't beat around the bush even when discussing touchy subjects.

"I think we should move into the keep." Evidently, he'd decided to stick to his blunt style.

God, did it sound tempting. "I can't. You know my father needs his familiar environment. We've talked about it before."

Andrew's lips tightened in that determined expression he got when he thought she was unreasonably stubborn. "He seemed perfectly fine to me during his stay at the keep. In fact, I think he was happier there than I've ever seen him here. He had William and occasionally the Guardians to keep him company and occupy him with this and that. He had Okidu serving his every whim. Did he complain about anything?"

Not even once. "He thought we were on vacation."

"So we keep telling him that. Or, if you want, you can take him with you when you go to work, and he can sit around here for a few hours. There are so many advantages to moving there, especially with regard to your father. In the keep, there is always someone who can watch him; if not William, then someone else. Even Okidu, or Onidu, Amanda's butler."

Nathalie pulled her hand out of his and raised her palms. "We can't live with your sister and her husband. It was fun for a little while, but it can't work as a permanent arrangement."

"I'm sure Kian can find an apartment for us; if not in the same building, then in one of the neighboring ones. The clan owns half of the high-rises on the street."

Yeah, and she could just imagine the rent—five thousand dollars minimum. Probably more. Those were luxury apartments for rich business people, not struggling coffee shop owners. True, thanks to Jackson and his crew she wasn't struggling as much as before, but she wasn't wealthy. Not even close.

"We can't afford a place like that." She shushed Andrew when he opened his mouth to protest. She knew what he wanted to say. That he was earning a good income and that combining their resources would be enough to pay for a fancy place like that.

"You're still making mortgage payments on your house, right? Can you afford rent that is probably over five grand a month? I know I can't because I have to make mortgage payments on this place whether I live here or not."

"So I sell my house. You're right, the mortgage is eating a third of my monthly income, and without it I can afford the five thousand dollar rent on my own."

She didn't want Andrew to give up his house. He loved the place, even though he was spending hardly any time there. "Your house represents your biggest asset, and it doesn't make financial sense to sell it. Besides, what if the rent is even more expensive than five grand? Can you afford it then?"

With an indulgent smile, Andrew shook his head. "Sweetheart, listen to yourself. You're looking for all the excuses in the world why it can't work instead of thinking of a way to make it work. Why?"

That was a dumb question. Because she was scared, that's why. This was another big decision, another upheaval in her life that she wasn't ready for. Couldn't he allow her at least a few days to catch her breath?

She crossed her arms over her chest and pushed her chin out. "It's a big decision, and I don't want to rush into it. I'd rather play devil's advocate and flush out all the possible problems."

"You're right. Let me put your mind at ease. Can you listen for a few moments without losing your cool?"

What cool? She'd lost hers a long time ago, when he'd been teetering between life and death, and she hadn't regained it since. But she nodded, letting him speak his mind.

"Instead of selling my house, I can rent it out. And you can rent out the apartment over the shop as well. In fact, I suggest you offer it to Jackson and his friends. Boys their age crave independence. They are going to love it, provided it's cheap of course."

Nathalie wanted to argue, but there was nothing more to argue about. Everything he'd said was true and made perfect sense. Rationally, she knew that moving to the keep was a good decision, one that would improve their lives, even Papi's. And yet, it was an extremely difficult step for her to take.

It meant taking for granted her new family's willingness to help with her father. She found it hard to internalize that help was out there—offered with no strings attached, just from the goodness of people's hearts.

It was true, though. She'd witnessed it herself. Even Bridget, who should've harbored some animosity toward Nathalie for stealing Andrew away from her, had been incredibly helpful and supportive. And William, who hardly knew her at all, was taking care of Papi as if he was actually enjoying it.

Andrew chuckled. "What? No rebuttals?"

Nathalie let her arms drop. "No. You won the argument. Let's do it."

Andrew lifted his arms, palms up. "Hallelujah, praise the Lord."

"Shouldn't it be, praise Nathalie?"

"Indeed it should." Andrew got up and pulled her to her feet. "Let me take you upstairs and praise you until the angels sing. Correction, just one angel. My Nathalie."

22

ANDREW

*E*verything was different at work. Andrew felt as if he'd been gone for a decade and not just a few days. The big office space he shared with four other agents looked and smelled different, the agents looked and smelled different, and so did he. Not the smell part, he'd gotten used to his own scent, but everyone noticed that he wasn't the same.

Most of the guys just cast him surreptitious glances or told him that the time off had agreed with him, but at the end of the day his luck ran out. As he stepped out into the corridor and joined several others who were waiting for the elevators, Tim walked over.

"Are you wearing platforms, Spivak? Because I swear that you are taller than you were before your vacation." Tim looked him over with the critical eye of an artist. "And take a look at this skin, baby soft." He pinched Andrew's cheek.

Andrew slapped the guy's hand away. "If you value your fingers, buddy, keep your hands to yourself."

The threat was effective, and Tim stuck his hands in his pockets. As an artist, he needed his hands in good working condition and was obsessed with protecting them from harm.

"Have you gone to some rejuvenation spa? Because if you did, I want the name."

That worked with the story Andrew had prepared in case anyone inquired about the changes he'd undergone. "Yeah, exactly. It was a gift from my fiancée. Massages all day long, and spinal realignment. Apparently, my poor posture made me look shorter than I actually was."

Tim's eyes narrowed into slits. "What are you talking about? You always had fantastic posture, Spivak."

Damn Tim and his sharp observation skills.

"I kept my shoulders squared, an old habit from my time as a Marine, but according to the chiropractor, the vertebrae in my lower back were compressed."

That bull-crap answer seemed to satisfy Tim. "I want the name and phone number of that spa. That's my destination for my next vacation. If they can make me look taller, I don't care how much it costs."

"I'll have to ask Nathalie. It was some weird French name I can't even pronounce."

"Thanks."

"See you later, Tim."

As soon as Tim walked away, Andrew released a breath. The problem with lies was that they usually meant more lies. Now he'd have to come up with a story about the nonexistent spa burning down to the ground or some other shit like that.

The elevator door opened and he stepped in, pressed the button for his parking level, and leaned against the mirrored back wall. The car made its way down, stopping at nearly every floor. People were going home. Most he knew in passing, a few he nodded hello to. Then as the doors opened at the gym level, he saw someone he actually wanted to talk to.

Roni, the hacker, was outside in the hallway, waiting for the elevator going up.

Andrew stepped out. "Hey, Roni, how are things going for you? You look good, kid."

He wasn't lying. Since Andrew had last seen him, Roni must've been working out vigorously. His arms looked a little less scrawny, and he was standing tall instead of hunching over.

The kid grinned. "I asked for a personal trainer, and the boss assigned me one. The guy tortures me every day, but if I look good, then it's worth it."

"You do. And I'm not saying it just because I need another favor."

"What is it?"

"Just one more check on the same thing. I need to know when was the last time she made a withdrawal. My friend is heading out there, and it will make his life easier if he knows when to stake out that bank."

"No problem. I'm glad to help." Roni transferred his gym bag to his other hand.

That had been too easy. Roni wasn't the type to offer something for nothing.

"I need a favor too," Roni murmured while looking down at his sneakers.

Here it goes. "What is it?"

"Can you hook me up with Sylvia again?"

Right.

Andrew leaned and whispered in Roni's ear, "That was a one-time deal. I'm not a pimp."

"No, not like that. I mean, only if she wants to. I don't have her number, and she doesn't have mine. So maybe there is a chance she would like to see me again? Like for coffee or something?"

There was so much hope in the kid's voice that Andrew hated to disappoint him. There was probably no chance in hell Sylvia wanted to have another go at the geeky kid with an attitude. It would be futile and embarrassing, but he was going to ask.

"Are you allowed to leave? Or are you still confined to this building?"

"I can meet her for dinner or at a coffee shop. My handler will have to be there, of course, but he'll give me space if I'm with a girl. He's a decent dude."

Andrew clapped Roni on the shoulder. "I'll see what I can do. I'll call her tonight, and if she is agreeable, I'll set up a time and a place for you to meet the following day. Good?"

Roni looked as if he'd just won the lottery. "It's better than good. Thank you. And I'll check on your lady friend and her visits to the bank."

"Good deal." They shook on it, parting when Roni stepped into the cab going up.

Andrew called Sylvia as soon as he cleared the parking garage and got reception.

She shocked him. "Sure, I will be happy to see Roni. I was wondering why he didn't ask for me. The poor kid desperately needs a friend. I'll text you the details of a place I like."

Sylvia was genuinely interested in meeting freaking Roni again, so much so that even over the phone Andrew had no doubt she was truthful.

"You're awesome. Text me the time too."

"I will. Thank you, Andrew. It was a nice thing to do."

Not really, but whatever. He would let her think he had done it out of the goodness of his heart.

As Sylvia terminated the call, another one came in. Andrew smiled at the gorgeous face staring at him from the screen and accepted it. "Hello, sweetheart, I'm on my way home."

"That's great because we need to be at Dalhu's in less than an hour."

Fuck, he'd forgotten all about it. "Do I have to dress up?"

"Of course, you do. I want us looking our best."

"We didn't buy a new suit."

Nathalie sighed. "I know you're going to hate it, but we need to borrow one from Kian. There is no time to go shopping, and your old one doesn't fit. I'm going to call Syssi right now, and have her bring one to Amanda and Dalhu's place."

"Fine." Andrew really hated borrowing clothes from his brother-in-law.

When he got home, Andrew grabbed a quick shower and even let Nathalie gel his hair into place. "I look like a gangster from the thirties," he said once she was done fussing with it. "And I'm packing too." He glanced down at the bulge in his pants.

Nathalie had showered before him, and the only items of clothing she had on while playing with his hair were a tiny pair of see-through panties and a matching bra.

She kissed his forehead, which brought her breasts so close to his nose he could feel the vapor coming off her damp skin. Unable to help himself, he reached with his hands and cupped both.

"They are getting bigger every day," he murmured before planting a gentle kiss above one swell and then the other.

"I know, right? That's the best side effect of the pregnancy. I feel buxom, sexy." She waggled her breasts in front of his face.

Andrew circled her tiny waist with one arm and delivered a hard smack to her butt cheek with his hand.

"Ouch! What was that for?"

"You are always sexy, and I love this butt." He palmed both cheeks and gave them a squeeze. "You don't need larger breasts. Everything about you is perfect the way it is."

She slapped his cheek playfully. "You're such a sweet-talker. But we don't have time for any hanky-panky. Let me get dressed." She removed his arm from her waist and turned around.

Her panties were the almost thong type, a narrow strip of fabric in the back leaving most of her beautiful ass exposed. His smack had left a very faint imprint on her left butt cheek. Sexy as hell. He wanted to adorn her right cheek in a similar way, but was afraid she wouldn't react favorably.

Maybe some other time.

He almost came in his pants when she bent at the waist to pull out her new, red dress from the plastic bag on the floor.

"What are you doing to me, woman?" he croaked, shifting his position to try and relieve the pressure on the club in his pants.

Turning her head with a wicked smirk on her beautiful face, she winked. "Payback, sweetheart."

The woman was a witch. With her gorgeous ass high in the air and her long, luxurious hair hanging down to the floor on one side of her head, she was sin and temptation personified.

"Ooh, you just earned yourself another smack." He was up and delivering a loud slap to the other cheek before she had the chance to cover what she was so carelessly flaunting.

"Stop it! Andrew! What has gotten into you? Are you suddenly into spanking?" She tried to sound upset, but he could tell she was having as much fun with it as he was.

Cupping both cheeks in his hands, he massaged them gently and kissed her neck. "You call this a spanking? Those were love taps."

"Aha. Whatever. Now leave my ass alone so I can get dressed. And put your shoes on. We need to get going."

With a sigh, he let go.

Half an hour later they were standing in the vestibule in front of Amanda's penthouse doors.

"How do I look?" Nathalie asked.

"I would rather show you than tell you, but then I'll mess up your makeup and hair, and you'll get mad at me. You're stunning, baby. And I'm the luckiest guy in the universe to have you. I can't believe some other schmuck didn't snap you up a long time ago."

She grinned, her red-painted lips forming the most beautiful shape. "That's because I was waiting for you."

"Damn right you were." He lifted her hand and kissed her knuckles.

The door opened to reveal Amanda and her mocking smirk. She braced one hand against the doorjamb and put the other on her hip. "Are you going to come in anytime soon? Or should I close the door and keep listening to you lovebirds sing each other's praises?"

Nathalie blushed and Andrew knew why. Just as he'd promised, last night he'd *praised* her into several screaming orgasms. Muffled by a pillow, naturally. Damn, they really needed to move. He loved that his woman was a screamer, and he hated that she wasn't free to do so.

Dalhu's tall frame appeared behind Amanda, and he pulled her aside, tucking her under his arm as if she was a dainty little thing and not a six-foot-tall woman. "Come in, guys."

"Thank you."

"Follow me," he said as he strolled down the hallway to one of the bedrooms.

"Wait," Amanda called. "Do you guys want something to drink?"

Nathalie turned around. "Not yet. I don't want to smear my lipstick."

"Give me a holler when you do."

"Nice," Andrew said as they entered Dalhu's new studio. It seemed that Amanda had had a wall knocked down between two bedrooms, combining them into one big, open space. There was a staging area with an armchair and some soft velvety fabric draped on a wooden contraption behind it. Several lamps were aimed at the chair, but they were turned off. Hopefully, Dalhu didn't intend on turning them all on. If he did, they would be baking from the heat.

"The suit Syssi brought is hanging on the hook in the bathroom. You can change in there." Dalhu pointed to a door.

When he was done, Andrew stepped out of the bathroom and looked at himself in the tall mirror Dalhu had put up on one of the walls. "I look damn good in a designer suit." The fit wasn't perfect, but it was better than any other suit Andrew had ever worn—including the tuxedo custom made for him for Syssi's wedding. He just filled the thing better now.

"Stop admiring yourself and get over here." Dalhu waved a hand toward the chair Nathalie was sitting in.

"How do you want to do it? With me standing behind the chair, looking regal? Or should I take the chair and have Nathalie sit on my lap?"

Dalhu shrugged. "It's your portrait, you guys decide."

There was only one person here who was going to make any decisions, and it sure wasn't Andrew. Even an old bachelor like him knew that it was the lady's call.

"Nathalie? What would you like?"

She pushed up to her high-heel clad feet and tugged on his hand. "I want to sit in your lap. I want our kids to look at this portrait and know how deeply in love their parents were from the very beginning."

Andrew heard Amanda sigh in the living room and murmur, "That's so romantic."

He had to agree.

23

NATHALIE

Nathalie's face was getting numb from holding the same expression for the past hour or so. The rest of her wasn't doing so great either. Andrew hadn't voiced any complaints yet, but his arm, the one holding her, must've gone numb. Her macho guy was probably waiting for her to say something first.

Andrew would let that arm fall off before admitting that his pregnant, mortal fiancée was tougher than him.

Fortunately, women didn't suffer from that particular mental affliction, and she was definitely done for today.

Nathalie let her face relax. "Can you give me a push up, Andrew?" she asked.

"Certainly, my love."

She stifled a snort at his relieved tone and pushed all the way up to her feet. "We are done for today, Dalhu. I was getting numb all over." Lifting her arms over her head, she did a couple of side stretches, remembering too late that her dress wasn't long enough for such a maneuver. Her arms dropped, and she put her hands on her hips for a couple more.

"Do you want to see how the portrait is coming out?" Dalhu asked with a shy smile.

Cute.

A guy who would've terrified her if she bumped into him on the street, a huge ex-mercenary, was acting like a little boy showing his mom a drawing he'd made and hoping for her approval.

"Sure, if you don't mind. Some artists don't like showing their work in progress. Only when it's done."

"Then it's good I don't consider myself an artist."

Yeah, right. Of course, he was. Like most people, Dalhu was shielding his ego by pretending he didn't put any stock in his talent.

He stepped aside as Nathalie walked around the easel and took her first look at his work.

"It's beautiful, Dalhu." In the hour or so they'd been posing for him, Dalhu had finished sketching their outline and started adding detail to their faces. She wondered if Dalhu had captured Andrew's real expression or had allowed himself artistic license. The love and pride radiated from the canvas. This was exactly how she wanted their future children to see them.

"Let me see." Andrew came around, but she grabbed him for a fierce kiss before he had a chance to see anything.

"What was that for?" he asked when she let go of him.

"For the way you look at me." Nathalie pointed at the picture.

As he glanced at the portrait, Andrew's eyes skimmed over his own outline without really looking and focused on hers. He frowned as if he didn't approve.

"What? You don't like how Dalhu drew me?"

"Oh, I like the way you look, what I don't like is how he sees you."

"What do you mean?" She cast a worried glance at Dalhu. By the amused look on his face, the guy seemed to know what Andrew was talking about.

Andrew pointed at the drawing, first at the swell of her breast and then at the curve of her hip.

"I think I look sexy."

"Exactly."

"Relax, Andrew. I view Nathalie with an artist's eye. There is only one woman for me, and you know it."

"In here, I do." Andrew pointed to his head. "But in here, I don't." He pointed to his chest.

Dalhu chuckled. "You want to talk about it? I'm avoiding visiting Amanda at work even though I'm not under house arrest anymore. I know I'll go postal seeing all the ogling looks I'm sure she's getting from her horny students. And the funny thing is that I'm not even the jealous type. I trust Amanda completely. I just hate thinking about what goes on in those little punks' dirty minds."

"Fuck, I hadn't considered the ogling customers my Nathalie will have to deal with again." He turned to her. "You can't work at the coffee shop anymore."

She patted his arm. "Down, Andrew. You're talking nonsense. I'm thirsty, and I'm going to take Amanda up on her offer."

Amanda wasn't in the living room when they got there, and Dalhu played host, pouring some carbonated water for her and scotch for Andrew.

"She is probably in her office. I'll go get her." He left them sitting at the counter.

Andrew took a sip then put his drink down. "Sorry for before. I didn't mean it. These immortal hormones are difficult to control."

Poor guy. He was having a hard time adjusting to his new physique. It was good Andrew had such a strong personality, otherwise the change would have affected more than his body. He would've become a different man. Funny how people didn't realize that their personalities were influenced by their body's chemistry, and not controlled solely by the command center up in their brains.

"I know, baby. I'm not mad, just amused."

Andrew opened his mouth to say something when they heard someone knocking on the door. He leaned back and glanced at the corridor. "Should we answer it, or give Dalhu a holler?"

"Both. I'll open the door, and you get them. On second thoughts, a holler is a better idea. God knows what they are doing in there."

"You're right. He should've been back already."

There was another knock, and then the door opened, saving Nathalie the effort.

Kian strode in as if he owned the place, which in a way he did, and Syssi was right behind him with a frown on her face. "You should wait to be invited. You hate when people barge into our place, and yet you're doing the same thing."

"I knocked." He walked over to the counter. "You guys look fancy." He gave Andrew a look-over. "Nice suit."

Not for the first time, she'd noticed that Kian was barely looking at her, and he didn't offer his hand for a shake either. At first, she'd assumed he was indifferent to her, but now she was starting to suspect it was the standard protocol between immortal males. Giving too much attention to another man's mate was apparently considered rude.

"It sure is. It's yours." Andrew offered his hand, and Kian shook it.

"You look gorgeous, Nathalie." Syssi leaned in and kissed her cheek. "You should always wear red."

"That's what Andrew says. But I think it's too flashy for everyday wear."

Syssi shook her head. "It's not. But we all have our little quirks and habits. For me, it's skirts and dresses. I feel weird if I wear anything other than pants to work."

"Hey, guys." Amanda finally decided to show up. "Let's move to the living room so everyone can sit." She shooed them away from the counter.

"Onidu! We have guests."

Her butler rushed out of his room, buttoning his jacket on the go. "Yes, mistress. Should I serve hors d'oeuvres?"

"That would be lovely." She turned to her guests with a dazzling smile that a few weeks ago would've made Nathalie's gut clench with envy. "Who wants a drink?"

"I want one, but I can't have it." Nathalie pouted.

Amanda tapped a finger on her red lips, and Nathalie wondered if she was always wearing lipstick, even at home. "I can make you a non-alcoholic cocktail."

"No, thank you. I'm fine with the sparkling water. I don't need the empty calories."

"As you wish. Andrew, I see you have your poison. How about you, Kian?"

"A beer."

"I'd like one too," Syssi said.

"I'll get it," Dalhu offered.

A moment later he returned with four bottles and handed one to Kian and one to Syssi, then put the third one in front of Andrew. "For later."

"So tell me, how is it to be back home?" Syssi asked. "Miss us already? We certainly miss you. The penthouse feels empty without you."

With a grimace, Nathalie cast Andrew a pointed look. She didn't want to bring up the subject of an apartment in the keep.

"We need a larger place," Andrew said without preamble. "I was wondering if we could rent an apartment here or in one of the neighboring buildings. We didn't consider a move before because of Fernando's condition, but he surprised us with how well he adjusted here. We could use help with him. Someone to keep an eye on him so Nathalie and I can have a breather."

Nathalie's cheeks warmed. This was exactly what they'd discussed the day before, but asking for help taking care of her father was embarrassing as hell. He was her responsibility.

"You can't rent an apartment in the keep," Kian said.

Nathalie's cheeks blazed hotter. She hadn't expected a refusal.

With a smile tugging at her lips, Syssi punched her husband's arm—not gently, given his wince. "He is joking, you guys. What he means is that you can have an apartment here. No rent required."

They were offering Andrew and her charity. As if asking for their help with her father hadn't been humiliating enough. "Andrew and I can afford to pay rent. We are not rich, but we are not destitute either. Don't treat us as a charity case."

Nathalie was itching to get up and walk out the door. She wouldn't, of course; she wasn't ungrateful and rude. But Andrew's relatives were making her very uncomfortable.

Amanda snorted. "I don't pay rent. No member of the family does. Kian built this building as a safe haven for all the clan members he is responsible for. If they choose to live elsewhere, they have to pay for their lodging, but not here. Don't forget that he used clan resources to build this, not his own money. The building belongs to the clan."

Great, she'd gotten pissed off for nothing.

Andrew rubbed a hand over his jaw. "Define clan members for me. Because I don't think I am. Only Annani's descendants and their spouses can claim that honor."

"Let me answer that." Kian stopped Amanda. "First of all, as Syssi's brother and an immortal, you are part of the family. But you're right; we didn't adjust the law to cover your situation yet. We will, though. I don't want any ambiguity. I'll talk to Edna and have her prepare a draft. The thing is, even if your status is not a hundred percent clear, Andrew, yours, Nathalie, is. You are Bhathian's daughter, and therefore Annani's descendent. In fact, it was a gross oversight on my part, as well as your father's, not to realize that you should receive a share of the clan's profit like every other clan member who turned twenty-five. We owe you five years of unpaid dividends."

Talk about speechless. "But you didn't know I existed! You didn't account for an extra person, whatever money was earned during those years was already divided between whoever was on the books."

"Let me worry about the accounting, Nathalie."

Damn, when Kian used that tone, it was impossible to argue with him. Nathalie glanced at Syssi, wondering if he had the same effect on his wife.

He had an effect on her all right, but of a different kind. Syssi's eyes were glazed with passion, and her cheeks were flushed. Kian's commanding tone was a major turn-on for his wife.

They were such a cute couple. Well, maybe cute wasn't the right term.

Nothing about Kian was cute. Problem was, a well-matched couple sounded too clinical. A passionate couple? A loving couple?

Andrew nudged her. "Penny for your thoughts?"

"What? Oh, nothing really. Thank you, Kian, Syssi, Amanda, Dalhu, you are all so wonderfully generous."

Dalhu raised his bottle. "I'm not. I'm still charging you for the portrait, and I regret giving you a discount. You can afford the full price now."

Nathalie wasn't sure if he was joking or not.

"*Mesdames et messieurs*, the hors d'oeuvres are ready." Onidu put a large oval platter on the coffee table. A moment later he returned with six small plates and six tiny forks. "*Bon appetit.*" He bowed and retreated.

"So how is it going to work?" Amanda asked. "You're going to commute to your coffee shop every day?"

"Yes. Jackson and his buddies are going to run it, and I'm going to come in only for a few hours a day. Andrew doesn't want me to exert myself."

Syssi nodded with approval. "He is right. Especially when that belly grows larger."

Andrew rubbed his neck the way he did when he was uncomfortable saying something. "Maybe you should stop working altogether. Financially, you no longer need to. Only if you enjoy it."

Nathalie shook her head. "I wouldn't know what to do with myself all day long. I love baking, and I love interacting with customers. What I hated was the grueling routine. I had no life to speak of. I was waking up at four in the morning and collapsing at nine. That's no longer the case. Thanks to Jackson and his crew, I can take it easy and enjoy myself."

Andrew nodded and pulled her closer, kissing the top of her head. "Is she the best, or what?"

Nathalie rolled her eyes. It was nice to have an adoring guy gushing about every little thing you did and said, but it was kind of embarrassing in company. "Stop it, Andrew, you're making me blush," she whispered, forgetting it was futile. The freaking immortals could hear a butterfly flap its wings in the other room.

Braving a glance at her new family, she was relieved that most of the indulgent looks were directed at Andrew and not at her. A man in love was allowed to make a fool of himself over his woman.

The only one who wasn't smiling was Kian. He appeared deep in thought. "I'll give you Ingrid's phone number." He pulled out his phone from his pocket. "You should call her and schedule an appointment. She can show you all the available apartments to choose from. Andrew, I'm sending you the contact."

Andrew's phone pinged. "Got it."

Kian put his phone back in his pocket and lifted the mostly full beer bottle to his lips, took a short swig, and lowered it back to the table. "I have an idea I want to run by you, Nathalie," he said, training his intense gaze on her.

She was getting used to the immortals' strange eyes, but the intensity that was unique to Kian still managed to unnerve her. "Yes?"

"What if we open a coffee shop like yours right here in the building? Most of the lobby is a wasted, empty space. We can section off part of it and build you a trendy and elegant place."

Wow, that was one hell of an offer. One she unfortunately couldn't accept. Not unless her five years of back dividends amounted to a small fortune. Because that was what building a fancy coffee shop in a high-end building like this would cost.

She shook her head. "I have no idea how much I'm getting in those dividends you've mentioned, but I'm sure it's not enough to cover the cost of something like this. Besides, I don't know if it's a financially viable idea. Spending so much money could only be justified by very favorable profit projections."

Was she imagining it, or was Kian looking at her with newfound respect?

He grinned. "It's a pleasure to talk business with someone who actually understands it. The thing is, I'm not thinking profits here. I'm thinking about a nice place for our people to hang out at, where they can grab a quick bite, or sit down with a cup of coffee and shoot the breeze. We have nothing like that, and I think it would improve the quality of life here. I'm willing to finance the entire building project, and you can collect the profits from whatever you sell."

When she tried to object, he raised his palm to shush her. "If it makes you feel better, you can pay the clan a symbolic rent."

Tempting, it was very, very tempting.

"What am I going to do with my other location?"

He shrugged. "Either close it or give it to Jackson and collect a share of the profits. From what I hear, he can run the place with minimal input from you."

"I'll have to talk to him. I think he would love to have the old place to run as he pleases, but I'll probably need his help with the new one."

"Well, you have plenty of time to figure it out. It would take a month or so to build the place."

"A month? I thought something like that would take much longer."

"Not really. We are not even going to build walls to enclose it because the ceiling is too high. It's not a complicated project."

"What about the kitchen?"

"We can use the commercial one in the basement for the baking, and have only a prep area upstairs."

Nathalie had no more objections. Apparently, Kian hadn't lied when he'd said a coffee shop at the keep was something he'd spent some time thinking about. Either that or he had a very quick mind.

"Well, what do you think, sweetheart?" Andrew asked.

"I love it."

24

ANANDUR

"Lana." Anandur accepted the collect call. Ever since she'd called him from Mexico that first time, he'd been jumping every time his phone rang. It was good his immortal body was immune to coronary disease or he would've dropped dead from the stress by now.

Why the hell did he care so much?

He didn't love Lana, and the rest of her crew were barely tolerable, but he felt responsible—especially for Lana. If anything happened to her, it would be on him.

"We have a problem," she said.

He gripped the phone tighter, the metal casing groaning from the pressure. "What's going on?"

"We have cargo. Four."

They weren't on a private line, and she was right to be cautious, choosing her words carefully.

"The same as always?"

"Yes, but this time also customers on board."

Fuck and double fuck. That complicated things. "How many?"

"Also four, each purchased one for himself, and they be here until next stop."

"They are getting off at the next port?"

"Yes."

"Good. We can wait."

"No. They take cargo with them."

Anandur raked his fingers through his bushy curls, pulling out hairs and welcoming the pain. Maybe it would help sharpen his focus. "What's the next port?"

"Acapulco."

"How long will it take for you to get there?"

"We go slow. Three days, maybe a little more."

"We'll be there before."
She sucked in a breath. "Anything we should do?"
"Absolutely nothing. Business as usual."
"Okay."
"Be well, Lana."
"You too."
As soon as he disconnected the call, Anandur speed-dialed Kian. "I need to see you right away. Lana just called."
"I'm in my office."
Three minutes later, Anandur pushed the door open, strode into the office, and took a seat in front of Kian's desk.
"Do you want me to come back later?" Shai asked Kian.
"No, stay. Take the files to the conference table. You can work there until we are done."
Shai nodded and lifted the stack of files from Kian's desk. Tucking them under his arm, he grabbed a notepad and a pen in his other hand and walked over to the oblong conference table.
"Shoot," Kian said.
"They have cargo."
"Damn."
"And customers on board."
Kian banged his palm on his desk. "What the hell is he doing? Running a bordello aboard his yacht?"
"I think the customers wanted a taste before finalizing the deal. Lana said that they would be taking the girls with them when they disembark in Acapulco in three days. That's our window of opportunity. We have to move fast."
Kian ran his fingers through his hair. "I need to call Turner. We need a human crew to handle the customers."
Anandur narrowed his eyes at Kian. "What do you mean by handle?" Kian was a bloodthirsty bastard, but he usually managed to control those urges.
Kian chuckled. "I wish there was a market for male sex slaves. It would've been the perfect payback. But I guess throwing them in jail will get similar results. Even hardened criminals don't tolerate pedophiles and slavers. They'll get what's coming to them."
Anandur nodded. "Are you going to make the call now? Time is of the essence."
"Yeah, but knowing Turner, he will take his sweet time answering. I'm not sure if he's really a sociopath with no emotions whatsoever or just a great actor. As far as he is concerned, nothing is ever urgent. Things get done at the pace he thinks they should be done and that's it."
"That's good. He keeps a cool head under pressure."
"Yeah, that's true. But I have a problem with purely analytical people who keep emotions out of the equation. The mind can come up with pretty convoluted stuff if it isn't guided by at least some feelings."
"Way over my head, Kian. I'm not one for deep thinking and philosophizing. This is a conversation you should have with someone smart, like Edna, not me."
Kian waved a dismissive hand. "You don't fool me for a moment with that dumb act. I know you have a good brain under all that red hair."

Anandur dipped his head. "Thank you."

Wow, a compliment from Kian was as rare as a smile from Bhathian. Perhaps he should look for the guy and see if he could get a smile out of him. Two positive outcomes increased the possibility of the third one being positive as well.

Damn, it seemed Dalhu's stupid superstitions had managed to infect him as well.

25

ANDREW

"What do you think, Papi?" Nathalie opened the door to his new room.

"Is this the same hotel room we stayed in before?" He asked while trudging to the BarcaLounger Okidu had been kind enough to schlep from Syssi's penthouse down to their new apartment.

"Not the same room, but the same building."

He lowered himself carefully, bracing his weight on his hands to help his weak leg muscles and achy knees on his way down. He sighed when he sank into the soft comfort of the chair. "This is such a good easy chair. I wish I had one like this at home."

"We will be staying here for a while, and you can enjoy it to your heart's content." She was expecting a rebuttal, but her father found the remote and got busy flipping channels on the big flat screen hanging on the wall.

"Do you want your door closed or opened?" Nathalie asked as she stepped out.

"Closed, thank you," he said without sparing her a glance.

That went way easier than she'd thought it would, which meant that the shit storm was still waiting to happen. She wasn't that lucky. Instinctively, she rubbed her hand over her belly, a mini panic attack stealing her breath away.

Whatever it was, it had better not touch her baby.

Nathalie closed her eyes and willed herself to calm down. Stress was bad for the baby. She was silly and superstitious. Of course, she was lucky. She was blessed beyond belief.

She was getting married to a man who was better than any dream she'd ever had, was expecting a beautiful and healthy baby, was opening a new business, and she was about to live like royalty in a most gorgeous apartment.

Ingrid had shown them several of the already furnished ones that had originally belonged to the timeshare portion of the building. She'd explained that most of the apartments she was readying for incoming clan members were smaller, with only one or two bedrooms. After all, with very few exceptions, most lived alone.

That entire floor was getting annexed for what comprised the clan's living quarters, and as Andrew and Nathalie had walked from one apartment to the next, a bunch of technicians had been rewiring cameras in the wide corridor.

The layouts and furnishings of the apartments on this level were almost identical, but this one had the best view. A living room and a dining room shared one big space, with a bank of windows overlooking the city. In addition, there were three bedrooms and three bathrooms, a laundry room, and a kitchen with a walk-in pantry—a true luxury.

The only things she'd brought from her old home were a few pictures, pillows, Papi's favorite throw, and clothes.

There were walk-in closets in all three bedrooms, and the master's was as big as her entire bedroom in the old house. The best part, however, other than having a room in between the master and her father's, was the master bathroom. It had a bathtub big enough for two and a shower big enough for four. Not that she was planning on inviting anyone other than Andrew into that shower.

Nathalie sat on the king-sized bed and flopped back. So soft. She spread her arms over the coverlet and closed her eyes, letting her other senses take over. Everything smelled new and clean.

Lovely, but it didn't smell like home.

She was so used to the slightly moldy scent of the old building's walls, to the food smells clinging to the furniture, to the odor of rotting trash wafting from the overturned trash cans in the back alley, and illogically, she missed them. They represented something that was hers.

Theoretically.

Practically, the bank owned most of it. Her equity in the place was less than a third. Still, it was more hers than this beautiful apartment in this brand new building.

Syssi tried to convince her that it belonged to her and Andrew, but it didn't. Even if she accepted that in some small way she owned a share in the clan's net profits and its assets, she had a hard time with this communal ownership thing. The building supposedly belonged to the clan, and as such, each member was entitled to an apartment. Logically, she understood what it meant, but in her heart she didn't feel like it was hers. She hadn't earned it; she didn't work for it; so how could it be hers?

"Are you taking a nap, sweetheart?" Andrew walked in with a bunch of trash bags overstuffed with clothing and shoes.

She sat up. "No, just checking out the bed."

He dropped his load inside the closet and stepped out. "And what's the verdict? Is it fit for my queen?"

"Come and check for yourself." She patted the spot next to her.

Andrew glanced her way longingly but shook his head. "I'd better not. You know what would happen if I get in bed with you."

"You'll fall asleep?" she teased.

"No. Your father is going to schlep the rest of the stuff up and walk in on us."

For a moment she thought he'd meant Papi and got confused. "We shouldn't refer to Bhathian as my father with Papi around. He might overhear and get upset."

"You're right." Andrew bent at the waist and planted a kiss on her lips. "Just a little advance on what I plan to deliver later."

Sweet Andrew, always hungry for her. She was indeed lucky. Hopefully, he would still find her sexy and desirable when she was big as a whale. A little snort escaped her throat. She shouldn't worry about that. Andrew had been a walking hormone before his transition; now he was a squadron of hormones folded into one. He would want her no matter what she looked like.

Or not.

What if he started lusting after other women?

Stop it! Andrew loves you, and he will never look at another woman the way he looks at you.

Again, logic was saying one thing, while the jealous Godzilla living inside her was whispering hateful things in her ear.

Nathalie shook her head. The Godzilla was imaginary and easy to banish, and luckily no real ghosts had paid her a visit in a long time. She wouldn't have minded a chat with Mark, she kind of missed him, but it was nice to have silence in her head, to be alone with her thoughts.

Maybe it was the pregnancy.

Who knew what a baby was aware of?

Perhaps pregnant women were off limits for ghosts, and she was looking into nine months of reprieve.

Yay!

Energized, Nathalie got up and headed to the closet. Their stuff wasn't going to jump out of the bags and magically arrange itself on the shelves.

She was done with one bag when Andrew came over with a new load. "These are your dad's things. Where do you want me to put them?"

She pointed to the far corner of the closet. "Put them there. I'll sort them away after I'm done with ours."

He offered his hand and helped her up, then pulled her in for a gentle hug. "Take it easy, Nathalie. It doesn't need to be all done today. You need to pace yourself." He placed a warm palm on her tummy. "You need to be mindful of the little one in here."

Silly man. She was just at the beginning stages of the pregnancy, and the little one was probably invisible without a microscope. She was perfectly fine working the same as she'd done before. But unless she wanted a long lecture, she'd better humor him. "I will."

He lifted a brow. "Promise?"

Damn, he knew her too well. "I promise. The moment I feel tired, I'll stop."

"I guess that's the best I'm going to get from you, so fine. I'm going to the house to pick up more clothes. Do you want anything from there?"

In fact, she did, and for some reason had felt shy to ask. But now that he brought it up… "Your grandma's china. It's so beautiful, and it would be a shame to leave it there to collect dust, or worse, for your tenants to break it."

Andrew smiled. "Consider it done. And it's our tenants, not mine. My home is your home."

"We are not married yet."

He grabbed her chin between his thumb and forefinger and gave it a little shake. "In everything that matters we are. A pagan ceremony performed by a superior being who isn't really a goddess is not what will define our commitment to each other."

"You're right. We should get married in a civil court."

Andrew rolled his eyes. "Stubborn woman. Do you really want to?"

"Of course. I want to be legally married. We are having a child. She would want her parents to be married for real."

"As you wish."

Smart man. She wasn't going to budge on that even though the idea of a civil marriage had just occurred to her.

"Well, that's the last of it," Bhathian said as he walked in with more trash bags. By the shape of them, they contained pillows and blankets and other bedding, which she now realized wouldn't fit her new, king-sized bed. She should take it back and let Jackson use it.

The boys had been ecstatic about having the place for themselves, especially since she'd offered it to them as a bonus and wasn't going to charge them rent.

"You can leave those in the hallway," she told him. "You guys are probably thirsty after all this schlepping back and forth. Let's get something to drink." She motioned for them to follow her to the kitchen.

"Do we have anything?" Andrew asked.

She turned her head around and smiled. "A full fridge thanks to your sister and her trusty butler. "

Syssi had thought of everything, making sure they didn't need to go grocery shopping for at least a week.

Nathalie opened the fridge and pulled out two beers for Andrew and Bhathian and a Perrier for herself. She handed the beers to the guys, then watched with envy as they gulped them down. A cold beer would've been wonderful. She unscrewed the top of her soda and took a long sip. Not as good, but good enough.

"Can immortal females drink beer while pregnant?" she asked Bhathian.

"I don't know. You'll have to ask Bridget." He emptied the bottle and threw it into the recycling bin.

"Well, I'd better say my goodbyes now. I'm flying out to Rio tonight."

Nathalie pulled him down to her and kissed his cheek. "Good luck."

Andrew clapped him on the back. "Roni said that he'd done something so he would get a notification whenever there is activity in Eva's account. Don't ask me to explain what or how because I didn't understand most of it. But in any case, he is going to call me as soon as there is any activity in that account, and I'm going to call you."

"Good deal." They clasped hands.

"Are you going to make it to the wedding?" Nathalie asked just to make sure. He'd said he would, but it couldn't hurt to ask again.

"I wouldn't miss it for anything. If we are lucky, I'll have your mother with me; if we are not, I'll resume the search after the wedding."

Nathalie nodded. "Don't feel bad if you can't find her."

He nodded in agreement, but his expression told another story. "Take care of my baby, Andrew."

"Naturally." Andrew wrapped an arm around her shoulders and pulled her close.

Bhathian smiled, which was almost shocking because he practically never did. "I'm happy for you. You look good together." He rubbed his hand over his jaw as if not sure what to do or say next. "Well, I'll see you at the wedding." He turned around and walked out.

"I'm going to miss him," Nathalie whispered, suddenly sad to see him go.

She should be glad. Bhathian was going to find her mother, something she'd been praying for ever since Eva had disappeared.

She couldn't help feeling anxious, though.

What if something happened to Bhathian? What if she never saw him again? What if he disappeared from her life the same way her mother had?

Her fear was irrational, she knew it, and yet she couldn't help it.

Andrew hugged her even closer, then kissed the top of her head. "He is going to be okay, baby. Bhathian is a powerful immortal, one of the strongest, deadliest creatures on earth. You have nothing to worry about."

26

KIAN

"When are you going to be done?" Syssi poked her head into Kian's home office.

"When I decide I'm done. It's not like this shit ever ends." He pointed to the stack of files he'd brought with him from his underground office. He was still working the same insane hours as before, but for some reason dividing his time between the basement and his home office made a difference. At home, he could work barefoot, in a pair of old jeans that were softened by endless wash cycles. He could also take breaks and have a snack in the kitchen with Syssi, or just have Syssi.

Life was good.

Andrew and Nathalie moving into the keep was another source of satisfaction. He liked having his family near him. Not necessarily interacting with them—who had the time or the patience—but knowing they were within reach and safe, gave him much-needed peace of mind.

"Please decide soon. I want to bring Andrew and Nathalie a housewarming present."

"Can't you do it without me?"

She shook her head. "You're coming with me. It would be rude not to."

"What did you get them?"

She smirked. "What do you think? A cappuccino maker."

Naturally. His wife's new hobby, or rather obsession. "Good choice."

"Right? I thought so too. By the way, did you call Sari?"

"About what?"

"The wedding, silly. Don't tell me you forgot."

Fuck. He did. Alex and the Russians had taken over his cognitive ram. Between talking with Turner and planning a coordinated extraction involving several units working together on foreign soil, a nice little thing like his brother-in-law's wedding had been shoved to the to-do-later file of his brain and then forgotten.

"You should have reminded me. I'll call her right now." He glanced at his watch. It was early morning in Scotland, but Sari should be up already.

"Blame the wife, why not?" Syssi murmured as she turned to go.

"Wait! Don't you want to be here when I talk to her? Discuss details?" What did he know about weddings?

"No. Just see if she is willing to do it and close on a specific date. I'll call her later with the details. There is no point in discussing the particulars before she agrees. What if she says no?"

He frowned. "Why the hell would she refuse?"

Syssi shrugged. "Maybe they are in the middle of remodeling the ballroom? You've said they are renovating the castle. Or maybe she has a vacation scheduled? You shouldn't take a yes for granted."

"Fine."

She blew him a kiss and sauntered away, her pert little ass swaying enticingly from side to side. He was tempted to drop everything and chase after her, get his hands on that beautiful ass.

Damn, she would shoo him away if he didn't make the call first. He picked up the receiver and dialed Sari's private line.

"Kian, what's wrong?"

He grimaced. Sari assumed something had happened because he only called when disaster struck or there was some kind of emergency, and he needed her help.

"Nothing, everything is fine. For a change, I'm calling with some joyous news."

He heard her puff out a breath. "That's a relief. I could use some good news for a change."

"Remember Nathalie? Bhathian's daughter?"

"Of course."

"She is marrying Andrew, Syssi's brother."

"Congratulations! Am I invited to another wedding?"

"Actually, I'm calling to see if you could host it. I don't feel it's safe bringing everyone over here again."

"Sure! I'll be happy to. When?"

"Six weeks, less if you can manage it. I was supposed to call you about it a few days ago, but I got distracted by other things."

"What's the rush? Don't get me wrong, I can do it, but a little more time could've been nice."

"Nathalie is pregnant, and she doesn't want it to be obvious when she walks down the aisle. You know how women are, she wants the dress to look good."

"I understand. Any specific instructions? Or am I free to do as I please?"

"Syssi will call you later with Nathalie's wish list. I don't think it will be anything grandiose. She is a very down to earth kind of girl. Nathalie, I mean. Syssi too."

He felt bad about dropping the task in Sari's lap. If she was as busy as he was, and he had no reason to think she wasn't, planning a wedding was the last thing she needed to be added to her load.

"I'm sorry I'm burdening you with this, but I see no other choice. Not if we want the entire clan to attend."

"Don't worry about it. I'll have my assistant take care of all the arrangements, and if she needs help, she knows where to get it."

"That's good. Makes me feel less guilty."

Sari chuckled. "Not so fast. You're still guilty of not calling more often."

"Ditto, sister mine. You can pick up the phone as well."

Sari laughed before disconnecting the call. They were so alike, Sari and he; workaholics, obsessive, driven. Syssi was his balance, the antidote, the one who forced him to slow down and enjoy life. He wished Sari would find someone like that too.

With a sigh, he pushed his chair back and got up. It was time to end his workday and go socializing.

What a concept…

"Oh, good, help me out." Syssi thrust the big box into his arms. "Hold it while I tie the ribbon around it."

She'd wrapped the box in some shimmery paper, not an easy feat given the size of it, and was now arranging an elaborate bow with the gold ribbon she'd used to hold it all together. A complete waste of time since it would get torn and thrown away in a few minutes.

"Why are you fussing with this so much?"

She lifted a brow, giving him that look women use when their men question something they consider self-explanatory. "You can't bring a gift unwrapped."

"Why not?"

"Because wrapping it nicely means you care. And that's even more important than the gift itself." She finished the bow and took a step back to admire her work.

He shrugged. "If you say so. Ready to go?"

"Aren't you going to change into something that's a little less worn out?"

"Nope."

Syssi put her hands on her hips and tapped her foot on the floor—Amanda's style. "How about shoes?"

"We are just going across the hall."

The tapping got a little faster. "Humor me. It's not polite."

The exchange reminded him of another conversation during which he'd admonished Amanda for walking into his home office barefoot and wearing a nightshirt.

Damn, he would look like a hypocrite. "Fine. If it will make you happy." Kian put the box on the kitchen counter. "I'll be back in a minute."

27

ROBERT

Robert collected his tools and handed them to the shift supervisor. The guy put them in the lockbox. "I'll see you tomorrow, Robert. Enjoy your evening."

"You too." Robert wiped the sweat off his brow with a handkerchief, then returned it to his back pocket. If he intended to keep the job, he would need more work clothes.

Not that he had a better alternative.

Carol's talk with whoever was in charge back home hadn't gone as well as she'd hoped for. What they were offering was a comfortable cage. He could live with Carol in an apartment in some secure building, but he wouldn't be allowed to leave. They promised they would find him something to do, but they didn't specify what.

Thanks, but no thanks.

He liked his newfound freedom too much to give it up so soon.

Frankly, he'd expected as much. Carol was naive and an airhead. What had she been thinking? That her people would accept him with open arms and give him full privileges because he'd saved her?

He knew they would suspect it was all a trick to infiltrate their stronghold. Hell, in their shoes he would have thought the same. But the fact remained that there was nothing for him there.

His only option was to stick to his original plan and convince Carol to marry him.

To achieve that goal, though, he would need to make an effort to appear more exciting. During lunch he'd talked with some of the guys he worked with, sharing his troubles, or rather a modified version that he hoped would fit a normal human couple. Chatting casually about personal stuff with other men had felt surprisingly good, making him feel less alone in the world.

Doomers didn't share much. They talked about battles and who killed the most, or which hookers were the best. No one ever talked about what bothered him on a personal level; like how to win a woman's heart.

The guys had told him he should take Carol out to nice places. Wine her and dine her and buy her presents. Apparently, that strategy worked with their wives and girlfriends. The thing was, these guys were the providers in the relationship and not the other way around. His so-called girlfriend would have to foot the bill. His next paycheck wasn't until Friday.

Still, it wouldn't hurt to try their suggestions. If it worked fine, if not, then not. The worst that could happen was spending too much of Carol's money in a fancy restaurant.

Later, when he got back, Carol wasn't in their room. She'd left a note; something about going out to buy new periodicals to read.

Robert glanced around at the messy room. There were fashion and gossip magazines strewed about every surface, and he knew there were more in the bathroom.

It was obvious that Carol was bored and needed to find something to do. Robert flinched. The problem was that her idea of keeping herself busy was doing someone, not something.

She got back when he was getting out of the shower. "Hello, handsome," she purred, her eyes roving over his nude body.

At least there was that. She liked the way he looked.

"Hello to you too...gorgeous," he tacked on at the end.

According to the guys, complimenting your girlfriend as much as possible was the best way to win her over. Jorge had said it was even better than giving her presents.

Given Carol's broad grin, the guy knew what he was talking about. Jorge's other pearl of wisdom was that nothing trumped great sex, and as a tutorial he'd suggested that Robert watch a couple of his favorite porn flicks.

As if an immortal male Robert's age needed tutoring. But just to cover his bases, he'd watched them on the bus on his way to the hotel.

She sauntered to the bed and sat down, patting a spot next to her. "Come here."

A perfect opportunity to practice what he'd learned.

Instead of sitting where she told him to, he walked over and pushed her back on the bed, then covered her with his body.

Her eyes sparkled. "Did you miss me, big boy?"

"I did, desperately." He smashed his mouth over hers and kissed her until she couldn't breathe.

It started as an act, repeating a line from one of the clips, but he was getting into it. His shaft was bursting with the need to be inside her. But maybe it wasn't his acting that was arousing him so, but her response to it. He hadn't seen such an expression of joy on her face since, well, ever.

If it made her that happy, he could keep acting. "You're so beautiful, I can't keep my hands off of you." He touched her everywhere, stroking, kneading, pinching. She watched him with hooded eyes, breathless, as he pulled her T-shirt off and roughly pushed her shorts down. His fingers found her liquid center, and he slid two inside her, then three on the next thrust.

Carol gasped. She wasn't used to such rough treatment from him, her tight channel squeezing forcefully around his three thick digits. Was he hurting her? Or was she enjoying the rough play? He'd better find out.

"Do you like it?" he whispered in her ear, then nipped it.

"Yes," she breathed.

Mindful of her suffering at Sebastian's hands, Robert had been treating her with extra care, but it seemed she was ready for things to get a little rougher, more intense. Perhaps it was a good sign. Maybe it meant that she was over her ordeal.

Without pause, he pulled his fingers out and speared her with his cock, shoving all the way in while still holding her down.

She orgasmed on the spot.

Holy Mortdh.

Robert had never been so rough with a female before, would have been appalled witnessing such a thing. But then he'd been dealing with mortal females. Fragile, breakable.

Carol only looked like a china doll, but she didn't like being treated like one. On the inside, the female was diamond tough.

For once, Robert didn't hold back. He fucked Carol with such gusto that the mattress slid off the box springs, landing partially on the floor while the box spring remained in place. He didn't stop. If she wanted a rough fuck, he was going to give her one to remember.

The whole thing lasted less than ten minutes, and when he sank his fangs into her neck, he didn't try to be gentle either. Not one of his best performances, but Carol wasn't complaining, and that was all that mattered according to Jorge.

"Listen to your woman, bro," he'd said. "Watch her body and find out what she likes, then do it even if you're not sure about it. If she loves it, so will you."

Smart guy.

Several long moments later, Carol opened her eyes with a blissed-out expression on her face. "Wow, Robert, is it really you?" She patted his back as if checking to make sure. "You're not some doppelgänger?"

What or who the hell was a doppelgänger?

"No. It's still me." He pulled out in a gush of liquid. Damn, he must've emptied one hell of a load into her. "Get showered and dressed. I made a reservation at the Wynn hotel's steakhouse for seven."

She narrowed her eyes and slapped his bicep. "Now I know for sure you're a doppelgänger. What have you done with my Robert?"

Her Robert?

It had a nice sound to it.

"Come on, silly woman. There is no time for games. Unless you want to forget about the reservation and save the money for something more important."

She smirked. "Okay, now you've proved that you are still you."

An hour later, they exited the taxi and walked into the fancy lobby of the Wynn.

Carol took his hand and tugged. "Come on, I'll show you the high rollers' tables. The really big money is behind closed doors, naturally, but it's interesting to watch the guys in the enclaves too. For some reason, there are very few women who gamble at the tables. By the way, do you happen to have some precognition talent? Because if you do, you can make a killing here."

He shook his head, not understanding what she was talking about. The noise level in the casino was deafening, and the gamblers emitted a nasty smell he wasn't familiar with—a mix of anxiety and excitement with a hefty dose of greed.

Carol tugged on his hand again, pulling him down to her. "Look over there." She pointed. "That's a high roller for sure. Four bodyguards. I've never seen one with so many."

The man she was pointing to was indeed surrounded by four burly guys. About a hundred feet or so ahead, the five were walking in the same direction he and Carol were heading. Perhaps the high roller was on his way to the steakhouse as well.

The bodyguards dwarfed the guy they were protecting, and yet there was an unmistakable air of power around him. Of medium height and build, his posture relaxed, the man walked with the fluid gait of a gymnast or a dancer—his arms swinging slightly as if he was listening to some catchy tune and moving them in sync to the music.

There was something familiar about the man. Robert had seen that exact kind of walk before…

He grabbed Carol's elbow, turning her around, and whispered while propelling her forward, "Don't say anything and don't look behind you. Walk a normal walk."

"What's going on?" she whispered back.

"Not now, later." He gripped her arm even tighter.

"You're hurting me," she hissed.

He eased his grip, but only a little. Once they cleared the entry doors, he kept walking, Carol's high heels clicking on the sidewalk as she tried to walk as fast as he did.

When they were about a thousand feet away from the Wynn, he dared to look behind him. A relieved breath whooshed out of his lungs. They hadn't been followed.

"Can you talk now?" Carol's voice shook.

"Keep walking. We'll catch a taxi at the mall."

After another few minutes, he glanced behind him again and finally relaxed. "The guy you saw. I think I know him."

"Who is he?"

"If he's who I think he is, that's Sharim's father."

She glanced up at him with questioning eyes. "Who's Sharim?"

"Sebastian. That's his real name."

A violent shiver went through Carol, and she listed to the side. She would have fallen if he hadn't caught her. For a moment, he considered lifting her into his arms and carrying her the rest of the way, but that would've attracted too much attention.

Instead, he tucked her under his arm, propping her against his side. "You have nothing to worry about. He is not a sadist like his son. I heard that he is an even-tempered guy. But that doesn't mean that he won't kill me on the spot if he recognizes me, and then thrall all the humans around to forget it. He's one of

Navuh's own sons, and they're very powerful immortals with abilities the rest of us could only dream of."

Carol shivered again, her slight body trembling all over. For a split second, Robert entertained the notion that she was worried about him, but then dismissed it. More likely, she feared recapture. They were both in danger, and it was best to get out of there as soon as possible.

The line for the taxi at the mall was no shorter than the one at the Wynn, but at least they were a safe distance away.

Hopefully.

Fifteen minutes later, they were sitting in a yellow cab and heading back to the MGM.

"Do you think he is looking for me? For us?" Carol whispered. She was clinging to his arm like a frightened kitten, her sharp nails digging into his flesh. He'd been wrong to assume she was over her ordeal.

Not even close.

"Not likely. He's too important for a retrieval mission. I'm surprised he was allowed to leave the island. The other sons, the generals, only leave for short military excursions and only when accompanied by a battalion of soldiers."

Carol tightened her grip on his arm. "I know why he is here; revenge."

She was trembling so hard Robert wished he had a blanket to wrap her in. "I don't think so. We are not important enough. But one thing is certain; with him here, we need to get out of town. It's too risky to stay."

Carol nodded her agreement.

The random encounter with Losham had put things in perspective for Robert. He'd been deluding himself thinking he could strike out on his own and make a home with Carol away from all other immortals. If he could accidentally bump into Navuh's son and top adviser in Las Vegas, he wasn't safe anywhere. And what's more, he couldn't guarantee Carol's safety either.

"Do we rent a car or steal one?" he asked as they exited the taxi.

"Rent. The monster never learned my last name, and Carol is a common given name."

"Let's stop by the front desk and see if they can get us a car."

She nodded. "Where are we going?"

To the only place that was safe. "You're going home. I'm accepting the deal your people are offering me."

28

ANANDUR

Anandur cast Onegus a sideways glance. "I have to hand it to Kian; the guy knows how to get things done in record time."

The chief Guardian tapped his fingers on the car's armrest. "Money is a great expeditor."

They didn't have all the details yet and would get another briefing once they met up with Turner's crew, but at least the major logistics of arranging the various modes of transportation had been solved.

It was early afternoon, and the drive to the clan's airstrip was pleasant—after they had cleared the goddamned city traffic, that is.

Onegus snorted and crossed his arms over his chest. "Turner was no doubt invaluable to that effort and cost accordingly. The bastard knows people turn to him only when things get too complicated for anyone else to handle, and his pricing reflects that."

"Yeah, the dude holds a monopoly on mission impossible. Imagine the movie scripts he can write."

Onegus shrugged. "Turner doesn't strike me as the creative type. Dry toast has more personality."

"I don't know about that. You have to think creatively to plan impossible missions."

As Anandur parked the car near the clan's airstrip, the jet they were going to use was already out of the hangar, ready and waiting for them.

It was such a waste of time to drive all the way out there. If not for Kian's paranoia, they could've used a chopper and gotten picked up from the keep's rooftop. The boss had gotten it into his head that there might be more criminals and traitors among his clansmen and that Alex might not have been working alone. A chopper would have raised questions; like who had arrived or who was departing and why. Kian preferred to keep their mission low key, with as few people involved as possible.

Total crap, but it was a blessing in disguise.

To keep things hush-hush, Kian wasn't joining them, which Anandur was grateful for. A civilian pilot, one with a real license, was going to fly the jet to Mexico. With all due respect to their regent's capabilities, no one who learned to fly with the help of a computer game should be allowed to pilot a real craft.

Not with passengers, that's for sure.

They got out of the car, and Anandur locked his baby up, then tossed the keys to Jeff, the hangar supervisor. "Take good care of her."

"Don't worry, I won't take her out on a joy ride... more than once a day."

Anandur pointed a finger at him. "I find a scratch on her, and your baby gets double."

Jeff had a love affair with his Cessna and treated her with as much care as Anandur his Thunderbird. The dude flipped him off, and as he walked away, he tossed Anandur's keys in the air then caught them mid-flight.

"Don't say I didn't warn you," Anandur called after Jeff, then slung his duffle bag over his shoulder and followed Onegus to the waiting jet.

A few moments later, their pilot revved the engines and they were off. The jet was one of the smaller ones and could seat five in addition to the pilot. The transport that would take the yacht's crew together with the scumbag, Onegus, and Anandur back to Los Angeles had been chartered from a private Mexican airline, and it would be waiting for them at the Acapulco airport.

Once they were up in the air, Anandur pulled a couple of beers from the mini fridge and handed one to Onegus.

"Thanks." He flicked the top off and lifted his bottle in a salute. "To a successful mission."

They clinked bottles and for a couple of moments drank in silence.

A frown furrowing his brow, Onegus put his beer down on the pullout table. "Doesn't it strike you odd that Alex is departing from his usual routine? Did Lana mention prior incidents of customers on board?"

Anandur shook his head. "No. From what Lana said, and also Amanda, I got the impression that he never invited men."

"That's what I thought. What do you think made him change his tactics?"

Anandur shrugged. "More money would be my guess. Maybe the buyers offered to pay more if they got to sample the merchandise before taking it off his hands."

"That would mean that the girls aren't thralled unconscious this time."

Anandur scratched his beard. "I wonder if they are thralled at all. He might have told them that it was a yacht party, with some rich dudes who would wine them and dine them and buy them presents once they arrived at Acapulco."

Onegus cast him a doubtful look. "You think this was enough to convince a bunch of girls to spread their legs for strangers?"

Anandur chuckled. "Onegus, my man, they do it for much less. Have you ever had to work at getting a girl at a club? They practically throw themselves at us."

Onegus flashed him his movie-star smile. "That's because we are so handsome."

"Maybe. But I've seen dudes who were below average in that department succeeding with not much more than nice clothes and a thick wallet. That and buying a girl a few drinks was enough."

"We'd better communicate this to Turner's men. In addition to being mindful of the female crew, who know what's going on and will take cover, we will now have a bunch of untrained civilians that can and will get in the line of fire."

Onegus raked his fingers through his hair. "I didn't want to even consider it, but I think we will need to use a chemical incapacitating agent."

Bad idea. The thing worked like a charm, silent and efficient, but also potentially deadly. Not as in a remote chance of one in a thousand deadly, but in a staggering ten to twenty percent. Unacceptable, unless all other methods of rescue were estimated to yield even more casualties.

In the somber silence that followed, Anandur tried to come up with better solutions. Trouble was, he had a hard time estimating their success. They had no way of knowing what the situation on board the *Anna* was. They might be all hanging around the grand salon, or sunbathing on the top deck, or lingering in their bedrooms, each guest entertained by a girl. The most likely scenario was a combination of all three.

A tactical nightmare.

"I'm calling Kian. I don't know if he and Turner considered the possibility that the girls are up and around, intermingling with the men." Anandur pulled out his phone.

Onegus shook his head. "I'm sure they did. Neither is the type to overlook such an obvious possibility."

One never knew.

Everything had been rushed, and plans had been hastily drawn. No one was infallible. Not even the infamous Turner. Besides, Anandur doubted Turner cared about casualties. To him, it was a question of numbers and probabilities, not individual lives. "I'd rather call and make sure." He dialed Kian's number.

Kian listened patiently for about thirty seconds then cut him off. "We are taking it for granted that the girls are with the men. The details are not ironed out yet. I'll call you when we finalize the plan."

"We don't have time."

"Yes, we do. We flew a drone out from Acapulco, and it caught up with the *Anna*. At her current speed, she is still a day away from reaching the port. Alex and his guests are evidently in no rush."

"We have drones in Mexico? I wasn't aware of that."

"A few months back we sold a couple to a local customer. I called and asked for a favor in exchange for a substantial discount on future orders."

"Good. So does it mean Onegus and I have the night off?"

"You wish. You are to rendezvous with Turner's team and go over the plan."

29

LOSHAM

For no apparent reason, Losham felt a peculiar prickling at the back of his head and turned around. Scanning the crowded Wynn casino, he spotted a tall, dark-haired guy holding a small, curvy blond by the elbow and rushing her out.

There was something familiar about the guy. Losham closed his eyes for a moment, letting his brain scan rapidly over every male he'd ever met. With his eidetic memory, nothing and no one was ever forgotten, but it usually took a second or two to retrieve the information. The other problem was that he didn't see the man's face. From the back, though, he looked a lot like Sharim's second in command, whatever his name was.

It must've been someone with a similar build.

It couldn't have been his son's second.

Sharim and everyone else at that compound were dead.

Burned to ashes.

Losham turned his head back and resumed walking in the direction of the restaurant he'd been heading to, but then he stopped and looked again.

The guy had also moved the same way Sharim's second had. Ungraceful for an immortal. His strides were heavy and his posture stiff, not fluid like that of most immortal males.

On the other hand, it was fairly common for a large human male. *Pathetic creatures, these humans.*

Losham shook his head. Grief was playing tricks on his otherwise infallible brain. Logic dictated that Sharim's second was dead, like the rest of his son's men, and not gambling in a casino in Vegas.

"Is there a problem, sir?" one of his bodyguards asked.

"No. I thought I saw someone familiar. Let's proceed."

Immortals were a superior breed, even such dumb meatheads as the males comprising his guard. They should be masters of this world, not fugitives living in secret, manipulating affairs from behind a smokescreen.

One day they would be.

He'd been working tirelessly toward that goal, but it was difficult. Not because humans were as numerous as ants while immortals were an endangered species. That was just one side of the equation.

The other was Navuh: a stubborn son-of-a-bitch who thought himself a god.

His father was charismatic, Losham had to concede, but as far as intelligence and cunning went, he couldn't hold a candle to Losham.

He let out a quiet sigh. Unfortunately, Navuh was indispensable. You couldn't lead people with smarts alone. Same as their inferior counterparts the humans, immortals needed a leader who could whip them into a mindless frenzy and unite them around a common goal, no matter how idiotic. A leader was the glue that held them together.

Without a charismatic central figure, their camp would dissolve into several militias, each headed by one of Navuh's power-hungry sons. In no time, the infighting would decimate their numbers.

As much as Losham despised the pompous despot, Navuh had to stay. That elusive magnetic quality, the dramatic instincts that made his father the perfect central figure, were not something that could be learned or imitated; they were innate, and they were extremely rare. There had been only a few such leaders throughout human history. Their power over the masses had been astonishing. Not even the gods could've managed to sway millions using only the power of their personality and a few motivational speeches.

Losham would have to keep dancing circles around Navuh, seeding ideas in his head and making him believe that he came up with them on his own.

From the corner of his eyes, Losham caught a shimmer of a dress, covering something delightfully curvy, and when he glanced her way, she cast him the unmistakable come-hither look.

A hooker.

Sin city was full of them. This one was working the casino floor, a cheapie—good enough for the goons protecting him, but Losham had more refined tastes. A high-end service was delivering a first class trio to his suite tonight.

As much as he sneered at human males, Losham had no problem with the females. Very pleasing when well paid.

Useful.

A beginning of an idea began germinating in his brain. Sharim and his predecessor's method of attempting to capture immortal males had its merits, but they had gone about it all wrong.

Endless patrolling of night clubs and bars in the hopes of finding an immortal male was like looking for a needle in a haystack with a table fork. Instead, the smart thing was to lure those males into a trap.

As with his people, most of these males weren't young. They had been frequenting whorehouses for centuries. But those establishments were not as prevalent and accessible as they used to be.

If he built them a quality one, they would come.

Not one, a chain.

A high-class chain of brothels run by humans who were enthralled to follow

Losham's instructions. He remembered Sharim telling him about a special sex club he'd been a member of—a place that catered to his deviant needs. It seemed there was a demand for places like that, and both those who wanted to inflict pain and those who wanted pain inflicted upon them paid hefty membership fees.

A sweet deal, and a perfect cover-up.

Who said that only deviant sex had to be practiced in a club like that? He could create clubs that catered to everyone. The vanilla crowd as well as the spicy crowd, or whatever the deviants called themselves.

And everyone would pay membership.

Naturally, he would keep a supply of beautiful hookers on hand, and let the men believe they were members just like them. The membership the others would pay would be steep enough to cover the expense.

Losham grinned. He liked this plan. Loved it, in fact. And selling the idea to Navuh would be a piece of cake. His greedy father would love a new profitable business that doubled as a trap for immortal males.

The idea was solid. The only missing part was a detection method that didn't involve Doomers circling the premises. Perhaps hidden cameras would be enough. Extremely well-hidden. After all, if a male flashed a pair of fangs and it was caught on camera, there was no need for any other type of detection.

There was another benefit to the membership club formula. It might be far-fetched, but what if it lured immortal females as well? Logic dictated that immortal females' sexual appetites matched those of the males, and therefore they also had to satisfy their needs with random mortals.

The thing was, their detection was even trickier than that of the males. As far as he knew, their fangs were tiny and didn't elongate, and he had no idea if they liked to bite or not. The only sure telltale sign was their superior strength. But again, it wasn't as if they flaunted it indiscriminately.

Still, a remote chance of snaring a coveted immortal female was better than none.

30

DALHU

Crouching, Dalhu snapped several pictures in quick succession, concentrating on Nathalie's dress. He didn't need Andrew and his lovely bride to pose for endless hours if he could capture their clothing on camera. As it was, they were getting impatient. "Just a few more," he said.

"I think you have enough." Andrew lifted Nathalie an inch and repositioned her on his lap.

Dalhu let his camera arm drop by his side. "Now why did you have to do that? You messed up the folds in her dress. They are not the same as before."

"My leg is getting numb."

Lifting the camera back up, Dalhu pinned Andrew with a hard stare. "No, it's not, you are an immortal. Be a man and sit still for a few more minutes."

He'd made good progress with their portrait, but he was leaving for Hawaii later that evening and wanted to continue the work there. At this stage, with Nathalie's face and hair done, and Andrew's almost there, he could complete the rest using photographs instead of live modeling. Capturing the exact shade of their clothing wasn't as important.

"You really shouldn't take work with you on your vacation," Nathalie said for the tenth time. "You should enjoy your time off with Amanda."

Dalhu still couldn't believe Kian had agreed to let him go. All he had to do was ask. It seemed he was indeed a fully-fledged member of the clan now. Except for one thing—no share in the profits. He still needed to earn his keep. But it didn't bother him. He wasn't a member by birthright and therefore didn't deserve a share of the clan's extensive fortune. He had all the riches he could have ever dreamt of. A female to love and who loved him back, a place to call home, and an occupation to help heal his soul and push the darkness away.

He snapped another picture. "Amanda is going to be busy getting the rescued females settled. I'm sure I'll have plenty of free time on my hands."

"Are you done?" Andrew grumbled.

"Yes. You can get up." Dalhu took the camera, a fancy piece of equipment Amanda had surprised him with, and hooked it up to his laptop to upload the pictures.

Gently, as if she was a delicate flower, Andrew lifted Nathalie off his lap and helped her stand. Once he was sure she was steady, he stretched.

The girl looked tired. While snapping pictures, Dalhu had noticed the dark circles under her big, brown eyes. He supposed it was to be expected in her condition. Not that he had any reference to judge by, but it made sense. Her body was working double duty now, doing everything it had always done while also building a new life.

Quite miraculous.

He glanced at Amanda who passed by the studio's open door with another suitcase in hand, wondering how he would feel if she was with child.

Crazy with worry, that's how.

From the little he'd learned while listening to Bridget talk about immortal pregnancies, he'd surmised that there was no risk to the mothers. If anything went wrong, their bodies' rapid healing took care of it. But miscarriages were common, which was especially devastating given the low conception rate.

Amanda had already lost a child and had barely survived the tragedy. Losing another would shatter her to pieces.

If contraception were an option for immortals, he would have used it. Not that he didn't want to have children, he would have loved nothing more, but risking Amanda's mental health wasn't worth it. Not to him.

"Darlings," she called while passing by again. "I hate to rush you, but Dalhu hasn't packed yet. We need to go."

Andrew pulled Dalhu into a quick embrace and clapped him on his back. "Enjoy your vacation, Dalhu. See you in a few days."

Nathalie smiled. "Have fun," she said, patting Dalhu's arm on her way out.

He cast a worried glance at Andrew, but apparently, the guy didn't mind the small token of affection his fiancée had shown Dalhu. Kian was so much worse. He got angry if anyone's eyes lingered on his wife for too long—and what he considered too long was about a half a second.

Dalhu frowned. It was strange that he'd never experienced jealousy or possessiveness toward Amanda. It seemed he was the odd immortal in that regard. The only thing that bothered him about other males leering after her was that they didn't deserve to even think about her, let alone have the nasty thoughts he knew they had. It was akin to sacrilege. Mortals shouldn't have these kinds of thoughts about a goddess.

Amanda wasn't as openly affectionate toward him as Syssi and Nathalie were toward their mates. And yet he had never doubted her, or her love for him. He was as sure of it as he was of his own. She'd never mentioned a wedding either, and it was fine by him. The last thing he needed was to be the center of attention with several hundred clan members eyeing him with suspicion. He wasn't naive; not everyone had accepted him wholeheartedly.

"Dalhu!" she called from their walk-in closet. "Don't just stand there, get moving! Do you want me to pack for you?"

Not a bad idea. "Would you, please?"

She marched into the studio and put her hands on her hips. "When I offered to do so this morning, you said you'd do it. I could've been done with it hours ago."

Amanda looked magnificent when she was angry, and Dalhu couldn't help himself. He pulled her against his body and kissed her until her body went soft in his arms. "I'm sorry. I got carried away with the portrait, which I still need to pack carefully because the paint is wet. And then there are the rest of my supplies."

When she lifted her eyes to him, there was only love in those twin blue lakes. "Why are you taking so much stuff with you? We are only going for a few days."

"As I told you, I want to paint a Hawaiian sunset and sunrise because they are magnificent. Besides, it may take longer. You said so yourself."

She lifted her chin and kissed him lightly. "Okay. But when I say stop, you drop everything, and we go out to have fun."

A chuckle bubbled up from deep in his belly. "Was there a time when I didn't? I always do what you want."

Her cheeks pinked and she rolled her eyes. "I wish. You never say no, but you use all kinds of delaying tactics."

"Oh, yeah? Give me one example."

She waved her hand at the room. "You were supposed to be done hours ago, and everything should have been packed already."

She had a point.

He kissed her forehead. "I need to retain some male dignity, woman. Besides, what's the rush? The plane isn't going to leave without us."

They were taking the largest of the clan's jets, and he was looking forward to experiencing the luxurious mode of transportation. Regrettably, they would be sharing the ride with the rescued females, and he would be exiled to the cockpit, out of their way. After what they'd been through, a male his size might look too intimidating to them.

A pity. He would've loved to join the mile-high club.

"I know, but I don't want a group of twenty-four women waiting for us."

He sighed. "I wish we were flying by ourselves."

Her eyes sparkled as she asked, "Why? Did you have some naughty ideas?"

"Uh-huh."

"Don't worry, darling." She winked. "Leave it to Amanda. I'll find a way."

His woman was the best. "I love you," he said.

"I love you too. Now hurry up and pack your supplies. I really don't want to be late."

31

NATHALIE

"How is Tiffany doing?" Andrew asked when Nathalie came back from saying goodbye to the girl, as well as to the rest of the women who were leaving for Hawaii.

She sat next to him on the couch, kicked off her shoes, and tucked her feet under her. "Excited, a little anxious. This is going to be her first plane ride."

Andrew wrapped his arm around her, and she rested her head on his bicep. "What did Vanessa tell them about the trip? Were they already thralled?"

"No, not yet. Amanda told them about this great job opportunity in a luxurious new hotel, with lodging and training included. She then asked each one of the girls if she was interested. Vanessa wanted to make sure they were told about it without influence to gauge their responses."

"And?"

"Unanimous excitement. Come on, who wouldn't want to move to Hawaii with a guaranteed, well-paying job?"

"Not me."

"Why not?"

"Because I love it here. Just look at this apartment. And most of the people we love are within an elevator ride."

Nathalie snuggled up to Andrew and pushed her hand under his T-shirt, resting it on his warm skin. "Yeah, I don't want to go anywhere either. Syssi showed me the movie theater in the basement. We should try it out."

Andrew kissed her forehead. "You know what we haven't done yet?"

Stifling a chuckle, Nathalie sighed dramatically and asked, "What?" Knowing Andrew, whatever it was, it surely had something to do with sex.

He leaned and whispered, his hot breath tickling her ear. "We didn't try sex in the tub yet."

"Nor did we try the kitchen counter..." she added.

"Or the lounge chair on the balcony outside our room."

"Pervert."

Andrew released an offended puff. "Get your head out of the gutter, woman, I was talking about sunbathing."

Yeah, right.

She looked up at his smirking face and arched a brow. "Really?"

"No, not really."

Andrew was so predictable, but in a good way. She wouldn't want him to change a bit.

"We have to wait until my father is asleep."

"I think he already is. I hear snoring from his room."

Nathalie sighed. With his new and improved hearing, there was no doubt that what he heard was true. "He must've fallen asleep in the BarcaLounger. I'd better check up on him."

"While you do that, I'll fill the tub."

"Sounds good."

As she'd suspected, she found Papi asleep in his chair. He'd reclined it fully, so it was almost flat. The television was still droning in the background, but she didn't turn it off. Papi slept like a baby with the television on but woke up the moment it was turned off.

Instead, she picked up the blanket that had slid down to the floor and covered him, then snatched a pillow from the bed and tucked it under his head. Satisfied that he was comfortable, she tiptoed out and closed the door quietly behind her.

Once again, as she walked the twenty feet or so from his room to the master bedroom, Nathalie felt like skipping with joy. Finally, they had some privacy.

Her grin grew wider when she found Andrew lying in the rapidly filling bathtub, his magnificent nude body a vision to behold. For a moment she just gazed at him, getting her fill of his masculine yumminess.

"Are you going to just stand there? Or are you going to join me?"

Damn his hearing. He'd known she was there, ogling him. As if the guy needed any more fodder for his ego.

She made quick work of shedding her clothes and walked over to the tub. "Is the water hot?"

She lifted a foot over the rim and dipped her toes. It was slightly too warm for her liking. She remembered reading somewhere that it wasn't good for the baby.

"Could you add a little more cold water, please?"

Andrew made a face but did as she asked.

She waited a few moments for the water to chill and lifted her other foot over the rim. "That's more like it."

Nathalie lowered herself into the water and sat across from Andrew. The tub was so wide that they could lie side by side without touching, but what was the fun in that?

Andrew was of the same opinion. "What are you doing over there, love, come here," he said tapping his muscular chest.

"Much better," he said as she laid her back against his chest, her head resting comfortably on his hard muscles.

"How are your breasts? Still tender?" Andrew cupped them gently.

Nathalie loved her new larger boobs, they looked great, but she missed the sensation of Andrew's fingers, tugging her tight buds. He was always gentle, but now even the slightest touch hurt too much to be pleasurable.

"Unfortunately, yes."

"Poor baby." Andrew circled his thumbs over her areoles, avoiding her stiff nipples. "How about my tongue? If I lick very gently?"

His cock twitched against her backside. The idea of licking her nipples was apparently turning him on.

She sighed. "I like lying like this. I don't want to turn around. Maybe a little later." She wiggled her butt, giving his hard length a rub.

"I like it too," he whispered and leaned to kiss her neck in the spot where it met her shoulder, then nipped a little, letting his new fangs scrape against her skin. She was getting used to them, and fear was the furthest thing from her mind when she felt them press against her skin. In fact, she was kind of craving a bite. Not that she was going to admit it to Andrew, not yet.

One of his large hands abandoned her breast and slipped lower to cup her center, his middle finger parting her folds. She was wet for him; his hands on her breasts had been enough to turn her on.

The moan she let out was unrestrained, and it felt damn good not to worry about making noise.

"You like that, baby?"

"Yes, please, more."

His finger slipped into her, then was joined by another while his thumb pressed against her clit.

"Yes, just like that." She rubbed her butt against his cock.

Andrew hissed into her ear and caught her chin, twisting her head around and taking her mouth in a hungry kiss.

The sound of water splashing out of the tub made her turn back. "Oh, my God, we are causing a flood." She leaped to turn the faucet off, while Andrew opened the drain.

Nathalie looked at the big puddle on the floor. "Our second week at the keep, and we are already causing destruction. They are going to kick us out."

"It's nothing." Andrew stepped out of the tub and grabbed a towel. He dropped it on the floor and let it absorb the water, then used another one to mop up the rest. In a few moments, he had the situation under control and was ready to get back inside.

She grimaced. "Sorry, it kind of spoiled the mood for me to keep fooling around in the bathtub. How about we dry off and continue in our nice king-sized bed?"

Andrew grabbed a fresh towel and spread it out for her to step into. "Your wish is my command, my lady. I'm your humble servant."

"Humble my foot." She snorted as she stepped into the large bath sheet he was holding up. Andrew wrapped her in it, and then lifted her into his arms.

32

ANDREW

As he lowered Nathalie to the bed, Andrew waited for her to climb under the covers before taking the towel he'd wrapped her in and drying himself off.

"My hair is wet, and I'm wetting the pillow," she complained.

"I don't really care, baby. All I want to do now is to lick you all over."

He dropped the towel on the floor and dove under the covers with her. Her skin was cold against his, and he hugged her close to warm her up.

"Your body is always so warm," she mumbled into his chest. "It's like snuggling up to a furnace."

"Glad to be useful."

She felt so small in his arms, fragile, and for a moment, his heart skipped a few beats as it was seized by worry. Damn, despite Bridget's reassurances that Nathalie was strong and healthy, that uneasy feeling wasn't going to leave him until she woke up on the other side of her transition.

On some subconscious level, Andrew wished she wasn't pregnant. It would've made everything so much easier—an unpleasant and disturbing thought that he pushed away as soon as it materialized. The child was a blessing. He should never think of her as anything less than a miracle. Nathalie would be fine and so would their daughter.

"Did the flood spoil it for you too?" Nathalie moved her thigh to rub against his deflated manhood.

"No, of course not. It was cold," he lied. No reason to tell her he was worried. Nathalie needed him to be strong for her. "But keep rubbing me like that a few seconds more and see what it gets you."

She smiled mischievously. "I'll do better than that." Her soft hand closed around his hardening cock, and Andrew forgot what caused him distress a moment ago. Up and down and back up again her palm went, until he was as hard as a wooden club. A few more and he would embarrass himself all over her hand like a teenager.

"Are you warm enough?" he asked a moment before flinging the blanket off Nathalie and exposing her sexy, nude curves to his ravenous eyes.

"I was," she complained.

He covered her with his body, kissing her long and deep before sliding down to pay careful attention to her nipples. Just as he'd promised, he lapped gently at each turgid nub, his hands plumping her breasts just as gently.

"Okay?" he asked between licks.

"Perfect," she breathed, arching her back and offering him more.

He took one nipple between his lips, applying the barest of pressure, and then resumed his licking. Nathalie's fingers raked his hair, encouraging him to continue, but he had other plans. With a last feathery kiss to each peak, he slid further down until his mouth was aligned with her mound.

For some reason, she had her legs closed, and all his tongue could reach was the top of her slit—right where her little clit begged for his attention.

After a few seconds of his ministrations, her thighs separated, and he pushed them further apart to expose her petals.

"Lovely," he smacked his lips. "My favorite nectar." He speared his tongue into her opening.

Nathalie gasped, her bottom lifting up. Andrew slid his palms under it and cupped each cheek, massaging lightly in sync with his tongue.

It seemed Nathalie had forgotten that she was free to make as much noise as she wanted now, and for a minute or two her moans were subdued.

Either that or he wasn't doing it right for her.

Andrew redoubled his efforts, pressing two fingers inside her as he lashed at her clit with his tongue. Nathalie hissed, then let out a deep, throaty moan before erupting in a scream loud enough to shake the entire building.

Or at least that was how it sounded in his ears.

God Almighty, the woman had lungs. Andrew was positive that not only Fernando had heard his daughter, but so had every immortal in the building. Any moment now, he expected the front door to burst open with Guardians rushing in to save the poor woman who screamed as if someone was going at her with a butcher knife.

As she sucked in a breath, no doubt filling her lungs for another scream, he surged up and covered her mouth with his—his shaft aligning with her entrance completely coincidental.

Nathalie took it to mean he meant business and pushed up. The head glided effortlessly through her wetness, and he lost it, growling into her mouth as he pushed all the way inside her with one powerful thrust, ramming against her cervix.

Nathalie hissed, but he wasn't sure whether from pleasure or discomfort and forced himself to hold still. "Did I hurt you?"

She shook her head. "It's nothing. Don't stop."

So he'd hurt her.

Damn, the guilt had a very disconcerting effect on him, and he experienced something he'd never experienced during sex before.

Andrew went soft.

Nathalie wrapped her arms around him. "What's the matter, baby?" She sounded worried, which doubled his guilt. Not only did he hurt her, he was also probably offending her by his very unmanly reaction.

Andrew lifted his head and looked into her loving eyes. "I'm sorry. I hurt you, and I'm mad at myself. The guilt is delivering an appropriate punishment."

She grabbed his cheeks and brought his head down for a kiss. "Silly boy, who do you think you're punishing? I told you it was nothing, and it's not the first time that it's happened. You are big, baby, and I love every delicious inch of you, fucking me like you can never get enough."

And... he was back.

God, it was such a turn-on to hear Nathalie talk dirty. It was as if she turned into a different woman. Gone was the sweet, good girl, replaced by a sultry seductress. Only with him, though. No one else would ever get to see that side of her.

Moving slowly, he was careful not to surge all the way, keeping his thrusts slow and shallow and stoking the flames one tinder at a time.

"Please, Andrew, don't tease me," she murmured, clutching at his shoulders and digging her sharp nails into his flesh.

He could never deny her anything, not in this or anything else. Increasing the tempo, he was careful not to hit her cervix again, but it was getting increasingly hard to control his movements, especially with Nathalie lifting up on every thrust, meeting him halfway.

"God, Nathalie, you're killing me..." Andrew hissed through clenched teeth as he let go, pounding into her like they both needed him to. With a shuddering groan, Nathalie's sheath convulsed around him, and his seed erupted.

Andrew went still, every muscle in his body tensing as he poured every last bit into her, some primitive instinct guiding him to empty it all as deep inside her as it would go.

Nathalie's climax went on and on, until Andrew collapsed breathless, at the last moment rolling off her but bringing her with him. As they lay sideways, their bodies pressed against each other's, Andrew was reluctant to withdraw, but even though he was still hard, he wasn't going for another round.

Nathalie wouldn't have objected, but then she wasn't as careful with herself as she needed to be in her condition. She needed him to make sure she didn't overexert herself.

A few moments later, she started moving against him, prompting him to continue.

He clamped his hand on her butt to still her. "None of that, baby. You need to rest."

She arched both brows. "Says who? I'm not tired."

"Says I." He pulled out.

With a sigh, Nathalie rolled onto her back and covered her eyes with her arm. "Don't tell me you're going to be like that the entire nine months. You're going to drive me nuts."

Andrew got out of bed and walked over to her side. "Come on, sweetheart, let's get showered." He snaked his hands under her knees to lift her up, but she slapped at his chest. "I can walk."

"Okay..." He backed off.

As Nathalie swung her legs over the side of the bed and stood up, her body swayed a little. Andrew caught her and held her against him. She let him for a couple of seconds, then pushed against his chest.

"I'm fine."

Reluctantly, he let go, and she stepped around him, heading for the bathroom. A glance at the rumpled sheets stole his breath away.

There were blood spots everywhere.

Panicking, he called after her, "Nathalie!"

The urgency of his cry brought her running back. "What's wrong?"

"Look." He pointed at the bed.

Her hand flew to her mouth. "Oh, my God. What is that?"

"Blood!" He waved his hand.

"I know that is blood. But whose?"

He glanced at her inner thighs then at his deflated shaft, and sure enough, there was blood on both.

"We need to call Bridget."

Nathalie nodded, looking just as scared as he felt.

Andrew made the call, then did a quick wipe down with a washcloth and got dressed. He waited for Bridget in the living room while Nathalie grabbed a quick shower.

Less than five minutes later, there was a knock on the door, and Andrew rushed to let the doctor in.

"Hello, Andrew, where is Nathalie?" Bridget asked in a calm tone as if she was on a social visit.

"I'm here." Nathalie walked in, looking white as a ghost.

Bridget sat down and motioned for Nathalie to join her on the couch. Nathalie sat on the very edge.

"Tell me what happened."

"There was blood on the sheet." Nathalie's voice quivered.

"How much blood?"

"I don't know. What is considered a lot?"

"Was there a puddle or just a few stains?"

"A few small stains."

"Did you experience any cramps?"

Nathalie shook her head.

"Yes, you did," Andrew reminded her.

She waved a hand. "That wasn't a cramp, just a little ouch."

"Care to explain?" Bridget said.

Nathalie's cheeks pinked, and she looked at Andrew. He wanted to tell her that this wasn't a good time to be shy, but figured she was shaken enough. Besides, he had no problem saying what needed to be said.

"During penetration, I bumped against Nathalie's cervix, and it was painful for her. After that, I was cautious, but we got carried away toward the end. Nathalie didn't experience any more pain, but I suspect it was the work of the endorphins."

Bridget smiled and patted Nathalie's hand. "You have nothing to worry about. During pregnancy, extra blood flows to the cervix, and any bump against it may trigger a little bleeding. It's normal, and is not a cause for concern."

Nathalie slumped against the couch pillows. "That was one hell of a scare."

Andrew squeezed in between his fiancée and the sofa's armrest, wrapping his arm around Nathalie's shoulders. She was still tense, and Andrew decided to lighten the mood. "I agree. It was terrifying. I thought there goes sex for the next nine months…"

Her small fist delivered a playful punch to his bicep. "You're such a cad, Andrew, I don't know what I see in you."

"A hunk of a man, baby. You're after my irresistible body."

That earned him another punch.

Bridget laughed and pushed up to her feet. "Now that we have determined that the emergency wasn't really an emergency, I'll leave you kids to fool around." She pointed a finger at Andrew. "Gently, mind you."

He nodded. "Absolutely."

33

ROBERT

It was late at night when they'd arrived at Carol's home, a small cottage in a nice, middle-class suburb. The inside was just as unassuming—a small living area with a fake fireplace, a kitchen that was open to the living area, two tiny bedrooms, and one bath. Not what he'd expected from a wealthy clan member.

Still, he wouldn't have minded living there with her. It felt like home, or what he imagined a home should feel like. With where and how he'd grown up, his only points of reference were movies.

"Should I bring our things from the car?" He followed her around, not sure what he should do next.

"No. I'm going to call first and see if they want us to come in right away."

"Couldn't it wait until morning?"

"No. I don't want to get in trouble again."

"Again?"

She waved a hand. "I did a few stupid things in my time, and I didn't like the consequences."

That was interesting. Was his Carol a troublemaker? He wouldn't put it past her.

"What did you do?"

She picked up the receiver and dialed a number. "It's a story for another time."

Drumming her fingers on the counter, Carol waited for her call to be answered. When it finally was, she didn't start with a hello. "Brundar, we've just got to my place. What do you want us to do?"

She had called this Brundar fellow a couple of times from the road. Robert found it strange that her fitness coach was her liaison to whoever was in charge of the clan in Los Angeles.

"I'm coming to get you," Robert heard the guy say.

"What about the rental, and what about our stuff?"

"I can take the Doomer, and you can stay and take care of it, or you can come along, and I'll have someone drop you off at your place tomorrow."

Robert bristled. *The Doomer has a name, and he saved your friend's ass.*

"I'm coming with Robert."

The guy disconnected without another word.

"When he gets here, we'll transfer what we have in the rental to his car. I'll come back for the rest of my stuff tomorrow." Carol avoided his eyes as she spoke, and he wondered what she was feeling guilty about.

Whatever it was, it was too late to back out now. Besides, he would rather be a prisoner of the clan than get captured by the Brotherhood. There was no doubt in his mind where he would fare better—even if Carol's relatives planned to torture him for information.

They waited in strained silence, and when a car finally slid into Carol's driveway, Robert was glad to get out of there. The driver got out and met them halfway. He didn't look like what Robert had imagined a fitness instructor would look like.

The man standing in front of him was a Guardian. Robert was willing to bet his life on it. Even though no weapons were clearly visible, he could tell the guy was packing, a lot, everywhere. And the way he carried himself was with the surety of a man who feared no one.

He heard Carol gasp when the guy offered his hand for a handshake and wondered why. Had she been expecting a pair of handcuffs?

"Welcome to the clan," the guy said while Robert clasped his hand. "You have our gratitude."

It was on the tip of his tongue to say that they had a strange way of showing it, but he had a feeling he should tread lightly with the man standing in front of him. Despite his almost feminine beauty, Brundar exuded a deadly aura. Cold eyes, not even Sebastian's eyes were that emotionless, and that flat, robotic tone...

This wasn't a male to trifle with.

Robert nodded, and Brundar immediately withdrew his hand as if he couldn't wait to sever the contact. Robert's lips tightened into a thin line. The guy probably couldn't stand touching a filthy Doomer.

"I'm glad to see you back home," Brundar greeted Carol with a slight dip of his head. No handshake, no embrace, and Carol, who was a touchy-feely sort of girl, didn't initiate any either.

Robert realized that he'd misinterpreted the guy's reaction. Brundar didn't like physical contact, and Carol was well aware of it. That was why she had gasped when the Guardian had offered his hand to Robert. It must've been a big deal for Brundar.

Robert felt a lot better.

"If you pop your trunk, I'll transfer our things from the rental," he told Brundar.

The guy nodded and pulled out a remote key from his leather jacket's inside pocket. The vehicle's back door lifted, and Brundar helped transfer the stuff without saying another word.

When Carol locked her front door and got in the back seat, Robert wasn't sure if he should join her or sit up front with Brundar. His dilemma was solved when Brundar pulled a syringe out of his other pocket.

"I need to knock you out for the drive." He hesitated for a moment before adding an explanation. "We can't trust you yet, and our location is secret. I'm sure you would've done the same in our position."

Yes, he would've, but it was a small consolation. "Am I going to be held prisoner?"

"Only until we question you and determine your true intentions."

Robert frowned; that didn't sound encouraging. "Are you going to torture me?"

"You have my word that no harm will come to you."

"But I'm still going to be put inside a prison cell."

Brundar shook his head, his long blond hair fanning around his disturbingly beautiful face. "You will be staying together with Carol in a very nice underground apartment."

"A fancy cell."

"Exactly."

Well, it could've been worse. He motioned at the syringe. "How do you want to do it?"

"Get in the back and put your seatbelt on."

As Robert got in and buckled up, Brundar leaned and without much preamble stuck the needle in his throat with the precision of an experienced medic. Robert felt a sting, then something cold entering his bloodstream, and then nothing at all.

34

AMANDA

*A*n air of excitement suffused the shuttle as Amanda and her crew got comfortable for the ride. The flight had been uneventful. But regrettably, there had been no opportunity to join the infamous mile-high club. With no privacy to be had aside from the one and only bathroom, she'd given up on the idea. Twenty-five females on board, twenty-six if she counted the captain, guaranteed that there had always been a line to the coveted porcelain throne.

Besides, Dalhu had spent the entire flight in the cockpit. It wasn't so much that he'd intimidated the girls, not after Amanda had introduced him as her boyfriend, but that he'd felt awkward as the only male among so many women.

She chuckled. Her unflappable, courageous warrior was intimidated by a bunch of human females. Even now, sitting next to her on the bus, he seemed uncomfortable, mostly physically, though. At six foot eight, he was too tall to fit in the narrow space between seats. His knees bumped against the back of the one in front of them, and he was forced to sit sideways, stretching his legs into the aisle.

"Pardon me." Yet another female stepped over his legs to get to a friend sitting in the back.

Amanda cast her an annoyed glance, and the girl blushed, scurrying away. Were these supposedly traumatized females stealing looks at her handsome mate?

She didn't like it. Not at all. It had started in the restaurant they had stopped at for lunch. At first, just a few quick glances that could've been interpreted as curiosity, but some had not been so quick. The chits were getting bolder by the minute.

In a huff, Amanda crossed her arms over her chest.

"What's the matter?" Dalhu asked.

"I think half of the hussies on this bus have the hots for you, and it pisses me off."

"Shh, they'll hear you," he whispered in her ear. "And I think you're imagining it. I'm flattered by your jealousy, though." There was a satisfied smirk on his face she wanted to wipe off.

"They can't hear me; they are human. And I don't care if Vanessa or Gertrude can. Maybe they will tell the horny bunch to keep their eyes off what's mine."

"Sorry, can't do that," Vanessa chirped from the back of the bus.

Dalhu looked way too smug, Vanessa wasn't helping, and Amanda's finger itched to flip the therapist off. Except, she had an image to uphold. She was there to provide help and guidance to these women, which necessitated keeping an image of professionalism and refinement.

About an hour later, the bus came to a stop at the employee lodging area of the hotel grounds. Everyone filed out, and Dalhu helped the bus driver take the luggage out and put it on the sidewalk. Twenty-two identical rolling suitcases, two different ones that belonged to Vanessa and Gertrude, a crate with Dalhu's work in progress, and Amanda's three designer trunks. It might've seemed excessive, but she'd packed Dalhu's things together with hers, and they were taking the space of at least half of one of the trunks.

While the girls were scrambling to figure out which suitcase belonged to whom, she stepped aside and pulled Dalhu out of the way. "I'm going to stay and get them settled. Do you want to come with me, or do you want to go to the hotel and come back for me when I'm done?"

"I'll go to the hotel."

Her man was so relieved to get away that he hefted the crate under his arm and pushed all three rolling suitcases ahead of him with the intention of getting there on foot—over a mile of uphill trek through the hotel's enormous parking lot.

Stifling a laugh, she called after him, "Wait!"

When he turned to look at her, there was fear on her warrior mate's face. Poor thing. He probably thought she'd changed her mind and wanted him to stay.

"Take the go-cart," she said, pointing at the vehicle parked a few feet away.

"Is it ours?"

"Of course. The keys are in the ignition. When you get there, look for Paul, he'll show you around."

"Sounds good to me." He loaded their things into the go-cart, kissed her cheek, and was out of there with screeching tires. Well, not really screeching—only in her imagination.

"Did everyone find their suitcases?" She waited a couple more minutes while the last few stragglers located their luggage. "Follow me."

The hotel itself was no doubt lovely, and Amanda couldn't wait to see it, but it would have to wait for later. Right now she was more interested in the employee quarters, where her charges would begin their new lives.

Per Vanessa's instructions, no one was there to show them around. Instead, the chaperones had familiarized themselves with the layout by studying the blueprints.

The four three-story buildings were located behind the sprawling parking lot in the back of the hotel, further inland. No ocean view, but other than that, fabulously appointed. Every apartment had four bedrooms, two bathrooms, and a living room with a kitchen. Outside, the four buildings shared a private swimming pool and a large grassy area for employee use only.

Since the hotel wasn't due to open for another month, her girls were the first personnel to arrive. That would give them an entire week to themselves before the other employees showed up.

In preparation for the long and grueling task of thralling her charges one at a time, Amanda commandeered the manager's office, and Vanessa the currently empty employee lounge.

It was going to be long and exhausting. The script they'd come up with was designed to fill several weeks of lost time. Not something that could be accomplished quickly or with more than one person at a time.

In fact, the plan called for two stages.

Amanda was going to do the heavy lifting with the lengthy scenario, adjusting it to fit each girl. Vanessa was going to take it from there and check if it had been absorbed and hadn't created undue confusion. Gertrude's job was to escort each girl, starting with Amanda's office, through Vanessa's approval, and out to the other side of the building. The ones already thralled and those who were still in line were not to mix until the last one had gone through the process.

Three and a half hours later, Gertrude escorted the last one out, and Amanda collapsed, clutching her head. The last time she'd suffered a headache this bad had been after her vodka-drinking competition with the Russian crew of the *Anna*.

Fates, she hoped the surly bunch was okay. Amanda had grown fond of Geneva, the captain, and the others weren't so bad either, especially when drunk.

"You look like shit," Vanessa said as she entered the office.

Amanda grimaced. "Thank you."

"I mean it. You should go and get some rest. Gertrude and I can handle it from here. The bus will arrive in a few minutes, and there is no need for you to come eat dinner with us."

"What if someone has a relapse? This was tricky as hell."

"I can handle it, Amanda. You've done your part."

Well, she had done the right thing and offered, but she wasn't going to keep arguing when all she could think of was the beautiful bed waiting for her in the presidential suite, and Dalhu's capable hands massaging her all over.

"You're right. I'm exhausted. I don't think I could perform another thrall if my life depended on it. I'm all tapped out."

With a smile and a hand wave, Vanessa left and closed the door behind her. Enjoying the quiet, Amanda rested her cheek on the desk for a few moments, then pulled out her phone and called Dalhu.

"I'm ready to go." She added a sigh.

"You sound awful."

"I feel even worse."

"I'm out the door."

She'd known Dalhu would drop everything to come get her, he always did. "I'm waiting."

This time she was pretty sure she heard the screech of tires a moment before Dalhu burst through the door with a frosty can of Cola in his hand.

She hoped it was as cold as it looked. "Sweetheart, you're a sight for sore eyes."

"Me or the Coke?" He handed her the can.

"Both."

As Amanda popped the lid, the fizzing sound of the soda was the sweetest she'd heard all day. She drained the entire can then produced a very unladylike burp. "Sorry about that."

Dalhu waved his hand in dismissal, and she realized he'd picked up the gesture from Kian. The two were getting closer. They were almost friends; a miracle, considering her brother's initial vehement hatred toward Dalhu.

"How are you feeling?" Dalhu asked.

"Much better, thank you."

"Are you hungry? Do you want to grab something to eat, or can you wait a little?"

Hmm, she wondered what he had in mind. If it was a tangle between the sheets, she didn't mind postponing dinner for an hour or two. "I'm still full from lunch." A little white lie so he wouldn't insist she had to eat first.

His face lightened with a big smile. "Sunset is in fifteen minutes. Paul explained it's very precise here. You have to be on time or you'll miss it. We can take a walk on the beach and watch it."

After the grueling day she'd had, there were a number of things she would've preferred doing other than walking on the beach, but this was Dalhu's first visit to Hawaii, and he deserved to get his fill of its beautiful sunsets and sunrises.

She smiled at her mate. "Sounds lovely."

35

CAROL

"Is he still out?" Brundar asked ten minutes into the drive.

With his head resting on her shoulder, Robert's deep breaths were tickling her neck.

"Like a light."

"Tell me if it seems like he is waking up."

"I will."

Carol felt strange about the unexpected role reversal. Holding Robert's big, unconscious frame from slumping forward, and adjusting his lolling head so it would rest on her shoulder and not hang loosely from his neck, she felt protective of him. Her inert motherly instincts must've flared into life. He was her charge now, and she would take care of him the way he'd taken care of her.

A frown creased her brow when she realized that during their time together she'd grown accustomed to relying on him. Not that it had been evident in their day-to-day life in Vegas. She had money, and he didn't, she was familiar with the environment, and he wasn't. And yet, having him around had made her feel safer than she'd ever felt before.

Robert was a warrior, big and strong, and although he didn't exhibit violent or aggressive tendencies, quite unusual for an immortal male, she knew he must've possessed them to survive the numerous battles he'd fought in. If the need arose, like it had when she'd fallen victim to the sadist, Robert would be there to protect her. There was not a shred of doubt in her mind that he would fight to the death to keep her from harm—even though he didn't love her.

She wasn't his fated mate, and yet he treated her as one.

Would it be so bad to keep him? Even exclusively?

With her natural inclinations and her colorful past, she couldn't imagine what life would be like with a single male, and one as unexciting as Robert to boot. But dependable and loyal had its merits. Besides, she'd survived these last few weeks without her addiction to sex and excitement kicking into hyperdrive.

Come to think of it, none of her other addictions had bothered her either. Not once had she felt like getting high, or numb, which was surprising given how incredibly bored she'd been. And things with Robert hadn't been so great either. They'd argued and bickered like some old human couple.

A bump in the road had Robert's head sliding off her shoulder, and she pushed it back, cupping his cheek to hold it in place. Hanging from his slightly parted lips was a drop of drool, and she absentmindedly wiped it off with her thumb. Poor guy. He'd allowed Brundar to render him as vulnerable as a newborn kitten, basically putting his life in her hands.

Carol tried to figure out what was it about having him around that soothed her soul—enough to forgo her assorted variety of crutches.

Not being alone?

Carol hadn't felt lonely before; she had plenty of friends and relatives after all, to hang out with. They were all single and destined to remain that way, so there was never a shortage of people to talk to, or invite over, or go out and have fun with.

Having a ready and willing sex partner at her disposal?

She'd never suffered a shortage of those either.

Then what?

Someone to always have your back, she heard a voice whisper in her head. She had a whole clan to rely on. But it wasn't the same, was it? Having a mate, even not a fated one, was different.

"Still out?" Brundar asked again.

"Yes. How long?"

"Less than five minutes. Are you sure he is not faking it?"

She chuckled. "He's not." Robert would not have known how.

He was still unconscious when Brundar parked the car in the clan's underground parking, kept sleeping through the wheeled gurney ride to the basement, and rolled to his side with a sigh when Brundar lifted him off the gurney and put him in bed.

Carol was starting to get worried. "Wasn't he supposed to wake up already?"

Brundar shrugged and headed for the door. "Everyone reacts differently," he said before stepping out and locking her inside with Robert.

If she wanted out, he'd told her she would need to call security, and someone would open the door for her. Until Robert was proven trustworthy, this was how things were going to be.

Not fun.

She glanced at the bar and sighed. There was an under-cabinet fridge, a microwave to heat things up, and even a Nespresso machine, but there was no stove and no pots or other utensils to cook with. Cooking would have to wait for now. A pity, she was in the mood to whip up something amazing and show Robert what she could do, maybe even invite Brundar and show off a little.

Other than the lack of a proper kitchen, however, this place was a palace compared to the tiny solitary-confinement cell Kian had thrown her in after her last drunken tirade in a bar. It looked like one of the luxury suites in an upscale hotel, the kind she'd stayed in only when she'd scored with some rich dude who had footed the bill.

This one, though, had some additional perks. Like a PlayStation and a bunch of games stacked high in the entertainment cabinet, or the narrow bookcase loaded with what looked like hundreds of movies. She pulled out a few, checking for titles she hadn't seen yet. Most were action flicks she had no intentions of watching; Robert would probably have fun with those, but she found a few romantic comedies too. She was about to search the next shelf when she heard a groan from the bedroom.

Robert was waking up, and by the sound of it, his forced respite hadn't been pleasant.

Peeking into the bedroom to check whether he was indeed awake or groaning in his sleep, she saw him lying on his back and clutching his head.

"Do you have a headache?"

He answered with another groan.

"Let me see if I can find some painkillers," she said even though there was a fat chance she would. Immortals didn't normally suffer from headaches, but she'd often felt achy after a workout and had taken some Motrin for it. She probably wasn't the only one who didn't like to tough it out. Incredibly, she found a bottle of Motrin in one of the drawers in the bathroom. The vanity was stocked with a good variety of items she was planning on checking out later.

"Here you go, sweetie." She handed Robert a bunch of pills and the glass of water that she'd filled up in the bar.

He took the pills and looked at them as if they were poison. "What is it?"

"Just Motrin. They will help with the headache."

He shook the pills in his hand. "Why so many?"

"You've never taken any?"

He shook his head.

"You're a big guy and an immortal. We need way more booze than humans to get drunk, and the same is true for pills. Don't compare these to those you've given me. They are not in the same league. Motrin is a very weak painkiller."

He cast her one more suspicious glance before throwing the eight pills she'd given him down his throat and chasing them with several big gulps of water. Putting the empty glass on the nightstand, he started fumbling with the buttons of his shirt—his fingers clumsy and uncoordinated from either the headache or the side effects of whatever Brundar had injected him with.

"Let me help." She swatted his hands away. His shirt was off in seconds, and Carol continued with his belt and his zipper. "Lift up," she commanded, pulling his pants off when he complied.

"Now get under the covers." She waited until he did and then tucked him in.

"Aren't you coming to bed?" he asked groggily.

"I'm going to grab a quick shower first."

There was no response other than Robert's breathing getting deeper.

36

ROBERT

Robert woke up with Carol's curvy body pressed against him, her back to his front, her sweet butt a perfect cradle for his morning stiffness.

She hadn't always slept in the nude.

The first few days after their escape, she'd slept in what looked like men's pajamas. It had been one of the first items she'd purchased. The top, which was a couple of sizes too big, was long-sleeved, checkered, and buttoned in the front. The long pants pooled on the floor and had caused her to stumble more than once. She'd forgone those first, sleeping only in the long top and panties, then the top had been replaced by a T-shirt, and then nothing at all.

That had also been the first night they'd had sex.

He'd taken it as a sign of recovery, or maybe her trust in him, when she'd admitted she liked sleeping in the nude and snuggled up to him.

Eyes still closed, he smoothed his hand over her soft skin, following the dip of her waist to the curve of her hip. She was so small. When awake, Carol seemed bigger for some reason.

She sighed and turned around, planting a closed mouthed kiss on his lips. "How is your headache?"

Headache? "What headache?"

She chuckled. "Good. I'm glad you're feeling okay."

Carol had thought he'd been joking, but he really didn't remember anything. His last memory was shaking hands with Brundar, after Carol and he had arrived at her house late last night. Then he remembered the syringe. Was it last night?

And where the hell was he?

Robert lifted his eyelids and looked around the room. The lights were off, and if there was a window in the room it was tightly covered, but he could still see well enough in the dark to appreciate the luxury.

"This is nice," he said.

Carol chuckled. "Yeah, I know. They gave us the royal prison cell."

"This is a cell?"

"Not exactly. It's more like a luxurious apartment with a locked door. From the outside."

Yeah, he'd been prepared for confinement. Not a crappy cell and iron bars, after all he'd saved one of their own and deserved some gratitude, but not something so luxurious. Apparently, the rumors about the clan's wealth hadn't been exaggerated.

"How long have I been out?"

"Long. We got here at about three in the morning, and it's after nine."

Six hours of sleep. Must've been the effect of whatever Brundar had injected him with. He was surprised no one had paid them a visit yet. They must've known he and Carol were still sleeping.

As Robert lifted his eyes up to the ceiling and saw the camera, anger bubbled up from somewhere deep in his gut. The fuckers watching the feed had seen Carol naked.

"There is a camera up there," he pointed.

"I know. I saw it when Brundar brought you in. It's off. But the one in the living room is on."

"How do you know it's off?"

"Someone spray-painted the lens with black paint."

Robert felt the tension leave his shoulders. "I need to thank that someone. Other than me, no one should see you nude."

She snorted and slapped his chest. "Don't be silly; they are all my cousins. They can see me naked all they want." And to prove the point, she got out of bed and sauntered to the living room where the camera was on.

"Where are you going?" Robert called after her.

"To bring a change of clothes. Brundar just dumped everything in the living room, and I was too tired to put it away last night." She brought two duffle bags and dropped them in the walk-in closet. "Aren't you going to help?"

Not bare-assed, he wasn't. Robert pulled on his jeans and followed her to the living room. "Leave it. I'll take care of the rest. Go get dressed."

She cast him a look he found hard to decipher, shrugged, and sauntered back to the bedroom, her round bottom swaying enticingly with every step. He would've followed her if not for the damn camera.

She was naive if she thought her clansmen were oblivious to her feminine charms just because they were related. Humans married their cousins, so that couldn't have been too big of a no-no. Not to mention the stories about sexual abuse by fathers or uncles or even brothers.

Robert couldn't fathom anyone doing such a thing to his own blood, but there were plenty of perverts out there, and as proven by the sadist, immortals weren't immune.

He picked up their two other bags and carried them to the closet when the phone rang. Carol picked up the one in the bedroom.

"Yes, sure. Give us fifteen minutes." She hung up.

"Brundar called to say they are coming to ask you some questions." Pretending to search for something on the floor, she avoided looking him in the eyes.

What was she hiding?

Damn woman. He should remember that Carol only looked naive and innocent. Anyone strong enough to withstand what she'd been subjected to and not reveal every last detail of her life, had a heart of a warrior.

"Who are they?" he asked as he pulled out a shirt from his duffle bag.

She closed her eyes and took in a fortifying breath. "Kian, the clan's regent, and Edna, our judge."

They were sending the big guns, impressive. "What about Brundar?" The warrior seemed to regard him favorably.

"Probably."

Robert narrowed his eyes at her. "He is not your fitness instructor, is he?"

The corners of her lips lifted in a small smile. "He is my instructor alright, and what he teaches requires me to be fit, but I'm supposed to do it on my own."

What could a Guardian teach Carol that required her to get in better shape? Not that there was anything wrong with the shape she was in. Robert liked her soft, padded body.

Unless...

No, the idea was ludicrous. There was no way Carol was training to become a Guardian. Yes, she was tough, but she was also lazy and undisciplined—definitely not Guardian material.

Robert chuckled. "You're in the Guardian program, aren't you? You've been holding out on me," he teased.

She gasped. "How did you guess?"

He winked at her attempted joke. "Your fighting moves betrayed you." He imitated one of her bored poses.

"You don't believe me?" Carol bristled.

He shook his head. "Prove it to me. Show me your moves."

She worried her bottom lip and then shrugged. "It's a self-defense class, and if I'm good, I can graduate to the program."

Even a class like that was not something he would've expected Carol to join willingly.

He lifted a brow. "Do you want to?"

"Not really. I enjoy taking the classes because it's something to do, and I'm good at some of the stuff."

"Good for you. It's important to have basic fighting skills." He wanted to ask her more questions, but it had to wait for later. They needed to get ready for their important visitors.

They were dressed and ready when the knock came, but they hadn't had enough time to make coffee. He wondered how formal these guests were, and if they would mind him using that Nespresso machine. It looked simple enough to operate.

The door swung open, and for a moment Robert was confused, his eyes following the stout, strange looking man entering the room and carrying a large tray. He looked distinguished enough in the suit he was wearing, but the clan's regent wouldn't come in with a tray.

Must be a servant.

Robert's eyes darted back to the door and those following behind the servant—a tall, striking male and a plain-looking woman with the wisest eyes

Robert had ever seen. He didn't know who impressed him more, the regent or the sage.

"Hello, Robert." The guy offered his hand and Robert shook it. "I'm Kian, and this is Edna."

She offered her hand too, and Robert shook it with utmost care. Her hand was so delicate that it seemed breakable. "Thank you for helping our Carol." She smiled a sad smile that reminded him of that famous painting, The Mona Lisa.

When Carol came forward, Kian pulled her into his arms for a quick embrace. "You gave us a big scare, girl. Don't do it again."

She chuckled. "I don't intend to."

The women embraced next, and Robert couldn't help noticing that Carol had been more at ease in her regent's arms than in Edna's. Had they been lovers? A surge of jealousy clouded his vision, but then he shook it off. Carol had told him that clan members didn't hook up with each other, and he had little reason to doubt her. Especially since Sebastian had said the same thing.

Then again, there were always the deviants.

Taking a quick sniff, Robert was relieved. No one in the room smelled of arousal or hostility. Suspicion, though, there was plenty of that in the air.

The servant cleared his throat and waved his hand at the coffee table, bowing slightly at the waist. "Coffee is served, mesdames and messieurs."

"Thank you, Okidu," Kian said as he took a seat in one of the chairs facing the couch. Edna took the other, leaving the sofa for Robert and Carol.

The servant bowed again. "Would there be anything else, Master?"

"I'll let you know if there is. You may leave."

The regent turned to Robert. "We owe you a debt of gratitude, Robert. You can name your price."

Offensive jerk. As if Robert had rescued Carol for personal gain. He'd sacrificed everything for her. His home and his so-called family, as shitty as they had been, were forever lost to him, and he was left with nothing.

He put his hand on Carol's thigh. "My prize is sitting right next to me." He held his breath as he waited for Carol to refute his claim, saying that this was only temporary until she fulfilled her promise to him.

Kian nodded in approval. "I appreciate your nobility, but let's be practical. You've abandoned your brethren and the only home you've ever known. I'm well aware that you couldn't have taken anything with you, and that you need our help in starting a new life."

Unfortunately, Robert couldn't afford a proud refusal. "I need papers to work legally in the States, and if you can help me find a job, I would really appreciate it. In the meantime, though, I'm asking for asylum. By rescuing Carol, I became a deserter. You can imagine what would be done to me if I were ever caught." He wasn't going to spell it out with Carol and Edna in the room, but he saw understanding in the regent's eyes. The man was a warrior. "I have no doubt they are searching for me, but maybe with time they will give up."

Kian chuckled. "No one is looking for you, Robert, because they think you are dead."

Robert frowned. "Why would they?"

"You didn't tell him?" Kian asked Carol.

She shook her head. "I was afraid to." She lifted her palm when Kian's features darkened and he eyed Robert with suspicion. "Don't get me wrong, Robert is a kind and considerate male; a miracle given where he comes from, but these were his friends. He only hated his sadistic boss."

A shiver went through her, and Robert instinctively wrapped his arm around her shoulders. Whatever her deception was, she'd done it out of fear.

"What happened?" Robert directed the question to Kian.

"Before you helped Carol run, we were planning a rescue operation. When she called to tell us that she escaped, she mentioned the other women held captive at the base. We attacked, liberated the women, and destroyed the monastery."

"What happened to the men?" It was a stupid question, but he had to ask.

"You will be glad to know that your sadistic commander is dead, but most of your friends are not. There were some casualties, naturally, but the rest are in stasis."

"Stasis?" He had no idea what that was.

Kian shook his head and lifted his coffee cup. "I can't believe they don't teach you guys the most basic stuff about your own immortal bodies. You know that other than death by venom you cannot die unless your head is cut off or your heart is removed from your chest, right?"

Robert nodded.

"Stasis is a suspended state achieved by injecting your enemy with venom but not until his heart stops completely. In that state, the body can survive indefinitely and be revived in some distant, utopian future when our peoples achieve peace or at least learn to coexist."

Robert snorted. "Never going to happen."

Kian's handsome face twisted in a grimace. "That's my opinion as well, but I'm overruled."

The overruling must've come from the goddess. That was what happened when a female was in charge. Females were soft-hearted. Not that he was ungrateful. Thanks to her, the lives of his friends had been spared.

Robert felt conflicted. On the one hand, he was glad no one was coming after him; on the other, he mourned those warriors who were his friends. Even if not technically dead, they were just as good as.

But he was happy that the captives were free and even happier that the sadist was no more.

Aside from getting captured, Robert's biggest worry had been the fate of the other girls. With Sebastian's favorite whipping toy gone, his ex-commander would've probably killed them. Carol was indestructible, but they were not.

"Penny for your thoughts," Carol said, her pixie face pinched with stress.

Robert clasped her hand to reassure her he wasn't mad. "I'm glad Sebastian is dead, and I'm glad the girls are free. I'm not happy about my friends being in stasis, but it's better than being dead."

Kian looked puzzled. "Who is Sebastian?"

"My sadistic ex-commander."

"I thought his name was Sharim."

"It was. He gave himself a new one when we came here. Mine isn't Robert either, but I want to keep it."

"What's your real name?" Carol asked.

He shook his head. "It belonged to a different man. That male is gone."

He saw approval in Edna's eyes. She hadn't said a word throughout the entire conversation, and he was starting to think that she had only come to observe.

The regent was the one who would conduct the interrogation. He shifted his eyes to Kian. "You wanted to ask me some questions."

"I think we've covered the basics." He glanced at the woman. "Edna is going to perform her own kind of evaluation."

Robert turned to the woman. "Ask away."

She smiled her sad smile again and pushed to her feet. "Carol, would you mind changing seats with me?"

"Sure, no problem." Carol looked as puzzled as he felt, but did as Edna had asked.

The woman sat next to him, her knees almost touching his, and lifted her hands. "Give me your hands, Robert."

Not knowing what to expect, he did.

"I'm going to probe you, and it's going to feel uncomfortable unless you open up to me and let me in. I'm not a mind reader, I can't read thoughts, but I can read emotions and intents. That's why Kian brought me here."

Robert braced himself for whatever was going to happen next. He had nothing to hide, but there were things he'd done that he wished he hadn't. Not that he'd had a choice. Still, he was man enough to accept responsibility. He could've disobeyed orders and paid for the refusal with his own life. He'd chosen to live.

Edna's presence inside his head was indeed uncomfortable. Remembering her instructions, he tried to relax and let it happen. The pressure eased, feeling more like a gentle flow. Robert closed his eyes.

"I need you to keep your eyes open," Edna said.

"Okay." He lifted his lids with an effort.

She took forever. By the time it was over, he felt lightheaded and nauseous. Edna looked drained.

"So many layers." She smiled weakly. "Your countenance is deceptive, Robert. You give the impression of being a simple man, but you're not."

From the corner of his eye, Robert saw Kian tense. What the hell was she talking about? He *was* a simple man, and her words were making him look bad in Kian and Carol's eyes. It sounded as if he was some kind of a mastermind who was hiding who he really was.

"It's not that you're hiding something, it's more that you're hiding from something. I can't tell you what it is, though. You need to figure it out for yourself. You care for Carol and would always protect her, but you don't love her. Not yet."

She smiled at Carol's crestfallen expression. "Not every love ignites with a flare, some start as a spark and need a lot of tending to grow."

Carol nodded.

What was it with that woman? Carol wanted him to love her while she'd stated over and over again that she didn't love him?

"What about the Brotherhood?" Kian interjected, clearly not interested in hearing about love and flares and other romantic nonsense.

Edna shifted her wise eyes to the regent. "Robert has no ill feelings toward the Brotherhood. Not everything he did for them sits well with him, but he is okay with most. I've gotten the impression that he regrets losing that way of life. But that's not unusual for someone who suddenly finds himself displaced."

Kian waved a dismissive hand. "What's the bottom line, Edna, can he be trusted or not?"

"I don't know."

The regent looked disappointed, but not as much as Robert.

"What now?" he asked Kian.

"We have another way to test you. But he won't be available until the evening."

"He, as in the guy who is going to torture me?"

Kian chuckled. "The only torture he is going to inflict on you are his corny jokes. Prepare to suffer."

37

ANANDUR

Onegus had received the update early in the morning, and he and Anandur headed out to meet up with Turner's team.

Their first meeting had been last night, and the introductions had been made in a rented shack of a house that was to serve as their temporary base for this mission. Thanks to the case of Coronas Anandur had bought on the way, he'd gained the men's approval even before they had a clue as to who he was and what he could do.

Their commander, however—a guy named Javier who didn't speak a word of Spanish, or much English for that matter, and communicated mainly through a variety of grunts—hadn't been too thrilled about the booze before a mission.

Anandur had disliked him on sight. Sticklers for the rules were, as a rule, not his favorite people.

Even more annoying, the guy had gotten it in his head that he was the leader of this mission and could give orders to Onegus and him. Anandur would've told him to shove it if not for Kian's explicit instructions to cooperate with the humans.

"Listen up," Javier called for everyone's attention.

"Here is the plan."

Wow, the guy could actually speak.

Onegus and Anandur had gone over the update several times before arriving at the shack; it had been concocted by Turner, no doubt. The guy's logic was solid, there was no argument about that, but Anandur wasn't thrilled about the increased risk to the crew and the new victims Alex had collected on the way.

"Overtaking the yacht while the cargo and the customers are still on board is too risky. We have to assume that the customers are armed, and the women, crew and cargo alike would be used not only as human shields but as a means to gain the upper hand." Javier paused and unfolded a nautical map, then pinned it to the wall so everyone could see.

Grudgingly, Anandur had to agree. However, he was more concerned with Alex than the mortal criminals who could be disabled with a thrall. The first thing the scumbag would do was to grab a girl and threaten to snap her neck if his demands weren't met.

The operation would be over before it ever began.

"According to the inside information that Anandur provided, we know that the customers, together with their purchased cargo, plan to disembark in Acapulco. We let them. Our team will follow and apprehend the customers on land and free the women, while Onegus and Anandur will wait for the yacht to depart and catch up with it at sea, using a stealth-blade helicopter."

He pointed at the map then looked at Anandur. "Make sure the yacht is in international waters before you board."

When the briefing was done, Javier approached Onegus. "You sure the two of you are enough to apprehend the owner of that boat? What if he grabs a woman and hides behind her? You need a sniper. Any of you good with a gun?"

"I am." Onegus flashed Javier one of his charming smiles, but it didn't do a thing for the guy. His lips remained tightly pressed, and his frown deepened. The dude needed to lighten up.

"Two men are not a team. I've been in this business long enough to know that. Unexpected shit happening is the norm, not the exception, and having backup is the only way to go."

Damn, the dry stick was right. Problem was, any human assist they brought along would freak out when fangs and super strength made an appearance, rendering them useless.

Onegus smiled again. "I'll confer with my friend and let you know what we decide."

Javier nodded his approval. "Take your time. The yacht is not expected to arrive until evening."

On the shack's front porch, and out of human earshot, Onegus rubbed his hand over his light stubble. "He is right. I think we should get another Guardian here."

Anandur sighed. "We could use someone like Arwel. Even a drunk immortal Guardian is better than a couple of human soldiers. But with Bhathian gone, the keep is left with only Brundar, Arwel, Yamanu and Kri. These are not good numbers. I don't feel right pulling another Guardian away from there."

"Agreed. The next question is whether we take a couple of humans with us or not. Instinct tells me not to. This is between us and one of our own. We just have to hope that the Russians will be smart enough to stay out of the way."

"Let's hope so." Anandur followed Onegus inside and watched him deliver the news to Javier. The guy wasn't happy, but ultimately it wasn't his call.

"What are you going to do with the customers?" Anandur asked.

Javier's smile was chilling. "They belong to us. It's part of the compensation."

Onegus and Anandur exchanged looks, then both shrugged. Whatever Javier was planning to do with these lowlifes, it would be a fate they no doubt deserved.

"Javier, one more thing you should know before we part ways. The girls you free may not cooperate with you. They may even think that they are going with the customers willingly. Knowing the perpetrator, we suspect that he drugged and hypnotized them. Hold them here until we arrive so we can check what was done to them."

Javier's brows lifted. "Hypnotism? You guys think I buy that crap? It's all make-believe."

"It's real, my friend, believe me." Anandur clapped the man on his shoulder. "I can demonstrate. If you want proof, that is."

Javier looked like he might but then shook his head. "I don't give a fuck one way or the other. I trust Turner, and I'll follow his instructions whether I understand them or not. My job is to catch the bad guys, free the girls, and bring them here, and then take them home. I don't need to know anything else." He walked away with a disgusted expression on his severe face.

"Spoken like a true soldier," Onegus said quietly. "Admirable."

"Are you jealous? Would you like us to be such an obedient bunch and not ask any questions?" Anandur teased.

"I can dream."

38

ANDREW

A strong sense of déjà vu assailed Andrew as he watched the display above the elevator doors, the numbers getting smaller as he neared the dungeon level of the basement. Not that the posh apartment Amanda and Dalhu had shared way back then looked anything like the word implied, but it still held the new Doomer behind lock and key as securely as any prison cell.

Once again, Andrew's lie-detecting skills were needed, and he wondered whether the transition had sharpened or diminished them. He hadn't had a chance to put them to the test yet.

Without paying attention to where he was going, Andrew's feet carried him to the right place, and he knocked on the deceptively ordinary-looking door. The thing and its jamb were reinforced to withstand an immortal male's strength. The Doomer couldn't break free.

Andrew was curious to meet this latest defector.

The guy was either a hero or a mole, and it was Andrew's call that would determine the Doomer's future. He was used to the burden of responsibility. His lie-detecting skills had been put to good use during his long years of service.

Kian opened the door and Andrew walked in. As first impressions went, the Doomer looked like a decent fellow; clean-shaven, his eyes betraying his worry but lacking hostility or deceit. He was about Andrew's height, the new post-transition one, and had an average build for an immortal male; wide shouldered and muscular, but lean. Like their human counterparts, only those who pumped iron religiously bulked up into bodybuilder territory.

"Robert the hero, I assume." He offered his hand. "I'm Andrew."

The guy looked embarrassed as he shook it with a strong hand.

"Carol?" Andrew tilted his head sideways to peek behind the two big males blocking her from view. He'd seen pictures of her as part of the briefing for her rescue mission, but he'd never met her in person. Like every other clan member, she must've been at Syssi's wedding, but they hadn't been introduced, and he didn't remember her.

She was even prettier than her picture, with a riot of blond curls cascading around her small face, and big blue eyes. When she got up to greet him, he was surprised at how soft she looked. About Syssi's height but a little more padded than his sister, she was the classic temptress; childlike yet sexy, innocent looking but tough as nails. She had to be to come out unscathed from her ordeal. Still, he was well aware that warriors carried scars on the inside as well as on the outside, and Carol might be scarred as hell and just hiding it well.

"That's me. The big troublemaker who caused a war."

"You were just the catalyst. It was bound to happen with or without you." He offered his hand, and she shook it.

Her smile was genuine. "Thanks for letting me off the hook."

"Shall we begin?" Kian asked. The guy had no patience for small talk.

"Do I need to sit next to him?" Robert asked Kian.

Andrew took a seat across from the Doomer. "No, you don't. I'm curious why you asked, though," he said.

"Edna," both Kian and Carol answered.

"Oh, so I'm an afterthought…" he teased. "You brought the big guns first."

"You weren't here in the morning." Kian apparently had taken his affront seriously.

Andrew didn't mind. On the contrary, it was good practice to hear another expert's opinion. "What did she have to say?"

"She was undecided."

Andrew glanced at Robert again, searching for what had been missing from his first impression. For Edna to be unsure, the guy had to be complicated as hell. And yet, he seemed perfectly ordinary. Luckily for Andrew, looks could be deceptive but words, when spoken to his face, could not.

"Okay, Robert. I'm going to ask you a bunch of questions, and I want you to answer them as truthfully as you can. Think of me as a lie detector, just better."

"You can do it? Discern a lie from truth?"

"Without exception."

Robert pointed at Kian. "And he trusts your judgment?"

"Completely," Kian answered.

The guy grinned happily. "Then I'm good. I was worried you guys would never believe me."

"Truth," Andrew said. "Do you want me to ask the questions or do you want to do it?" he asked Kian.

"Go ahead. You're the expert."

"Very well. First, Robert, I want you to tell me a lie." Andrew needed to test his skill before proceeding.

"About what?"

"Anything. What color are my eyes?"

"Blue."

"You were supposed to lie, Robert."

"Sorry." The guy rubbed his neck.

"What's my hair color?"

"Brown."

Damn, the guy was either not so smart or had a real hard time lying. "Again, you were supposed to lie."

"Okay, but you need to ask me something that isn't as obvious. I can't help it."

What could he ask Robert that the guy would be inclined to lie about?

Something about Carol, he wouldn't want to say anything negative about her. From the briefing, Andrew knew that she was a pothead, but Robert might not know it. What else? She didn't work, didn't volunteer, and spent most of her time hanging out with friends and clubbing.

"Is Carol a hardworking person?"

Robert hesitated. "Yes," he finally answered.

A clear and resounding lie. Hallelujah. "That was a lie. Congratulations."

"Hey, not nice," Carol pouted.

Kian crossed his arms over his chest and lifted a brow.

"Fine." With a huff, she mimicked his pose.

It was time to start the serious questions.

"Why did you rescue Carol?"

"I couldn't stand the torture. She was so brave, but I was afraid her mind would snap, and she would become catatonic. No one can go through what she did, day in and day out, not even a trained warrior, and not lose his mind."

"Truth."

Kian shifted in his seat, and Andrew had to avert his gaze. The guilt was as overwhelming as it was irrational. If they could've been faster, they could've spared her days of torture. But that had been impossible. They had done all they could.

"Did you know that by helping her you were leaving everything behind for good?"

"Yes."

"Truth. You had no ulterior motives?"

"I did. The most compelling motive there is. An immortal female of my own."

"Truth. Did you demand from Carol that she be with you in exchange for your help?"

"I did. I asked for three months, hoping she would grow to care for me and consider staying."

Andrew glanced at Carol. She looked conflicted, as if she hadn't made up her mind yet.

"Truth. How did you like your life in the Brotherhood?"

Robert shrugged. "It was all I knew. I hated the battles, even though I did what was required of me. Getting the second in command position with Sharim was a reward, and it worked out fine until he started torturing the first girl and then Carol. I hated him then. I wanted him dead."

"Truth. Was there anything that you liked doing?"

"Since Sharim's wasn't a real combat unit, he put me in charge of all the administrative work and procurement. When he started collecting girls, he put me in charge of seeing to their needs. I liked doing that. I'm organized and methodical. I was good at it."

"Truth. If you could, hypothetically, would you go back to the Brotherhood?"

This time Robert didn't answer right away. It took him a couple of minutes.

"Depends on whether Carol decides to stick with me. I'd rather be in the Brotherhood than alone. If I could have a different commander, that is."

"Truth."

Andrew looked at Kian, checking if his brother-in-law was satisfied with Robert's answers.

Kian lifted a finger, indicating he was taking over. "Unlike Andrew, my questions are more direct and require a yes or no answer."

Robert nodded.

"Are you a mole?"

"No."

"Truth."

"Did you come here to gather information about us?"

"No."

"Truth."

"Would you ever consider selling information about us to gain access to the Brotherhood or for any other reason or purpose?"

"I'm not that stupid."

"I need a yes or no answer."

"No, I would never disclose any information about you or your clan for any reason you can think of. I'm not a mad dog. I wouldn't bite the hand that feeds me."

"Truth."

Kian clapped his hands on his thighs. "Okay then. He pushed up to his feet and waited for Robert to do the same. "Welcome to the clan, Robert." He offered his hand.

"That's it? No more questions?" Robert asked as they shook on it.

"I don't have time now. But later we will discuss what job you can take on. You're not completely free yet. There is a probation period during which you'll be wearing a locator cuff and will be restricted to the keep, but you no longer need to stay here. I'll have Ingrid find you an apartment upstairs."

"Thank you." Robert shook Kian's hand again, then shook Andrew's. "And you too, Andrew. I appreciate you coming here to help me out."

"You're welcome, but I did it for this guy, not you." Andrew pointed at Kian. "Now, if my services are no longer needed, I would like to bid you farewell and go up to my fiancée who I haven't seen since morning, and who is waiting for me impatiently."

Kian offered Andrew his hand. "Thank you, as always, invaluable." He slapped Andrew's back.

"What do we do now?" Carol asked.

"You wait here for William, who is going to bring the cuff, and then for Ingrid to show you to your new place."

"Thank you." Carol gave Kian a quick hug and then hugged Andrew. "You too."

"No problem." Andrew kissed her cheek, belatedly remembering that immortals were funny about other males touching their mates, him included. He glanced at Robert, but the guy was either too relieved at the moment to notice or didn't share that affliction.

39

ANANDUR

The wait was nerve-wracking.

The human team was spread out, hiding in several strategic locations around the harbor and waiting for the customers and their purchased human cargo to disembark.

Until the yacht left the harbor again and their part in the mission began, Onegus and Anandur were stuck waiting in their hotel room.

For lack of more productive things to do, Anandur watched the live feed from the drone following the yacht. At least he would know exactly when it docked. The big question was the time of departure. Tonight or next morning, and if it stayed overnight, would Lana attempt to contact him?

Anandur could only imagine how betrayed the crew must feel. They'd been expecting a rescue by now. Lana was probably cussing him out, using every Russian curse known to man. With a sigh, he glanced at the laptop screen again.

A moment later, Onegus stood up. "I'm going to take a nap. Wake me up in an hour, and then you go. Watching that thing serves no purpose. The yacht is not going to move any faster. In fact, there is no reason for you to stay up either. Kian or William are going to call us when the boat finally docks."

"What if they think the same thing?"

Onegus lifted a brow. "Kian? William? I don't think so."

With that his commander toed off his boots, lifted the comforter off one of the beds, and crawled in. Thirty seconds later, his breaths slowed and deepened.

Lucky bastard. Anandur wished it was that easy for him. He tried, but it was no use. Too anxious and too agitated, he couldn't sleep even though it was the second sleepless night in a row. Not a big deal. He could go without for another forty-eight hours and still subdue one fucking civilian without anyone's help. So why the hell was he so worried?

It made no sense.

Maybe it was a premonition? If Syssi got them, others could as well.

He was being ridiculous.

What was next? Calling the tarot hotline and asking for a reading?

When the call finally came, Anandur was still wide awake, while Onegus was sleeping like a baby and ignoring his cellphone.

Anandur grabbed it. "What's up?"

"Where is Onegus?" Kian asked.

"He is right here, snoring."

"Well, good for him. Just wanted to let you know the boat will be docking in about half an hour. You should get ready."

"Why? We need to wait until she leaves again."

"I want you to check on the girls immediately after Turner's team gets them, and do whatever you need to help them out. I don't want the girls waiting around for your return. The sooner they get home, the better."

"What if the yacht leaves while we are busy with the girls?"

"You'll still have plenty of time until she reaches international waters. Your pilot is ready to take off on a moment's notice."

"Okay. I'm going to wake Sleeping Beauty up and wait for Turner's team to report."

What Anandur really wanted to do was hoof it to the harbor and take part in the action, maybe get a word to Lana. But like an obedient soldier, he was following orders. Which in this case meant he wasn't going to do anything stupid.

More than two hours had passed by the time Javier called. "We got them. Four girls and three scumbags."

"Anyone hurt?"

"The fourth scumbag. Do you care?"

"No, not really. How are the girls taking it?"

"Hysterics. We locked them in one of the bedrooms, and we are awaiting your arrival. I hope you know what you're doing because those are four terrified little girls."

Anandur's blood froze in his veins. "What do you mean little girls?" he growled in a voice that could barely pass for human.

"Sixteen, maybe seventeen. I didn't ask. They shriek like banshees whenever anyone gets close."

"Son of a bitch," Onegus spat.

Too distraught to try and sound human, Anandur handed Onegus the phone. Little girls. He was going to kill Alex, slowly. There would be no trial for that dirtbag motherfucker.

"We'll be there in fifteen," he heard Onegus say

Anandur trained his eyes on Onegus, the twin projectors illuminating his commander's face. "I can run faster than that."

Onegus frowned. "You need to take a deep breath and calm the fuck down. I've never seen your eyes glow like that. Javier might be mistaken. Or he might have exaggerated to get a quick response from us. Sixteen or seventeen could easily be eighteen or twenty."

Not that it made much of a difference. An eighteen-year-old girl was still a child in Anandur's eyes, but the reality was that most girls that age were already sexually active, which made it just a little less atrocious. Not as far as the intentions of those men, but as to the girls' own perception of what had happened. Partying on a luxurious yacht, they had no idea what fate had been awaiting them.

Anandur stomped his feet into his boots, grabbed his wallet and his watch and headed for the door. "I'm waiting in the car," he called out to Onegus, who had rushed into the bathroom. As from this morning, their gear was stored in the helicopter, and they had nothing to take with them from the hotel.

A few minutes later his commander slid into the passenger seat of their rented car, and Anandur took off. By the grace of Lady Luck, they reached their destination without getting pulled over by the police.

There was a communal sigh of relief as they entered the living area of the small house, though audible only to their immortal ears. Each of the men had probably thought he was the only one glad to see them come in and do something about the four hysterical girls.

"Follow the sobs," Javier pointed to the second door off the hallway. "They think we are the bad guys, and that we murdered their boyfriends and are going to do inconceivable things to them."

Anandur wasn't surprised.

The girls had been under the impression that they were on vacation and going out with guys to party in Acapulco. Instead, they'd been attacked by a bunch of commandos, their so-called boyfriends subdued, and all of them taken to what looked like an abandoned shack.

The key was in the door, and as Onegus twisted it in the lock and depressed the handle, the shrieks got louder. When he pushed the door open, they found the four girls huddled in the corner like a pile of scared kittens.

"Look at me," Onegus said in a soft voice that nonetheless carried a tone of command. He was already working the thrall, pushing it as a gentle wave to induce calm.

A handy little trick Anandur would've loved to master. Unfortunately, his thrall was pitifully ineffective, especially on humans who had whipped themselves into a frenzy.

The shrieks stopped, and four pairs of red-rimmed, teary eyes looked up to Onegus.

He crouched, perhaps in an attempt to look less intimidating, and smiled. "You are safe, and you are going home to your families."

One gathered the courage to ask, "Who are you people? And why did you kidnap us?"

He pointed to the living room. "These men, the ones you are terrified of, rescued you from a horrific fate. The men you were with were not nice guys. They didn't mean you well. They purchased you from the yacht owner either for personal use or for resale."

"Oh, my God," one of the girls whimpered.

"What do you mean purchased us?" the brave one asked even though he saw understanding dawn in her eyes.

"We've been monitoring his activity for a while now. He tempts pretty girls like you to come on board and party, then sells them to sex-slavers."

She glanced at the shocked expressions of her friends and shook her head. "I can't believe we were that stupid. What were we thinking? We were on vacation in Cabos, a little getaway to celebrate the end of finals week, and this really handsome guy invited us to his yacht, and we thought nothing of it..."

Naturally, they had been under Alex's thrall.

The fact that these were college girls, not sixteen- or seventeen-year-olds, was a huge relief. Anandur thanked the merciful Fates.

"He drugged you. That's why you didn't question anything and followed him without thinking, and he kept drugging you while you were on board." Onegus gave them a plausible explanation. "Look around you. Do you have a purse with you? Luggage? Would you have followed these men you thought were your boyfriends without a purse, a phone, a passport, or some other form of identification?"

The girls exchanged glances, then shook their heads, the horrifying realization dawning on their young faces and leaching the color out of them.

The one who had done all the talking was the first one to bounce back. "So you're from the government? Like the FBI?"

Onegus shook his head. "We are a secret private organization dedicated to stopping this horrendous trade." Minute by minute, Onegus's calm tone was melting away the girls' anxiety.

Anandur watched the stress leave their faces. The leader who'd asked the questions even got up and sat on the bed, and then the other three joined her.

Onegus was doing a wonderful job, his gentle thrall unraveling Alex's and adding a hefty dose of reassurance.

"Here." He handed the leader a few sheets of paper and a pen. "Write your names and home addresses, and these guys out there will take you home."

She took the papers and handed them out. "Are you going to accompany us?" she asked hopefully.

"I wish I could, but we still need to apprehend the yacht owner and bring him to justice."

The girl smiled for the first time. "Good luck. And if you need me to testify against him, I'll be happy to."

"Thank you, we might call on you, but we probably won't need to. We already have enough evidence to put him away for eternity."

And wasn't that the truth—eternity having a whole different meaning in Alex's case.

40

LOSHAM

Nothing helped Losham's melancholy. Not the pretty girls, not their soft hands on his body, not even their gasps and their moans and their whimpers.

The only time he felt like doing anything at all was when he was plotting revenge. And the more he plotted, the more ambitious in scope his plotting became. His father, the exalted Navuh, would be very happy with him. For once, Losham's need for revenge aligned with Navuh's ultimate goal of world domination.

Losham had used to scoff at his father's grandiose ambitions, not to his face, naturally. Navuh wouldn't have executed him, he was too valuable, but a beating and prolonged torture were a given.

He often wondered if Sharim had inherited his deviant tastes from his grandfather. Navuh's private harem was inaccessible even to his sons, ensuring no one knew what went on in there. For all Losham knew, his father could've been even worse than Sharim.

Navuh's offspring hadn't been raised by their mothers. The five sons he'd fathered had been taken care of by nursemaids and tutors. The daughters had been given into the care and tutelage of the other Dormants.

To father dormant sons who could later transition into immortality, Navuh's private harem must've been comprised of immortal females, and not ordinary Dormants who had been turned by Navuh either, but the daughters of gods. Navuh's five sons possessed abilities almost as powerful as their father, which meant that they were of much purer blood than the rest of the men whose genetics had been diluted by generations of breeding with humans.

Losham would've loved to have known his mother. If she was still alive, that is, and hadn't been executed for displeasing his father in some fashion. Losham must've inherited his brilliant mind from her. Navuh was smart, but not nearly as smart as Losham.

Sitting in the antechamber to his father's reception hall, Losham glanced at the huge portrait of Navuh. His father cut an imposing figure, and it was on Losham's advice that he had it hung there and not in his private residence as had been his original intention.

Anyone cooling his heels in the waiting area was forced to look at the intimidating male who seemed to be staring at them from the canvas. Combined with the long wait, by the time they were admitted they were properly subdued.

Obviously the portrait had no effect on Losham, and he didn't mind sitting and waiting for hours until his father deigned to see him.

That form of humiliation didn't work on him either.

Navuh could pretend all he wanted that he was too busy for an audience with Losham, his top adviser, but Losham knew exactly what the despot was doing behind the imposing double doors.

Absolutely nothing.

Losham, on the other hand, had everything he needed to keep working while appearing inactive and resigned. The gears in his brain kept turning at an uncommon speed, while his memory ensured that none of his conclusions was ever forgotten. Everything was stored and organized in the appropriate compartments.

A side door opened and Navuh's secretary emerged, but he knew the guy hadn't come to escort him in. Losham hadn't been waiting long enough.

The secretary bowed his head. "His Excellency, Lord Navuh, is very busy today. He will see you as soon as he can." The man bowed again and scurried back through the side entrance to the reception room; the one dedicated for servant use.

Up until Sharim's untimely demise, Losham hadn't been interested in taking over the world of humans. There was no need, no real gain to be had, just a lot of headache and additional work. It was better to be the puppeteer and manipulate the human leaders to do the work for him.

History was abundant with various despots who had striven to achieve that goal, but even though some of them had commanded armies of hundreds of thousands of soldiers, ultimately they had all been defeated.

Contrary to popular belief, what humans referred to as good usually triumphed over what they referred to as evil.

What those despots had lacked, though, was an adviser as brilliant as Losham. He wasn't presumptuous, nor was his ego overinflated. He'd known most of those leaders and their closest lackeys personally. Some had been highly intelligent, but Losham was in a league of his own.

His biggest asset, though, something none of them had had the luxury of, was time.

He could plot and plan, then plot and plan again, setting things in motion, then sit back and wait to see his machinations come to fruition.

And that was his second biggest asset—patience.

An asset the great Navuh lacked.

That was why his father would not approve of Losham's plan unless he presented it with a slight variation: The estimated timeline.

Losham wanted Annani and her spawn gone, eradicated, and whatever they'd given the humans destroyed, annihilated.

It wasn't logical. He'd run through the scenarios of possible outcomes, and none of them were good. In fact, destroying Annani and humanity's technological and social achievements was detrimental to the Brotherhood's future. The new technology and global communication made life much easier, even for Doomers.

Destroying it served no other purpose than the need for revenge.

The side door opened and Navuh's secretary emerged, his robe flying behind him as he rushed over. "Our exalted leader will grant you an audience now, but Lord Navuh regrets to inform you that he can spare only ten minutes of his valuable time."

It was the same nonsense every time; a posturing Navuh apparently couldn't do without. Not even once had his father cut their meetings short. He was too smart not to listen to everything his best advisor had to say.

Instead of rolling his eyes, Losham assumed a respectful expression and bowed his head. "Our Lord's wishes must be obeyed. I'll keep it brief."

41

ANANDUR

"Ready?" Onegus asked, his voice coming out of the speaker inside Anandur's headset. The helicopter pilot had switched to silent mode almost immediately after takeoff, but it was still pretty noisy in the cabin.

They hadn't followed the boat until it became late enough for Alex to be asleep, and with international waters only twelve nautical miles or so from the coast, it meant that the *Anna* had passed that line hours ago.

The high altitude of the drone following it ensured that even immortal ears couldn't detect it by sound. The helicopter's silent mode, however, wasn't silent enough. If awake, Alex would hear it, and the mission would be compromised. The moment he realized that he was under attack, the jerk would use the crew as a shield.

Anandur didn't know the guy well, but anyone who could sell people into sexual slavery wouldn't hesitate to snap a woman's neck, which meant a long swim. The pilot was keeping the craft steady about three nautical miles away from the yacht.

Fortunately, the water was warm.

"Ready," he replied.

Onegus went first, rappelling down and jumping the few remaining feet into the water. Anandur went next. Given the mild temperature they'd decided to forgo wetsuits, which would've restricted their movements. Now that he was in the water, Anandur regretted not putting at least a sleeveless top on. The straps holding his equipment secured to his back chafed like a son of a bitch.

Onegus was a powerful swimmer, but so was Anandur, and it took discipline not to turn this into a competition. It reminded him of the trek up the mountain not so long ago, when Kian and Andrew had butted heads about Kian rushing ahead of the humans who couldn't keep up. Shockingly, Anandur had been the one to talk sense into those two. A lot had happened since. Funny how centuries could pass with nothing significant happening, not as far as the clan's future, that is, and then suddenly everything was changing at an unbelievable pace.

An hour later they caught up to the boat.

With practically no wind, and waters as calm as could be, they were banking on the captain engaging the autopilot and going to sleep. The boat's slow speed was a good indication that that was indeed the case.

The good news was that there were no lights in the common areas or the other rooms on this side of the yacht. Hopefully, both the crew and Alex were sleeping in their own beds and not having an orgy at his cabin.

Not a far-fetched scenario according to Amanda.

She'd been their main source of information about the crew and their habits as well as the yacht and its layout. After searching the boat from top to bottom, looking for the drugs she'd suspected Alex of smuggling, Amanda was well familiar with where everything was and who slept where and with whom.

Anandur unstrapped the grappling hook launcher and glanced at Onegus who had done the same. The hooks were going to make noise; there was no way around it. They had seconds to get to Alex before he grabbed a crewmember.

Onegus nodded and pointed his launcher up toward the railing. "On three. One. Two. Three." They shot at the same time, their hooks clunking noisily against the metal railing. Damn, unless the scumbag slept like a dead man, there was no way he hadn't heard that.

Anandur gripped the rope and climbed faster than a monkey, arriving a second ahead of Onegus. This time, he wasn't straining his muscles to the extreme in competition with his superior, and the prize wasn't satisfaction over winning. He was competing against time, and the prize was getting the crew out alive.

Their bare feet made hardly any noise as they ran toward Alex's cabin, arriving within seconds at his door. As planned Anandur burst in, while Onegus covered him with a throwing knife in each hand.

"Fuck, Alex isn't in his bed," Anandur gritted before running for the bathroom, his heart pounding in his chest not from exertion but fear. Alex must've grabbed whoever had been sleeping with him and dragged her in there.

But there was no one in the bathroom either.

Could he have slipped Turner's watch and stayed in Acapulco?

Alex could've done so easily if he'd suspected their presence, thralling whomever he'd bumped into to forget he'd ever seen him. He'd pulled a similar trick with the private investigator in Marina Del Rey.

"Not in the closet," Onegus said.

"Not in the bathroom either."

Damn, the possibility of Alex giving them the slip was gaining credence. Nevertheless, the safety of the crew demanded that they ascertained that Alex wasn't on board first.

"Fucking hell, I wish we could split up," Anandur said as they left the owner's suite. One could rush to Geneva's cabin on the upper deck, the other to the crew quarters on the lower deck. But assuming Alex had a gun, they needed to cover for one another. A bullet in the right place might give Alex enough time to either escape or deliver death with a blade. Working together, one of them could take the bullet while the other jumped Alex.

"Geneva first," Onegus said and broke into a sprint. It made sense. Her cabin was the closest.

Again, Onegus covered while Anandur burst through... and was greeted by a barrel of a gun. But it wasn't Alex who was pointing the thing at his heart. It was a blurry-eyed Captain Geneva. Sitting in bed and clasping the weapon with two steady hands, she meant business—provided her ancient Russian handgun would actually fire. The thing belonged in a museum.

"Put the gun down, Geneva. We can't find Alex. Is he on board?"

For a second or two, her eyes traveled the length of his mostly bare body, still wet and dripping water on the carpet, then shifted and gave Onegus the same once-over. She shook her head. "Anandur, you shit-head, we thought you weren't coming."

"I'll explain later. First, answer my question."

She waved the gun, and both he and Onegus instinctively ducked. "Of course he is here, where would he be?"

"You sure he didn't slip out and stay in Acapulco?"

"Pfft, if he did, then he is still swimming. He was here before I went to bed."

"Fuck, let's go, Onegus."

"Where are you going?" she called after them.

"We need to find him before he grabs one of the crew and uses her as a bargaining chip," Anandur answered while grabbing the handrail on the glass staircase and using it to swing himself to the level below, then repeating the same move to descend another level. Onegus was right there with him as they ran to the first crew cabin and burst through the door.

Two startled women jumped out of bed, and a moment later the rest of the crew rushed out into the hallway, gawking at the two half-naked, wet men.

"Anandur!" Lana called and threw herself into his arms, kissing him on both cheeks. "You came." Then she scowled. "Two days late!" and she delivered a slap that would've knocked out a human.

He caught her hand as she prepared to deliver another one. "You can beat me up later. First, we need to find the scumbag. He is either swimming toward shore or hiding here somewhere."

Light footsteps running down the stairs had everyone whip their heads around, but it was just the barefoot Geneva, still clutching her gun.

"You found him?" she asked.

"He is not here." Damn, they had a problem. If he was still on board, hiding somewhere, Alex could sneak up and grab one of the girls while Onegus and Anandur searched for him. And telling them to get into one room and lock the door wouldn't help either, not unless it was reinforced.

Anandur cast a glance at Onegus, who was probably thinking the same thing. "We need to call the chopper and have them airlifted."

Brilliant idea, but someone had to take the yacht back to the harbor, and neither he nor Onegus had ever driven a boat like this. Give him an oar, and he could row with the best of them, but this modern day behemoth was too complicated to figure out on his own.

Geneva snorted. "I'm not leaving. I'm the captain."

Anandur cocked a brow at Onegus. "What do you think?"

"That the chopper can take only five. I thought they could maybe squeeze together, but I think there would be a weight problem."

The Russians weren't small women. Tall and heavily muscled, they probably weighed the same as average-sized males—Marta possibly more.

"Okay, Geneva, you stay, but the three of us stick together, understood?"

Her lips forming a tight line, she nodded. "He is just one man," she said, but he heard the uncertainty in her voice. The woman was too smart not to notice Alex's peculiarities. She knew something was up with him, just not exactly what.

Onegus hailed the helicopter pilot and relayed the plan. The women would be taken to Acapulco and wait for Geneva to bring the boat back, hopefully with none of them hurt and Alex subdued.

The women got dressed and were ready to go faster than Anandur expected, and as the group emerged on the upper deck, the chopper was already hovering above with the rope dangling down and dragging over the wooden planks.

"Can you climb the rope, or do you need to be pulled?"

The women were athletic, but rope climbing required a lot of upper body strength. If they couldn't, he would have to go first and pull them up one by one, then go down again, which would leave Onegus and those waiting below exposed.

Lana harrumphed. "Watch." She jumped up and grabbed the rope high, letting it fall on the outside of her leg then stepping on it using the opposite foot to anchor it. Her weight distributed between her arms and her feet, she climbed at an admirable speed.

"Okay, I'm impressed, who's next?"

"I go." Renata jumped and caught the rope, climbing just as expertly as Lana had.

Sonia went next, then Kristina, and the last was Marta.

The women must've had military training. No mud-wrestlers learned to climb rope like that. For the first time, doubt drifted through Anandur's mind, and he questioned the whole mud-wrestling tale.

They should've checked the Russians' story. He couldn't believe no one had thought to do so. Except, what reason could the women have to lie? It wasn't as if the profession of mud-wrestling prostitution was such an honor badge.

"We should check the closet," Geneva said as the helicopter took off.

"I did," Onegus said.

"Did you check behind the fake panels?"

"No. But don't you need to close them from the outside?"

She shrugged. "I don't know if he is hiding in there, and if he is how he managed to close the panels from the inside. But if it were me, I would've used the best hiding place on this ship. Don't forget that he thinks the crew is loyal to him and will not rat him out. Unless someone knows there is a hidden compartment behind the false wall, no one would think to check there."

Good point.

Onegus turned on his heel and headed for the stairs, with Geneva following close behind him.

Anandur caught her arm to get her attention. "We go in there together, but if I tell you to get out, you don't wait even a split second to do so. The thing we fear the most is Alex grabbing a hostage. If he is in there, Onegus and I can handle him, but I don't want you to become collateral damage. Understood?"

She nodded.

"I want to hear you say it, and for the love of your God, don't try to be a hero."

She cast him a quizzical glance. "I'll get out of the way. You have my word."

"Good." He clapped her on the shoulder.

The ridiculously large walk-in closet housed the equivalent of a clothing store, and none of the items were from Wal-Mart like Anandur's. He wasn't familiar with the cost of men's high fashion but estimated that tens of thousands of dollars had been spent on this wardrobe. Maybe even more. Such a waste.

He pointed Geneva to a safe corner, far from the entry door, where no one could grab her from behind without going through Onegus and him first. Then the two of them pushed the clothing aside to clear a wide section of the back wall.

Alex's scent was all over the place, but it didn't mean he was on the other side of these panels. The scent lingered on his clothes, even the laundered and dry-cleaned stuff.

Examining the seams between the panels, they didn't find any that looked uneven or warped. Maybe Alex had used one of the panels closer to the side walls, not the center ones.

With that in mind, Anandur pushed the clothes back to the middle and away from one side, but these panels also looked undisturbed. Maybe they should stop pussyfooting and just pry them out and see whether he was there or not.

Onegus started clearing the other side, when Anandur heard the unmistakable sound of a gun being cocked. He leaped at Onegus to get him out of the way, but he was a split second too late. The bullet tore through the fabric paneling and into Onegus's chest.

As the commander hit the floor, Anandur shouted to Geneva, "Get down!" and dropped over Onegus to shield his body from the volley of bullets that followed, spraying the closet. Some went into the walls; others ricocheted off the harder surfaces.

A moment later the fake wall exploded, and Alex leaped out, holding a gun in each hand and shooting straight ahead to clear the way. In another split second, he would realize that his targets were down on the floor and then it was game over.

Anandur did the only thing he could to turn the barrels away from Geneva. He grabbed Alex's legs and pulled, toppling the scumbag to the ground. What he hadn't expected was the guy's quick reflexes.

Alex turned mid-air, landing on his ass instead of his face, and pointed the gun at Anandur's head with an evil smirk and a glint in his beady eyes.

Damn, it was going to hurt. But if Anandur moved out of the way, the scumbag was going to shoot Onegus.

Alex must've realized Anandur's dilemma, taking a second to gloat before pulling the trigger. That second was his downfall.

A shot that was louder than all of those that had come before it was fired from behind, hitting Alex in the back of his skull. He dropped, his head hitting the floor.

Geneva lowered her gun and closed her eyes. "I'm sorry I killed him, but it was either him or you."

"Thank you for saving my ass, but he is not dead. Yet."

He should probably thrall her now.

She frowned and walked closer, placing two fingers where Alex's pulse was supposed to be. "He is dead. What about your friend?" Voice calm, Geneva was all business. Who was she? What was she? No civilian would act that casually after killing a man.

"Not dead. Just injured."

To prove him right, Onegus groaned and turned on his back, clutching his chest. "Son of a bitch, that hurts."

"He needs a doctor. Call the helicopter back."

Fuck, he needed to think fast. Amanda had said the Russians were so guarded that they were difficult to thrall unless they were drunk. Anandur had trouble thralling even a willing subject, let alone a resistant one.

Onegus could probably handle her, but he was in no shape to do anything other than lie on his back and moan in pain until his body repaired the damage, which would take another ten minutes or so. Alex's head injury would take longer, but Anandur still needed to cuff him as soon as possible, and it would be damn hard to explain why he was putting handcuffs on a dead man.

"Geneva, there are things you don't understand, and I can't explain. What I need you to do is go up and change course to bring this boat back to Acapulco."

"What about them?"

"Leave them to me. I know what I'm doing."

Geneva pinned him with a hard stare then shrugged. "No problem. I don't need to know." She turned around and walked out of the closet. "The less I know, the better," he heard her murmur as she left the cabin.

Definitely ex-military. Or maybe the KGB?

Anandur pulled a pair of reinforced handcuffs from one of the many compartments in his waterproof equipment belt and cuffed Alex's hands behind his back. He grimaced as he checked the injury. It was a nasty one, shredding part of the skull and doing a number on the inside, but the bullet had already been pushed out, which meant healing was progressing well.

Onegus sat up and caught the bullet as it fell out of his chest, then put it in his belt. "A souvenir." Holding a hand over his injury, he pushed up to his feet and headed for the bathroom. "I'm going to wash up. Can you find me something to wear?" He waved a hand at the racks upon racks of clothing.

"Sure, any preferences? Italian couture, French?"

"Surprise me."

"Yes, dear."

After securing Alex's ankles with another pair of handcuffs, Anandur pulled a couple of T-shirts, jeans for Onegus and pajama bottoms for himself and joined the chief Guardian in the bathroom.

The guy had done the smart thing, taking a quick shower and washing off not only the blood from his chest but the ocean water as well. Anandur handed Onegus the clothes and jumped in the shower for a quick wash down of his own.

It felt good to pull on clothes over a clean body.

Grabbing several washcloths, he dipped them in warm water, then went back to the closet where he'd left Alex and cleaned the guy the best he could.

Onegus shook his head. "This scumbag doesn't deserve it."

"I know. I'm not doing it for him. I don't want Geneva and the others to see it. I still need to convince the astute captain that her shot wasn't fatal."

"Don't worry about it. I'll take care of her and the others."

"Good luck. You heard Amanda; the super-suspicious Russians are resistant to thralling."

Onegus flashed him one of his charming smiles. "You really think any female can resist this?" He pointed at his pretty-boy face.

42

KIAN

"How did it go?" Syssi asked Kian when he returned from collecting the crew's testimony.

The boat's crew, together with the two Guardians and the accused, had flown to Los Angeles the morning following Alex's capture. Kian had the women stay together in an apartment a few miles away from the keep. The building belonged to the clan, but it was only a rental asset owned by a subsidiary; no direct connection to the clan.

Taking Syssi by the hand, he led her to the couch and pulled her onto his lap. "Now everything is great." He nuzzled her neck. "I love coming home to you."

She smiled. "You're funny. You work from home and hardly ever leave the keep. It's me that comes home to you."

"Semantics." He kissed her softly, hoping she'd drop the subject and continue to more pleasant topics—the kind that didn't involve talking.

But his Syssi wasn't going to let it go until he told her everything she wanted to know. Better get it out of the way.

"So what did they say? Do you have what you need for the trial?" she probed again.

"We already have more than enough to convict Alex ten times over, but I took Edna with me to run a light probe on them."

She frowned. "Why? Did you think they would lie?"

"No, but Anandur got a little suspicious. He said that they didn't act like civilians during the mission. Too cool-headed and disciplined. At some point, they must've had military training."

"So?"

Kian rubbed a hand over his jaw. "They never mentioned it. Why tell Amanda about the mud-wrestling and the prostitution but not about military service?"

"Do you think they might be spies?"

"No, it doesn't add up, and Edna confirmed that other than their part in Alex's trade, she sensed no guilt in them. It seems that they are telling the truth about wanting a new life as legal aliens doing legal work. They might be deserters from the Russian army. That would be a better explanation than the mud-wrestling story."

Perhaps he was paranoid, but Kian was contemplating having Andrew ask the Russians a few questions. Just to make sure.

"You're right. Does it matter?"

"To us? No."

"Didn't they want citizenships, though?"

"They were happy enough with the alien status, and it sure as hell wasn't easy to pull off either."

The truth was that their testimony was superfluous at this point. Enough incriminating evidence had been collected by Turner's team, who'd questioned the four girls and the lowlifes who'd purchased them. But a deal was a deal, and Kian wanted to give the Russians what had been promised without them feeling like they hadn't earned it.

"When are they leaving for Hawaii?" Syssi asked.

"Tomorrow. Anandur is escorting them."

"I wish we could go," she said with a wistful look on her face.

Kian smoothed his palm over his wife's long hair, hating that he couldn't give her everything she wanted. He wouldn't have minded a tropical getaway with his beautiful Syssi, away from the keep and the clan and the responsibility that came with his job. But someone had to do it, and that someone was unfortunately him. Or fortunately, depending on who you asked. "We are going to Scotland soon. It's a mini vacation."

Syssi scrunched her nose. "I would love to see Scotland, but three days, including travel time and a wedding, is not enough to do any sightseeing. We'll probably never leave the castle grounds. But I'm excited about exploring it. Amanda says it's beautiful."

The truth was that he hadn't visited the Scottish keep in so many years he would probably have trouble recognizing it. Sari had been renovating the place extensively, one section at a time—specifically the windows and doors, plumbing and electrical systems, the bathrooms, and of course top of the line security measures.

"We will go to Hawaii some other time when things are less hectic here."

Syssi's face twisted in a grimace, but it only made her look cuter. "As if that is ever going to happen. If it does, we wouldn't know what to do with ourselves."

True. And how pathetic was that?

"It is what it is, love. Nothing I can do about it. Besides, you're busy too, especially now with Amanda gone."

Syssi sighed and rested her cheek on his chest. "I can't wait for her to get back to the lab. She makes running it look so effortless while it's anything but."

He rubbed her back. "If you need help, don't be shy and ask for it. Hannah is a capable girl. I'm sure she can ease your load."

"Not really. It's the juggling of university research and our own for the clan. And now we have William's game to integrate as well."

"Can I do anything to help?"

She lifted her head and kissed his lips. "That's so sweet of you to offer, but you'd be just as lost as I am. Amanda has been doing it for such a long time now that she doesn't need to stop and think before tackling every little issue."

Proud of his baby sister, Kian nodded. He knew she was a gifted teacher, but it was good to hear that she was also a great manager.

As Syssi cupped his cheek, running her thumb over his lips, Kian took it as a sign that the time for talking was over and pushed to his feet with Syssi in his arms.

"Are you sure I need to be present at the trial tomorrow?" she asked as he carried her to the bedroom.

He could understand her reluctance to participate. It would be difficult to hear the testimony and even more difficult to vote on the sentence, but he was going to ask for the most severe one they had, entombment, and a unanimous vote was needed. Local clan members would be present physically, and those abroad would vote virtually.

"I'm sorry, sweetheart, but there is no way around it."

She pouted. "Can't you give me special dispensation? Aren't you the boss?"

So now he was the boss. Funny.

Outside of the bedroom, he found himself saying 'yes, dear' more often than not, which was fine by him. Whatever made his Syssi happy, he was more than glad to oblige. She loved submitting to him sexually, but she also loved that he never argued with her over anything. Whatever she wanted, however she wanted it, she got it.

As long as it was up to him, it was hers.

There had been only one point of disagreement between them about what she'd considered extravagant gifts, but they had worked out a compromise. The next super-expensive piece of jewelry he'd buy her would be on their fifth wedding anniversary. In the meantime, she wanted gifts that were more about the heart than the wallet.

Problem was, he had no idea what she'd meant by that. Hopefully, not love poems or other crap like that because then he was screwed. Spending money was so much easier than coming up with ideas.

43

ANANDUR

"It's beautiful here." Lana threaded her arm through Anandur's as they strolled along the beach.

"Yes, it is." He hoped she wasn't attaching any romantic meaning to it. He'd merely wanted to say goodbye properly, not rekindle what had never been between them. He liked her, the sex had been awesome, but that was it.

He glanced at Amanda and Dalhu who were strolling a little ahead of Lana and him, leading the procession of those who wanted to see the sunset—which was everyone except Geneva.

They had their arms wrapped around each other, her hand lovingly stroking his back. Anandur couldn't help but compare their relationship to that of Kian and Syssi, or that of Andrew and Nathalie. The two other couples were so in love that the air between them sizzled, melting into rainbow-colored goo, not to mention their crazy rush to get married.

Not these two.

On the surface, both appeared more reserved, their expressions of love more subtle—like this little backrub Amanda was giving Dalhu. But whoever had been privy to what they had gone through to be together knew that only true love could've motivated two people to go to such extremes.

"Penny for your thoughts," Lana nudged him.

Considering that he was saying goodbye, he couldn't share his musings with her. Bringing up the subject of love was a bad idea. "I'm glad you like it here, and that you and your friends are getting along with the other trainees in the program."

It had been Amanda's idea to include the crew in the training the other women were going through in preparation for their jobs at the hotel. He'd thought she'd lost her mind and had told her as much. It was like putting an ex-rapist, even a reformed one, together with rape victims.

She'd dismissed his concerns.

The other women had been thralled to forget what had happened to them, and the Russians were too ashamed of their part in Alex's trade to ever bring it up. Just to make sure, though, he'd warned them against ever talking about it with anyone, reminding them that they could still go to jail for their part in the crime.

Lana and the others had sworn to take it to their graves.

Hopefully, that wouldn't be anytime soon. They had a new lease on life, and he wished them success in achieving their dreams.

"I hope you'll be happy here. Find a nice guy, start a family," he said, and then glanced at her almost fearfully, not wanting to see her hurt.

She nodded, looking thoughtful but not sad. "God willing. I always wanted children."

"Oh, yeah? How many?"

She pretended to think about it, looking up to the sky and holding a finger against her lips. "At least ten, maybe twelve."

"Seriously?"

She laughed. "No, but four is good."

"You know, raising good kids is not easy. Some grow up rotten despite your best efforts."

Like Alex.

His mother was a good person, and what he'd done had broken her heart. It had been difficult to watch her on the monitors, as she'd cast her vote. She'd looked so defeated, so devastated, crying inconsolably when he'd been taken to the catacombs.

Her pleading to make it merciful had convinced Edna to reduce the severity of the punishment. With the help of Brundar's venom, Alex had been put into his tomb already in stasis instead of suffering through many days until his consciousness faded. He didn't deserve the mercy. It had been granted to his mother.

One thing was sure; any wistful thoughts Anandur had ever entertained about becoming a father were gone. Even if one day the Fates smiled upon him and brought him his one true love, he wouldn't want children with her.

Lana shrugged. "There is a saying in Russian about people making plans and God laughing at them. It doesn't sound good in English. But you understand, yes?"

He nodded. "Shit happens all the time."

"And good things too. I want to say thank you, Anandur. I know you helped us to get information, but I also know what you give us is more than it was worth."

"You're welcome. But the thanks should go to my boss. He was the one who came up with the idea of letting you run the dinner cruises for the hotel."

"I know, and I said big thank you to Kian, and the others did too." She chuckled. "He didn't like the hugs and the kisses on the cheeks. Maybe we are not the type of women he likes?" she asked hesitantly.

Go figure women.

She didn't mind that Anandur had been using her to get incriminating information on Alex, but was hurt thinking Kian didn't find her or her friends attractive.

"Kian is a newlywed, and he has eyes only for his wife. You could've been the finalists in the Miss Universe competition, and he would've felt awkward about getting hugs and kisses from you. Besides, the guy is crazy jealous and hates it when any man even looks at his wife for more than a second. He would've exploded if some strange guy hugged her. So, naturally, he thinks the same is true for her."

Lana sighed. "So romantic. I hope I find a man who will love me like this."

Shit, now he was feeling like an ass. "I'm sorry that I can't be that guy."

She shook her head. "It was nice. Especially the sex…" She winked. "But I didn't feel butterflies in my belly when we were together or cry when you were away. It wasn't love."

"Hm, butterflies and crying. I'll file it under what to expect when falling in love."

A pair of pale blue eyes pinned him with a hard stare. "You laugh because you never loved a woman. When you do, you call me and say; Lana, you were right."

44

NATHALIE

"I'm starting to show," Nathalie groaned, observing her profile in the mirror. From the front the change wasn't noticeable, but from the side the bump was pretty obvious.

She smoothed her hand over her protruding middle. The seamstress was coming to do the final fitting, and she was willing to bet the dress was going to be too tight in the waist.

"Don't be silly, your belly is just as flat as it was before." Syssi waved a hand. "It's all in your head. You're a month and a few days pregnant. The baby is still smaller than an almond."

Syssi was kind, but the scale didn't lie. Nathalie had gained a pound and a half since last week. "My pants are starting to feel tight."

Syssi smirked. "You know, when they say that you should eat for two when pregnant, I don't think they mean it literally."

There was a knock on the door. She was expecting the dressmaker, but it was Bridget, her other bridesmaid. Syssi and Bridget were getting their final fittings too. Amanda, her third, had gotten her own dress, which was fine by Nathalie. She didn't want them to look the same anyway. They had agreed on a color, but each had chosen her own dress design.

"Hello, girls." Bridget entered the master bedroom and closed the door behind her. "Why the sad face, Nathalie?" She sat on the bed, watching Nathalie's reflection in the mirror.

"Just look at it," she said as she rubbed her middle again. "The whole rush was so I wouldn't show at my wedding."

"Pfft, it's probably gas."

Syssi gasped. "Bridget!"

"What? I'm a doctor. Intestinal gas is natural and nothing to be ashamed of."

Nathalie frowned, thinking about the burrito she'd had for lunch yesterday. Maybe she was bloated because of the beans? But what about the weight gain?

A muffled cellphone ring sounded somewhere in the room. Nathalie scanned for the source, but then remembered it was still in her purse. She'd rushed home to make it in time for the fitting and dropped her stuff on the dresser instead of pulling the phone out and charging it. The battery was probably in the red zone. It had been one of those days in the coffee shop, and her plans to leave early and avoid stressing over getting home on time had been thwarted.

Syssi tossed her the purse, but the ringing stopped. A few seconds later it resumed.

She pulled the phone out and glanced at the number.

It was Bhathian.

Her heart somersaulted in her rib cage. Did he have news about her mother? Had he found her?

That would be the best wedding present ever.

"Hello?"

"Nathalie." His voice sounded gruffer than usual, and her heart sank down to her gut. Bhathian didn't have good news.

"What happened?" she asked, choking on the words that left her constricted throat and went out of her dried-out mouth.

"Eva gave us the slip again. Someone else had been withdrawing money from her account."

"Can't you ask them if they know where she is?" What she meant was; thrall them to get her mother's whereabouts, even if whoever was doing the withdrawals was reluctant to share that information. There were all kinds of rules governing who could be thralled and who couldn't, but she was certain that these were extenuating circumstances.

"I did. Sister Juliana of the Casa de Martinho orphanage said that Eva donates her monthly salary to the orphanage and has been doing so for six years. They have a signed authorization."

Nathalie's legs felt wobbly, and she sat on the bed next to Bridget. "Maybe someone in the orphanage knows where she is?"

"I went there and asked. No one has any information about her."

She hesitated only a moment before asking, "Did you make sure they were telling the truth? I know they are nuns and all, but they might be protecting her anonymity."

"There was no deception. They really didn't know."

"So it's a dead end."

"I'm afraid so."

"Are you coming home?"

"I already have a plane ticket to Scotland. I'll stay until then and just hang around. Maybe the Fates will smile upon me."

She nodded. "The Fates already did. We found each other. Finding her has been a long shot. Don't let it get you down, Bhathian. We have plenty to be grateful for, and we shouldn't tempt fate by not showing our appreciation for the gifts we've been given."

He sighed. "I have such a smart daughter. You must've inherited it from your mother."

His words cheered her up a bit, and she smiled. "I love you too."

She heard him suck in a breath and realized it was the first time she'd told him she loved him.

"I love you, Nathalie. You've brought sunshine into my dreary life."

Tears stung the back of her eyes. Papi used to call her his sunshine too. She was so fortunate to have two fathers who loved her.

"I guess I'll see you in Scotland?"

"You sure will."

"Goodbye, Bhathian." It had been on the tip of her tongue to call him Daddy, but it was too soon. She still felt like she would be betraying Papi.

"I'm so sorry." Bridget patted Nathalie's knee.

With their bat-like super hearing, they must've heard Bhathian's grim news as clearly as she had while holding the phone to her ear. There was no privacy with these people.

"Me too," Syssi said. "Do you want a glass of water?"

"Yes, please." Her mouth felt so dry that her tongue was sticking to its roof and her words were coming out slurred.

Syssi left and a moment later came back with a tall glass of water. She handed it to Nathalie. "The seamstress is here. Should I let her in? Or do you need a moment?"

Nathalie gulped half the glass on a oner and hiccupped. "Sorry about that. Let her in. There is nothing like trying on a beautiful dress to chase a bad mood away."

Bridget high-fived her. "When the going gets tough, the tough try on clothes. In my case it's shoes."

The dress was gorgeous, and her new plump breasts looked amazing in it. Question was, whether the snug waist would fit.

It did, but the seamstress had pulled the zipper up with difficulty.

Nathalie groaned, her belly muscles straining the seams to bursting. "I knew it. It's too tight."

The damn tears she'd barely managed to contain after Bhathian's call were threatening to spill out. Her mother was not going to be at her wedding, and now she was also too fat for her dress. In a week, she was going to have a protruding belly, and her dreams of a white wedding would be crushed.

It wasn't about hiding her pregnancy.

She didn't care if the whole clan knew she and Andrew were expecting. It was about a silly girl's dream of wearing a beautiful princess-style dress with big fluffy skirts and a tiny waist.

"It looks great," Syssi said.

"Yeah, but in a week's time I might not be able to squeeze into it at all."

The seamstress, Mrs. Bella Shultz, shook her head and pushed her horn-rimmed glasses higher on her nose. "You need to be comfortable at your own wedding and not squeezed like a sausage. I'm going to let it out a little, but this is the last modification." She pointed a finger at Nathalie. "I'll bring the dress tomorrow. You'd better watch what you're eating until the wedding. No beans, no cabbage, no cauliflower, not even bread. Anything that causes bloating is out."

Bossy old lady, but she was right. From now and until she walked down the aisle, Nathalie would be eating salads with no dressing and dry chicken breasts.

Yum...

45

ANDREW

*E*xhausted after the long flight from Los Angeles to Edinburgh, Nathalie had fallen asleep as soon as they'd gotten comfortable in the limousine. At first the drive had been smooth, but as they neared the castle it had gotten bumpier, jolting Nathalie's head, which was resting on Andrew's shoulder.

If not for Syssi's irrational fear of a helicopter ride, they could've already been at Sari's keep. Frankly, though, he was grateful. Andrew hated the damn things. Then again, he hadn't ridden in one since his transition so his weird reaction to helicopter takeoffs and landings might be a thing of the past.

He'd test it some other time.

Syssi hadn't been too happy about flying in the clan's private jet either, but Kian had managed to convince her that it was just as safe as a commercial airliner. He must've believed that because Andrew would've known if he'd lied, but the truth was that flying in style was riskier.

The small planes weren't as safe. Still, he'd chosen not to say anything, and neither had Brundar or Anandur. They either didn't know or had preferred to keep quiet.

"I can't believe the old man is still sleeping," Anandur whispered from Andrew's other side.

Nathalie had been worried when Fernando hadn't woken up throughout the entire flight. She'd stayed awake to watch over him, checking every few minutes if he was still breathing.

"The sedative Bridget gave him knocked him out. It was a relief to see him wake up when we landed, even though he went back to sleep as soon as we got into the limo."

"It's a damn shame we only get to stay a few days. Most everyone is already there, partying and drinking." Anandur leaned away, giving Andrew a little more room.

Andrew adjusted Nathalie, so she rested more comfortably against him.

"Kian can't leave the keep for longer than that. As it is, I don't know how he has the guts to entrust its safety to the human security team. It makes me uncomfortable as hell."

Anandur chuckled. "Safety is an issue for him when he has to protect people, not things. And all of our people are here."

"True."

"I heard the guys in the office threw a surprise bachelor party for you."

"It wasn't anything fancy. Just pizzas and beers at Barney's."

Anandur leaned in close and whispered, "What about the strippers?"

"There were none. To the horny bastards' great disappointment, Barney refused to allow strippers at the bar." Andrew could just imagine the tantrum his fiancée would have thrown if there had been naked women at his party.

"That's a shame." Anandur leaned back and crossed his arms over his chest.

Absentmindedly, Andrew wrapped one long strand of Nathalie's dark chestnut hair around his finger, then let it spring back and uncoil. Beautiful hair. Beautiful woman. She was going to be a magnificent bride.

He'd stolen a glimpse of her wedding dress when the seamstress had dropped it off. It was a huge fluffy number with endless petticoats, lace, and little pearls sewn all over. Nathalie had refused to let him see her in the dress before the wedding because according to some stupid superstition, it was bad luck.

Andrew wondered at her convoluted logic. She'd come to every fitting he'd had for his new custom-tailored tux, and that had somehow been okay. No bad luck involved.

Damn, his back itched, and he couldn't scratch it without disturbing Nathalie. "How much longer?" he whispered.

"Almost there," Anandur answered.

It seemed like they were climbing higher and higher up the mountains, the serpentine Highland road dangerously too narrow for the large limousine taking them up to the castle. It was dark, there were no lights on the road, not even the headlights of other cars, and the asphalt hadn't been fixed in a long time, probably since it had been first laid. The road was so full of potholes that it was a wonder Nathalie could sleep so soundly, or that Kian could type away on his laptop.

Syssi was reading a book, her glowing eyes providing the illumination. Must've been an exciting story. It was just too weird. He was still getting used to the various quirks of their new physiology.

The limo made another sharp turn, and he had to brace himself not to slide over into Anandur. If he were still human, Andrew would've been anxious. But the limo's driver was an immortal, and his eyesight and reflexes were just as exceptional as Andrew's, probably better. He was in total control of the vehicle.

A few minutes later the road ended in a short bridge. Across from it loomed the castle walls, but the massive gate had been left open and the limo glided by, going through the inner wall gate and into the castle grounds proper.

The sprawling stone building was surrounded by grassy lawns and flowerbeds. Andrew was impressed. Unless those Scottish immortals had thralled some human gardeners to take care of their greenery, they must've been into horticulture.

He kissed Nathalie's forehead. "We are here, baby. It's time to wake up."

She lifted her head and looked out the window.

Illuminated by a clear moon, the castle and its gardens must've been clearly visible even to Nathalie's human eyes, but she didn't say anything. Was she still sleepy?

"What do you think?" he asked.

"That I'm dreaming. It looks like something out of a fairy tale."

Andrew chuckled. "I don't know about that. I always imagined fairy-tale castles as gloomy and imposing. This one looks inviting." Only three stories high, not including the attic or the basement he was sure a building this old had, it was wide but not tall. The windows must've been new because they were large and ornate.

Several people spilled out the front doors and rushed to greet them. He must've met all of them at Syssi's wedding, but he only remembered Kian's other sisters, Sari and Alena, and a few of the Guardians who'd come back to help with Carol's rescue.

Lots of hugs and kisses and a few happy tears later, they were escorted to their rooms and left alone to freshen up. Nathalie's father was in a room across the hall, close but with no shared wall, thank you very much. Although with how thick the walls were in this old stone structure, the soundproofing between rooms was probably damn good.

"Look at this bed." Nathalie walked over to the monstrosity that had stepping stools on both sides to climb onto it. "Why do you think they made it so tall?"

Andrew shrugged. "It's Scotland. It gets really cold here in the winter. Maybe the further it is up from the floor the less drafty it gets."

"I don't think so. Not with this fireplace. You can stand inside it."

Just for the fun of it, he did, then peeked inside to see if it was the genuine article or a modern imitation. It was the real thing.

He walked back and took Nathalie's hand. "Come on, baby, let's freshen up. They are waiting for us with dinner."

Andrew would've gladly skipped the meal and jumped into the inviting bed for a quick romp with his beautiful bride, cuddling with her under the ultra-thick comforter and sleeping for a few hours.

But he couldn't be rude to the people who had organized his wedding and had also paid for it. He'd argued that he wanted to cover at least part of it, but Kian wouldn't hear of it. When Andrew had asked for Sari's phone number, Kian had refused to do that either.

The fight over who would foot the bill hadn't ended there. When Andrew had called his parents, his dad had thrown a fit over it as well. He'd said that he was happy that his two children had found the loves of their lives, but he'd insisted that he wanted to pay for the wedding. At least one of them.

He'd even demanded to talk to Kian.

His dad's efforts had been just as ineffective as Andrew's. There was no reasoning with his stubborn brother-in-law. His father had even threatened not to come to the wedding, but Kian had called his bluff.

Tomorrow, when his parents arrived, Andrew would have to smooth things over between his dad and Kian, or the two stubborn mules would keep arguing and upset Nathalie.

He wasn't going to let it happen.

She would have her princess-in-a-castle dream wedding, and nothing was going to tarnish her day.

With a sigh, he opened the door to the adjacent bathroom, and his jaw dropped. "Nathalie, you have to see this."

She pushed by him. "Wow. This is like something straight from a fairy tale."

Someone had gone all out with that bathroom. Whimsical murals adorned the walls and the ceiling, ornate porcelain legs supported the bathtub and the vanities, and everything that could've been possibly gilded was. Gilded mirrors, gilded faucets shaped like swan necks, and gilded towel holders: A Disneyland-style, fairy princess bathroom.

"Do you think they did it for us?" The tired look gone from her face, Nathalie's eyes sparkled with excitement.

"Kian mentioned that they were renovating the castle a section at a time. Perhaps they did this one after hearing your wish for a princess-style wedding."

Nathalie turned in a circle and laughed. "That's why Sari was so eager to escort us to our room. I was wondering why she was so bubbly, but I assumed she was the easily excitable type, which didn't really make sense. Her job here is the same as Kian's in Los Angeles. You need a level head to hold a position like this."

The gesture was so over the top that he didn't know how to react. What do you say to someone who has done so much for you?

A thank-you just wasn't enough.

Nathalie seemed to ponder the same problem. "How are we going to thank her for this?"

Giving Sari his firstborn was out of the question but… "Maybe we can name our daughter after her? Just the middle name, that is."

Nathalie smiled. "I like it. Sari. It's a unique name. It sounds exotic."

Andrew grimaced. "It sounds like an Indian dress."

"What if we spell it differently?"

"We could, but I still vote for saving it for the middle name."

An idea had been brewing in Andrew's mind for the past week, but he was waiting for the right time to approach Nathalie about it.

His hand reached for the pendant he was wearing under his shirt. He'd picked it up from the jeweler the morning of their flight and hadn't shown it to Nathalie yet.

Andrew didn't feel like it was a proper substitute for the tattoo that he'd carried on his body. The white gold pendant, hanging from a thin chain around his neck, was just a piece of jewelry, not a memorial for his friends.

But if he named his daughter Phoenix, Andrew would not only pay tribute to their memory, but in some small way invite them to share in his legacy. His immortal daughter would carry their unit's symbol into eternity.

He hoped Nathalie wouldn't object.

A disturbing thought must've crossed her mind because Nathalie's smile wilted. "We shouldn't talk about names until the baby is born. It's bad luck," she whispered.

Andrew gathered her into his arms. "When did you become so superstitious?

First the dress that I wasn't allowed to see, and now this baby naming thing. Is it something new?"

She nodded into his chest.

"Why?"

"Because I'm scared. I feel like I've been too lucky and my luck is about to run out. I have all I've ever dreamed of, and I'm afraid of losing it." Her words came out in a shaky whisper.

Wrapping his arms tighter around her, Andrew kissed the top of her head. The truth was that he had no words of reassurance for Nathalie because he'd often felt the same. As if happiness was a rare commodity, a finite resource, and if you had a lot of it, fate or God or the universe wouldn't let you keep that much for yourself. Some would be taken away.

Instead, he said the only thing that was the honest truth and was hers to keep forever. "I love you, Nathalie. And I always will."

46

NATHALIE

Nathalie's full bladder demanded her attention, waking her up far too early for someone who was supposed to still be jet-lagged. She wanted to stay cuddled with Andrew under the blankets, but it refused to be denied. Seven or eight weeks pregnant, and she was already suffering every imaginable symptom.

Was it because she was older?

Thirty wasn't that old for having her first baby. Women were starting families at an older age now. Heck, her own mother had been forty-five when she'd gotten pregnant with her. But like everything else in Nathalie's life, it seemed nothing ever came easy.

Which reminded her that Andrew's parents were due to arrive. Beside her Andrew was snoring lightly, looking calm and content as can be, while she felt like throwing up, and it had nothing to do with morning sickness.

Nathalie was a nervous wreck, but it wasn't marrying Andrew that had her panties in a wad, or even imagining walking down the aisle with hundreds of people watching; it was the prospect of meeting Andrew's mother.

God, how she wished she could indulge in a glass of wine or two to calm the jitters. If everything had gone according to schedule, Andrew's parents had arrived at the airport about half an hour ago, and the helicopter sent to pick them up would be landing at the keep shortly.

Just great. The dreaded first meeting with her future mother-in-law had to occur the morning of the wedding.

Dr. Anita Spivak, the accomplished and saintly pediatrician, intimidated the hell out of her, and that was even before she'd met the woman face to face. Nathalie didn't know what was more impressive about Andrew's mother, the fact that she was a medical doctor, no small achievement by any standards, or that she was volunteering in Africa, a dangerous and unforgiving place.

She would be so unimpressed with her future daughter-in-law. A baker who didn't finish college and had gotten pregnant out of wedlock. What if Anita suspected Nathalie of doing so on purpose to entrap Andrew?

Ugh. She'd better take care of that bladder.

Barefoot, she padded to the bathroom and took care of that first, then debated whether to go back to bed or jump into the shower.

She was too strung up to fall asleep again.

Too much was going on.

As if the upcoming meeting with Andrew's parents weren't enough, Bhathian's connecting flight had been canceled. The last she'd heard from him, he'd said he was scrambling to find an alternative. Hopefully, he would make it on time to the wedding.

If not, she was going to make everyone wait.

As per Bridget's instructions, Nathalie didn't wash her hair. Appointing herself as Nathalie's stylist, Bridget was going to wash it later. Amanda had put herself in charge of her makeup, and Syssi was going to help with the dress and whatever else was needed.

Wrapped in a thick towel, Nathalie went back and nudged Andrew, feeling a little guilty about waking him up after only a few hours of sleep. "Andrew, wake up, baby, we have tons of things to do."

His lips lifted in a smile. Opening his eyes, Andrew moved with that new unnatural swiftness she was starting to get used to. In a second, her towel was gone, and she found herself under his big, warm body, his morning erection poised at her entrance.

"Good morning, gorgeous." Andrew buried his nose in the hollow between her neck and her shoulder. "You smell so good." He kissed the soft spot then nipped it, sending shivers straight down to her center. Any other morning, she would have loved to continue their play, but not today. She was too stressed.

"We can't, Andrew. Your parents will be here any minute now, and you're still in bed. You need to get up."

He swiveled his hips, the tip of his shaft sliding against her wet entry. Damn, even when stressed out of her mind, the man never failed to turn her on.

"How about a little quickie? Two minutes. I promise."

Nathalie slapped his shoulder. "Save it for the wedding night, tiger. Now hop into the shower and get ready."

"Yes, ma'am." Andrew made a pouty face as he rolled off her, then pointed a finger at Nathalie. "I'm holding you to it, and I'm going to collect even if you are exhausted and fall asleep."

Nathalie climbed down the insanely tall bed and collected her towel from the floor. "I promise, I won't. And if I do, you have my permission to do wicked things to me while I'm out."

"Ooh, kinky, I like." He waggled his brows.

"Gross, if you ask me, but fine." She wrapped the towel around her body and headed for the closet. Andrew was still at the same spot she'd left him, no doubt ogling her ass. Incorrigible. But as always, he managed to make her feel better. "Get moving, Andrew, we don't have all day."

He was done in less than five minutes. If there was one thing that years of military service had taught Andrew, it was how to use time efficiently in the bathroom. She didn't want to know what else it had taught him. But as long as it had kept him alive she was grateful for it.

"Ready?" He clasped her hand.

"As ready as I'm going to be."

Andrew peered down at her face and frowned. "Why are you so anxious? You're not getting cold feet, are you? Because if you do, it's too late. I'm marrying you even if I have to do it caveman style." He pulled her along, his long legs quickly eating the distance between their room and the main staircase.

She had to strain her leg muscles to keep up. "Oh, yeah? And what's that? I've never heard of a caveman wedding."

"Because there is none. I'll throw you over my shoulder, proclaim in a loud voice, so every male in my tribe hears me, that you're mine, and carry you to my cave, where I tie you to whatever cavemen use for bedposts and have my wicked way with you."

If it were only that simple.

But then she wouldn't have her dream wedding.

She tugged on his hand to get his attention. "Slow down, Andrew. I can't walk that fast."

"I'm sorry, baby." He stopped and wrapped his arm around her waist. "You walk at whatever pace is comfortable for you, and I'll follow your lead."

"Thank you."

The helicopter pad was in the back, next to the stables and the barns and a large vegetable garden. Sari's people must've either striven for self-sufficiency or liked to keep busy with farm work.

It was a beautiful, cloudless morning, and the long walk was invigorating. Andrew kept his promise and didn't rush ahead, giving her plenty of time to look around. Whenever the doors of a barn or a stable were open, Nathalie peeked inside, curious to see the animals, but only a couple looked like they were used for that purpose; most housed a more modern form of transportation—cars.

At the helipad, they joined Syssi and Kian.

"I'm so excited." Syssi pulled Nathalie away from Andrew. "I can't wait for my parents to meet you. They are going to love you."

"You think so? Why? I'm no one special."

Syssi's eyelids peeled wide. "Are you kidding me? The girl who managed to put an end to Andrew's bachelor status? My mother is going to kiss both your hands and thank you."

That was nice to know. Apparently, any female would do, as long as she managed to drag Andrew to the altar. On the one hand, it was a relief to know that she didn't need to be anybody or prove anything to be accepted; on the other, it was an insult because she didn't need to be special or wonderful or anything other than someone with ovaries.

"Besides." Syssi leaned and whispered in her ear. "You're a knockout, and you can bake. A killer combination."

That was much better. Hopefully, Syssi's parents would share their daughter's opinion.

47

ANDREW

"You look beautiful, sweetheart." Andrew kissed Nathalie's cheek, careful not to dislodge the huge rollers Bridget was putting in her hair.

Nathalie made a face. "I look ridiculous, but thank you."

Andrew glanced around and chuckled. Their bedroom suite had been converted into a bridal command center, bustling with activity and saturated with estrogen.

He was definitely not invited, and his presence was tolerated with the understanding that he was just picking up his tuxedo and going to Kian and Syssi's suite—headquarters of the groom and his best men.

Kian had promised Cuban cigars, and the best Scottish whiskey money could buy. Great, but Andrew would rather have stayed with his bride and watched her getting ready.

Even with a helmet of rollers that made her look like an alien spacewoman, his Nathalie was stunningly beautiful. And to think she'd been worried his parents wouldn't like her. Who in their right mind wouldn't? She'd enchanted them by simply being herself.

She was perfect.

"Andrew, stop standing there like a doofus and move it." Syssi gave him a gentle shove.

"I don't get why I need to go. Kian stayed with you before the wedding, and you guys walked down the aisle together."

He'd caught a guilty look on Nathalie's face before Syssi shoved him again.

"I need to pick up something from my room. I'll be right back," Syssi called to the girls as she opened the door and walked out with him. "You shouldn't complain, Andrew. Nathalie just wants a traditional wedding."

He swung the tuxedo bag over his shoulder. "I was just teasing."

"Don't. Not today. She is too stressed. Bhathian called earlier."

"I know. He should arrive more or less on time."

"If everything goes well, he is scheduled to land in an hour. Which means he'll be here in two or more. I told Nathalie that forty-five minutes' delay is not a big deal, and that everyone would just spend more time schmoozing, but it didn't do any good. She is still stressing."

Andrew sighed. "This was supposed to be her dream wedding. I thought she would be floating on a cloud. I don't get why she can't relax and enjoy herself."

Syssi kissed his cheek. "Don't worry about it. Go and have fun with the guys. The girls and I will take care of Nathalie. We can't give her wine, but we will get her to loosen up with some goofing around."

"Can you videotape?"

She slapped his back. "Get out of here already."

"Didn't you need to get something from your room?"

"Nah, it was just an excuse to escort you out. See you at the altar, big brother."

Cigar smoke and male laughter greeted Andrew as he opened the door to Kian's suite. The guys were out on the balcony, but they had left the French doors open, and all the smoke was getting inside.

Sari was going to kill them for stinking up her castle.

"Andrew, my man, I have a cigar with your name on it," Kian waved him over. He hadn't been joking. A red bow was tied to the big-ass cigar, with his name printed on it.

"A bit much? Wouldn't you say?" He took the cigar and the cutter Kian was handing him. Andrew had asked the guys not to throw him a bachelor party, and this was the compromise; a wedding day guys' get-together.

"Don't look at me. I sent this clown to buy them." Kian pointed at Anandur.

Anandur shrugged and took another swig from a bottle of whiskey. "Seemed like a good idea when the sales girl offered to personalize the cigars. Gave me more time to admire her bosom."

Arwel chucked an empty cigar wrapper at him. "I'm sure you did more than admire it."

Anandur huffed. "A gentleman doesn't tell."

"Too bad you're not a gentleman," Kian said.

Anandur arched a brow. "Have you ever seen me treating a lady with disrespect? Give me one example."

Kian frowned but came up with nothing.

"Aha, you can't. I'm a perfect gentleman." With a slight bow, he handed his bottle to Andrew. "And I'm even sharing my booze in a very gentlemanly manner."

Andrew pushed the hand with the bottle away. "Keep it. I'd rather have a beer."

The guys went silent as if he'd committed blasphemy.

"Beer? On your wedding day? Shame on you, Andrew," Arwel slurred, letting his thick Scottish accent take over, and handed him an unopened bottle of whiskey. "Don't drink it all. Your lovely bride will not be happy if you show up drunk." He finished his declaration with a burp.

48

NATHALIE

Nathalie's phone rang, but there was no way she could reach it. Her beautiful dress required careful maneuvering around furniture. Besides, her nail polish was still wet.

Syssi answered. "Bhathian. Are you calling from the airport?" He must've responded in the affirmative. "Great, we are waiting for you." She smiled at Nathalie and gave her the thumbs up. "No. No way. Nathalie won't let us start without you," she told him. Bhathian must've argued because Syssi kept shaking her head. "I can't give her the phone, she has wet nail polish on." Syssi rolled her eyes as she listened. "A suit is fine. Not everyone is wearing a tux."

From Syssi's side of the conversation, Nathalie surmised that Bhathian didn't have a tux. "Tell him he can come in jeans if he wants to. I don't care. As long as he is here for the ceremony nothing else matters."

Syssi smiled. "He says he loves you."

"Tell him I love him too."

Naturally, Syssi didn't have to say anything because he'd heard her. In this room, Nathalie was the only one who'd heard just half of the conversation. She would have to endure that, and other human limitations, for the next seven and a half months.

"He is going to be here in about an hour," Syssi said for her benefit.

"That's great. Just half an hour delay." Nathalie waved her hands in the air to speed up the nail polish drying and hardening. She hadn't planned on having her nails painted, preferring the natural look of a good manicure, but when Amanda got something into her head, there was no changing her mind. It was better to just go with it.

The second coat of nail polish and the topcoat were dry by the time Bhathian called to say he'd arrived and was downstairs waiting with everyone else.

Bridget and Amanda fussed with some last minute unnecessary touch-ups to

Nathalie's hair and makeup, while Syssi went to get Fernando, who'd spent the afternoon watching William and some of the local boys play video games.

Nathalie had been so worried about Papi's reaction to another new place and new people, but he surprised her with how well he was handling everything. If she hadn't known better, she would have thought he was improving. Sadly, the doctors had told her that dementia wasn't curable, and the best she could hope for was to slow its inevitable progression.

The door opened, and Papi walked in, looking debonair in his tuxedo.

His face lit up, and he clasped her hands. "My Nathalie! You are the most beautiful bride I've ever seen. You look like a princess."

A tear stung at the corner of her eye, but she was afraid to touch it and ruin Amanda's masterpiece. "Excuse me, Papi." She pulled her hand out of his grasp, grabbed a tissue, and gently dabbed at the tiny drop.

"Hey! No crying, girl!" Amanda waved a finger at her.

"I'm trying, but it's hard not to get emotional with all these crazy hormones floating around."

Amanda smiled wickedly. "You leave me no choice. I'll have to walk behind you and tell you annoying jokes. And if that doesn't work, I'll have to kick you. You can't get mushy while pissed."

Fernando frowned. "No one kicks my daughter."

Amanda smiled sweetly. "I was just joking, Fernando. I love Nathalie." She leaned in, as if to air kiss Nathalie's cheek, and whispered in her ear, "I'm so going to do it." Out loud she said, "Big smile, girl. Show Andrew and everyone else how happy you are to become his wife forever and ever."

Amanda might have meant it as a tease, but it had been exactly what Nathalie needed to hear. She and Andrew were getting married, and everything else, small or big, was inconsequential. Still, she was grateful that Papi was there, and that her biological father was there as well.

As the bunch of them spilled out of the bedroom, Nathalie glanced at the ornate, tall ceiling and couldn't believe she was getting married in a real castle.

The curving staircase was magnificent, but she wondered how she was going to manage the descent in her full dress. Real princesses and the actresses playing them must've trained for hours perfecting the skill of walking gracefully with their heads held high and not getting their feet tangled in their skirts.

"Girls?" She glanced at Amanda and then at Syssi.

They understood immediately, and each picked up a side, together with the countless petticoats under it. Luckily, the staircase was built on a grand scale. The three of them, including her dress, could stand side by side.

When the last step was behind her, Nathalie felt like she'd overcome the final obstacle. From now on, everything was going to be wonderful. The smile came naturally; a big grin everyone would see even from under her veil.

Amanda and Syssi let go of the skirts, and Papi took his place at her side. She threaded her arm through his, and together they waited a few moments for the bridesmaids to enter and join the groomsmen.

It was good Papi wasn't paying attention to the details because the ceremony was only loosely based on the traditional one. For starters, one of her bridesmaids was married, and then the three had entered together and not one at a time. The thing he was sure to notice, though, was that a woman was officiating. A glowing, otherworldly woman.

The first notes of *Here Comes the Bride* sounded from the pipe organ, and Nathalie patted her father's arm. "It's our cue, Papi, let's go."

As they entered, a hush fell over the assembled company. They advanced at an easy pace toward the altar, where Andrew was grinning from ear to ear and looking more handsome than ever.

You're stunning, he mouthed.

Nathalie grinned back, her eyes trained on her man to the exclusion of everyone else, including the small, glowing figure up at the altar.

"Look, Nathalie," her father whispered in awe. "An angel came to marry you. You two are blessed."

"Yes, we are, Papi."

49

ANDREW

"Good morning, Mrs. Spivak," Andrew said jokingly and kissed Nathalie's warm cheek. The pagan ceremony hadn't called for a name change, and he wasn't sure Nathalie wanted to take his even after the civil one. But it was fun to say.

Nathalie groaned and turned around, presenting him with her best asset. Poor girl. She'd been exhausted after the wedding and the reception, and he hadn't had the heart to hold her to her promise.

His Nathalie had gotten her dream wedding, and she'd had fun.

After discarding the petticoats that had been weighing her down and restricting her movements, she'd gotten comfortable and danced the night away. Toward the end, her feet had been so sore that he'd had to pick her up and carry her up to their room. Not that he hadn't planned to do so anyway.

Andrew would've let her sleep the day away, but people were leaving and wanted to say goodbye.

"I don't want to get up," she moaned. "Every muscle in my body hurts."

Damn, his plans for morning sex with his wife would have to wait. He pressed his erection to her luscious behind. "I'm sorry, sweetheart, but you have to."

"Why?"

"Because my parents are leaving and want to say goodbye, and so are Syssi and Kian and many others."

She turned back around. "Is anybody staying?"

Wrapping his arms around her, he cupped her butt cheeks and gave them a gentle squeeze. "Dalhu and Amanda are flying out tomorrow, and Bhathian the day after. I think that in three or four days we will be the only ones left."

She smiled a sleepy-eyed smile. "And we will be off on our honeymoon."

He kissed her soft lips. "What do you want to do first? Explore the countryside or stay in bed for a few days? I vote for staying in bed."

"I'm sorry about last night. I didn't keep my promise."

He rubbed her back. "You were exhausted. I would've been an asshole if I didn't let you sleep."

She sighed. "If I were immortal, I would've had the energy. But as a human, I can't keep up with you."

The last thing Andrew wanted was for Nathalie to feel less than perfect the morning after their wedding. "As an immortal, odds are you wouldn't have gotten pregnant. After the transition, fertility rate drops to an almost zero level. We've been given a precious gift. The extra wait is a small price to pay."

More than anything, Andrew hoped that he wouldn't be proven wrong. So many things could happen between now and then, but he refused to let worry spoil the moment.

"I know. I'm just tired and achy and envious. You are strong and healthy and gorgeous, and you're going to stay like that, while I am going to get fat and even more tired. It's unfair."

"What can I do to make it up to you?"

She shook her head. "Ignore me. I think I'm moody because I'm crashing from yesterday's high."

"I don't mean right now. For the next eight months. Is there anything I can do?"

"Just keep loving me and telling me I'm beautiful even when I look like a hippo."

"That goes without saying, and my princess is never going to look like a hippopotamus."

"An elephant?"

"You're going to look like a beautiful woman who is pregnant with my child."

That seemed to appease her, and a small smile bloomed on her face. "Is it true that men find pregnant women sexy?"

"I don't know about other men, but I find you incredibly sexy. You want me to prove it to you?" He pressed his erection against her belly.

Regrettably, he didn't get the response he wanted. Instead, Nathalie reached for his pendant. "It came out perfect."

"It's okay, but it's a poor substitute for the tattoo."

"What else can you do? Nothing will stay permanently on your fast-regenerating skin. Do you want me to get one?"

"A tattoo? No way."

She pouted. "Why not? I can have the experience and then it will fade away after the transition, same as yours."

"But that's exactly the point. It will fade, so why bother. I have a better idea, but only if you agree."

"Shoot."

Andrew hesitated. Nathalie would not refuse his request even if she didn't like it. If he thought she'd only agreed for his sake, he would scrap the idea himself. "What do you think about the name Phoenix?"

"For our daughter?"

He nodded.

"It's beautiful, but I told you that I don't want to name her until after she is born."

Andrew released the breath he'd been holding. Nathalie had spoken truthfully. She really thought the name was beautiful. "How about a list of potential names? Is that considered bad luck as well?"

Thinking it over, she first frowned and then shook her head. "I think it's okay. So we have two for the list; Sari and Phoenix."

"Phoenix and Sari. Sari would be on the list of middle names."

Nathalie snuggled closer and kissed his neck. "I think Phoenix is perfect, and it will definitely go to the top of the list."

"You are the best, my Nathalie." Andrew closed his eyes and gave a silent prayer of thanks for the gifts he'd been given.

First and foremost, for the gift of life—his human one. He'd been spared when so many hadn't. He hadn't expected to survive and yet he had. Same for immortality. He hadn't expected to come out alive on the other side, and yet here he was, healthy and strong.

But maybe he'd been given those gifts not because he'd wished for them or earned them, but because Nathalie had. She was so much more deserving than he.

It made perfect sense.

God or fate had entrusted Andrew with Nathalie's well-being, and he was going to spend his days and his nights making her happy, holding her, and loving her, for as long as they both lived. Which, hopefully, meant as close to eternity as it got.

The end... For now...

Ready for Eva & Bhathian's story?
COMING UP NEXT
Dark Guardian Trilogy

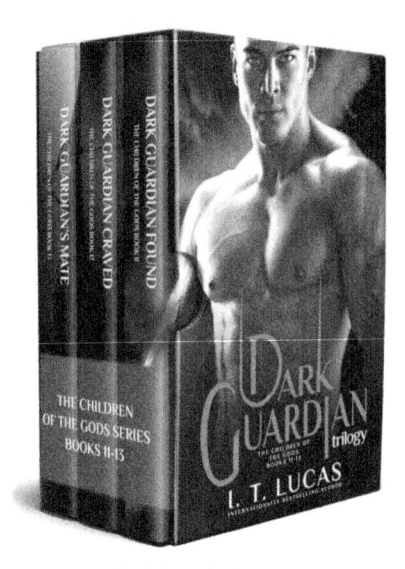

Read the enclosed excerpt

INCLUDES:
11: DARK GUARDIAN FOUND
12: DARK GUARDIAN CRAVED
13: DARK GUARDIAN'S MATE

Dear reader,

Thank you for reading the **Children of the Gods series.** If you enjoyed the story, I would be grateful if you could post a review for **Dark Warrior Tetralogy** on Amazon. (With a few words, you'll make me very happy. :-)

DARK GUARDIAN
EXCERPT

EVA

5 years ago
Bayshore Towers
Tampa, Florida

"Please don't cut me, I'll do anything, please…"

Eva sat bolt upright in bed, whipping her head around to look at the man sleeping next to her. Did he hear that?

A split second later the cobwebs of dreams dissipated, and she remembered who and what she was. Fifty years of living with that shit, and she was still waking up every morning thinking she was a normal human being and not a freak with supernatural senses.

No one aside from her could hear the pleading coming all the way from the other side of the corridor. Not unless they were in that same apartment with the bully and his terrified victim. The luxury building had excellent soundproofing between the residences, ensuring the privacy of its wealthy occupants—ordinary people couldn't hear a thing from the neighboring apartments. But Eva was as far from ordinary as it got. She'd learned to tune out most of the intruding sounds, like the guy snoring next door, but the urgency and distress in the girl's voice had managed to penetrate her shields.

The nearest article of clothing Eva could see was her one-night stand's dress shirt. Lifting it off the floor and shrugging it over her shoulders, she debated whether to wake Wilbert Whitmore the Third and tell him to call the police.

No time.

Not even to find her panties. They must be hiding somewhere under the bed.

A girl's life was on the line and every second counted. Besides, Eva could probably handle the situation on her own. After all, she was a trained DEA agent, and subduing some drunkard bastard shouldn't be too difficult. Never mind that the last time she'd had any training was thirty-something years ago. Hopefully, the moves she'd learned were still hardwired into her brain, and the muscle memory was still there. As to her level of fitness, she had nothing to worry about—along with the enhanced senses, her body had somehow mutated into a never-aging, fast-healing, efficient machine.

Saving the girl should be easy, but it needed to be done quickly. Eva was there on an assignment, and couldn't afford for Mr. Wilbert Whitmore the Third to start asking questions. She was supposed to be a random hookup, and not some superwoman playing hero and saving young girls from bullies. Ideally, the rescue would be done in a few minutes, and she could get back in bed, pretending that nothing had happened. There was a fat check waiting for her if she coaxed more details out of Wilbert about the business deal he was negotiating on behalf of his father.

A quick in and out. Scare the shit out of the guy, get the girl away, and that's it. Nothing overly ambitious or fancy.

Not bothering to fasten more than the minimum number of buttons necessary, Eva grabbed a candleholder from the coffee table, a container of mace spray from her purse, and a lock-pick set from a hidden compartment in her left boot.

Prepared to snoop around Wilbert's apartment, she'd brought the tools of her trade. Seducing him hadn't been part of her original plan, but one thing had led to another, and she'd ended up going home with him instead. It wasn't her normal mode of operation as a corporate spy—hooking up with her targets wasn't part of the deal—but the guy was single, decent-looking, and she hadn't been with a man in over a month. The decision had been easy. A sweet deal, actually. While charging her client extra for going above and beyond their original arrangement, she'd scratched a troublesome itch.

Wilbert had passed out too soon to satiate her hunger, but that was nothing new. Most men didn't. In fact, she could remember only two who had, and both of them had been jerks. Her record with men sucked, including her cheating, lying, ex-husband.

But at least none of them had been physically abusive. Not that Eva would've tolerated even a hint of violence.

As she rushed to the scene unfolding in the apartment down the hall, her footfalls almost soundless on the luxurious carpet, Eva was once again reminded that things like that were tragically common. When she'd first started her detective agency, she'd dealt mainly with gathering evidence on cheating spouses. Her clients hadn't been the downtrodden variety, and yet in some cases she'd discovered that spousal abuse happened behind their fancy closed doors. As evidenced by what was going on right there, in one of the most prestigious addresses in Tampa, violence and bullying existed in the most affluent of places, crossing lines of social standing, level of education, and financial means.

"You little bitch, I'll do whatever the fuck I want to you. I own you."

"Please, Marty, I beg you, I'll be good. I'll do anything you want, please!" The girl was sobbing hysterically.

With an efficiency born of years of practice, Eva picked the lock and dropped her toolkit on the floor before the guy finished his next sentence.

"Damn right, you will. Because I'm going to teach you a lesson you're never going to forget."

Eva didn't need X-ray vision to know that the psycho was about to cut the girl. Mace in one hand and candleholder in the other, she burst in and rushed toward him. The element of surprise worked to her advantage. Regrettably, the size of the room didn't. Even as fast as she was, she couldn't cross the distance fast enough.

Looming over the kneeling girl, her hair fisted in one meaty hand, a switchblade clutched in the other, the guy had his back to the door. But even though he was clearly high on something, his reflexes were intact. Still holding onto the girl's hair, he turned around and pointed the knife at Eva.

At the sight of his half-naked would-be attacker, the snarl twisting his lips transformed into an evil smile.

Idiot.

He had no idea who he was dealing with. To him, Eva was just another female he could easily terrorize.

Big mistake, mister.

Eva kicked the door, and it slammed shut behind her. There was no going back. She was committed to wiping that grin off the asshole's smug face.

Holding his gaze with a smile of her own, she closed the rest of the distance in one leap and brought her candleholder down on his wrist, sending the knife clattering to the floor. The idiot hadn't expected her to move so fast, and the surprise in his eyes quickly turned into a murderous rage. With another smile, she lifted the mace and sprayed.

Bellowing his pain and fury, the guy dropped the girl and clutched at his face.

"Run!" Eva commanded.

But the girl didn't move. As soon as the jerk had let go of her hair, she'd crumpled down to the floor.

Did she pass out?

Her face was badly bruised, and blood was oozing from a shallow cut on her cheek, but those were superficial injuries—not enough to cause loss of consciousness. Except, the bastard might have done more damage than that. If he'd kicked the girl, she might have internal bleeding or damaged organs. Broken ribs were also a possibility.

That complicated things.

Eva's plan had been to scare the guy and help the girl get away, but the situation had turned out more complex than the run-of-the-mill domestic violence case.

This wasn't a normal couple. Not that beating up and cutting a partner could ever qualify as normal.

It was more than that, though. The girl lying unconscious on the floor looked underage, and the guy was a brutal thug with a lot of money.

The thing was, the bastard didn't seem as out of it as Eva had initially suspected, and he didn't look scared either. In fifteen minutes or so, he'd get over the temporary loss of vision and give chase.

Already, he was trying to grab her, reaching for her blindly. "I'm going to fucking kill you, bitch. You can run all you want, but I'm going to find you, and

I'm going to cut you into tiny little pieces and send them one at a time to your family. And I'll do the same to that little bitch." He pointed at the girl on the floor.

An involuntary whimper betrayed the girl. Apparently, she wasn't passed out, just pretending to be.

Eva shuddered. The vehemence in his tone suggested those weren't empty threats. She wasn't afraid for herself, there was no way he could ever find her, but the girl was another story.

She would have to whisk her out of there and hide her. Make her disappear. The thing was, Eva needed more time than a fifteen-minute head start.

"Did you hear me?" The guy was practically foaming at the mouth. "I'm going to cut you up piece by piece, and I'm going to start with that little shit." He pointed at the floor. "While you watch. And then I'm going to do the same to you."

Eva wasn't the type to lose her temper, and her training had taught her to ignore taunting, but this one was pressing all her buttons. Every one of her suppressed motherly instincts was screaming at her to protect the young girl.

As the guy leaned forward, his hands grasping air while he tried to grab her, again, she glanced at the candleholder still clutched in her hand and, without giving it any thought, swung it full force, hitting the thug at the back of his skull. A sickening crashing sound followed, and he fell forward like a toppled tower and stayed down.

"Did you kill him?" the girl whispered.

"I don't know," Eva admitted. That hadn't been her intention—she'd only meant to knock him out to give them enough time to escape—she hadn't realized how much muscle she'd put behind that swing. Not that she was sorry to end the scum's life.

Not at all.

A monster like that didn't deserve to live and harm people just because he could.

The lack of remorse surprised her. Eva had never killed before, and taking a life should've shocked her. But it didn't. In fact, all she felt was enormous satisfaction. She'd just made the world a better place.

Later, she'd pray for God's forgiveness.

Crouching beside the prone body, she checked for a pulse.

There was none.

"He's dead." She glanced at the girl. "Are you sorry?"

The girl huffed out a breath. "The only thing I'm sorry for is that it wasn't me with that candleholder. I should've done something like that a long time ago, but I was too scared."

"I'm glad you didn't. He would've killed you."

The girl didn't look strong enough to lift the heavy candleholder, let alone swing it with deadly force.

An unnatural force.

Even in the hands of a strong man, the thing shouldn't have fractured the guy's skull.

"What do we do now?"

Good question. She could call the police and claim self-defense. Accidental manslaughter. The thing was, even if they believed her, which was doubtful, Eva couldn't afford the publicity a case like that would garner. All her careful planning and ingenious track-covering would be blown to hell.

No way.

She could disappear, but what about the girl?

"What's your name?" As partners in crime, they should at least get to know each other's names.

"Tessa." The girl got up on shaky legs and offered her hand.

"I'm Veronica." Eva chose one of the many different names she used.

"Thank you, Veronica. You should go. I'll say that I did it. I'm dead anyway." Tessa sounded like an old woman resigned to her fate, not a young girl with her entire life still ahead of her.

"What do you mean, you're dead anyway?"

"Martin is... he was a major drug dealer. Whoever takes his place in the organization will make sure to finish me off to teach the others a lesson."

Poor girl. She wasn't making any sense. Probably the trauma.

"Others? Like the other girlfriends or wives?"

"Slaves. Martin bought me."

Yep, definitely trauma. And if not, whatever the story was, this wasn't the time or place to discuss it.

"Get dressed. If you have a scarf and sunglasses to cover your bruises, wear them. Don't take anything. I'm getting you out of here."

The girl's shoulders slumped. "I have nowhere to go."

For some reason, Eva had been expecting that. Tessa had that lost, helpless and hopeless look about her. "Nonsense. I'm taking you home with me."

Tessa opened her mouth to say something, but then she shut it and ran to do as she was told.

Smart girl.

Eva grabbed a dishrag from the kitchen and wiped the candleholder clean, then repeated the process with the door handle. By the time she was done, Tessa had come back with a scarf wrapped around her head, hiding her bruises and cut cheek, and a pair of big sunglasses covering her swollen eyes.

"Follow me. Keep quiet as a mouse until I tell you it's okay to talk. Got it?" Eva said as she closed the door using the dishrag. She was going to keep the damn thing with her until she could burn it.

The girl nodded.

Back at Wilbert's place, Tessa waited by the door as Eva put the innocuous-looking candleholder on the coffee table.

As she left the girl on the couch to go retrieve her things from the bedroom, Eva had the passing thought that for years to come neither Wilbert nor his guests would suspect what that decorative piece had been used for.

Thankfully, Wilbert was a sound sleeper and didn't wake up as Eva gathered her stuff and tiptoed out.

She'd left him a souvenir, her panties that were lost somewhere under his bed, and a note with a phone number to call her. In order to collect her fat check, she still needed to get more details about the deal he was cooking. Wilbert would call, she had no doubt about it. He'd want a repeat of the mind-blowing sex.

This side gig as a rescuer, or perhaps vigilante, shouldn't affect her performance on the job. Eva's reputation as one of the best corporate detectives in the area was on the line.

The Present

"Tessa, have you confirmed my flight reservations and checked me in?" Eva asked more out of habit than necessity. Tessa was an excellent personal assistant—organized and methodical—and there was no way she'd forgotten.

Tessa's smile was part sweet and part indulgent. "Your first-class seat on Copa Airlines to Rio De Janeiro is confirmed. It leaves as scheduled at six forty-five."

"Thanks. You're the best." And so was her client who was footing the bill for the ticket and the luxury hotel.

The first time Eva had flown to Rio had been on an assignment for the same client, except it hadn't been about his business. The guy had hired Eva to spy on his much younger wife, whom he'd suspected of cheating on him while visiting her family. The client had been so relieved when Eva reported the woman innocent, that he'd paid her a nice bonus and had been using her services to spy on his business competitors ever since.

Eva owed him for introducing her to that lucrative niche market. The pay was much better, and no family drama. Win-win for Eva.

"You're welcome, and thank you for the compliment."

"It's well deserved. You're a life saver."

"Ditto."

Five years ago, when Eva had rescued her and taken her in, Tessa hadn't known how to use a computer: shocking for a sixteen-year-old, though understandable given her tragic circumstances. But she was smart and had caught up quickly, joining Eva's crews of misfits, as she liked to call her employees, slash tenants, slash adopted family. They could never replace her Nathalie, but to Eva, Sharon, Nick, and later Tessa meant much more than just people working in her detective agency.

She treated them as if they were her kids, which they thought was hilarious because Eva looked no older than twenty-five.

God, it was hard to believe she'd just celebrated her eightieth birthday—probably because most of the time she felt as young as she looked.

"You should start getting ready," Tessa said.

"I know."

"Here, I made you a list of things you need to pack. You always forget something." She handed Eva a printed page.

At the top of the list, the words PHONE CHARGER were typed in capital letters. Without fail, Eva always forgot to pack it and had to buy a new one at the airport.

"Did Sharon say when she'd be back?" Eva hated to leave without saying goodbye.

Tessa smirked. "She'll be here. Don't worry. She knows you want a hug before getting on a plane. And Nick is going to drive you to the airport."

"Good."

Instead of obsessing about leaving her "kids" home alone, she should be excited about visiting Rio after all that time.

Eva hadn't been back since pulling the clever maneuver almost seven years ago, leading whoever was after her all the way to Brazil, only to discover that her trail ended there. She'd gotten on a plane to Rio with her real passport as Eva Vega, but had returned to the States with a fake one. And the best part? All expenses had been paid by her paranoid client.

Lucky for her, the man who'd been in charge of producing the good stuff for the government back in her day was still alive. She'd approached him as Eva's daughter and told him a sad story about an abusive ex-husband who was after her. Having had a huge crush on Eva when she was still with the DEA, the guy couldn't refuse a plea from a daughter that looked like her identical twin. At a bargain price, he'd supplied Eva with several fake identities that were good for international travel.

Finished packing her suitcase, Eva threw the charger into her large satchel so she wouldn't forget it later. Her various passports, as well as other documents, were locked in a safe behind the mirror in her bedroom. She pulled them out, trying to remember which one she'd given Tessa to make the reservations. Veronica Soren? Melinda Bechek? Or was it Rachel Daigle?

The office was located at the front of the house, but instead of walking over she dialed Tessa's number. "Who am I this time?"

Tessa chuckled. "I don't know how you do what you do with such a shitty memory. You're Melinda Bechek."

"Thanks a lot. I give you compliments, and this is what I get back," she teased.

"Yeah, yeah. You know I love you. Sharon and Nick are back."

"I'll be there in a moment."

Eva closed the suitcase and hefted it off the bed down to the floor. Thankfully, the checked luggage weight limit for first class was generous. Her various disguises took up a lot of space, especially the padded one she used to make herself look old. Her makeup case alone weighed close to five pounds.

As Eva rolled the suitcase into the front room, Nick took it from her. "I'm going to put it in the trunk."

Sharon pulled her into her arms and squeezed. "Have a safe trip. And be careful."

"I always am."

Tessa was next, wrapping her skinny arms around Eva's waist. The girl was so small that she still looked like the sixteen-year-old Eva had found years ago. She'd tried to fatten her up, but nothing worked. Tessa couldn't gain weight no matter how hard she tried or how much food she consumed.

"I'm going to miss you," she said.

Yeah, she was going to miss all of them. They managed to plug a portion of that big hole in her heart. The missing piece that belonged to Nathalie.

Eva wanted to see her daughter so desperately, it was a constant physical pain. Leaving Nathalie had been the hardest thing Eva had had to do in her life.

But she'd done it to protect her daughter. If she were ever discovered for the mutant she was, Eva wouldn't be the only one they would experiment on. They would want her child as well. Whoever they were. She didn't know whom she was hiding from, but she knew enough to stay hidden.

"One week is not that long. I'll be back before you know it."

Compared to the seven years since she'd last held her daughter in her arms, seven days was indeed nothing.

BHATHIAN

"Hey, Bhathian, what's up? You look in a nastier mood than usual." Anandur dropped his tray on the table and pulled out a chair.

"Bug off." Bhathian took a long swig from his beer. He should've known better than to take his lunch break in the keep's café, or Nathalie's as they all referred to it, the clan's new favorite place to hang out.

It was like waving an open invitation for unwanted company.

He wasn't in the mood for socializing. Hell, lately his dreary disposition had gotten worse. Bhathian had never been a cheerful sort of chap, not even in his youth, but he hadn't been grim. That first turn for the worse had come about thirty-one years ago when he'd let Eva slip from in between his fingers. Then six months ago, when he'd finally gotten a thread of information about her and followed it all the way to Rio, his hopes of getting her back had been shattered. Her trail ended there.

The woman was very good at running and hiding, leading him and whoever else she believed was after her to a dead end.

The sad part was that Eva was running from phantom shadows produced by her own mind. Not that Bhathian could fault her for that. The woman had no idea how and why she'd turned immortal and was terrified of anyone finding out, probably suspecting that the government or some secret organization had tampered with her genes.

If Eva had known no one was after her, she wouldn't have felt compelled to disappear and could've stayed in touch with their daughter.

But that was water under the bridge. By doing such an excellent job of covering her tracks, Eva had doomed herself to eternal running. She'd never learn the truth about herself, and he would never get the chance to make it up to her for deserting her in her time of need.

Dimly, Bhathian was aware that he was wallowing in self-pity, but he lacked the fortitude to pull himself out of that sinkhole, offending the Fates by his lack of gratitude. They had been kind enough to let him find the daughter he hadn't known he had—a dormant daughter who would soon join her immortal family as one of them. Not having to watch his child grow old and die while he lived on, he was already luckier than any other immortal male.

As soon as she delivered his granddaughter, Nathalie would go through the transition.

Bhathian couldn't wait for either.

The grandchild would be his chance to experience everything that he'd missed while his daughter had been growing up. And as soon as Nathalie recovered from giving birth, her husband was going to induce her transition, making her indestructible. The gnawing fear Bhathian was suffering every moment of every day while she was still a fragile human would finally be put to rest.

Damn, he'd been so sure he was going to find Eva and give being a family a try.

Naive wishful thinking.

Even if he had found her, he doubted Eva would've wanted anything to do with him.

He'd messed up big time.

After that one fateful hookup they'd shared over thirty-one years ago, when Eva had found him and told him she was carrying their child, he'd offered to pay for an abortion. When she'd refused, he'd offered her money.

No wonder Eva had disappeared and had never bothered to find him again and tell him about his daughter.

The guilt sat heavily on Bhathian's shoulders.

He should've suspected that Eva was an immortal, and not only because he'd been drawn to her like he'd never been drawn to any woman before. Her resistance to thralling should've been a big clue.

Except, it had never even crossed his mind because it was impossible.

The idea that she'd been a Dormant who'd been unknowingly turned by a random immortal male was preposterous. There were no other immortals aside from his clansmen and their sworn enemies, the Doomers.

When Bhathian had come back from Brazil empty-handed, he'd interrogated every male of his clan. But looking at Eva's picture, none of them remembered ever encountering her. And it wasn't as if a male could've forgotten a woman like her. She was unforgettable.

As for the Doomers, over thirty years ago there had been none in the area.

That left the incredible possibility that it had been some random immortal who'd somehow survived the ancient cataclysm that had wiped out their kind, or a descendant of one.

Was there another secret group of immortals outside the two warring camps?

Except, Bhathian and his clansmen had been searching for centuries, and had never found even one. And yet, someone must've turned Eva. She'd been a carrier of the immortal genes, but she'd been born human.

He'd seen her birth certificate.

"So, Nathalie is getting big." Anandur put his half-eaten pastry down. "I don't think she should be on her feet for so many hours a day. I thought Andrew told her to cut it down to four."

Bhathian glanced at his daughter. She was standing behind the counter, so her seven-months-pregnant belly wasn't on display, but he had to agree with Anandur. The child growing inside her wasn't small. Nathalie had already gained in excess of thirty pounds, and from now on the growth would just accelerate.

How the hell was she going to give birth to such a big baby?

Dr. Bridget should suggest a cesarean delivery. Ever since Nathalie had announced her pregnancy, Bhathian had read every book he could find on the subject, and it seemed that it would be much safer for both mother and baby not to go the natural way.

The thing was, Nathalie had dismissed his concerns, calling him a worrywart.

"Do you think a daughter of mine is going to follow her husband's instructions? She's doing whatever the hell she wants." Bhathian crossed his arms over his chest. He was proud of her independent spirit, but he wished she'd listen to reason from time to time. A talk with Dr. Bridget seemed like the best way to go. She was the only one who could talk some sense into Nathalie.

"I see." Anandur lifted the small cappuccino cup and took a few sips, then put it down and bit into his second pastry.

What was that about? Anandur was like an old yenta—an unrepentant gossiper. "What do you mean?"

Anandur rolled his eyes as he swallowed. "Isn't it obvious? When Nathalie first opened the café, Andrew used to hang around here and help her out every free minute he had. Have you seen him lately? Because I haven't. The only way I know that he comes home at night is seeing his car parked next to mine."

Bhathian cast another glance at Nathalie and frowned. Her smile looked a little forced. He'd noticed that before but had assumed it was the effort it took to work long days while hauling around that belly.

On second thought, it couldn't have been about the pregnancy. Nathalie was doing very well, considering the size of the baby, even thriving, and she was excited about becoming a mother. Her new coffee shop in the lobby of the keep's high-rise was a huge success, full of immortals who were either too lazy to cook for themselves, or just liked hanging out with fellow clan members.

Were Andrew and Nathalie having marital problems?

Not the social type, even Bhathian had noticed that Andrew never showed up in the gym or joined the guys for beers anymore. But that was understandable. The guy had a very pregnant mate at home and didn't want to leave her alone to hang out with the guys.

Up until recently, Nathalie used to invite Bhathian over once or twice a week, and he would spend some time with both Andrew and her. But she'd stopped doing so lately. She was too exhausted after work. Besides, he saw her every day at the café, so there was no need.

Anandur must've heard something. The guy was always snooping for gossip and could extract information from the most reluctant sources. "If you know something, just spill it."

Anandur shook his head. "Sorry, man. I don't. But I can smell trouble. I think you should talk to her. Or maybe give Andrew a call at work."

Uncomfortable with the subject, Bhathian glanced around to check if anyone was paying them any attention. Thankfully, Anandur had been uncharacteristically low key, and it seemed that those sitting around them were busy with their own conversations and tuning everything else out.

"I'm not going to stick my nose where it doesn't belong. They are both adults and can work out whatever problems they have on their own." The idea of approaching Nathalie or Andrew with questions about their marriage horrified him. Bhathian had a hard enough time with regular conversations, let alone touchy subjects.

Anandur took another sip from his cappuccino. "Do you think it has to do with his fangs? They should be fully active by now, venom and all. I know I would be frustrated as hell if I had to fight the instinct to bite."

Frustrated was too mild of a word for that. Bhathian couldn't imagine doing so on an ongoing basis. If that was the problem, then it was a huge one, and Andrew needed help.

He ran his fingers through his hair. "The only solution I can think of is an induced coma. That or stasis."

"I agree. Andrew should do it before he loses it and bites Nathalie."

Bhathian knew Andrew would never harm Nathalie or their unborn child intentionally, but immortals often had trouble controlling their animal urges. Especially a newly turned immortal like Andrew. "They shouldn't be left alone in the same apartment."

"Yeah, but who is going to tell them that?"

"Bridget."

Anandur nodded. "Are you going to talk to her?"

Bhathian pushed up to his feet and threw his empty bottle into the trash bin. "I was planning on seeing Dr. Bridget about something else. I might as well bring this up while I'm there."

Dark Guardian Trilogy

Includes:
11: Dark Guardian Found
12: Dark Guardian Craved
13: Dark Guardian's Mate

THE CHILDREN OF THE GODS SERIES

THE CHILDREN OF THE GODS ORIGINS

1: Goddess's Choice

When gods and immortals still ruled the ancient world, one young goddess risked everything for love.

2: Goddess's Hope

Hungry for power and infatuated with the beautiful Areana, Navuh plots his father's demise. After all, by getting rid of the insane god he would be doing the world a favor. Except, when gods and immortals conspire against each other, humanity pays the price.

But things are not what they seem, and prophecies should not to be trusted...

THE CHILDREN OF THE GODS

1: Dark Stranger The Dream

Syssi's paranormal foresight lands her a job at Dr. Amanda Dokani's neuroscience lab, but it fails to predict the thrilling yet terrifying turn her life will take. Syssi has no clue that her boss is an immortal who'll drag her into a secret, millennia-old battle over humanity's future. Nor does she realize that the professor's imposing brother is the mysterious stranger who's been starring in her dreams.

Since the dawn of human civilization, two warring factions of immortals—the descendants of the gods of old—have been secretly shaping its destiny. Leading the clandestine battle from his luxurious Los Angeles high-rise, Kian is surrounded by his clan, yet alone. Descending from a single goddess, clan members are forbidden to each other. And as the only other immortals are their hated enemies, Kian and his kin have been long resigned to a lonely existence of fleeting trysts with human partners. That is, until his sister makes a game-changing discovery—a mortal seeress who she believes is a dormant carrier of their genes. Ever the realist, Kian is skeptical and refuses Amanda's plea to attempt Syssi's activation. But when his enemies learn of the Dormant's existence, he's forced to rush her to the safety of his keep. Inexorably drawn to Syssi, Kian wrestles with his conscience as he is tempted to explore her budding interest in the darker shades of sensuality.

2: Dark Stranger Revealed

While sheltered in the clan's stronghold, Syssi is unaware that Kian and Amanda are not human, and neither are the supposedly religious fanatics that are after her. She feels a powerful connection to Kian, and as he introduces her to a world of pleasure she never dared imagine, his dominant sexuality is a revelation. Considering that she's completely out of her element, Syssi feels comfortable and safe letting go with him. That is, until she begins to suspect that all is not as it seems. Piecing the puzzle together, she draws a scary, yet wrong conclusion...

3: Dark Stranger Immortal

When Kian confesses his true nature, Syssi is not as much shocked by the revelation as she is wounded by what she perceives as his callous plans for her.

If she doesn't turn, he'll be forced to erase her memories and let her go. His family's safety demands secrecy – no one in the mortal world is allowed to know that immortals exist.

Resigned to the cruel reality that even if she stays on to never again leave the keep, she'll get old while Kian won't, Syssi is determined to enjoy what little time she has with him, one day at a time.

Can Kian let go of the mortal woman he loves? Will Syssi turn? And if she does, will she survive the dangerous transition?

4: Dark Enemy Taken

Dalhu can't believe his luck when he stumbles upon the beautiful immortal professor. Presented with a once in a lifetime opportunity to grab an immortal female for himself, he kidnaps her and runs. If he ever gets caught, either by her people or his, his life is forfeit. But for a chance of a loving mate and a family of his own, Dalhu is prepared to do everything in his power to win Amanda's heart, and that includes leaving the Doom brotherhood and his old life behind.

Amanda soon discovers that there is more to the handsome Doomer than his dark past and a hulking, sexy body. But succumbing to her enemy's seduction, or worse, developing feelings for a ruthless killer is out of the question. No man is worth life on the run, not even the one and only immortal male she could claim as her own...

Her clan and her research must come first...

5: Dark Enemy Captive

When the rescue team returns with Amanda and the chained Dalhu to the keep, Amanda is not as thrilled to be back as she thought she'd be. Between Kian's contempt for her and Dalhu's imprisonment, Amanda's budding relationship with Dalhu seems doomed. Things start to look up when Annani offers her help, and together with Syssi they resolve to find a way for Amanda to be with Dalhu. But will she still want him when she realizes that he is responsible for her nephew's murder? Could she? Will she take the easy way out and choose Andrew instead?

6: Dark Enemy Redeemed

Amanda suspects that something fishy is going on onboard the Anna. But when her investigation of the peculiar all-female Russian crew fails to uncover anything other than more speculation, she decides it's time to stop playing detective and face her real problem —a man she shouldn't want but can't live without.

6.5: My Dark Amazon

When Michael and Kri fight off a gang of humans, Michael gets stabbed. The injury to his immortal body recovers fast, but the one to his ego takes longer, putting a strain on his relationship with Kri.

7: Dark Warrior Mine

When Andrew is forced to retire from active duty, he believes that all he has to look forward to is a boring desk job. His glory days in special ops are over. But as it turns out, his thrill ride has just begun. Andrew discovers not only that immortals exist and have been manipulating global affairs since antiquity, but that he and his sister are rare possessors of the immortal genes.

Problem is, Andrew might be too old to attempt the activation process. His sister, who is fourteen years his junior, barely made it through the transition, so the odds of him coming out of it alive, let alone immortal, are slim.

But fate may force his hand.

Helping a friend find his long-lost daughter, Andrew finds a woman who's worth taking the risk for. Nathalie might be a Dormant, but the only way to find out for sure requires fangs and venom.

8: Dark Warrior's Promise

Andrew and Nathalie's love flourishes, but the secrets they keep from each other taint their relationship with doubts and suspicions. In the meantime, Sebastian and his men are getting bolder, and the storm that's brewing will shift the balance of power in the millennia-old conflict between Annani's clan and its enemies.

9: Dark Warrior's Destiny

The new ghost in Nathalie's head remembers who he was in life, providing Andrew and her with indisputable proof that he is real and not a figment of her imagination.

Convinced that she is a Dormant, Andrew decides to go forward with his transition immediately after the rescue mission at the Doomers' HQ.

Fearing for his life, Nathalie pleads with him to reconsider. She'd rather spend the rest of her mortal days with Andrew than risk what they have for the fickle promise of immortality.

While the clan gets ready for battle, Carol gets help from an unlikely ally. Sebastian's second-in-command can no longer ignore the torment she suffers at the hands of his commander and offers to help her, but only if she agrees to his terms.

10: Dark Warrior's Legacy

Andrew's acclimation to his post-transition body isn't easy. His senses are sharper, he's bigger, stronger, and hungrier. Nathalie fears that the changes in the man she loves are more than physical. Measuring up to this new version of him is going to be a challenge.

Carol and Robert are disillusioned with each other. They are not destined mates, and love is not on the horizon. When Robert's three months are up, he might be left with nothing to show for his sacrifice.

Lana contacts Anandur with disturbing news; the yacht and its human cargo are in Mexico. Kian must find a way to apprehend Alex and rescue the women on board without causing an international incident.

11: Dark Guardian Found

What would you do if you stopped aging?

Eva runs. The ex-DEA agent doesn't know what caused her strange mutation, only that if discovered, she'll be dissected like a lab rat. What Eva doesn't know, though, is that she's a descendant of the gods, and that she is not alone. The man who rocked her world in one life-changing encounter over thirty years ago is an immortal as well.

To keep his people's existence secret, Bhathian was forced to turn his back on the only woman who ever captured his heart, but he's never forgotten and never stopped looking for her.

12: Dark Guardian Craved

Cautious after a lifetime of disappointments, Eva is mistrustful of Bhathian's professed feelings of love. She accepts him as a lover and a confidant but not as a life partner.

Jackson suspects that Tessa is his true love mate, but unless she overcomes her fears, he might never find out.

Carol gets an offer she can't refuse—a chance to prove that there is more to her than meets the eye. Robert believes she's about to commit a deadly mistake, but when he tries to dissuade her, she tells him to leave.

13: Dark Guardian's Mate

Prepare for the heart-warming culmination of Eva and Bhathian's story!

14: Dark Angel's Obsession

The cold and stoic warrior is an enigma even to those closest to him. His secrets are about to unravel...

15: Dark Angel's Seduction

Brundar is fighting a losing battle. Calypso is slowly chipping away his icy armor from the outside, while his need for her is melting it from the inside.

He can't allow it to happen. Calypso is a human with none of the Dormant indicators. There is no way he can keep her for more than a few weeks.

16: Dark Angel's Surrender

Get ready for the heart pounding conclusion to Brundar and Calypso's story.

Callie still couldn't wrap her head around it, nor could she summon even a smidgen of sorrow or regret. After all, she had some memories with him that weren't horrible. She should've felt something. But there was nothing, not even shock. Not even horror at what had transpired over the last couple of hours.

Maybe it was a typical response for survivors--feeling euphoric for the simple reason that they were alive. Especially when that survival was nothing short of miraculous.

Brundar's cold hand closed around hers, reminding her that they weren't out of the woods yet. Her injuries were superficial, and the most she had to worry about was some scarring. But, despite his and Anandur's reassurances, Brundar might never walk again.

If he ended up crippled because of her, she would never forgive herself for getting him involved in her crap.

"Are you okay, sweetling? Are you in pain?" Brundar asked.

Her injuries were nothing compared to his, and yet he was concerned about her. God, she loved this man. The thing was, if she told him that, he would run off, or crawl away as was the case.

Hey, maybe this was the perfect opportunity to spring it on him.

17: Dark Operative: A Shadow of Death

As a brilliant strategist and the only human entrusted with the secret of immortals' existence, Turner is both an asset and a liability to the clan. His request to attempt transition into immortality as an alternative to cancer treatments cannot be denied without risking the clan's exposure. On the other hand, approving it means risking his premature death. In both scenarios, the clan will lose a valuable ally.

When the decision is left to the clan's physician, Turner makes plans to manipulate her by taking advantage of her interest in him.

Will Bridget fall for the cold, calculated operative? Or will Turner fall into his own trap?

18: Dark Operative: A Glimmer of Hope

As Turner and Bridget's relationship deepens, living together seems like the right move, but to make it work both need to make concessions.

Bridget is realistic and keeps her expectations low. Turner could never be the truelove mate she yearns for, but he is as good as she's going to get. Other than his emotional limitations, he's perfect in every way.

Turner's hard shell is starting to show cracks. He wants immortality, he wants to be part of the clan, and he wants Bridget, but he doesn't want to cause her pain.

His options are either abandon his quest for immortality and give Bridget his few remaining decades, or abandon Bridget by going for the transition and most likely dying. His rational mind dictates that he chooses the former, but his gut pulls him toward the latter. Which one is he going to trust?

19: Dark Operative: The Dawn of Love

Get ready for the exciting finale of Bridget and Turner's story!

20: Dark Survivor Awakened

This was a strange new world she had awakened to.

Her memory loss must have been catastrophic because almost nothing was familiar. The language was foreign to her, with only a few words bearing some similarity to the language she thought in. Still, a full moon cycle had passed since her awakening, and little by little she was gaining basic understanding of it--only a few words and phrases, but she was learning more each day.

A week or so ago, a little girl on the street had tugged on her mother's sleeve and pointed at her. "Look, Mama, Wonder Woman!"

The mother smiled apologetically, saying something in the language these people spoke, then scurried away with the child looking behind her shoulder and grinning.

When it happened again with another child on the same day, it was settled.

Wonder Woman must have been the name of someone important in this strange world she had awoken to, and since both times it had been said with a smile it must have been a good one.

Wonder had a nice ring to it.

She just wished she knew what it meant.

21: Dark Survivor Echoes of Love

Wonder's journey continues in *Dark Survivor Echoes of Love*.

22: Dark Survivor Reunited

The exciting finale of Wonder and Anandur's story.

23: Dark Widow's Secret

Vivian and her daughter share a powerful telepathic connection, so when Ella can't be reached by conventional or psychic means, her mother fears the worst.

Help arrives from an unexpected source when Vivian gets a call from the young doctor she met at a psychic convention. Turns out Julian belongs to a private organization specializing in retrieving missing girls.

As Julian's clan mobilizes its considerable resources to rescue the daughter, Magnus is charged with keeping the gorgeous young mother safe.

Worry for Ella and the secrets Vivian and Magnus keep from each other should be enough to prevent the sparks of attraction from kindling a blaze of desire. Except, these pesky sparks have a mind of their own.

24: Dark Widow's Curse

A simple rescue operation turns into mission impossible when the Russian mafia gets involved. Bad things are supposed to come in threes, but in Vivian's case, it seems like there is no limit to bad luck. Her family and everyone who gets close to her is affected by her curse.

Will Magnus and his people prove her wrong?

25: Dark Widow's Blessing

The thrilling finale of the Dark Widow trilogy!

26: Dark Dream's Temptation

Julian has known Ella is the one for him from the moment he saw her picture, but when he finally frees her from captivity, she seems indifferent to him. Could he have been mistaken?

Ella's rescue should've ended that chapter in her life, but it seems like the road back to normalcy has just begun and it's full of obstacles. Between the pitying looks she gets and her mother's attempts to get her into therapy, Ella feels like she's typecast as a victim, when nothing could be further from the truth. She's a tough survivor, and she's going to prove it.

Strangely, the only one who seems to understand is Logan, who keeps popping up in her dreams. But then, he's a figment of her imagination—or is he?

27: Dark Dream's Unraveling

While trying to figure out a way around Logan's silencing compulsion, Ella concocts an ambitious plan. What if instead of trying to keep him out of her dreams, she could pretend to like him and lure him into a trap?

Catching Navuh's son would be a major boon for the clan, as well as for Ella. She will have her revenge, turning the tables on another scumbag out to get her.

28: Dark Dream's Trap

The trap is set, but who is the hunter and who is the prey? Find out in this heart-pounding conclusion to the *Dark Dream* trilogy.

29: Dark Prince's Enigma

As the son of the most dangerous male on the planet, Lokan lives by three rules:

Don't trust a soul.

Don't show emotions.

And don't get attached.

Will one extraordinary woman make him break all three?

30: Dark Prince's Dilemma

Will Kian decide that the benefits of trusting Lokan outweigh the risks?

Will Lokan betray his father and brothers for the greater good of his people?

Are Carol and Lokan true-love mates, or is one of them playing the other?

So many questions, the path ahead is anything but clear.

31: Dark Prince's Agenda

While Turner and Kian work out the details of Areana's rescue plan, Carol and Lokan's tumultuous relationship hits another snag. Is it a sign of things to come?

32 : Dark Queen's Quest

A former beauty queen, a retired undercover agent, and a successful model, Mey is not the typical damsel in distress. But when her sister drops off the radar and then someone starts following her around, she panics.

Following a vague clue that Kalugal might be in New York, Kian sends a team headed by Yamanu to search for him.

As Mey and Yamanu's paths cross, he offers her his help and protection, but will that be all?

33: Dark Queen's Knight

As the only member of his clan with a godlike power over human minds, Yamanu has been shielding his people for centuries, but that power comes at a steep price. When Mey enters his life, he's faced with the most difficult choice.

The safety of his clan or a future with his fated mate.

34: Dark Queen's Army

As Mey anxiously waits for her transition to begin and for Yamanu to test whether his godlike powers are gone, the clan sets out to solve two mysteries:

Where is Jin, and is she there voluntarily?

Where is Kalugal, and what is he up to?

35: Dark Spy Conscripted

Jin possesses a unique paranormal ability. Just by touching someone, she can insert a mental hook into their psyche and tie a string of her consciousness to it, creating a tether. That doesn't make her a spy, though, not unless her talent is discovered by those seeking to exploit it.

36: Dark Spy's Mission

Jin's first spying mission is supposed to be easy. Walk into the club, touch Kalugal to tether her consciousness to him, and walk out.

Except, they should have known better.

37: Dark Spy's Resolution

The best-laid plans often go awry...

38: Dark Overlord New Horizon

Jacki has two talents that set her apart from the rest of the human race.

She has unpredictable glimpses of other people's futures, and she is immune to mind manipulation.

Unfortunately, both talents are pretty useless for finding a job other than the one she had in the government's paranormal division.

It seemed like a sweet deal, until she found out that the director planned on producing super babies by compelling the recruits into pairing up. When an opportunity to escape the program presented itself, she took it, only to find out that humans are not at the top of the food chain.

Immortals are real, and at the very top of the hierarchy is Kalugal, the most powerful, arrogant, and sexiest male she has ever met.

With one look, he sets her blood on fire, but Jacki is not a fool. A man like him will never think of her as anything more than a tasty snack, while she will never settle for anything less than his heart.

39: Dark Overlord's Wife

Jacki is still clinging to her all-or-nothing policy, but Kalugal is chipping away at her resistance. Perhaps it's time to ease up on her convictions. A little less than all is still much better than nothing, and a couple of decades with a demigod is probably worth more than a lifetime with a mere mortal.

40: Dark Overlord's Clan

As Jacki and Kalugal prepare to celebrate their union, Kian takes every precaution to safeguard his people. Except, Kalugal and his men are not his only potential adversaries, and compulsion is not the only power he should fear.

41: Dark Choices The Quandary

When Rufsur and Edna meet, the attraction is as unexpected as it is undeniable. Except, she's the clan's judge and councilwoman, and he's Kalugal's second-in-command. Will loyalty and duty to their people keep them apart?

42: Dark Choices Paradigm Shift

Edna and Rufsur are miserable without each other, and their two-week separation seems like an eternity. Long-distance relationships are difficult, but for immortal couples they are impossible. Unless one of them is willing to leave everything behind for the other, things are just going to get worse. Except, the cost of compromise is far greater than giving up their comfortable lives and hard-earned positions. The future of their people is on the line.

43: Dark Choices The Accord

The winds of change blowing over the village demand hard choices. For better or worse, Kian's decisions will alter the trajectory of the clan's future, and he is not ready to take the plunge. But as Edna and Rufsur's plight gains widespread support, his resistance slowly begins to erode.

44: Dark Secrets Resurgence

On a sabbatical from his Stanford teaching position, Professor David Levinson finally has time to write the sci-fi novel he's been thinking about for years.

The phenomena of past life memories and near-death experiences are too controversial to include in his formal psychiatric research, while fiction is the perfect outlet for his esoteric ideas.

Hoping that a change of pace will provide the inspiration he needs, David accepts a friend's invitation to an old Scottish castle.

45: Dark Secrets Unveiled

When Professor David Levinson accepts a friend's invitation to an old Scottish castle, what he finds there is more fantastical than his most outlandish theories. The castle is home to a clan of immortals, their leader is a stunning demigoddess, and even more shockingly, it might be precisely where he belongs.

Except, the clan founder is hiding a secret that might cast a dark shadow on David's relationship with her daughter.

Nevertheless, when offered a chance at immortality, he agrees to undergo the dangerous induction process.

Will David survive his transition into immortality? And if he does, will his relationship with Sari survive the unveiling of her mother's secret?

46: Dark Secrets Absolved

Absolution.

David had given and received it.

The few short hours since he'd emerged from the coma had felt incredible. He'd finally been free of the guilt and pain, and for the first time since Jonah's death, he had felt truly happy and optimistic about the future.

He'd survived the transition into immortality, had been accepted into the clan, and was about to marry the best woman on the face of the planet, his true love mate, his salvation, his everything.

What could have possibly gone wrong?

Just about everything.

47: Dark Haven Illusion

Welcome to Safe Haven, where not everything is what it seems.

On a quest to process personal pain, Anastasia joins the Safe Haven Spiritual Retreat.

Through meditation, self-reflection, and hard work, she hopes to make peace with the voices in her head.

This is where she belongs.

Except, membership comes with a hefty price, doubts are sacrilege, and leaving is not as easy as walking out the front gate.

Is living in utopia worth the sacrifice?

Anastasia believes so until the arrival of a new acolyte changes everything.

Apparently, the gods of old were not a myth, their immortal descendants share the planet with humans, and she might be a carrier of their genes.

48: Dark Haven Unmasked

As Anastasia leaves Safe Haven for a week-long romantic vacation with Leon, she hopes to explore her newly discovered passionate side, their budding relationship, and perhaps also solve the mystery of the voices in her head. What she discovers exceeds her wildest expectations.

In the meantime, Eleanor and Peter hope to solve another mystery. Who is Emmett Haderech, and what is he up to?

For a **FREE** Audiobook, Preview chapters, And other goodies offered only to my VIPs,

JOIN THE VIP CLUB AT ITLUCAS.COM

TRY THE SERIES ON
AUDIBLE

2 FREE audiobooks with your new Audible subscription!

THE PERFECT MATCH SERIES

Perfect Match 1: Vampire's Consort

When Gabriel's company is ready to start beta testing, he invites his old crush to inspect its medical safety protocol.

Curious about the revolutionary technology of the *Perfect Match Virtual Fantasy-Fulfillment studios*, Brenna agrees.

Neither expects to end up partnering for its first fully immersive test run.

Perfect Match 2: King's Chosen

When Lisa's nutty friends get her a gift certificate to *Perfect Match Virtual Fantasy Studios*, she has no intentions of using it. But since the only way to get a refund is if no partner can be found for her, she makes sure to request a fantasy so girly and over the top that no sane guy will pick it up.

Except, someone does.

Warning: This fantasy contains a hot, domineering crown prince, sweet insta-love, steamy love scenes painted with light shades of gray, a wedding, and a HEA in both the virtual and real worlds.

Intended for mature audience.

Perfect Match 3: Captain's Conquest

Working as a Starbucks barista, Alicia fends off flirting all day long, but none of the guys are as charming and sexy as Gregg. His frequent visits are the highlight of her day, but since he's never asked her out, she assumes he's taken. Besides, between a day job and a budding music career, she has no time to start a new relationship.

THE PERFECT MATCH SERIES

That is until Gregg makes her an offer she can't refuse—a gift certificate to the virtual fantasy fulfillment service everyone is talking about. As a huge Star Trek fan, Alicia has a perfect match in mind—the captain of the Starship Enterprise.

Also by I. T. Lucas

THE CHILDREN OF THE GODS ORIGINS
1: Goddess's Choice
2: Goddess's Hope

THE CHILDREN OF THE GODS

Dark Stranger
1: Dark Stranger The Dream
2: Dark Stranger Revealed
3: Dark Stranger Immortal

Dark Enemy
4: Dark Enemy Taken
5: Dark Enemy Captive
6: Dark Enemy Redeemed

Kri & Michael's Story
6.5: My Dark Amazon

Dark Warrior
7: Dark Warrior Mine
8: Dark Warrior's Promise
9: Dark Warrior's Destiny
10: Dark Warrior's Legacy

Dark Guardian
11: Dark Guardian Found
12: Dark Guardian Craved
13: Dark Guardian's Mate

Dark Angel
14: Dark Angel's Obsession
15: Dark Angel's Seduction
16: Dark Angel's Surrender

Dark Operative
17: Dark Operative: A Shadow of Death
18: Dark Operative: A Glimmer of Hope
19: Dark Operative: The Dawn of Love

Dark Survivor
20: Dark Survivor Awakened
21: Dark Survivor Echoes of Love
22: Dark Survivor Reunited

Dark Widow
23: Dark Widow's Secret
24: Dark Widow's Curse
25: Dark Widow's Blessing

Dark Dream
26: Dark Dream's Temptation
27: Dark Dream's Unraveling
28: Dark Dream's Trap

Dark Prince
29: Dark Prince's Enigma

Also by I. T. Lucas

30: Dark Prince's Dilemma
31: Dark Prince's Agenda
Dark Queen
32: Dark Queen's Quest
33: Dark Queen's Knight
34: Dark Queen's Army
Dark Spy
35: Dark Spy Conscripted
36: Dark Spy's Mission
37: Dark Spy's Resolution
Dark Overlord
38: Dark Overlord New Horizon
39: Dark Overlord's Wife
40: Dark Overlord's Clan
Dark Choices
41: Dark Choices The Quandary
42: Dark Choices Paradigm Shift
43: Dark Choices The Accord
Dark Secrets
44: Dark Secrets Resurgence
45: Dark Secrets Unveiled
46: Dark Secrets Absolved
Dark Haven
47: Dark Haven Illusion
48: Dark Haven Unmasked

PERFECT MATCH
Perfect Match 1: Vampire's Consort
Perfect Match 2: King's Chosen
Perfect Match 3: Captain's Conquest

The Children of the Gods Series Sets

Books 1-3: Dark Stranger trilogy—Includes a bonus short story: **The Fates take a Vacation**
  Books 4-6: Dark Enemy Trilogy—Includes a bonus short story—**The Fates' Post-Wedding Celebration**
  Books 7-10: Dark Warrior Tetralogy
  Books 11-13: Dark Guardian Trilogy
  Books 14-16: Dark Angel Trilogy
  Books 17-19: Dark Operative Trilogy
  Books 20-22: Dark Survivor Trilogy
  Books 23-25: Dark Widow Trilogy
  Books 26-28: Dark Dream Trilogy

ALSO BY I. T. LUCAS

BOOKS 29-31: DARK PRINCE TRILOGY
BOOKS 32-34: DARK QUEEN TRILOGY
BOOKS 35-37: DARK SPY TRILOGY
BOOKS 38-40: DARK OVERLORD TRILOGY
BOOKS 41-43: DARK CHOICES TRILOGY
BOOKS 44-46: DARK SECRETS TRILOGY

MEGA SETS

THE CHILDREN OF THE GODS: BOOKS 1-6—INCLUDES CHARACTER LISTS

THE CHILDREN OF THE GODS: BOOKS 6.5-10—INCLUDES CHARACTER LISTS

TRY THE CHILDREN OF THE GODS SERIES ON AUDIBLE
2 FREE audiobooks with your new Audible subscription!

FOR EXCLUSIVE PEEKS AT UPCOMING RELEASES & A FREE COMPANION BOOK

Join my *VIP Club* and gain access to the VIP portal at itlucas.com
CLICK HERE TO JOIN
(or go to: http://eepurl.com/blMTpD)

INCLUDED IN YOUR FREE MEMBERSHIP:

- **FREE** Children of the Gods companion book 1
- **FREE** narration of Goddess's Choice—Book 1 in The Children of the Gods Origins series.
- Preview chapters of upcoming releases.
- And other exclusive content offered only to my VIPs.

If you're already a subscriber, you can find **your VIP password** at the bottom of each of my new release emails. If you are not getting them, your email provider is sending them to your junk folder, and you are missing out on **important updates, side characters' portraits, additional content, and other goodies.** To fix that, add isabell@itlucas.com to your email contacts or to your email VIP list.

Printed in Great Britain
by Amazon